JUNE BETHUNE

Nashid Ali

Cover and Illustrations by Heather Workman

Original Property of Nashid Ali

Table of Contents

Dedication		5
The Winniper Family Tree		6
An Untitled Poem		7

Wicked Winniper Winters – December to February

POV	Date	Page
Thomas Winniper, Sr.	Wednesday December 31, 1890	9
Teresa Winniper-Townsend-Kane-Bethune	Tuesday January 1, 1946	53
Christina Kane	Thursday February 26, 1948	103

Hopeful Springs – March to May

POV	Date	Page
Olivia Newton Winniper	Monday March 13, 1950	149
Kenneth Bethune, Jr. a.k.a. Kenny	Wednesday April 4, 1956	200
Jazz Lancaster	Tuesday May 2, 1961	243

Love in the Summers – June to August

POV	Date	Page
June Bethune	Sunday June 16, 1963	337
Lucy Lancaster Cashman	Saturday July 4, 1965	373
Duke Winniper	Thursday August 18, 1966	429

An Empire Falls – September to November

POV	Date	Page
Thomas Winniper, III	Monday September 16, 1968	487
Thomas Winniper, Jr. a.k.a. Papa Winniper	Wednesday October 29, 1969	661
Nancy Winniper	Tuesday November 23, 1971	692

Dedicated to my 10th Grade English Teacher,
Mrs. Tina Margaret Holley. R.I.P.

The Winniper Family Tree

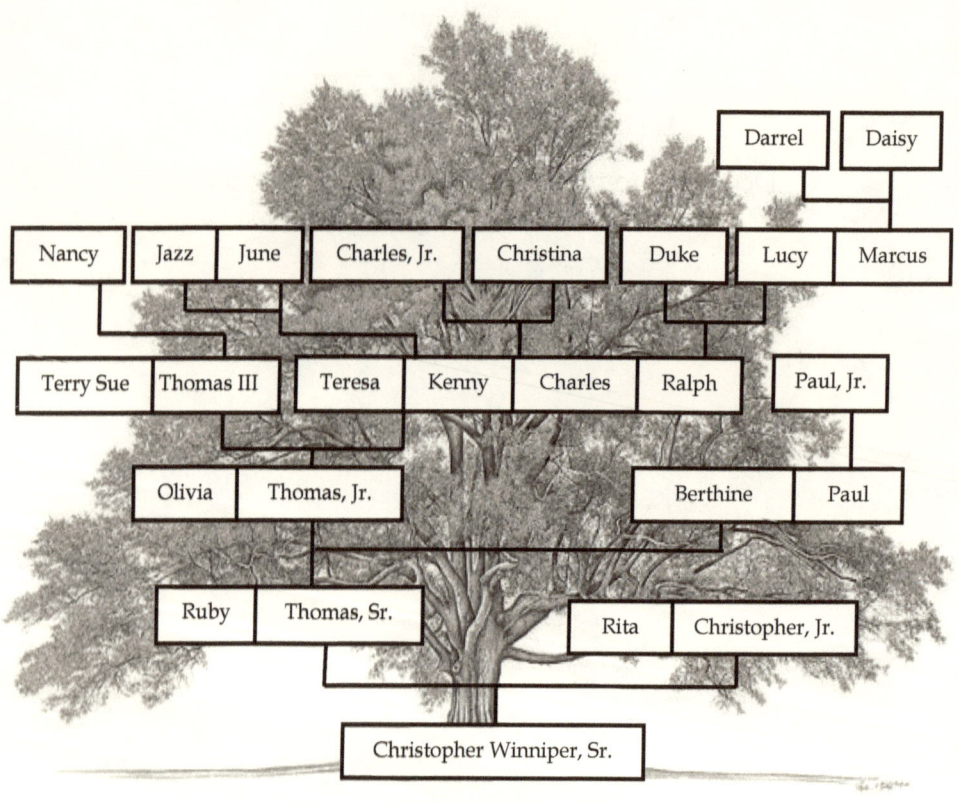

They hunt her as killers,
   faces gnarled with glaring,
         grizzly teeth.

And she bleeds,
   falling to the ground,
     her eyes trembling next to him.

One tear from the sweet,
   young, and innocent
         June Bethune.

One bloodied smile,
   from her to him,
       as they meet their doom.

Wicked Winniper Winters

DECEMBER 1890

Sunday	Monday	Tuesday	Wednesday	Thursday	Friday	Saturday
	1	2	3	4	5	6
7	8	9	10	11	12	13
14	15	16	17	18	19	20
21	22	23	24	25	26	27
28	29	30	31 ★			

Wednesday, December 31, 1890

<u>Thomas Winniper, Sr.</u>

Mention these miracles
When spinning those tales that
Make women wail
And wish for more jails to
Send those men who offend
And contend that
A woman's money and time
Are not her own to spend.
Trapped in themes
Of concept and commerce,
The Winnipers war
Wondering who lit the bomb first.
The terse smirk and shirk,
Unable to hurt worse,
Trapped in a curse
And this verse of much worth.

Thomas Winniper, the youngest heir to the Winniper Family Estate, has usurped his older brother's rightful inheritance and now, he plans to become more successful than their deceased father could have ever dreamed. Thomas munches on the last crumbs of a buttered slice of rye bread while envisioning his future. He will leave a much grander legacy than the dead bread king of South Dakota. In his humblest opinion, he is an up and coming business giant of the expanding American Midwest.

At age thirty-eight, the aspiring enterpriser sits in his father's old wooden rocking chair inside the family's drawing-room. In his lap, he cradles his pregnant wife, Ruby, while celebrating the coming New Year with his older brother, Christopher, Jr., and his sister-in-law, Rita. Violet, the Winnipers' Sioux maid, stands silently beside the liquor cabinet, awaiting any and all instructions. While basking within their family's massive, and masterfully designed, 56-room mansion, the Winniper brothers prepare to seize an opportunity to acquire the ownership rights to a recent oil strike and Thomas believes that destiny has delivered this opportunity directly to their doorsteps.

"Christopher, my boy, I don't care if the whole damn village is down there..." Thomas glares over a fresh glass of whiskey, savoring the burn already in his gullet. "I'm getting that oil. And there ain't a damn thing them Injuns can do to stop me!"

"It's our land, Thomas." Christopher, Jr. concurs, omitting certain logic of ownership while saturating his throat with brandy on ice, spitting a cube back into his empty glass. "*Bleh*, we can do what we want."

"Soon, Christopher." Thomas takes another swig of whiskey and pats his wife on her thigh. "Of course, we should share the wealth with our wives..."

"Thomas, don't be crude." Ruby laughs into her husband's shoulder and rubs her stomach joyfully, smiling like the world is not watching. Her long red hair falls over his chest and he tugs her hips, holding her a little tighter. "Whatever you make will be for the baby."

"Not if it's a girl!" Christopher, Jr. laughs, nudging his wife with his empty brandy glass, his eyebrows arching in expectation. "Only men can inherit; that's the law."

"It's a stupid law!" Rita adds sharply while grabbing her husband's hanging hand and removing his foggy brandy glass from his grip. She then dutifully walks toward Violet and hands her the glass; the maid then retrieves a round bottle of Armagnac brandy from the liquor cabinet as Rita broods through the room. "Someone should change that law!"

"But we mustn't argue with Uncle Sam, dearest," Christopher, Jr. scoffs sarcastically, hooking his fingers over his head like horns. "The government knows best!"

"Unless it's taxes," Thomas jokes, tugging Ruby's side playfully with his left arm wrapped around her waist. "Or regulations, or what they did with our slaves in Tennessee."

"Yes, sir, brother, things used to be much better." Christopher, Jr. reminisces upon times he's too young to remember, a nostalgic bigot, still wishing for old nooses. "Pappy had over 400 slaves when they passed that emancipation indoctrination. He lost that entire inventory; how can Uncle Sam account for that? It's like they owe us this oil, Thomas, right?"

"No one owes anyone anything," Thomas growls through his beard, still eyeing his wife as his main concern. Their eye contact consumes much of his concentration, her curves controlling another considerable portion. Yet, somewhere within his heart, his ambition continues to firmly grasp a small amount of self-entitlement. "We're going to take what we deserve and not ask anyone for permission."

"But I hate that you're going to be gone tonight," Ruby pouts, pushing her bottom lip over her chin and dropping her head with sad, sullen eyes. "We should be celebrating the New Year."

"Yes, I hate it, too, but business is business. We got to put that oil fire out! The new zoning laws take effect at midnight, we better control that land before sun-up. Plus, I have an appraiser scheduled tomorrow for the drilling specs." Thomas laughs from deep inside his throat, rocking in his chair with his wife in his lap; he continues to rub her stomach softly, hoping his son can sense him within her womb. "Anyway, the baby ain't due for a month or two. You and Rita should be fine tonight. Violet can tend to you."

"We'll be more than fine! I'm going to get your pregnant wife drunk!" Rita yells as Violet hands her Christopher's brandy glass, filled to the brim with potion. After inspecting the glass and taking a long sip, Rita smiles and stares wickedly at Thomas. "I'll get her double-drunk, once for her and another for the baby!"

"Or, you'll just get yourself drunk twice," Christopher, Jr. peers at his wife. "Woman, bring me my brandy!"

"Come and get it," Rita responds with a look that makes her insolence tolerable to Christopher, Jr. Thomas often views her as a strumpet or siren who seduced his brother, but while watching Christopher, Jr. bend to her beck and call, Thomas realizes what their father must have also realized: some men will always be fools for women. Ruby leans into Thomas, whispering into his ear.

"I...I'm just..." She hesitates, moving her face to his, staring into his eyes for a moment away from all reality. "I'm worried about you."

"Oh, don't be, Ruby." Christopher, Jr. interrupts, breaking their romantic concentration as only a brother can. He removes his pistol from the holster and points it in the air. "Me and my little brother are war veterans; them Injuns will buck when they see what we got for 'em."

"Make sure it's loaded," Rita jokes, walking to her husband and handing him the brandy glass; he ignores her instantly while he happily eyes the mixture swishing within his hand. She moves close enough to whisper, yet her voice remains loud enough for Thomas and Ruby to hear. "Sometimes...when we're alone...you forget."

"Um..." Christopher, Jr. stammers and looks over his shoulder to Thomas and Ruby, who both watch quietly, expecting retaliation. He turns back angrily, raises his drink, and taps the bottom of the glass to his wife's forehead, moderate jabs, over and over. "I'm...always...loaded. And...don't...mock...me."

"Ow! Never, sweetheart," Rita replies and rubs a sore spot on her forehead before cowering toward the family's 1770 Victorian white sofa and taking a seat farthest away from her husband. She grabs a nearby wine glass of Merlot from a marble top coffee table and turns to Ruby, covering her sad eyes with sarcasm and forced decorum. "I do love being a Winniper woman."

"As do I," Ruby agrees, actually believing her words; she squeezes Thomas's arm, and he holds her closer, often a signal of his masculinity and purpose—he is her protector, the key to her prominence.

"Thomas, all I'm saying is..." Christopher, Jr. begins while taking long gulps of brandy, "...surely, the Good Lord did not intend them Sioux...to end up living on a damn geyser full of oil. I mean, it's spouting out of a hole! Black gold!"

"What's your point?" Thomas asks sharply, hoping to cut through his brother's rhetoric.

"My point is simple, baby brother. This is our land, this is our country." Christopher, Jr. walks closer to Thomas and Ruby, almost hovering over them with his brandy glass loosely gripped in his fingers. "Those Sioux are devil worshippers, and God wouldn't want some devil worshippers getting rich off his land. This is America!"

"No, I reckon he would not," Thomas agrees, while taking a sip from his whiskey glass. "The old man gave them that territory a few decades ago, some agreement with the government, but they still live off our farmland, profiting from our harvest...and now they strike oil!"

"This is a test, Thomas. God is testing us and you heard what happened at Wounded Knee. They did it right, kill 'em all!" Christopher, Jr. struts around the room, waving his pistol and brandy, forgetting which is which, firing the glass and sipping from the gun barrel. "Them Sioux ain't legal citizens, and they can't do a thing. We get that land back, and it's ours in the good state of South Dakota. We've been gracious for letting them stay on our land this long!"

"Just be careful...I feel like you're going off to war all over again," Ruby adds, placing her head on Thomas's shoulder again. She is a baby with a baby inside her womb. "I've heard dreadful stories about those *Ghost Dance Sioux.*"

"Oh, they're harmless. It's almost sad my father didn't find the oil before he gave them the land." Thomas insists, reaching for his Enfield rifle laying on the rug and checking the loaded .58 caliber barrel with his pregnant wife still in his lap.

After narrowing his eyes and surveying the weapon amidst the backdrop of Ruby's expanded curves, he realizes his mindlessness and quickly places the rifle back on the floor and unholsters his father's Colt 1851 revolver, another family heirloom bestowed upon the younger Winniper son during his valiant service in the war. Thomas knows how the sight of the revolver sours his brother so he often unholsters the weapon before any coming ordeal. He asserts his power while opening the barrel and counting six loaded .36 caliber bullets.

"One, two, yep, it's a good thing Pa left me in charge to make sure we get what we deserve."

"Pappy did always make a mess of things; you know I was supposed to have that gun." Christopher, Jr. complains, moving over a bundle in the corner and retrieving a large rope. His eyes brighten at the thought of future possibilities. "Can we hang some of them?"

"No, we won't have time." Thomas responds smugly, grunting and sliding the revolver back into his jacket holster; he lightly pats Ruby on the hip, and she rises as a trained animal. He stands beside her and holds her in his arms for a moment, staring into his wife's eyes and feigning a semblance of love. "We need to be quick about this…I want to spend the New Year with my wife."

"Your wife would love nothing more than that," Ruby coos softly, but waves of concern brush over her forehead in wrinkles and creases. "But what if things don't go as planned?"

"Well, that's why we have guns…" Thomas retorts as he pats his father's gun with a laugh. "I have Pa's Colt, my war rifle, and the sheriff and Will boy are bringing the entire militia. More than enough so you don't have to be scared."

"I'm not scared. Especially with Will boy and them crazy Bethunes," Christopher, Jr. adds, mentioning the Winnipers' business partner and fellow Indian War veteran William Bethune. He is another legacy baby, dreaming of destiny and dynasties in the Midwest. "You know those Bethunes won't hesitate to blast one of them Sioux if they get unruly."

"Well, just hope you do your part," Thomas chides his brother. "I remember you ducking a lot during the war!"

"Now listen here…" Christopher, Jr. raises his pistol momentarily before placing the small sidearm in his holster. He then raises his brandy glass in his left hand and points his wetted index finger at Thomas. "I fought just as long and hard as you did; just so happens, you got all the credit."

"Do you think these Sioux will just lie down?" Rita asks, interrogating Christopher, Jr., upset that he lavishes so much attention upon his brother. "They have sharecroppers living down there too…they know…"

"I know all about who's there and what they know. Christopher, maybe you should spend more time controlling your wife." Thomas rustles his coat over his shoulders, tucking his rifle in a sling. "I spoke to Johnnie earlier. He's been helpful with uh…*developments.*"

"He's a good boy. He and Violet love coonin'," Christopher, Jr. remarks while eyeing Violet contemptuously and mimicking his little brother, throwing his coat over his shoulders in the same rough move. He shoves his rifle in a similar sling, a little less convincingly, an imitation at best. "I hope the good help is passed along for generations to come."

"Well, I promised them that they could stay," Thomas continues to move about the room, checking the colt in his jacket holster and anxiously patting his rifle. Violet remains silent next to the liquor cabinet, she knows her place well. "They'll have to move closer to the estate while the oil refinery is built."

"You did what?" Ruby asks, walking closer to Thomas, yet, still not daring to imitate Rita and interrogate her husband "I thought we would fire the blacks—along with those Sioux natives! I want them all away from our property before the baby comes!"

"I told you, dear, Johnnie's helpful, and Violet's his wife." Thomas raises his hand to impede Ruby's consternation. "The man has a family to feed like the rest of us, and at present date, his familial goals align with mine. We will always need servants, and his children will be loyal to us. Darling, this oil is going to make our family wealthy beyond our wildest dreams. We can afford to sprinkle crumbs for the ants."

"Just a moment, Thomas; I agree with your wife." Christopher, Jr. pushes in between Thomas and Ruby, pointing back and forth between the two. "They should all be off our land."

"*Our land?*" Thomas asks, poking Christopher, Jr. with his finger. "The old man left it all to me, big brother. I own all the responsibility, all the problems, all the wealth. Legally, you don't even own that shack you call a house."

"Pa' built that cottage before we…It should be me in this big house!"

"Oh, please don't start arguing, Thomas," Ruby intervenes between her husband and his brother, seeing the beginnings of a new confrontation. "Not tonight."

"I'm sorry, dear," Thomas concedes, placing his hands on his wife's arm and glancing between her soft, alluring eyes and Christopher's cold, jealous stare. "My brother and I will behave like Winniper men, right, Christopher?"

"Of course," Christopher, Jr. confirms, ruffling the sleeves of his coat and walking away. "He's always right, Ruby."

"And look, Ruby, think of it this way," Thomas begins, backing away from his wife so that she may see the caliber of man she married. "After we eradicate these pests from our land, we'll increase our family's value and trade our liabilities for greater assets. The 20th century is right around the corner, and the world's entering an industrial age. With oil, we can do business around the globe!"

"Oh, please don't talk business," Ruby moans, clutching her stomach and sitting on the sofa. "It makes me dizzy."

"Why yes, me too!" Rita feigns, placing one hand to her head and taking a long sip of Merlot from her glass. "Our delicate female skulls can't possibly contain all the know-how to understand economics."

"Still boring people with your anecdotes?" Christopher, Jr. remarks to his wife. "Just like in grade school."

"You're right; it is like we're back in grade school," Rita retorts, taking another long sip from her wine glass and savoring the taste before rolling her eyes to Christopher, Jr. "And I'm still smarter than you."

"And you still follow me home every day."

"Okay, break it up you two," Thomas orders, moving between his brother and sister-in-law. "Come on, Christopher. We need to meet Sheriff Cobb. If we hurry, we can come back and celebrate with our wives."

"I don't know if that's a good thing," Christopher, Jr. grumbles, taking a lasting gulp of brandy. "I don't want to hear her screaming about how she can't do anything because she's a woman…"

"And complaining about how much I despise you when you drink." Rita interrupts while leaning back defensively so that she is closer to Ruby on the sofa.

"Listen, if we follow the plan," Thomas begins, standing in the middle of the room, looking between Christopher, Jr., Rita, and Ruby, "we can be home before midnight."

Thomas walks to the sofa, kisses Ruby, and cocks his war rifle, not sure which he loves more—his guns, his wife, or his family's sofa. The Louis XVI sofa is a Winniper heirloom; originally shipped directly from the Palace of Versailles, his father had it transported to South Dakota when he moved the family from his childhood home in Tennessee. Thomas looks over the sofa and thinks of Louis XVI, a king in a lineage of kings, and he dreams that, one day, Thomas XVI will reign supreme over the kingdom built by his forefathers. The Winnipers haven't lacked for anything since they arrived from Europe with the first Puritans, migrating North and South through the originally colonies before mass-producing grain, wheat, yeast, and bread on their farmlands in Tennessee.

Thomas now views himself as the next in line to take hold of his family name and do what God wills; he prays only to achieve more than his predecessors—the dream of any noble prince, to be the greatest king in a great lineage of great kings. Glancing over his wife, his weapons, and his prized possessions, he feels the pangs and the longing for more before turning away to grab a nearby knapsack. He delicately hoists its strap over his right shoulder and gently rests the bag against his waist.

"What's that?" Ruby asks as Thomas and his brother exit the drawing-room; Thomas pauses and turns back to his wife. He opens the sack and reveals a large jug of clear liquid.

"In case we get thirsty." Thomas smiles and turns away, rejoining his brother and walking through the mansion. The brothers exit out the back door toward the forest behind the Winniper Family Estate. Thomas quickly forgets his wife and focuses on the conquest.

"Why don't you let me get George and the boys?" Christopher, Jr. asks, stepping over brush and bushes. "They'd love some of that moonshine. We could..."

"No," Thomas interrupts without turning to his brother, while maneuvering through twigs and branches. "Sheriff Cobb is already meeting us with the militia. We can't afford any mistakes. Courthouse opens tomorrow, and we need to control this land and clog the oil geyser by morning."

"You're right there, brother," Christopher, Jr. agrees with a big smile, happily following his brother through the thickets. "No telling how big them industries can be."

"We'll have more money than Midas." Thomas laughs, thinking of the black gold. "I have big plans for our family, Christopher."

"I still can't believe them Injuns struck oil! I'm glad Pappy left you in charge, little brother. You knew exactly what to do," Christopher, Jr. confides sincerely as he and Thomas move through the forest, holding their rifles in front of them, just in case. "You s'pose we could let the Injuns live? Maybe they'll leave peacefully."

"I doubt they'll leave without a fight." Thomas continues to march through the woods, clutching his rifle and hopping over a small stream, the unofficial property line between the Winniper Family Estate and the Ghost Dance Sioux reservation. "And we can't leave witnesses."

"Why not, Thomas?" Christopher, Jr. asks from behind his brother, following Thomas's every move and maneuver through the trees and brush. "What do you think is gon' happen?"

"Well…it could be worse than Wounded Knee. More bad publicity could stall our Westward Expansion. We'll have to say it was a revolt. The Injuns crossed into our property and we drove 'em back and took back the land." Thomas explains his plot callously, still not looking back, focused on pressing forward; riches and power lie ahead. "These Sioux let the blacks and Mexicans live on their reservation…no telling who knows by now. We don't want any newsmen coming to our land asking the wrong questions."

"Just our luck those Injuns would strike oil on the land we gave them," Christopher, Jr. goofs, catching his coat on a thicket; he tugs and pulls his sleeve until he finally rips the fabric free. "But couldn't we just buy the land back?"

"Why buy what we can take, Christopher?" Thomas sneers as he sees Sheriff Cornell Cobb, Sr. smoking a cigar through the woods, while standing among several armed militiamen. The brothers approach the sheriff, his son and deputy, and their cohorts. Thomas whispers to his brother, without care or concern. "Now, stay quiet, y'here?"

The Winniper brothers walk through the end of the woods and stand amongst the sheriff and his men. In the distance, a plume of smoke billows from the Sioux village.

∞

During the Westward Expansion, the Winniper family and other Dakota proprietors sold the government the land for the Sioux reservation, but once wildcats and oil drillers began profiting from several nearby strikes, well, two rabbits couldn't occupy the same hole. Until his death, their father respected their past agreements with the Sioux and the sharecroppers, hiring them to work on the Winniper farm, harvesting wheat, corn, and enough vegetables to establish a local farm empire, as the Winniper patriarch so desired—and he encouraged his sons to desire the same. Inheriting their father's sense of manifest destiny, his sons, especially Thomas, dreamed that the Winniper name would loom large throughout the U.S.—America's first family.

Crowned after his father's death, the younger brother with the more mature dreams, Thomas abandoned his father's agreement and implemented a plan to take their land back from the Sioux reservation. First, he began to charge the sharecroppers rent to live on their farmland, causing some to move to the Sioux village. Over time, the Sioux found their reservation barren; the dry land couldn't sustain more homes, mouths, and water demands. A loyal Winniper worker living between the Sioux village and the Winniper plantation, Johnnie Robinson, acted as an intermediary between the displaced sharecroppers and the overburdened Sioux village. After receiving their pleas, he approached Thomas Winniper to barter a deal for the Sioux to produce vegetables on his farmland and use the nearby stream on the Winnipers' property. Like a cat coaxing a bird from its cage, Thomas Winniper gladly agreed to loan the Sioux vegetables, bread, and more, and he also allowed their women to use the Winnipers' stream. Advantageous to Thomas's ambition, the agreement turned the Sioux and the sharecroppers into new and renewed slaves, impoverished by debts that compiled with interest.

During the winter months, Thomas and Christopher, Jr. increased the prices for their vegetables and bread and only offered access to a water well near the stream, for an additional tax. Slowly, more and more of the Sioux men began to catch the sharecropper truck to the Winnipers' farmland, each working off his family's debts alongside the blacks and Mexicans.

A veritable conglomerate of the impoverished, the blacks and browns suffered through mutual anguish every day on the Winnipers' farm, until two days ago. After no one from the Sioux village caught the sharecropper truck, leaving Johnnie Robinson without any help on the farm, he rode a horse from the Winniper family's stable to the Sioux village. When he returned, he told Thomas Winniper the most extravagant news: the Sioux natives had struck oil. In fact, the Sioux hadn't *struck* oil; out of ego or tradition, a Sioux craftsman carved a new, redwood totem pole for the village, and, after removing the old totem pole, a black liquid began to shoot from the hole. The Sioux men, some dreading the morning trek to the Winniper farm, stopped to watch the liquid spurting from the ground, while wondering what it was.

As Johnnie explained to Thomas, and Thomas explained to Christopher, Jr., William Bethune, and Sheriff Cobb, someone lit the spout on fire, believing it could be oil, and it's been burning ever since.

∞

For the past two days, the Ghost Dance Sioux have rejoiced and danced around the fiery spout, believing it is a sign from their gods, beckoning the Sioux tribe to channel their ancestors in a Ghost Dance ritual.

As they stand in a thin clearing, watching the smoke ascend into the night sky, Thomas can hear drums beating in the distance; he looks to Sheriff Cobb, who removes a watch from his pocket and glances at the time through squinted eyes.

"You're late, we've been waiting." Sheriff Cobb complains boldly, forgetting his place, or maybe he has yet to learn the new pecking order in South Dakota.

"Sorry, Sheriff," Thomas apologizes, while extending his hand to the grumbling, insolent man who stares down and slowly takes the gesture. "You know how a pregnant wife can be. The baby's due any day now."

"Oh, yes I remember those days." Sheriff Cobb laughs, glancing to his deputy son. "When Junior here was born, his mother couldn't get enough rhubarb."

"That's right, I remember that," Christopher, Jr. chimes in. "I think she ate our whole harvest that year."

"Hey…" Cornell, Jr. interrupts while poking his chest out toward Christopher, Jr. "What are you saying about my Ma?"

"Calm down, son. He didn't mean anything by it." Sheriff Cobb pulls his son away from the Winnipers, smiling with pride. "Excuse him. The boy's got his daddy's temper."

"Quite alright, Sheriff," Thomas smiles, hoping his wife conceives a similar son, dreaming of teaching his seed to become a man in moments like these. "We're going to need all the firepower we got, tonight."

"Yes, the boys and I will walk with you this way," Sheriff Cobb explains, pointing toward the Sioux village and the smoke plume. "William and his group have already circled around back…"

"Do you think that'll be enough?" Christopher, Jr. asks, poking his head between Thomas and the sheriff. "Thomas, you said no one can get out."

"Twenty red-blooded Americans should be enough for any war." Sheriff Cobb confides, cocking his rifle. "Plus, we've got guns."

"My thoughts exactly," Thomas growls, eyeing his Enfield rifle and remembering bloody nights like these; the smell of death is already in the air.

"I'm glad Congress passed that law banning coloreds from carrying firearms." Christopher, Jr. adds. "Ain't nothin' patriotic about a fair fight."

"One day, we'll get Congress to pass any law we want, Christopher." Thomas predicts. "And Sheriff, after tonight, you and your family will never have to work again. I can assure that."

"Well, that'd be nice, Thomas, but I think my family wants to play a more *disciplinary* role in our new town," the sheriff beams brightly. "The boys and I think very highly of you and your family…if your father was alive…"

"I'm sure he'd be proud," Thomas espouses confidently, walking toward the Sioux village. "Let's get going, gentleman, I promised the wife I'd try to be home by midnight."

"Yes, sir," Sheriff Cobb agrees, turning to his son and fellow henchmen. "Let's go, boys. Make sure you're locked and loaded…tonight, we do God's work."

"Gon' make you proud, Pop! I wish I had my trumpet!" Cornell, Jr. cheers happily, lifting his rifle and joining his father as they trail the Winniper brothers, all marching toward the large smoke plume that drifts over the trees. The drums pound softly in the distance, the ground trembling slightly in mild rumbles; the stories of the Ghost Dance Sioux's rituals fill the men's minds, knowing the tribe makes human sacrifices if their gods desire blood.

Thomas Winniper begins to make his way through a wall of bushes and trees that separates the Sioux village from the forest and the stream on the Winniper property. Crouching behind his brother, Christopher, Jr. slips through the natural barrier, followed by the sheriff, his son, and the Dakota militia.

∞

Established after the Indian Wars expanded west to Dakota, the militia formed the principal resistance to the Sioux and Cherokee who once dominated the region. Whenever Sheriff Cobb encounters a problem beyond the means of himself or his deputy, he and William Bethune round-up the militiamen, their rifles, and, if need be, he wheels out an old canon that the Bethune family brought from Tennessee.

As young men, the Winnipers fought beside the Bethunes to defeat the Sioux in South Dakota; the two then split much of the land amongst themselves and their fellow-men. Over the last year of conflicts between the Americans and the Natives of the Midwest, as the Dakota militiamen passed away in battles and feuds, most of South Dakota has become consolidated within two estates: the Bethunes and Winnipers.

The two families are now the most powerful land owners in the young state. After receiving the news from Johnnie Robinson, Thomas met with his brother and William and they devised a plan to reclaim the Sioux village and the oil. When the time for implementation arrived, Thomas enlisted Sheriff Cobb to round up the militia for a massacre to rival Wounded Knee.

Simply put, the Winnipers and Bethunes understood that the American way would soon become industrial, emphasizing business over morality, and so, all the principles their fathers professed no longer applied. A new American West expanded past the Mississippi River, and any agreements made with the Sioux could not hinder America's sense of manifest destiny: the rich must get richer.

∞

With comparable slices of the pie, the sheriff and the Dakota militia trounce through the forest as equal assassins; though they all understand that the Winnipers and Bethunes will facilitate any and all business, the rats remain content with cheese. As the ground begins to thunder underneath their feet, the heat from the fire warms their faces.

"God, I can already feel the flames!" Christopher, Jr. complains in the hot darkness, trying to see through the tall grass. "Those damn Injuns are burning our profits..."

"Keep quiet!" Thomas barks, pointing his gun at his brother for a moment before turning back through the trees. A bright orange light pierces through the night as if the sun has risen from the ground. Thomas pushes his way through, reaching the edge of the woods surrounding the Sioux village. Small animal-skin huts and wooden shacks stand throughout the enclosed community, gated by God's forest, yet fated to be concealed. In the center of the village, the Sioux men and women dance around the ignited oil spout. Shooting fire in the air, the gasoline geyser rises over 20 feet, pluming high into the sky.

Several Sioux men beat drums, and the sharecroppers stand nearby, watching the spectacle in bewilderment. Far across the village, where the woods and Bethune property begin, Thomas can see one dim lantern, a signal from William that he is in place. Thomas crouches within the thick stalks of grass and turns back to Christopher, Jr. and Sheriff Cobb.

"Everyone get down!"

"I think I stepped on a frog," Christopher, Jr. whines, crouching beside his brother and peaking at the Sioux dance ritual. "What are those nitwits doing? They're burning all the oil!"

"That's why we're here." Thomas smiles as he opens his knapsack. "Sheriff, do you see that lantern in the distance?"

"Uh...no." Sheriff Cobb squints over the tall grass, through the villages toward the woods. "Wait, yes, I do see it. I must be getting old."

"That means Will boy's in place," Thomas continues, slinging his rifle over his shoulder and removing the jug of moonshine from his sack. "Now when this starts, there's no going back. Are your boys ready?"

"Well..." Sheriff Cobb turns to his son and the other militiamen. "Boys, are you ready?"

"Locked and loaded, Pop!" Cornell, Jr. cheers enthusiastically. "They all gon' die."

"Yep," the sheriff chuckles and turns back to Thomas. "I think they're ready."

"Then let's go." Thomas begins to rise from the grass but the sheriff grabs his arm momentarily.

"Um, Mister…Mr. Winniper," Sheriff Cobb stammers. "Maybe we should wait until they finish their…ritual…"

"*Their ritual*?" Christopher, Jr. repeats in confusion. "Do you want to dance, too, sheriff?"

"No, it's just…I've seen these Sioux do some…some sick, devilish work," the sheriff adds. "That ritual…that dance is the *Ghost Dance.*"

"Say what?" Christopher, Jr. asks, holding his rifle to his chest and stepping toward the sheriff. "Listen here, Cornell, don't tell me you believe in that witchcraft?"

"Heavens no, sir," Sheriff Cobb confirms, placing his hand over his heart. "I was raised Protestant, in a good church."

"Then what's your worry, Sheriff?" Thomas asks, while moving away from the men. "God will protect us."

"You're right, sir," the sheriff calls behind Thomas, trying to keep his voice below the tall grass up ahead. "It's just that…"

"Be a good Christian, Sheriff," Christopher, Jr. interrupts, passing the sheriff and putting him in his place, behind the Winnipers, ignored and unimportant. The sheriff's son approaches his father, creeping toward the high grass with the militiamen in tow.

"You said yourself this is God's work, Pop," Cornell, Jr. recalls, looking back at the militiamen. "What are you afraid of?"

"Afraid?" The sheriff grabs his son's collar and backhands his face sharply. "Remember how to speak to your father, boy."

"Sorry, Pop." Cornell, Jr. hangs his head and lowers his voice. "Guess I got carried away."

"It's okay, son. We both did…" Sheriff Cobb pats his son's shoulder, sharing a moment of conciliation before the coming commotion; the militiamen stand by idly, awaiting their next move as Thomas and Christopher, Jr. move ahead toward the Sioux. "Let's go, boys. Stay low and keep your guns ready."

The sheriff and his son follow Christopher, Jr. and Thomas toward the Sioux bonfire. Dancing around the high fire spout, the Sioux dancers chant incantations over the men's drumming, and the ground beneath their feet rumbles in rhythm. The trees around the village sway from side-to-side, all the limbs shaking to the Sioux dancers' hips; Christopher, Jr. trips over a fallen branch.

"Dammit!" He grimaces as his head bounces off the ground; slapped with grass and mud, sweaty muck coats his face. Thomas kneels over his brother and grabs his hair tightly, pulling his head out of the mire.

"I told you to keep quiet, boy." Thomas glowers over his brother angrily as the militia catch up to the brothers; the Sioux still remain entranced in their ritual ahead. "You're not going to ruin this for me."

"For you?" Christopher, Jr. pushes his brother away and tries to rise to his feet. "I..."

Before he can finish, Thomas punches his brother in the mouth, reasserting his dominance and reminding his brother that amnesia has consequences. Christopher, Jr. falls on his backside and those coming questions of masculinity enter his mind—the big brother forced to play a smaller role in the Winniper family's destiny.

"I told you keep quiet." Thomas stands over his brother threateningly, one fist cocked over him while the other hand holds the jug of moonshine.

"*Boys, don't fight,*" a familiar voice cries, circling around the militia. "*You always fought as children.*"

"Who said that?" Thomas asks, searching the militiamen's faces.

"Said what?" Sheriff Cobb whispers, crouching within the thick grass and glancing to the Sioux ritual.

"Was it you?"

"No, sir."

"*Turn away, my sons,*" The voice continues to circle around the militia; the drums boom under their feet as a cold wind whips over their skin. "*Turn away.*"

"Who said that?" Thomas asks, looking at Christopher, Jr. "It sounds like..."

"Pappy..." Christopher, Jr. finishes his brother's sentence.

"Hello, boys." Christopher Winniper, Sr. appears over his sons' shoulders, standing between them and the Sioux celebration in the distance. Their father is dead in living flesh; his skin has withered like worn white leather, and his hair is strained, sweaty, and stringy like when he passed away in the mansion's master bedroom. Christopher, Sr. smiles at his sons before frowning with disappointment. *"It's good to see you, and it's bad, too."*

"What are you doing here?" Christopher, Jr. asks, wiping his face with his right sleeve, rising to his feet, and standing close to his brother, although he remains almost a full step behind. "Are you seeing this, Thomas?"

"Seeing what?" The sheriff asks. "Who's there?"

"Our father." Christopher, Jr. whispers, turning back to the militia. "He's standing right there."

Sheriff Cobb looks to his son and shrugs with his gun still in hand.

"Don't bother with them," Christopher, Sr. explains, stepping closer to his sons. *"They can't see me."*

"Hold it." Thomas aims his rifle at his father, peering over the old man's features. "Don't move another inch."

"Who are you talking to, Thomas?" Sheriff Cobb continues to question, staying low within the tall thicket.

"It's our father," Christopher, Jr. repeats in shock, his eyes growing wide with amazement. This time, he continues to stare at his deceased father, while taking another step so that he is farther behind Thomas. "He says you can't see him."

"Well, I told you we should wait until them Injuns are done with that Ghost Dance!" The sheriff yells, forgetting his place again, yet this time, he remembers quickly. "I mean, uh, are we still going through with this or not? Junior and I need to get home to his mother."

"Calm down," Thomas commands himself and the sheriff, still staring at his dead father in disbelief, yet he is unwilling to reveal his fear to his brother or anyone else. The new king swallows his apprehension and begins to move past his father's ghost toward the celebration ahead. "Let's go."

*guns not included

"*No, wait, son,*" his father calls behind Thomas, reappearing in front of his son, between the Sioux and the militia. "*I didn't give you control of the family so that you could ruin it! Don't go through with this. It'll be very bad for you…for both of you.*"

"What do you mean?" Christopher, Jr. asks, peaking over Thomas's shoulder.

"*These Sioux…*" Christopher, Sr. begins, "*these Sioux have powers…I gave them this land because…*"

"Times change," Thomas murmurs quietly, while stopping in his tracks, still perturbed to speak with a ghost. "Our business needs to expand."

"Pop…" Cornell, Jr. kneels close to his father. "You believe he's really talking to a ghost?"

"Could be, son," the sheriff responds softly, removing a pouch of tobacco from his front pocket. "I saw one of these Sioux bring a deer back to life. Ever since, there ain't nothing I don't believe."

"*Boys, take a moment,*" Christopher, Sr. implores, moving closer to his sons. "*You have two beautiful wives, a child on the way. I left you both with more than enough to enjoy life…but, if you do this, you will end up like me…filled with regrets.*"

"What do you have to regret, Pop?" Thomas asks his father. "You were a self-made man."

"*I regret giving you that revolver, Thomas. I've seen what happens with it! I regret making you lord over your older brother. Yes, I made myself into a man…*" Christopher, Sr. grins wryly and shakes his head, "*…but I raised two boys who are marching to kill a village of innocent people. There are children over there…and you'll kill them for what? Money? Power? Respect?*"

"All of the above, sir. We have a right to it all, Papa, and you gave me that right!" Thomas returns his father's guile with his own, moving past his mentor; the student has become the master. "What's done is done. Now, let's go, Christopher."

"*Son, please don't! You'll curse our family. You'll curse our bloodline!*" Christopher, Sr. shouts to his son as the militia passes; he reappears in front of Thomas who continues to walk through his father's spirit. "*You have no right to kill these people! They are innocent! They are all innocent! God gave them that oil! God gave them their powers! Let them celebrate in peace!*"

"Thomas…maybe we should listen," Christopher, Jr. whispers frightfully to his brother as they crouch through the thickets while approaching the Sioux dance ritual. The clouds swirl with the oil fire's puff in a purple and grey smog that spreads across the starry sky. "He's a ghost, he must know…"

"If he could stop us, then he would." Thomas continues moving toward the fire. "He can't tell me what to do anymore. He's dead."

"But the Sioux…" Christopher, Jr. stammers, creeping beside his brother. "What about their powers?"

"Are you afraid?" Thomas snidely challenges his brother, crouching lower as they approach the Sioux dancing around the fire and the ground continues to shiver in trembles and quakes. "You can leave; I'll keep the land, the oil, the glory…"

"No…" Christopher, Jr. interrupts. "I'm here…I'm staying…with you, little brother. Like you said, what's done is done. Lead the way."

"Good, now here, take this jug." Thomas turns over his left shoulder and raises the jug of moonshine. "Don't drop this shine and crawl ahead until I tell you to stop."

"What?" Christopher, Jr. questions. "What do you want me to do?"

"I added some of that glycerin the old man used in the wars," Thomas explains with a smile, happy to have a few useful lessons from his father. "You're going to throw it in that fire."

"But…" Christopher, Jr. pauses, looking back to Sheriff Cobb and the militia as they crouch nearby. "What about them?"

"This is our land…" Thomas implores, shoving the jug into his brother's chest. "When they tell stories about this night, do you want to be the one who stood around or do you want to be the hero that led the charge? All the shame from your past erased in one throw. It's my gift to you brother, for your loyalty, but I can do it for you if you want…"

"No, I can do it!" Christopher, Jr. affirms sharply as he puffs out his chest, adjusts his rifle over his shoulder, and grabs the jug firmly with both hands. He crouches and moves away from his younger brother, hunching down on his belly as he begins to crawl toward the edge of the tall grass where the Sioux dance and sing around the fire spout.

Beside the dancing circle, the men continue to drum and chant along with the dancers. Across the village, Thomas can see William's lantern dimly lit in the distance and a few figures hide amongst the trees. Christopher, Jr. reaches the edge of the tall grass and looks back to his brother.

"Wait there," Thomas whispers, holding up his open palm to his brother and taking another look at the lantern, hoping William and his half of the militia are ready for the coming carnage. He then turns back to the sheriff and the militia with a nod. "I'll pay a dollar per head. Leave no survivors."

"Yes, sir," the sheriff responds joyously, turning toward his son and the militia. "You hear that, boys? A dollar per head, that's better than goose hunting."

"I'm gon' buy Ma' a fur coat." Cornell, Jr. asserts, imagining the garment hanging from the edge of his rifle.

"You leave that to me, son." The sheriff cocks his weapon, preparing for war. "You just stay safe out here."

"Yes, sir."

"We're ready when you are, Mr. Winniper," Sheriff Cobb announces assuredly and Thomas turns back toward the Sioux dance ritual, taking a moment to absorb the chanting, dancing, and ceremony. In the corner of his right eye, Thomas sees his father, standing beyond the dancing circle. The ghost begins to walk among the women and men before dissolving into the fire and billowing above in the smoke.

"*You'll curse our family. You'll curse our bloodline.*" His voice echoes through the clouds, carried in the wind. Thomas cares less for his father in this moment than he did during his father's life—a casualty of causality. Thomas has always longed to become the patriarch with the power and inheritance to demand any portion, principle, or prospect in the United States. And with all his ambition coursing through his psyche, Thomas signals to his brother, running a finger across his neck and pointing to the fiery spout, knowing his brother has always been the better pitcher, or, at least, he is the better patsy for collateral damage.

"Here we go," Christopher, Jr. whispers as he rises from the edge of the grass and hurls the jug toward the ignited oil spout. The Sioux continue to dance and shout in their ritual, conjuring ghosts and praying to fire gods that certain ancestors appear in the flames. Since the oil spout sprang from the Earth, the Ghost Dance tribe has praised their gods and expressed thanks through song and ritual, never stopping, never softening the chants or slowing the dances for their fiery blessing. Some of the sharecroppers sit amongst the ritual, no doubt watching the women, while others sleep in the nearby huts and shacks—Will boy will take care of them. In total, the troops must eliminate about fifty men, women, and children before the Winnipers can enjoy the spoils.

Thomas and the militia watch the jug sail through the air, an unnoticed dove floating on invisible wings, concealing all its horror. Even with the pounding drums and stomping feet and clapping hands and swishing bodies and cocking guns, the world seems silent. A blessed child could be born in this moment, bathed in a sweet, smoky wind; everything, absolutely everything, feels so blissful before the fall. The jug dips into the center of the fire and shatters the ground within, igniting a firebomb of exploding glass, dirt, and rocks—an instant massacre.

"*Mihinga!*" The women wail as their bodies quickly rip to shreds; the drums stop and those still alive stare at the carnage, wondering what to do before filling the air with a new sound…screams, loud, unrelenting screams.

"Take aim!" Thomas orders while raising his rifle and turning to Sheriff Cobb. A Sioux boy runs from the inferno, hopping over Christopher, Jr. Thomas approaches the boy quickly, aiming with clairvoyant precision. "Stop right there!"

He fires a shot through the boy's chest and the boy's body drops immediately; the child will sleep forever, put to bed by a greedy reaper. Thomas grabs a .58 caliber bullet from a pouch on his hip and reloads the rifle while walking over his crouching brother.

"Glad you don't miss, baby brother," Christopher chides, watching two more children run from death to death; Thomas and the sheriff shoot them down with precision. Bodies burn betwixt the dead as the Sioux continue to fall; those still alive, fill the air with screams. The militia advances around the roaring fire spout, corpses lay scattered in a murderous mosaic.

Thomas and the militia continue to shoot and shoot and shoot; Thomas pauses for a moment to see William and his militia moving from hut to hut, invading, excavating, and eviscerating any life within. William and his militia consume like a wildfire, igniting every shack in their path, burning each home to the ground, and polluting the air with more screams. Thomas continues to shoot and kill the Sioux men, women, and children as William and his militia advance toward the center of the village.

"These Injuns are running too fast!" Thomas screams to William, trying to reload, aim, and shoot in one motion, but his father's Confederate-issue rifle jams, locking in place with a bullet stuck in the chamber. After realizing he only has time to aim for wound shots, Thomas straps the rifle over his shoulder, unholsters his father's revolver, and begins to fire upon fleeing legs and knees.

His shots drop more Sioux bodies to the ground, wiggling worthlessly, which doesn't warrant any remorse from their attackers; only woe mingles within their torment. Thomas takes a moment to enjoy the carnage while retrieving a handful of the .36 caliber bullets from his jacket pocket and loading six more into the revolver's chamber. He feels as though he has all the time in the world, not like during war. The Ghost Dance Sioux are mostly unarmed; they've lived in peace until now.

"That one's getting away!" William yells, aiming far in the distance for an elderly man, slinking away with a leg wound.

"I got him in my sights," Thomas adds, aiming true, remembering his service in the first Indian Wars. He would wait for days upon a perch.

∞

And when the enemy invaded, the murderers looked in mirrors, brothers shooting brothers. Initially, war bothered him, killing brown men who looked so familiar, but over time, the violence satiated a deeper desire for self-importance. His head count became a mating call.

∞

Tonight's conquest feels surprisingly similar; Thomas squeezes the revolver's trigger with familiarity and pierces the old Sioux man through the skull. The man wilts clumsily, knees folding inward and his back slumping to the ground, gunned down as he still tries to escape. His limbs shake, twitch, and then stop moving entirely.

Thomas scours over the slaughter, Sioux bodies burned and bullet-riddled, lying in desperate escape paths from the once lively dancing circle. Their ignited shacks crumble around the smoky village. The screams turn to whimpers and even those begin to fade within the howling winds. Thomas sees a dying Sioux woman, crawling from her burning, collapsing wooden shack and he takes a step toward her while his brother continues to delight in these war games.

"Whew, this is more exciting than when I crashed my Motorwagen on Winding Way!" Christopher, Jr. notes, firing at a nearby oil patch, igniting another blaze that leads to the spouting fire within the Sioux village. The celebration and the people have surrendered to the force of madmen seeking to profit from their blessing. "There ain't too many more of 'em left, Thomas! We might be home by midnight!"

"We still have more work to do…have to put the fire out!" Thomas yells back to his brother, walking closer to the woman who still crawls from her hut. She drags her crushed body with her arms, grimacing and grunting through each pull and pant. Thomas smiles at her pain, raises his head to the moon, and guesses the time could be around ten o'clock. Indeed, he has enough time to finish his hostile takeover and return home to celebrate the New Year with his pregnant wife.

Within this murderous moment, blood coating his world, he still finds time to think of Ruby, the same as he did during battle; he never forgot his courtship. Her image would flash before his eyes, and he would remember her smell, only briefly, before coming back to reality and seeing his prey, his kill, the enemy. Whether Sioux, Apache, or any other kind of Injun, they remain the same to him—objects to destroy for glory. Thomas raises his revolver and aims at the wounded woman, struggling and straining to lift and carry her crippled body another inch further from the fires which burn everywhere—she is unable to see the inevitable. Thomas cocks the revolver, sliding a bullet into the barrel, and he aims true.

"Don't move. It's over now."

"Please…" the Sioux woman begs, frozen on the edge of her burning shack. "Don't, Mista Winnie-purr! My husband…he wurk…for you!"

Before Thomas can respond, a wounded, badly burned, Negro sharecropper appears in the doorway of the collapsing shack holding a small pistol; he fires one shot that misses Thomas, but, from behind, Thomas can hear a muffled scream. He turns to see his brother fall to his knees from a bullet wound through his neck.

"No! Christopher!" Thomas shouts, turning back to the man who then fires another shot that strikes Thomas's shoulder and passes through his back. The impact hurls his body backwards and he stumbles onto his rear and the butt of his rifle. He uses his left hand to steady his fall while his right hand still clutches his revolver. Thomas raises the weapon and fires a shot through the Negro's chest; the wounded sharecropper places his hand over his heart and falls backward into his burning home. The weary wooden foundation crumbles underneath him and the roof's charred, oak planks fall on top of him as his wife shrieks from the ground just beyond the porch. Thomas struggles to his feet and aims his revolver at the crippled, Sioux woman.

"*Mihinga! Minhinga! Omikaya! Omikaya!* Please…help!" She begs, her fear freezing her between her dead husband and her own death, uncertain which horror is worse. "Please…don't…don't…don't kill me!"

"Your nigger husband killed my brother," Thomas growls as he stalks over the Sioux woman, venom seething through his teeth. "You had no business race-mixing with his kind anyway…"

"Please don't, Mista Winnie-purr! I wurk fer you before I get pregnant! She's a baby girl…I know!" The desperate, Sioux woman frantically grasps her barely protruding stomach. She wears a bone choker with the skull of a rodent in the middle, symbolizing her status as a sorceress. Having been in the midst of a ghost dance ritual, she still wears her bone choker and her beaded firegod bracelet. Her body fills with terror and torment while lying near her husband's corpse, as her dying family drowns within burning ash, charred wood, and blood-soaked dirt. She is pathetic and weak in the eyes of a tyrant. "I no cause no trouble! Let me live for my baby! You already kill everyone!"

"Not everyone." Thomas quips without hesitation, a murderer with too many sins; he adjusts his father's revolver within his grasp and aims toward her heart.

"Then I curse you…and your family! In the name of all who have died here, tonight!" The Sioux sorceress yells, removing the firegod bracelet from her wrist, raising it in front of her, and beginning an incantation. "You kill me and take our land, you and your family will never be happy until you die and your family leaves this land! You may gain wealth but you never be happy. Your pregnant wife, she pregnant, right? Your family regret what you have done here tonight!"

"Every family has problems," Thomas laughs, pausing in the moonlight, thinking again of his brother, his wife, and their coming child.

"No, *shey sheem, shey sheem,* your seed will have many burdens, too. Your baby, your wife…if you kill me…she have my baby, too…yes, *Gonawey, Gonawey sheem*…your wife…all the mothers of your children…have painful labor, they have two babies…but…one child have my blood…the blood of those you killed here, tonight…yes…*Gonawey, Gonawey sheem…*"

The badly burnt Sioux sorceress pauses during her spell, desperate to squeeze every ounce of vengeance through each breath while she lies meagerly in the mud. Hearing her rant, several riflemen crowd around Thomas and laugh at the spectacle, waiting for their leader to put this lunatic squaw out of her misery. Her sacrifice has led her to a sinister plot, a fortuitous narrative formed from the spirit of her slain tribe.

"I curse your family, Win-per; I curse your blood and your gun and your…"

Thomas squeezes the revolver's trigger and shoots her clean through the heart, caving her chest inward and choking her speech; her arms give way and she falls headfirst into the murderous muck beneath her. She dies while murmuring into the grime; her body shivering in the cold, night air, a few feet from her Negro husband—two shades of brown with matching kill shots.

The militiamen rejoice at the sight and scatter to collect any and all available rewards from around the burning village. The sorceress's final words dissolve amongst the nightmare as the night air sporadically fills with sharp screams and smoldering shacks. There are still some lastingly wretched victims to attend to before the night's work is done.

For the next hour, the ecstatic men prepare to cap the spouting oil fire while continuing to finish the slaughter, firing upon anything that moves or groans within target range. Thomas doesn't venture near Christopher's corpse which lies lonely amongst the massacred Sioux—a ghostly white mass amongst the brown skin and dirt. Midway through his cleanup duties, Thomas hears hooves galloping in the distance; the sound echoes over the open Dakota plains and reverberates under the dry soil, while the corpses quiver on the surface of the burning village.

"Who's that?" William Bethune yells from across the village, drawing his rifle and running to Thomas's right side. The two point their weapons toward the approaching rider barreling through the darkness. "Are you expecting more help?"

"No, just you," Thomas answers quickly, raising his eyebrows, tilting his head to the right, and inspecting William's behavior with a king's suspicions. "You didn't make any other deals, did you?"

"Of course not, but...I did consider killing you and taking the land for myself."

"Mista Winniper!" the rider yells from ahead. "Mista Winniper!"

"Hold your fire." Thomas commands while pausing, putting his ear to the sky, and raising his head over the sounds of the dying, the wounded, and the insatiable, murder-hungry militiamen as they transition the remaining Sioux from life to death.

"Mista Winniper! Mista Winniper" The horseback rider wails loudly while he rumbles into the village atop one of the Winnipers' black stallions.

"It sounds like Carl." Thomas narrows his eyes and walks closer to receive the rider, Carl Potter, the Winnipers' local messenger boy. He's only good for a day-long journey, anytime longer without supervision and he turns to moonshine or any available intoxicant. He is a sullen, twelve-year-old immigrant from Württemberg, Germany; his father died in battle while fighting alongside Thomas and Christopher, Jr.

∞

36

The brothers convinced their old man to hire Little Potter and bring him to the Winniper Family Estate. Christopher, Sr. was so enthralled with Thomas's growing military reputation that he welcomed the boy among his family without any further consideration. The old man's service in the Confederacy embarrassed him, not because he advocated slavery or secession, but because they lost. Both shame and fear made his memories bitter and he sought a new name and identity in the Dakotas.

Thomas and Christopher, Jr. had ambitions of improving the family's war record and becoming heroes in the Indian Wars, but only Thomas proved worth the merit in battle. He could shoot and lead better than his older brother, and he understood the concept of conquest. He commanded a small regiment throughout much of America's Westward Expansion into the Dakotas, working with local militias, ex-unionmen, and even an occasional Confederate relic.

∞

Throughout his childhood, Carl has watched the Winnipers increase their wealth and property claims; their empire has risen around him; yet, still only twelve, he, like most people his age, questions his future, uncertain if his steps along *these* pathways are the wisest. He sees himself as a servant, and he fears any alternative.

"Sir! Sir!" he screams, before noticing the fiery carnage, the burning bodies, and the random gunshots still popping off around the village. "My Jesus, what happened here?"

"Carl, get on with it!" Thomas demands furiously, grabbing the horse's reins and turning Carl away from the village's interior where the oil fire still blazes amidst the forsaken dance circle.

"You have to come quick, sir!" Carl yells, glancing frenziedly around the massacre. "Miss Ruby having the baby! Her water broke and Doc Morton on the way!"

"But...but...she's not due for weeks." Thomas stammers in shock before turning his head and looking back at the dead Sioux sorceress who cursed him. Her eyes are still open, staring into the dirt where her family died. He casts aside any notion of guilt and turns back toward Carl. He steps to the side of the horse, but again, he looks back over the dead bodies and thinks of reloading one more time to take care of a shivering child in the distance. No remorse, no resentment, he only sees obstacles in the way of his goals, but his wife, his family, and his son are central keys to achieving his dreams for their empire.

"Sir, where is Master Christopher?" Carl asks fearfully, horrified by the sights and screams as every few seconds a militiaman aims and shoots another would-be survivor. The tall burning oil stack still roars in the center of the village, but there is no more dancing, no more joy. "I still can't drive the car, sir; and Johnnie, he helpin' the misses. Sir, didn't your brother come with you, tonight?"

"He's around, now move back," Thomas orders roughly, pushing Carl back on the tall horse and hopping upon the saddle in front of his servant. He grasps the reins tightly and scans over his newly acquired land once more. He ignores the patches of murdered browns and imagines the oil refinery that he will build pumping money from the oil fire. He smiles in triumph and pulls the reins quickly. "Yah!"

Thomas kicks the horse upon both sides and the stallion bolts from the burning shacks, ascending smoke, and smoldering bodies. They race up the solitary path normally used for the sharecropper truck on the commute to the Winnipers' farm, riding away from the woods.

The stallion storms thunderously through the beaten dirt path, the Dakota oak trees hanging over their heads and the moon shining above. In the distance, the church bell begins to ring loudly, signaling midnight; Thomas knows he has secured the land but he fears the cost.

His child is on the way and he hopes to have a son and enjoy a moment of happiness within a night of gloom. He thinks nothing more about the curse; he does not see the night clouds circling ahead. Steering the horse through the Winnipers' open property, Thomas turns down the massive entrance toward the family's mansion and Carl holds on tightly.

Passing their eastern fields and rows of bushes, Thomas barrels the horse through the driveway until he reaches the front of the Winnipers' mansion, where Johnnie runs down the steps toward them. Thomas hears his wife scream from their master bedroom window and he dismounts the horse in stride.

"Godspeed, sir!" Carl calls from behind as Thomas frantically runs past Johnnie, hurrying up the front steps, opening the door, and rushing into his home.

"Johnnie, put that horse back in the stable!" Thomas shouts, dropping his rifle and removing his jacket and pouch while climbing the steps. Hearing his voice, Violet opens the door to the master bedroom and approaches Mr. Winniper with a deeply concerned look on her face.

"She very sick, Mr. Winniper." Violet murmurs, holding her arms out over her stomach. "Belly boom boom. Very big now."

"Get out of my way," Thomas growls, covered in Sioux blood, neither caring nor concerned whether Johnnie told her the plot to eliminate her village. He saved their family and sacrificed her people to the Winniper family's dynasty.

"Sir, your coat...stains all over. Look like blood." Violet mentions, pointing her finger at the deep red splotches on Thomas's coat as he storms past her. No doubt, she's more concerned about cleaning the stains from his coat than the origin; though if she only knew...she may be thankful and destroyed in the same moment.

Thomas enters the master bedroom where Dr. Morten leans over Ruby while she cries in bed, laying upon pillows and blankets, sweating on the sheets, and drenching the fabric into a soggy mess. Rita stands next to the bed, pacing frantically.

"I don't know what happened," She stammers, fear running over her forehead in wrinkles. "She was fine earlier, I-I didn't give her nothing to drink. I swear."

"Violet!" Thomas calls over his shoulder, ignoring Rita completely. He forgets that she is now a widow. Violet hurries into the room behind him, standing at attention in the doorway. "Get more towels, some cold water..."

"Make that hot water, sir!" Doc Morten demands, squeezing his palms together before scratching his head.

"Right...get hot water, towels, and tell Johnnie to bring the crib from downstairs."

"Yes, sir," Violet responds quickly and runs toward her duties. Thomas removes his bloodied coat, throws it to the floor, and strides to Ruby's side. She lies on her back in pain, exhausted and filled with fear. Her eyes dart around the bedroom and she struggles to speak when she looks at him. He takes his wife's hand slowly, softly, in sharp contrast to the coward who killed children only moments ago—the violent hypocrite.

"Ruby..."

"I-It h-h-h-hurts, Thomas…" She shakes violently, and he reaches around her back and holds her shivering body in his arms. "Something else is in me…something's wrong…"

"You'll be okay. Just breathe…" He tries to comfort her, rocking her in his arms "Doc, how bad is it?"

"I-I don't know," Doc Morten stutters, adjusting his glasses and looking over Mrs. Winniper. "I've never seen anything like it."

"What do you mean?" Thomas asks, wiping his wife's pale face, her breathing exasperated and flushed.

"Well…her stomach…has grown considerably in the past hour. I…" Doc hesitates and Ruby shrieks in pain.

"Ah, the baby's coming!" She yells, her throat growing raspy. "I…I can't…"

"Sh, rest yourself. Don't worry. I'm here now. Violet!" Thomas yells, straining his neck to throw his voice out the door and down the hallway. He then stares at Rita across the bed. "Make yourself useful, woman! Get some water!"

"There's water on the nightstand," Ruby gasps, clenching her throat. Rita runs around the bed, retrieves the pitcher of water, and fills a clean glass from the nightstand. She then hands the glass to Thomas and takes a moment to hold his attention.

"Thomas, where is Christopher?"

"Um…he had to stay behind…and…uh…*clean up*. Here, Ruby, drink." Thomas answers Rita with a quick lie and turns away toward his wife. He doesn't want to address his brother's death and distract himself from his child's birth; he tilts the glass with his right hand and lifts Ruby's head with his left hand. She struggles to lift her arms, trying to grasp the glass and help guide the water to her lips. She manages one solitary sip, wetting the tip of her tongue but she continues to shake, seizing in his arms; he feels her spine snapping underneath him.

"I-I-I can't t-t-take this, Thomas. I…I think I'm d-dying," Ruby stammers feverishly, unsure of her words, questioning her mortality. Her body has somehow been betrayed in the past hours. "I-I-I th-th-think I…I'm s-s-s-seeing g-g-g-ghosts."

"Listen, you'll pull through. Think about the baby." Thomas places the glass on the nightstand and holds his wife in his arms; the hero is still in costume. "Remember you wrestled that bull down in Nashville before we moved west? All those Southern boys were too scared, but you, you've always been strong, Ruby."

"But, I-I...I'm scared, Thomas," Ruby weeps openly, drenching her cheeks, hoping to hold back some of her desperation, but the dam breaks. "I feel...cold...*evil* spirits...all around me. Don't y-y-you s-s-see th-th-them?"

Ruby screams violently, and her body begins to shake in Thomas's grasp. Her stomach does feel...*larger*; he places his arms around her waist, trying to calm her. His pregnant wife, the bucking bronco, seizes in her husband's arms as her face stretches with torment, her pain overcoming her voice.

"Doc, what's happening?"

"She's having very heavy contractions, Mr. Winniper. Her stomach is under a tremendous amount of pressure." Doc relays matter-of-factly, still more concerned with her bulging stomach while he wipes his glasses. "She may have eaten or drank something to induce labor. She should give birth any minute."

"She didn't drink anything, I swear."

"Rita, shut up! No one's talking to you! Doc, Ruby knows better. She didn't drink anything. She wasn't due for weeks."

"I know, Mr. Winniper. I checked her yesterday," Doc continues, walking towards Ruby's legs and spreading them in the center of the bed. Ruby gasps at his brashness but she continues to wince in agony. "Tonight, her stomach is so big...it looks like she giving birth to twins. She's completely dilated, effaced at roughly...midnight, probably after."

"But why is she in so much pain? What happened to her stomach?" Thomas asks as Violet enters the bedroom carrying towels and another pitcher of water; Johnnie follows his wife with a white, wooden crib, a Winniper heirloom where Thomas, Christopher, and their father once slept.

"Well...I can't rightly say, Mr. Winniper..." Doc Morten begins, interrupted momentarily by Ruby's screams. "Sometimes the Good Lord just wants the baby to come early. Any disturbance can trigger an early delivery. Do you know of anything that may have happened in the past few hours? Was your wife upset about anything?"

"Ah, no! Stop talking about me like I'm not in the room!" Ruby screams, clutching her husband's arms as Doc Morten continues to inspect her. Thomas searches around the room for any suspicious eyes as Rita, Violet, and Johnnie watch in silent horror. Ruby's cries bring him back to the trauma at hand. "Doc, pull this baby out, please!"

"Almost, dear," Doc encourages. "Push a little more; the baby's got to breach the head and shoulders."

"I hope you're happy, Thomas!" Ruby snarls, striking her husband in the shoulder. "You wanted a son so bad! You did this to me!"

"You don't mean that, Ruby." Thomas pleads with his wife, attempting to comfort and distract, cradling her upper body while Doc Morten attends to her lower half. "You wanted a child, too. You'll be fine, sweetheart. Everything will be perfect. We got the Injuns' land tonight, honey. We'll have everything we want."

"I want this pain to end! God, why?" Ruby yells, opening her eyes widely to her husband before clenching her face in pain. "Doc, please! Please, help me!"

"Just keep pushing. The head is out," Doc explains calmly. "Mr. Winniper, please try to keep your wife calm."

"*Keep me calm?*" Ruby repeats, growing even redder in the face, filled with anger. "I'm not a child! I'm in pain! And you're not helping!"

"Honey, please, try to…" Thomas begins, but his wife screams wildly in his ear, abusing the moment, forgetting the demure woman that she was earlier in the evening, and exorcising every ounce of pent-up aggression.

"I can't take this! Please, Doc!" Ruby screams, beginning to shake again in her husband's arms, clenching his biceps in her grasps; her body tenses and flexes in spasms. "Pull it out!"

"We can't force the process," Doc urges, still looking between Ruby's propped up legs. "There could be considerable damage. Let nature take its course. I see the chin and a bit of the neck!"

"God, why?" Ruby asks again, staring aimlessly into the ceiling with darkening eyes. "What did I do to deserve this?"

"Ruby, calm down, you'll be fine." Rita encourages from the side of the bed.

"You're almost there. Push!" Doc urges emphatically and Ruby screams, pushing with all her might. She clenches her husband's shirt tightly before her body goes limp. "Yes, he's out! It's a boy!"

"Ruby, you did it!" Thomas exclaims, as Doc Morten treats the child, the boy beginning to cry. Thomas feels his heart flutter at the sound in a way that men never speak of; and he looks down to his wife as the angel who has delivered another blessing to the world. "Sweetheart, you did it! You're okay!"

"Wait…" Doc whispers and looks closely between Ruby's legs. "Violet, take the boy."

He continues to stare in amazement as he holds the baby over his shoulder. Violet gently grasps the newborn and cradles him against her left shoulder before slowly carrying him from the bed. Thomas nervously looks over the doctor's crazed expression.

"What is it?" Thomas asks, leaving his wife's side and moving around the bed to stand behind Doc Morten, Jr.

"I-I…" Doc stammers in disbelief, rubbing his forehead with his wrist, hoping to massage the confusion from his brain. "I…think there's…uh…another child. It's…it…uh…is breeching…feet first…" he announces finally, still stunned, seeing a dark brown foot beginning to peek through.

"*Feet first?*" Thomas repeats in similar shock, looking to his wife with instant suspicion, forgetting the curse, but she lays silent within her sweat and tears, limp and unconscious. "Ruby? Ruby, are you okay? Doc, what's wrong?"

"Sh-sh-she…she probably just fainted," Doc stutters, obviously overwhelmed by the sight between Ruby's legs. He exasperatedly moves back around the bed and grabs Ruby's wrist to check her pulse. "Her pulse is very weak…"

"She's not breathing." Thomas joins Doc Morten's side and holds his finger to her nose, feeling no air or sign of life. Rita, Violet, and Johnnie continue to watch quietly, crowding around the Winniper cradle, protecting the young Winniper son from all the death surrounding his birth. Thomas crouches down closer to his wife, remembering a similar stance when awaiting the Sioux slaughter; he holds his wife's head as delicately as he held the jug of glycerin and moonshine. "Ruby, wake up, please! You…you can't leave me! I have everything we could ever want! You have to wake up!"

"Mr. Winniper…" Doc drops Ruby's wrists and stares at Thomas, taking another moment to remove and rearrange his glasses. "Your wife…the child…what should I do?"

"What do you mean?"

"I…uh…I think there's another child on the way, sir. I can see the feet. It's odd…a miracle maybe, I've never seen anything like it…but your wife must've had twins all along." The doctor shakes his head confoundedly and motions over Ruby's stomach before returning his hand to her wrist. "Should I deliver the second child or treat your wife?"

"You can't do both?"

"If I treat your wife, then the child will likely die," Doc explains. "And even if I treat your wife, she may still die given the...complications. She was in an extraordinary amount of pain, sir."

"Treat my wife," Thomas demands, fearing the Sioux prophecy, surmising the other child is a girl, and believing one son is enough to carry a legacy. His wife could produce more sons; a daughter would only bring outsiders. He looks over his wife and for a moment he sees the dying Sioux sorceress at the edge of his revolver. "Ruby, please wake up."

"Step aside," Doc murmurs, angling Thomas away from the bed and moving closer to Ruby's chest. He places his palms over her heart and then pumps on her chest, trying to revive her. He places his ear to her mouth, hoping to hear any sign of movement in her throat cavity or lungs, but he hears none. "Come on, Mrs. Winniper. Violet, bring a wet towel!"

Violet takes a concerned look at the Winnipers' son in the family crib and rushes to grab a clean towel. She drips the towel into the pitcher of water near the bedside and hands it to Doc Morten. The doctor lays the towel on Ruby's forehead and resumes pumping her chest, if not for true effect than at least for the show.

"Wake up, Mrs. Winniper!" Doc Morten wails loudly with sweat forming over his eyebrows. Rising from the bed and standing behind Doc Morten, watching his dying, possibly already dead wife, Thomas hears murmurs and coos from the nearby crib. Becoming intrigued, he turns and walks over to see his heir amidst Rita and Johnnie. They remain silent, both in awe and obedience. Thomas looks inside the crib and his son looks into his father's eyes with the same eyes, and the two can see themselves in one another.

Thomas reaches into the crib and picks up his son; the boy cries sharply and Thomas continues to pat him, but the boy won't stop crying, noisily, painfully, even angrily, into his father's ear, just like his mother did moments ago. Thomas places the babe back into the crib and gazes at his son, who seems so innocent and so distant from everything his father has now become. Thomas feels a shrill up his spine and he eyes Rita and Johnnie for inquisition; seeing none, he turns back toward the true tragedy. He walks to the bed where Doc Morten still huddles over Ruby, checking her pulse without response. "She's gone, sir."

"What? That's all you can do?" Thomas asks, standing over Doc Morten threateningly, an instinct when a Winniper receives bad news. "You don't have any more…"

"Sir, sometimes…" Doc pauses, readjusting his glasses over his eyes and taking a moment to glance at Ruby. "Sometimes life has complications."

"But, you barely did anything, Doc!" Thomas broods while moving closer to the doctor and his dead wife and staring between the two. He doesn't know which problem to address first or what to do after; for the first time, life has overwhelmed the Winniper heir. "Surely, you have some gadgets in your bag! Send for someone else! Violet…"

"Sir, she's gone." Doc pats Ruby's still hand, moving away from the corpse, giving a free path between Ruby and her husband. "The pain was just too much. Only Jesus could bring her back."

"*Jesus?*" Thomas repeats, unable to consider the possibility, a murderer calling upon Christ, hoping to save a life; his hypocrisy becomes clear as he looks over his wife's body. "That Sioux squaw said…"

"But…" Doc begins, moving around the bed. "There's still time to save the other child."

"Yes…please do." Thomas sobs for a brief moment, wiping his eyes and wondering if Rita will think less of him for crying during this lapse in control. He's always concerned for his appearance, even in mourning. His newborn son continues to wail inside his crib, without end, a sign in the Winniper home that something is wrong. "Save the child if you can. The boy won't stop crying."

"That's common with newborns, especially twins. They've been together for seven or eight months; they don't like to be apart." Doc affirms with a hand wave, leaning back toward Ruby's legs. Thomas crouches over the bed next to her and cradles her body under his left arm, holding her right hand gently. She already looks like a ghost, if not from labor then death has applied its own shade. Doc Morten spreads her limp legs and applies pressure inside. "I can try tugging on the feet."

"Please be gentle, Doc," Thomas sobs softly with tears in his eyes, still caring more for his wife than another child. He drops her hand to wipe his eyes, looking over to Johnnie standing over the baby's crib. "What are you here for, Johnnie? Go back to the stable! I'll have Violet call you if you're needed!"

"Yes, sir," Johnnie answers quickly, exiting the bedroom in a hurry. He pauses briefly for a moment at the door, looking down at the floor. "I'm sorry for your loss, sir… and…uh, uh…congratulations on the son, sir."

"Violet, close the door behind him…and check on my son," Thomas orders and Violet closes the door behind Johnnie, taking no time to wave or say goodbye to her husband, obedient first to her master, her employer, her job. She moves over the crib where the Winnipers' son still cries loudly. Rita continues to stand next to the crib, amidst the melee, worried for her own husband, but believing that he will arrive soon.

Rita chooses to distract herself with her new nephew and she lifts him into her arms but he continues to howl. His head bobs around aimlessly, his eyes searching for solace he may never find, at least not in this mansion. She places the babe back into the crib, ever so softly, before raising her index finger to her left ear, rubbing the sore, beaten drum within, worn from the baby's shrill.

"I've got both feet…come on…come on…I see it's…it's a girl!" Doc Morten declares cheerfully, hoping to find a ray of light at the end of the tunnel. Slowly, he removes a brown Sioux baby tenderly from between Ruby's pale legs and holds her upside-down by her feet. "Here she is!"

"Be gentle, Doc," Thomas implores the doctor, still looking over his wife's dead face, wiping her drenched brow but unwilling to close her eyes. Doc Morten raises the child for a moment before cradling the babe gently and turning away from Thomas. The doctor still stares over the child in awe of her complexion. Thomas hears her soft coos, fragile and faint, and he strains his neck trying to see the baby. The doctor's bulky shoulders shroud the newborn in mystery and Thomas continues to move his head and neck trying to see his second born. "Hey, let me have a look! Do you think you she'll be okay?"

"Uh, well…I need to…uh, check…" Doc stammers, reaching for his bag and fumbling through the contents, "she's barely breathing."

"God, you took my wife," Thomas whispers, raising his head to the ceiling as his wife once did. Violet watches in silence as the doctor pumps his thumb on the babe's chest. "Please, God save…"

"She's a little darker than I'd expect." Doc observes, pausing his efforts and eyeing the child more closely. "A lot darker, really."

"What do you mean?"

"Well…" Doc tilts his head, "she looks…uh…*like a Sioux.*"

"What? *'A Sioux'?*" Thomas repeats, still unwilling to believe the Sioux sorceress's curse, after the clear evidence lies dead in his arms. He rises from her side to walk around the bed as Rita moves closer out of curiosity. They both stand over Doc Morten's shoulders to behold the work of God. In his arms, the doctor cradles a newborn, bright-eyed baby girl, brown olive skin coated lightly in drying blood and placenta, black hair with soft curls, little strands of heaven. She is beautiful, innocent, but both Thomas and Rita stare in horror at a dark brown Sioux girl born as if conceived by two Sioux natives.

Thomas's eyes widen and his face fills with wonder, shock, and anger. The Sioux sorceress's words flash through his mind and his body tenses in rigor mortis rivaling his dead wife. He absorbs the tragic carnage. He knows the curse is real. His wife lies dead in their master bedroom, their newborn son cries uncontrollably, and his doctor holds a cooing, colored baby, born from the same mother as his white son. "Doc, please, tell me, *how is this possible?'*

"Well, I didn't want to presume, sir," Doc begins, rolling his eyes toward Ruby and momentarily accusing the deceased as he looks between the mother and child. "But sometimes a woman has needs outside the home…"

"What are you trying to say, Doc?" Thomas interrupts, grabbing Doc Morten roughly by the back of his shirt collar even while he cradles the baby. "Are you suggesting my wife, *my wife*, was unfaithful?"

"No, no, sir! Please don't take offense." Doc pleads, placing the newborn baby girl into Rita's hands and standing to face Thomas. "It's just…sometimes two men can impregnate a woman but I've never seen anything like this. From your wife's symptoms before…and now a white boy and an Injun girl, born to the same mother. It's…it's…it's either infidelity or, like I said before, it's a miracle."

"How dare you, Doc? *A miracle?* You call *this* a miracle? My wife is dead!" Thomas growls while pointing at Ruby's lifeless body and walking toward Rita. He observes the Sioux baby girl, still cooing softly in Rita's arms, and he remembers the curse, the dying pregnant woman's last words. Her baby girl now whimpers in the arms of the wife of the man her husband killed—is this pure vengeance or pure justice? The baby yawns and wipes her eyes with her small hand and Thomas twists his face in a deadly scowl, recalling his brother drop to the ground, choking to death from a wound to his throat. This baby represents that pain; his sins are sown into her skin. "She's a curse. One of her kind did this to us. I want it gone."

"Well, sir, I think…"

"I don't pay you to think, Doc." Thomas interrupts, placing his hand on Doc Morten's shoulder and pulling him away from the scene. The two men pass Violet and his newborn son, who still wails in his cradle. "You're no longer needed. I don't want to hear any more about it. "

"But, Mr. Winniper…" Doc begins to protest, trying to regain his leverage against Thomas's forceful push. The Sioux baby girl begins to cry in Rita's arms, hearing her brother, both fearing for their futures if separated. "She's a living being, an innocent…"

"My wife was innocent."

"Sir, please don't do this!" Doc continues to fret, stepping from side-to-side and stealing glances at Rita and the Sioux baby girl. "Rita, I can find a home for her! No one has to know!"

"Doc, I'm asking you nicely to leave. It's my child. I'll do what I want with it." Thomas continues to force Doc Morten from the bedroom, pushing the doctor when momentum alone isn't enough to carry him away. "Have your wife send me a bill tomorrow and add a tip for your discretion. I have big plans for you and for this town, *Doctor* Morten, and I don't want them interrupted…*by anything.* Do you understand?"

"Yes, Mr. Winniper." Doc Morten concedes, hearing all the potential points of profit and knowing the Winniper money may soon be the strongest currency in the nascent Dakotas. Still a duty calls in his mind and he leans against the doorway once more to catch a glimpse of the lamb before the slaughter, envisioning a horrible fate. "But…"

"No 'buts', Doc. Wait downstairs and I'll have Johnnie boy give you a lift back home when he's done." Thomas orders sharply, ushering Doc Morten out of the bedroom. "Violet, close the door behind the good doctor."

"What about your wife?" Doc protests as Violet holds the door open for him.

"Ruby's with Jesus, Doc. Like you said, only he can save her now." Thomas affirms, turning away from the doctor and walking toward his wife. "I'll have her portrait made…and she'll have a plot in the family grave…and one day, I'll join her."

"*And the child?*" the doctor asks, hoping for inclusion, hoping for the same solace as the newborn boy in a lonely crib. Both still try to steal one last glance at the Sioux baby girl fidgeting and squirming in Rita's arms. Both her brother and Doctor Morten fear Thomas's next steps—her first and last moments of life seem near. "What will you do with her?"

Thomas pauses, staring from his wife, to his newborn son and daughter, to Rita and Violet, and finally resting on the doctor. For the first time, Thomas sees himself in the doctor's glasses; his eyes are swollen from crying more tears than he ever thought a man should cry but he never imagined this level of despair and joy mixed into one night. All the triumphs and tragedy burn around him like a Sioux village in an oil fire. "I'll do anything to protect my family, Doc. Now, you have…a goodnight."

"G-g-goodnight, sir." Doc Morten stammers, tilting his hat to the man who holds the key to future fortune. "I'm terribly sorry I couldn't do more."

"Thank you, Doc. Go home to your wife and son." Thomas sighs, walking toward Rita and taking his Sioux daughter into his arms, the baby cooing happily for a moment in her father's arms, unknowing the wolf will bite. "And remember, not a word about this…not even to your wife. I know she's a gossip. If I hear one word, you and her, and your son, well…"

"I understand, sir."

"Goodnight."

"Goodnight." Doc repeats, patting his left leg to spark his feet into action. He begins shuffling from the doorway, leaving the master bedroom in silence and shame. Rita and Violet stare at Thomas as he holds his wide-eyed daughter.

Thomas walks through the room to where his son cries in the Winniper family crib, the noise is almost deafening. When Thomas stands over his son so that the son may see his twin sister, the boy stops crying and stares at his brown mirror image in his father's arms. Thomas looks back and forth between the Sioux baby girl and his now cooing, doe-eyed son, and he can see the resemblance. They are two of a kind, linked from birth; they smile the same, coo the same, they are the same. They are both his children, both Winnipers. He knows he could raise his daughter if he willed it so, but, he thinks of the scandal, the hardship, and the impossibility. He turns to Violet, stretching his daughter away from his chest.

"Take this to the haystack inside the barn…tell Johnnie to burn it." Thomas commands, watching Violet's eyes widen as she looks over the newborn child. "And you make sure he does it. I've killed enough of *your people* tonight. Tell Johnnie, if he doesn't do it, his Injun wife won't be able to bury her kin…she'll be dead with them."

"Please don't, sir. I-I'll do as you say." Violet bows obediently and takes the Sioux babe from her master's arms. Thomas's son begins to cry furiously within his crib, and Thomas stares blankly at his heir while Violet creeps toward the bedroom door. She pauses and turns once more, her face welling with tears, but Thomas shoos her away with his hand.

"Hurry, and don't come back until it's done. Rita, you go find Carl." Thomas barks more orders while turning away from his sister-in-law, walking to the bedroom dresser, and hurriedly searching for a cigar within one of the many drawers. "Carl will take you to where Christopher is. Tell him to take you both home after."

"Yes, Thomas," Rita responds softly, completely forgetting her previous insolence with his brother and behaving under a domineering force. She wilts to his power, unknowing how he betrays her emotions. He could tell her that she is a widow, but he is so fixated upon his own mischief that he has no room to care. She looks back into the master bedroom, almost daring to speak but she relents, swallowing whatever words she dreamed to muster before exiting the room.

The Winnipers' son still cries in his crib, his mother dead in her bed, and his father clutches his shoulder wound in his right hand as he removes and lights a long cigar with a match in his left hand. Smoking a cigar after the birth of a son is a father's right, as the boy will learn soon enough.

Christopher, Sr. often recounted the story of smoking a cigar after each son's birth. Naturally, Christopher, Jr. and Thomas dreamed of doing the same, finding a woman that they loved maybe not as much as their father loved their mother, but just enough to procreate yet not enough to respect.

∞

The goal has always been to bear sons who grow to honor the Winniper name and carry the family legacy beyond their father's dreams.

Thomas Winniper, Sr. inhales the fantasy that he was never meant to realize; the smoke billows from his lips, and he feels all the regret his father's ghost warned him to avoid. Inside the barn, Johnnie burns a heap of chicken bones wrapped in wool cloth while Violet creeps away to a wooden shed in the west end of the estate and stashes the Sioux infant inside before returning to the mansion. Staring at his dead wife and hearing Thomas, Jr. wail incessantly, Thomas, Sr. knows that he has created a personal hell. The future that he orchestrated has now trapped him in a circumstance that he cannot control. How can his family build a legacy if each birth brings a twin Sioux? One white son must suffice and any Sioux children that come from the Winniper bloodline must be eliminated in secrecy.

"We've got a lot of work to do, boy. This is no time for tears…men must be strong." He puffs emphatically, his eyes turning red in the thick smoke as he strolls over the crib and looks down upon his crying son, unknowing how to console his heir, unwilling to pick up his own child. He simply stokes his cigar while standing over his son. "You're my son, Thomas Winniper, Jr. and one day, you will be the king of my empire and everyone in the world will know the name…Winniper."

JANUARY 1946

Sunday	Monday	Tuesday	Wednesday	Thursday	Friday	Saturday
		1 ★	2	3	4	5
6	7	8	9	10	11	12
13	14	15	16	17	18	19
20	21	22	23	24	25	26
27	28	29	30	31		

Tuesday, January 1, 1946

Teresa Winniper-Townsend-Kane-Bethune

I see rivers and oceans, or is it black gold?
I hear justice and freedom, or is it control?
And I smell souls in the stratosphere, or are we alone?
And I don't know how we've gotten here,
Or is it our home?
Welcome to Winniper County,
Where women are tamed
Where secrets remain chained
To minds seeking claim or fame
With women's words treated as foreign and absurd,
Given the choice to speak, but never to be heard.

Teresa Winniper-Townsend-Kane-Bethune broods in her living room as she questions both her third husband, Kenneth Bethune, Jr., or simply, Kenny, and her decision to wed him, a young American loafer. All her emerging doubts stem from his latest mistake: he forgot the evening bread, again.

∞

When Teresa was a child, her father always ensured that she and her brother enjoyed fresh bread with dinner. Her father, Thomas "Papa" Winniper, Jr., son of the Midwestern oil pioneer, Thomas Winniper, Sr., and grandson of the bread king of South Dakota, Christopher Winniper, Sr., was born on the inaugural day of Winniper County when his father defeated the Sioux uprising, seized their land, and established the Winniper family's oil empire.

As he learned of his father and grandfather's legacy, Thomas Winniper, Jr. grew into his own patriarchal model and became "Papa" Winniper, an ode to all values and principles of Winniper masculinity and fatherhood. Teresa and her brother, Thomas III, adored their Papa but they also grew accustomed to his many demands.

∞

Papa Winniper has halted an entire dinner party until the help finished baking a fresh loaf from the Winniper family's wheat harvest. The family and guests sometimes growl under their breaths but they never protest too loudly. Papa Winniper has always been, in fact, a boy, an heir, a gentleman with much power whose social grace has often been assumed in his family lineage.

Now, Teresa's convinced that if she and Kenny ever find time to entertain a house-warming at their modest two-story home, their guests will gossip about the declining civility in the Winniper bloodline.

Refusing to live at the Winniper Family Estate, Teresa and Kenny have moved their family to a quaint burb within Winniper County, still living close to her father's wealth, amassed over three generations of Winniper male enterprise. Although Teresa has grown to despise her family's money and the secretive stipulations surrounding her pregnancies, she still believes in family.

∞

A fool who sought some security, she rushed into two marriages and bore twins within each marriage. Her mother stashed her Sioux newborns in secret with a family friend while Teresa raised her white babies with their respective fathers—until the music stopped.

When she left her second husband for Kenny, she hoped his youth would bring her true harmony. She prayed that Kenny's innocence, young and dumb, could wash her family's sins away. It did not. His youth became a crutch. She merely asked him to bring a few items from the market and he couldn't even remember to do that.

∞

She suspects that he purposefully forgot. Kenny has become an alcoholic, addicted to her never-ending supply of financing. Like a jack of all vices, he has acquired habit after habit, fixation after fixation, from cars to gambling.

∞

Once, Teresa and Kenny took a Cognac-and-cocaine-filled trip to Monte Carlo, leaving the children, the ones she can acknowledge and raise in public, with her parents at the Winniper Family Estate. Papa Winniper enjoyed the time, indoctrinating his grandchildren into the Winniper way of life, power, and privilege while the May-December couple travelled in a private jet and found their way to the crap tables soon enough.

Kenny blew through their entire cash stock and all her bond notes the first night, figuring the roulette wheel would eventually land on *Red 23*. It did not. Teresa soon became a revolving door, passing from the bank to the casinos on an endless circular conveyor, supplying Kenny's fix as he bet and rolled, cursing every unlucky outcome. Kenny only realized his mistake after the incident, unaware of just how heavily his greedy blunder would affect their marriage.

∞

Both born under ladders, it would seem, Teresa now doubts Kenny and their modern marriage, a powerful, thirty-five-year-old matriarch and an eighteen-year-old playboy. The same nagging, self-destructive questions creep into her mind: *Why me? Why him? Why anything?* Walking through their home, Teresa ponders her existence as if she were standing on a limb, not knowing if she'll jump or if she'll reach for a branch to save herself. She assumes that God truly wants to drive man wild with the things he does not know, and she looks through her quaint home, past her husband, over to her daughters Christina and June.

The sisters pillage through a large closet as the family's maid fumbles over towels and blankets, helping the girls prepare for an afternoon swim and picnic at the Winniper Country Club.

∞

Teresa kept Cleotha as a provision from the settlement of her second divorce, a symbol of suburban success.

∞

The Negro maid lives on the third floor without much care for a private life. She cooks the meals, cleans every room, prepares the children for school, and performs all the traditional motherly duties, assisting Teresa as an adjunct to her matriarchy.

Forced to accept the pressure of suburban appearances, Teresa feels the need for perceived perfection, valuing the family moments that she never experienced as a child at the Winniper Family Estate. Now, she fills her life with the essential compassion and unconditional care that was once denied to her. These needs overpower her very being, consuming an already weakened consciousness. She is the Winniper daughter with more invested in her meaningless marriages than any career or hobby; the circumstances have denied her the life that would allow her to accept, acknowledge, and raise both her Sioux and white children.

∞

When she was a late teen, Teresa tried to appease her father, allowing him to choose her first husband—a submission essential for the perfect Winniper woman. As an ambitious importer-exporter, Ralph Townsend ingratiated himself with Papa Winniper during business trips to Dubai and the Far East. Over the years, he helped the Winniper tycoon develop oil recruits in foreign lands and he established partners in Third World huts and shacks, claiming to *bring industry abroad*. As Teresa aged and Papa Winniper sought a suitable groom for his only daughter, Ralph became an adequate candidate, a discrete dependent willing to keep the family secrets while expanding the Winnipers' reach across the world. On paper, Ralph was the perfect son-in-law.

Papa Winniper planned and promoted the marriage as if it were a concert; guest invitations and press releases dispersed around the edges of the western region, the Dakota king's daughter marries a potential oil heir—rich people getting even richer. Ralph tried his best to convince Teresa that his motives were genuine, based in romance and not finance. He feigned interest in flowers instead of future stocks, cars instead of commerce, and homes instead of heuristics. Ralph's efforts evolved to define his personality, so she never believed him and she never enjoyed his comforts.

Following the birth of her first pair of twins, when she and her mother began their deception to save her Sioux child, Teresa still felt like a monkey stuck inside a cage. No matter where she went inside Winniper County, she would notice onlookers passing by and she imagined them mocking her social captivity. Even if these slights were only figments of her imagination, the ridicule was still real inside her psyche. After giving birth to three pairs of twins, Teresa has lost control of her anxiety, knowing the secrets she must maintain in order to protect the Sioux children she may never know.

∞

"I'm going to the market for bread!" Teresa announces loudly through the house, quickly grabbing the keys to her father's old, blue Spoister, remembering how she charmed Papa Winniper so that he willingly gave her the broken-down vehicle. Teresa then charmed Thomas III so that her brother fixed the car without cost or trifle. Emerging into womanhood, she learned how to manipulate a man with batted eyelashes and inflated trills in her voice; she spun the men closest to her into a web necessary for any sense of domestic control. Regardless, she feels empty, unwilling to relent the larger control in her marriages to receive any number of cars or material goods. For Teresa, life means more than things; still, things make her feel better. "I'll just get a Marley loaf and be right back!"

"Terri, wait!" Kenny calls from down the hallway, making his way toward his wife at the door. "I'm sorry I forgot to go to the market. My Ma' came by earlier with a problem and I...uh...uh..."

He stands close to her, rubbing her arms and Teresa smiles brightly, smelling bourbon seeping from his skin and thinking her husband is most attractive when he apologizes. His eyebrows stretch to the sides of his forehead and his eyes widen, searching pitifully for reassurance that the world doesn't hate him.

"It's okay, sweetheart." Teresa calms Kenny's worried look by placing her hand on his cheek. She is now a mother of seven. "I know you have a lot on your mind."

"I do…" Kenny whimpers, "…it's been hard…*knowing*."

"I know, dear." Teresa continues to stare into her husband's eyes, seeing another child needing a mother, not a man needing a wife. "It's been hard for me, too."

"And…I'm still sorry about Monte Carlo…" Kenny murmurs, lowering his head in shame. "…I know we've blown through a lot of money."

Distributing the blame between them, he raises his eyes only to measure her scorn, but Teresa simply looks over her husband's sad face, unable to judge her last hope for love.

"Money isn't the problem," she confides honestly, but she quickly closes the gate, locking away any notions of confronting her deeper marital issues. "Baby bro' will probably give me a loaf for free anyway."

"I would hope so." Kenny continues to hold his wife's arms, massaging her with his thumbs softly. "Between Thomas and your father…"

Teresa places her finger over Kenny's lips abruptly. She believes that words which will hurt the one who speaks them are best left unsaid. Kenny never seems to realize how much his sporadic energy affects his outlook on life.

∞

His eccentric gambling binge at the Monte Carlo was one continual, compulsive bet: *Red 23* at the roulette wheel. Whether the years of Bethune wealth had finally crippled him or his newfound responsibilities as a father and husband had proven too much to bear, he snapped into a realm of loss where he wouldn't or couldn't stop betting and repeating over and over, *"Red 23 skidoo"*, miss, *"Red 23 skidoo"*, miss. When Teresa asked him to explain, he only said that *"23 skidoo"* was something his late father said. Kenneth Bethune, Sr. passed away when Kenny was only nine years old and Kenny's mother assumed the role of patriarch and matriarch until Teresa took the part, no audition necessary.

Eventually, Teresa refused to give her husband any more funds for his gambling binge, a decision that elicited tears from a clown. Kenny began crying in the casino like a sullen child, pouting over money that has never been used for such vices in a Winniper household. She lost respect for his manhood because he had fallen so far from her father's image. A man she despised still controlled how she saw every man in her life; now Teresa looks into her husband's eyes, seeing a usurper where she once saw a savior.

∞

"Let's not argue...there are always ears listening in this house." Teresa glances around her husband to see Cleotha next to her daughters. Cleotha quickly turns to a nearby basket, picks up the laundry, and walks away toward the kitchen; Christina looks away toward a nearby window, but June continues to stare blankly at her mother. Though she is only four years old, the family's sadness affects her more profoundly than her older siblings. While both Duke and Christina trudge through life, absent their respective fathers, June lives with both of her parents, yet she often mopes around the home, inexplicably sad as if she lost something that she cannot remember. Teresa has never understood how her children have matured with such different personalities. Each feels their mother's torment, the separation, unable to explain why being a Winniper feels so hard, so cold.

The family still doesn't understand the curse, why the Winniper twins are born both Sioux and white, newborns crying so loudly, weeping in anguish, victims since birth—they all wailed within their first moments of light, except for June. Teresa remembers when her youngest daughter was born.

∞

She didn't cry. She merely cooed softly and grabbed her mother's finger, holding it tightly. June looked at the world around her with curiosity in her eyes; she had no fear.

∞

As June has grown, her eyes have continued to widen brightly, taking interest in anything that catches her attention. While Teresa stares at her daughter, she still sees that newborn wonder in her baby's eyes, but that sadness, the kind Teresa sees in the mirror, is there, too. For a moment, Teresa thinks of June's twin brother, Jazz, and tries to visualize what he must look like now after four years; she wonders if he has the same, conflicted eyes.

"I'll be back soon, June. Don't forget your goggles for the pool." Teresa smiles at June while looking over her daughter's face. "Watch over your brother and sister while I'm gone."

Pointing at June, Teresa squints her eyes and scrunches her face in a patrolman's scowl, giving the four-year-old toddler assurance that she is in charge.

"What about me?" Kenny asks coyly while grabbing Teresa's hips, a devilish smile forming on his face. "What should I do?"

"Nothing. June can watch over you, too." Teresa pats Kenny's face tersely, looking over his shoulder to June, who smiles brightly while reaching for her big sister's swim floaties.

"I'll pack these for Christina!" June declares, hopping to her feet and running upstairs. Her steps pitter-patter quickly to the second floor as she laughs loudly. "Duke, I'm in charge!"

"That's our baby girl," Teresa whispers to Kenny, smiling in half-minded joy as she remembers Jazz, the Sioux baby boy who may never know his mother. "Okay, I'm off to the market! I'll be back in a flash!"

She leaves her husband stranded without a kiss and bustles out of the doorway in haste, converting her annoyance into vigor and forgetting his absent-minded ways so that she may accomplish a quick, but necessary task. She considers that the carbohydrates in the bread will give her children much-needed nutrients; sacrificing their nutrition for her husband's sheer laziness, well, that's not something a Winniper woman does.

Surely, if Teresa desired a chauffeur, a butler, and another maid, she could hire all the help in South Dakota to tend to the family of five's every need. Indeed, she could even move the family to the Winniper Family Estate and live in luxury with her parents. But she knows that life at the estate is not life; trapped in a Winniper observation chamber, **_their wealth and secrets prove that freedom is free_**. As Teresa opens the car door, the faint smell of oil catches her nose. The old Spoister always smells like a race track, and she attributes the fumes to her father's old antics on Suicide Gorge near the cross-section with Winniper Road.

∞

Even while becoming a mild-mannered American tycoon and an international oil export extraordinaire, Teresa's father always had a widely discussed wild side in both business and racing. On Saturdays, Thomas Winniper, Jr. would race anyone and everyone who challenged him, whipping around sharp turns and steep hills without real concern for his life.

He epitomized a Winniper man, and his father always taught him that being a Winniper man was like having a contract with Jesus—a glorified self-appeasement agreement. A Winniper man has a God-given right to always be successful and always take what a Winniper man wants. Papa Winniper's exploits were so notorious that he even earned his own series of race games at the town's most celebrated holiday—the Winniper County Founder's Day Parade, the first day in January.

Starting in 1891, January 1st became Winniper County Founder's Day, a festive parade, an extravagant event where all the citizens of Winniper County gathered to celebrate the day that Thomas Winniper, Sr. and his militia defeated the Ghost Dance Sioux uprising, seized their land, and established Winniper County with the support of William Bethune and their respective militias. Shortly after the victory, Thomas, Sr. founded Winniper County, harvested the family's oil land, established the Winniper Family Holding Company, and became the richest man in the emerging Midwest.

Over fifty years later, the town still celebrates Winniper County Founder's Day, minus Teresa and her modest family. The Winniper Family Estate is worth billions, and their wealth and influence help the family control an entire county devoted to their name and leadership. The Winnipers became an established powerbroker in South Dakota; Thomas Winniper, Sr. taught his son everything he learned of farming, oil, and cheap labor. In his father's image, Thomas, Jr. became "Papa" Winniper and later expanded the family business beyond South Dakota, stretching to all the American coasts until the world came within reach.

The Winniper Family Holding Company soon became a financial backer to oil strikes, oil wealth, and oil wars all over the world, and the Winniper family enjoyed many blessings, though their lives remained mired in secrets. Over three male generations, Thomas Winniper, Sr., his son, and Teresa's brother, Thomas Winniper III, have quietly locked the truth behind the Winniper births with an inherited understanding that the Winniper men must eliminate any threat of exposure and burn any possibility of shame into unrecognizable ashes when necessary.

∞

Teresa sits in the front seat and explores her car briefly, reminiscing on past times, and a brief regret passes over her as she starts the ignition. Often, the choices she makes never seem right or wrong until it's too late to change the outcome. She loses herself in the now, the unalterable present, but still, she lingers on the *"what if"*. Considering the causal nature of spacetime, Teresa once dreamed of a reality that now seems inevitably deterred by what her name requires of her and her family. How can wealth ever be free? Earlier in the day during the annual Winniper County Founder's Day Parade, Teresa experienced a blessing that quickly became a nightmare: a chance to see her forgotten children. She could not linger long in that land of *"what if"*, fearing that the moment could deliver a fate she would be unable to flee—repercussions of inherited understandings.

An eternal exculpation within a human heart can never remove the traces of self-persecution; the Winniper family forever tainted itself after killing its own. Along with her family, Teresa endures circumstances determined by powers outside of their control. She knows these circumstances well enough; she is content to mask her deeper quest for more knowledge, content to enjoy half of her children and retrieve a loaf of bread for their dinner.

∞

The Spoister purrs gently as she reverses down her small cobble driveway in their quaint suburb. She and Kenny searched high and low for a suburban retreat in Winniper County, where their neighbors are just as rich and their Winniper "celebrity" seems common amongst mutual arrogance. Although her family has built a business dynasty in Winniper County that attracts potential partners around the world, she has never desired any overambitious attention.

∞

In quiet truth, she was fond of romance and her family's money enticed many suitors, but even at a young age, Teresa believed in true love. She yearned for someone who would accept and cherish her…and all her children. Despite going through two unsuccessful marriages and two costly, if not deadly, divorces, Teresa still returned Kenny's advances with an unbridled mix of affection and compassion. Yet, after she conceived and gave birth to her third pair of twins on June 9, 1941, she reluctantly parted ways with Jazz, returned to her suburban home with June, and avoided any sexual acts which might lead to another conception with her young husband.

∞

Now, Teresa fears having to abandon any more of her Sioux children; she can no longer contain the guilt of bearing brown babes who are then left with a family confidant and hidden in secrecy without the love or touch of their white mother. The anguish surrounding these circumstances has eliminated any fondness she once had for romance. As a middle-aged frump, Teresa pines for the children she will never raise and the sex she will never have with her lively husband. Remembering Kenny is only twenty-two years old, she does her best to quench his thirst without conceiving more children, fearing his betrayal if his needs are not met at home.

When the children are soundly sleeping in bed, and the queen and prince let the entire world evaporate, only their love is left, and it feels real, moving deeply between the two. Somewhere beyond the moments when she must correct his mistakes or funnel money into a bad investment, she still loves Kenny. His youth keeps him naïve and innocent, though he has experienced similar hardship. She continues to gamble her love on him as he gambles her savings and accrued assets, leveraging her family's ever-expanding wealth. And through it all, she is sure that he still loves her, or, at least, he loves the freedom that she provides from his mother, Tallulah "Tilly" Bethune. A married man and a father, he cannot be trifled with by the woman who once ruled over his childhood. In reality, Teresa is a bodyguard and he is her gigolo. Both accept one another as co-stars of their weird performance. Teresa plays a damsel in distress, while Kenny portrays a suffering leech. A castaway Bethune heir living with a weary Winniper woman, both seeking protection from an overbearing mother and a demanding father, respectively; both run from their parents' expectations for each of them to portray their designed characters with pride and aplomb. They are sacrificial lambs to American productivity.

Driving through Winniper County is an upper-class adventure, an education in suburban planning: roads covered with black gold. Papa Winniper dictates a detailed maintenance schedule and ensures the entire county remains in immaculate condition, especially the most social areas, such as the Winniper Pavilion where Thomas Winniper III runs his Winniper Market.

∞

Underwhelming his father, Thomas III chose agriculture over industry, utilizing the Winnipers' farm harvest to support a fresh market in the center of town. Though the Winniper citizens held Thomas III in their collective arms as the boy savior who brought a central market of fresh produce to the community, Papa Winniper still viewed his son as a would-be black sheep, second only to Teresa in terms of disgrace. She had eclipsed anything Papa Winniper would tolerate from a woman, let alone his only daughter.

As the siblings aged, Thomas III survived as an afterthought to his sister's madness; when they were children, Papa Winniper would bellow orders while Thomas III hid behind Teresa. When they were adults, Papa Winniper would still bellow orders, but Teresa would no longer listen. Even before her marriages, she would rage loudly, rant and rave if necessary, and run away from the estate when she wanted. Papa Winniper had no recourse; she had called his bluff and he could no longer control her antics, leaving Thomas III as the lonely brunt of his father's failed expectations.

Teresa loves her brother and their father sure enough. Throughout the years, she has visited the estate often, where dinner parties and Sunday brunches are frequent occasions, but, of course, Papa Winniper has always kept his money in circulation—the bank never, ever closes. Whether for his children or for potential profits, the Winniper Family Estate has always crawled with family, friends, and business elite who hope to scratch a dollar or two from the money tree.

Despite being Papa Winniper's eldest male heir and living in the Winniper family's mansion for most of his life, Thomas III has never enjoyed much access to his father's inner circle—the business partners, managers, and lawyers receive more welcome as passing strangers. Papa Winniper saw his son as a liability and a follower, some sissy who always cowered behind his sister or fainted under pressure. Though Teresa could only become a wife and nothing more, Papa Winniper secretly respected his daughter's backbone. Her unwillingness to accept his truth made her an interesting foe; his daughter would always say *"no"* when everyone else in his world would only say *"yes"*.

She would often stand up to him over dress choices, school lessons, and social gatherings, just to get her way. It seemed everything that he wanted for her went against what she naturally desired for herself. Her father appreciated her tenacity while lamenting its absence in his son. Teresa's grandfather taught her Papa that a Winniper man takes what he desires for himself as a familial right destined by God; and Papa Winniper, in turn, preached these values to his son, but Thomas III never committed to the task.

When Teresa ventured across the world and searched for answers to the hard questions of the Winniper family's curse, Thomas III joined his sister for a while but eventually returned to the womb of the Winniper Family Estate. Defeated at home and abroad, he established the Winniper Market, content to aid his hometown community in any way he could, becoming a public savior and a town clown for silent ridicule—the fallen Winniper heir, doing his best in circumstances that no one truly understands.

Born only a year apart, Thomas III and Teresa each had a Sioux twin, sacrificed for the Winniper family's bottom line. Faced with the same loss that her children feel now, Teresa and Thomas III each developed a uniquely, rebellious nature. Whereas Teresa sought to devalue their father and every influence he had in her life, Thomas III focused on minimizing himself in his father's eyes, making his character completely contemptible to the ambitious tycoon. Before and between her marriages, Teresa and Thomas III would frequently leave Winniper County and travel the world just to take pictures, talk to locals, and collect artifacts to show their parents. They loved showing their family and friends all the places they had visited and telling them about all the kinds of people they met while listening to their audience's shockingly stupid amazement:

"Those Greeks sure are tall."

"Why do those women wear beads on their head?"

"The Negroes have their own country?"

"How do those Chinamen get up so high in them trees?"

To the Winniper family's worshippers, it was unfathomable that two capitalist country bumpkins would travel so far away from their domestic security. The privileged siblings left the nest and sailed across the world just to visit foreign lands and snap pictures of natives; however, for Teresa, the escape became the only way to search for truth. No tribe could explain the family's curse, but many shamans, monks, priests, and chiefs laid their hands upon Teresa and Thomas III, hoping to cure what proved incurable. Secretly, her mother and father believed the knowledge that their daughter sought was important for the entire family because they each pined to explain their family secret. Even Papa Winniper had only received few answers from his father— *"A burden is a burden; we bear it as best we can"*. And after she bore Duke and Lucy, a white boy and a Sioux girl, and then Charles and Christina, a Sioux boy and a white girl, Teresa became desperate to understand the family's continual conception of white and Sioux twins. Nothing in the medical or spiritual world could explain it.

These circumstances had also plagued her mother, Olivia, and even Papa Winniper admitted that his father only told him that he, too, once had a Sioux sister, who died along with his mother during childbirth. For Teresa, separation anxiety fueled her to find answers and closure. Even in the midst of her ponderings, she knew she could not allow her father or her husband to kill her Sioux babies. Once, she dreamed of a way to fix the cure so that she could bear a normal family, one child at a time. Teresa and Thomas III spent a small fortune, searching the globe and scouring through jungles, villages, and cities in hopes of finding any knowledge of the Winniper women's condition. For years, Teresa continually asked the questions, hoping for a resolution.

She wondered, *"Why me?"* and *"Why our family?"* but she never found any answers. She felt like God never heard her cries and she began to doubt God's existence in a world with so many questions.

∞

As Teresa speeds through Winniper County's winding dirt roads, she passes two Negro children at a lemonade stand, a grandfather figure in overalls sitting close by underneath a short, wide oak tree. He tugs his cap slightly as she passes, his face wrinkled from age and heat, and Teresa continues down the road, passing Doc Morten's home and office, the timber red roof over a dilapidated oak house covered with dried leaves.

Another Winniper County legacy, Dr. Xavier "Doc" Morten, Sr. began his practice providing physical examinations, pediatric services, and personal house calls to many South Dakota citizens in the late 1800s. Fifty years later, his son, Doc Morten, Jr. now applies his father's trade in the same home. Much like Papa Winniper, Doc Morten, Jr. sought to eclipse his father's success. In addition to serving the county's private needs, Doc Morten, Jr. also serves as the county medical examiner and performs necessary autopsies when warranted, especially when the death occurs under the suspicion of foul play. Paramedics and first-responders instantly transfer the deceased to the doctor's exam room inside his home.

The Morten family's old oak home provides a morbidly beautiful background for death and childbirth; the faded wooden front porch still has a hole where Papa Winniper stomped around so hard the day Duke and Lucy were born. He was ecstatic to have another male heir, one to replace Thomas III, but he was sadly upset that Teresa's travels had not produced a cure to their curse. She still gave birth to an unwanted Sioux girl; and though her intentions had always been to keep both children, her father's expectations quickly became apparent. Her mother, maybe in desperation to save the family, concocted a plan, lying to both sides to protect the whole.

∞

Teresa admires how her mother has remained loyal to them all, but she still regrets the circumstances and the decisions which led her to give Lucy away to a family friend. It is a day Teresa never wishes to remember, but she is unable to forget the loss of one twin when she looks into the eyes of the other. She turns her mind to better times as the dirt road turns into pavement and the Winniper Pavilion comes into sight up ahead. She remembers when the property was only a grassy knoll with a man-made pond in the middle. Her father brought the family to the site with a couple of business partners, swaying his hand over the property and baptizing the land under the South Dakota sun, his sweat cleansing the earth. Teresa truly believes that no one ever planned for people to build a town in Winniper County, but the Winniper and Bethune families merged their militias and led a few other properly placed pawns to pioneer a small South Dakota county with simple means and simple ways.

Historically, the Winnipers have controlled every facet of the quiet community since the county's inception on January 1, 1891. Law enforcement, judges, council members, prosecutors, and every pair of boots in the labor force have marched to the beat of the Winniper oil refinery—the vitality of South Dakota itself. Like a black heart spilling every drop of blood needed to keep America and several overseas nations alive, the oil refinery has become a global trough, which the Winnipers and Bethunes have manipulated for personal and financial gain. Implementing his father's instructions and harkening to a base need for the Winniper male to conquer, Thomas Winniper, Jr. has transitioned the family's growing importance in global business into a social codependence that has allowed him to enforce any international or domestic law or penalty that he deems appropriate for practical or impractical purposes. His control has also created the leverage to hide a secret that could ruin his family name if exposed to the public—a secret Thomas Winniper, Sr. always warned his son could never be made public, even at the cost of blood.

∞

The founder of Winniper County, the architect of the family's oil grab, made sure his only son would be willing to kill or even die to protect the family and conceal the Winnipers' Sioux children. After Papa Winniper and Olivia conceived Teresa and her Sioux brother, the Winniper heir faced a decision his father chose for him long ago. Although he has never discussed the predicament or his decisions, Teresa has realized that his power came at the price of his innocence. Murdering babies gives morality a horrible complex. She has watched her father demand obedience from his employees, defend his methods no matter how cruel, and deny any freedom to anyone within Winniper County at his discretion. And as he consolidated his power over the American landscape and cemented the Winniper Empire into the world's economic and political power structure, all the family's partners and clients submitted to the new regime, desperate to be counted present and fed private or public contracts under the shade of the Winniper tree. Teresa's father knows how to compensate well for compliance, a trait which makes her obedience even more difficult. Life could be so much easier if she were to truly abandon her Sioux children and forget they exist for better or worse. The benefits far outweigh the risks.

For all its quaint corruption, Teresa has never experienced or heard mention of any violence or wrongdoing inside Winniper County. The lawmen and militias from the past transformed easily into high-ranking county officials and a full-fledged police force, protecting the county borders and Thomas, Sr.'s bottom line asset—the oil. Over the years, the need for immediate security has become less and less apparent and the community ascended into more luxurious forms of society. Sheriff Cornell Cobb, Jr. was also the best musician on the force. A wartime trumpet player, he had enough time to pick up the fiddle on duty. Most citizens think of the sheriff as a frilly civil servant, more concerned with profits of finance than serving the community. Another inherited post, Cornell, Jr. ascended to public service as a deputy for his father, who taught his son to always keep a close watch on whatever the Winnipers desired.

Even as a young man, Cornell, Jr. joined his late father in the coup against the supposedly savage Ghost Dance Sioux, and the wealth shared from the spoils catapulted the Cobb family to public prominence as the founders of the local police force. Next to the Winnipers, Bethunes, and Mortens, the Cobbs are a common legacy within the South Dakota elite; they are champions of the oilman's moral code as long as they adhere to the Winniper doctrine—protect the family at all costs.

When Teresa began partying and socializing around town, creating more fights than fairytales, Sheriff Cobb, Jr. would arrive on the scene and play his fiddle in the middle of the crowd until everyone went home. He called it *"keeping the peace"*. The sheriff created the ephemeral sense that nothing would ever change and all would remain well in Winniper County; a higher power watched over their movements and controlled the damage done.

Indeed, there has always been a Winniper eye observing all actions within the county line. First, Thomas Winniper, Sr. closed much of the county while constructing the steel barges that fortified the Winniper oil refinery. Soon after, the entire town began to buzz with prospects from all over the country, creating orders, conducting negotiations, and signing contracts for Winniper oil. Throughout his second life as a single father, his business networks created the means by which Thomas Winniper, Sr. established his county bylaws, separating any external riff-raff from business within the borders of his property.

As the wealthiest landowners in the region, the Bethunes and Winnipers turned the town into private property that the families patrolled and protected with extreme prejudice to outsiders. Anyone asking too many questions would be immediately expelled. Thomas Winniper, Sr. trusted very few people, ensuring most of his loyalty to those present with him on the day he defended his property from the ransacking Sioux.

Teresa often heard Sheriff Cobb, Jr. explain what it was like to defeat the enemy protecting the ones he loved. The small battle became a war in Winniper County folklore—it was the day the truth died. Although the Cobbs have always been comparatively close to the Winnipers, Sheriff Cobb, Jr. still does not know about the Winnipers' curse. When he was younger, some of the other riflemen relayed the dying words of a Sioux sorceress that Thomas, Sr. shot through the heart with his Colt revolver. After hearing the stories, Cornell, Jr. and his father cared more about what happened to the high metal 1851 revolver than the dead Sioux woman. That gun may have been worth a few hundred dollars at the time. In truth, the Cobbs were merely hired henchmen and guards; neither Thomas, Sr. nor his son gave the family much consideration beyond protecting their assets within Winniper County. When Thomas Winniper, Jr. assumed the patriarchal duties of the Winniper Empire, the sheriff became even more irrelevant in their ever-expanding, international power grab.

As Thomas Winniper, Jr. met with kings and warlords from around the world, he delegated much of the business properties within America to his financial manager, Freidrich Potter, and Freidrich, in turn, delegated these orders to the estate's accountants, lawyers, and brokers. Admiring his business acumen, personal wealth, and family visage, the people of Winniper County, envisioning the patriarch of old, began to affectionately call Thomas, Jr. by the nickname "Papa".

∞

It was and still is true that Thomas, Jr. modeled himself perfectly after his father's wishes. The only emerging difference between Papa and his predecessor has been that Papa does not like to micromanage. He is always far too concerned with the bigger picture; he never evaluates his employees beyond the bottom line, and he never cares much about the daily goings-on within Winniper County as long as the money keeps rolling in, and everyone, truly *everyone*, behaves according to his orders.

Papa may attend a popular wedding as a favor to a colleague or host a charity event at the estate to influence public opinion, but Teresa's father has never truly enjoyed anything about the public life except the applause and respect; and he has forced his family to take a similarly narrow viewpoint toward engagement with the common folk. Behind his recalcitrance, Papa faces the difficult challenge of expanding the family empire while hiding the bloody secrets surrounding their wealth.

∞

Papa had hoped Teresa would submit to marriage and motherhood and Thomas III would attend to business or intellectual pursuits, but Papa could never deter his daughter and he could never motivate his son. When Teresa became desperately driven to escape from Winniper County, she convinced her brother to join her traveling mania and tribal indulgences. Teresa and Thomas III never restrained their pursuits, a true Winniper trait, and while the county line became a physical representation of Winniper dominance, Papa Winniper could not control Thomas III or Teresa as Thomas, Sr. had once controlled him. Whether inside or outside of Winniper County, Teresa dragged Thomas III through the streets and terrain of the world as if it all belonged to them, and Papa Winniper could do nothing to dissuade her until Thomas III returned to the Winniper Family Estate. After losing her traveling mate, Teresa eventually returned to Winniper County but she never relented to her father's wishes. Even though she has married three times, she has never truly settled down.

By all accounts, the little town of Winniper County seems perfectly quaint, with all the trimmings of segregated civility, but, underneath the prim and proper values, bigoted hearts beat within those who still dream of owning slaves. Many Winniper County settlers moved from the Winnipers' farmland in Tennessee after the Civil War, waiting until the late 1860s to release most of their Africans into servile sharecropping. Teresa spent much of her time as a child trying to understand why one kind of people would hate or enslave another kind of people if they are all the same species. As she continued to ask questions many of her family and friends could not answer, Teresa looked to the maids and workers at the Winniper Family Estate and never noticed any difference between their service and hers. They were all victims under a cruel master, born and bred to be cogs in the machine; and she vowed never to raise her children to see any human as better than another.

It is amazing how youthful intentions turn into adult reckonings, and the reality within Winniper County's small town culture left little hope to dream for social integration or racial equality. As she matured and married to bear both Sioux and white children, Teresa realized that her Sioux babies would never be welcomed in the Winniper community, and if the community knew the truth, the entire family would be ostracized. Her father would be a king thrown from his throne, everything would come crashing down; thus, Teresa became trapped between her will to protect her entire family and her inner longing to save her family from the same ignorance that infects those who would persecute them.

∞

Teresa battles her notions of independence and society as she wonders how each of her children will develop when they are older and they begin to search for answers outside the womb. Will they mimic their mother and become frightened? Will they become lost in questions, hopelessly searching to complete themselves? Teresa drives toward the emerging Winniper Pavilion, thinking of her childhood as a game that she never finished: continually unraveling the Winniper secret in a never-ending mystery, holding a key to the future, but needing a door to the past.

∞

She scoured over the county, country, and world, looking for clues and traces of any known cases similar to the Winniper women's conception. With constant miscues and countless wrong turns, Teresa's efforts never led to a sensible answer: no one ever knew how the Sioux and white twin births could keep happening and all the efforts to fix her pregnancies proved in vain after each Sioux child was born.

∞

Teresa speeds through the uneven, yet paved road covered with gravel pits and leftover rubble—the Winniper citizens barely have a week to enjoy a smooth new pathway until oil trucks and motormen start zooming up and down the paved road and dirt paths as they head from the oil refinery to the coasts and beyond. While creating a veritable center of commerce in Winniper County, Thomas Winniper, Sr. monopolized much of the American oil and export industry in the early 1900s. Now in the late 1940s, his prodigal son, continues expanding the empire beyond American boundaries while simultaneously remembering to keep the Winniper County roads buzzing with business. Following his father's example, Thomas "Papa" Winniper, Jr.'s local investments bolster public support and garner the cooperation necessary to silence any outsiders.

Nowadays, Teresa often wonders what tourists think of Winniper County. Do they stop for a moment to enjoy the small town setting? Or do they recognize their home town's simplicity and pass by with fast familiarity? Humans seldom enjoy what they don't miss and seldom appreciate what they already have. Ingratitude is, seemingly, a human curse, but as Teresa speeds into the Winniper Pavilion, she feels a ticklish, tingling warmth that she once longed for when home was only a memory.

∞

While traveling through the Nairobi, her heart would long for Winniper County, proving she was a victim of her father's domestic programming or maybe just a child away from home. She would stare at the night sky for hours and wonder if her father, mother, or brother would look at the same stars later in the evening.

Teresa often fantasized about home in those days. Her nostalgia altered her perspective; before he left, whimsical chats with Thomas III made being a Winniper seem like a blessing and their father became a man of principle, forced to make tough decisions. He wasn't such a bad man after all. But when she returned to the Winniper family's mansion, she justified her mistakes in marriages and genetically blessed children. Duke, Christina and June needed a mother, and Teresa accepted the task with pleasure. She adored her white children, and she wanted to do everything she could for them. Marrying a few times never hurt the Winniper reputation as long as there was a marriage to accompany any childbirth. June being the latest, it became imperative for Kenny and Teresa to assuage appearances throughout the engagement and pregnancy.

∞

As a valiant theatrical effort, the Winniper family has bonded together convincingly enough to display their strength and humility while hosting dinner parties and attending every charity event. Papa Winniper insists that his wife and Thomas III show their plastered-on smiles to all the gossiping guests and chatty partygoers. Although she avoids such trivialities, Teresa recognizes that these social gatherings within Winniper County are a testament to the insecurities of their wealthy, always needing friends, judging their opinions, and gauging interest in potential ventures. The Winniper enterprises and investments control a large constituency of new business owners hoping to capitalize on the financially fruitful location and the consistent commerce. Papa Winniper offers only the best rewards to the slickest oil producers, manufacturers, and distributors. Even at the Winniper Pavilion, an array of clothing stores, carnival-style vendors, and novelty shops glisten in the midday sunlight and perfectly accessorize the Winniper Market—the centerpiece to the monstrous Winniper buffet of South Dakotan hospitality.

The Winniper Market stands directly in the center of the pavilion, a common hourly rental for community events and bake sales. Many Winniper citizens frequent the market because it is the only source for fresh produce unless they harvest at home after paying for a county permit. Making the pilgrimage to the Winniper Market is an accepted alternative; families meander around the aisles, collecting their groceries and chatting with Teresa's brother. Thomas III is the town's grocer and community foil. Known throughout Winniper County as the male heir who fell farthest from the tree, the community treats Thomas III as their son, chiding him about finding a wife, producing a male heir of his own, and living up to his Winniper family legacy.

Many citizens love his adorable anecdotes and his simple-minded, South Dakota charm, but in a Winniper world of large commerce, Thomas III has underachieved. He is still an afterthought, small peanuts in the Winniper circus, or maybe a sad clown.

∞

Thomas III's reluctance to take the reins of the family business resulted in his father pushing him aside. Teresa often felt that Papa Winniper wasn't patient enough with Thomas III. Their father disqualified his only son the moment he refused to jump into the Bethune's lake at age five.

A fun family visit turned into a goaded moment of mental trauma when her brother fainted on the dock, Tilly Bethune screaming for her maid to bring ice, and all along Papa Winniper stood over his unconscious son, unwilling to help him. Kenneth, Sr. sat quietly in a lawn chair at the edge of the dock, narrowing his eyes before staring out over the lake. Papa continued smoking a cigar with a disgusted scowl over his face, thinking his son would never be man enough.

Several years later, when Kenneth Bethune, Jr. was born, Teresa wondered how his father treated him, questioning whether the man closes to her father dealt with his first male heir in the same fashion. Later, after his father passed, she found out that Kenny's mother Tilly had ruled the Bethune family with a heartless fist. She shepherded negotiations, maneuvered takeovers, and executed many corporate conspiracies with Papa Winniper.

∞

Tilly Bethune is a woman within a man's arena, but her wealth, legacy, and alliances have given her tremendous power.

∞

By studying his mother, Teresa found answers to her questions about Kenny's upbringing; Tilly had chosen to wield her matriarchal authority without regret and she sacrificed members of her family to prove her loyalty to Papa Winniper. Thus, Teresa pities Kenny in the same way that she pities her brother—both victims, as all humans are, of circumstances and life.

As Teresa and Thomas III became teenagers, the Winniper family's resentment ran deep between the siblings and their father, though they never held any malice toward their mother, Olivia. Both children viewed their mother as a silent civilian and sometimes a patron saint. In either regard, she is an innocent hostage caught within the Winniper web, while using whatever leverage she may have to protect her children and her family's interests.

∞

Papa Winniper has never made explicit concessions to his wife, his son, or his daughter. If circumstances lead him to investigate his suspicions, he could quickly learn that Teresa's Sioux children are alive and residing in Winniper County. His darling wife has aided their survival; his ever-obedient son has also helped when he could find time away from trysts with cashier girls. Thomas III has even often brought the children produce from the market and the family's farmlands.

With this revelation, Papa would likely kill the entire family and start fresh; but, while feigning complete ignorance of all their deception, Papa has continued to help support Teresa and her "legitimate family" while also allowing Thomas III to use the family's harvest to supply the market.

∞

In some ways, helping his son build the produce market to serve the Winniper community brought the two closer together. Thomas III provided a successful foil that humanized the old patriarch to the townspeople: even the king had a fool for a son. The mutual dependence between them became a concession that proved more socially advantageous than either man had first understood.

Thomas III convinced his father to finance the Winniper Market and hire a family owned construction company to build the tented carnival-like structure over an old Winniper hemp field. Before the construction, Teresa and Thomas III learned their Great-Uncle Christopher Winniper, Jr. cultivated hemp, tobacco, and wheat at his cottage home near the Winniper family's mansion. Unfortunately, he died during the Sioux uprising, but Thomas Winniper, Sr. dedicated the fruits of the seized land to his brother's memory and gave a small percentage of the oil profits to Christopher's widow Rita. She remained at the Winniper family's mansion, helping to care for Thomas, Jr. until she passed away shortly before the boy began grade school.

Under Thomas, Sr.'s ambition, the Winniper family business grew into an expanded American enterprise of moneymaking ventures by mass-producing oil embargos, hemp trades, tobacco exchanges, crop distribution channels, and by never forgetting their financial roots—wheat farming. Growing up at the estate, with their farmlands close by, Thomas III and Teresa always loved the smell of fresh bread. Several servants would harvest the wheat, bake the dough in the kitchen, and fill the mansion with a familiar aroma: love, butter, and home. Leaving Tennessee as true masters of the yeast art, Teresa's Great-Grandfather Christopher Winniper, Sr. raised slaves, sharecroppers, countrymen, and his sons to produce the largest bread outpost in South Dakota, a business feat surpassed only by his youngest son and only surviving heir, Thomas Winniper, Sr.

After Thomas Winniper, Sr. defeated the rampaging Sioux tribe and harvested the oil strike, he developed the Winniper Family Estate into an American capital of industry. Once renowned for the goods and produce from their Winniper farmland, Thomas Winniper, Sr. had always plotted to turn the Winniper name into a powerfully profitable machine. His vision was so influential and important that the South Dakota Governor, Author C. Mellette, helped Thomas, Sr. receive the local charter for the creation of Winniper County on January 1, 1891.

During his makeshift speech, Thomas Winniper, Sr. dedicated the coming oil wealth to his brother, and, of course, he remembered to endorse the governor's coming re-election, though Governor Mellette never ran. While traveling through South Dakota libraries, Teresa read several new articles alluding to rumors that her grandfather Thomas Winniper, Sr. bribed and manipulated Governor Mellette to certify Winniper County and all of its conspicuous bylaws for business and private property; she also uncovered that her grandfather even paid many of the would-be Winniper citizens to attend the inaugural Winniper County Founder's Day Parade.

Though he saw them as sheep from his flock, Thomas, Sr. ingratiated himself with the citizens, just enough so that they would view him as an affable messiah; little did they suspect that the entire county, their homes, and all their businesses rested on his private property. After securing the rights to the largest oil strike in American history, Mr. Thomas Winniper, Sr. became, from that day henceforth, the undisputed oil king of South Dakota. Throughout the years, some of the Winniper citizens grew to detest Thomas Winniper, Sr.'s constantly flagrant intrusions into their private lives. New zones here, emergency road work there, he moved families and business around in Winniper County like pieces in a board game because he never understood personal, professional, or public boundaries—everything was his. As a man who felt forced into many hard decisions and who sought only the best results for his business success, his family affairs began to dissolve into nothingness, a black hole of bottom line judgments.

Although Thomas, Sr. directed much of his ruthlessness toward his business enemies and any government legislator seeking to meddle in his pockets, he also reserved a certain spiteful amount of anger for his only son. He would often chastise Thomas, Jr. for his childish tendencies and common phobias; he punished his son for crying or resisting hard work. It became a staple of his manhood for Thomas, Jr. to sit in the cigar room through late nights with his father and listen to business heads yawn about mergers and acquisitions. Quite sensibly, Thomas, Jr. grew into a shrewd business monarch in order to fulfill the wishes of his father; "Papa" is the modern version of Thomas, Sr.

Papa Winniper responds coldly to any opposition, obsessively driven by the ambition to advance the Winniper family's acclaim and bring death to any who might oppose them or expose their secrets. As a stern and stubborn father, Papa Winniper has tried to transform Thomas III into the same image of manhood. Thomas, Sr. had explained all the necessary traits for a successful Winniper man and Papa had complied and adopted these principles into his success; but, when Papa Winniper tried to do indoctrinate Thomas III into the ways of the Winniper man, Papa saw his efforts fail to produce promissory results in his heir. Accepting his failures as a father, Papa then permitted Thomas III to become a sideshow, by helping his son establish a produce market that would eventually become the epicenter of a large commercial pavilion that now sits in the center of the entire town—a central circus ring for a forsakenly privileged clown.

∞

Teresa drives into the Winniper Pavilion parking lot after passing under a large stars-and-stripes banner with the words "Winniper Pavilion" painted in white letters on the front. Country onlookers stare at Teresa's sleek blue Spoister, ogling this Chicago-style car and its infamous driver. Over the years, Teresa has become increasingly desensitized to colloquial trappings and social inequalities; oddly, the only thing she appreciates about her father is the luxury of his money. Truthfully, Teresa has never held a job nor lifted a finger in labor; though admittedly, many of the *established* women in Winniper County have never worked either. The well-to-do seldom have knowledge of work's function, leaving their minds with very little knowledge of anything else. Teresa parks her expensive automobile amidst watchful eyes and she forgets her dissenting thoughts in order to resume the demure aptitude necessary for a Winniper woman: her mother calls it "the will to survive God's humor".

When Teresa opens the door and steps from the car, she no longer feels at home. She struts down a runway with eyes surveying her chic baby blue heels and middle-aged frame. The hisses and innuendos surrounding her character have often run wild, unfiltered by her or her family. While walking through the bustling parking lot, Teresa adjusts her oval sunglasses and her turquoise flowered sundress, ignoring the leering looks while her childhood wish for invisibility creeps into her mind. She keeps her head down, giving no eye contact, no chance for a hello. Long ago, she and her parents abandoned any attempts to restrain the wild actions of their deceptive daughter within the confined Winniper County community. Regardless of their reasons or intentions, people talk, and no matter what Teresa had done to start the rumor mill, no matter how the Winnipers' reacted or attempted to manage the gossip, the results were always the same—one lie or another always became folklore.

She reaches the wooden framed entrance and stealthily steps past the hay barrels and fresh fruit carts in front of the market. To the right of the entrance, Teresa can see Sheriff Cobb, Jr.'s patrol car parked awkwardly on the curb, barely giving customers room to walk on the sidewalk. Teresa continues to stroll through the front entrance of the Winniper Market, hoping for the best but always expecting the worst.

Inside Thomas III's market, customers scramble through the aisles, picking carved cantaloupes, fresh breads, chopped cutlery, butchered beefs, and generally germane goods. Teresa often tells Thomas III that his market looks more like a baseball field with customers running from base to base, hoping to return home before an imaginary outfielder throws them out. Whenever Teresa stops by to visit her brother, she immediately reverts back into a little girl, standing on her tip toes and stretching her neck, searching for the boy who could never hurt her. She notices a newly hired, nubile cashier fumbling through her duties at one of the checkout lines. No doubt she is another high-school recruit for Thomas III to cherry pick, although his efforts prove mainly harmless. Thomas III is notorious for never sealing the deal with any of the women around town, though he has his share of greedy seductresses. He plays along and Teresa never questions him beyond settling down, hoping that one day he'll give her a niece and nephew. Maybe then, he will finally stand up to their father.

"Hey thur, Ter'! Where's ya been hidin'?" A squirrelly voice beckons below her and the familiar chops of old man Potter's gums send chills up Teresa's spine as his scraggly fingers playfully poke her hips. Carl Potter was once the Winniper family's errand boy, and he and his son, Freidrich, still serve the family diligently, in any servile capacity. Teresa turns to face the old man and smiles sweetly. She almost knocks him over after bumping into his small frame with her chest. His eyes grow as they fill with depraved amazement and he catches his balance with his polished, wooden cane. "You know my boy has been workin' pretty close to yur pa'. It's mighty nice to see you, *as always.*"

"Hi, Carl." Teresa groans, already getting annoyed with her gooey-eyed admirer. "I haven't been hiding, just very…very busy, marriage, kids, you know?"

Teresa continues to look over and around Carl, searching for that brotherly protection that Thomas III provides in moments of crisis and, when appropriate, he forgoes his personal advantage like when he joined her to travel the world.

"You lookin' fer Tommy boy, my dear?" Carl asks, his eyes still resting directly on Teresa's pert chest. Having worked for the Winnipers since he was a boy, Carl has never left the tit, aging into a seventy-one-year-old market hand. He is no longer much use in this emerging age of technology; he survives on whatever Papa Winniper provides, and when Thomas III opened his market, it seemed only sensible for Carl to join the circus and accent the act however he could. Teresa looks down at the aged deviant, takes a step away, and lifts his chin slightly until his eyes connect to her eyes.

"Yes, I am looking for Thomas," she confirms softly, smiling brightly to cover her assertive nature. The idea of ripping Carl's head off his frail body crosses her mind with a secret cheer, but she concedes her fantasy to ask the old man to point her in the right direction. "Do you know where he is?"

"I sure do!" Carl raises his palm and wipes his forehead, smiling with gums as if he won the tooth lottery. He straightens his back as much as he possibly can and points in the opposite direction toward the produce section. "He's just past the lettuce, over yonder in the bread aisle!"

"Oh, perfect," Teresa coos happily. She turns away from Carl without another word, walking away from the perverted relic and toward the bread aisle at the far right of the market. "That's exactly what I need."

"Come back and see me 'fore ya leave!" She hears Carl's gums chomp greedily and she doesn't turn to respond; a momentary fantasy of his disembowelment is enough to quell her revulsion. When she was a child, Carl passed his hungry eyes over her body, prodding her with inappropriate pokes whenever possible. Teresa remembers when she became *ripe*, he even petitioned her father to agree to their marriage; yet, as Teresa would later find out, her father would never agree to any marriage that didn't meet his standards. Papa had always intended to secure her within an approved union that he could control from beginning to end.

The ceiling lights dim toward the far east of the Winniper Market as the sunlight barely stretches to the edges of the bread aisle. Teresa continues to glance around the section, until finally noticing Thomas III hunched over a crate of assorted bread. He holds an onion loaf above his head, inspecting it with one eye and then another before placing the bread back in the crate.

"Hey, baby brother!" Teresa yells down the aisle, again arching in her heels while waving to her brother in her best adolescent sister impression. He raises his head and his smile reassures her that today is a good day; he may give her a whole week's worth of free bread. "I'll take whatever's free, Thomas!"

"Everyone pays!" Thomas III retorts with a hearty chuckle, looking back over the bread in his crate. "Nothin' is free in this world, sis, you know that!"

Always teaching, even within jokes, Thomas III inspects the already thoroughly inspected bread as Teresa walks happily toward him. She hugs him tightly and smells their father—bread and sunlight waft into her nostrils. In her mind, her brother becomes their father, holding her closely as he did when she was his little princess after coming home from some large business deal and ordering a fresh loaf from the kitchen.

"Always bake a fresh loaf when I arrive!" He would bellow a bread edict to the nearest house servant. Teresa pulls away from Thomas III, hoping that she does not see her father's maniacal eyes in her brother. She doesn't; somehow, Thomas III is still innocent.

"It's good to see you, Thomas. I saw Sheriff Cobb's car out front, is he around?"

"Uh…no…uh, I haven't seen him, but, it's good to see you, too, sis. We missed you at the founder's parade today." Thomas III drops his head while raising his eyes to his sister; he is still the sheepish little brother. "Papa was askin' for you, he felt pretty sore about you and the kids not showin' up. You know how he is about public appearances."

"Well, we're leaving soon…things will be different." Teresa hides the understanding they both share, knowing what plans exist but unwilling to acknowledge the elephant in the room. "I want…I *need* them, Thomas. I thought about going to Berthine's cabin today while everyone was celebrating, I knew they'd be there, but…I'm scared. I think Papa knows…"

"I…uh, he hasn't said anything to me. He's too busy with dollar signs to notice much else. And he still hasn't given me great-granddaddy's revolver. He says I have to earn it." Thomas III moves closer to his sister, dipping his head to look her in the eyes. "He does miss you though, in his own way. We all do, but, you can't go visit your other children. Me and Mama check on 'em when we can, but, it just wouldn't be safe, for them or you."

"You're right, I do know…all too well." Teresa begins to eye the bread loaves, remembering June and Christina sitting at home waiting for her return. "I'm hoping you can give me a Marley loaf for dinner tonight."

"Main course, appetizers?"

"Salad."

"And I can only assume you want the best price, too?"

"Papa's special price…" Teresa laughs, envisioning the old man ordering loaf after loaf from the family kitchen. "Do you remember?"

"*Free.*" Thomas III returns Teresa's laugh with a smile, sharing a common joke between siblings and remembering all the times their father negotiated, conned, or bribed a vendor or colleague for free services or merchandise, always at his *special price.*

"Well, take a look here, grab what you like." Thomas III moves aside and sways his arm over the large bread cart. Teresa giggles joyfully to show her appreciation, and she leans over the cart, smelling the aroma. Hawking over the bread assortment, she notices one large Marley loaf with a lumpy deformity in the middle and dives in for the grab.

"I'll take this one." She snatches the oddball Marley loaf from the bunch, and Thomas III eyes her curiously with a laugh.

"You had to pick that one, huh? You always pick the bad one."

"Bad is just a state of mind, right?" Teresa chuckles and holds the bread up to the light. "I like bad; sometimes bad is fun. Remember when you tried to fly?"

She smiles wickedly while reminiscing about the time she convinced Thomas III that he could fly if he tied his bedsheet to his waist. To this day, she almost wets herself with the vivid memory of her little brother running off the barn roof and jumping off the edge. For a few seconds, Thomas III really could fly, and then gravity took hold and he landed flat in the animal depository, falling deep within the putrid, fecal pit for all the farm animals.

"Sometimes being bad is fun; sometimes it's not." Thomas III joins Teresa in a laugh while lifting another large, lumpy Marley loaf from the cart and handing the bread to her. "Take this one, too. How are the white kids?"

"They're good…" Teresa responds quickly, smiling to herself as she smells the bread and thinks of home. "Very loud, obnoxious, and spoiled, but we are doing pretty well."

"And the new husband?" His question comes with both eyebrows raised suspiciously, anticipating Teresa's convoluted answer. "How's he treating you?"

"Kenny and I were married almost two years ago, and, sadly, he's not so new." Teresa rolls her eyes and pulls strands of her blonde hair over her eyes. "But he is doing well, too; we're adjusting to the family life. We are in love. We make it work."

"Does he know about the others?" Thomas III questions his sister and she attributes the brotherly interrogation to her absence from their family gatherings.

∞

Since her rushed marriage to Kenny and June's birth, Teresa made it a point to distance herself from family, attempting to create a new nest and home, where she, her children, and her husband could be safe from the past. Fearing that her father somehow uncovered her betrayal, she chose to move away from the estate while remaining near enough to feed from the Winniper wealth.

∞

"Did you tell him about Jazz? Did you tell Kenny that you plan to leave?" Thomas III asks, continuing to prod his sister for the truth.

"Yes…" Her voice falls into the bread loaf, attempting to gather her answer. She looks into her brother's eyes, locked between the lie and the truth. She realizes why she avoids her father, frequents her brother's market less and less, and laments every visit to her family's estate.

Missing her Sioux children more and more and struggling to hide her postpartum depression, Teresa feels trapped within a world of deceptions with her life and family at stake. The father who could embrace all her children would rather kill them. He would kill Teresa if he knew she had not only betrayed him but she also told her husband about the Winniper family's curse.

∞

The Sioux babies should've been killed and her husbands should've been deceived, but Teresa and her mother conspired to save the babies and conceal them in a cabin near the old Sioux village at the edge of Winniper County. And then, there's Thomas III, her hero, the one person she completely trusts to protect her because he has never taken advantage of her, even at the risk of his male ego. As they struggled under their father's thumb, her brother never sacrificed her emotions for his personal gain or pleasure.

∞

Though Papa Winniper still sees his son as weak, Teresa leans into her brother, feeling his arms steady her weight—he is her crutch. She inhales the comforting smell of home and releases herself from the world of lies in order to experience a moment of clarity.

"It's been tough, but, you know…I just want to live with all of my family. I'm glad they're alive, I thank God every day, but…I need to see them."

"I know, it's hard for all of us." Thomas III agrees, placing his hands on his sister's shoulders. "But, you shouldn't have told Kenny. You shouldn't have trusted him. I'm trying to protect you…uh…I've tried my best to…"

"I know you have, Thomas. But Kenny is Jazz's father, too. He kept asking, wondering why I'm being so cold towards him. He thinks I don't love him anymore. He has a right to know the truth. I don't want to lose him, too!" She realizes her brashness and quickly lowers her voice, while changing the subject. "Speaking of the joys of married life, when are you going to move out of the mansion and start your own family, little brother?"

"God no, have you seen the new cashier, Terry Sue? I hire too many pretty girls to ever domesticate!" Thomas III chuckles under his breath before considering his true fear. "I'm never having kids, Teresa. I don't want to find out if I have the curse in my blood, too. I'd have to do what Papa did or...do what you've done."

"H-have you seen them recently?" Teresa asks sheepishly, dipping her head to smell the two loaves of bread; she remembers a serene sense of home. "I mean, are they okay?"

Her voice shakes like a coward, too reluctant or remorseful to recognize the children that she will never be able to completely love. She relies on subtle messages from her mother or brother, experiencing postpartum pangs every time she hears more.

"I bring them food when I can, Teresa." Thomas III confides, still staring at his sister, worried for what could come from disobeyed orders. "They're doing just fine by the looks. The baby boy, um, Jazz, he's growing fast; four years old, he's already started playing the guitar."

Thomas III smiles brightly, and the thought of her youngest son playing the guitar like his twin sister June almost shatters Teresa. Her knees grow weak underneath her, troubled by the revelation.

"That's...*nice*. June is very creative, too..." She mumbles, stretching an awkward smile across her face, but Thomas III notices her inner turmoil. He wraps his arms around her gently and squeezes twice while she shivers in his grasp. She tilts her head away from Thomas III and wipes away a tear with her left index finger.

"Stay strong, sis," Thomas III whispers, while holding Teresa. "You did the right thing...with all of them."

His words reassure her momentarily, yet the image of her Sioux children, playing only miles away, causes tears to well in her eyes.

"No, don't cry, Teresa. You have to remain strong...for your family." Thomas III continues to whisper into her ear. He realizes her predicament better than she; Papa Winniper could kill Teresa, her mother, brother, husband, and all her children in one afternoon, if he desired. Teresa rarely fears her father, but Thomas III has grown with a healthy paranoia for the man who is capable of murderous deeds.

"Sis...you have to protect yourself and your children. God knows what Papa would do if he found out...*you have to protect yourself.*" Thomas III repeats emphatically.

Teresa looks into her brother's eyes, considering the necessary mechanisms to conceal their family's secrets, and suddenly, the hug seems less endearing: they are two fools sailing in a drowning boat. Teresa pulls away slightly and continues to wipe her eyes.

"You're right, Thomas. But I can't leave them there. I'm going to find a way to bring my family together. Even if we have to run away, I don't care what Papa does. It's *my* family." She sobs openly, dabbing her eyes with her fingertips before looking around the aisle and noticing a few customers staring idly. In their minds, they plant a new gossiping tree, sprouting lies, rumors, and half-truths about the Winnipers' crazy daughter. "I better leave before the whole town knows what I'm crying about."

"What's done is done, sis. I doubt you'll make it home before they crucify you." Thomas III jokes sarcastically, and the passing thought brings a dark cloud into Teresa's mind. The adult siblings often muse about the Winniper family folklore in South Dakota, the untrue tales of the wonderfully wacky Winnipers. Teresa remembers that after Papa wrecked his 1928 DeSoto race car on Suicide Gorge one Christmas morning, the entire church began to believe and spread the gospel that Papa could never die. They testified that he must be a blessed king of God who will live forever.

Legend has it that Papa Winniper lost control of his DeSoto, spilled over a tight curve, and fell off a steep cliff. Exasperated spectators, many avid churchgoers, hiked down the cliff and found the car in pieces at the bottom of the tree-filled gorge. After an extensive search and rescue mission with the entire county foregoing their Christmas Day celebrations to search for the town's benefactor, they eventually found his unconscious body hidden in a red oak tree about fifty yards from his demolished car. There are conflicting accounts on how Papa actually came down from the tree; in his version, he regained consciousness and climbed down himself, but several old-timers still recall hoisting ropes and scaling ladders to pull the lifeless millionaire down to safety.

Papa Winniper has often recounted this story as a mark of his valor and youthfulness, but Teresa and Thomas III have never believed much of their father's words. The extravagant folklore surrounding the family has exposed a tragedy in the shadow of their torment—no matter how bright the moment, gloom will always follow. Thomas III continues to look at his sister; she believes that he cares for her well-being. He also understands the power of fiction.

"Maybe you should go, Teresa. I think you've said enough. You know, my customers love to gossip."

"Papa still calls them *'peasants'*. All the wealthy have their own farmlands like we do so only *certain types* shop *here*. And their gossip has never bothered me; it's the truth that really hurts. I think their fairytales are kinder than the truth."

"Fantasy is always better than reality, sis, because the consequences aren't real." Thomas III counters and gives her shoulder a soft pinch. "But will you be okay to drive home? You can't cry and drive. We don't want you to have an accident."

"I'll be fine. We're having a picnic at the country club." Teresa giggles happily, imagining herself as a good mother, providing her children with a privileged meal in a privileged environment. "We'll let the kids get tired in the swimming pool."

"Make sure Christina remembers her floaties," Thomas III reminds his sister, flapping his arms like a wild chicken. "She's no good in the water."

"I have another daughter to remember those. June's at home packing them now." Teresa turns her thoughts back to her wonderful suburb filled with quaint lies, and she senses an unsettling wave of regret wash over her body. "Well...uh, I'm off, baby brother. Um, don't work too hard, okay?"

"Who? Me?" Thomas III chuckles while pointing to his chest as Teresa turns away. "This place practically runs itself."

Waving his arms over the Winniper Market, Thomas III treats the small grocery store as if it is his kingdom. Teresa unexpectedly snickers at the managerial man who was once her impish, confused brother. She wonders if Papa will ever appreciate Thomas III and take pride in the kind of man that his son has become without feeling shame for his son's shortcomings. Teresa begins to walk away, still feeling that warm longing for home. She forgets all her worries about what her father potentially knows and she looks back to her brother as he resumes searching through the bread cart, inspecting each loaf according to his father's standards.

"It was good seeing you!" she calls childishly, seeking a lasting reassurance that her one constant relationship will not desert her. "You're still my favorite person in the world, baby brother."

"Ha, you're my favorite, too, big sis." Thomas III smirks awkwardly, squinting through his eyes under the dim ceiling lights. The store customers still flock aimlessly around them, taking whiffs of the conversation. "I'll come by the house soon. Maybe we can have a party."

He performs a comical shuffle, and Teresa giggles at the thought, an adolescent sister returning to temporarily appease her fears. She glides through the market, spying Potter in the bakery with one of Christina's grade school classmates. Teresa thanks God that the old perv is momentarily distracted, and she slinks from the market, sneaking quickly through the parking lot.

After she enters the Spoister and drops the bread loaves in the passenger seat, she places the key in the ignition but her hand pause. She begins to envision her Sioux children. Often, she ponders the impossible until it seems real, and what she lost, what she never did, and what she never could possess all combine to become a vision in front of her eyes. Woe to her imagination, she starts dreaming about the Sioux babies that she abandoned for lack of better options. She forced herself to deny her children while adhering to God's law—a noble sacrifice, her mother said. Olivia had suffered after having her Sioux babies taken from her following Teresa and Thomas III's births.

∞

Within her worldwide excursions, Teresa continued to search for a cure, or at least an explanation, to the Winniper family's affliction. Although their pregnancies would pass peacefully and seem easier than the pregnancies of others, when the day of birth arrived, every Winniper woman would bear twins: one boy, one girl, one white, one Sioux. For three generations, Teresa, her mother, and Teresa's late grandmother Ruby Winniper all bore two children of a different race and gender, both Winnipers, but, in the end, the ambitious Winniper men decided to kill the Sioux babies and raise the white babies in the lap of Midwestern suburbia's luxury.

On the surface, the Winniper family epitomizes the absolute best of everything. Though Thomas Winniper, Sr. could never explain or resolve the biological phenomena, the choice became clear when his dying wife conceived twins, one white boy and one Sioux girl. Only his son should survive. And when it came time for Papa Winniper to conceive with Olivia, whether a Sioux boy and a white girl or a white boy and a Sioux girl, the end was always the same. God or chaos chose the odds but the Winniper men chose their fate with each dead Sioux newborn. The surviving white newborn would always cry incessantly, forever mourning the loss from birth through death and beyond.

In order to quiet a town filled with gossip, all the Winniper men have concealed the family secret since it began with Papa's birth in 1891. The fear of being shamed, exposed as intermixed with Sioux blood, has compelled Teresa's parents and grandfather to eliminate any trace or evidence of their Sioux offspring. To date, Teresa, her grandmother, and her mother are the only known women to bear such twins, and as she travelled the world, seeking enlightenment or solace, she found neither.

Though their global treks meandered through exotic habitats filled with dangerous creatures, perilous adventures, and indigenous cultures, she never found an answer for *"Why?"* And after she returned, Papa introduced her to Ralph Townsend, who soon became her first husband. Teresa consented to the marriage out of weakness and bore biracial twins, Lucy and Duke. Despite her best efforts to remain loyal to all the strands of her family, her first marriage quickly dissolved into the typical Winniper web of deception. When she tried to tell Ralph about the family curse and the Sioux girl stashed nearby, he became more of a liability than an asset and Papa dealt with him accordingly.

With her second husband, Charles Kane, Teresa bore twins, a white girl and a Sioux boy, Christina and Charles. They were a cantankerous pairing even from the beginning; they cried the loudest when separated. Much like her first marriage, her relationship with Charles ended in the same turmoil with the twist of a new, young lover, Kenny Bethune.

Shortly after meeting Kenny two years ago, Teresa bore twins originally conceived in a tryst with the well-known Bethune bachelor. Her affair with Kenny was an elitist rebellion that produced another pregnancy and another Sioux child that she couldn't possibly keep. But her mother had executed a cunning plot to keep Teresa's Sioux children safe from Papa Winniper. She even convinced a family friend to raise the children in secrecy, risking the lives of even more innocent people.

Instead of following her father's wishes, her mother conspired with Berthine Lancaster, the Winniper house maid, to raise Teresa's Sioux children across the woods from the Winniper Family Estate. Teresa insisted on naming each of her children, hoping to reunite her family later in life and convince her Sioux children that she has always loved them.

∞

Her mother and Thomas III visit the children in secret, posing as an old friend and a family benefactor, taking whatever vegetables and clothes they can spare, and passing along updates to Teresa when possible. All along, Teresa has recognized how her mother enjoys a secret pleasure in their deception. Right underneath Papa Winniper's nose live three Sioux grandchildren that he has never known, but the women understand and fear that if their patriarch ever learns the truth, or worse, if he ever believes the truth could be exposed to the public, blood will surely run from any number of murders.

Nostalgia and circumstance make Teresa's heart pump faster as she drives out of the Winniper Pavilion parking lot. The seemingly inevitable disaster swells within the pit of her stomach and she remembers the anguished moments of conception when her babies were born. The pain of childbirth has paled in comparison to living without three of her babies. So vivid, only two years earlier, Teresa went into labor with June and Jazz during a fabricated day-vacation, giving her enough time away from Kenny to meet with her mother and Doc Morten, Jr. in secrecy—the unexplainable being too difficult to even comprehend.

Her misgivings and sins still twist her heart in a lifetime lost to a genetic trait, or, a genetic fate, or, is it a genetic mistake? She finds sadness in self-defeat, reckless metaphors making moments of rebellious tantrums; she exercises her freedom. The apex of such exercise is her ability to destroy herself, to willingly challenge a murderer's wrath.

Perhaps, in an unconscious effort to cause her own demise, Teresa's eyes blankly drift from the road ahead. Her attention tilts to the Winniper Pavilion fading in her rearview mirror, and she mistakenly gives into an angry impulse, one too many times, seeing the pavilion, the market, and the entire community as chains connected to her wealthy name. She can't help believing that her privileged, tormented life is an inherited mistake. And while her personal lament distracts her from the road, a rusted, blue Ford T truck that looks exactly like her brother's model appears behind her. Unnoticed, the truck speeds up quickly behind Teresa's Spoister. A few car lengths behind them, the sheriff's patrol car follows the Ford T closely, ensuring that the loose ends will be tied tight. For her last moment, all is reasonably lucid; she laments but she still heads home to her husband and children, but then, the familiar Ford truck violently slams into the Spoister's rear bumper like a battering ram created specifically to shatter her common life. The impact pulls Teresa from her frustrations and she quickly realizes that she is in danger.

She clutches the steering wheel tightly and tries to control her car, but the balance tilts between the front and rear tires. She glares frantically into the rearview mirror to see her brother driving his truck's front plate into her bumper. Thomas III glares through the windshield with a scornful sorrow in his eyes as he aims his car and aggressively rear-ends Teresa's Spoister. Her head smashes into her steering wheel abruptly, her chin careening off of the wooden console. She understands this moment only as a memory, a victimless crime that she initiated herself long ago.

There is only a feeling of lovely nothingness, her car rocking from side-to-side, and she drifts between conscious reality and darkness. Her father's Spoister careens violently off the road, and she feels the entire world swirl around her body. The car collides with a tree and the crash shatters the windows. Her head hits the steering wheel again as glass showers her hair and her face and the light...oh, the light to behold...

As the dust and fumes settle, Teresa leans against the steering wheel, gasping for air as she twists her head to the left where she sees her brother's truck creep slowly alongside the wreckage. His face is pale, numb, and drenched in cold sweat. He stares at her blankly with the eyes of a boy who once played her hero when they were children, but he does not save her today.

Teresa sees the ghost of a red-haired woman, wrapped in a bloody bedsheet, sitting in the passenger seat beside Thomas III. The woman weeps but then smiles sadly when she sees Teresa take her last breath, hoping to comfort her coming kin through her transition to death.

...................................*in*...*out*..............
..

And then, there is nothing.

∞

She awakes in a cold room, lying on a frigid metal bed. Rising to her elbows spiritedly, her lungs fill with what she believes is air; yet, her breath remains still, unlabored and motionless. She looks down over her arms, legs, and feet, her body still clad in the same turquoise sundress; one mangled blue heel shoe rests over her left foot. A sigh of relief washes over her body. The flash fades over her senses and she now stares at the metal bed, seeing her lifeless body as an adjacent door opens slowly.

"I don't know how long this will take, sweetheart." Doc Morten, Jr. enters the frigid room with his wife Marilyn following behind him, tugging on his lab coat. Along with being Winniper County's most popular doctor, he is also the medical examiner, hired as another inherited minion within the Winniper web, forced to cover-up secrets as the county coroner.

"Well, you promised we'd play bingo tonight!" Marilyn points her finger sternly at her husband. "I'm going to hold you to it, Morty!"

"I hope you do." The doctor smiles brightly and mockingly attempts to bite his wife's finger. A notorious flirt, drunkard, and humanitarian, Doc Morten, Jr. is also known for his selfishness.

Raised under his father's tutelage, he attends to Winniper County's medical needs, perfectly willing to give anyone as much care as they want as long as they can afford him; and in Winniper County, South Dakota, everyone can afford extra attention. If a mother thinks her child has measles, Doc Morten, Jr. will confirm the diagnosis and prescribe cold towels, castor oil, and elephant pills while entertaining the tyke with jokes from the latest newsreel. If an oil rig worker thinks he broke his back on the job, Doc will confirm his lawyer's statement and testify in court—for a nominal fee, of course.

As a source of pride and celebration, Doc Morten, Jr. is a very popular personality in Winniper County; however, his wife, Marilyn, is commonly disliked for her gossiping nature and her callousness when dealing with surviving family members. Many relatives, next of kin, and widows find Marilyn crude when she dishes details about the deceased. Most recently, she told half the Winniper Baptist Church choir that the deceased Deacon Phillips had bus tickets and a letter to "Raul" in his jacket pocket. Some of the Winniper citizens wonder if Marilyn attains her information through Doc Morten, Jr. or infiltrates the exam room on her own volition, but as she flirts with her husband, heedless of Teresa's corpse, she behaves like a snoop out for a scoop, unconcerned for the privacy or respect of the dead.

"Well, hurry up!" Marilyn impatiently flails her arms over Teresa's corpse, taking glimpses of the deceased's torn dress. "Get on with it!"

"I think you should leave first, Mary."

"I ain't goin' nowhere!" Marilyn barks loudly. "There's been a murder, Morty! Someone attacked this woman in our town! What if it's a serial killer?"

"Keep your voice down, Mary. There's no need to shout." Doc Morten, Jr. steps around his wife and grabs several tools from a nearby dark oak desk. "Teresa probably just ran off the road."

"Nope, this is definite foul play, Morty. *It's a tragedy.*" Marilyn pouts, leaning into her husband and looking up to his face intently. "Do you know how hard it's been not to tell anyone about their family? Those babies…"

"Yes, but you can see the consequences right here before us, darling. Besides, they pay us well enough." Doc Morten, Jr. looms over her body and smiles coyly as he grabs her wide hips. "Now go on, and git. I can't concentrate with you in here. Your beauty is too distracting."

"Nice try, buster." Marilyn points her index finger toward her husband's mouth, daring him to resist her. "You're not getting me out of here."

"Oh, yes I am." The doctor attempts to bite his wife's finger again but she recoils quickly. "You know you bring out the animal in me, Mary. Now get out of here!"

"No! I ain't goin'!" Marilyn yells sternly, placing her hand on Doc Morten, Jr.'s chest and pushing him playfully. "You'll have to throw me out!"

"That's fine, sweetheart." Doc Morten, Jr. grabs Marilyn's hand swiftly and pulls her weight toward him as he lifts her over his shoulders. "Have it your way!"

"Put me down, Morty! Put me down!" Marilyn's legs flail wildly as her husband carries her out of the room. Teresa hears him fumble up a flight of stairs as Marilyn screams. "Morty, stop! Don't drop me!"

A resounding thud echoes above her, followed by a door slamming loudly, and Doc Morten, Jr. lumbers down the steps and re-enters the exam room.

"Doc?" Teresa speaks delicately, feeling nothing, fearing the finality of the unquestionable truth. Doc Morten, Jr. moves across the checkered linoleum floor and stands over Teresa's tattered body. "Doc, can you hear me?"

"What'd they do to you, Teresa?" the doctor asks quietly while Teresa's arms and legs lie over the sides of the metal slab; her limbs are badly bruised with glass embedded in her skin. As her ghost moves closer to her dead body, watching in shock and confusion, she stands next to Doc Morten, Jr. and he begins to weep softly, mustering up a few tears for the girl he helped bring into the world.

"Is this real?" She passes her hand over the doctor's head, testing her existence, but she can only feel nothingness. Her spirit drifts from her center like the warmth from a recently used stove. "Tell me that I'm not dead, Doc. Please, can you hear me?"

"I never believed a word your father said about you…" Doc Morten, Jr. turns away to retrieve his surgical tray filled with incision tools, gauze, and a small record player. He gently adjusts the album in the record player before looking back toward Teresa's corpse. "I know you and your ma' saved those babies, but he didn't have to do what he done."

The doctor starts his record and Beethoven's "Moonlight Sonata" fills the examination room, a procedural necessity for postmortem music therapy. He believes the dead can hear the music and find peace in the end.

"This is real…I'm dead." Teresa feels death's finality closing around her from all angels and angles. "I'm dead…and my brother killed me."

As she looks around, she focuses on a mesmerizing darkness that begins to loom along the edges of the room. Faint voices surround her yet she remains still while standing beside the oblivious doctor; she only wants one thing: her family. Teresa backs away from the darkness but her end consumes the room while she dreams of her suburban home, hoping to escape the room and avoid watching the coming cuts to her corpse.

"You know I have a job to do, Teresa. For the safety of my family, I have to follow your father's orders." Doc Morten, Jr. adjusts the pair of white cotton gloves over his hands and grabs a large scalpel and syringe. "Your death was the result of a tragic accident…caused by…uh…*exhaustion*. Yes, that's it. You fell asleep at the wheel."

Teresa steps away from the doctor, staring at him in horror before running from her corpse on the table. Embracing the darkness, she passes wildly through nothingness, trying to find her children—all of them. She thinks of her home in the suburbs of Winniper County, the well-planned Winniper County roads with Dutch duplexes and quaint cottage homes. Without proper lighting, the residential streets would seem ominous in the evening, but the neighbors' son Rudy gets paid $10 a day to turn on the oil lamps that hang over each home's mailbox. Rudy's parents, the Chamberlains, refuse to pay him so their light is rarely on even after he returns home. Thinking of these intricacies to the setting, Teresa runs through the aimless streets, searching for her home. Seeing the front door, she races down the small driveway in a panic and bursts through the front door. There is an eerie silence that is unfamiliar.

She stands as an unseen ghost in the foyer. The house lights are off and the impending doom of the moment becomes a siren that blares throughout her reality: she hears sinister alarms coming from upstairs. Teresa runs up the staircase, passing the picture of her sitting with her brother at Café Demur in Rome.

∞

She wore her white champion suit and he wore his Winniper County College sweater even though he had foolishly dropped out of school one year earlier, only three courses shy of completing his degree. Papa Winniper thought his son's failure was just another display of his ineptitude, but Teresa knew that Thomas III had purposely failed to meet their father's expectations. The old man had grand plans for his college-educated son, but her brother was more afraid of his future responsibility than an honest day of work. The Winniper Market became an adequate consolation for the son who had never impressed his father; yet, Thomas III still obeyed Papa Winniper, perhaps clinging to any opportunity to prove his worth.

∞

The sirens continue to shriek noisily as Teresa reaches the second story; she sees Duke and Christina pulling June by her arms and legs. June squeals deafeningly; her cries infuse with the sirens and Teresa feels the world around her begin to collapse. Even after their mother's passing, Christina and Duke still struggle to love their little sister; they show affection through aggression and convey discontent through violence.

"Stop, Duke! Christina, stop that!" Teresa screams mutedly, though the force of her angst shakes the walls. Suddenly, Kenny opens the door to their master bedroom and Duke promptly drops June's legs. June stifles her cries and the sirens cease for a moment, until Kenny yells at the children, blasting another round of alarms throughout the modest 2-story home. Teresa cannot understand her husband; his jumbled words sound as if he is yelling through a faulty loudspeaker.

"Kenny?" Teresa begins to walk slowly toward her erratic lover, and his words become clearer as she moves closer to him.

"...it's my fault..." Kenny sobs uncontrollably before turning away, wailing frantically, and slamming the door behind him. Teresa walks through the door as he plops into bed amidst empty liquor bottles and framed photos of her. She lies down next to her husband, a gentle ghost with a wallowing widow.

"Stay strong, Kenny," Teresa whispers in hopes that he can hear, feeling that the certainty of her death is still too difficult for either of them to digest. She rests her translucent hand over his forehead, unseen in the air and tries to wipe his hair softly. "Think of the children..."

"Why did she have to die?" Kenny's question lingers in the room, unanswered in life or death. "I betrayed her. Mama was wrong. I should've gotten the bread. She will never let me be a man!"

"Kenny...what do you mean? I..." Teresa remains frozen while lying on the bed; once again, dark nothingness creeps into the edges of the room. "I never thought..."

"It was her father. He caused all of this!" Kenny continues to sob, pounding his fists into the mattress; the empty liquor bottles clang against the picture frames creating a macabre percussion melody. "He found out that we were leaving...and he killed her...but...who told him?"

"Be reasonable, Kenny," Teresa consoles without touch, hoping to reach across the living threshold so that her husband can sense her presence. "Think about our family. You have to protect our children."

"And she left me here! I'm twenty-two, with three kids...and only one is mine!" Kenny's exacerbated worries shake the bed as he shifts his body and his anger continues to spill through his rant. "And she left me with that father-in-law! He might kill me, too! What am I going to do?"

"There's no one else to take care of them, Kenny," Teresa pleads with Kenny but he still cannot hear her and he remains stoic in bed. His cheeks droop groggily as his eyelids bat up and down, struggling to remain open throughout his drunken stupor. Teresa has seen this desperate look upon his face many times. "Kenny, you have to be stronger. You can't let Papa have them. You have to…"

"I-I-I c-c-can't l-l-leave…" Kenny's words slur drunkenly. "At l-l-least, not until that old man p-p-ays f-f-for w-w-what he d-d-done! He's g-g-goin' to p-p-pay, Teresa! As God is m-m-my w-witness, he'll pay!"

Teresa smiles amidst the tragedy, happy for some solace in the afterlife. She believes in Kenny's resolution to see her family through to better days.

"Thank you, Kenny."

"Besides, as l-l-long as I r-r-raise these kids, th-that horrid old fart will need me! He don't want nothin' to happen t-t-to his p-p-precious grandson." Kenny slams his palm violently on the mattress, and Teresa jumps from the bed as her world shakes again. Kenny's eyes shut completely and his entire body lies comatose amidst the empty liquor bottles and framed pictures. He is an embarrassing familial patriarch. Teresa flees back into the hallways as Kenny's words fade in her consciousness.

"As God is my witness, he'll pay."

In the hallway, Christina and Duke leave June whimpering on the floor while they engage in a disconnected discussion, bantering back and forth though Teresa cannot discern their sentences. Duke storms into his room and looks back over his shoulder as June calls to him.

"Go…funeral…"

"Mom…hi…" Duke abruptly slams the door, leaving June alone while Christina walks into her bedroom. June drops her head sadly before rising to her feet and walking away toward her guitar at the end of the hall. Teresa stands silently in crumbling disbelief; her world, her family, and her life fade around her, existing beyond her reach but within her spirit. She struggles to maintain focus on her battle with the darkness as absolute nothingness creeps deeper into her consciousness; yet, she is still not at peace.

Teresa feels an unsettling need to see *all* of her children. She can hear Christina close her bedroom door and June sits alone in the hallway, strumming a lonely guitar with her fingers. The ever-enveloping darkness continues to consume Teresa's surroundings, but she quickly avoids death's coming end and runs into the last strands of light in her visible consciousness. She flees frantically from her fate, while thinking about her Sioux children and their home—Berthine's cabin.

Teresa turns her thoughts to the extensive dirt pathway that stretches through the wheat and crop fields of the Winnipers' farmland. She moves quickly through the miles and miles of real estate surrounding the Winnipers' oil reserves and the forgotten Sioux village where Berthine's small cabin sits quietly in the middle of a clearing within an oak forest. The old Sioux village is an appropriate ghost town, an afterthought amidst the Winniper family's oil wealth and farming profits. Winniper County has completely forgotten the sins of its origin and their secrets remain hidden within the forest.

Time starts to feel like a fly, landing wherever necessary to survive. Teresa passes through columns of tall oaks until she sees the white, wooden steps that lead to the Berthine's modest oak cabin. The handcrafted oak doors create a sense of timeless decorum, and Teresa flies into the home, imagining her Sioux children all together, awaiting her as if their mother had only stepped out for a moment.

And suddenly, she whispers in acceptance, "I am home."

FEBRUARY 1948

Sunday	Monday	Tuesday	Wednesday	Thursday	Friday	Saturday
1	2	3	4	5	6	7
8	9	10	11	12	13	14
15	16	17	18	19	20	21
22	23	24	25	26 ★	27	28
29						

Thursday, February 26, 1948
Christina Kane

Play me a song to keep my heart in tune;
Remember the tale of Jazz and June,
Where love untouchable, a truth unfound
Turns heaven and hell upside down,
And 'morrow lies within warm arms,
Dreaming of passion's poisonous charms,
And peace is not hard to find
As they sing together, forever in time.

Christina Kane sits in her family's living room, puffing her cheeks and looking out the window. Now, at age nine, she never enjoys spending time with her siblings and stepfather. Maybe, she could be at Burger Town with friends, but a steady rain has ruined all her plans to skip the evening's family dinner at home. She wishes the downpour would stop; rainy weather is rare in Winniper County where the sun seems to always shine—except today.

Filled with glistening sunlight, the man-made streets and immaculate driveways form a traveler's brochure of American suburbia. Christina has always felt that Winniper County is the most beautiful place in the entire world even though she has never left town long enough to compare anywhere else to her home. In their brief interactions, her grandfather has ensured her that she and her siblings have no reason to ever leave, no reason to stray too far from his reach or the luxury and leisure that he can provide for them. Carefully proportioned sidewalk-to-street ratios perfectly pave the upper class community with manicured grass lawns that match the manicured toes perched prominently on pristine porches. The haughty housewives and money-grubbing mistresses use their overlooking eyes to stare across the sidewalks and into nearby homes, observing the grandeur while judging each family's status within the town's wealthy hierarchy—the symbols and evidence of which stretch far down any road in any direction of Winniper County.

When walking around her neighborhood, Christina often views her suburb as a bountiful destination for the rich and richly influenced. She wonders why anyone would ever leave Winniper County; it seems like the perfect place for a girl to become a housewife to a sturdy, strong, and faithful egomaniac like her stepfather, Kenny, or her estranged, biological father, Charles. She hasn't seen her father since he left her mother, but she had hoped that after her mother's death, he would come to claim her—he did not.

Christina continues to stare out to the soaked world and wonders what most teenagers wonder: *Why, oh why am I here? Why can't I leave home? Why does it always rain when I want to go outside? Why does Mrs. Chamberlain always leave her husband's Ford convertible uncovered after she drives it?*

A British oil trader, Ronald Chamberlain comes home every day and complains until his throat is sore about his car being uncovered; and even if Christina is listening to music or hiding from her siblings or her stepfather, she can still hear Mr. Chamberlain howling from inside his duplex next door.

"Sheila! I've told you time and time again, put the cover over my car!" Mr. Chamberlain wails after arriving home in his Porsche, a more practical car for his daily commute. He often speeds down the block and squeals into the driveway, anxious to get home after a hard day working at the Winniper Brokerage Firm—a subsidy of the Winniper family's parent corporation, the Winniper Family Holding Company. "I've told you and told you, but you still don't seem to learn! I may just brand it on your forehead while you sleep! I bet if I burn the words on your forehead, you'd cover the car then!"

"Oh, bollocks!" Mrs. Chamberlain's Yorkshire accent emphasizes her high-pitched shrill. When not in her presence, Christina always imagines Sheila Chamberlain, a tall, buxom blonde, as a fairy princess in a grand, flowing dress, complete with a jeweled crown and a bedazzled wand. Mrs. Chamberlain flutters around her home, scantily clad in revealing outfits, hilariously defenseless against her own ridiculous nature—a fairy without her tale. "It's just a bloody conver'ible! You can buy ten more in town if you like! It's not like you don't have the money! Who cares?"

"I care, Sheila! I care very much!" Ronald counters aggressively, unbuttoning his tie and loosening his sleeves. "My father built that Model HC! If my mother saw how you treated it, she would absolutely die!"

"Good! I hope she comes over soon!"

"Take that back, Sheila!" Mr. Chamberlain pleads as though this argument hasn't happened countless times before. "My mother loves you, and I will not have you disrespecting her!"

"*Loves me?*" Mrs. Chamberlain retorts, stomping around the car and falling to her knees in the driveway. "Your mother detests me, and she killed Mumford!"

"She didn't mean to kill your dog, sweetheart!" Mr. Chamberlain explains. "You have to understand, Jewish women don't like German shepherds, dear. I told you not to buy him."

"But she hung him outside with an extension cord!" Mrs. Chamberlain mimes the noose around her neck and makes herself the victim, hoping to heap her sorrow upon her husband so that she can become blameless for the bird feces on his prized convertible.

"She thought he was a persecutor!" Mr. Chamberlain tries to comfort his wife while Christina usually assumes her post at the window, watching intently, filled with aspirations of becoming a scientist who may one day study the Chamberlains as test subjects. "I told you she was sorry…and I bought you a new dog!"

"A new dog? Scruffy is a mouse!" Mrs. Chamberlain continues her pity party, shuffling aimlessly around the driveway in tears. "You bough' me a li'l rodent, a chi-chi!"

"It's called a *chi-wa-wa*, darling, and they're all the rage in Hollywood. Joan Crawford has three!" Mr. Chamberlain continually adds, holding up the small pup. The Chamberlains often neglect their pet and allow the mutt to defecate throughout the neighborhood. Rudy purposely allows the chow to soil the well-kept lawns so that he may dutifully clean the mess for an extra tip on his street light route.

"We're not in Hollywood! I don't care what Joan Crawford has!" Mrs. Chamberlain always becomes irate when her husband, or any man in her presence, mentions another woman. She fears competition for male attention and loathes the idea of any challenge. Her pouting has built a nice platform upon which she can shout her tragedy to the world. "I wanted a big dog and I loved Mumford, and there's not a damn thin' you, your mother, or that car can do to bring him back!"

Around now, Christina usually watches Mrs. Chamberlain storm into her home, followed by Mr. Chamberlain. Often times, Christina would also hear a door slam, or a chandelier crash, or even a small explosion. Christina has since learned that the explosions come from homemade pipe bombs produced by Rudy. For Christina, watching Rudy Chamberlain evolve into a malcontent teen has become an independent study of a spoiled American youth. As an only child, Rudy has received everything his heart has desired, but he has never been happy with anything that he has received.

∞

Considering his eccentricities, Christina once pitied Rudy; she felt that he never had a chance. **Any child who receives that much attention inevitably thinks too highly of himself**; and, in doing so, Rudy's mind became incredibly centered on one thing: his own pleasure. Unlike most good, clean, Christian-American teenagers, Rudy never developed inhibitions or even moral fears. He simply did not care about his future, his faith, or even his eternal soul. In class, Rudy would profess his love for Satan, Hitler, Buddha, Jesus, and Robert Johnson all in one sentence. This, however, is not the reason for Christina's contemptuous attitude toward the young Chamberlain heir, but rather, Christina despises Rudy's penchant for using her house as a test site for his explosive, and often illegal, scientific experiments.

Sneaking over, under, and in through the top of her home, Rudy would creep, crawl, and climb into every nook and cranny he could find, only to steal, smash, electrify, and/or detonate whatever his mischievous mind desired to destroy at the moment. Originally, Christina thought she and Rudy would become great friends because they shared a mutual love for science. She dreamed of becoming an archeologist and traveling the world like her mother, while he dreamed of explosives and high-impact reactions.

Over the years, her passion and proximity have made her an easy target for Rudy, who favors being more competitive than compassionate. The night before Rudy and Christina's 3rd grade science fair, Rudy cut a hole through her attic and crept down to her family's living room where he glued a miniature, plastic man within Christina's science project: a volcano model of Pompeii. She spent weeks constructing the three-dimensional landscape complete with a newspaper and clay volcano. Rudy's last-minute contribution went completely unnoticed.

Christina entered her Pompeii model into the science fair the next day, unaware of the coming catastrophe. As she presented her science project to the parents, teachers, and students passing by her display, Christina began to catch a whiff of a rotten, foul smell. Despite the odor, she continued her presentation without pause, explaining the Battle of Pompeii and the caustic volcano that wiped out much of the population; yet, as she continued, onlookers started to become more and more revolted by her science fair project and the smell lingering from within the replica.

Looking around, Christina still could not discern the fecal odor. Hearing the whispers that began to build around her science project, she looked within her unassuming town of Pompeii. Smack dab in the middle of her volcano landscape, under the cover of a pineapple tree, which she had handcrafted from her mother's pottery clay and painted with her brother's watercolors, Rudy's miniature man had become inappropriately automated, dropping his pants and defecating small pellets of dog feces on the tree's fallen pineapple fruit. Christina later learned that Rudy spent weeks planning to sabotage her science project. He collected feces from around the neighborhood, loaded the excrement into a syringe, and then injected the stool into the miniature toy, or, as Rudy called him, "Diarrhea Man".

Needless to say, their teacher promptly disqualified Christina from the science fair and their principal suspended her from school for a week. Whereas most students could not have executed such a mischievous plot without bragging to a friend, Rudy had no friends, and he never mentioned his gag to anyone. He left Christina complaining about a ghost intruder who had somehow sabotaged her science fair project and subsequently ruined her 3rd grade report card with her first and only non-A. She had always excelled, but a suspension and a B seemed to doom her chances at becoming a scientist. Time has revealed that the 3rd grade science fair was merely one instance among many during which Rudy Chamberlain's crooked creativity brought misfortune into Christina's life. As a result of all his boyish pranks, she could neither trust nor care for Rudy; in fact, she has often wished for his demise.

∞

Christina thinks that if he were dying from an unknown disease and only she could cure him, she would stand directly in front of him and joyfully watch him die a slow death.

"Christina! Christina, come help me!" Kenny screams from the kitchen like a lost child in a supermarket. Though she is Teresa's second child, sharing no blood relation to her mother's third husband, Christina is the eldest female in the household, and the only one who notices her stepfather's fragility. While her brother and sister remain in their respective seclusion, still dealing separately with their mother's death, Christina tends to Kenny's widowed sensitivities, knowing that he is, in fact, the oldest child in the home.

Like cold fiberglass, Kenny easily shatters under pressure; he has never completely bolstered the family under his patriarchal power following Teresa's death. Only Christina seems to care and coddle his uselessness, which makes her the only one in the home who accepts his weakness and his incessant need for a maternal figure's help, even when that maternal figure is a nine-year-old spinster-in-training. Kenny is a twenty-four-year-old adolescent who still enjoys being babied, even by his children.

"Christina! Please help!"

"Coming!" she calls through the living room, standing from her perch in the window as God's urine continues to cascade from the heavens. The consistent rainfall soaks Mr. Chamberlain's convertible with reckless abandon and wide, wet puddles accumulate throughout the interior. Christina anticipates a pending argument with verbal fireworks and she smiles to herself while walking through the family's dark living room. She stops to rearrange the pictures over the fireplace, placing photos of her in front, transitioning Duke's pictures to the back, and folding June's baby pictures face down—a common posturing tactic in the household.

∞

Christina barely remembers living with her father, Charles Kane, before he divorced her mother after her affair with Kenny. Both Duke and Christina lived with their respective fathers briefly before their mother moved on, finally landing with Kenny whom she loved until her death. Duke and Christina never knew their mother's reasons for leaving their fathers and Christina doubts her mother could have even explained. Teresa always seemed like an enigma, undefined and uncontrolled; her mother was certainly unlike any of the other mothers that Christina met at school functions. Sure, Teresa attended the science fairs and parent-teacher meetings, but Christina felt as though her mother always had something better to do. She was a distracted mother, though she tried her best to look the part. Teresa would dress up so much more than the other mothers; she wore sparkling diamonds, bright sundresses, and high heels as if she were attending a far more important event than a bake sale. Christina fondly reminisces upon these moments, looking over the pictures of her mother while smiling about the better days when life seemed simple.

∞

"Christina!" her stepfather beckons again from the kitchen. "Come help me, please!"

Presumably, he has heard her rearranging the picture frames; Kenny is very edgy about the children mentioning their mother or even looking over the old pictures in the dimly lit living room. He once tried to take the pictures to the attic, but the children protested, cried, and actually bonded together against him. It was then that he realized their collective strength—the Winniper offspring. Knowing that he could never stay close to the family's fortune without the children's compliance, he returned Teresa's pictures to the living room mantle and he became a servant to the children's collective will. He is a guardian in name only. Christina enters the kitchen through the side door that leads to the living room, and the smell of broth and garlic immediately hits her nose.

"*Eck*, what is that?"

"It's dinner, chicken broth!" Kenny announces proudly, placing his fists on his hips like a superhero. "Sheila...uh, I mean, Mrs. Chamberlain gave me the recipe. She says it's healthy."

"*Mrs. Chamberlain*? I've never seen her cook a day in her life!" Christina treads cautiously through the kitchen, keeping her nose far from the boiling pot of broth. "She has a maid, a butler, two cooks, and two sous chefs! Her cooks even have their own cooks!"

"Christina, don't be so crude! We once had a maid, too, if you remember, *Cle-o-tha*. Besides, Mrs. Chamberlain is a very nice lady; she's been very kind to us over the years." Kenny scolds softly, after referring to the Negro maid that he fired following Teresa's death. He places his arm around his stepdaughter's shoulders and his greasy oven mitt swipes against her cheek, lightly coating her chin in dust, oil, and broth. "Sheila's helped me in *many* ways after your mother passed."

He steals a look into Christina's eyes to investigate whether she understands his innuendo.

"I'm sure she has…" Christina remarks slyly, more so to let her stepfather know that she understands more about his exploits than he would like her to acknowledge. As a precocious child, Christina once envisioned her family as a normally functioning organism, sharing and growing together as one, yet, since her mother's death, their five-part harmony has become a discontent quartet, in which each voice seeks its own solo and never carries the right pitch. And, to use another metaphor, the household has become a Domestic Bureau of Investigation in which Christina, Duke, June, and Kenny hunt for the evidence to expose each other's secrets and crimes, in order to gain leverage in their constant attempts to alleviate any individual responsibility to keep the family façade alive and well. If Kenny can lie about his relationship with Sheila, Christina can turn over pictures in the living room, Duke can stay out all night without calling home, and June can lock herself away in her room, strumming her guitar and singing her songs about nothing: no one has an obligation to love inside a house of lies.

Although Kenny has sole ownership of the family's duplex, he has never controlled the movements within. The children don't walk on eggshells, or attempt to hover and hope not to alarm Kenny to their whereabouts. They've never cared about feigning respect; Kenny is an afterthought in terms of discipline or supervision. Even now, as Christina opens an overhead cabinet and retrieves the dinner plates, utensils, and napkins to prepare the table for his chicken broth, she knows her two siblings are somewhere in the house, yet she hears nothing upstairs.

She lifts her head to hear above her stepfather's ramblings about his squawk stew. The first floor is the silent foundation of the discordant household, yet, secretly in separate bedrooms on the second floor, a fifteen-year-old boy paints macabre portraits of car crashes and a six-year-old girl stretches her small fingers over an acoustic guitar, looking back and forth between the strings and a chord chart, trying to strum a new chord. Both youths normally indulge in their respective arts after arriving home from school, conjuring up whatever visage or inspiration that the day has brought into their minds, but they mutually avoid Kenny.

Christina is the only one who can tolerate him consistently, maybe for want of a paternal figure in her life. She secretly thinks that neither Duke, June, nor her stepfather has a true plan or life goal. To her, they seem to lack a common future; individual escapes seem inevitable. The family of four simply lives to endure the day's drama, impatiently passing through these moments in the nest egg. They believe that tomorrow will be a little better, as long as they can survive today.

As Christina walks through another side door into the adjacent dining room, she begins to position the plates and utensils in their proper place. She remembers how her mother taught her to set the table when they still lived with her biological father. She believes that her mother knew all along that Christina would be the one who cared for the family in her absence. Christina's anger was, and still is, a deceptive act to disguise her vulnerability. It is only during these calm, maternal moments, when the world stops for a simple nurturing task, that Christina can remember her mother fully, with both joy and sadness. She thinks that these moments mock her mother's memory. Setting a table, staring at old pictures that now mean nothing, she invents the lessons that her lackluster mother thought were important for any woman to know. The irony brings a wry smile to Christina's face; her mother taught her how to set the table for a family that didn't even attend her funeral.

∞

"It's too cold outside!" Christina protested as a selfish and sorrowful seven-year-old.

"Yeah, that's right! It's too cold!" Duke repeated in agreement. Although he is the oldest of his white siblings, born almost six years before Christina, Duke is an instinctual follower. He gravitates toward submitting his personal will to appease those closest to him. Whatever his friends do, Duke wants to join in, and however his friends feel, Duke feels the same way.

"Mom wouldn't want us to catch a cold," Christina suggested to her siblings, beginning to convince them for the first of many times as the hierarchy emerged following their mother's death. "You know what? For the sake of Mom, I'm not going!"

In that moment, the logic felt morally empowering as she pushed by June and stormed toward her bedroom; Duke finished the job with a quick remark and entered his lair, leaving June alone in the second-floor hallway. The cohabited space between their bedrooms had devolved into a labyrinth of rag dolls, army replicas, unclaimed dirty clothes, paint canvases, art supplies, and an overturned filing cabinet that vomited twenty years of marriages, motherhood, and memories. June remained in the hallway while Duke shut his bedroom door with a slam.

"You wouldn't catch me dead at her funeral!" Duke yelled from inside his room.

"I heard that!" June wailed in the hallway. "Mom!"

"Mom is dead, June. She's never coming back!" Christina barked from her bedroom door, eyeing her little sister with a newfound hatred that has lasted ever since. "And it's all *your* fault!"

"I'm telling my father!" June spoke too soon. Duke's bedroom door flung open, and he charged toward his little sister. He still wore his work clothes from the night before, and from the smell of his trousers, Christina assumed he hadn't washed his uniform in many weeks. His faded, cheese-covered slacks smelled like soggy burgers from his crummy part-time job at Burger Town. He loved the joint so much as a kid that he pleaded with Papa Winniper to let him work there. Duke wanted to get close to the source of those oily, ooey-gooey meat patties. The foul stench of old beef consumed his room and crept into the hallway, but, Christina joined her noxious brother and advanced toward their little sister without pause. Since June's conception, she has been the object of Christina's childhood contempt. June brought along an infantile stepfather who stole Teresa from Christina's biological father and June has always seemed to gain favor at Christina's expense.

"If you go near Kenny's door," Christina snarled over June, "I'll break you in half."

"And I'll break the other half," Duke added, hurrying next to Christina's side. The two elder siblings hovered threateningly over their little sister. "I'm sick of you whining to that drunk!"

"Don't touch me!" June recoiled defensively as her siblings descended upon her arms and legs. Christina and Duke began to strike their sister with welts, muffling her screams as best they could amidst the attack. A common tactic within the household, the elder siblings found it easy to overpower their baby sister. As a natural second fiddle, Duke has always considered Christina to be the alpha dog, which has given her free reign to insult and assault June whenever she has deemed necessary.

"Ugh, you smell like that crappy burger village, Duke!" Christina yelled while striking her sister in the shoulder.

"It's called Burger Town!" Duke replied as they began to grab and pull June's legs and arms. "And I only make the fries! So I smell like fries!"

"AHHH!" June squealed in pain while Christina pulled her hair sharply, stretching her scalp and forehead.

"I like their milkshakes," Christina remarked, taking a moment to release June's hair before punching June in the arm.

"You only like the milkshakes because I give them to you for free," Duke clarified, as he and Christina once again grabbed and pulled June's arms and legs in a vicious stretch hold. They maliciously tortured their baby sister without care for her safety or well-being.

Once, Duke and Christina watched a newsreel about Texas Klansmen who used horses to pull a Negro man apart by the limbs. After seeing such brutality, the two siblings began to corner June at any waking moment and yank her limbs until she would scream loud enough to alarm their mother or rouse Kenny from his binge drinking. That particular day, Kenny had planned to drink himself into an alcoholic coma and forget his wife's funeral, but, for June, her siblings' abusive torture had suddenly turned her silent mourning into a high-pitched expression of her physical torment.

"AH!!!" she bawled in the sharpest pitch of fear to ever pierce a human ear. "Daddy, help!"

"June, shut up!" Christina cackled above June, pulling her baby sister's arms roughly while looking back toward the master bedroom.

After receiving the news of Teresa's murder and viewing the body the day before, Kenny locked himself in their lonesome bedroom. The images of his shattered wife lying lifelessly on the medical slab haunted his thoughts—the medical examiner and coroner, Doc Morten, Jr. had not done a good job cleaning her wounds; Kenny assumed that the doctor's wife distracted him from his duties. The car accident severely disfigured Teresa's torso, and her face remained tattered from shards of glass even after the doctor's autopsy. Kenny struggled to hold his stomach during the viewing; he had never observed such carnage, not even in the war reels before a picture show. And as he gasped at the gashes and scars on a face that was once so beautiful and so innocent, Kenny saw vengeance for all their lies and deception. Papa had exacted his revenge upon Teresa's beauty. Kenny stared over her marred cheeks and bone protrusions, knowing he could never replace her. Their fantasy love was truly over.

Though he was a known alcoholic and a trust-fund reject before meeting Teresa, her love had helped him prioritize his habit. Consenting to their marriage as a down payment, Kenny willingly sacrificed his bachelorhood and settled into the monotony of home life; but, when he married Teresa, the eighteen-year-old Romeo was ill-prepared for domestication. He performed well in matters of newlywed romance, but he never embraced his role as a father or stepfather. Sadly, his apathy has no bounds; Kenny has neither enjoyed nor embraced June or his stepchildren. From toddler to tyrant to teen, all three youths have always seemed kinder and smarter than Kenny. In some way, each child exemplified the excellence of their Winniper blood. Duke's artistic eye for drawing, Christina's scientific proclivity, or June's musical virtuosity, Teresa's children had more skills than Kenny ever possessed. Duke, Christina, and even little June have always wielded similarly sinister mind states that question everyone and calculate everything, while identifying weaknesses to exploit for personal gain.

"Yea, June, stop crying!" Duke growled, following Christina's lead and pulling June's legs. "We're just playing!"

June continued to scream as only a little girl knows how, while she summoned a few pathetic and pitiful tears—the definitive damsel in distress.

"Stop! You're hurting me!" June screamed loudly and Christina, the elder and angrier sister, opened her heart slightly, easing her grip momentarily. Before their mother left the house to die, Teresa reminded June to pack the swimming floaties for Christina and June still had them on her arms a day later. Christina turned her head from side-to-side, investigating each end of the hallway, looking left to their parents' bedroom and then right toward her own. She finally brought her glare back to June and continued to numbingly stretch her baby sister to the brink. "Christina, please! I won't tell!"

While June begged her big sister to release her arms, Christina continued to ignore her pleas, glowering unaffectedly at her squealing sibling, still unwilling to love her. Christina was not always notorious for her crookedness, cowardice, or caution. Initially terrorized or neglected by her older brother, her biological father, and then by Kenny, Teresa pitied her middle child. She often tried to quell Christina's anger by coddling her, coaching her, and trying to mentor her through those rainy days spent staring out the living room window. Yet, despite Teresa's best efforts, Christina grew to resent her mother's methods with regards to her parenting skills, her cavalier attire, and especially her choice of men. Christina began to fear that one day she, too, would fit her mother's mold, and abandon her dreams of research laboratories and magical reactions in order to chase uncaring men and romantic fantasies.

∞

Physically, Christina has always been quite frail; her thin, strawberry blonde hair resembles both her mother's blonde and great-grandmother's crimson hue. Her Uncle Thomas has often remarked that Christina looks more like Teresa than June, but Christina could never tell whether her uncle meant his comments as compliments. He frequently laughs after his remarks, no matter if he meant to be funny.

"The mailman delivered the wrong mail. {*laugh*}"
"You should take it to your neighbor. {*laugh*}"
"I've never even had a neighbor. {*laugh*}"

Born with elitist guilt and a bad sense of humor, Uncle Thomas has become a scratched record, a soul that never sounds right and never catches the rhythm of life. Whenever he chooses to check on his late sister's family, he awkwardly enters the home, interjecting into the family discord and inspecting their natural disharmony.

During her uncle's visits to their modest, suburban abode, Christina braces herself for a myriad of sappy comebacks and half-hearted gestures. Christina inherited Thomas's lack of social fluidity, yet she is also dissimilar to him, in that, while he allows his verbal record to skip constantly, Christina silences her song before giving others a chance to truly listen.

She is like her late mother in that way; Christina has become guarded, forcing herself into a cocoon of pseudo-maternal instincts. She tries her best to supervise her siblings and stepfather, but she fears losing herself in the disturbance, the ridicule, and the repercussions from her failure. These doubts are parts of a predestined anxiety, the predetermined paradox of the abandoned child. How can a daughter replace the mother who never was much of a mother at all?

Although she performed well in her science courses, Christina seldom learned anything within the classroom. Instead, she resigned herself to the library and read book after book on her course subjects. She would then return to the classroom and ask the teacher question after question until the teacher could no longer answer. Even at a young age, Christina cherished challenging the establishment, proving to herself that her vulnerability as the middle child would end one day—the day when she learned to maneuver and manipulate men like her mother. It would seem that after Teresa's death, Christina gained all the strength she needed to hold dominion over their household, but very little of that power has translated to the outside world.

∞

"AH! Stop, Christina! I didn't do anything!" June continued to plead as Christina tugged on June's arms roughly. Duke loosened his grip on June's ankles before dropping her legs momentarily. June's lower body fell to the floor with a thud.

"Pick her back up!" Christina cackled loudly, resuming her grip around her sister's wrists. "Mom's gone now! We can throw her down the stairs!"

"Yes, I've been waiting for this!" Duke bellowed, grabbing June's ankles and lifting her legs from the floor. Christina looked down to June, who stared up to her sister with frightened eyes. Christina heartlessly urged Duke to hurry up, and they lifted June's squirming body from the floor. Christina could hear June's frail bones cracking and grinding like metal locks and latches, clanging out-of-place.

"I love our family time!" Duke jokingly remarked, while looming over June as she tried to free herself. "I think our baby sister is getting stronger!"

"Where do you think you're going?" Christina belted as she clutched June's arms tighter. "You belong to us now!"

"Stop! I won't say anything to my daddy!" June pleaded furiously, trying to struggle free from the pain. "I don't want to go to the funeral!"

"I don't believe you!" Christina yelled, holding June's arms angrily as June kicked free from Duke by blasting him in the gut with her right heel. The blow caused Duke to lose his balance, and he stumbled clumsily against the hallway wall, shaking the second-floor.

"Help!" June yelled. "Help! Daddy!"

"She kicked me!" Duke doubled over in pain, clutching his stomach.

"Shut up, Duke! Grab her!" Christina ordered, struggling to keep her grip on June's arms while Duke fumbled to his feet and raised his hand over June's face.

"AH!" June screamed before Duke could cover her mouth, and her shrill shook the cream hallway walls. The door to their parents' bedroom swung open violently; Kenny stood there possessed, dressed in faded polka dot boxers. A crimson bed comforter soiled in alcohol, tears, and urine draped over his shoulders like the cape of a super-less hero.

"S-s-top wha-chu doin' or I will ki- you like I k-k-k-kill Teresa! It's my fault! My mother m-m-made me do it! Oh, Teresa, w-w-why? Why? Oh, w-w-w-w-w-why?" Kenny swung his fist in the air, his body careening against the sides of the doorway.

Christina and Duke dropped their sister and stood stunned as June collected herself on the floor. She rubbed her knees, ankles, wrists, and shoulders tenderly, feeling the soreness from her siblings' torture. Christina stared at June with piercing eyes, fearing that her little sister would milk Kenny's grief in order to elicit some form of parenting. He stumbled farther into the hallway and swung his arms wildly above his head.

"My father was n-n-never around! I s-s-swore I wouldn't b-be like him..." Kenny placed his liquor-soaked hand over his sorrow-soaked heart. "I s-solem...s-slolem...s-sloppily s-swear, I won't leave you...*you brats!* But I...don't w-w-wanna hear wuuuuunn soun'! Don't even b-b-reathe no more...or I will k-k-kill you clean! We've d-done it before! And I d-d-don't f-feel anything...f-for anyone...anymore."

June stood between Christina and Duke with shared shock and awe, experiencing a curious conundrum, in that, she felt loyal to her father, but she also knew her debt to her siblings. Even as a toddler, June knew she could not survive alone with her alcoholic father, so she unhappily sided with her tormentors and stepped behind them, shielded away from her drunken father.

"What are you talking about, Kenny?" Christina asked out of curiosity, taking a step forward to observe her stepfather. "You're drunk!"

"No, I'm not! I d-d-did it! We s-s-set y-y-your m-m-mother up! Like a m-m-mob hit from the p-p-picture shows! Your g-g-grandpa k-kept it all...all in the family! Y-y-your uncle, m-m-my mother, m-m-me...Kenneth Beth-thune Junior...*her husband*...I d-d-did it, too! Or, it was what I didn't do! We killed y-y-your mother!"

"It was an accident, Kenny. Doctor Morten came to the house and told us all about it! You would know if you came out of that room!" Christina moved decisively in front of June and Duke, filled with her mother's sense to protect her feeble brother and naïve sister, even if she was only saving them for herself.

"Don't believe a word of it! They never wanted us to be happy!" Kenny held his hands up to God in protest. "We w-w-were leaving! We were g-g-going to be a family! But I…I helped them…lure her to the market…I d-did what m-my mother told me…like always, *like always*…It wasn't hard for your mother to b-believe that I just…forgot the bread. We're j-j-just…just pawns in our families' game. Your mother and I…and all you…*children*…we're all c-caught in this Winniper Oil Empire…b-but…we're far…f-far from…n-n-nobility. The c-c-crown makes us do h-h-horrible things…and t-t-t-tell ourselves r-r-reasonable excuses, and more excuses, and still more…reasonable…they were reasonable…excuses, *right?* Is there s-such a thing, Teresa, m-m-my b-b-b-beautiful angel? I d-d-don't know…"

His voice faded under his drunken breath; he swung his arms under the comforter and the stench of two-day-old grief billowed down the hall.

"Ugh, Kenny! Take a bath!" Christina mocked, wiping her hand in the air. "And where's Cleotha?"

"You smell worse than me!" Duke quickly added, looking to Christina and remembering his instinct to follow. "Yea, and where's Cleo? I'm hungry!"

"I fired Cleotha! She was your mother's maid!" Kenny countered sharply, still waving his arms under his smelly comforter, and flapping his pungent wings—a caped con-artist. "I'll p-p-probably g-g-go to hell f-f-for what I've done! And I'll n-n-never s-s-see your mother again!"

"But, what about the funeral?" June added, serving in despair, assuming her father would return. "Are you going?"

"*What funeral?* I don't have money to pay for that!" Bingo, Kenny countered with a typical volley. "I can't afford that; we'll b-b-bury her in the spring!"

"Grandpa is paying for it," Christina chided, a low blow to her stepfather's ego. She has always been willing to attack the man who stole her mother from her much wealthier father, or so she remembered. Her mother chose a boob over a boon and quickly felt the consequences.

"What? Who told Papa to…" Kenny grumbled under his comforter, "…how dare he? She…she's *my* wife…that…that's not allowed!"

"He kept calling, and you've been in your room," Christina reported with a scornful scowl. "We didn't know what to do! Our mother just died!"

She could see his ego sink farther than he could stoop to pick it up. His teetering world gently fell off a widowed cliff. Kenny was a beaten man.

"You shouldn't have let him plan the funeral! He...j-j-just wants...to c-c-c-cover...his tracks! He's the c-c-c-cause of all of this!" Kenny mourned sadly, scuttling back toward the master bedroom he once shared with his wife. "Never trust your grandfather, kids! He's...he's an *evil* man!"

He slammed the door, and Christina could hear him flop back into the bed as the liquor bottles clanged against one another.

"Teresa, why?" he whimpered from within the bedroom walls. Christina and Duke stared at the door blankly before looking back at June and listening to her father's sobs. "Why? Why?"

"What about the funeral?" June asked Christina and Duke. "Who is going?"

"You are," Christina answered quickly and punched June in the shoulder as she slithered back to her bedroom. "You can tell us how it goes."

"Yeah, write it down, whiz kid," Duke mockingly wrote in his palm before pushing June against the wall and re-entering his lair. "Like all those stupid songs."

"Tell grandma I want more presents for my birthday this year!" Christina yelled back from her bedroom doorway. "One gift isn't enough!"

"Christina's right," Duke added from inside his room as June regained her fragile composure and listened to her selfish siblings. The harshness in their words filled her young mind with disbelief and disgust.

"I want at least three paint sets this year!"

"Say hello to Mom." Christina slammed her bedroom door tersely, and she could hear Duke close his door, too, and begin rummaging through the wooden cabinet along his adjacent wall—a secret hiding place for war comics and nudie magazines. From inside her room, Christina could hear June sit in the hallway and strum her guitar, shocked, confused, and destroyed by the family that no longer was a family. Desolate and withdrawn for the rest of the morning, June still found the courage to attend their mother's funeral after a long car ride with her grandparents.

June returned that evening and told Christina how their grandfather remarked that he trusted Doc Morten, Jr.'s findings but he also believed Kenny could be a suspect in any possible foul play. Papa Winniper said that Kenny and Teresa planned to run away from Winniper County and take *his grandson* with them. When their grandparents arrived to retrieve whoever was willing to attend the funeral, they neither exited the car nor ordered their driver to approach the door to the embarrassing duplex. Their black limousine simply waited while June, a four-year-old, exited the house alone, tiptoed down the front steps, and marched along the cobblestone walkway until she reached the car parked in the driveway.

After enduring her siblings' torture earlier that day and strumming her tears through her guitar, June became determined to attend her mother's funeral, in spite of her father, brother, and sister. She dressed herself in her Sunday best and attended the funeral without any of her immediate family by her side. When she entered the limousine, her grandmother briefly smiled and extended her gloved hand to lightly brush June's blonde curls away from her face. Her uncle Thomas III lowered his head and cried; he couldn't look her in the eyes. Her grandfather, irreverently silent, stared at the duplex's front door and released a sharp grumble before promptly telling the driver, *"Step on it."*

June later told Christina and Duke that there were no preachers or pallbearers at the funeral; the entire ceremony lasted a little longer than it took for the cemetery groundsmen to lower their mother's crimson casket into the ground.

In her will, their mother requested that a New Orleans jazz band play during a short, funeral procession. Afterwards, June couldn't stop describing the music. June said the sounds spoke to her, but Christina never understood the importance, or, she never really cared. Following the funeral, June would often fantasize about moving to New Orleans and singing in a jazz funeral band; she thought it was beautiful how the music grieved for the dead and celebrated life at the same time.

The few guests parted ways as two gravediggers lowered the creaking wood-framed casket into the six-foot plot. Still a child, unfettered by her grief, her mother's tragedy, or her father's joyless alcoholism, June stood silently with her grandparents, hoping the horribly peaceful moment would linger on, knowing the miserable insanity waiting for her at home. And when June returned to the family's disappointing duplex, she was the star of the household. She was the lone member to journey to their mother's funeral, the chief storyteller to relay the finality—their mother was, in fact, dead. For Christina, her mother's death meant that she could stop pretending to love her siblings and Kenny.

And over the years, Kenny and the children have routinely avoided any moments of congregation within their *suburban home*. The kitchen, living room, and upstairs hallway have become awkward sites where the family feels forced to revisit their shared loss while remembering the mother, wife, and woman who tied them all together.

∞

They mostly hide within their bedrooms like preferred, prison cells, all trapped in the suburban myth. Even now, as Kenny attempts to cook a family dinner and Christina attempts to prepare the table, they continue to avoid their pain, trying to capture any remnants of their innocence before tragedy descended upon their household.

"June! Duke! It's time for dinner!" Kenny bellows from the kitchen before speed walking into the dining room with the bulbous steel pot of stew in his mitted hands. He takes a moment to savor the scent as he proudly hovers over his newly seasoned-to-smell soup.

"Are you sure it's ready?" Christina asks, in her most motherly tone, remembering that she is the family's matriarch and supreme ruler. At nine years old, she believes ten will be the age she ascends intellectually. She is already smarter than her siblings and stepfather but she wants to prove to her grandfather that she can be just as valuable as Duke. "I learned in science class that..."

"I'd be more appreciative if someone had cooked dinner *for me!* And that same someone stayed around when I didn't have a father." Kenny interrupts coldly, stepping past his stepdaughter and placing the pot in the center of the oval, oak, dinner table. He stares over the empty table chairs and furrows his eyebrows. "Where's everybody? Why are they taking so long to come down?"

Christina always detests his questions, as if she, the middle child, is accountable for the whereabouts of her siblings. She is not sure if Duke and June share a mutual disdain for her, but she has never loved her brother or sister, and she knows for a fact that she has never and will never like them.

∞

As a toddler whose father abandoned her, Christina learned the rewards of family and wanted none of them; she feared the inevitable insanity of power struggles and sensitive secrets. Gaining adult insight from her quiet grandmother, her demanding grandfather, her misguided mother, her absent father, and Kenny, an alcoholic and dependent stepfather, she donned a cold demeanor as a temporary fix until she can separate from all her connections. After her mother's death, Christina only wanted to leave Winniper County. She wanted to go outside in the rain and fly beyond the horizon and feel the real world without the safety net of her grandfather's money.

∞

While Duke seems all too willing to live under the Winniper family's wealthy tree and June is too young and naïve to care about much beyond her stupid guitar, Christina identifies herself as a scapegoat of their inheritance, blinded by passion, happy to be unhappy and willing to wallow in self-pity or self-doubt. Science and study sometimes mix with her soul and create a concoction of jealousy and self-hatred for the man she can never become.

"I don't know why they aren't coming downstairs, *Ken*," Christina answers coyly with a shrug, her customary answer. Her stepfather huffs dramatically, puffs her cheeks, and rolls his eyes. "Honest, Kenny, I don't!"

"Even if you did know, would you care enough to tell me?" Kenny asks slowly and deliberately, although, Christina can tell he doesn't want to hear the answer. Knowing the truth, she ponders whether to crush Kenny's pathetic heart. She abandons any notions of chastisement; remembering her mother, her compassion shields him from her contempt, for now.

"I honestly don't know, *sir*." She shrugs apologetically. They could play this game forever; however, disinclined to diminish these delicate dinner moments, Kenny leaves his stew on the table and storms by Christina. He stomps into the foyer and stands at the bottom of the staircase. Christina follows him, looking at several of her Uncle Thomas's photographs still hanging on the walls of the hallway between the dining room and the foyer. All her mother's adventurous pictures belong to moments between marriages, when Teresa and Thomas III would visit exotic locations from the Far East to South America. The pictures show their mother in her happiest moments.

∞

Teresa lost incremental pieces of her adventurous side with each respective marriage. Following her second marriage and Christina's birth, Teresa began taking fewer risks. She travelled more infrequently and cared less and less about being an individual. During her first two marriages, Teresa posed as a model mother for Duke and Christina, accepting her role as such. And then, Kenny ruined her efforts when he stole her away during a moment of mutual weakness. Their tryst began as an adult affair between longtime friends, as he often proclaimed. The changed man, who has brewed the broth, was once Teresa's boy toy, thirteen years her junior. He was her third and final attempt at holy matrimony. Her marriage to Kenny became her farthest excursion into domesticity. She genuinely poured her heart into their union and she tried to protect their family when they moved to their quiet suburban home, amidst the Winniper County populous at a reasonable distance away from her father's estate. Teresa believed her family could be far enough from her father's control while remaining close enough to his money, but she miscalculated and the results were catastrophic.

∞

"Kids, come down for dinner!" Kenny hollers up the staircase, straining his neck as far as he can. He pauses and listens to a long, lingering silence. "June! Duke!"

Still, nothing.

"Hurry up and come down, or I'm comin' up!" Christina commands thunderously, launching her voice up the stairs where the treble bangs against the walls and the bass knocks against the bedroom doors of her siblings. Her voice echoes throughout the house and elicits an immediate reaction. She hears two doors open and shut quickly and the rapid steps of forced family time rumble through the second floor hallway and cascade down the stairs.

The little, blonde, six-year-old descends first, leading the way for the submissive, hawkish, fifteen-year-old boy, who still wears the same smelly trousers from work. June bounces to the bottom of the steps before looking up blankly to her father.

"Hi, sweetie! How are you?" Kenny asks June brightly, but she slides around him quietly without a word. "Good. Glad you could make it."

He mumbles above her and stares into the corner, dejected; he imagines himself as a child placed in timeout. In his peripheral, he can see his daughter nestle under Christina's arms, a new Winniper reigns.

"Hey, kiddo." Christina brushes June's hair, falsely endearing herself while Kenny watches himself in the corner. "How was school today?"

"Horrible, I don't like math." June grumbles under Christina's touch, leaning further into her spiteful sister and wrapping her thin arms around her sister's waist. "I don't want to go to school."

"If we lived with our *grandfather*, we wouldn't have to. He says Winniper women aren't supposed to go to school." Christina empathizes satirically with June, extending her bottom lip and lowering her head to her baby sister. Both sisters then share a momentary glance toward Kenny, who stares at his daughter and stepdaughter, wishing he could be a part of the cool crowd. Christina leans closer to June, while looking at Kenny with a less than genuine smile. "I can help you with your homework after dinner if you like."

"Let's make this dinner fast," Duke scoffs roughly, jumping to the bottom of the stairs with a thud. He stands proudly in his Burger Town employee shirt and black slacks before slithering past Kenny with little recognition. "I still have to go to work! The old man said he won't release my trust fund 'til I'm eighteen!"

"You seem to like that job, Duke," Kenny remarks while extending his hand to rest on Duke's shoulder. As the youngest male heir grows into a *Winniper man*, Kenny has tried to ingratiate himself with the would-be king, with little results. "You've been working there for years, I remember you begging your grandfather to work there when you were ten. You got any plans for what you want to do after? You know, after you do inherit all that money?"

"Yep, I got big plans! I'm goin' to buy every fast car I can find and I'm never goin' to work again!" Duke throws his hands into the air and attempts some athletic détente, avoiding any further contact with Kenny but accidentally knocking down a framed picture of his mother and Uncle Thomas standing over a lion's carcass. "I might buy Burger Town though. Promote myself to cook so I can work with Earl."

"But you're not a cook," Christina adds quickly with a scowl, thinking of Duke's disgusting, yet entertaining, friend. "Earl told me you're still mopping the kitchen."

"Yep, and that's why I said 'promote', sis. One day, you're going to listen to what I say." Duke pauses for a moment, ignoring Christina's glare and placing the picture of his mother back on the wall. "I got big plans."

"But, if you're the owner, then you can't *promote* yourself to cook, right?" Christina continues to test Duke's logic, but June interjects between her brother and sister after hearing the conversation's direction and fearing an argument among the two siblings sworn to protect her from her father.

"Hey, *Dad*, the food smells great." June remarks falsely, having learned from her sister. "Uh, what is it?"

Taken back by his daughter's empty compliment and still unfamiliar with her newfound falsehood, Kenny proudly saunters through the foyer toward his stew in the dining room.

"Well, it's a recipe, Shelia…uh…" Kenny fumbles over his words while walking along the walls, lightly nudging the pictures, and almost knocking them over again. "It's a new recipe. Mrs. Chamberlain gave it to me."

"I bet she did," Duke murmurs angrily as the family moves into the dining room; his eyes dart away from his sisters. "She's a tramp."

"Excuse me?" Kenny asks with his eyebrows raised, walking away toward the piping hot pot still on top of the polished oak table. "What'd you say?"

"He said 'I bet she did'," June reassures him, always the young moderator, desperate to keep the peace in her sad world. "Missus Chamberlain's a nice lady, Daddy."

Again, June displays her adolescent inability to understand sarcasm, nuance, or posh in any way, shape, or form. Because of her innocence, naiveté, and constant sorrow from always missing her mother, most people simply follow along with June's miscues. Her preserving blonde cuteness mesmerizes them, her American debutante mannerisms charm them, and her princess position subdues them, although they do not know her struggle within the world of Winniper family consequences. Kenny stares at his daughter, lost in her wonder for a moment.

"Yes, June, she is pretty nice."

"Nice *and* pretty," Duke jests with a smile as the family gathers around the dining table, taking seats in a specific order; there's still a Winniper hierarchy here. Christina waits for her siblings to sit down, eyeing her brother and sister before ensuring their submission.

"Who's ready to eat?" Christina waves her hand over the table, reviving their mother's memory and awaiting a response. Kenny and June sit promptly; Duke follows obediently and hoists his nose over the broth before tucking a felt napkin into his collar.

"Everyone's ready, Christina. Food is fuel for the body and spirit!" Kenny comments heartily, raising his tonality into a chipper, American Dad visage as he tries to excite three uninterested youth.

Christina hears a low velocity explosion next door at the Chamberlain's home. She thinks that if their neighbors ever came over for dinner, they would enjoy it, especially if certain secrets found their way into pleasant conversation. Seeing inside the zoo without helping the animals is like watching a disaster without helping the victims; the Chamberlains could excuse themselves, their home life, and their volatile son, simply by thinking *"At least we're not Kenny and those kids, right?"*

Christina imagines the quaint, suburban banter next door— *"Hello"*, *"I want"*, *"I need"*, *"Give me"*, *"Got it"*, *"Thanks"*, *"I need more"*. The colloquial exchange satisfies the social order; yet, within the Winniper-Bethune household, even *"Hello"* receives jeers and angry stares. Only semi-genuine pleasantries occur when Papa Winniper makes a rare visit to the sorrowful suburban home of his deceased daughter. His appearances always garner the most attention from their nosey neighbors; the Winniper County residents treat Papa like a king visiting his subjects. His *"Hello"* always receives the highest regard and the warmest welcome from anyone he encounters. A South Dakota oil man, the townspeople love that his boots are always dirty and his pockets are always full. When Papa visits, Kenny usually receives a small financial handout from his father-in-law, usually with strict instructions for the money's appropriation—groceries and no liquor. The lawyers will handle the rest. Kenny knows that Papa Winniper cares more about his grandson than the totality of Teresa's family. The girls are an afterthought at best.

The animosity between the widowed husband and his weary father-in-law has led the former to seek a new arrangement that benefits both parties. The drunkard wants to return to his liquor and, in exchange, he plans to return a prized possession to the family's benefactor. Ultimately, Kenny has realized that he cannot be a father to his daughter or his stepchildren.

∞

Caught within this conundrum, Kenny used this year's Winniper County Founder's Day Parade to approach Papa Winniper with a proposal. In very little time, he and the old man agreed to an arrangement that will deliver Duke, the family's youngest male heir, to the Winniper Estate so that Kenny, the ill-equipped bachelor, may return to his single life.

∞

And now, on the eve of his plan's fruition, Kenny smiles over the dinner table, playing the fatherly ruse while struggling to disguise his enthusiasm for freedom.

"Today has been a great day! I hope you each had a great day, too!" Kenny exclaims happily, convincing himself that his kindness is genuine. The three youths scan one another's faces, each searching for a savior, anticipating who will break the uneasy tension—none do. Kenny sighs heavily and prepares to continue drudging through the family dinner. The awkwardness of their family time continues to permeate the room through an oddly unnatural aroma that wafts from the chicken broth.

"Don't you feel it, kids? There's something in the air! It's been a really, really great day!"

"Yay...let's eat." Duke callously grabs the handle of the soup ladle and delicately dips it into the broth. He carefully gathers as many pieces of chicken as possible, but he looks around momentarily as if daring anyone at the table to challenge his gustative dominance—none do. He is the real alpha male, his grandfather's favorite fruit, so he takes his rightful share.

Duke slops the ladle's contents into his soup bowl, filling it full of chicken and very little broth. He glances around once again before taking another large helping and passing the ladle to June. As usual, having watched and learned from Duke or Christina, June knows exactly what to do—she drops two helpings of mostly chicken-and-no-broth into her bowl before handing the ladle to Kenny.

"Oh, I'm okay. Here Christina, help yourself." Kenny holds the ladle for Christina who sheepishly grabs the neck with tentative hands. "Eat up."

Christina quickly darts her eyes toward her siblings, questioning her starving submission—how dare she become vulnerable to hunger? She usually refuses to eat anything under their roof, but, because the rain caused her to miss joining her friends at Burger Town, she feels a thunderous gurgle in the pit of her stomach. She tentatively dips the ladle into the soup while searching around the table for any accusations. Even eating can be a sign of weakness. She longs for a chance to escape from the dinner table, almost as though she's afraid of what may happen if she consumes Kenny's meal. She ignores her anxiety and pulls the ladle from the broth, serving herself a modest portion with a proper proportion of chicken-to-broth.

Again, she investigates her siblings' faces for approval, like a puppy learning a new trick or an inmate flexing muscles during rec time. No one knows how Christina became so tentative during social situations; her insecurities have manifested into pure malice and she remains constantly on edge within her unraveled household. She intimidates for fear of intimidation from her brutally boisterous brother or her absently amiable stepfather.

Given her status as the oldest female in the home, she is the natural maternal substitute for Teresa, and it is no wonder that June has grown to idolize Christina. June emulates her big sister like a daughter imitates her mother. June has become a child with a similarly withdrawn nature, mirroring her sister's temperament; they both rebel against anything that would restore the house to a home.

Christina quietly hands the ladle back to Duke, and the siblings share a glare and confirm their mutual disdain; yes, she sees the animus in the mirror. The image is so clear that it's frightening.

∞

Forced to interact throughout years of their mother's marriages, divorces, and heartaches, Christina and Duke united over their common angst like prisoners held captive in a war camp. Although Duke was already six years old when Christina was born, she quickly outmaneuvered him for their mother's affection—that is, until three years later when Teresa eloped with Kenny, and both Duke and Christina moved aside for June.

∞

"Thank you, Christina." Duke smiles deliberately, campaigning for her reassurance and he receives a slight glimmer of respect. Both siblings see each other as castaways from the same shipwreck. Duke, the older and stronger brother, has always used Christina as a crutch, especially when dealing with confrontation, and Christina has used Duke to buffer her contempt for Kenny. Duke and Christina have defied much of Kenny's nonsensical attempts to be their father and they spurn the constant burden of mending their broken home. As the years continue to pass slowly, Christina whines and complains to their grandparents and uncle almost every time they visit. Duke has remained a content mute of sorts, keeping his mouth shut while dreaming of the lavish toys that he will own once he ascends into their grandfather's good graces.

∞

After Teresa left Charles for Kenny and gave birth to June, Duke and Christina became defensive toward their new stepfather and sister. Possessing few truly aggressive traits, Duke acquiesced to Christina and she became their natural leader. She became self-assured as she tried to conquer their fears of inadequacy. Before June could speak, Christina would try any trick imaginable to take her mother's attention away from the newborn, but, over time, Christina and Duke bonded through their mother's neglect as covariant atoms from a disbanded molecule. Christina often explains life through science; she envisions her mother as a conflicted quantum force which departed from the world too soon.

Following her mother's death, Christina portrayed herself as the rising leader of the much maligned household. The renegade Winniper-Bethune clan, lost in a suburban sea with a drunken twenty-something father of three. Christina began to see her siblings and stepfather as pawns, while wondering if her grandfather will ever save them from each other or if he will sacrifice them for a greater masterplan.

∞

Grabbing the handle from Christina, Duke again dips the ladle confidently into the chicken broth and removes not one, not two, but three healthy helpings. He stares intently at Kenny, daring him to challenge his emerging dinner table dominance. As Duke grows older, he has become tougher to control while he inches closer to the date of his trust fund disbursement.

"Wow, you must be hungry, son," Kenny remarks in a senselessly wholesome expression that makes Christina hate him even more, but, in this soon-to-be-mocked moment, she plays along as a necessity to retain her position as the cool, calculating, and controlled leader of her household. For her siblings, she's an example of perseverance through hardship—at least, that is how she portrays herself as she writes her legacy in her mind. Kenny continues to beam brightly while watching the children taste the broth. "Have more if you like. I ate a ton while I was cooking it!"

"Well, I am hungry…it's been a long week," Duke mumbles between each bite, shuffling the food in his cheeks. "I'm just…happy…to have…time…to eat!"

Each member of the household maintains a level of mystery because the family uses information of one's whereabouts as leverage toward domestic dominance—who can't do the dishes or doesn't have time to take out the trash. The excess in family chores and responsibilities necessitates espionage in the home, especially between Christina, Duke, and Kenny. At six, June is still too young, too cute, and too innocent to play these war games. Although he is a louse in almost all respects, Kenny protects his baby girl from any hard labor, but, Christina knows that soon June, too, will join the fray of family espionage and extortion. It's in the Winniper blood to use disinformation and interrogation on a small, family-sized battlefield.

Four individuals imitating a family, they often intersect at awkwardly-angled ambitions in order to investigate the motives of each other's movements; but, when the truth comes to light, instead of sharing love, care, or compassion, each family member manipulates and contorts their discovery for personal gain. Suddenly, a liar or a thief has time to dust the cabinets or sweep the kitchen.

∞

A poignant example of leverage within Kenny Bethune, Jr.'s happy home occurred about a year ago when Christina discovered Duke's secret crush on Mrs. Chamberlain. He even went so far as to sneak into the Chamberlain's backyard and leave a gift for her in their old dog house. One day, Christina caught her brother crawling into the diminutive wooden shed; he stayed inside only briefly before quickly exiting and creeping away. She waited until he snuck back into their house before ducking and diving between their adjacent backyards to retrieve the item. When Christina tiptoed into the dog house, there was a felted, crimson jewelry case sitting atop a moss-covered water bowl.

On the box, there was a small note written on lemon paper: *"To my Sheila–From Duke"*. Christina rolled her eyes in disgust, foregoing any perceivable appreciation for how ordinary Duke had always been. Much like June's adoration provided Christina with a mother's confidence, Duke's constant submission to her in times of difficulty or simple stupidity gave Christina an inflated sense of self-importance. The middle child, a girl no less, became the center of strength in a chaotic household.

And while Christina managed their stepfather and the loss of their mother, Duke never went out of his way to impress anyone or achieve anything—there was no need. No matter what Duke did, he always knew he was a male Winniper; Papa had told him as much. His trust fund and inheritance have always been right around the corner so he never worried about self-sustenance—there is still no need.

In his exclusive social circle life, he had only one loyal, best friend, Earl Bethune, Kenny's mutually wayward little cousin; and within the home, Duke had at least one person that would always follow him, June, and one person that he could always follow, Christina. And Christina happily manipulated Duke and exploited all his actions.

∞

To Duke, Christina has always been a very comforting standard for the hell bound. Their sorrow-stricken family has always felt cursed, and even within the inferno, Duke has always known that he has both a minion and a leader in his two sisters. Presumably, while June can always play the victim within their broken home, Christina has ascended into their mother's role and she bears the responsibilities of the woman who betrayed them all.

∞

Crawling further into the dog house, Christina picked up the red jewelry case from the water bowl and noticed the label underneath: *Cartier.* For a moment, she imagined their mother opening the case and receiving a gift from one of their fathers. When Christina opened the felted top, she smelled their mother—warm bread and the setting sun. Her Rita-crested diamond necklace sat within the case's satin center—a gift from one of her husbands, or maybe a gift to herself, which was common. Teresa always loved the lavishly explainable and unreasonably expensive, a charm that Christina admired in her mother. Her mother enjoyed a sense of reckless abandon that fueled her appreciation for money, morals, and, dare she say, men. Though Teresa seemed to despise the family's wealth, she still indulged in the luxuries of their oil empire.

∞

Like her mother, Christina believes it is her right as a Winniper woman to have beautiful things on her body, in her house, and anywhere else that she desires. When no one is home, Christina often searches through Teresa's bedroom closet, still filled with evening dresses, furs, and an endless array of shoes. Christina imagines her mother's past joy during moments spent marveling at her own beauty. The jewelry, clothes, and accessories are among many of the Winniper family's blessings, yet, within the Chamberlain's dog house, any material extravagance would seem very cheap and eagerly misplaced.

∞

The felt case, the diamond necklace, the smell of their mother, they all reminded Christina that a life once lived so lovingly in the lap of luxury had dissolved into a begrudging comedy, within which, her brother simply gave away their dead mother's possessions to the whore next door.

Christina took her mother's belongings and Duke's note, crawled from the dog house, and stormed back to their house with far less care for who heard or saw than when she entered. (Damning information always supersedes discretion in leverage battles within the Winniper family.) Christina's brash bravado dared any onlooker to question her motives while she stomped through the backyard, determined to expose a thief. As Christina entered the home through the backdoor, her initial inclination was to tell Kenny and blow the lid off Duke's scandalous intentions towards the neighbor's wife, but she paused and developed a keener sense of manipulation than most people ever learn in life. Quietly and calmly, Christina crept upstairs to Duke's room and knocked on the door.

"Who is it?"

"It's me! Open up!"

"Go away, science geek! I don't have any candy!" Duke yelled from within his room. Christina has always been somewhat of a candy pest, but, that night, she had a more pressing proposition.

"I don't want any candy, *big bro'*. But now that you mention it, maybe I'll go ask Kenny for some and I'll be sure to show him Mom's necklace that you tried to give Mrs. Chamberl-" Before she finished her sentence, the bedroom door flung open and Duke pulled her inside hurriedly.

"Don't touch me or I'll tell!" Christina's protective stance became slightly more effective when she held the necklace case between her body and her brother. "I swear, I'll tell him you're giving away *our* mother's jewelry!"

"Shh, you're always overreacting. Calm down, sis." Bingo. Whenever Duke called her *"sis"*, or addressed anyone without a derogatory undertone, she knew that *he knew* he had lost. Cordiality, courtesy, and general compassion are not free commodities in their household.

"What is this?" Christina asked knowingly, raising the necklace case to Duke's face. "What were you thinking?"

"Don't worry about it." Duke tried to grab the case but Christina threatened to punch him and Duke cowered in fear. "It's just a necklace! You know...for a present."

He stammered under her cocked fist, glancing to his sister as she looked over him authoritatively, mocking his vulnerability. His boyish stupidity infuriated her; he was always so inconsiderate, a mildly artistic loner, mostly stoic and uninterested unless he's trying to impress someone.

"How dare you, Duke? You shouldn't..." Christina paused, seeming to retreat while instinctually feeling that chastising her older brother was alien to her being. Though she promptly began to play her mother's role, she never fully believed her lines. "Mom would be so hurt..."

"Save it, *Christie.*" Duke stood tall for a moment of defiance and poked out his narrow chest. "Mom's dead, and she doesn't need that necklace or any of the jewelry in her closet. So I don't want to hear about it."

"Well, maybe Kenny wants to hear about it." Christina made a move toward the door, but Duke grabbed her arm gently, almost pleading for her to stop.

"Wait, Christina, I'm sorry! Please, sis," he apologized quickly, letting go of her arm and resting his hand on her shoulder. "It's just, you know...well, you don't know, you're too young...but when you get older, you'll meet someone, and you'll do what she's doing to me."

"What is she *doing* to you?" Christina eyed her brother curiously, sensing a new, adult world beyond her understanding.

"I can't talk to you about that," Duke responded coldly, and Christina shot him another glare: he cowered in his place once again, remembering his vulnerability in this pressing matter of extortion.

"Tell me, Duke."

"Well, she's not *doing* anything to me...*yet*. But you see how she parades around over there in all those tight clothes. She's driving me crazy!" Duke emphasized, walking away from his sister and staring anxiously at his hands. "I want her so bad, Christina. But she says I'm still too young."

"Did she ask you for the necklace?"

"No...I mean, she asked for something nice."

"What? '*Something nice*'? And you give her Mom's necklace?"

"It's all I could afford," Duke uttered under his breath. "It's not like Mom will miss it. And Mrs. Chamberlain has really big..."

"You're a pig, Duke." Christina charged closer to her brother, reaching out and grabbing his collar roughly with her left hand while still holding the evidence of his betrayal in her right. "Have you given her anything else?"

"No..."

"Don't lie to me, Duke, or I'll tell Kenny!" Christina wrung his neck with her fist, clenching his collar, trying to keep her voice down. Even amidst her anger, Christina feared that June or Kenny may overhear their conversation and their inquisitive ears would never ignore this kind of juicy gossip-drama inside their boring, drab home. "Have you given her anything else?"

"Um, well...she said she liked a pair of Mom's earrings." Duke rolled his eyes, avoiding Christina's glare.

"So you gave them to her?" She pushed him further into his room so that his back hit against his dresser, knocking over several toy soldiers and a wishful, unused can of shaving cream. Duke braced himself against the dresser, the older brother crushed into rubble by his bullying younger sister. No telling the lengths he would go to appease her and gain her approval, even at the risk of embarrassing himself.

"I'm sorry, sis. She was over one day looking through Mom's closet, and I said she could borrow them." Duke crumpled above his sister, completely broken before her; yet, he still looked down at her while she held him up by the collar and drilled a hole into his head with her persecuting glare. "Don't look at me like that, Christie! I can get them back!"

"*Borrow?*" she growled, taking offense to his insolence. "How dumb can you be? How do you expect to run Grandpa's business if you're this stupid? How long ago did you give them to her?"

"Um, it was last summer."

"Duke! Mom died barely a year ago…and you're already giving her stuff away!" Christina began to thrash Duke around the neck, wrenching his collar and striking him with the jewelry case in her right hand. "What is the matter with you? Stop giving away our mother's things!"

"I told you, Sheila's got a hold on me!" Duke pleaded in a desperate tone that Christina had never heard from him; she suddenly believed that either Mrs. Chamberlain had blackmailed her brother with a horrible secret, or Duke truly convinced himself that he was powerless against her *mature* charms. "I'm sorry, sis. I just have this…*urge*…and I can't say no to her. It'll happen to you, too…"

These revelations turned Christina's stomach in knots, and she felt an emotional nausea that began to build in her gut.

"You make me sick, Duke. You really do." Silence passed between them, brother and sister lost in their roles, and within the pause, they were equal, until Christina resumed her matriarchal portrayal. "I don't want to see you near Kenny and Mom's bedroom. If Mrs. Chamberlain ever comes over here, you better keep her downstairs, or I will tell Kenny everything. And you better get those earrings back before the end of the week or I'll go get 'em myself!"

Christina stared at her big brother; her glare became a toothy shark bite of judgment that he never saw coming. The pain of her indignation hurt more than a mere flesh wound. It was in that moment that Christina fully transformed into the mother of the house, protector of Teresa's legacy. Christina carried a prideful sword and a shameful shield. From then on, Duke knew clearly where he stood within her regime: a princely pawn under the watchful eye of his manipulative younger sister, too stupid to defend himself from his own insecurities.

"I…I'm s-s-sorry, Chris-t-t-tina," Duke stammered pathetically, losing the confidence and timber in his voice. "I r-r-really…really am so s-s-s-sorry."

Looking pitifully at his sister, he begged for her forgiveness. He had committed a sin against the family, an unforgivable betrayal of their fallen matriarch. After her passing, Teresa became a saint; Kenny and the children created a shared mythos of a devoted mother and loving wife and they each tried desperately to keep her legacy alive within a morbid household of missteps, miscues, and misgivings. The picturesque possessions and memorialized memories have helped the family remember her, but these images have also fueled their illusion as they remember the woman as she never was. When Duke gave Teresa's belongings away to some troglodyte next door, he knew how badly he would hurt his sisters and his stepfather. He had tried to replace their American queen with a foreign housewife who had always coveted Teresa's jewelry. No matter how much money Mr. Chamberlain earned, he would never be a Winniper; and Mrs. Chamberlain barely waited for Teresa's casket to drop before she started crossing the line both figuratively and literally.

For his crimes, Christina refused to offer Duke any consolation or absolution. She planned to use his treachery against him for years and she exited her brother's bedroom triumphantly. She walked to Teresa and Kenny's bedroom and opened through the door without pause. Caution was unnecessary because Kenny was nowhere in sight, a usual occurrence at night. If he had any money left after visiting the bar, he would eventually lose it all at a crap table or roulette wheel. Papa Winniper kept him and the family on a strict allowance, yet, Kenny always complained that he never had enough to satisfy his appetites. Christina returned the necklace and the jewelry case to her mother's dusty dresser, which was covered in soot, adorned with all of her children's framed pictures, and stamped with the final note that she had left for Kenny—the note that he conveniently overlooked on the day when he "forgot to go to the market".

Ken, can you go by the Market when you wake up? Tom will give you a fresh loaf for our family picnic this eve. Love, T.

Their mother had no idea of the repercussions for marrying such a buffoon. While staring at her mother's personal memorial, Christina began to worry about her own fate in love and marriage, but she remembered her task, concealed Duke's treachery, and left the master bedroom. She did not know that many devious deeds were still yet to come and these future scandals would require her discretion in order to save her family from itself and protect the Winniper Empire.

∞

Christina suddenly realizes that her mind has wandered into the past for too long and she wonders if the others have noticed her daydreaming during dinner, or, maybe, they're lost in their thoughts, too. June and Duke continue to sip their broth in silence while Kenny paws the ladle, stirring the chunks of chicken within the steel pot; they're all stuck in this mundane moment. Though the surviving members of the household have continued to coexist after Teresa passed away, the children and Kenny have distanced themselves from one another. June has become almost completely detached from her alcoholic father: the smell alone drove her away.

For the past two years since Teresa's death, Papa Winniper has kept the family together under their suburban roof. Spread apart by deception, bound together by lifestyle, these dinner table moments constantly force Kenny and the children to confront their mutual need for that Winniper family wealth. Kenny refuses to work and he's too prideful to ask his mother for support, so the family unites under a silent agreement—love is only a weapon. As they sit within their contemporary ritual, they see Teresa in one another and they hate each other for being a constant reminder of the one they all lost. She was the one who held their family together and she ultimately taught them the most important life lesson for any Winniper: love can cause more violence than hate.

Christina glances at Duke and catches a glimpse of a humble smirk across his face. Maybe, he is simply content to fill his belly, or, maybe, he is secretly happy to enjoy his time with the family. Kenny motions for Duke to grab the soup ladle and serve himself another helping. Duke raises his eyebrows in eager surprise and chuckles under his breath.

"You sure, you don't want none, Kenny? Sheila makes a pretty good stew!"

"No thanks!" Kenny answers quickly, pushing back his seat and hopping to his feet. "I had three bowls just making it! Eat up; I forgot the bread, again!"

He rushes into the kitchen, and the mood deflates as the siblings acknowledge their shared reality. They briefly stare at one another across the dinner table before they disengage in earnest disinterest.

Christina darts her eyes toward her brother and sister while they resume swallowing their soup. Duke greedily spoons his portions into his mouth, eyeing the unguarded ladle inside the still steaming pot. He's already plotting his third helping. June matches his pace, using her napkin between sips and wiping drool and soup from her chin. Reluctantly, Christina raises her spoon from her bowl, timidly tests, and eventually tastes a small sip of soup before swallowing.

Often, long after Duke and June finish their meals, Christina remains at the table, cautiously nibbling her food or sampling her drink. Sometimes, Kenny forces Duke and June to stay with Christina until she finishes eating and then all the siblings clean up the dishes and dinner table. On these rare nights when Kenny flexes his patriarchal muscle, Christina still takes her time. As a habit, she maneuvers a ruse to foil any of Kenny's assumed fatherly deeds. When Kenny or her siblings want her to hurry, she slowly raises her spoon at a tepid tempo like an old conductor waving through an adagio melody, controlling every movement. All along, Christina has used their languished dinners as a common platform for interrogation.

"So, Duke, where were you this morning?" Christina asks Duke smugly. He completely disregards her question and refuses to raise his eyes toward his sister. "Wendy told me you were at Harrah's party last night."

Wendy Davis is a known gossip, but, of all Christina's school acquaintances, Wendy is her closest friend. Papa Winniper has explained how the family should use their relationships, so Christina views Wendy's "friendship" as a weapon worthy of exploitation, especially when aimed at her brother and sister. Wendy's value as a gossiping gal, squawking and talking throughout the entire town, is substantially greater for an antisocial chemistry nerd like Christina. With plots and secrets in mind, Christina smiles with sinister intentions as she continues to prod her brother for more information.

"I didn't hear you come home. Seems like you were out all night, I bet you were with a special someone." Christina glances at Duke curiously and even June understands her hustle. Another game is on the horizon; the winner still has to live here and the loser suffers just a little more. "Have you reunited with your *old* girlfriend? And I do mean *old*."

"Oh no, he wasn't with Sh-uh...*her*," June interrupts the impending onslaught, fending off Christina on Duke's behalf. She is the baby sister coming to her big brother's defense. As much as she admires and idolizes Christina, June also treasures her brother because he is her masculine protector from her wayward father. June gives Duke a playful nudge on his elbow and he drops his spoon into his soup.

"Ow!"

"Duke went racin'. He's going to be a driver and a painter. Tell her, Duke."

"Racin', eh?" Christina asks coyly, glancing back toward the kitchen, trying to hear any movement to ensure that Kenny is still occupied. "Racing and painting what?"

"I'm going to race cars and paint pictures of them!" Duke contorts in his seat, grabbing his spoon from his soup. "I'm a better drawer than most of the kids at school and when I can drive, I'll have Grandpa give me one of his old race cars! They got that new NASCAR professional racing! I'm going to try out!"

"*Try out*, eh? Have you told Grandpa about this, Duke?" Christina inquires; her eyebrows rise in a questioning stare. He remains silent, a cloud descending upon his dreams. Papa Winniper may indulge his grandson's interest in fast cars because he considers it a sign of masculinity, but, Papa won't allow his only grandson to compete in a deadly sport and risk the Winniper name dying on a race track. "Come on, Duke, you should tell Grandpa the next time he visits. Don't you think he'd want to know?"

Looking back and forth between June and Duke, Christina pauses from the shock of her exclusion; her maternal role has its solitary moments. She rarely desires inclusion within her siblings' lives due to her disinterest or her personal insecurities; either reason will do. Their silence halts her momentum, and June seizes the conversation.

"Christina, why can't you relax?" June asks boldly, yet her little voice barely peaks above her bowl after she sips a large spoonful of soup, most of which dribbles down her chin. She speaks through swallows as she eagerly dabs her face with her napkin. "When I runaway…to New Orleans, I bet…you'll be right behind me! You're so…nosey!"

True, but over the years, an animal develops habits and senses necessary for its survival. June still exists in a fantasy where people accomplish their dreams because society allows those dreams to manifest as a product of hard work or talent. Christina often worries about how June will fare in the real world. The dreaming diamond could be crushed into a lump of coal.

"While you're lost in New Orleans, I'll be an archeologist in Pompeii. I'm going to get paid to do research and ask questions and look at clues…and…and I just know Duke is up to no good!" Christina explains emphatically before pausing, pivoting her shoulders toward June, and pointing her spoon across the table. "And *you*…mind your elders! At least your father is here for us! My daddy hasn't even seen me or talked to me in years!"

Christina's thoughts of her father disrupt her rhythm and disturb her temperament. Her eyes become cloudy as Duke slurps a final, extravagant sip of broth before dropping his spoon in his empty bowl.

"Why are you so difficult, Christina?" Duke speaks deliberately, lingering on each word while throwing sand at a concrete wall. Because of the years of neglect from her father, mother, and stepfather, Christina is impenetrable. A challenge only makes her walls harder to penetrate and tougher to climb. Seeing this, Duke stares at her with contempt. "You're a real curse sometimes."

"What did you call me?" Christina goads Duke to revive his insult in hopes that Kenny will reappear on cue. She wonders what is taking him so long with the bread, but her thoughts return quickly to Duke's comments.

"I called you…" Duke's words flounder in his mouth and his eyes dance from side-to-side. He suddenly loses consciousness and his head bobs awkwardly on his neck until he slams face first into his soup bowl.

"Oh God! Duke!" June shrieks as she jumps up from her seat and leans over her older brother. She shakes his shoulders and pulls his lifeless head from the bowl before looking at Christina in confusion. "What happened? What did you do?"

"I didn't do anything!" Christina yells from her seat, refusing to move. She's either too afraid to acknowledge the moment's urgency or she simply doesn't care about her brother's well-being, especially after his insult. "Whatever it is, he had it coming. Go get your father!"

"Kenny! Come help! Duke, wake up, please!" June continues to shake Duke furiously and Christina feels a strange rush move over her body. June appears to feel the sensation, too, as her spine shakes and her eyes roll back into her head.

"Christina, I…I…don't…so…good…feel." June stumbles over her words and clutches her stomach. "My…tummy…is…"

Suddenly, little June falls limply to the floor with a modest thud. Her petite, six-year-old body crumples behind Duke, who still remains comatose in his seat at the table.

"June!" Christina finally rises and struggles to walk around the dinner table toward her brother and sister. Christina glances dazedly around the room until her eyes land on the smoldering broth pot. On cue, Kenny re-enters the dining room with a workman's whistle in his mouth and a roll of duct tape in his right hand. Christina begins to slip between a drug-induced fantasy and her surreal reality as her head bobs uncontrollably. "Kenny, what's…happening?"

"You're going to your grandpa's home! And I'm getting the hell out of Winniper County!" Kenny boasts wickedly as she succumbs to the forces pressing upon her consciousness. She falls to floor, no longer feeling the strength to resist the darkness. In the last light, she sees Kenny dancing around the dining room, holding a thick, yellow rope, the duct tape, and a pair of scissors. He happily steps over Christina as she tries to elicit words through her last conscious breaths and he pauses to look down upon her. "I really hated being your father. I see why Charles and Ralph never came back."

"But…wh…what…about June?"

"What do you care? She's your baby sister and you let her to go to Terri's funeral alone. Hell, we all did."

"You...never...loved...us..." Christina fades between light and darkness as Kenny kneels over her and leans closely to her face. His six-year-old daughter lies comatose just behind him and, even in the end, he still ignores her.

"I did love your mother, but it wasn't enough. So you remember that...I'll never see you again, but you remember that. Love is never enough."

"You're...psychotic..."

"Am I? I bet your grandpa won't even tell you what happens until you get pregnant. Teresa didn't tell me until after June and her twin were born!" His breath smells like vodka and cranberry juice. With her last moment of consciousness, Christina glances directly into Kenny's eyes; grey clouds form around her peripheral vision, but Kenny's words fill her mind with confusion.

"June...doesn't have...a twin."

Hopeful Springs

MARCH 1950

Sunday	Monday	Tuesday	Wednesday	Thursday	Friday	Saturday
			1	2	3	4
5	6	7	8	9	10	11
12	13	14	15	16	17	18
19	20	21	22	23	24	25
26	27	28	29	30	31	

Monday, March 13, 1950
Olivia Newton Winniper

Take a moment to sip clarity and redefine the norm,
A wedding of Calamity and Chaos
In God's changing form,
Believe as though deceived
By an intellect great and large,
Achieve as though relieved by a new power in charge,
The untrained eyes
Search for understanding perception
While a master's pupils dilate,
Determining imperfection,
The feeling of completion, in family and in life,
Escaping the coronation of Calamity and his wife.

Clue: Thomas "Papa" Winniper, Jr. = Calamity
Question: If Calamity is her husband,
          then who is Chaos?

Olivia Newton Winniper rarely experiences a dull moment in life because she seldom acknowledges her mediocrity. Putting little value in her thoughts or actions, she lives a life of wealth and ignorance. While walking through an unusually emerald forest, she notices the sprouts beginning to burst from the brittle branches of the oak trees along the border of the Winniper Family Estate. At age fifty-six, Olivia loves the way that the large trunks line their gardens and the immense driveway; the trees form a blockade at the edge of the estate. The oaks create a fluorescent barrier between the estate and the common folk; her husband calls it a *natural fence.*

Whenever Olivia walks through their expansive property, she feels Teresa's spirit throughout all 560 acres, especially when she passes her children's old playhouse.

∞

Once Teresa and Thomas III became old enough to have adventures around the estate, the former country shed quickly became their favorite hideaway. Thomas III would act like a fireman or cowboy and Teresa would be a damsel in distress. Back then, Thomas III dreamed of becoming a hero. Olivia loved that her son believed he would become a good man, but, she knew that his father had other intentions. And though Teresa acted demure during her childhood games with her brother, she was always a rebel at heart.

Very early into Teresa's childhood, Olivia knew that Teresa would have problems in her father's world. Papa had clear plans for his family, though he rarely discussed them with his wife; he trusted that she would support his decisions and she always did. Olivia understood her role and she tried her best to fulfill her duties as a wealthy wife and mother.

∞

While walking by the shed, Olivia peeks into the small wooden playhouse and remembers her children frolicking inside.

∞

Though Olivia loved Thomas III, she also pitied her son because he was always under his father's thumb. In the beginning, there was only Teresa and Papa gave Olivia more responsibility over raising their daughter while he waited for her to produce a son. When Thomas III was born, he became his father's most prized possession, so, in turn, Olivia held a special affinity for Teresa; she enjoyed watching her firstborn mature from a bouncy baby girl into a troublesome toddler.

As Teresa aged into a young woman, she would often retreat to the shed, searching for solitude so that she could dream of leaving the estate for good. She brainstormed about starting her own wheat cropping business while reading agriculture books and drawing sketches of farming systems. After she agreed to her first marriage and gave birth to Duke and Lucy, she learned about the family's curse and she began retreating to the shed more frequently, hoping for inspiration to find a solution to the biracial twin pregnancies—she was always an optimistic problem-solver.

∞

The grass amongst the trees has grown tall in the four years since Teresa's death; the surrounding shrubs shade the trailer-sized shed where Teresa and her brother would escape from "being a Winniper".

∞

They sought refuge from their name and claim throughout their childhood, and they even hid here long after they became adults. Olivia rarely saw her children once they matured enough to roam the county and travel the world. Most of their family time involved jousts and jests between the siblings to procure money from their strict father, who would decide their allowance, based upon certain performance criteria for their groveling. Papa had a strict rubric to judge his family, but his monetary rewards were worth his ire, so the children thought. As Teresa and Thomas III aged, Olivia became an afterthought to them, but she always protected her children and their interests as best she could.

After he killed Teresa, Thomas III stopped visiting their country shed. He thought he saw her ghost in one of the windows. The weeds and grass grew like monsters that guarded over the area. This part of the grounds became an allegory of Teresa, utterly abandoned by the family. The forest at the edge of the Winniper Family Estate slowly consumed the childhood haven; voluminous weeds and winding vines tangled, negligently unkempt. With a simple order to one of the landscapers, servants, or sharecroppers who worked on the estate, the Winnipers could have easily had the entire area shaved, crafted, and arranged into any desired, outdoor manicure; but, without a will, there's no way.

∞

Interestingly enough, Olivia doesn't mind the tall, thin grass rising above her waist. She enjoys the feeling of growth during the spring and summer. The extra foliage helps her abandon her fear. Concealed in a large overcoat, brown gloves, and a pair of Teresa's hiking boots, Olivia treks through the estate and into the forest—a mature lady on a mother's mission. Truly, no matter where her steps take her in life, the grass will continue to grow and the tree leaves will shine under the sunlight. Over her many years, Olivia has found comfort in the continuous harmony that is nature; whereas, humans, acting unnaturally or inhumanely, have continuously introduced discord into her life, her family, and her world.

Up ahead, through a clearing in the forest, she sees the log cabin that belongs to her longtime friend, a Sioux woman named Berthine.

∞

Johnnie Robinson, Berthine's black father, originally built the cabin in the late 1800s. Thomas Winniper, Sr. allowed Johnnie boy and his family to remain in the forest between the site of the Winniper family's oil refinery and the family's mansion. Two families on one man's property, the former serving the latter, all nestled happily inside the Winniper County lines that Thomas, Sr. established in 1891.

In her old age, Olivia only remembers speaking with her deceased father-in-law in passing, at formal occasions, long before she married Thomas, Jr, a.k.a. "Papa", but, now, she often sees the old man in her husband. Papa has always emulated his father's wrath and ambition; and as he has aged, he has chosen the most violent means to achieve his father's power-hungry agenda.

∞

Olivia Newton met Thomas Winniper, Jr. where most Winniper County children meet their future mates—during Sunday bible study at Winniper Baptist Church. Matched early in life by families of mutual greed and ambition, Olivia's parents quickly groomed her to become Mrs. Thomas Winniper, Jr. As the time approached for the Winniper heir to choose his bride, the town believed the decision came down to two women who had spent their respective lives preparing to vie for his affection and purse: Olivia Newton and Tilly Bethune.

Daughter to William Bethune, Tilly began her life much like Olivia, groomed for marriage and motherhood, the vehicles that advance a family's status and wealth. Whereas Olivia Newton depended upon and loathed her family's greed, Tilly Bethune and her father embraced every ounce of the blood money that they gained from the Winniper family's oil. Although rumors flew that Thomas, Jr. and Tilly were childhood sweethearts, his father had always secretly detested the Bethune family. Thomas Winniper, Sr. enjoyed a healthy rivalry and lucrative partnership with William and while a marriage between their children seemed advantageous to both families, Thomas, Sr. always feared that the Bethune family could someday usurp his family's power.

Because the Newtons and Bethunes raised Olivia and Tilly inside the church of God and oil wealth, both families were firmly cemented in Winniper County's elite circle. The choice for the town's future queen depended upon Thomas, Jr.'s personal taste, because his father had passed away before the prospect of nuptials. Thomas, Jr., Olivia, and Tilly were still in secondary school when Thomas Winniper, Sr. died from a heart attack.

Instead of being prudent and handing his oil and farming enterprise to a trust or bank, Thomas, Sr. bequeathed his entire estate to his son. Prepared for the throne, the prince quickly left school at the age of fifteen and became one of the wealthiest men in the world. In 1907, Thomas, Jr. became the majority share owner of a holding company worth $450 million. Thomas, Jr. expanded the Winniper Family Holding Company into a global investment firm, manipulating and profiting from every major industry including oil, steel, agriculture, media, finance, manufacturing, trade, and estate planning. Throughout his success, he remained loyal to his father's wishes and he allowed Johnnie Robinson, his wife Violet, and their daughter Berthine to remain within their cabin in Winniper County. As a child, Papa adored the jovial Mr. Robinson and Berthine always admired the Winniper family. She, Thomas, Jr., Olivia, and Tilly grew up so close in proximity that they felt as though they were pseudo-siblings, raised together, but separated due to circumstance. Time created distance and disengagement from these notions, and Thomas, Jr. became a man who saw no equal to himself, so the women around him inevitably became secondary.

∞

Olivia remembers visiting Thomas, Jr. and Berthine at the Winniper Family Estate; they were all happy, though they did not know why.

∞

Berthine, a Sioux daughter of a black sharecropper, and Olivia, a white daughter of a wealthy, Confederate banker, often played with Thomas, Jr.— the girls always united against the boy. Olivia and Berthine watched little Thomas help Johnnie remodel the Robinsons' cabin. It was a wonderfully boisterous undertaking for a privileged youth and an uneducated black man. In those days, Papa Winniper was only "Junior"; though his princely prospect already began to burden him, he was a much more relaxed as a child. Back then, he still enjoyed spending time with people. While they reconstructed the modest cabin, both Thomas, Jr. and Mr. Robinson grumbled and bragged at the same time, claiming mastery over the smallest task.

"You see how I shave dese plank edges," Johnnie Robinson boasted while wiping sweat from his brow. "Dat curve right dere is a perfectly fit to withstand rain or snow! God himself could sneeze on dis here cabin, and it would stand straight up!"

Berthine's father was prone to using hyperbole and he occasionally over-embellished his talents. Johnnie played a pivotal role in Thomas Winniper, Sr.'s discovery of the oil within the Winnipers' land; though his deeds and his loyalty gave his family a sense of security within the shade of the Winniper family tree, Berthine later learned that her father's actions haunted him throughout his life. He, too, faced the Winniper family's paradox, in which, he sacrificed his humanity in order to save his family.

Over the years, Johnnie amassed a sharecropper's fortune from the Winniper Family Estate, living as a faux king with his Sioux wife and daughter despite his field hand upbringing. Although very few people understood Mr. Robinson's deeper need to succeed as a poor black man in South Dakota, his sacrifices cost him dearly. When they were children, Berthine once told Olivia that Johnnie and Violet suffered frequent night terrors. During these episodes, Berthine's parents woke up while wailing and sweating, sometimes in unison, as if they had shared the same nightmare.

Every few months, either one or both of her parents rose from a turbulent sleep, screaming desperately until someone living could assure them that they were alive and their nightmare was only a dream. Once they calmed down, neither would ever reveal what prompted their fear. They only told Berthine that they loved her and that she was their only child. She grew up believing that her parents suffered from flashbacks of a traumatic event that ingrained itself so deeply into their psyche that the memories disabled their innocence. Though they lived peacefully within the oak forest of Winniper County, they never had peace, no matter how much or how little of the Winniper family's wealth trickled into their small wooden cabin.

∞

Weaving through more weeds and wickets, Olivia continues to make her way through the forest, the rugged terrain rolling under her well-worn hiking boots. Many wanderers become lost between the oil refinery, the cabin, and the Winniper Family Estate.

∞

When Olivia visited the master house with her parents, she spent hours playing games in the high forest stalks. She, Thomas, Jr., Berthine, and sometimes Tilly, ran to and fro between the mansion and cabin, crawling over and under fallen trees, but never entering the oil refinery. They heard stories about the oil refinery being built upon a Sioux ghost town; Berthine and Thomas, Jr. believed the property was haunted. Even as children, Olivia and Tilly believed whatever Thomas, Jr. believed; their competition began early in their childhood.

For years, the Winnipers and Newtons joined the Bethunes and the rest of Winniper County for the January 1st Winniper County Founder's Day Parade. They would relish invites and regards to celebrate Thomas Winniper, Jr.'s birthday privately and as Olivia and Thomas, Jr. grew older, the elite families learned more and more about the events that transpired on the day Thomas Winniper, Sr. supposedly found his oil.

Members of the privileged few bragged about a murderous coup, whispering in small circles to ears of mutual culpability. They shared secrets inside boardrooms and cigar lounges filled with the Winnipers, Bethunes, Cobbs, Newtons, Mortens, and ancillary players like the Allen family, legal henchmen at best.

∞

The Winniper County Founder's Day Parade celebrates the triumph that has become a local folklore. How much one knows about the night their county's benefactor unexpectedly became a father and tragically lost his brother is a measure of their inclusion within the elite town's exclusive company.

The oral history, as recited within the Winnipers' inner circle, explains how sometime before Thomas, Sr. struck oil, a local Sioux tribesman became upset with a town store clerk who refused to serve him.

∞

No one knew what the Injun wanted, but apparently, he and the clerk began to fight and the Sioux man died during the fracas. At the time, it wasn't a crime to kill a Sioux or any native. All across the nation, American law did not recognize the native tribes as legal citizens and thus, the law and the American people treated the natives as foreign savages. The law did not apply to them, so there was no need for a trial.

The injustice infuriated several native families in the old Sioux village and they began to burn several acres of the Winniper family's wheat harvest on the night Thomas, Jr. was born. According to Winniper County folklore, Thomas, Jr.'s mother went into labor while his father battled the disgruntled Sioux natives and stopped them from burning his crops. The family's maid Violet promptly sent Carl to Doctor Morten, Sr.'s home while she tended to Ruby Winniper. When young Carl Potter ran into the doctor's home to tell him of Ruby Winniper's condition, Doctor Morten, Sr. seemed to care more about the burning cropland than the woman in labor.

After learning about the violent uprising, Doctor Morten, Sr. tried to alert the town militia, hoping they could stop the Sioux and protect the Winniper family's lucrative harvest. He was completely unaware that Thomas Winniper, Sr. had already commissioned the Bethune and Cobb militias to seize the real prize. The most "in" members of the inner circle learned that, all along, Thomas Winniper, Sr. had planned to seize an oil discovery that had occurred inside the Sioux village and he fabricated every ounce of the public story in order to satiate the press and justify the massacre of the Ghost Dance Sioux. And, as the story goes, the riches from the Winnipers' oil secured the loyalty of the families that helped Thomas, Sr. defeat the Sioux. Their shared wealth spawned the South Dakota oil industry and they gave birth to an American oil empire capable of ensuring profits and elections.

∞

In particular, the Winniper and Bethune wealth has always financed a majority of Winniper County's economy and South Dakota's political payoffs.

∞

Once she married Thomas, Jr., Olivia learned more of the remaining truth. During the melee at the Sioux village, Doc Morten, Sr. travelled to the Winniper Family Estate after receiving word that Ruby Winniper was in trouble. In the peaking hours of dawn, Ruby died after spontaneously giving birth to Thomas, Jr. and a twin Sioux sister while the Bethune and Cobb militias secured the oil strike and burned the surrounding Sioux village to the ground.

Thomas, Sr. and his henchmen had murdered the tribe and, while Thomas, Sr. returned to his wife's side, the henchmen capped the oil spout and buried the bodies in one mass grave.

∞

Glancing back and forth between the long grassy field and the lush oak tree forest that separate Berthine's cabin from the Winniper Family Estate, Olivia wonders if humans grow like these plants and trees, waiting to be cut down or trampled upon by life's indeterminable circumstances. Surely, the Sioux did not deserve to have their land taken from them, but if they hadn't, she would not have the life that she does. The weight of an old woman's worries wears upon her weak and weary ankles. She hastens her steps through the edges of the forest and makes her way toward a narrow, wooden bridge.

As Olivia crosses the bridge, she stares over the stream that separates the site of the old Sioux village from the Winniper Family Estate. The smell of fresh apple pie drifts over the plains and Berthine's baked goods beckon just ahead through the trees. Olivia's eyes grow wide as the scent enters her nostrils; she absorbs as much as she can while remembering those days long ago when life seemed so innocent. They *were* children, once—she, Tilly, Berthine, and Thomas, Jr. Though time has turned her husband into a cantankerous old bigot, Olivia remembers when he enjoyed simple pleasures like freshly baked bread. Olivia has always apologetically appreciated the luxuries of their privileged life; she has eaten more than her share of delicious sweets. Her mouth instinctively waters after dinner because her programmed palate expects dessert, a dish she has never gone without. Dessert has always been her childish reward for hosting and attending dinner parties, charity events, birthday celebrations, and other social rituals in Winniper County.

The amount of care and decadence that the local bakers spend on their baked goods is an art of construction. Only the most capable masters receive the patronage to invest the time and effort into the craft. Winniper County celebrations are notorious for producing the most flavorful cakes, pies, cookies, and pastries, especially at the Winniper County Founder's Day Bake Off.

Though she remains relatively reclusive, Berthine is a master of baking in the highest form. She never enters the competition and she only cooks for her family, so she has become Olivia's secret treasure. For the old friends, eating together creates a mysterious need for mutual satisfaction, and Olivia wonders if Berthine would ever endanger her family and expose the truth about Teresa's Sioux children. Olivia's brief fear threatens her faith while exposing her paranoia; she inhales deeply and quells her mortal worries as she remembers her moral duty as a mother and grandmother. All things must come to pass.

Olivia does not believe that she has enough courage to end her family's secrecy, nor does she know if she would, even if she could. As a woman of oil wealth, Olivia feels adequately entitled to ignore her conscience and indulge in her desires. She ensures her survival by eating and she assuages her tastes by eating *well*. Every so often she does appease her inner voice, especially on her Sioux grandchildren's birthdays. Olivia hikes through the forest to the cabin, after providing Berthine with whatever she needs to cook and bake the largest meal possible for the children.

Since Teresa's death, over four years ago, Olivia has spent more time with her Sioux grandchildren. After Kenny delivered Duke, Christina, and June to the mansion, Papa has kept more of a watchful eye around their home, but she still finds time to journey away from the estate. She only visits Berthine's cabin when her husband is overseas on business, because she knows that the risks and repercussions could be fatal if someone discovered their secret. Papa still refuses to accept any alternative arrangement for dealing with the family's blood curse.

∞

Implementing his father's indoctrination and following his father's instructions, Thomas, Jr. had Doctor Morten, Jr. dispose of Teresa and Thomas III's respective Sioux twin. Thomas, Jr. believed his father—a dying Sioux sorceress had cursed the family so that the Winniper women endure a painful labor and give birth to Sioux and white twins. Even now, he waits for Duke, Christina, and June to mature into relationships, knowing the axe must swing upon each brown bundle of joy.

Thomas Winniper, Sr.'s instructions were clear: the Sioux children can never survive. They should never live beyond their first breaths and dispose of them as discreetly as possible. And lastly, eliminate anyone, who threatens to expose the family's curse, regardless of name, title, or relation.

∞

The son has implemented these murderous means; Papa believes his decisions have saved the family, ensured their legacy, and camouflaged the conspiracy behind their oil wealth. From the Winniper male perspective, he has kept both the secret and the lie intact. Thomas, Jr. and his father chose to kill and conceal their family's truth while raising an empire and exalting their Winniper legacy. The hypocrisy of their wealth has become more than Olivia can bear mentally and the time that she spends away from the estate, sneaking to Berthine's cabin, has proven most therapeutic, even soul-cleansing.

During her trips through the forest, she feels as though she reclaims her innocence; the clouds form the faces of her youth. When away from the mansion, she rediscovers a carefree understanding that only young children can have, unburdened by regrets—whatever may come will be their destiny. She sees her family's saga as a fated battle between good and evil, rich and poor, love and hate, and all the polar paradigms that pervade the world's perception. Their story is the story of the world, itself.

Olivia reads books and news articles to her Sioux grandchildren during her visits, testing their knowledge and intellect while comparing them to their white counterparts. Her observations challenge her own sensibilities. She hopes her Sioux grandchildren can see beyond their skin, beyond their poverty, and beyond how others may view them. Every night she prays that living with a Sioux pseudo-mother will help them appreciate their heritage and their place in life.

Tasting love in Berthine's cooking and experiencing warmth from the outside world during Olivia's visits, maybe they will understand that family is a different concept for them; yet, in order for her Sioux grandchildren to have any family, or any semblance of normalcy, they must age and prosper in secrecy, hidden from her husband. Though a silent pact maintains peace, complete trust and compassion don't exist once a Winniper man feels that he must protect his name. Despite the fact that Papa Winniper lacks confidence in his heirs, the fifty-nine-year-old man still fights to hold the Winniper family's gleam in the public eye. He hopes Thomas III or Duke will rise from their respective doldrums and shine a youthful light upon the family's legacy so that the county and the world will remember who butters their bread and whom they should respect for years and generations to come. Papa Winniper may never accept Thomas III, but Olivia knows that Thomas III and Teresa have inspired their father.

∞

Papa saw his children chase answers to the difficult questions of their family's curse. He funded their worldwide excursions, secretly hoping they would find a cure to make the family whole. Internally, Papa struggled to contain his optimism and pride.

Thomas III and Teresa would return from traveling the world and spending their father's money, and, their tanned skin glowed with freedom and sunlight. Papa Winniper would beam brightly along with his adult children, proud of their adventures. They had been somewhere, done something, and met new people, which was more than Olivia had ever done. When her children returned, they had so many stories and new memories that Papa and Olivia would listen to them talk on and on for hours. These were the only moments in their adult lives when the children actually enjoyed their parents' company. After Papa arranged for Teresa to marry the notoriously boring Ralph Townsend, her trips became less frequent, and noticeably less adventurous, and she spent much less time at the mansion.

For the next few years, the family seemed relatively at peace with all pertinent members living in harmony through a divorce and quick marriage to her second husband. Teresa did her best to love Charles Kane and raise Duke and Christina in Winniper County, while Thomas III began dating and ditching every wealthy debutante that Olivia sent to his market. But then, in early spring 1941, Olivia noticed Teresa's stomach—a bulbous bump that naturally grabs a mother's attention.

Olivia asked her daughter, who initially denied the bump, but, after much prodding, Teresa confessed to having an affair. She revealed to Olivia that the father was Tilly Bethune's playboy son, Kenneth Bethune, Jr. A well-known fool and sole male heir, Kenny habitually depleted his Bethune trust fund. He invested his time in gambling debts and pool hall hustles instead of oil racketeering and finance schemes. The antithesis to the reluctant, fearful Thomas III, Kenny didn't run from his inheritance due to fear or insecurity; no, Kenny ran from an easy fortune because he found more value in his own destruction.

Teresa begged Olivia not to tell Papa about the affair or the pregnancy, and, as a Winniper woman familiar with their many secrets, Olivia understood her daughter's plight. Olivia made the proper arrangements for a very discreet divorce and an immediate wedding, coaxing Papa to give his only daughter away for the third time, in order to prevent any further scandal. The ordeal seemed to have a happy ending until the day the babies arrived…

Before Teresa's first pregnancy, Olivia attempted to explain the family's curse to her daughter as best as she could. She made the secretive arrangements with Doc Morten, Jr. and she planned to handle the entire ordeal without Papa's interference. When the moment came, Olivia pulled her husband's Spoister around the back of the Winniper Family Estate, snuck Teresa through the kitchen and patio, and drove to the Mortens' mansion faster than her husband could have ever raced in that speed demon.

Though he rarely speaks of his racing days, Papa Winniper was once a daredevil in his own right, but he could have never matched the urgency Olivia felt in those moments while pressing her pedal to the Spoister's floor. She pulled over to an adjacent side street and walked with Teresa in the dead of night to the Mortens' personal care facility inside their massive mansion.

∞

Olivia often remarks to Berthine that the Morten family practice has been the most successful business in Winniper County for years. They suckled from the Winniper family name, and rightly so. The late Doc Morten and his son have been essential to concealing a secret that only a few *living beings* outside of the Winniper family know—and none will tell.

Though Thomas, Jr. never discusses trivial topics like money or legacy with his wife, Olivia knows that the Morten men have received excessive overpayments for silence and social discretion. For two generations, the Winnipers have spent time and money concealing the dark curse of their bloodline, dating back to the day Thomas Winniper, Jr. was born on January 1, 1891. Since that day, the Winniper births have been blessings and curses, and the women and the Sioux children have become collateral damage to the Winniper family's financial success.

∞

When Teresa and Olivia arrived at the Mortens' mansion, they quickly snuck through the garage into a rear entrance next to a well-kept veranda. Doctor Morten, Jr. ushered them into his home and his wife Marilyn waited in the doorway of his exam room. She hurried them inside, swiftly shut the door behind them, and closed all the curtains.

∞

Normally, the floor-to-ceiling windows provide an expansive, relaxing view of the Mortens' decorated backyard. The Mortens pride themselves on their Victorian vegetable garden and their country house, state-of-the-art laboratory, where the late Doctor Morten and his son have concocted their own medicines.

∞

Expecting new memories and old karma, Olivia checked the lock on the exam room door, adjusted the curtains, and nervously joined Doctor Morten, Jr. as he helped the mother-to-be lay down in bed.

"Teresa, stay calm," Olivia whispered softly over her daughter. "The babies have to take their time."

"I don't want them to take their time!" she grimaced, holding her stomach tightly. "They need to come out now!"

Teresa desperately clenched Olivia's hand, reminding her mother of how she had reached for Papa Winniper with the same sense of panic. Olivia clutched his hand and dreaded what might happen next. When Olivia gave birth to Teresa, she saw pure terror in her husband's eyes. Papa feared that his wife would die during childbirth like his mother. A breech-birth death, Ruby bled too much during labor; she couldn't be saved, but her son survived while his father ordered Violet and Johnnie Robinson to execute the boy's twin Sioux sister. Thomas, Jr. always worried that one day his wife would suffer his mother's fate and his anxiety began to influence all his decisions and actions.

While observing her daughter's tensing cheeks, Olivia questioned her resolve to watch Teresa endure so much pain. She doubted her past submission, thinking back to when Papa executed their Sioux children years ago. Unlike Ruby, Olivia was alive and lucid when she left the Sioux babies to her husband's disposal.

Choosing to ignore her doubts and focus on the children she could love publicly, Olivia raised Teresa and Thomas III in the comfortable wealth of the Winniper Family Estate. Teresa and Thomas III became her consolations and Papa Winniper never mentioned exactly what he'd done to their Sioux newborns. Much like Olivia's vow to Teresa, Papa had promised that he would care for their Sioux children and deliver them to a home where they would be safe. It took only one look after the deeds were done for her to know that his promise had never received serious consideration.

∞

The silent truth of her dead Sioux babies has created more weak links in a long chain of lies that has enslaved the entire family.

∞

"Now, do as your mother said and stay calm, Teresa." Doctor Morten, Jr. wheezed while Marilyn hustled around the room frantically, gathering tools and placing towels on the medical bed. "When we tell you to push, you'll need to bear down with your perineum muscles and push the baby through the..."

"Doctor Morten!" Olivia hissed over the doctor's shoulder, her face twisting gruesomely at his descriptive instructions. "I believe we can escape the...*medical talk.*"

"Argghh!" Teresa yelled vociferously, releasing her mother's hand and tightly grasping the bed's headboard. "When can I push?"

"Soon, darling, just let the doctor tend to you," Olivia gently encouraged her daughter and rubbed her hands over Teresa's arm. "It's not easy having two babies at once. And this is your third pair!"

Looking down at Teresa, knowing and empathizing with her daughter's pain and frustration, Olivia asked herself what all the Winniper women must wonder during labor: "*why me?*" She conceived twice, but Olivia never had anyone to comfort her. She was unable to confer with another Winniper woman who conceived twins before her—only her late mother-in-law could have understood her dilemma. Olivia vowed that she would be there for her daughter to help her through the pregnancy, calm her during the labor, and coach her through the aftermath.

"You have to pace yourself, Teresa," Olivia added tenderly, attempting a reassuring smile, one she had planned for years. When Teresa became pregnant and bore Duke and Lucy, Olivia delivered Lucy to Berthine's cabin in the middle of the night. Reluctant to be seen on the main roads, she drove along the dirt pathways of the Winniper family's oil refinery until she reached the woods between the Winniper Family Estate and the old Sioux village. She parked the Spoister and carried the newborn girl to Berthine's cabin; Lucy was the first Sioux baby survivor, a living stowaway hidden under Papa Winniper's nose, inside a cabin that he helped build.

Six years later, Olivia delivered Charles to Berthine, which was much more difficult because both Charles and Christina wailed immediately after their separation. They were instantly torn from joy and comfort. Because Teresa gave birth to Charles and Christina during the day, it was impossible to keep Charles quiet long enough to hide him at Doctor Morten's home. In a rush, Olivia left the home with Charles swaddled in her arms. She drove back to her family's estate, parked at the edge of their driveway, crept through the oak trees, and placed the crying Sioux baby boy into an old fireman's helmet inside Thomas and Teresa's country shed.

She couldn't think of another place to keep him safe from the groundskeepers, landscapers, and housemaids, so she wrapped the newborn in a purple, cotton blanket and placed him on top of a bale of hay. His screams muffled as he cried from within the shed, whimpering, cold and alone. At nightfall, Papa Winniper retired to his office suite with several attorneys and cigars, unconcerned with Teresa or his newborn granddaughter at Doctor Morten's house. She had not conceived another male heir, and worse, she had given birth to another Sioux baby. He wanted to avoid the responsibility so he mistakenly trusted and assumed that the women had destroyed the evidence completely.

Olivia excused herself under the guise of being tired from the day's joy and heartache. She snuck back into the playhouse, scooped up Charles from within his makeshift manger, and brought him to Berthine's cabin.

∞

Lately, Olivia has worried that the early trauma of their separation still affects Charles and Christina. Both twins have grown to become equally sinister and cold, by far crueler than their siblings. They mirror each other's malice though they still have never met. Though they now live less than two miles apart, none of Teresa's children know about the existence of their respective twin.

∞

After Papa paid Kenny to drug and deliver Duke, Christina, and June to the estate, Kenny left town with the neighbor's wife. Kenny eloped with Sheila Chamberlain so quickly that he didn't even say goodbye to his mother, Tilly.

∞

Olivia has maintained a superficial relationship with Tilly over the years; their roles have shifted and, while Olivia has become a meek housewife, Tilly has controlled the Bethune family's interest in the Winniper Family Holding Company and she has become a powerful business partner for Papa Winniper.

∞

Though Tilly never discussed Kenny's elopement, Olivia knew his betrayal hurt his mother in the same way that Teresa had hurt her father. It's difficult for a parent to realize that their child is a liar—the image in the mirror is too real.

∞

Using a comparative analysis, Olivia has recently noticed some peculiar similarities between Teresa's white and Sioux twins. Raised separately since birth, having never met nor known of the other's existence, each pair shares an intangible bond. They are unique counterparts, true doppelgängers in character and personality. At age eighteen, Duke is an insecure, loud mouth, while Lucy has the confidence to control her quarrelsome brothers, though she has never spoken a word. At age eleven, Christina is a ruthless tyrant while Charles is a sneaky democrat; both will stop at nothing to get their way. At age eight, Jazz is already a natural musician and June can never stop singing the blues.

∞

"Why can't I have my children? Why can't I be with them?" Teresa asked repeatedly during her last labor. Crying through tired eyes, she worried about Charles and Lucy. In her hysteria, she began to fear her father's cruelty if he found out that they had survived. "Take me to Berthine's cabin."

"No, we've been lucky with the other two, Teresa," Doc Morten, Jr. replied abruptly while continuing to move around the medical room. "You will keep *your* child, and we will..."

"*I will* take care of the *other* child..." Olivia interrupts sharply, still rubbing her daughter's arms and trying to transmit some comfort through her fingertips. She leans closely to Teresa and whispers, while gently squeezing her daughter's skin. "Berthine is taking good care of Lucy and Charles. Your children are fine. Now, you focus on delivering two more. One day, you'll see. Just be patient."

"But why can't I keep them, Mama? I want all my children...together." Teresa wept wearily, rolling her exhausted eyes in a daze. "I want my family. I want to see them."

"No, you can't, sweetheart," Olivia raised her thumbs to wipe her daughter's cheeks. "Someday it will be different, I promise."

Olivia leaned into her daughter's shoulders, hovering over Teresa and staring into her eyes sharply. Her daughter may have been the strongest Winniper woman of them all; she bore six children in total. Maybe her anguish was the worst to endure; it may be better for a mother to die during childbirth than to live without her child.

"I want someday to be today, Mama. I can't let another child go..."

"Teresa, stay calm...you chose to have this affair. We did as best we could with it. You knew...you've known all along, which is more than I can say for myself." Olivia pacified her daughter's cries, briefly, while rubbing her hand over Teresa's forehead and smiling with a motherly illusion—her attempt to redeem past indiscretions. "I'm sorry that this is the way your father chooses to handle this, but we, women, we do as we must. I know you are scared, but you *can't* be scared *right now.* You're bringing two lives into this world; don't let their first moments be filled with fear."

"I don't think I can do it," Teresa stammered, begging her mother for a different outcome. "I get so depressed afterwards...I have to keep both of them, please."

"Teresa, think of your children, *all of them.*" Olivia nodded reassuringly as Doc Morten, Jr. completed his set up by sliding a large aluminum tray next to the medical bed. Marilyn laid several towels over Teresa's straddled legs and Olivia tried her best to hide her fear. "What would Duke and Christina think after so many years? If you bring home the other baby, how are you going to explain that without adding more lies and endangering everyone? It's just best to keep things the way they are. Doc is right, you've been luckier than most."

"Okay, ladies, I believe we are ready." Doc Morten, Jr. stepped around Olivia and positioned himself at the foot of the bed. He leaned forward between Teresa's ankles.

"Whenever you like...begin to push," he instructed while maneuvering a long two-pronged tool under the towels that covered Teresa's legs.

Olivia stared over Teresa with concern, reading her daughter's face for any doubt or trepidation. Teresa's eyes remained soft and resolved, understanding her circumstance: the cursed Winniper women were either tragically doomed or pleasantly blessed to conceive Sioux and white twins in a small South Dakota town of their own creation.

∞

They are a family trapped in their own social cage. Olivia has often wondered how such a trick could be possible. Papa has told her several wild tales of an Indian curse and the oil strike that his father stole from the Sioux natives, yet, Teresa and Thomas III travelled all over the country and the world, and they never found a religion, tribe, or scholar that knew anything about such an affliction or curse. Never has anything like this even seemed possible; and thus, the Winniper women have succumbed to their best instincts over the years. Olivia has found a way to save some of the family's Sioux offspring. For the time being, Teresa's children are safe from public scrutiny. She is proud that she helped her deceased daughter ensure the safety of her children. Olivia plans to continue to conceal the Sioux children at Berthine's cabin as long as the arrangement does not tarnish the Winniper family name.

Now, as a mature woman, Olivia appreciates the need for reputation. She understands how one's legacy can acquire resources, allies, and favors alike.

∞

Long ago, Olivia forgave God and submitted to an understanding that *the world is as it was meant to be.*

∞

The Winniper family must survive without the excuses of the poor or weak. She believes that in order to endure their misfortune, they must remain wealthy enough to hide it. Hence, the Winniper women risk their family's survival by removing the Sioux babies from Papa Winniper's clutches and rearing their white heirs within his Winniper wealth—a family displaced for the sake of family. How else could they all survive within the circumstances of this world?

∞

"Are you ready, Terri?" Olivia asked, but her daughter looked at her blankly, leaving the question unanswered. Teresa took a moment to stare at nothing; her glare became glazed over as if she was peering into bright lights.

"*Teresa?* Are you okay?" Olivia leaned forward into her daughter's line of sight and titled her head, trying to gain Teresa's attention. She shook Teresa's hand quickly and Teresa's head propped up abruptly, blinking out of her trance.

"Y-yes, I'm ready." Teresa grasped her mother's hand and repeated their mantra for self-reassurance. "I just have to be patient. Someday, it'll be different. I just have to be patient. Be patient."

"Yes, be patient," Olivia whispered, glancing to the doctor, nodding, and raising her voice. "But now, you need to push, sweetheart."

"But, it hurts." Teresa grimaced slightly, urging her body to mobilize.

"Come on, push!" Olivia encouraged her daughter, holding tightly to her hand.

"It's worse this time! They're monsters!" Teresa yelled, caught in a cliché. For over an hour, she reenacted a poorly-lit scene from a horror film she saw in the 30s; the hideous footage showed a child being born.

"Push harder!" Doc Morten, Jr. cheerily added from the edge of the bed; a happily disengaged bystander, he kept taking peeks at his wife's skirt, and Marilyn enjoyed noticing her husband's attention.

"God, help me!" Teresa clung to her mother's hand firmly.

"I see the crown," Doc Morten, Jr. proclaimed, reaching for more tools from his tray. "Keep pushing!"

"Aaaahhh, I can't!"

"You're doing great, Teresa." Olivia smiled, praying that the moment would be over soon, yet still knowing another child waited for the same ride. "Keep pushing, keep pushing!"

"The shoulders are next!" Doc Morten, Jr. exclaimed, reaching his hands between her legs. "This is the hardest part. Come on!"

"Push, Teresa!" Marilyn urged from the sideline while shaking her hips for the home team.

"It hurts so much!" Teresa screamed, releasing Olivia's hand, balling her fist, and pounding on the mattress of the medical bed. "Get this kid out of me!"

"Your baby...is...a...boy!" Doc Morten, Jr. explained as he pulled a brown baby boy from under the towels and held him upside down as the infant's cries filled the room.

"I hear him!" Teresa screamed joyously, reaching her weary arms out over her stomach. "Let me hold him, please!

"You can't keep this one!" Doc Morten, Jr. confirmed casually, wrapping the baby in more towels. He then handed the child to Marilyn, who gently placed him in a nearby wicker basket. Olivia wanted to go to him, but she didn't want to excite Teresa.

"I want...to...see him," Teresa sighed in exhaustion. "I want...to see...*Jazz*."

"It's best that you don't," Doc Morten, Jr. replied, repositioning his knees at Teresa's feet. He then looked to Olivia for support and confirmation. "We don't want her to get attached to *that* one. She still has one more to pop out."

"He's right, Teresa." Olivia patted her daughter's head lightly, wiping her moist hair and smiling at the child who never faked sick and never played dead. Teresa was always strong. She was always filled with life, but her pregnancies took a toll on her spirit. "Try to rest before the second one comes."

"I can't, Mama, it hurts. It's worse this time…"

"Well…" Doc Morten, Jr. leaned forward, working between Teresa's legs, fidgeting with his tools, and causing Teresa noticeable displeasure. "It seems the next one might be on the way…*now.*"

"But, I'm not ready!" Teresa proclaimed frantically, knowing the pain from the twin births and remembering her father's stories about her deceased grandmother. Though Thomas, Jr. rarely discussed the loss, he couldn't escape the guilt that his mother bled to death after giving birth to him. His personal demons made enduring Olivia's pregnancies especially difficult so he only completed the ordeal twice. Papa was content after Thomas III's birth, but it was Teresa, who endured three pregnancies, after knowing the consequences and still believing in love. As she struggled to find the strength to produce her sixth child, she looked to her mother for help. "I'm not ready, Ma'. I can't do this!"

"Yes, you can, darling. Is there any bleeding, Doc?" Olivia asked, leaning over Teresa's shoulders.

"No, no more than usual." Doc Morten, Jr. peered under the towels and keenly inspected ground zero. "Whenever you're ready, Teresa, give 'er a push."

The doctor raised his head above Teresa's legs and nodded confidently. Olivia grabbed her daughter's hand gently and began to coach her through the pain. After another hour, Teresa finally gave birth to one healthy, white baby girl: June Bethune, daughter to Kenny Bethune and Teresa Winniper-Bethune—the blessed child of two powerful empires.

Immediately after June's birth, Olivia wanted to send word to Kenny, but she had to take the Sioux newborn to Berthine and return without arousing suspicion. Teresa passed out from fatigue shortly after June's birth and by the time she awoke, her Sioux baby boy was gone. Kenny and Papa stood over her inside the Mortens' medical room, yet, neither man knew about Jazz's survival. Kenny beamed over his blonde, beleaguered wife, gently cradling his first child in his arms.

"You did it, sweetheart. We have a little baby June, just like you wanted. Can we name her June *Tallulah* Bethune after my mother?" he asked with a drunken smile, unable to resist drinking before seeing his firstborn. While Kenny held June softly and Papa grumbled, uncaringly doing his duty, because June was not a male heir. Olivia sat sullenly in the corner of the Mortens' medical room. She was an exhausted orchestrator of another successful Winniper hoax; all the lies remained intact and the castle still shined brightly in the moonlight. By returning from Berthine's cabin before the men had arrived, Olivia had kept the Winniper family's curse concealed after another secretive birth. Even Marilyn has quenched her urge to squeal. Her mouth has remained shut for years; but, prophetically, while watching Teresa cradle June in her arms, Olivia listened to the newborn girl crying a sad melody and she knew the arrangement would never be enough.

Though Olivia couldn't predict the exact lengths to which her daughter would go to unite her family. Teresa never shared her plans to destroy the illusory serenity that the Winniper name had created for her. Olivia did have one thought creep through her mind after Jazz and June's birth: *Teresa will never accept being away from her children and her children will never accept being away from each other.*

They were family; they would always have a connection to one another, especially to their mother. Olivia knew that mother's intuition well. Worse than knowing that her children had died, Teresa knew that her children were alive and well, and another woman raised them as their mother. As Teresa's despair grew more apparent, she pulled away from the family and she supposedly plotted to run away with Kenny and her children. Whether or not she had real plans, Olivia quickly understood her own short sidedness.

Even though they survived, Teresa couldn't bear her Sioux children growing up away from her, outside of her home, and ignorant of their real family. It was only a matter of time until their arrangement came undone; somehow Olivia's attempt to save her family through more secrecy had still failed. Olivia wondered if Papa was right: was it better to kill the Sioux babies? Did Thomas, Jr. and his father save the family and their brown children from a life of torment?

During Teresa's last labor, Olivia wrapped her arms around Teresa's shoulders and her daughter felt lost, incomplete, as if half her life existed elsewhere and she could never enjoy anything entirely. Teresa stared up at her mother with contempt and callousness and Olivia knew then that she had compromised her daughter's life for a tragic oversight in her personal character. The family's legacy outweighed Olivia's children and she accepted their deaths as necessities under the circumstances. Olivia willingly lost herself while raising Teresa and Thomas III; yet, for Teresa, her children far outweighed any legacy because they were alive. They were real, far more real than the legacy itself, much more in need of a mother, and she needed her children. On the silent drive to Berthine's cabin, Olivia contemplated…

∞

Turning her thoughts from hurtful memories, Olivia continues hiking through the grassy field toward Berthine's cabin. She reaches the cobble stepping-stones at the edge of the forest and remembers how they hopped along these stones as a child, back before the cabin was truly full.

∞

When Johnnie Robinson originally built the cabin, it was solely for his family. In 1909, he became sick, several church members moved into the cabin to aid Berthine and sit by his side. Her mother Violet had passed away the year before from a sudden stroke in the middle of the night. The church family loved the Robinsons so much that they donated one of the old church pianos to Johnnie because he loved the hymns. A few burly deacons helped transport and lift the brown church piano into cabin's main room and every Sunday until he died, the choir came to the cabin and sang for Johnnie. One of the church members who frequented the cabin was a Negro sharecropper named Paul Lancaster, and, while reading scripture and chatting by her father's death-bed, Berthine and Paul fell in love. They said their vows on the same day that Johnnie Robinson passed away—he gave his daughter away with his dying breath.

Within the oak cabin, Paul and Berthine Lancaster lived comfortably as happy newlyweds. Johnnie Robinson had accrued a considerable amount of savings after collecting the Winniper family's scraps over the years. These morsels of oil wealth had provided a secretly privileged life for a Negro-Sioux family in the late 1910s, complete with a quaint South Dakota cottage. Violet had told Berthine not to have children; she often warned her daughter without fully explaining her worries, but Berthine believed her mother and she never conceived with her new husband. The draft for World War I ended any nuances of a dream life for many families, and the Lancasters shed their pound of flesh. As the government began to enlist young men to serve on the battlefield, Paul answered the call at the tender age of 25.

∞

Olivia remembers when Papa held a small dinner for the Lancasters at the Winnipers' mansion.

∞

It was the first and only time that any colored mouths had eaten at the Winnipers' dinner table. Berthine was so nervous that she dropped her soup all over her lap. The guests at the dinner party, Berthine, Paul, Papa, and Olivia, laughed and relaxed and the night went along peacefully and cordially, as if the evening could have become the norm.

∞

The Winnipers have rarely ever discarded class and rank, but, with Paul being shipped off to the largest war in history, Papa and Olivia forgot the small things and enjoyed the time they shared with an old friend and her departing husband as if they were one family. In truth, both Olivia and Thomas, Jr. have always treated Berthine like a sister; they were all raised so closely and, yet, so far apart.

A supposedly Sioux-Negro hybrid, Berthine has always looked more like her Sioux mother than her black father. Olivia believes that her childhood playmate could have been a part of the Winniper family. Maybe Berthine really is a lost Sioux baby—fortunately, for her, she has survived; she could have been killed at birth.

Olivia often tries to merge her husband's logic into her everyday routine, though it rarely works. Her hypocrisy runs especially rampant in her diet; she eats to console the contradiction of a powerful family with secrets like these. If the lies are chains, then they are constantly tightening and the Winniper family has begun to choke itself. How can she find better times?

When thinking only of herself, Olivia believes her past happiness is impossible to rediscover because the present is continually changing from *what was* into *what could be*. How can she bring those moments of her childhood into the present? How can she ever reclaim that joy when the world around her has not only changed, but it has also changed her?

∞

Paul Lancaster never came home from the war, and Berthine was left with a broken heart and the responsibility of burying her husband.

∞

She often wears his army tags around her neck; sometimes, she still needs the closure and the comfort of being close to him.

∞

Even though her father's savings had allowed her to live comfortably within the cabin between the Winniper Family Estate and the oil refinery, Berthine asked Olivia to hire her to work at the Winniper family's mansion, shortly after Paul's death. Berthine seemed to channel her mother's spirit, taking on Violet's old routine from her many years of serving the Winnipers. Berthine hustled around the house, busying herself with sewing, knitting, cooking, cleaning, and doing whatever handiwork the Winniper family could offer in addition to their regular maids' daily chores. The other slaves, er, *servants*, tolerated Berthine due to her grief; it was written all over her face that this widow needed to work. She needed something to care about beyond herself.

∞

For her part, Olivia has always been sympathetic; moreover, following Paul's death, she bonded more closely with her childhood friend and the two women harmonized their spirits in *many ways*—at least, when appropriately away from respectable circles.

∞

Before Olivia married Thomas, Jr. and became an official Winniper woman, she enjoyed watching the small blues functions in the haunted, desolate Sioux village. She sometimes convinced Tilly, Thomas, Jr. and another mutual friend, Donny Rupert, to hike through the woods and visit the ghost town where only a few sharecroppers remained enslaved to the Winnipers' oil refinery. Most of the others still till in the fields of the Winnipers' farmland. Olivia, Thomas, Jr., Tilly, and Donny often snuck through the Winnipers' vast estate, creeping and crawling under and over fallen trees throughout the forest until they smelled the campfires burning at the edges of the forgotten village. Through a few more trees, they could see and hear the Winnipers' oil refinery, a symbol of the family's power overlooking the last relics of a massacred people.

For these small blues functions in the village, the workers, their women, and any other contributing hoot congregated during an evening on the weekend, usually Saturday night. When her father fell asleep early and her mother was at the estate, Berthine joined them, and the five of them would inch as close as they could and listen for that old twangy guitar. Sure enough, a Negro woman always started *singing* with that low, throaty Ma Rainey voice, *"Good Lawd, Good Lawd"*. Olivia loved how those women could sing.

∞

She has never felt bias or anger toward anyone because she has always felt awkward and meek while being herself. She has never formed a real self-image.

∞

Born into the Newton family's investment legacy and raised to ascend into the Winniper fold, Olivia often felt like her parents had already planned her life, and she went along with their plans rather passively. When Olivia was a child, obeying her father was a prerequisite for a wealthy daughter of status. After she and Thomas, Jr. married, William Bethune forced Tilly to marry her younger half-brother, Kenneth, Sr., a child that Mr. Bethune conceived with a mountain hooker while on a deer hunting trip in the Black Hills.

Sadly, William Bethune had several illegitimate sons in Winniper County, and Tilly would have married any of them upon their father's command. Even though Kenneth, Sr. was considered a bastard by most of Winniper County's social standards, William Bethune still gave his eldest male heir his last name in order to keep the Bethune wealth in the family. Though, at the time, Mr. Bethune clearly underestimated Tilly's abilities.

While the Newtons and Winnipers consolidated their power into one enormous, industrial-investment empire, the Bethunes remained an ancillary kingdom while working in tandem with the ruling hierarchy in the Dakotas. The families' respective power actualized a successful outcome, produced from their collective will. They shared a sense of destiny; and, once she became a Winniper woman, Olivia quickly understood the distinction between the mirror and the image.

∞

So now, she eats to satisfy and accentuate the paradox of their power because what she has digested and tolerated inside her body, mind, and spirit has altered her form, her perception, and her understanding of herself. She has changed from an inquisitive extrovert, who loved the blues and the thrills of life, to an insecure child protector, a portrait of a good, obedient wife, who lies to her husband, her family, and her community. She is the only one who truly knows all the pieces in the play; she interacts with Papa, the children, Thomas III, and Berthine, but she is not the puppet master. No, she is just another puppet, dancing to a tune that she does not control.

With a wooden cabin, post-to-post clotheslines, a shallow water well, and a vintage garden, the remains of the old Sioux village provide a primitive footstool to the oil refinery in Winniper County. Over the trees, Olivia can see the smoke billowing from the steel dispensary. The metal for the machinery is manufactured in Pittsburgh, plugged into the South Dakota soil, and connected to the eager oil below. All the wealth flows directly into the family's hands and the estate dolls out the appropriate payments to the county and corporation's most loyal and valuable servants.

∞

And while Thomas Winniper, Sr. and Thomas, Jr. amassed great wealth from the oil strike which was once on Sioux land, the sharecroppers and estate workers still live in poverty, under the shadow of the Winniper family's luxury.

∞

Within Winniper County, the few blacks, Sioux, and Mexicans coexist in a miserable fairytale at the lowest level of the social totem pole. Olivia hopes that her Sioux grandchildren's upbringing within Berthine's home encourages them to employ an appropriate level of tolerance, which will allow them to coexist within their arrangement. As they age and see people, they must always accept their circumstances beyond race and mistakes. Although Olivia knows her husband and her family have made mistakes in the past, she takes some comfort in the fact that Papa silently allows Teresa's children and Berthine to survive in her cabin just outside the lavish Winniper Family Estate. He must have his suspicions, but he knows his duty if he uncovers the deception.

As long as all parties keep their respective distance, all is forgiven, in order to avoid further honor killings, spared and unspared. The yearly harvest from the farmland is enough to feed the entire county and Thomas III provides plenty of extra goods, though Berthine grows her own crops as well. The yields all over town provide yard work and maintenance for some of the remaining migrants seeking success in South Dakota's booming economy. A starved, surviving cohort of poor people struggle and strive to relocate to Winniper County because they have run out of better options.

As the cobble-stepping stones turn into a pebble walkway leading to the front porch, Olivia can already hear the little critters excitedly buzzing around inside Berthine's cabin.

"Give it back!" Jazz's little voice squeaks from inside the house. "It's mine!"

"I had it first!" Charles' slightly huskier voice retorts sharply, and Olivia hears a loud thud. A smile forces its way across her lips as she nimbly hoists her frail, tender frame up the three porch steps. Presumably hearing her ascension, the front door opens quickly and two overjoyed, bright-eyed brown faces peer outside. Teresa's youngest boy, eight-year-old, Jazz, and his eleven-year-old brother, Charles, smile happily and wrestle at the door, fervently tugging a guitar between them.

"Olivia!" The boys exclaim in unison, realizing a new prize, dropping the guitar, and running to the grandmother they believe is just a family friend. Before she can completely situate her balance on the last step, the boys hug her closely, pulling her weight firmly onto the creaking, yet still sturdy porch.

She laughs to herself that her husband is probably still proud of his role in remodeling the cabin. She beams over Jazz and Charles, sons to Kenny and Charles, Sr. respectively, while wondering how these boys will fair without knowing their fathers.

∞

Charles Kane never met his Native American son. Much like Ralph, Charles had been an absent father, consumed in work and triumph with his newfound Winniper family connections. So after her evening tryst with Kenny, and when her monthly visitor never arrived, Teresa felt no allegiance to her second husband. She named Charles after Mr. Kane to spite him, just in case the two should ever meet and notice a resemblance. Once Teresa divorced her second husband and married Kenny, she hoped the Bethune bachelor and their new beginning would deliver the love that still eluded her, but her circumstances still trapped her and her entire family—something Olivia only realized after her daughter's murder.

∞

Olivia remembers when Teresa came to the estate, sneaking in through the garage, hoping to remain unseen by the many servants who also act as spies for Papa Winniper—a man who has always been keenly aware of any movement in Winniper County, especially within his home.

∞

When she was a child, Teresa told Olivia that the Winniper Family Estate was like a fortress with guards as housekeepers and cells as bedrooms. Olivia could never convince her daughter that everyone in the family had a duty to ensure that their secrets remained tightly locked within their proper place, untampered and undiscussed.

Upon hearing of Teresa's affair and her third pregnancy, her first out-of-wedlock, Olivia did her best to aid her daughter and conceal her sordid affair from their respective husbands. Hoping to avoid more scandal, executing a quick divorce and marriage to Kenny, and secretly controlling every detail of their continued arrangement with Berthine, Olivia deceived Papa Winniper for the third and final time. She saved Jazz and whisked him away to Berthine's cabin.

∞

All along, Papa Winniper has ignored any inkling that Teresa's Sioux children are still alive, but Olivia knows that he may just be biding his time.

∞

Jazz and June's birth was an especially secretive scenario because Teresa vowed that she would never become pregnant again after giving birth to Christina and Charles. She promised that she and Charles, Sr. would remain unhappily married; yet, after two years of dull romance, at age twenty-nine, Teresa seduced a seventeen-year-old loose neck after she saw him during a fated encounter at a filling station. Kenny walked past her wearing black-rimmed sunglasses, a Vegas waiter's jacket, and worn Converse shoes; she instantly recognized him, Mrs. Bethune's baby boy, but he had a peculiar smile, Teresa thought. Why did he act so proud and poor?

Teresa immediately followed this rascal, leaving Charles, Sr. engaged in a conversation with the gas pump attendant. Little did Charles, Sr. know, his wife was stumbling into a hornet's nest. The wayward son of the Bethune dynasty, Kenny could have wielded the wealth of one of the most privileged families in South Dakota. His mother had secured the Bethunes' seat at the Winnipers' round table, but Kenny chose recklessness and impulsivity. Tilly still ensured that the commoners treated her son like a prince, but the elite social circles secretly considered him to be a pariah. His heart-throb status conflicted with the good Christian values of free market capitalism.

Amongst each other, Tilly and Papa Winniper openly loathed Kenny's unambitious loafing. They had no use for a scapegoat, at least not yet. When the opportunity presented itself for both Teresa and Kenny to anger Tilly and Papa, they quickly slept together. Winniper County's Romeo and Juliet recklessly engaged in an affair that could have crumbled both kingdoms without proper mediation. Teresa played with firearms in both hands; aiming directly at her heart, she had only intended to hurt herself, but there has been collateral damage which still affects the family.

Unfortunately, Olivia's daughter never believed her mother could orchestrate a speedy transition between divorce, marriage, and childbirth while Papa judged and scrutinized their ever action. Teresa felt that they could not escape his influence, no matter how hard they tried. Often, Olivia would catch her daughter speaking too freely, almost revealing her Sioux children to her father, but, Teresa always stopped herself, knowing the truth could lead to the children's deaths, and maybe even her own. Growing up with her father's protection, Teresa became adept at understanding the lengths he would go to defend his name and avenge his ego if he felt undermined.

On New Year's Eve, Papa ordered his minions to collapse an entire coal mine in West Virginia with 39 workers still inside, just because the senior workmen had threatened to strike. Papa profited from the tragedy; he had placed an insurance policy on the mine during the prior fiscal year. Like Teresa, Olivia knew his treachery; the sweet boy had become a violent man and she even admired his malice to some degree.

∞

Thomas "Papa" Winniper, Jr. has always been a calculating individual, willing to do anything to get what he wanted—a true alpha carnivore.

∞

Trapped within the Winniper family's wheelhouse, Olivia knew she could never outright tell her husband the truth and expect her grandchildren to survive. Her silence declared a muted truce, but, after June and Jazz were born, she also realized that Teresa couldn't uphold the women's side of the arrangement. Teresa couldn't stand being away from her children for much longer. She was a mother stuck between two homes with neither filling her heart completely.

Teresa never told her mother the truth about her feelings and never expressed her desperation because she knew her mother had risked so much to arrange for Berthine to care for her Sioux children. Olivia expected Teresa to understand and accept that there were no alternatives, but Teresa could not follow her mother's logic or her father's commands. She chose a different path, hoping to run away with her entire family; yet, those spies, ones as close as a sibling and a husband, delivered a swift verdict and an execution at Papa's behest. He was the man who sealed her fate, and, less than five years after June and Jazz were born, their mother was dead.

∞

When Olivia visits Jazz, Charles, and Lucy, she hopes Teresa somehow sees how much Olivia cares for her Sioux grandchildren and knows that they are still loved even when their real mother is gone. As the boys hug Olivia's waist tightly, she feels their warmth and their endless supply of youthful excitement. They don their Sunday best with faded brown slacks, plaid button-down shirts, and red suspenders. Olivia enjoys these visits more and more, not only because she can escape from her maniacally, chaotic mansion, but also because she has a chance to admire these children and Berthine.

The Lancaster family lives so simply, so cleanly, but they are poor compared to the Winnipers. Berthine and the children survive in relative isolation from the rest of Winniper County, quietly inhabiting the remnants of the sacred Sioux village along with the estate's spared, subservient sharecroppers. While they reside in a handcrafted country cabin, the Lancasters never want for food; Olivia and Thomas III help as much as possible. Mother and son scuttle toiletries and produce from the market and the farmland with Papa's silent consent—inculpable ignorance. Of course, the patriarch never ventures beyond his castle without pressing business or a scheduled public appearance. He no longer travels for pleasure or curiosity.

After years of playing in the forest as a boy, the man no longer visits the forgotten Sioux village or Johnnie's cabin. Though Papa could easily send eyes and hammers to destroy the quaint cabin, he has ignored Berthine and her children, leaving him free to act under the illusion and leaving the family free to live in peace, at least for the moment. As is, the secrecy keeps Teresa's children alive and safe. Even Olivia conceals the fact that she is their biological grandmother and she sacrifices the full culmination of her rightful place in their lives in order to have any place, in any life, at all.

"My, my, my, you two have grown!" Olivia pats Jazz and Charles on their heads as they beam brightly, staring up to her with excitement. A brief flash of reality flutters over her back and she looks over her shoulder towards the forest, fearing a minion sent to watch or worse. The same social constrictions that confine these children to their small, isolated cabin also limit Olivia to these brief, reticent visits with her Sioux grandchildren. She exhales, tells herself to enjoy the time that she has with her family, and laughs over the boys, smiling at their youthful joy and placing her hand over Jazz's cheek. "Eight and eleven years old, my, how time flies!"

"I'll be nine in June! Hey, that's a puuurty necklace! You look like a magazine model!" Little Jazz exclaims jubilantly, referring to Olivia's white pearl necklace, a keepsake from her family's fortune. She often sleeps with the pearls still clicking around her neck. Recently, when she visits, Jazz has made it a point to notice her necklace—the only material sign of her wealth. He's beginning to read more magazines and his interest in popular culture mirrors a little blonde girl sulking over her guitar, confined to the Winniper family's mansion. Often, Jazz and June remind Olivia of each other, their mannerisms, their fantasies, and their love for music; she imagines that if they ever meet...

"Why, hello, Olivia! Boys, give dear Olivia a chance to get inside!" Berthine orders happily, winking at Olivia and instantly reassuring her old friend. In one instance, Berthine's presence calms any lasting worries that Olivia may have for the moment. She sees a mother, the steward of the house; maybe Berthine needed the children more than they needed her. A distant image of her former self, Berthine raises Olivia's grandchildren in a happy house of love under her very watchful eyes. Over the years, Olivia and Berthine have trusted one another more and more with their respective secrets, risking their lives as elderly women to provide a better upbringing for the Sioux offspring of the Winniper family.

∞

As old women, Berthine finally confided in Olivia and told her about the only time Violet and Johnnie Robinson spoke of the night that Papa was born. Her parents told her that Thomas Winniper, Sr. ordered them to burn and bury a brown baby girl inside the barn, but they couldn't do it. Instead, they took the child home, kept her hidden for years, until it was safe to raise her as their daughter, whom they named Berthine. Berthine became a part of the Robinson family, and Thomas, Sr. never questioned his long time servants. Berthine grew up as a friend to Thomas, Jr., ignorant to the fact that he was, and still is, her brother. She didn't know until just before her mother died that she shared the blood of the wealthiest family in America.

When her adoptive parents finally entrusted her with the knowledge of her origin, they did so knowing that Berthine could never reveal her identity, for fear that she would be killed—a fate she had escaped long ago. They had risked their lives to hide her in their cabin and later, fake an orphan adoption to explain her growing presence. Besides allowing Thomas, Jr. to spend time working with Johnnie, Thomas, Sr. rarely had time to pay much attention to the Robinsons.

Still, for the rest of their lives, Johnnie and Violet had night terrors while dreaming about being murdered for their betrayal. Imagine the Sioux child who grew up so close to her twin white brother; all those years, her adoptive parents couldn't tell her or the boy for fear that he may one day finish his father's orders.

∞

In truth, Berthine shares more in common with Teresa's children than Olivia or Teresa knew when they began the arrangement.

∞

It was fortuitous that Olivia loved Berthine so much when they were children. The two shared a bond as young girls that evolved as they matured into complex women.

∞

They both have needed each other to protect the ones that they love most. While gazing at Jazz and Charles, Olivia knows that Berthine has loved and cared for her great-nephews and niece. Berthine has raised Teresa's children as only a mother could, fulfilling a role she never enjoyed with her late husband, Paul.

"They're fine, Berthine." Olivia coos over her grandsons.

"See, Mama. Everything's fine!" Charles responds to Berthine's command and grabs Olivia's hand playfully. "Come on, Olivia, Lucy's inside waiting."

Jazz mimics his brother, grasping Olivia's other hand and leading her toward the doorway. In a flash, Lucy appears beside Berthine, runs past her, and descends upon her grandmother. Having never spoken a word, Teresa's only Sioux daughter grins brightly, revealing all her teeth. Lucy's childish exuberance reminds Olivia of Teresa. Olivia envisions her daughter as a toddler, bouncing around the estate with her little brother, laughing and screaming, innocent in days of their youth.

∞

Olivia watched Teresa become more cynical with age, especially after her first twins were born. While raising Duke and resisting any further advances from Ralph, Teresa could never fully focus on her newborn or her marriage. She said she felt incomplete without her Sioux daughter. Hearing of Lucy's inability to speak made her life even more miserable. No monitoring system or channel of communication would suffice; Lucy has never spoken a word and no one in the family understands why.

One quiet night per year, Doctor Morten, Jr. comes to the cabin to check the children, but he has never given a clear cause for her affliction. After learning about her daughter's disability, Teresa expressed her concerns to Olivia and Thomas III, but, her mother and brother agreed that Teresa could never visit the children, and Teresa obeyed for fear of the repercussions. Living through relays from two confidants never satisfied her. She hinted about fleeing town, leaving with her children and Kenny, and even those whispers proved fatal because, though she needed her children, Papa Winniper believed that even after she had them, she would never stay hidden. Teresa's wild child ways always made her a risk; she could easily, and unintentionally, expose the family secret. Her mixed family would still attract attention in the 1940s while living anywhere in America.

The consequences for Teresa's whispers came to fruition when she died, or rather, when Thomas III killed her and Sheriff Cobb, Jr. ensured that he completed the job. Olivia knew who gave the order, and she feared that her husband would send the wolves to Berthine's cabin, despite his fondness for her and her home. Following their daughter's funeral, Olivia begged behind closed doors, willing her husband to spare himself more blood. She knew her husband had become weary of his burden, the murders, and the secrecy; he didn't want his grandchildren's blood on his hands.

Saving Teresa's Sioux children from his malice, Olivia promised Papa that their grandchildren would always remain ignorant of their true identities and their rightful inheritance. As only a sincere woman can, she convinced him that Jazz, Charles, and Lucy will never learn that they are part of one of the most powerful oil families in the world—their brown skin bleeds Winniper blood. After burying his daughter, Papa was exhausted from concealing the family's curse and mourning the children he had lost. He mumbled a soft consent, a quiet agreement though Olivia knew she could never completely trust him.

Bringing Teresa's *legitimate* children to the family's estate helped assuage Papa Winniper's restless bloodlust. He became a proud grandpa, a role that suited him nicely, in fact. Olivia was able to see a side of her husband that few people see, a slight benevolence that he often hides for fear of seeming weak. Because Papa Winniper considered Duke as his only chance for a successful male successor, having his grandson and granddaughters inside the family's museum-like mansion occupied his patriarchal sensibilities. Teresa's *acceptable* children removed most of his concerns toward any outliers from his reckless daughter's life and untimely death. Though she had done much harm, Teresa had also produced Duke, who may one day become the king of the Winniper family's oil empire.

∞

Still, Olivia tries to visit her Sioux grandchildren during birthdays and other opportune occasions. They only know her as Berthine's longtime friend and an elderly benefactor to the Lancaster family. Giving charity and compassion as compensation for their circumstances, Olivia does her best to pay her respects to her grandchildren, hoping to absolve her soul in God's eyes. She fears the consequences of her own actions while hugging Lucy, lost in moments of principle, thinking about how Teresa damned herself.

"Happy birthday!" Olivia cheers as Lucy hugs her tightly and pulls her grandmother through the doorway and into the cozy home. The family embraces amidst the warm, oak, cabin—living room, kitchen, and dining room all-in-one convenient, domestic space. A handcrafted, oak dining table, an old brown church piano, a stretch purple, wool throw rug, and a wooden, rocking chair decorate the all-in-one. A thin hallway across the main room leads to two bedrooms—one for Lucy and Berthine, the other for Jazz and Charles. Berthine's entire cabin could fit inside any of the 56 rooms within the Winnipers' mansion.

After celebrating Duke's birthday during breakfast and leaving him to enjoy time with his friends, Olivia has crossed the forest to share his twin sister's birthday with her brothers and her adoptive mother. Lucy has lived with Berthine since birth and she has never, ever, left the concealed confines of the forest near the ghostly quiet, Sioux village in Winniper County.

Although, at age eighteen, Lucy has matured into an olive-skinned beauty, she still cannot speak. She secretly dreams of seeing the world but she has only seen pictures in books and magazines. She only knows what Berthine has told her. An obedient child, she always adheres to Berthine's strict orders; she rarely leaves the cabin for play, and she always returns home before sundown. Lucy's bright brown eyes, however, lead Olivia to believe that her granddaughter has never missed nor wanted for anything. She has Teresa's youthful innocence, the glow that a wealthy girl has before realizing the responsibilities of being a wealthy woman. Though she dreams of traveling, Lucy has no real concept of a greater life experience or the responsibility that comes with status, class, and enlightenment; yet, for all human spirits, nothing is ever bright enough when our dreams have the light of God.

"We baked Lucy a cake!" Charles announces emphatically while walking beside Jazz and the boys join Olivia in a hug around Lucy's waist—she has become the guitar. She is adept at handling their games and controlling their tempers; their big sister has always provided a comforting ear.

∞

After Charles was born during Teresa's second marriage to Charles Kane, the family's secret became a true burden. Having already experienced the initial trials of deception during her first marriage and the twin births of Duke and Lucy, Teresa tried to explain the curse to Charles, Sr., hoping honesty would help assuage any anger. Mr. Kane became so upset that he would have burned Charles, Jr. but Olivia and Papa ensured their son-in-law that the family eliminated their mistakes with extreme prejudice.

∞

Now, little Charles has survived longer, and proven himself to be much smarter than his late father.

∞

Mr. Kane was a businessman who blindly followed Papa Winniper and played the gullible fool as his wife enticed a younger man. The humiliation that Charles, Sr. endured because of Teresa's tryst with Kenny was enough to cast him away. Neither the town nor the family questioned his disappearance.

∞

Unlike his father, Charles, Jr. is not a follower; Olivia wonders how long Winniper County will contain him. He is already a tactful miscreant who often questions Olivia's presence, constantly interrogating her relationship with Berthine. On the cusp of his teenage years, Charles realizes that his life has only prepared him to work as a sharecropper.

∞

Even after establishing himself as a hardworking apprentice at the Winniper family's farm, he found that the menial position and hard labor didn't suit him, and he quit the program after the summer.

∞

Innocently enough, Charles has concocted an understanding of his situation that makes him behave differently than Lucy or Jazz, and his ideas and ambitions have led him to sneak away from their close-knit cabin whenever possible. He often seeks factory mistresses and house maids. The boy is already very fond of any girl willing to bat an eye his way.

∞

Recently, Olivia saw her grandson kissing a sharecropper's daughter while working in the Winnipers' wheat fields, mere moments away from his twin counterpart.

Olivia feared that Charles and Christina would somehow meet, but he never wandered away from his kiss, and, to this day, he has never learned the truth of his family's isolation in Winniper County. He rarely questions their circumstances, except when it comes to Olivia. Unlike his siblings, who may feel the same, Charles challenges that incredible and irking discomfort, hoping to understand what he does not know.

"Olivia, how old is you? I mean, *are you.*" Charles asks inquisitively, quickly correcting himself and looking over his shoulder for Jazz. "*Are you* older than Mama?"

"Mama won't tell us," Jazz adds, giving a stern look to Berthine. Olivia laughs at their interest and shrugs her thin shoulders.

"Well, I can understand why she won't tell." Olivia jests, glancing to Berthine with a nod; women should never tell but Winniper women should never, *ever* tell. "Your mother is a little older than me but only a little. She was born...well, I'll let her tell you that, but I was born on May 29, 1893. Can you do the math?"

"Wait, let me do it!" Charles demands brightly, raising his hand as if in Mrs. Burk's elementary class for the sharecroppers' children in the old Sioux village. The grade school volunteer cannot offer much beyond the basics of American education, but children bred to work in fields don't need much. Charles begins to count on his fingers, before glancing around curiously at the rest of the family. "I been workin' on my math-a-ma-tics."

"We're going to be here a while," Jazz interjects while giggling and hitting Charles's hands. "Let me try!"

"No, I got it! I'm older than you!" Charles retorts, turning to Olivia with frantic eyes; the boys always keep each other on their toes. "1893, right? And it's 1950 now...so, that's uh...60...um 56 years old! Yep, Olivia is 56 years old!"

"Correct, Charles! I am 56 years...*young.*" Olivia swallows slightly as the words escape her mouth. Charles smiles joyously at his successful calculation, ignorant of Olivia's slight discomfort. Very seldom do women her age embrace their *wiser years*, but, in this moment, while surrounded by the children that her daughter never knew, she feels a need to embrace the time that she has left. She hopes that one day her family will live with complete openness and truth despite how impossible both may seem.

"Wow!" Jazz muses alongside his big brother. "If Olivia is 56, then Mama has to be at least 60 years old."

"Hey, watch it little one. I'm never getting old! Olivia and I are going to live forever." Berthine croons sweetly, wraps her arms around Olivia, and hugs her friend tightly. The two women know that Berthine could never share her real date of birth with the children. She couldn't even explain how they came to her without a husband or man in the home.

Maybe the children are still too young to ask the wrong questions. Though Charles is obviously coming of age, maybe Lucy's silence has been a blessing that influences her younger brothers to accept their insignificant cabin-life. Olivia and Berthine exhale in one another's arms, two women baring the weight of an entire family. Berthine tilts her head toward Olivia's ear and holds her friend tenderly.

"Jesus told us to walk in good faith, children. I pray we all still have a lot of living to do."

"What were you and Mama like when you were children, Olivia?" Charles wonders aloud, yet he eagerly moves to her side. There is a pause as Jazz and Lucy listen for Olivia's answer, hoping to find some connection between the past and the present.

"Well, we...uh...we were a lot like today. We were friends from the start, very much like sisters. We were kind and we took care of each other," Olivia confides sheepishly, refusing to let the children see an old woman blush. "We also listened to blues...when we could..."

"Oh, I love the blues! Have you ever heard any bands from New Orleans?" Jazz asks with his head raised to his grandmother, awaiting an answer to cure some nagging intrigue.

"What do you mean?" Olivia responds for clarification but also pausing at the thought. June has often asked about New Orleans and music, and here, her twin brother, unprompted, mentions the same obsession.

"Well, I heard some of that blues on the radio and they said that there was a big party there," Jazz dances around the room, describing the scene matter-of-factly. "And there's a lot of people dancin'. The party is named after someone named Marty! Marty Graw!"

"Watch your tone, little boy," Berthine barks while placing Lucy's double chocolate fudge cake on the table and glancing at Olivia. "I swear he's got that music in his bones."

"*Marty?*" Olivia looks around the room and shrugs her shoulders toward Charles and Lucy, trying to understand.

"He means Mardi Gras, ma'am." Charles explains while shaking his head at his little brother. "We got a little radio box in our room. Mama gave it to us for Christmas so we can listen to some of the bands and broadcasts, but he doesn't understand everything he hears."

"Yes I do! I can play some of the songs on the piano!" Jazz proclaims proudly, stopping his dance and pointing his finger straight in the air. "One day I'm going to move to *N'orleans*, become a blues musician, and I'm never coming back!"

"Boy, I told you to stop playin' that music in this house." Berthine warns, "This is a Christian household. My father would roll over in his grave if he heard that piano playing anything but a good hymn."

"But, Olivia just said you two listened to the blues when–"

"Mama, don't worry. Jazz is going to work for Olivia's family, just like the rest of us." Charles retorts, hurting himself with the insult. "Everyone from around the village works in the Winniper family's house or on their farm or in that oil rig! He'll never–"

"Alright Charles, that's enough!" Berthine exclaims while lighting a lone candle on Lucy's birthday cake. She knows that Charles's candor and tongue could place the entire family in jeopardy. "Now, let's sing 'Happy Birthday' to your sister and eat some cake!"

"But, he..."

"Lawd Jesus, have mercy! Let it go, Jazz!" Berthine stares sternly at the youngest, giving him a decision—cake or pain. "I know the Good Lawd say we should turn the other cheek but if my Paul were alive, God rest his soul, I don't know who he'd whoop first!"

"I'm sorry, Mama," Jazz concedes softly, moving around the dinner table, away from Charles so that he stands across from his brother while also remaining equally close to the cake. Olivia wonders if they are conscious of how much they compete with each other; and she worries that Charles may change Jazz into a dangerous cynic like him. He's already conscious of his circumstances and struggling with his future; Olivia fears that he may cause his own downfall like his mother and father.

"Is everybody ready to sing?" Berthine asks as the family crowds around the dinner table and hovers over the cake. "1, 2, 3!"

"Happy birthday to you!" they all begin to sing, smiling, cheering, and masking any notion of a looming deception. "Happy birthday to you!"

Olivia observes her Sioux grandchildren at the table and feels the same sense of loss that Teresa felt after Jazz's birth.

∞

Olivia removed the boy from the Mortens' exam room without giving her daughter a moment to hold him. Teresa never had a chance to see or touch her babies, and for that, Olivia feels remorseful; she thought she knew best.

∞

Though she and Papa Winniper believe that they have made the correct decisions for their family, Teresa's absence reminds Olivia that not all mistakes are forgivable, especially when children lose their mother, but worse when they lose their lives. For Olivia to stand amidst three Sioux children saved from the barnyard fire is a miracle that she hopes will last.

"Happy birthday, dear Lucy!" Olivia wishes Teresa could see and enjoy this song because Teresa was right all along. Rules and stigmas be damned, family should always stay together regardless of any deformity or difference between them. Olivia just wishes that she could have been strong enough to fight with her daughter instead of against her. She sees now that her family is worth dying for, even if it's only to see these children survive.

"Happy Birthday to you!" They all exclaim cheerfully in a boisterous conclusion. Lucy smiles her usual, full-faced grin and Teresa shines through. Teresa lives on through her children and her spirit radiates inside Lucy's joy as her oldest daughter becomes a woman.

"Make a wish!" Charles encourages Lucy, staring at the lone lit candle on the delectable chocolate cake. Lucy hesitates, afraid to believe for even a moment.

"Go ahead, Lucy!" Berthine urges, waving her hand over the smoking candle. "Whatever you wish for, you'll receive."

"So make it a good one!" Olivia adds with a guilty grin. She looks at the family that she saved and destroyed by arranging for the children's survival and forbidding their mother from seeing them. Lucy leans forward cautiously, while Olivia watches and absorbs the misfortune that she has caused in her grandchildren's lives. Even though they do not know her true identity, they still treat Olivia like a queen; she is another respected, matriarchal presence in their happy home. Realizing her mistakes, Olivia wishes she had acted differently; she longs to be worth the children's love.

Although Teresa's Sioux children shower her with adoration and affection, Olivia feels that she does not deserve their admiration. Lucy blows lightly toward the lit candle, and Olivia alters the moment in her mind, daydreaming that Teresa is here to know how much love she still has in this world. Olivia prays that Teresa knows her Sioux children have grown into complex and beautiful beings.

Sadly, even in 1950, the Winnipers still believe that the cold, hard world will never allow a wealthy family to have the same amount of power with Sioux children in their bloodline. Their elite class and their private shame collide within an international war zone that they have helped to create; still, no one would understand if their secret became exposed. The family's blood curse would consume public opinion; so they remain trapped in their own rules. Society and wealth cometh; love and truth be damned. Olivia hopes Teresa knows that she was right all along; and her parents have been either too weak or too stubborn to make amends for their mistakes.

∞

These rules weren't made to be broken, legacies weren't made to die; they should have never been made, never been built as monuments against the laws of God.

∞

Family and love should have come first, but the family has sacrificed these moments for a legacy that cannot exist beyond its own rules. As Lucy exhales and the candle flickers and exhausts; the ground underneath them trembles from a deep percussion like a loud drum has been struck beneath them. The cabin quakes and vibrates softly before settling; smoke wafts from the extinguished wick and Jazz and Charles cheer enthusiastically. They hoot and holler more than necessary, both probably happy to celebrate anything and have any source of relief from their forest doldrums.

"What did you wish for?" Jazz asks his sister eagerly.

"She can't tell, Jazz," Charles interrupts. "It's bad luck!"

"No, that's Christmas presents," Jazz counters; their voices begin to rise over one another—boyish bravado at its best. "You can't tell anyone what you want for Christmas, or you won't get it!"

"That's not right, either," Charles battles back, both locking intellectual horns again. "You can tell Santa what you want. How else would you get anything?"

"Relax, boys! This is not how good *Christian* children behave! Sometimes, I think that male pride is already preventing you two from fully accepting the ways of Jesus into your hearts." Berthine interrupts authoritatively. She motions toward the table and gently grabs a knife next to the cake. She pauses over the first incision, daring either boy to misbehave. "Now, I'm going to bless this here food so we can eat. Let's enjoy the time we have with Olivia."

"You're right, Mama," Jazz agrees, then turning to Lucy and rising to his tiptoes to whisper in her ear, "Lucy, what'd you wish for?"

Lucy takes a moment, glancing around to Charles and Olivia before pointing to her throat. Jazz inspects his sister in confusion.

"She wished for cake," Charles reads her face, moving closer to them. Lucy pauses and nods while avoiding eye contact, but her nostrils contort oddly.

"She's lying! Her nose is twitching! You didn't wish for cake, Lucy!" Jazz asserts loudly, raising his finger to her nose. Lucy giggles and shakes her head side-to-side before pointing to her mouth and trying to bring words to her lips.

"I..." she stammers and the family stills; a dead silence overcomes the main room. Berthine drops her knife on the cake and Olivia moves closer to Jazz and Charles, whose open-mouth expressions morph from shock to surprise to excitement. Their faces brighten eagerly as if Christmas has come early.

"Lucy's trying to speak!" Jazz exclaims, crowding his sister even more and staring up to her throat with wide eyes. She continues to tense her neck, and Jazz raises his hand to his sister's throat, massaging her voice box with his fingers. "Come on, Lucy, say something!"

"Give her some room, Jazz! Let her speak!" Charles commands as he nudges his brother and moves beside him, angling for position. They both begin to ardently poke and prod their sister, trying to push the words through her body. "You wished to speak, didn't you, Lucy?"

"I-I-I..." Lucy continues to strain, stretching and straining her unused vocal chords. The aura in the room briefly transcends time and the family exists in a suspended universe. Everyone stands on the edge of their toes, hoping Lucy finally sheds whatever mental or physical deficiencies that she has, but, she submits to the struggle and nods her head. She only opens her mouth one more time before closing her jaws in defeat.

"Don't give up! You've never said a word in your life and you just said I!" Jazz begs while rubbing his hand softly against his sister's throat. He then reaches for her arms, clenching her shoulders above him and stomping wildly around her feet. "We've never even heard your voice! This is a miracle! C'mon Lucy! Speak!"

"Just say something! Make a sound! Say anything!" Charles pleads along with his brother impatiently, clamoring around his sister and patting her back to make the words come forth. "Start off slow!"

"Boys, stop! Leave your sister alone! Lawd Jesus, it's just too much sometime." Berthine jeers at the commotion while placing her hands on the table and attempting to overcome her own shock so that she can prevent Jazz and Charles from heaping more pressure upon Lucy. "Let the girl enjoy her birthday!"

"But she was about to say something! You all heard her!" Jazz argues, staring at each of them and then turning back to his silent sister. Her eyes are now sullen, stuck within the girl she was and the woman she can become. Jazz grabs her hand softly and raises her palm to his check, trying desperately to make a connection. "She just needs some help! Come on, Lucy...we love you! We don't care what you say! Just speak!"

"Jazz, that's enough!" Berthine barks, glaring at Jazz before calming herself in Olivia's sight; the moment has become too large for the all-in-one room. Berthine takes a deep breath and ruffles her kitchen apron out of frustration. "Charles, bring your brother over here and make him sit down! I'm going to bring out my bible soon."

"Yes, Mama." Charles complies while gripping Jazz's right arm and pulling him away from Lucy. Olivia watches the family hierarchy with Berthine as the sheriff, Charles as the deputy in charge, and Jazz as the constant criminal. Lucy remains the silent bystander, standing near the table, staring over her chocolate cake while wrinkling her lips and forehead in frustration. Olivia can see her granddaughter trying to figure out her voice's mechanics; she continually strains her neck but grows shy when she notices Olivia watching.

"I wish I could come here more often," Olivia admits flatly, also reeling at the hope of hearing Lucy's first words. Suddenly, Olivia remembers that good things rarely happen to the Winnipers without bad consequences. "I'm sure it's hard with just the four of you."

A pause falls over the cabin as if she has mentioned an ignorable ghost.

"There aren't just four of us," Jazz responds very assuredly as Charles promptly tugs his little brother's arm and leads him towards his seat at the kitchen table.

"Jazz, be quiet," Charles snaps sharply, reaching for a chair and positioning it behind his brother. He steps back and stands behind his brother while pointing to the chair. "Now, sit down!"

"What does he mean?" Olivia asks nervously, looking back and forth between the children. None of them want to speak further to the point, and Olivia tilts her head toward Berthine, wondering if the *ol' girls* have one more secret to share.

"Oh, it's nothing." Berthine bristles in response to her friend's worries and she delicately grabs the knife from the cake and begins to cut a slice. She carefully places the piece of chocolate heaven on a tiny, blue and white ceramic plate. "The kids think they see a ghost every now and then; I think they've been listening to too many stories about the old village."

"But we do see her!" Charles affirms, eagerly scooting a chair next to Jazz and sitting down at the table. He folds his hands together and waits obediently for his serving, believing that if he continues to behave for a little longer, Berthine will serve him before Jazz.

"She's here right now!" Jazz defiantly lifts his head, eyeing Olivia to judge whether she believes him. For the moment, the family has once again forgotten Lucy, who still stands silently.

"Where?" Olivia wonders half-heartedly, not wanting to deter the boy's imagination.

"Right there!" Jazz points to the wooden rocking chair that rocks slowly in the main room's corner.

∞

Berthine told Olivia that the rocking chair was an old throwaway gift that Charles Winniper, Sr. gave to her father when he began working for the family. Johnnie said *Charlie Senior* brought the chair from Tennessee but when he arrived at his estate in South Dakota, he wanted all new furniture. Johnnie took the gift as a token of his loyalty, and he treated the family's trash like treasures for the rest of his life.

∞

The chair tilts eerily, back and forth, back and forth. The motion is steady, without wind or agent of force. Jazz waves happily and laughs at the chair as though he sees someone waving back.

"There's no one in that chair, Jazz," Berthine retorts, staring at the rocking chair.

"I see her!" Jazz proclaims, repeatedly pointing toward the rocking chair.

"Me, too!" Charles concurs and the brothers agree for a brief moment. "But I saw her first!"

"No, you didn't!"

"Yes, I did!"

"No, *I* saw her first," Berthine concedes with a grumble, continuing the cake ritual, slicing and serving, while glancing at Olivia and raising her eyebrows. Her look finally assures Olivia that the ghost is real. "She's wearing a blue sundress...with flowers on it...she reminds me of *someone* we knew..."

"She's always wearing that blue dress," Charles comments as all three children stare at the rocking chair which continues to sway steadily back and forth. Olivia stares in disbelief and glances to Berthine who nods her head. Even if Teresa's ghost sits in that chair, Olivia refuses, absolutely refuses, to see her. She won't allow herself to believe that her daughter's ghost is only a few feet away. Her face must convey her fear and Berthine realizes the possible outcomes of revealing any more.

"Kids, let's stop scaring Olivia, please. We've had enough *drama* for one day." Berthine finishes cutting the cake and placing five portions onto small plates. "Let's just enjoy the celebration and hope this cake don't ruin your appetites for supper."

The rocking chair begins to slow and Charles and Jazz turn back toward the table.

"She's gone," Jazz mourns sadly, hanging his head while arming himself with a nearby fork and reaching for a small plate of cake. Charles waits for Berthine to scold him, but she does not; and he resents her negligence as he grabs a plate for himself. Olivia continues to stare as the chair keeps rocking slower and slower before finally stopping with an eerily soft, and lingering, creak.

Olivia's eyes dart around the main room and she observes her grandchildren, while they eat their cake in a nonchalant response to the ghost sighting. Jazz and Charles greedily eye the rest of the birthday cake, elbowing one another to displace each other's eating rhythm. Olivia does not dare to ask any further questions about the ghost or the mysterious incident with Lucy; unlike little Charles, Olivia finds comfort in the unknown. The truth is the most unavoidable pain.

Lucy dips her head in momentary isolation, still feeling like the forgotten child. She remains standing while she tries, once more, to flex her newfound voice; she watches her brothers elbow each other playfully, and she begins to smile and giggle after realizing that they are both plotting over the rest of her birthday cake. She uses that momentum from her laugh to squeeze her vocal chords and maneuver a sound through.

"I-I-I-I-I…s-s-s-s-saw….h-h-h-h-h-her…t-t-t-t-too."

APRIL 1956

Sunday	Monday	Tuesday	Wednesday	Thursday	Friday	Saturday
1	2	3	4 ★	5	6	7
8	9	10	11	12	13	14
15	16	17	18	19	20	21
22	23	24	25	26	27	28
29	30					

Wednesday, April 4, 1956

Kenneth "Kenny" Bethune, Jr.

I forgot to forget my lady,
In the corners of my mind.
She was locked inside a memory,
In a dream that I can't find.
And I search my deserted thoughts,
Longing for whom I lost.
Dare I escape to find her forgotten face?
Or is that face the cost?
Serendipitous sirens signal a cause,
In superconscious pause;
She stands on a street sensibly
To a round of devilish applause.
And I hear my corroded cognition,
Coursing to see her true;
Dare I test to define her dress?
Or is her vengeance through?

Kenneth "Kenny" Bethune, Jr. yells painfully from his bed. Amputated at the knees, he spends most of his days whining like a colicky baby.

"Sheila! Sheila! Get some warm water!" Hoping that the former Mrs. Chamberlain hears him and returns quickly, Kenny strains his neck to the left and searches out the door and down the hallway while throwing the bed covers aside and pulling a wool blanket up to his waist. A thirty-two-year-old head case, the once infamous playboy lies crippled in a worn, dingy, and shaky Chicago bedroom. He lightly rubs his fingers over his knobbed knees; for a moment, he feels his absent toes tingling underneath the blanket.

"Sheila!" he screams hoarsely, his throat clenching and scraping like his words are dragging across sand paper. "These bed sheets are irritatin' my legs!"

Kenny leans forward to rub the nubs of his knees, agonizing over the sensation; a sharp sting vibrates through his nerves. He feels his lost limbs, the cut calves and the axed ankles of an amateur amputation. Sheila Chamberlain hurries into the bedroom, carrying a wash cloth and a bucket filled with steaming hot water.

"You don't have any legs, Ken!" Sheila counters furiously; the head scarf that she wears around her forehead to keep her hair out of her eyes has fallen awkwardly over her eyebrows. "Remember that?"

"Oh, hush; and hurry up!" Kenny waves his arm to swat at Shelia, but she dodges the blow. She adroitly moves around the bed and drops the bucket on the mattress with a splash. Some of the water jumps from the pot and scalds his right thigh. "Ouch! Be careful! You're burning me!"

"Quiet, darling. Just lie back." She takes a gentle tone that mellows his agitation and Kenny carefully leans back against his sweat-soaked pillows. Sheila dips the washcloth into the water, wrings the rag twice in her hands, and begins dabbing his stumps.

"We have to get new bed sheets," Kenny insists while pouting and looking away; Sheila sighs in frustration, disbelieving her circumstances.

∞

She never thought that a neighborly affair with a known adulterer would result in a life of exile.

∞

Now, she has lost most of her English posh, she can't return to Winniper County, and she may never see her husband or her son Rudy again.

"We can't afford anything new," Sheila complains. "Not until your mother sends another check in the mail."

She continues to rinse the wash cloth and lightly clean the worn stitches on Kenny's knees. She considers the prospect of petitioning the government to pay for his predicament; marshmallow rain drops seem more likely. She knows they are outcasts after Kenny made a deal with the devil to leave hell, but Sheila forgot to consider Kenny's gambling addiction.

∞

After dumping Duke, Christina, and June at the Winniper Family Estate, Kenny ran through more of Papa Winniper's payoff in a day with Sheila than he ever spent with Teresa. He abandoned every good person in his life—his daughter, his stepchildren, and his mother. Everything became a blur of casinos and cheap motels.

Chicago seemed like an appropriate place to call home, because it is the epicenter of old crime and illegal gambling—a swinger's town. Kenny lost a poor man's fortune with every hair-brained scheme that he concocted; he even tried to extort Papa Winniper for more money, threatening to return and reveal the Winniper family's guarded secret. His foolish plot cost him his legs, a warning from Papa Winniper to never again dream of exposing the family or crossing the Winniper County line. Kenny's mother took heed to Papa's threat; she saw the signs, yet she hoped to prevent her son from experiencing an early death. Kenny mistakenly believed his father-in-law would show mercy to him because he had delivered Teresa's children and thus, Kenny didn't worry about his safety. He even thought that maybe he and June could reunite down the road, once his demons subsided.

Although Teresa passed away after only two years of marriage, Kenny had learned much about the multifaceted arrangements within the Winniper family. Their silent secrets abide within rules of consequence and mutual moral decay; their fears derive from perception more than reality, he thought. Teresa and Kenny spoke about their twins, Jazz and June. Kenny never cared; he wanted to raise both, but Teresa told him the Winniper rule: the Sioux children must all die.

She was honest with him, behind closed doors; she shared the family curse and confessed that Teresa and her mother were hiding her Sioux children. When he arrived at Doc Morten, Jr.'s home and gathered June in his arms, everything else seemed mathematic and he played his role as best he could. Life was perfect. He had an affectionate older woman who cared for his addiction and allowed him to spend just enough of her money at the roulette wheel. Heaven couldn't be any sweeter and he rarely thought of his Sioux son, but then Teresa decided that she and Kenny would leave Winniper County with all of her children. She sealed her fate, and, after some coaxing from his mother, Kenny helped Papa and Tilly set up the car accident that ultimately killed Teresa. Kenny never atoned for his betrayal. He only remembered Teresa's warning—*there are no accidents in Winniper County.*

∞

That upper crest town has always been too small and too industrial to accommodate any personal ill will; no one deviates from the norm.

∞

Two years after his wife's suspicious death, Kenny's constant confusion and alcoholism led him to one conclusion: he could never be a father to June, let alone two other disrespectful, mean, and abusive brats. Although he never intended to repeat his late father's mistakes, he abandoned his only child without even saying goodbye. Cutting his losses after mourning Teresa for two years, Kenny decided to ditch his daughter and stepchildren so that he could elope with the neighbor's wife; at the time, he thought his decision was in everyone's best interest. Affairs came naturally to him, fatherhood did not.

As the excitement of his tryst with Sheila waned, Kenny once again began to make too many mistakes to remain happy. He lived recklessly enough to cause what Teresa had prevented: his self-destruction.

∞

Now, he lies defeated, consciously aware of his failure and unable to deny his role in every action that led him here.

"I-I-I don't think my mother w-w-w-will send anymore checks, Sheila," Kenny stammers and shakes nervously, afraid to look his lover in the eye. His gaze falls upon his stumps, a worse punishment than a woman's scorn. Sheila continues to dab the warm, wet towel over his wounds without pause and Kenny feels a momentary hope. Maybe…maybe their love is real. "Maybe we should ask Uncle Sam to help us with my…*disability.*"

"*Disa-what?*" Sheila repeats, her high-pitched British accent adds an extra twang to her disgust and she stops her therapy to stare straight into Kenny's eyes. Her eyes throw daggers whenever she senses his weakness and vulnerability. He lies in her feeding circle, and it's then that the lioness decides to pounce. "We're supposed to be rich! You Bethunes have just as much money as the Winnipers! Certainly not more, but you own part of that oil company!"

"But we can't go back home, Sheila. Even Mama can't protect me." Kenny waves his right hand over his missing legs like a showcase girl showing a client a new car: the spoils of victory. "Mama promised Papa that I wouldn't return, and you know what'll happen if…if…uh…"

Kenny's voice falters, and he senses Shelia eyeing him, summarizing his manhood in one sentence.

"Are you afraid?" Her question challenges his manhood and he tries not to hesitate.

"No…I-I'm not afraid." Kenny sticks his chest out but winces after straining his back. "Ouch, uh…no…I'm not afraid of anything…it's just…"

His words dissipate as the memory of a car door slamming on his legs flashes over and over in his mind—Sheriff Cornell Cobb, Jr. drinks a beer and laughs over him as the pain overcomes his spine and senses. The beer turns into a flute and the sheriff performs an illusionary solo.

"It's just what, Kenny?"

"Mama...Mama told Papa that we won't come back. That's the only reason the sheriff hasn't come and killed me, himself. We can't go back and Mama, she said she's still mad that I left in the first place! She told me I shoulda kept those brats...something about *strategy*. I don't even remember what they looked like or why I left. You told me we were in love...and now we're stuck here, Sheila!" Kenny turns away from the disgust on Sheila's face; the power women have had over his life still plagues his every waking moment. All his thoughts and actions must appease the feminine guile of any proximal woman. He can't imagine a living arrangement without conditions which position him as a woman's acquisition.

"Why did you leave then? You were worth more money in Winniper County." Sheila's stern tone cuts through the air and hovers over Kenny's head like a raised axe over a condemned man's neck. "You told me that you would take care of us!"

"I did...I mean...you and Mama said that Papa paid me a lot of money...but...*I* spent it too fast...and when I tried to get more...he...they...did...this..." Kenny mumbles, looking over his missing legs and imagining how they would feel. "And I can barely remember a damn thing but what y'all tell me and now you want to go back...they'll kill me, Sheila!"

"You said that before you asked for more money and they only crushed your legs!" Sheila flings the wash cloth at him and he tries to catch it, but he misses and the rag hits him in the face. He can smell the pus from his wounds mixed with the dirt from the floor. Lost in her own grime, Sheila groans gutturally, placing her right hand on her hip and pointing her left index finger at him. "This is all because of you and those damn kids!"

"Yuck! Watch it! You came with me, remember?"

"Why don't you let me go back?" Sheila asks quickly, pivoting, changing the subject, and daring him to challenge her. "I'm sure I could talk to Papa."

"No, Mama said he's not like that, Sheila. He only deals with a small circle. And Mama said he still kills some of *those* people." Kenny drifts away before looking back to Sheila. "We're leaving here soon anyway."

He reaches out to her and tries to wrap his hands around her waist, seeking some sort of assurance that his masculinity is still intact.

"Don't touch me!" Sheila pushes his hands away and steps back from the bed. "You told me we were going to get married in Morocco! Chi-ca-go is not Mo-roc-co!"

"I know, baby, and we are still going to Mo-rocky-o, baby!" Kenny implores desperately, half-man belly dancing in his bed, trying to entertain Sheila without falling off the bed. "We just stopped here to see the sites! We'll be Mr. and Mrs. Bethune very, very soon."

"Sure, I've heard *'we'll be'* too many times! When will we be where you said we'd be? When will we do what you said we'd do? We should own Morocco by now!" Sheila steps farther from the bed, pointing at him and his lost limbs. Her hand motions over his stubs and a wave of sorrow simultaneously washes over his body. Kenny stares at her, hoping for a sense of remorse, but she has none. Their romance is over. "You can't do anything! You can't see any sights! You can't walk! You can barely make love to me!"

"How can you say that?" Kenny whimpers in despair. He leans back in bed, folds his arms over his chest, and glances up to the cracked ceiling in their one bedroom apartment, remembering when they moved in two years ago. "Haven't I been through enough?"

∞

They thought their apartment was some romantic love shack, a Newport Avenue one-bedroom with holes and creaks just like the hideaways in the gangster movies.

Their cinematic dreams quickly became nightmares in South Side's shallow streets, dive bars, and art shows. Kenny had attempted to pursue gambling at the highest levels, but it's a lot easier to lie and cheat for fast money than to plan and work for it. He struggled from table to table, wheel to wheel, without learning any new skills or exhibiting any new luck; he had a miserable cloud following him that loomed larger night after night. A few months ago, while hustling late night in a random pool hall, Kenny enjoyed a momentous rally against several unknown and slightly under-developed challengers. He finally had an opportunity to showcase his talent for a competitive reward.

After leaving the humble establishment with an unusually large wad of money in his pocket, Kenny happened upon a young white woman in the street. She wore a long, grey wool overcoat with seemingly very little underneath; a fur pompadour rested on her head. She smiled sweetly, her red lipstick smeared against the edges of her lips and her blush smudged awkwardly over her cheeks. Suddenly, Kenny and the young woman were not alone and everything went black.

∞

He can't forget the images of her wicked smile and her overly made-up face—the lasting fragments of his shattered memory.

"Ken, baby, I'm sorry." Sheila interrupts his thoughts again, forgiving him with her eyes. "It's just hard to see you like this."

She moves toward the bed and leans in closely, but her conceit still keeps them apart.

"*'Hard to see me like this'*?" Kenny asks angrily, still stuck in his remorse. "It's hard *being* like this, Sheila! It's hard not remembering what happened and *knowing* that the police won't do anything about it!"

He feels the blood rushing through his body and his knee nubs ache as the creases of his wounds cling to his stale stitches. Sheila momentarily suspends her verbal assault and casually grabs the wash cloth to resume cleaning his open sores. Though they often fuss and fight, she has been great, delicately undertaking his care and monitoring his ego nonetheless. She finds a nearby roll of gauze within the bed sheets and begins to wrap new bandages over his stumps, holding the gauze tightly like Tilly taught her to do.

Still dealing with unresolved Mommy issues, Kenny constantly yearns for a woman to serve his desire and become his willing domestic slave/superior, depending upon the perspective. Whether in marriage, affairs, or childhood, Kenny has remained dependent upon the women in his life to protect him and care for him as he recklessly gambles and loses another bet.

∞

After surgery, while he recovered in the hospital, Kenny became even more dependent upon Sheila and his mother. Both women helped him recover pieces of his memory bit-by-bit. And though Tilly described his late father as a war hero from World War II, Kenny only has fleeting recollections of his father or much of his life before Chicago. He doesn't remember how he betrayed his wife and her children; he doesn't remember the Winniper family's secret. He only has a nagging feeling that he lost something, maybe someone important, but he has no real idea of the danger that surrounds him. Though, his chopped legs are a constant sign and a permanent reminder that he does not have the power to flee his reckoning.

"You should...uh, have more...faith...in the police." Sheila folds the pus-soaked rag and pats Kenny's head. She fumbles over her sensitivity and drops her words clumsily, unsure how to reassure Kenny. "Detective Steelers...said he's...looking at suspects."

"That detective is a first-class crook! He's probably on Papa's payroll!" Kenny throws his arms in the air, thinking of the South Side detective assigned to investigate Kenny's assault/attempted murder. "Plus, I still can't remember anything. I just know I saw a pasty-face whore in an overcoat."

"Yes, you told me over and over about the *'whore in the overcoat'*." Sheila drops the wash cloth in the bucket where it splashes within the bloodied water and sinks to the bottom among the other tattered rags. "Didn't that sketch artist draw her picture?"

"Yes, I kept it."

"Where is it?" Sheila stares over Kenny's pathetic face, and he seems dejected. Rejected by the world, he and Sheila are the exiles from the families that they abandoned and now they torture each other as a mutual punishment. "I'll get the sketch for you and you can whine to her!"

"No! Please don't! I couldn't take it!" Kenny clenches his butt cheeks tightly while closing his eyes and hoping to prevent any haunting memories of his attackers and the fur-hatted woman who brought him so much misery. "It took weeks for the nightmares to stop!"

"You were a much better man before, Kenny. You had this suave debonair attitude; I could tell you came from money the moment I saw you. Now you smell like piss and you can't stop sweating and whining…and lying around." Sheila reaches back into the bucket, retrieves a soaked rag, and continues to dab his wounds until Kenny calms down. She then sits at the edge of the bed and tilts her head back, exhaling in frustration and anxiety. The past year flashes through Kenny's mind, and he realizes how much time and effort he has taken from this once ravishing, buxom woman.

He barely knows her beyond her big breasts and her British accent, though he has listened to Sheila and his mother tell him about his past, his family, and even his personality. After using their help to regain some of his memory, he still understands very little of his former self. He simply follows orders and heeds warnings. He lives a life that has lost its momentum; he exists in a new beginning with nothing in sight. He can only see endless plains of possibility and peril.

"Maybe you should leave me." Kenny suggests, widening his eyes and raising his eyebrows to enhance the statement and make his concern clear. "How can you possibly love me? Look at me."

He raises his hands over his body, again showcasing the shell of his former physique. She can see his frail bones poking his skin, exposing his skeleton in odd places like his hips, ribs, and chest.

∞

Kenny had run on the track team in high-school; he knows this because his mother brought pictures, trophies, and medals to the hospital. According to the artifacts from his childhood, he was very active and very well-liked.

∞

Now, he remains in bed all day and night, stuck with another man's estranged wife, living in the Chicago fog far away from his family and friends, though he is unsure if he ever had any friends other than Sheila and his mother. Tilly hasn't told him much about his late wife and his estranged children, except that he betrayed them, though he had his reasons.

"Trust me, baby, I'm not goin' anywhere." Sheila leans in close so that their noses touch lightly. "Your mother pays me a lot of money to stay. I'm sure one of our checks will get here soon, if she knows what's good for her."

Sheila lightly kisses Kenny's nose. Her words sink into his consciousness, and he wonders whether she knows more than she has shared. The possibility of her dishonesty causes an anxious rush of more and more disconcerting notions:

Has my mother been lying the whole time?

How would I know?

Am I in danger?

Three thunderous knocks slam against the front door and rock the walls of the apartment. Sheila turns abruptly towards the hallway leading from the bedroom. She drops the wash rag on the bed, overcome by fear and curiosity; she takes a side-step to peer further down the hallway, searching for any possible coming chaos.

"Who could that be?" Sheila asks with intrigue pouring from her eyes. Now that she has grown accustomed to listless boredom with a cripple, she has become anxious for any form of excitement.

"I don't know. Are you expecting anyone?" Kenny questions her enthusiasm, glaring at her callously; suddenly, her mentions and musings about his mother and her money have made him defensive. He can't continue to hold his ego's weight with his frail arms, and his head hits the headrest with a thud.

"Ouch!" he yells while three more thunderous knocks shake the apartment.

"Oh, be still! Here, let me do it." Sheila leans over him and fluffs the pillow behind his head like a dog shaking a toy.

"Ow, take it easy!"

"Oh, stop being a baby! Be a man!" Her tone scolds Kenny, and he instantly sees his mother instead of Sheila. Another triplet drums against the front door and she pushes his shoulders back against the pillow. "Now just lie still."

"Are you sure you're okay to answer that?" he asks without sarcasm, but Sheila perceives a hint of disdain.

"As if *you* could protect me…I'll be fine, *sweetie.*" She smirks dismissively, steps away from the bed, and turns toward the bedroom door. Before she walks away, she tilts her head and murmurs under her breath, "Don't run away…"

"I heard that!" Kenny shouts behind her, but she does not respond. Sheila exits the bedroom and walks down the hall; she leaves his eyesight but he can hear her unlatch the top lock.

"Check the peep-hole first!" Kenny barks; Sheila often forgets her caution, a symptom of being too trusting or, perhaps, too jaded. She subconsciously assumes that everywhere is like her hometown of Harrogate in North Yorkshire. She easy assimilated into the privileged community of Winniper County. Sometimes she believes the world is a quaint country town with people behaving under a cloud of social acquiescence.

"Who is it? Delivery from where?" Kenny hears Sheila ask through the door and there is a murmur in response but the words are inaudible. He then hears the bottom lock turn. *"The jewelry store!"*

"Sheila, who is it?" Kenny continues yelling down the hallway and he stretches his neck and upper body to the left, searching for a response. The door opens creakily with a wild swing and slams against the wall.

"It's a delivery from…" Sheila's words fade, and Kenny hears a scuffle as several loud footsteps enter the apartment.

"Sheila! Sheila?" Kenny calls down the hall, hearing only silence in response. He sees a long shadow creep down the hallway and she appears before him – the young, fur-hatted woman from the night he lost his legs. Horror, pure terror seizes his body and his lips tremble during a frightened response. "It-t-t-t-t's y-y-y-you…"

His voice quivers from a mental malfunction, seeing the image of many nightmares: the eye shadow around her eyes, smeared lipstick, smudged blush, and that hat…fur with a fussy feather sticking from the brim. She no longer wears an overcoat; she dons a crimson and blue sundress, the colors splitting at the waist. A cream Chanel purse hangs over her shoulder as she stands in black high heels and juts her hips to the side, cracking that dangerous smile; she is the spitting image of someone he once knew though he can't recall who.

"Hello, Kenny. It's good to see you again. Your room still smells like a liquor cabinet." Having matured into a very polished, heavily made-up, and elegantly dressed eighteen-year-old, Christina casually strolls into the bedroom, confident in her kill. Her eyes dart around the small dingy room; atop the dresser are several, potential assault weapons: hairbrushes, curling irons, and shaving knives. Kenny's body is still frozen in horror; he has no fight in him. His knobbed knees are numb.

Standing a few feet away, Christina then glances to the nightstand next to Kenny's bed that is covered in pill bottles. An old copy of the Bible lies underneath a half-filled bottle of Butisol and an empty bottle of Jack Daniels—the Bible, the Butisol, and the Jack are the only weapons within reach.

"I see you still haven't put down the booze. The Bible looks new though." She takes a step closer to him and his body tenses as he raises his hands.

"Stay back!" Kenny screams at the top of his lungs. "Don't come any closer! Sheila!"

"What are you hollerin' for, Kenny?" Christina continues to move closer to him, sauntering toward the edge of his bed. She gently removes her gaudy fur hat and places it over two prescriptions of Panadol on the nightstand. "I'm not going to hurt you. I'm not mad at you for what you did."

"Wh-where's Sheila?" He asks nervously, before reaching across his body and timidly sliding the Bible from underneath the Butisol and Jack. Kenny takes care to put the bottles back on the nightstand, but after they are safely returned amidst the other elixirs, pills, and narcotics, he quickly turns his upper body toward Christina and clutches the good book to his chest.

A small piece of thin, wax paper falls from the book and lands in his lap. On the face is a police composite sketch of Christina. He looks back and forth between the sketch and Christina and he sees her as the devil. While holding the Bible between himself and his intruder, the Holy Book acts as a spiritual fortress of God's willpower that will keep him safe.

"And I know you won't hurt me because you can't! Mama said only God can judge me! Now, where's Sheila?"

"*Mrs. Chamberlain* is fine. She's in the other room with Duke and June. You remember your daughter, right?" Her words rest above his ears for a moment before diving into his conscious understanding. Kenny consumes the words, and he lifts his upper body to an upright position. She moves a step closer and quickly grabs the piece of sketch paper from his lap. "Did you tell the police about me?"

She observes her likeness before looking back at Kenny and questioning his convenient amnesia. She has heard stories from servants and minions, but she hasn't believed them, until now.

"I...I couldn't remember anything, except your face."

"So you really forgot *everything*, huh? You don't remember what you've done? You abandoned your daughter."

"*My what?*"

"It's true...and...well, I guess your darling mistress and your good mother didn't remind you that you have a daughter." Her fingertips travel curiously over Kenny's bandaged wounds, and he flinches under her unfamiliar touch. "We are just disposable pawns, Kenny. They use us to hurt each other, and I'm sorry for what happened to you, but you once had a family and then *you* abandoned us. I hated you for that, we all did."

"Mama told me I betrayed my wife and her children...but she never said I had a daughter of my own." Kenny's hand grazes over the Bible clutched against his chest and he looks into the young woman's eyes, searching for a speck of truth. "Who are you?"

"You really don't remember? It's me, Christina." Christina leans forward and looks into his eyes, also searching for that same speck. She tosses the sketch on the floor next to the bed. "I'm Teresa's daughter; Teresa was your wife? Don't you remember? Your mother didn't tell you our names? She didn't show you pictures?"

"No, she just showed me pictures from when I was a kid. She said I was happier, but I remember you. I remember you the night I got hurt! Your face is the one of last images that I remember clearly before...*ouch*...and then...*ouch*...Sheriff Cobb..." Kenny grimaces as all the pain, frustration, and anger rushes through his body, aimed toward this woman. Without thinking, his hands drop the Bible onto his lap; he reaches out toward her and wraps his palms around her throat. Kenny catches her off-guard, her neck strains for freedom, and her eyes open wide in shock. He sees her look of surprise as a refreshing break from the mundane. "You did this to me!"

"Ah! Let...me...go!" Christina cries while prying at Kenny's hands, but she cannot loosen his grip. His rage has given him superhuman strength. After months of adrenaline shots, the excess testosterone in his system pumps rapidly through his blood and fills his upper body with exuberant malice.

∞

Tilly hired trainers and physical therapists to help her son regain his upper motor skills, especially his grip and his arm strength. She also tried her best to re-indoctrinate him to the ways of family. His mother hoped that his amnesia may give him a chance to return to Winniper County. He couldn't expose what he could not remember, so she tried to give him a new history that explained his accident while also warning him of the dangers surrounding him. Sadly, Kenny couldn't shake all these old ghosts; and this woman within his death grip, she has shone through it all. She is his constant torment from a past life and he can never escape her image.

∞

"You're the reason I'm like this! You're the reason I have no legs and I have these flashes! I don't even know who I am anymore!" Kenny chokes her roughly. "What did that sheriff do to me? I remember him...and I remember you! How do you know the Winnipers?"

He screams so hard that his lungs feel like they are exploding through his throat. Christina continues to struggle and choke within his grip, furiously digging her nails into his hands between attempts to breath. He moves her neck away from his outstretched arms so that she cannot hit his face. She throws her elbows into his arms and momentarily jars his grip loose.

"I can't...breathe! Help!" she gasps, "June! June!"

Kenny regains his grip around her throat as he hears a few fumbling footsteps bound down the hallway and then June, now a mean-spirited fourteen-year-old girl, appears at the door. She wears a greasy, blue jean jacket and a flannel undercoat. Water from a sidewalk puddle dries at the bottom of her worn jean pants; construction sand and gravel dust cover her black leather boots. She has obviously been walking in the Chicago streets.

"Who are you?" Kenny barks, wondering if this mongrel girl has tracked the entire city into his apartment. June's perplexed face turns into fear at the sight of her amputated father, while he squeezes her sister's neck in his hands.

"Let her go, Kenny!" June steps cautiously toward the bed and reaches for his forearms. She rubs her fingers against his skin and her eyes relieve the idea of a threat; she instantly endears herself to him. "Dad, let her go."

Kenny instantly recognizes something familiar in the girl's tone and touch, and his grip around Christina's throat loosens slightly. She takes a few short breaths but she remains silent, watching the reunion.

"What'd you call me?" Kenny stares at his daughter with his mouth wide open. "Who are you?"

"I'll explain everything, just let her go." June continues to graze his forearms with her fingertips and his grip relaxes enough for Christina to squirm free. Christina falls to the floor and begins gasping for air.

"He...he...he almost killed me!" Christina rubs her neck tenderly, while breathing deeply, desperately pulling air into her lungs. Her dress had bunched around her waist during the struggle. She stands dizzily and readjusts the fabric to her frame before lifting the fallen straps back onto her shoulders.

"*You* almost killed *me!*" Kenny retorts, pointing a finger back and forth between his frail chest and Christina. He then looks at the teenage girl standing next to his bed; she stares sadly at his legs, sorry for the father she hasn't seen since she was six. He still doesn't know her true identity so he treats her with general disdain. "I don't know who you are, but this woman damn near killed me and..."

"We're here to help you, Kenny." Christina still gasps while stepping closer to the bed. "My name is Christina, and this is June. We're Teresa's daughters, but you don't remember that. All you remember is me. I shouldn't have been there that night but I wanted to get back at you. I wanted to see you hurt, but...I didn't want *this*. I'm sorry for what happened to you, but we're here to help you, honest. May I sit?"

Christina motions to a wooden chair in the corner closest to the bed. Tilly often sits there, reading the Bible or the newspaper to him while Sheila tends to whatever duties she can find available.

"May you sit? *Christina*, you say your name is, right? Why not? I couldn't stop you anyways so go ahead..." Kenny grumbles, realizing that he is not in any real position to resist. The girls may not see his vulnerability, but his battles with Sheila have taught him that a woman can be quite strong. He is unable to attack, unless one of the girls steps within striking range. "But, where's Sheila?"

"I told you, she's in the other room with Duke. They have some *catching up* to do." Christina answers with a giggle, remembering Duke's former crush on Mrs. Chamberlain and wondering how their reunion is going, especially given the fact that Duke can no longer speak. Suddenly stricken with silence on his eighteenth birthday, he hasn't said a word in over six years. Christina imagines what her hot-headed brother would say to Sheila if he could fire at will. "I'm sure she's safe, though. He sees her for who she *really* is, now. She really loves that beautiful necklace you bought her."

"What necklace? I didn't buy her anything!"

"We know..." June adds while walking across the room to the farthest corner, next to the oak dresser. She crosses her arms and leans against the wall, detaching herself from the conversation.

"We bought it for her...from you. We knew she would open the door for anything that shines; she hasn't changed much." Christina smiles and leans forward. "Listen, Kenny, you really don't remember us, huh?"

Christina looks into Kenny's eyes intensely, searching his mind for any recollection or recognition. Kenny has received this questioning glare from Sheila and his mother, but no one else from his past has ever visited him in the hospital or at home.

∞

His mother explained his isolation as a *consequence of his betrayal.* The Bethunes were perfect partners for the Winnipers; their mutual fortunes abounded from a will to do whatever was necessary to secure their legacies and Kenny had disrespected the bond that the two families had established many years ago. When he threatened to return to Winniper County if he did not receive more money to finance his tryst with Sheila, he crossed a sacred line.

∞

As additional punishment for his failed extortion plot, his Cousin Earl and the rest of the Bethune family have refused to visit Kenny; he is a forbidden exile, unable to return to the county that has made both families rich.

"No, I don't remember you, either of you. How do you know Sheila? How do you know my family? Do you work for the Winnipers?" Kenny asks frantically while glancing at June, who still leans aloofly against the wall. He fears the worst as he continues to stare curiously at the girl; he slowly tilts his head side-to-side and surveys her features from different angles. "She said you were…*my daughter*, and you just called me 'Dad' but…I don't have a daughter. Mama said my wife died and I abandoned her kids to be with Sheila. Mama says that women love me and I leave them."

"Your *Mama*…is not telling the whole truth, Kenny. Yes, our mother died, but, at least for a little while, you took care of us. And you did have a daughter with our mother. You were always a drunk, but you at least tried to do the right thing, until you abandoned us." Christina's voice trembles over her words. Kenny can tell that it's difficult for her to reveal the truth to him and hear it for herself. He turns his eyes to June, who nods reassuringly.

"That's impossible. What about Sheila? She told me my wife died in a car accident and I was stuck with her three kids." Kenny repeats the lie and challenges June to speak, staring directly into her eyes and daring her to question his resolve. Sinking deeper into the corner, June lowers her head in sadness and sits down against the wall. "I've only loved Sheila; I left my Mama for her. We moved from Winniper County and we're in love."

"No, Kenny. She is a bottom feeder…" Christina scoots the chair closer to the bed and leans forward toward Kenny, amused and yet annoyed at his memory loss. "Sheila and your mother have lied to you since your accident. They think if you don't remember the truth then you can return to Winniper County, but, you can never go back there. We're never going back either. Whether or not you remember, Kenny, you were married to our mother. Her name was Teresa."

"*Teresa?* I don't know anyone named Teresa! Is this some kind of extortion plot?"

"She died about ten years ago. And it was a car accident." Christina continues to explain as her eyes travel down Kenny's body to the bandages on his stumps. "Duke and I are her children from her first two marriages. During her second marriage to my father, you two had an affair and you knocked her up. By the time June was born, my father was gone, and you and our mother were married."

Christina's words continue to fall over Kenny like twenty pound rain drops, denting his manufactured world with damage he cannot ignore. He has always had his doubts about the stories Sheila and his mother told him. Even now, he struggles with a need for absolution as June's eyes stare up to him from the corner. She folds her knees against her chest, forming a ball of sadness and empathy, lacking bitterness and resentment for the father who left her. Kenny remembers these sad eyes in a brief flash, a daughter, blonde hair, and her mother's smile…*June.*

"But that's impossible, you're not…" Kenny pauses, filled with confusion while looking at the despondent teenager in the corner. "What did I do?"

"It was hard for all of us, Kenny. When our mother died, we had a lot of problems inside that house, but we all thought that we could make it. We thought you'd be there for us, at least until we were old enough to move out on our own. But you gave us to our grandfather." Christina explains, fighting tears as she thinks about the life she could have had. She remembers her dreams of becoming a scientist or an archeologist, and she recalls the feeling when Papa told her she could no longer attend school. "We understand why you left; we never treated you right, but, the way you did it…you drugged us. You were a coward, and you were cruel, even to your own daughter."

"I didn't do it. I didn't do it." Kenny repeats, trying to convince himself that this entire episode is another illusion. He looks to June, who glares back at him; she is a mirror image of despair. He sees his misery in her. "How do I know you're not lying? How do I know you are my daughter?"

"Look at her, Kenny. You raised her for six years, or at least you tried. We had a life. I thought I had a future. I was in school; I wanted to be a scientist." Christina pauses and clears her throat as if the information hurts her to divulge. The bedroom endures an awkward moment of silence for the research she will never attempt while Kenny glances back to June. She clutches her knees closer to her chest and sits against the corner, quietly observing her ignorant, and deformed, father.

"...I remember something...about you...those eyes. You look different though; you're older...angrier. You may look familiar, but...how could you be my daughter?" Kenny asks the question in his best detective tone, a trick the hospital orderlies taught him. Many people can learn, but learning *how* to learn is a different task entirely.

∞

Kenny spent hours reconstructing his cortex processing through cognitive rehabilitation treatment. He hoped and prayed with his mother that he would somehow regain ability to understand information; although, most of the information that he learned about himself and his family was false. When he couldn't understand fully, he taught himself to feign as if he did understand, when, all along, he was failing to understand mostly lies.

∞

"Tell me what happened from the beginning."

"Listen, Kenny, we don't have time. You need to come with us, we have to leave soon. You're in danger, and we're trying to help you." Christina implores flatly; she's conflicted, disgusted by the notion of helping her former stepfather, though she feels guilty for her role in his demise. "We don't have time for more questions. They're coming here to..."

"Take it easy, sis. He doesn't need to know that!" June calls from the corner, casting a hand in the air as if she can grab Christina's words before they reach Kenny. Christina rolls her eyes mockingly while June rises from her Indian style squat and continues to empathize with her long lost father. "We don't need to scare him. I just wanted closure. If he decides to come with us..."

"Closure is the last thing I want..." Christina jests with a joking smile before looking deeply into Kenny's eyes. "What about the money?"

"What money?" Kenny asks sharply, suddenly believing the entire act is a hoax. "Sheila! Call the police!"

"Our grandfather has been giving you money since you abandoned us..." Christina explains, pointing her finger accusingly at Kenny. "I think we should get some of that."

"Wait, *your grandfather?* You're saying Papa Winniper, the wealthiest man in America, is *your grandfather.* So what does that mean? This *Teresa*...I was married to a Winniper? And now you come expecting to get money from me?" Kenny summarizes the hoax to hear its absurdity. His belief fades completely as Christina scoots the wooden chair up to the bed and leans closely to his face. In his bedridden state, Kenny tries to lean away as far as he can without losing his balance. "You two are the worst scam artists in history. You expect me to believe these lies? Who sent you here? Sheila!"

"No one sent us." Christina glares directly into Kenny's eyes to clarify her seriousness and sincerity. "In fact, if Grandpa knew we were here, he might kill us, too."

"But we're moving down south, Dad," June adds, stepping forward and moving closer to his side, hoping for one last moment of reconciliation. "Do you remember how I always wanted to sing in New Orleans? I'm finally going. You should come with us!"

"Why would I come with you? How could I get there? Do you know how to care for a thirty-two-year-old cripple?" Kenny asks mockingly, motioning toward the dingy bedroom and his broken condition. "I'm going to stay here with Sheila. We're going to Morocco soon."

"Morocco is fine. I never wanted you to come along anyways." Christina chimes in with a sadistic joy in her voice. "But you should leave as soon as possible. Grandpa doesn't believe you lost your memory...and..."

"Sheriff Cobb is coming back." June explains frantically, having heard the conversations and the innuendo; her young ears have become adept at deciphering murder plots. "Grandpa is tying up any old loose ends and he's just biding his time. Grandma Tilly came to the estate a few weeks ago and she...she...your mother made a deal."

"What do you mean, *'my mother made a deal'?*" Kenny's tone rises as his urgency escalates and he senses the danger in their words. He observes their fear and hesitation and his own sense of dread increases in response. "What are you trying to say? My mother is a saint. She and Sheila have been taking care of me. They love me. Please, don't tell me differently."

"Love is complicated in our families, Kenneth. Your family and our family own the Dakotas and half the Midwest. Your mother and Papa have almost monopolized the entire U.S. oil industry." Christina describes their families with a modicum of pride, but she withholds any information her former stepfather could use to hang himself. Though Kenny cannot understand, his knowledge of the Winnipers' secrets has already placed his life in jeopardy. Christina tries to pull the wooden chair even closer against the bedframe as she leans over the side of Kenny's bed. "Our families have committed horrible crimes, and they'll do even worse to hide them."

She leans back triumphantly, having clearly etched a sketch for Kenny to see. Nodding to her sister, June takes her cue, reaches out, and grabs Kenny's left hand in her left palm.

"I know it's hard for you to understand, Dad, but you must leave soon. Take Sheila and go tonight."

"But…but we don't have any money. Mama hasn't sent her check."

"Dad, she's setting you up! Let us help you get out of here," June implores, squeezing his hand and placing her right hand on his shoulder. "We can leave now and head to New Orleans. We'll get lost in the city."

"That's insane, don't you see my condition?" Kenny points to his amputated legs. "I need Sheila…"

"Don't you see? She's probably helping them!" Christina claims, holding her index up in the air. "She's on your mother's payroll!"

"Sheila? No…I mean…sure, Mama sends her money but…she…she loves me. What we have is real." Kenny affirms confidently while removing his hand from June and reaching for the Bible still in his lap. "God put Sheila in my life. How could I survive without her? She…she loves me."

"No, she-she doesn't. She-she has received checks from y-y-your mother and our grandfather for y-y-years! I have p-p-proof." Christina mocks Kenny's stammer. She reaches into her purse and removes several stacks of paper. "I stole these bank receipts from Papa's office. These are bank receipts that date back to 1947. Our families have paid people to do their bidding all over the country, no matter how many bodies they leave behind."

Christina throws the receipts onto Kenny's thighs and he stares at the scraps in front of him. Several payment receipts read "Chamberlain, Sheila" on the invoice, and some of the receipts have the watermark seal of the Winniper Family Holding Company.

"What is the Winniper Family Holding Company?" Kenny asks with a blank gaze. Another scene flashes through his mind; he has received similar checks for a similar reason, though he cannot remember exactly when or why.

"It's one of the family businesses," Christina answers quickly, rising to her feet so that she stands above him in superiority. She recalls how he stood over her after he served a poisoned soup and she grows vengeful. "We should just leave you here to die. Don't you remember Winniper County, the exclusive, high-class community for exclusive, high-class people?"

"Yes, I…I remember, I remember…bits and pieces. We had a lot of secrets, but I don't…I don't remember…I promise."

"Don't you remember your payments for abandoning us?" Christina fires down upon Kenny, unable to withhold her anger any longer. "You thought you had a fortune but you spent it all anyways! And when you tried to get more, look what happened to you! I told you, we're disposable pawns, Kenny!"

"Christina, calm down! Can't you tell it's too much for him?" June raises her hand and gently touches Kenny's face; she smiles reassuringly, trying to re-establish a connection with her father. "I know you don't remember me, Dad, but…I know you tried your best. Mom tried, too. Money can make anyone do anything and I never believed either of you left us on purpose."

"Left who? Your mother left me!" Kenny's recollection falls weakly from his mouth and June notices that he can't handle any more truth. He simply repeats phrases because he is unable to process what he's already learned. Tears well in his eyes and his cheeks puff in desperation as coherent slivers seep into his consciousness. "She had another child…you…you had a brother that you didn't even know about. So many secrets…it hurts…it hurts real bad…to remember. They're all dead now…Teresa…"

"Calm down, Kenny. You're not making any sense. Don't cry." June lightly pats his forehead, trying any touch to convince him to leave with her. "Please come with me, Dad. We can be a family again."

"Just remember what I said…I never wanted you to come with us." Christina adds cantankerously while moving toward the door before turning back with a smile and then a sad frown. "But it's too hard to hate anyone so pitiful. You were a louse but you didn't deserve this. I am sorry I came with them when they hurt you; I thought I wanted to see it, but I'm sorry. I'm sorry all of this happened to you, Kenny…"

"Sorry? Why are you telling me this now?" Kenny pleads, still begging for absolution. His world has become so cold and so confusing. "You did this to me and you fill my head with lies!"

"*You* did this to yourself, Kenny." Christina answers sharply, pointing to Kenny's bandaged stumps. "When you left, you became an easy target. I was just a pawn to catch you off-guard when you thought you were safe. Grandpa used us both."

Christina reaches for her fur hat on the nightstand and motions to June that it's time to leave. Her sister nods in agreement; both are still ignorant of the real cost of Winniper womanhood. They do not know about the curse and Kenny can't remember enough to warn them.

"Let us help you, Dad." June pleads, continuing her last effort to reconcile with her father. A child should never question whether her father loves her; even worse, June has grown to love and hate herself and she sees this reconciliation as a chance for her to reclaim her childhood and regain some of her innocence. She still remembers a time before her mother passed, when the family went swimming and had picnics at the country club—a time when everything seemed fair and fun. "We can leave tonight and we can be a family again, you, me, Duke, and Christina."

"I don't know those people. And I don't know you." Kenny replies coldly, stretching his neck to search down the hallway but Christina blocks his view. She places her gaudy fur hat back on her head as Kenny twists his neck and upper body, trying to look around her. "I need to see Sheila! Whoever's in there better not be…uh…*touching* her!"

"He's already *touched* her! I think she *touched* him, first."

"Christina, please! Kenny, you have to get out of here, now! Sheriff Cobb and his men are on their way!" June squeezes Kenny's hand with an urgent frown, begging her father to change his mind. "Papa doesn't believe you'll stay away. He doesn't believe you lost your memory!"

"But my mother…she's coming to visit me. She'll protect me if…" Kenny hesitates before becoming noticeably angry; his skin turns red and he stares at June with a resentful demon inside his eyes. "Daughter or no daughter, you both can get out! I don't know you! I never *abandoned* you! It's all lies! You've all told me lies! Get out!"

"See, June." Christina goads happily, gloating as she bounces back and forth inside the room. Her fur hat almost tips off her head but she catches it during her rant. "I told you, he hasn't changed! He would do it again! He would abandon us, again! And you made me feel guilty for getting him back!"

"I just wanted to help," June mumbles resignedly, releasing her father's hand and stepping away from his bedside. Her eyes begin to water and her black eyeliner runs against her cheeks; she quickly wipes away the tears and turns toward her sister, falling into her sister's arms and shielding herself from Kenny.

"We're goin' to N'orleans, Kenny. June's goin' to be a big star. And we'll never think about you, again." Christina boasts, while holding her sister closely and swinging her head away so that she can whisper softly to June.

"He's not worth your tears. He's never been worth a damn one." Christina grabs June by the hand and gently pulls her sister toward the doorway. A flash appears in Kenny's mind—two little girls in a small home, one pulling the other, and an older boy following orders. Christina pauses at the door and looks back over her shoulder, soaking in Kenny's half-legged portrait, *The Pathetic Man.* She hates him as much now as she ever has; he has validated her scorn and vindicated her guilt. "Even though you betrayed us, we still tried to save you, Kenny. June never got over what you did and she still convinced us to leave Papa and come here. Your daughter's a saint and you never deserved her, or our mother. Let's go, June. He's a dead man and he doesn't even know it."

They exit the bedroom and disappear from Kenny's sight, but he can hear June crying softly down the hallway.

"I'm sorry, Dad. I'm sorry."

"Sheila!" Kenny calls down the hallway but he only hears murmurs and whispers and then a piece of tape rips loudly. "Sheila?"

"Ouch!" Sheila screams from the living room. "Duke, what's the big idea? You all better get out of here before your grandpa finds you! I remember you two girls!"

Kenny can hear a spine-tingling slap and more footsteps move through the living room as the front door opens and closes. Silence fills the apartment, and then Sheila's frantic footsteps rush down the hallway. When she enters the room, she holds the side of her face and winces during each step. She glances at Kenny without much care; their love shack is too small, and he is sure that she has heard much, if not all, of their conversation.

"One of those whores hit me! Don't worry, sweetie! I'm going to call the cops!" Sheila rushes to the nightstand, lifts up the phone, and dials furiously. "Did they hurt you? Are you okay?"

"I'm fine, they didn't hurt me. Don't call the police." Kenny looks up to her, but she ignores his request. He's so busy trying to get her to follow his orders that he doesn't notice the sparkling necklace around her neck. "I said *'don't call the police'*, Sheila!"

"Hello! Yes, we just had three intruders come into our apartment!" Sheila snitches hysterically. "Yes, they tied me up and put duct tape over my mouth! No, it wasn't a party! Yes, 51 Porter Street, thank you! And hurry!"

Sheila hangs up the phone anxiously and sits on the edge of the bed. She stares back and forth between the floor and Kenny, unsure which is lower.

"I told you not to call the police, Sheila."

"Sweetie, those Winniper trash just broke into our apartment, and you don't want me to call the police?" Sheila rants. "Those Winnipers have gone too far now! They just barged into our home"

"You let them in, Sheila," Kenny retorts, counting his blessings after past encounters with mysterious types. "They didn't want to hurt us."

"Yeah right, they just wanted to fill your head with a bunch of lies." With that, Sheila confirms his suspicions, and Kenny knows that while she was in the living room, she was listening to his conversation with the girls and thinking of an alibi to their claims. In this moment, he decides to become wise to all her lies and play dumb to the truth.

"I know, baby, but I don't believe a word they said." Kenny smiles sweetly and a noticeable ray of relief brightens her face. "You're my number one girl, and I don't care what nobody says about you."

"You don't? I mean, of course not." Sheila leans toward Kenny and presses a soft kiss on his sweat-greased nose. "Those Winniper girls are probably junkies by now anyways. I mean…uh…I'm going to check if they stole anything."

Sheila stands, but stops after seeing the sketch on the floor. Without a word, she reaches down, quickly grabs it, walks away toward the dresser near the corner, and places the sketch face down on the surface.

"They didn't take anything," Kenny asserts, scrunching up his nose in disgust. "They just…wanted to talk."

"You never know. Those Winnipers are very sneaky; I think that Christina snuck into my house a few…uh…I mean, you can never be too sure." She courses through the items on the dresser, lifting a hairbrush to her nose. "I think one of them touched my hairbrush."

"They didn't, Sheila," Kenny continues. "Calm down."

"What do you mean 'calm down'? How can I calm down?" Sheila whirls around and paces through the room, holding the hairbrush aggressively. "We're lucky to be alive!"

"They weren't armed. And *you* let them in." Kenny repeats and raises his arms accusingly, straining his back in the process. He contorts and kneads his back gently against his pillow, but the pain moves sharply through his spine.

"I was deceived!" She flaps her arms furiously while fingering her new diamond necklace. "I don't even know if this necklace is real…but it is nice."

"It looks expensive! They gave you *that*?"

"Yep, but I'm going to hide it before the police come!" She promptly unsnaps the necklace and removes it from her neck. "I could wear this if we ever go back to Winniper County. All the wives will be jealous!"

"Wait! You called the police on robbers that *gave* you an expensive necklace!" Kenny waves his arms to show his displeasure, using his only available limbs and appealing to her sensibilities. She holds the necklace up to the lone ceiling light in the room, gazing with wonder at the diamond array in front of her, admiring the shiny craftsmanship.

"Well, those girls could be dangerous. What if they come back?" Sheila steps closer to the bed and dangles the diamond necklace over his amputated legs. "And we can tell the police it was the same woman who attacked you. I heard you recognize one of them."

"The other said she was my daughter," Kenny mumbles before remembering that he doesn't remember. "I don't know if it was the young woman from the sketch, and I don't believe a word she said, anyways." Kenny's throat clenches tightly, and he swallows deeply, falling under the shimmering necklace's trance.

"That's why I called Detective Steelers," Sheila dreams affectionately; the detective's name causes a strong heat wave to creep into Kenny's stomach. The drunken detective is a belligerent, incompetent troll, poking his city nose into the crimes of high society. Detective Steelers has never truly believed that Kenny could not remember what happened. He has always wanted to angle for any leverage he could find in order to access the Bethune wealth; and Kenny has consistently caught this inebriated sleuth making eyes with Sheila.

"No, Sheila!" Kenny balls his hands into fists. He isn't sure if Sheila intends to leave him for Detective Steelers, but, the thought sends his body into overdrive and he feels blood rushing into his absent legs. "I told you I never want to see him again! I told you to never even mention him again!"

"But you said she was the same woman." Sheila nods her head matter-of-factly. "And he's assigned to your case."

"He's an idiot, Sheila! The man doesn't even believe me! I lose both my legs and he thinks I did it to myself!" Kenny's anger builds and he flails his arms around, adding to his upset demeanor. He overcompensates for his absent legs by overusing his arms. Sheila begins to pace nervously in front of the bed; she stops and taps her toes, combining sounds with Kenny's display of hand wrenching, arm flailing, and fist pumping. "I hate that man...and I hate that you called him!"

"Kenny, now *you* should calm down," Sheila insists, holding the necklace in her left hand while moving around the bed and patting Kenny on the forehead with her right palm. "Remember how you behaved when he came to speak to you in the hospital. He could have arrested you, but he didn't."

"He called me a cripple!"

"Well, that was after you threw your apple sauce at him!"

"Detective Steelers is a moron..." Kenny groans as he folds his arms and tilts his head away from Sheila's touch. "The man couldn't detect his own..."

Two booming knocks rock against the door and interrupt Kenny's insult.

"Oh, that's him!" Sheila stands on her tiptoes like an excited child; she then hurriedly rushes to the dresser and hides the necklace in the top drawer.

"Don't answer it! Don't open the door, Sheila!" Kenny shouts demandingly, filling his lungs with false feelings of dominion while swinging his arms above his head wildly. "Tell him to go away!"

"Now, watch your tone, mister!" Sheila turns and points at Kenny sternly. "I don't want you to cause any more trouble tonight!"

She turns back and checks her fading physique in the mirror. She flattens her kitchen shawl to suit her curves and she adjusts her head wrap above her eyebrows. Before Kenny can protest any further, Sheila rushes from the bedroom and, again, Kenny hears the top lock unlatch and the door swings open with a cheer.

"Hello! Come in!" Her words echo down the hallway and Kenny raises his body against the headrest so that he can hear them closely. "Thank you for getting here so fast."

"No trouble, nope, none at all, sweetie." The detective's boisterous voice barrels through the apartment and Kenny hears his footsteps thud into the living room. "Seems there was a struggle in here, maybe a little break-in occurred here tonight?"

"Yes, it was terribly awful." Their steps move down the hallway. "Ken is back here. Just follow me, detective."

"Don't mind if I do." His low grumble receives a giggle from Sheila as they saunter into the bedroom. Kenny lies feebly with his elbows propping up his body, anticipating an interrogation. Detective Steelers wears the same cheap outfit that he wore when Kenny met him in the hospital. The detective dons a faded black suit, brown church dress shoes, and a black tie; and everything smells like whiskey and cigar smoke. His wildly bushy moustache is a statement that Kenny has never understood.

"Hey there buddy, how you feeling?" Detective Steelers strides toward the bed and stands incredibly close, hovering over Kenny and asserting his dominance. He firmly places his hand on Kenny's shoulder and almost shoves him down into a lying position on the bed. "You look tired, maybe even a little scared."

"No, uh, I…uh, I'm fine, thanks." Kenny casually nudges the detective's hand from his shoulder and regains his balance with his elbows supporting his upper body.

"Can I get you something to drink?" Sheila offers the detective, forgetting any duty to Kenny as she auditions for a new role.

"That sounds greats, darling," Detective Steelers replies with a tilt of his head, noticing the way her kitchen shawl accents her hips. He pulls the wooden chair away from the bed and stares back at Sheila. "Brandy on the rocks, please."

"Um, well, at the moment, we don't have any more Brandy, no more liquor at all. Kenny drank the last of the whiskey earlier this morning and...we don't have a lot money right now. We only have water."

"It's straight from Chicago's finest sewers," Kenny adds smugly. "Feel free to find some brandy elsewhere."

"Oh, well, the water is just fine." The detective smiles in the way a jerk smiles at a pretty girl. He scoffs and sits down in the wooden chair; his superiors have programmed him to interrogate so he has the training to expose insecurities.

"I wish we did have some brandy. But I'll get the water." Sheila regrets her station in life before glancing at Kenny dismissively and turning away toward the door. The detective's eyes follow Sheila's wiggle as she walks out of the bedroom and sashays down the hallway, stopping once to look back over her shoulder and make sure that he is watching her.

"Enjoy the view?" Kenny interjects; when the detective's head spins around, he locks eyes with Kenny and stares coldly.

"What are you talking about?" Detective Steelers quips with an arrogant trill, daring Kenny to question him. "I was just stretching my neck. I'm a happily married man."

"Don't play coy," Kenny challenges, while raising his upper body against the pillow at his back. He sits up in bed and catches his breath. "You shouldn't be here. There was no break-in."

"Well, Sheila just called me in a panic. She said there *was* a break-in." Detective Steelers explains confidently and leans forward toward Kenny. "So either there was a break-in or she just wanted me to come over."

"Well, uh...there were people here, but...uh, she was mistaken."

"Was she, Kenny?" Detective Steelers slides the chair closer, unknowingly mimicking the chair's previous occupant. "Because there are still several *miscularities* in your case..."

"*Miscu-what?*" Kenny tries to repeat the detective's word, but he pauses after the second syllable. He believes that the detective invents most of his big city vernacular in the course of his drunken binges. The two men mirror one another, staring blankly into their similar selves.

"You say you saw some woman, a young woman, and then, you don't remember anything afterwards." Detective Steelers removes a pad and pen from the inside pocket of his suit jacket and he holds the pen closely to Kenny's face. "It all seems suspicious, Kenny. Are you sure this has nothing to do with…"

"Here you go, Detective." Sheila re-enters the room, carrying a large glass of water with no ice. Sheila glad-hands happily, giving the glass to the detective and her gaze momentarily lingers on his lap. "Sorry I took so long. And double-sorry, we don't have any ice.'"

"Thank you, Sheila." Detective Steelers grabs the glass with his left hand while holding his pad and pen in his right. He then raises the glass to his stache, takes a few slow sips, and swallows each gulp with authority, groaning slowly from either disgust or gratitude. He clearly hasn't tasted the city's drainage system recently.

In fact, the detective rarely drinks anything but whiskey, especially not water. He tepidly sips from the glass and he only tolerates the grains of dirt and mold in his throat because he knows how his presence disturbs Kenny. For a hardworking sleuth, any imposition upon the out-of-town elite is a thrill. Detective Steelers glances toward Kenny and chuckles as he wipes his mouth with his wrist. He places the glass on the dusty floor, takes his pen and pad into his hands, and looks Kenny squarely in the eyes.

"So there was no burglary tonight, huh? What about the night you got your legs crushed? I suppose that didn't happen either, huh? I imagine you grow legs as soon as I leave, is that it?"

"We've been over this before, *Detective*," Kenny begins, refusing to take the bait and instigate a longer visit than necessary. He plans to expedite the next report in the detective's failed investigation. Kenny speaks tenderly though he continues to overcompensate for his immobility by using his hands to articulate his sincerity. He waves his arms, and clenches and unclenches his fists, struggling to emit his trustworthiness "I don't remember what happened. It's all fuzzy. I was on my way home from a bar in the South Side."

"But you were dumped at Sacred Heart in the North Side, beaten so badly that the doctors had to amputate your legs at the knees. And you're trying to tell me the people who broke in tonight had nothing to do with that? Look what they did to you." Detective Steelers makes a chainsaw motion over Kenny's stumps, back and forth, simulating the amputation of Kenny's crushed legs. "They obviously kept you alive for a reason. Maybe they wanted to get money from you or your family."

The detective continues to run his hand over Kenny's stumps, looking to Sheila and assuring that she sees the pathetic piece of man she calls a lover.

"Kenny, tell him that the same woman came here tonight!" Sheila confesses, revealing that he has not been entirely forthcoming while usurping any authority he believed he had over her. He wonders about the amount of time she just added to the detective's visit. Kenny believes Sheila has mastered him, so that now she controls and manipulates him within the tiny world of their dingy, one-bedroom apartment.

He can't remember the last time they left their home; she refuses to help him into his wheelchair. She complains that people will stare. Inside their apartment, she keeps him under her thumb because her ears have honed the ability to listen around corners. Sheila is capable of hearing gossip over fences, into neighbor's homes, and even across state lines. Filled with spite and contempt, she walks over to the dresser, grabs the sketch of the woman, and holds it up to the light.

"Here she is! It was the woman from this police sketch!"

"Oh, really? Now, why wouldn't you tell me that, Kenny?" Detective Steelers gawks accusingly at Kenny. He lingers on his question, allowing the assumption to build a dissenting tension between the couple. Sheila strolls over to the detective and hands him the sketch. There is a long pause as he places his pen and pad in one hand and looks over the drawing. He then glances back and forth between Kenny and the picture, waiting for Kenny to speak. "She is a tart, isn't she? Well…what do you have to tell me about her, Kenny?"

Kenny narrows his eyes, squinting at the detective and Sheila, wondering if they truly care about his answer or if they simply want his submission. A traitor and a tormentor challenge his manhood and his honor, and he does not fully understand how his life has become this tragedy. All of the people around him would welcome his death. Feeling the weight of Sheila's disloyalty, his mother's expectations, and his own despair after suffering a brutal attack that he cannot remember, he buckles under the pressure.

"It was her," Kenny admits softly. "It was the woman from... *the night.*"

"Did she still wear that fur hat?" Detective Steelers scoffs as he retrieves his glass and takes a long sip. He closes his eyes sharply and dreams that the water is bourbon. Lost in this heave, he exhales after his gulp and snarls at the lack of inebriation. "I never bought that line, seems fishy."

"Yes, she did! She had the hat! What do you mean *'fishy'*?"

"I mean you're full of it, boy. The truth is that you're a snot-nosed punk who grew up with a silver spoon shoved in your mouth." The detective's words are so dismissive that he believes himself without fact. Detective Steelers nods convincingly and Kenny glances to Sheila, who offers no assistance. "You came to the big city, lost a game of pool to the wrong wise guy, and someone collected your legs as payment."

"But I remember winning that night..."

"Oh, now you remember..."

"Sheila, I told you not to call him!" Kenny shouts, emphasizing his irritation with his arms and Sheila looks to the detective with a desperate expression, playing the damsel in distress. "Don't look at him! Why don't you listen to *me* anymore?"

"Don't yell at her, buddy." Detective Steelers demands sternly as he gulps down the rest of his drink, holds out the empty glass, and looks to Sheila. "I think she's been through enough with you already."

"Would you like some more water?" Sheila asks innocently, dipping her shoulders away from Kenny and gazing dreamingly into the detective's eyes.

"I don't see why not, darling." The detective smiles slyly while peaking around her shoulder at Kenny, boring holes in his eyes, and forcing him to watch as he loses his lover from the sidelines during a game he can no longer play. "Sweetheart, a little tap water don't hurt a real man."

"*Darling…sweetheart?*" Kenny's anger grows as he repeats the detective's pleasantries; he pounds his chest twice while Detective Steelers continues to smile arrogantly. "Stop using your pet names on *my* wife."

"Oh, Kenny, stop. You know we've never been married." Sheila interrupts, attempting to deflate Kenny's fury, but she only antagonizes him. "Technically, I'm still married to Ronald. And the detective's just being polite."

"No, he's not being polite, and you keep encouraging him!" Kenny points to her sternly. She looks back and forth between the two men, finding comfort in only one. Kenny notices her indecision and grows even angrier. "We're still getting married in Morocco, right? I see the way you look at him!"

"Here, another glass, hun…please." Detective Steelers hands her the empty glass, and she looks into his eyes with a meek smile. "Let the boys work this out."

The detective returns her smile with a smirk from his cocky jerk face, and Kenny clenches his hands, riled up at the detective's notion of "*working this out*". Sheila glares at Kenny forlornly, giving him up as prey. She walks out of the room and leaves him alone with the brutish detective. Detective Steelers stands from the wooden chair and flexes his muscles inside his cheap suit. He then steps directly toward Kenny and stands over the bed with confidence; the detective is clumsily self-assured, despite his semi-drunken steps. Kenny assumes the detective had a few spirits before he arrived at the apartment and the water is a welcome dilutor in his stomach. Still, Kenny fears what this able-bodied man can do so, in preemptive defense, Kenny tenses his body and clenches his fists tightly.

"I tell you, if you lay one hand on me, I'll…" Kenny threatens weakly, knowing his current disposition. Detective Steelers calls his bluff, drops the sketch, the pen, and the pad on the bed, and the grabs the collar of Kenny's worn pajamas. The detective tightens his grip in both his hands, pinning the cripple under his arms.

"You'll what?" Detective Steelers snarls over Kenny, while ruffling his pajamas and pushing his chest further into the mattress. He leans his body weight against Kenny and growls like a rabid bulldog. "I could drag your no-legged carcass into jail right now. I'm an officer of the law."

"Take…your…hands…off…" Kenny gasps under the detective's grip, sinking further into the bed and smelling the stench that Sheila often complains about. They do need new sheets, a new mattress, and a new life. "Please! Help!"

"Tell me what happened that night! I don't buy a single word you say!" Detective Steelers lifts his fist above Kenny's face and his knuckles look like daggers ready to slice Kenny to shreds. "Why does Papa Winniper want you dead, Kenny? What did you do? What secrets do you know inside that little pea-sized brain? Tell me before it's too late! I hear they're coming back soon, do you think this woman showing up tonight was a coincidence?"

The detective grabs the sketch from the bed and shoves it into Kenny's face before resuming his bear-like assault and applying his full weight upon Kenny's chest. Kenny sinks so far into the mattress that he can only see Sheila's shadow, cast against the adjacent wall just outside the bedroom door. Her visage peeks into the corners of his left eye and he wonders if he sees a ghost; there's another flash in his mind, and he remembers someone he once knew.

"Teresa…help me…" Kenny squirms, but the shadow disappears as Sheila walks closer to the bed.

"No one can help you!" Detective Steelers shakes Kenny roughly, shocking him from his hallucination. The detective presses Kenny even further into the bed and Kenny feels like his body has sunk completely within the mattress. He is now as soiled and stained as their sinful bed. "You need to help yourself, boy! Tell me what you know!"

"I…don't…know…anything." He can barely speak under the detective's weight. Detective Steelers slowly grinds his knuckles into Kenny's chest, and the air squeezes out of Kenny's lungs. The sketch of Christina falls to the floor, a sad memory of a girl he never really knew. "She was just some tramp!"

"Stop lying, Kenny! You're impeding my investigation and my wallet!" Drool escapes from the detective's mouth as he yells over Kenny. Kenny struggles to gasp for air; and, in the corner of his eyes, he sees Sheila's loafer slippers next to the detective's wrinkly church shoes. "Tell me what you know, Kenny. You Bethunes must have something on the richest family in the world, or else you'd be dead already."

"Sheila...help..."

"Tell me what you know about the Winniper family! What are they hiding?" The detective's roaring voice cascades over Kenny, searching for an answer from anyone, anywhere. "Why am I being hounded by my superiors to leave your case alone? My lieutenant says you won't make it to summer!"

"I...I...I don't know..." The words barely escape Kenny's blue lips as he squirms to release the pressure and gasp for air. Detective Steelers leans forward, even closer than before, staring deeply into the eyes of the man he is willing to kill for answers, but Kenny remains steadfast. "Please...detective...I...don't..."

"I know...I know...you don't *remember* anything...right? You don't know anything, huh?" The detective whispers. "But I know something...Sheila's coming with me. I hear your own mother helped set you up that night. I hear you were supposed to die."

"What?"

"Sorry, I have to run." The detective grins cynically. "I wish you could join me, Kenny, but I hear you're going on a trip soon. Morocco, right?"

With that, Detective Steelers releases his grip, and the air rushes back into Kenny's body. The detective stands tall, stretches his back, and adjusts his suit. He turns and checks his demeanor in the mirror before looking towards Sheila and winking conceitedly. He raises his chest like a conquering Roman soldier and stomps toward the door, but he pauses, turns, and walks to Sheila.

"Thanks for your hospitality, *sweetheart*. I'll take that water to go." The detective grabs the glass of water from her hand and downs the entire drink in one slurp. "How about you and I talk for a second?"

He moves past Sheila and grabs her arm authoritatively without giving her a chance to respond. He leads her into the hallway but stops so that their exchange remains in Kenny's eye sight. He whispers to her softly and Sheila pauses under the detective's chin, breathing in his scent while he smells her hair.

After a moment or two, they break their not-so-subtle embrace and the detective walks away, heading through the hallway. Kenny hears the detective's clunky footsteps move through the living room before he opens the front door, leaves, and slams the door behind him. There is silence in the bedroom as Kenny still gasps for air while rubbing his throat and chest. Sheila returns to the doorway and watches him blankly, knowing that Detective Steelers has taken his manhood.

"He almost killed me," Kenny whimpers in bed, an impish shell of the boy toy that he once was. "I could've died again."

"Maybe you should...just get it over with," Sheila replies sharply with a newfound anger. Her tone is so hurtful that Kenny struggles to maintain what little composure he has left.

"What? Why would you say that, darling?"

"Don't 'darling' me!" Sheila shouts, creating drama where there was none; she needs a fight to prove that he is too weak to handle her. "You men think you can throw out a 'darling' or 'dear' or 'sweetheart' and get whatever you want!"

"But, sweetheart..."

"There you go! Sweetheart! Baby! Honey!" Sheila rants without provocation; she is an actress preparing for her final curtain call. "You men think every girl wants to hear compliments and pleasantries and they do, they all do. But I'm not a girl, I'm a woman...I have needs!"

"I-I know..." Kenny stammers, sensing his mother's presence and dropping his head instinctually. He feels shame and guilt but he does not know why and he cannot stop these emotions from filling him with doubt. "I-I-I can t-take care...of your needs."

"No, you can't, Kenny!" Sheila counters, confirming his fears that she has moved on. He no longer lights her fire, now that he no longer provides the mystique of wealth and power. He is a crippled man who needs more love and care than she ever planned to give him. "You can't even take care of yourself! I have to change your diaper! I just can't do it anymore!"

"I told you to let me use a bucket by the bed!"

"Then who would take that to the trash, Ken?" Sheila asks while wrinkling her nose at the imagined smell. "I'm sick of hauling your bowels around the apartment and taking the trash downstairs in the cold. I never did any chores with Ronald!"

"I'm sorry, Sheila," Kenny apologizes, continuing to hang his head, unable to muster any counterclaim. He is a beaten man. "I tried to be a better husband, or a better lover. I didn't know…"

"I know you didn't know…the detective's right. You won't make it a month without me." Sheila steps forward, sits on the edge of the bed, and places her finger over Kenny's mouth, stopping his pathetic mumblings. She's done hearing him, done seeing him, done feeling anything for him in the face of their mutual destruction. Her words sting, wound, and almost kill his spirit. She rises from the bed and walks quickly toward the dresser.

"You need me more than I need you and what kind of man needs a woman more than himself. You're not a man. You're still a little boy."

"How could you? 'Little boy'?" Kenny repeats, still in shock as he lifts himself on his elbows. He watches as she fumbles nervously over the dresser, making decisions about what to keep and what to leave. "What are you doing?"

"What does it look like, Kenny? I'm leaving you." Sheila responds curtly, removing the necklace from top drawer of the dresser. "I'll have Monty send for my things."

"Monty? Who is that?"

"Oh, Detective Steelers, silly," Sheila explains with a girlish smile. "He asked me to call him Monty now. I think it's cute."

"The detective?" Kenny continues to repeat her words. Once again, he is stuck in a daze where the information is too much for him to process. The mental trauma of the attack has made bad news more difficult for him to understand. Still a disillusioned child, Kenny uses his amnesia as an excuse for the naïveté which has always plagued him. "How could you leave me for him? After all we've…for him? He's married."

"That's why it doesn't feel so bad," Sheila admits, while turning and walking closer to the bed. "Think of it this way: somewhere across town, Mrs. Steelers is going to feel exactly like you. And somewhere in South Dakota, Ronald has been feeling just like you two are going to feel. This is not uncommon."

Sheila walks around the bed and pats Kenny's head softly, treating him like a dog that she is releasing to the wild to die alone.

"But what about getting out of here? We can go anywhere you want!" Kenny offers fearfully, feeling the coming absence in his life and knowing that he cannot survive without Sheila's care. He tries to convince her that they are in this predicament together. "Those girls said the Winnipers are coming for us."

"No, *sweetheart*," Sheila laughs, leaning closely to Kenny for the last time, inviting him to remember what he'll be missing before stepping away so that she is out of his reach. "They're coming for you and only you. Monty told me all about it."

"You can't leave me like this, Sheila," Kenny beseeches her, searching for an object to help him, something to extend his reach beyond the bed. He glances momentarily at the sketch still on the floor and all feels lost. "You just can't…"

"Oh please, *'you just can't'*. Are you sure, Kenny? Can't I?" Sheila mocks him for pleasure while backing out of the door with a wide smile. "I'm leaving you right now and no one can stop me!"

She turns in the doorway, just as the front door opens slowly. Sheila stands frozen as Sheriff Cobb, Jr. and several armed men walk casually into the apartment and march down the hallway. Tilly enters the apartment behind her small band of mercenaries as they back Sheila into the bedroom.

"I think *we* could stop you, dear…" Tilly chuckles while reaching into her fleece jacket pocket for an Upmann cigar. She obviously heard their conversation through the apartment's thin walls, but Tilly carefully removes a match and lights the cigar with two long puffs like she is in the midst of a movie scene. "Sheriff, have the boys take all the valuables and jewelry after we're done. Mister Winniper wants us to burn this here whole apartment buildin' down."

"Yes ma'am."

"What! Why? Let me leave first, please!" Sheila begs, clutching the necklace and moving back closer to the bed as the men continue to descend gradually and silently upon the doomed couple. "I should have left sooner."

"Mama? What's going on? What are you doing here?" Kenny asks knowingly, struggling to keep his elbows sturdy enough to hold his weight. "Did you bring money? You…uh, I'm doing better, uh, you could have mailed the check like usual, you know."

His mother, the sheriff, and the henchmen remain silent as they crowd around the bed, filling the small bedroom with guns, knives, and assorted weapons, all with murderous intent. Sheila crawls into the bed next to Kenny, and they both shake with fear as Tilly continues to puff on her cigar.

"I *really* should have left sooner," Sheila repeats and her mind fills with regrets as she crawls against the headboard so that she leans into Kenny, and cowers in their executioners' presence. "You can keep your money! I didn't want any of this to happen!"

"We don't always get what we want, sweetheart. I didn't want to marry my impotent half-brother. Six years of marriage and he never so much as touched me. But I was a good girl, loyal to my father—he wanted to keep the oil money in the family." Tilly puffs the cigar without remorse for the coming violence. She has made peace with her demons and a deal with the devil has given the Bethunes a long-term extension with the Winnipers. "You see, this is all about family. And if you can't put family first, well, then you're left behind, no matter who you are. I'm just glad your grandfather and the man you called your father didn't live long enough to see what you've become, Kenny. Do you remember your father? Do you remember what that gambling drunk said to you the day he killed himself?"

"No, Mama, I don't remember anything, I promise."

"I know, it shouldn't matter. He wasn't your real father, anyway. He knew it all along; he never had me, in that way, but…he played along with the lie because he had a son. But lies…they kill the weak. I suspect that's why he put a bullet through his skull. Do you remember that, son?"

"No, please Mama, I don't want to remember no more! I'm having a hard time understanding things tonight. Sheriff, your boys beat me up real good last time! I learned my lesson! I won't tell nobody nothin'! I mean, I lost my legs, isn't that enough? Please, Mama, I promise I won't tell no one what we done to Teresa, I'm mean…uh, I don't even remember what happened!" Kenny's memory begins to spill forward frightfully; he can no longer resist the images as his mind floods with moments from the past.

A weary man lies on his deathbed, holding a deck of cards or a pair of dice; he gives a slow wink and a soft smile before whispering his final words. Kenny stares up at his reapers but he can't manage the same wink or smile. He feels Sheila trembling next to him and fear grips their bodies as the gunmen glare at them with knowing finality. This reckoning is the consequence of a greater scheme that Papa planned years ago. Sad inevitability courses through the bedroom and descends upon the lovers who became disposable pawns.

"You can remember, Kenny. That's the problem; you're beginning to remember too much. Truth is, I'm proud of you for at least conceiving a child with Teresa. You were more of a man than your fake father, much less of a man than your real one. But, before you go, just tell Mama what your Paw-Paw said when he killed himself…and this will all be over."

Kenny sees the alternative ending, the one that Hollywood rarely approves, when evil finds the corrupted in debt and without means to survive. His worst fears have come to fruition before his eyes, and he is only left with the images of a mother who planned his murder, a father he never knew, and a daughter he once loved and lost, or maybe he never loved her or anyone else, including himself. It is in these revelations when a father should miss his child and call to her in his end, but Kenny stares blankly at his morbidly murderous mother and he remembers how his father faced a similar demise with a gambler's curiosity.

"He…uh…he said '*23 skidoo*'."

MAY 1961

Sunday	Monday	Tuesday	Wednesday	Thursday	Friday	Saturday
	1	2	3	4	5	6
7	8	9	10	11	12	13
14	15	16	17	18	19	20
21	22	23	24	25	26	27
28	29	30	31			

Tuesday, May 2, 1961

<u>Jazz Lancaster</u>

What is the probability
That two twins will meet?
The prophecy would be complete.
To repeat, the curse came from a dying Sioux verse,
Hidden in the seed 'til they conceive.
Indeed, a fee for the gallantry
That balances the browns on a phallic, white steed.
Horses, of course, no remorse when bred with force,
Raised without love for their source.

But in the report to God, hear a cry so odd,
The hope for two to try so hard and fly so far.
Forget the larks or the sharks that rip at their hearts
And wish to see their love fall apart;
And in disregard, the twins creep in the dark,
Sweet truth buried deep in their roots,
Sowing their rude youth in music uncouth:
If only they could meet, if only it were true...

Jazz Lancaster sees life as a fleetingly fast dream, a passing sadness that only leads to more tragedy, yet the pain always feels so good. His inner doubts deter his destiny, but he has faith that nothing can change God's will—he will succeed, someday.

∞

Though Berthine raised Jazz and his siblings over the graves of their slaughtered Sioux ancestors, she and the children practiced Christianity. Berthine's father, Johnnie Robinson, was an avid Baptist and he passed down the faith to her. Without much inherent defense, Jazz internalized Berthine's teachings and he believed everything that the King James Bible had to offer, until it could not offer a music career.

∞

Now, while living in New Orleans, Jazz remains faithful with a twist; he believes God's infinite powers will collaborate to define his legacy, but he's unsure exactly when his legacy will begin. He dreams of an intermittent existence when his fingers hit the keys or he sparks a conversation with a pretty girl, who actually returns his smile, yet, the dream cannot amount to reality. His imagination's touch eludes any actualization. At nineteen years old, he only feels his dreams when he performs; his art finds the stage and the people see, they hear, and they *experience* his fantasy coming to life.

A lone, Midwestern blonde sings onstage and Jazz observes her cream dress against her thin frame. His fantasy turns into reality a little earlier than expected. She croons softly over a dimly lit crowd, a blue light piercing her shoulders so perfectly that he swears her skin shines like a Winniper County sunrise; she reminds him of home.

Lonely and cold, he reminisces upon those simple mornings outside Berthine's cabin, while he sips a strong whiskey from a pint-glass and sits at the service bar of *Teezy's*, a Scapetown, New Orleans speakeasy. Resembling his late father Kenny, Jazz doesn't hold his liquor; rather, the liquor holds him. And just like his father, whom he never knew, Jazz has become an alcoholic who has succumbed to a pseudo-addiction that forms a crutch and allows him to ignore the family that he still does not understand.

He, Charles, and Lucy know that Berthine is not their biological mother, but she has never answered their questions. Because she raised them in relative seclusion, they have no one else to claim as their parents so they continue to play the game for lack of a better option. Though the three Sioux siblings live far away from Winniper County, they stay in contact with her so that she can provide guidance, protection, and assistance, often when they don't even ask. Jazz thinks she has some overarching duty to monitor and control them. He has tried to get away from her and his siblings, though he needs them all more than he would ever admit.

Although he has grown into a dashing, young man with steely eyes that pierce souls, Berthine and his siblings still treat him like a defenseless baby. They order him around and impose inconveniences upon him as they see fit because they want to keep him down. They know, in fact, he is a king, meant for greater deeds than being their loved one.

Jazz thinks that their adoptive mother raised them to believe her lies because the siblings fulfill her need for family. They're probably orphans from the Sioux village but Jazz can't be sure; he only knows that their story is incomplete.

∞

Though Lucy couldn't speak when they were children, after her eighteenth birthday, she told Jazz and Charles how someone brought them to the cabin. She didn't know who nor could she remember much beyond that, but the siblings quickly knew that Berthine was not their real mother. Berthine had casted herself as the noble matriarch, but she raised the children in a financially and socially segregated town where they never felt welcome. She hid them inside a small cabin of love at the edge of a forgotten forest because she believed that she had to protect the children from a community that would judge them harshly.

∞

Onstage, the young blonde's lullaby is the only sufficient distraction from his self-deprecation—he has found a new affliction. Her pitch is as sweet as ginger and her tone is moist like a delicate tongue lapping at his ear; sensual lips kiss his lobes and her smooth bluesy, melody pierces through the walls around his heart...

You say you want to be brand new,
I hear you want to improve;

But prepare for bad news-
It's just jazz; it's just jazz and June.

Stuck in those same ways,
Your life is the same haze
On an unnamed street that you can't pave,
And you're still stuck with no luck in a maze.

You say you want to be brand new,
You say you want to improve;
But prepare for bad news-
It's just jazz; it's just jazz and June.

She finishes as tenderly as she began and he wants to stand from his bar stool and give her a hand, but he's unable to find his balance. The mostly black audience members snap their fingers and deliver a lackluster admission of appreciation and her presence fades along with the echoes of her lyrical voice. She looks as out-of-place as he once did while standing amidst the Negro music scene—two odd ducks out of water. A white blues singer sticks out just as much as a Sioux jazz pianist in any Scapetown bar.

The boulders inside Jazz's suede shoes weigh down his admiration for her skills and he simply finishes his last sip and stares into his now empty whiskey glass. His iceless and hollow companion seems jealous at the attention he has given to the songstress. The patrons continue snapping their fingers while some light clapping patters through the dark dive bar. They acknowledge the colonizer with the courage to sing a cappella in Teezy's blues bar.

Scapetown usually isn't so nice to her kind or maybe, her kind isn't so nice to Scapetown; but she is Alice in a wonderland of her dreams, all alone, yet unafraid. Meanwhile, Jazz trembles in fear as if tonight will be the first time he has ever stepped onstage. He can't help envisioning his cozy cabin in South Dakota as he roasts under the service bar's neon lights. He only hopes, at the very least, not to embarrass himself so badly that the crowd rejects his play forever. Even the worst listeners will give a performer a few brief moments to prove himself before booing, unless they remember a previous bombing.

Although he has gained local notoriety as one of Scapetown's young, up-and-coming rhythm and blues pianists, he often wishes the patrons and critics would consider his developing talents as mediocre. Jazz thinks that he still has so much to learn; he is not confident enough, yet, and if he made more mistakes, then the crowd would understand his anxiety and maybe they wouldn't expect perfection. Their eyes, ears, and minds would recognize that even greatness can fall short of expectations.

The stage is noticeably empty as the blonde singer stands next to an unmanned custom-made black grand piano. She mutters a muted "thank you" and steps down into the scattered sea of black patrons. They are mostly Creoles who inspect her with differing intentions. Jazz assumes that some of the *bruthas* notice her young, ample curves and round rosy cheeks. They enjoy her sexual appeal while dreaming of what it would be like to conquer such a delightful specimen of femininity; but, consequently, their wives, girlfriends, and nightly whores have sharp knives carved for their men's eyes if they continue to stare at this white girl's thighs.

She silently moves through the crowd, swishing back-and-forth among the closely packed chairs and blue linen-covered tables. Finally, she reaches the service bar and stands near Jazz's bar stool perched against the countertop. A bulky white male and cliché suburban female, presumably the girl's brother and sister, approach her impatiently.

"Okay, June. Are you ready to go?"

"Hey, Christina…uh…so…h-how'd I do?" June asks self-consciously, crinkling her nose as if she's preparing for a blow to her self-esteem.

"Great, sis. I think the crowd really enjoyed you, right, Duke?" Christina replies quickly with a slight twinge of sarcasm peeking through her voice. She tugs her brother's jacket, but he remains silent while glancing around the room for any and all riffraff. Christina passes a mutual glare over the shackish bar before turning back to June. "Hey sis, it's dirty in here. Can we go now?"

"No, let's stay for a bit, Christina," June pleads eagerly, and Jazz can feel that tingle when someone glances at him nearby; her blue eyes tickle his sixth sense. "I want to see some of the other acts."

Jazz's heart leaps, tumbles, and sinks to the bottom of his stomach, and a familiar nausea fills his nerves and morphs every emotion into uncertainty. He's not sure if he should vomit or defecate, maybe ask for some water, or run for the door. Those frantic questions return about his life choices; being a Native American man in a white man's world without an education, his *legal* options for income are clear. The Negros and the Mexicans have shown him the path: he can be a day laborer, breaking his back for another man's pockets or a musician, tapping into whatever spiritual essence he has retained from his Sioux ancestors. His people were from the Ghost Dance tribe, and he feels the rhythm of their drums in his heartbeat. His life seems to have only two options for survival, though only one option includes any hope for happiness. Teezy, the bar's owner and host, steps onstage, grabs the mic stand roughly, and leans into the microphone with a heavy exhale.

"Alright, alright, alright, dat was a good song right thea, June!" Teezy claps twice for effect. "As I always say, anyone with da blues in they heart iz welcome to sing at *Teezy's*! Now, I'm not sure if June could handle the 'Friday Night Firepit'; it may be a little too hot! But, I do know our next performer could sign with any recordin' studio in town! I don't know what the boy is waitin' on, we all tryna git paid, but please, ladies and gentlemen, put your hands together…for the young sensation rockin' Scapetown with dem keys…he's known as…*Jazz Lancaster*!"

Jazz hears the claps but he tries not to register the sound. A sip of melted ice and whiskey in a 90/10 proportion temporarily helps to stop the clouds from forming around his creativity, but the rain is coming. He never plans the inevitably unpredictable rollercoaster when jazz improvisation meets technical skill. He just performs to his given talents. He often sits at the piano, wondering how God determines who will be what and whether humans have any say in the matter.

Having heard the arguments for free will, he still doesn't feel as though he ever had a choice. He's been a musician since he fought for his brother's guitar; he wanted it more than Charles. Often times, music has been his only escape while being confined to a small cabin inside a small village inside a small town. He is still an imprisoned victim of his birth, though he has never understood why Berthine kept him and his siblings inside their home, chained to such a short leash. In these moments of awkward reflection, when the crowd expects greatness and when he should feel the most excitement, he only processes the dread of returning home. He never wants to see that cabin again, nor hear about his ancestors' village or Winniper County. Still, the burden of doubt doesn't overwhelm him completely, and the boulders in his shoes sift through his soles as he rises from his bar stool.

Several recording scouts sit at candle-lit tables along the wall of the bar, taking notes on performances and reactions while waitresses apply for day jobs as secretaries, assistants, and mistresses. The recording scouts stare intently at Jazz and their expressions and calculations clearly surmise that his Native American look and his soul brother talent will make one of them very, very rich, but the commercial market still frightens him more than this little stage in *Teezy's*.

Jazz manages a weak grin as he pushes away from the bar, hoping to stave off any revelation of his fear; many believe his scowls and unkind demeanor are signs of arrogance. There are general rumors about the Sioux boy's disdain for common folk, but he's actually frightened of success and the relationships it brings. Although he knows that his family wants him to be successful, he struggles to remain close to them because he fears that he will disappoint them; and even if he does meet their expectations, he still won't trust them. Maybe he hasn't had enough whiskey. He thinks about ordering another glass for the walk to the piano, but the only excitement he feels is the possibility that his mistakes will finally amount to his failure. He could ruin all of his potential and bring peace instead of the coming chaos.

"Maybe they'll boo," he thinks. *"Maybe they'll walk out and never expect me to entertain or amuse anyone ever again. Maybe I'm only meant to disappoint them."* His thoughts wound his sensibilities momentarily, a profound defeat in hubris; he walks away from the bar and begins to shuffle through the crowd, feeling familiar pats and arm grabs. The crooked looks are from those who actually know him, fellow musicians he wouldn't work with. He could never sacrifice his desired sound to become part of a band; he demanded control of his art.

So now he trudges toward stage as a solo artist, placing one foot on the edge of the platform before looking back over his left shoulder. He sees June standing with her sister and brother at the bar. She looks lonely or, at least, she still seems out-of-place, even among her siblings, but there is a moment when her mesmerizing blue eyes connect with him and he feels an unfamiliar flutter in his stomach, different from the common form of a stage performance—an actual connection between himself and another person. She tilts her head to the side as he pauses to collect his thoughts, waiting to open the valve that releases his inspiration.

"Play something we can dance to!" a Creole crouton calls from the front row and several others join the appeal with grunts or yelps of agreement. There's no time for improvisation when the crowd demands appeasement; he is unable to disappoint, or rather, he truly values acceptance over self-expression—a setback for any artist to admit. And he knows that now is the time to bow in submission to the laws of this music jungle.

He steps onto the stage and positions the microphone stand next to the wide black piano as someone hits a spotlight on his eyes—Teezy has no talent for cues. Jazz flinches and swiftly sits at the squeaky leather bench behind the keys. Adjusting his vision to the light and leaning toward the microphone, he glances between the crowd's eyes; one lush from the floor takes a swig of his beer and yells into the ceiling. "Gaaaaad dog, c'mon boy! We wan' a dance!"

"Okay." Jazz whispers with little force or resistance, perfectly willing to escape into repetitive choruses and popular lyrics. While the piano keys will always be his first love, his goal is to become the real Elvis Presley. Though he can't play the guitar as well as Chuck Berry or dance as well as The King, Jazz continues to keep Charles's guitar for safekeeping, hoping someday he will reconcile with his brother after becoming the world's most popular star.

It's important for Jazz to surpass anything his brother could ever accomplish before resolving his issues with Charles on mutual terms. Jazz maintains regular contact with Charles and Lucy because they have helped him survive in New Orleans, but, his brother is distant, callous, and even dismissive. Jazz feels the need to live up to his siblings' assistance, but, in the same breath, he feels the fear of what his success will do to their family, given how Lucy's success has already changed their relationships—specifically, her relationship with Charles.

∞

Once he began performing regularly in Scapetown, Jazz asked several bar owners to purchase a flat-footed Lancaster piano from his sister. Lucy had become an accomplished entrepreneur in New Orleans. Once, his mute, older sister finally spoke, she evolved into a very progressive colored woman. She and Charles left Winniper County and arrived in New Orleans several years ago, before Jazz was old enough to travel. For years, they had listened to him rant about Mardi Gras parties, so they decided to beat him there. Berthine gave Charles and Lucy some money along with her blessing because she trusted them to remain safe as long as they remained together and she felt it was best for the children to leave Winniper County, as quietly as possible. They had become too beautiful or, maybe, too wild to hide.

As a young woman in the heart of the late 50s jazz and bebop scene, Lucy fell in love with the Creole culture in Scapetown and she used some of Berthine's money to buy a custom brass, French horn imported from a Creole trade company called Cashmen Exports—owned by Marcus Cashmen.

While walking home to the apartment that she shared with Charles, a Belgian horn player saw her newly acquired instrument, inquired over a price, and paid her double to buy the instrument on the spot. She had an eye for valuable instruments and she soon bought a custom piano and a vintage violin from the same trader, though she could not play a single note on any instrument.

Coincidentally, Lucy had chosen a rare niche commodity of custom Creole instruments and her investments attracted significant interest. So she sold a few more horns and then some posh pianos and her eye for artistic apparatuses became a popular statement for musicians and collectors alike. They had to have an instrument *"from Lucy"*. Lucy's stylish eye and simple demeanor turned her random interest into a reputable business that blossomed under her feet and made her a respected, small-time entrepreneur in Scapetown, New Orleans. Her success also made her an object of scorn for Charles, who missed competing with Jazz, because, against Lucy, there was no competition. She was the innocent, wide-eyed country girl making it in the big city of the South; and he became the heel, forced to turn bad in order to make good.

Quite simply, Charles couldn't handle the 9th ward speakeasies and the risqué nightlife as well as his sister. Charles used Berthine's money to run the streets, seeking self-destruction in the form of thrills and ghetto notoriety. Lucy used the money to buy and sell more horns, pianos, oboes, and strings while mailing some of the profits to Jazz and Berthine in Winniper County.

Throughout Jazz's childhood, his outwardly poor family somehow maintained resources beyond their visible means due to a modest inheritance from Johnnie Robinson and frequent handouts from Olivia Winniper. Her son, Thomas III, would visit the cabin when Jazz was a toddler, but neither he nor Olivia has visited the family in recent years. When Charles and Lucy left Winniper County and moved to New Orleans, they mainly relied upon each other for personal support, bonding over the struggle of finding one's way and using their shared fortitude as a resource of its own.

A few months after Lucy established her business, Charles forgot their bond or, more accurately, he stopped caring about offering any support to Lucy. He started his own enterprise, but he had a lower moral standard. While becoming a coldhearted, underground crook, Charles transitioned his daily life into nightly capers and he lessened his contact with Lucy, Jazz, and Berthine without even sharing his reasons. Secretly, he felt like a failure and he refused help from Berthine and Lucy because he feared how his family would treat him for being weak. Jazz understood his brother's seclusion. He's often behaved similarly; but, while Charles chose the illegal income options for the uneducated mice in America, Jazz worked tirelessly to cultivate his musical talent so that one day, he could capitalize on the legal options for the American children left behind in the rat race.

Three years ago, a highly competitive music scholarship from the New Orleans Music Reformatory finally brought Jazz to the South; it was a great reason for him to leave Winniper County before he turned eighteen and even Berthine couldn't stop him. She had to let go of her baby boy, and at age sixteen, the last of Teresa's Sioux children left Berthine's cabin.

Because Charles had already left their apartment to delve into underground crime, Jazz moved in with Lucy. He and Lucy always hoped Charles would return so Jazz slept on the couch in the two bedroom apartment, and he was never happier. He spent his nights and weekends, composing melodies and practicing on a piano in the living room, and during his day, he attended courses at an elite music school within the mecca of syncopated music. Slowly, his compositions became clear representations of his soul; his form began to take shape and his talent emerged whenever and wherever he played.

Every now and then, Charles would visit Lucy at their apartment or stop by Jazz's school performances, checking in from time-to-time and feigning interest in both his siblings' successes. Jazz ignored his brother's jealousy and Lucy used her youngest brother to replace her bond with Charles; she and Jazz filled a mutual need for one another. Lucy provided a safe nest for Jazz, free of charge, though his scholarship did help. She also nurtured his talents and connected him with her clients, many of whom were popular musicians and bar owners in the New Orleans music scene. Jazz was always true to himself, cantankerous, challenging, but also bright and witty. He and Lucy supported each other like she and Charles did when they first moved south. The New Orleans music scene became an extension of their home. Though Jazz and Lucy both felt strikingly out-of-place as Sioux natives in a mostly black and white crowd, together, they thrived.

∞

Jazz has often felt especially cursed with his given name as *Jazz Lancaster*, but, as Teezy told him, "boy, God made ya to play dis here music. Ya got dat Injun soul in ya!"

Teezy always had a way to make Jazz feel at home in a black underworld. He called Jazz a "Sioux soul brother" and his praise is the main reason that Jazz frequents his bar more than the other local establishments. *Teezy's* is also the closest to Jazz's new apartment.

With Lucy, her clients, and even Charles working in the shadows, "Jazz" has become virtually untouchable in the New Orleans scene. His talent has paved the way; his dedication has unlocked the force behind the local music scene on and off the dance floor. This young Sioux musician can play beyond his name, beyond his race, and maybe even beyond his skill-level. He calls to a spirit or god beyond this world; and he only recently began crafting his signature sound while mastering the piano after gigging around town and practicing relentlessly in Lucy's apartment.

∞

He never had an instructor while living in Berthine's cabin; he had her piano and Charles' guitar, but he had to teach himself how to play the music in his mind.

∞

Jazz often thinks about Teezy's words—only God could make him this way. His talent feels natural and unnatural at the same time. Still, as the seeds of his legend grow, he often carries an identification card to prove his legal name to doubters, women, security guards, and other performers. Amongst listeners and artists alike, he has become a walking Jesus in the underground blues scene—he is "*Jazz*", the Sioux native sensation, who plays soul music in Scapetown, yet he cannot save any souls, least of all his own.

∞

Although he has performed in Scapetown for more than a year, Jazz still rehearses nervously at amateur nights and open jam sessions, frantically fretting over keys that seem so friendly at home. Anxiety builds in his fingers while he sits at the piano, glancing over the black and white slabs and taking a moment to scan the crowd one more time as they wait, deadly silent. They jostle in their seats, preparing to see and hear and experience an artist at his craft.

The fingers in Jazz's right hand flutter over the keys in an impulse crafted after hours of practice. He improvises an ascending adagio, pressuring up the pitch scale to a climactic peak. Jazz loves the feeling of being on the edge of this musical mountain, sensing the sound and only the sound, pure as itself. Hanging upon one note, he lingers for a beat, glances again to the audience, and relishes the subtle control within the uncontrollable future when his improvisation may encounter mistakes that are fatal enough to finally disappoint the crowd and destroy his young career.

He slides down the keys to rest in the lower octaves, searching through the key signature; he thinks that his music can never sound sweeter than when he is alone in his room, and even a sold out stadium can't compare to the true freedom of solitude. There's no one to judge him, no one to criticize his flaws; when he performs for greedy eyes, his public phobia consumes his nerves. Even in these amateur exhibitions without professional stakes, his heart feels like it may burst as it beats inside his chest; his stomach turns topsy-turvy. The only solution is to ride the wave through his music and he peacefully places his mind into the harmony built from his song's soul.

"*I'm a travelin' minstrel…*" he begins to sing, feeling through the melody and striking the keys in rhythm. "*…dancin' to the beat! Whenever I'm around, you've got to move your feet!*"

He builds the chorus as the crowd catches the groove and begins to make room for the energy, carrying away chairs, moving tables into corners, and creating the space for them to let loose. This is the new tribal exuberance, the new Ghost Dance.

"And you can't help gettin' down...no, you can't help comin' 'round, the whole town is gettin' down, infected by my sound because I'm a travelin' minstrel..." The women begin to croon along with the contagious rhythm and the men take aim, feeling the feminine force in a carnal way that Jazz sometimes abhors for its debauchery, but he knows the crowd's indulgence is good for business. He can provide the music for their pleasure or their pain, but he chooses pleasure because he's had enough of the latter and the former brings more praise.

Lost in the repetition, Jazz can play for over thirty minutes nonstop; he becomes one with the rhythm while the gents gyrate for the ladies and sometimes the ladies gyrate back. The couples inch closer every eight measures and though Jazz doesn't dance much, if at all, he assumes the pleasure comes from the closeness itself. He's glad that he can play the piano well because a colored man who can't dance or play an instrument has no chance at romance in New Orleans.

Scapetown is a specialized breeding ground for musical excellence; some of the best business managers are women, and they are always looking for an eligible horn player or a new-in-town pianist who can headline a band. Jazz has met a few potential wife-managers, but the casual nature of these proposed partnerships leads him to question long-term relationships in theory and application. For the most part, Jazz thinks people are wicked. He only finds purity in creation; he believes that lies accompany all human interactions.

Still lost in his thoughts, his eyes wander around the crowd as he transitions through the second verse. *"Ladies, get down if you know how...might be a problem if you don't show out..."* His mouth moves in coordination with his fingers and his feet stomp the sustain pedal and clutch in rhythm, but his eyes travel aimlessly through the crowd until they rest on June.

He stares at her and she stares back at him, almost looking through him. She's not dancing or moving while even her brother and sister have a small groove in their shoulders; but, June just stands there like a statue within the moving world of the manipulated. Leaning her hips against the bar, she gazes into his eyes from so far away that he wonders why she feels so close. He's lost again, and he feels an unfamiliar tingle run through his spine—trains coming off tracks, his mind misplaces an inflection here and there. The nuances of jazz's syncopation suddenly confuse the beat in his feet, and he tries to regain his composure so that he can reassert his conscious decision-making over his fingers, but he has lost the rhythm—an improvisational sin.

"And I can't help-I mean, you can't help..." He flubs the line and raises his head from the piano to see the crowd still dancing and groping without noticing his error. They continue to grind against one another, drunkenly enraptured in the rhythm even after a slight lapse. He quickly glances back to June before silently vowing not to repeat his misstep. A miniscule mistake maybe, but he quickly resumes pace, propels the tune through the final chorus, and extends his improvisation into an exotic ending. Traveling up and down the scales, he wants to rush and end another bout with performance anxiety, though his ego encourages him to show off his talent for a special audience member at the bar.

The dancers stop moving and join the recording scouts and bar patrons, staring in shock and pleasure as Jazz wrecks their entire notion of movement. Consensual rhythm be damned, he flies through scales and dyads in degrees that only make sense when he records his music on the lithograph Lucy bought for him before he moved out of her apartment. He hopes to earn the money to repay her someday; his debt is his only current monetary motivation. He still fears being rich more than being poor; poverty is within his comfort zone because he's been poor all his life. As he moves into a lower octave chord progression, he finishes his song with a closing phrase that Dr. Frankford taught him after he arrived at the New Orleans Music Reformatory.

Now Dean Frankford, Jazz envisions his former mentor still enforcing strict modal chord progressions at his alma mater, but he's unsure if the prestigious, secondary school considers him an alumnus because he was expelled.

∞

His favorite professor never expected an *Injun* boy from Winniper County, South Dakota to obtain a high level of classical or technical skill nor maintain the confidence to showcase his talent in a professional exhibition. Jazz initially hated Dr. Frankford because he openly doubted Jazz as a piano student. Though he was smart, he lacked skill and he was extremely antisocial. The music school became a place for Jazz to flourish under the challenge of like minds and he humbled his musical palate under superior mentorship.

Dr. Frankford's obsessive nagging turned Jazz into a perfectionist, but Jazz still fears displaying his talent to more than a few drunkards at an amateur exhibition or a Friday night slew session of old has-beens.

∞

Teezy's "Friday Night Firepit" has become a rite of passage in New Orleans. It is a weekly jam session where careers are lost and won, a reckless gathering of Scapetown's best and most dangerous improv musicians. Even with this level of "heat", over the past year and a half, Teezy's bar has become a place of comfort and safety for Jazz. The loaded dive bar is a Scapetown relic known mainly for its past greatness and its cheap bourbon. Though he is too young, the tenders always fill his glass; his talent commands their respect. Jazz feels that the bar has provided a perfect platform for him to impress the locals, but it's also a false representation of him as an artist and a person. As an alcoholic, Sioux jazz musician, he is just as out-of-place in New Orleans as he is in Winniper County.

The custom Lancaster brand grand piano echoes over the crowd until their loud claps ruin his reverence. The fainting wisps of his song did well enough alone and Jazz thinks their adoration taints his purpose. He plays to hear, not to be heard, yet he considers his ultimate goal to turn music into a long-lasting career and secure a better livelihood for himself and his family—a sharecropper's scraps could never support those dreams. The resolve to never return to Winniper County is probably the only sentiment that Jazz and Charles have ever agreed upon, but they have chosen very different means to establish their respective careers. Charles is a crook, Jazz is a creator.

The crowd's cheers reek of their need for escape, one less moment spent suffering under Jim Crow. The blacks and browns enjoy a short vacation from their oppressive reality, but, amidst their escape, June continues to watch him from the service bar as if she can't see anything else. During his performance, she refused to dance along with the rest, preferring to keep her mind and body docked in demission. And even now, she leans her back against the service bar, refusing to clap; she only stares, thinking something, but he can't read her mind like the others.

Jazz surveys the crowd as he rises from the piano and descends from the stage, regaining his mortality and shaking hands with an eager recording scout whom he doesn't care to hear. He nods and dons the courteous smile that makes him seem mildly cordial. Jazz softly repeats "Thank you" and "We should meet soon", while traveling through the crowd and darting his eyes away from whomever to June, then glancing to whomever and then back to June. He reaches his stool at the end of the service bar and peeks along the countertop in her direction, while resuming his perch and dreaming of his next gulp. A Creole waitress promptly prances around the bar with enthusiastic zest.

"Great song, Jazz! You really killed 'em tonight! Teezy had me bring you a double!" She leans in close while gazing into Jazz's eyes, reaching to the countertop, and placing down two whiskey glasses filled with a lot of bourbon and very little ice. He looks between her curves and the glasses and a lusty wave fills his chest and flows through his toes and fingers. She notices the momentary lapse in his stoic nature and takes advantage of the opening. "You know, Teezy said you're kind of a lonely guy. I could help you with that sometime...I...uh...get off work soon..."

Her invitation lingers as a prelude to more carnage, but he envisions a long seduction, filled with those questions that he especially doesn't care about—*Where are you from? How'd you get here? What's your name?* None of the potential answers pique his interest; in fact, the idea of going through the nuances of such trivial conversation aggravates him enough to eliminate those fleeting pangs of desire.

"I'll let you know," he replies coldly, returning to his artistic, not-to-be-bothered mode. He grabs one of the glasses from the countertop beneath her looming chest without hesitating for sexual friction; and he hurriedly swallows the entire glassful in one, labored gulp. She grins, arching the corner of her lips, a betrayal of sorts; her body wants a mate that her mind does not comprehend.

Jazz believes that women like her only understand how to reap pleasure and pain from brief, physical intimacy; yet, she would undoubtedly and annoyingly struggle with questions of morality during the next morning's mental incursions—the pros and cons of casual sex. This Creole strumpet chuckles coyly while stepping away from him and walking back around the service bar with a swish in her hips that Jazz likes to watch. He remembers that he is a mortal, a young man filled with desires and aspirations. His eyes dart back to June, and the blonde singer giggles, presumably having watched his exchange with the waitress.

"June, can we go now?" Christina interrupts peevishly, tugging her sister's arm while trying not to attract too much attention. June averts her eyes from Jazz to glare at her exit-watching siblings, both maneuvering into position and standing over their baby sister with huff and puff faces.

"You can go, Christina," June answers rebelliously as her eyes return to Jazz. She turns her hips toward him, places her elbows on the countertop, and leans forward over the service bar, away from her siblings. "I'm going to stay awhile."

"We can't leave you...*here!*" Christina counters while grabbing June's arm, turning her body away from the service bar, and stepping in front of her field of vision. Jazz snickers into his watery glass and June catches him giving her a return diss for her giggles during his encounter with the waitress, but, actually, Jazz can't stop laughing at the back of Christina's denim jacket—a grungy Midwestern faux pas, patched with an embroidered logo of Route 66. She wears a gaudy fur hat, in the middle of a poor bar; the entire family is out of their natural environment, even more so than June. "You're not staying here alone, June! Duke and I will drag you out of here!"

"Let go of me! I'm not a child anymore!" June shouts, pulling her arm away from her sister's grasp and beginning to create a scene. "I'm almost twenty now! I can do whatever I want!"

She spills over her words while glancing back at Jazz and the two unknowing twins communicate with their eyes. Jazz knows her pain, her flaws, and her dreams, and they are all purely and genuinely *beautiful*. She is like him; she fights for her art, enduring the treacherous journey to achieve fantasies that were born long ago. Christina grabs June's left arm again and June struggles to pull free, but her sister holds tightly, two alpha females unwilling to relent.

"Duke, don't just stand there!" Christina growls while turning her head to her brother and eliciting his help. He silently moves behind June and wraps his arm around her right arm and waist, but June wriggles her right arm free and throws a hook into Duke's chin, dislodging two front teeth on impact.

Duke groans and winces while watching his teeth scatter on the floor, but, no words escape his lips as blood fills his mouth. He angrily lifts June off the floor and Christina tugs on her arms, trying desperately to subdue their wild baby sister.

"Let...go...of...me!" June continues to scream as she's held over the service bar and Jazz chuckles at the childishness of it all as he places his whiskey glass on the service bar and watches the drama unfold. A bloodied brother and a protective sister try to snare their wild-hearted sister—white minnows swimming in the colored pond of Scapetown, New Orleans.

Offering these moments of domestic and social escape, Scapetown has often served as an urban oasis from Jim Crow, where anyone who felt jazz in their veins could mingle with the majority Creoles, the subordinate blacks, the migrating Latinos, the last of the Natives, and even a few capitalist and/or kind-hearted whites and Arabs. Being a Sioux native, lost in the modern world of fast cars and faster money, Jazz has always laughed at the idea of the racial landscape in America being confined to *white* and *black*. So many Latinos look like blacks and so many Italians look like Arabs and so many Creoles look like whites; he has never cared much about race after growing up in a poor village amidst oil wealth and seeing all the colored workers serving one rich family. He understood early that race really doesn't matter in the end; money is the god of this world and money only respects itself.

∞

Growing up in Winniper County, Jazz became accustomed to seeing browns and blacks serving whites; the submission implanted in his brain as normal behavior. He believed that colored people were meant to serve. He even dreamed of working for the Winniper family until he went to Mrs. Burk's grade school, the only school in his deprived village. Learning to read alongside the other sharecroppers and servants' kids, Jazz realized he, Charles, and Lucy were somehow different from the other kids, even different from the remaining Sioux natives in other parts of South Dakota. His tribe had been special, but they were no longer living.

∞

He, Lucy, Berthine, and Charles are the only surviving members of the Ghost Dance Sioux, but none of them know what that truly means. They practice Christianity because they have no knowledge of their history or rituals.

∞

Being raised by a Sioux widow on the outskirts of Winniper County, in their makeshift sharecropper village on top of the bones of their ancestors, Jazz, Charles, and Lucy remained indoors so much that they rarely enjoyed the company of anyone outside of their isolated cabin. Berthine ruled their whereabouts like a prison guard, and she claimed that the children should always avoid making any trouble in Winniper County because of the town's violent past. Ignorant of the truth about the Sioux uprising, every year, Winniper County celebrates the defeat/slaughter of the Ghost Dance Sioux and the town holds a parade to commemorate the inauguration of the oil empire that Thomas Winniper, Sr. built on the Sioux's native land.

Jazz was happy to leave South Dakota behind, and after moving to New Orleans, he struggled with his shock as he witnessed whites, blacks, Creoles, and Mexicans playing together in all kinds of jazz, samba, and blues bands. He conceded that his favorite trumpet player wasn't Louis Armstrong, but rather a Dominican gentleman named Lenny Vargas who could samba dance while scaling any of Satchmo's latest improvisations. New Orleans artists like Lenny taught Jazz to look within himself, search his musician's heart, and find where the raw soul functions as a harbinger for improvisations.

∞

To Jazz, the ability to improvise is proof of self-awareness and artistic mastery; and the artistic world validates the product when artists and fans ask the question, *where does he find his inspiration?*

Jazz believes that the same God that blessed him has also blessed Dominican Lenny. The only difference between their approaches to musicianship is that Lenny feels much more comfortable and behaves more enthusiastically while performing in front of people. He never faces an ounce of fear; if anything, Lenny wants the crowd to fear him. During stage performances, he scours over the audience's faces, looking for fellow trumpeters. When he finds an unfortunate competitor, he shouts and dares the trumpeter to join him onstage. He keeps an extra horn waiting among many alternates. His main trumpet, the Tribega, sometimes cracks from extended exhaustion.

∞

While spending a month double-booking and double-headlining throughout the Scapetown music scene, Lenny broke his Tribega horn almost every night, while attempting some reckless dance move along with an even more reckless improvisation riff. It became a staple of his performance; he would blow until the climactic crack and then he would scramble offstage after his set and fix his talisman while traveling to a new club, ready to play the next set.

∞

Jazz has adopted a less formal relationship with his pianos and he plans to continue his bigamist artistry as long as his sister sells his mistresses. Lucy's entrepreneurial success and Jazz's musical prowess only add further symbiosis to their relationship because her highly regarded little brother continues to showcase his talents on the best Lancaster Pianos throughout New Orleans' many music establishments.

Lucy tries her best to keep the money in the family, sending Berthine what little money she can save from her profits. And after watching Dominican Lenny slave over his Tribega, dedicated to its pristine presence and purpose, Jazz knows that he has never felt connected to anything but the music itself. Though he loves his sister, brother, and mother, his life still feels like a dream within a dream, an unreal existence without motives or means. He fills a space in some forgotten place and performs a contrived role to an audience of onlookers and coexisting corpses.

Even though he is closest to Lucy, music is Jazz's only real companion. Their bond is the only relationship that he has cared to nurture and cultivate, but the traditions in marriage prevent them from sharing any nuptials. He imagines an artistic performance, marrying music on an empty stage, and although Jazz does not dare deny his desire for females, he does recognize that his first and only love may inadvertently hinder any chance of having a consistent lover or wife.

His partner would have to love music just as much; his toes tingle at the thought of a cosmic threesome. He wonders if he can be *Jazz Lancaster*, a fearless musician, and *Mister Lancaster*, a loving husband, and *Dad*, a caring protector. The thought makes him smile, but he catches himself while the siblings still fight; no one is noticing his daydreams. He grabs and sips from his second glass of whiskey and briefly imagines himself as a devoted partner and a noble father with musically talented children who would never tussle and wrestle in the middle of a blues bar like June, Christina, and Duke.

"Let go of me!" June wails, grabbing a fistful of Christina's hair.

"Let go of *me!*" Christina cries desperately and several bar patrons surround the tussling family while the two blondes jostle back and forth. Christina stomps over the floor as Duke continues to lift June up and down, in nauseating hurls.

"Ay, you clouds gotsta go!" Teezy bellows from near the stage as he breaks through the surrounding crowd. "Ay! Jimmy, break dem up!"

Teezy points to the bar's busboy, who leans casually with a broom under his chin while watching the skirmish. Jimmy tenses his body, shocked that Teezy noticed him gawking amidst the onlookers. His face looks like he just realized that, indeed, he is still at work, and he is unable to enjoy the show.

"I-I don't know, boss." Jimmy cracks a sly grin while staring at June. "Dey seem to be doin' okay, y'know what I mean!"

The drunken crowd laughs and there's a brief possibility that no one will intervene and stop the melee, but reason trumps the fantasy.

"Dammit Jimmy, if da police catch dese white folks fightin' in hea, dey goin' home and we all goin' to jail! Now break dem up or I'ma break *you* up!" Teezy balls his right fist tightly and cracks the knuckles in his left hand. He raises his head over the crowd and begins pointing at the various lushes and louses. His words have hit a metal truth that echoes around the bar, bouncing off the walls and falling into every brown ear. "And what y'all doin' standin' 'round watchin'? I brings y'all da best talent in dis hea city and dis how ya treat me! Ya can't even protect your own!"

"Hey, get them out of here, Jimmy!" a short, stocky man howls from within the crowd. "I got warrants!"

"Yea, you girls, uh, break it up!" Jimmy orders half-heartedly, moving towards June and Christina, glancing around to see if anyone notices his roaming hands as the two still tussle with fistfuls of hair.

"They all gotta go!" The Creole waitress chimes in, no doubt thinking of the tips she's losing as she helps Jimmy break the siblings apart. She moves past Duke and Jimmy and pulls Christina's waist away from her sister, causing her to release June into Duke's arms.

"Don't touch me! I'm a Winniper!" Christina yells heatedly and the crowd backs away; the name elicits fear even in these dark corners of the country. "Do you know how rich we are? We could buy all of you! I'll have my grandfather sue every one of you! Get away from us!"

"Chill out white girl!" the waitress implores, standing stiff with her palms up. Christina doesn't hold a real gun but the threat behind the name Winniper and her privileged presence in this underprivileged world, well, she must truly have a dangerously protective weapon in order to be so bold. "No one's going to hurt you. You're the one causing a ruckus!"

"Just take your asses back to Mayberry!" someone clowns from within the crowd, presumably a short male seeking some undeserved attention.

"Dey 'aint no Wenapuhs! They look like po' white trash," a gruff voice adds from far away, a corner rat at the pool table or just another drunk face. "If dey Wenapuhs, den I'm a Rockafella!"

"Who said that?" Christina glares madly over the crowd, terrified and outraged, as the patrons laugh and begin to whisper more insults, some not so benign. Jazz's ears perk up after hearing the word *Winniper*, the name makes his skin crawl and he feels a dragon's talon tickle his spine. He prepares to take another long swig of his second glass, but he can tell that the environment has turned, and the high society tourists are no longer welcome. He worries if the tide will turn for June as well, but, as Duke places her feet on the floor, she stands and stares down at the floor, embarrassed and ashamed.

"June, I can't believe you convinced us to come here!" Christina blasts, finally turning her vitriol where most appropriate. "Earl wants me and Duke to come back home! And I don't care if you come anymore!"

She motions to Duke, who clutches his bloodied mouth while sliding his tongue through the space where his two front teeth once belonged. Christina throws her arm around her brother's shoulders and the two siblings head for the door. The colored sea parts for these white refugees and they exit the bar like conquering heroes who accomplished nothing and learned nothing. June stands alone, amidst the surrounding patrons, lost at sea. She turns among the faces and feels the shame that may have been inevitable; she is a white rabbit that travelled down the wrong hole.

Still searching for that always precious absolution, she tilts her head to find Jazz still seated at the bar. Their eyes meet and she begs him to throw her a raft, to help her feel as though she belongs, but he only throws a disgusted smirk, an instinct he couldn't prevent. Her pupils hit the floor again, her head dips in disgrace and the moment is over, though, he hasn't quite absorbed his act of malice. Jazz finds her amusing, but he still doesn't grasp how important she is until she abruptly turns, runs through the crowd, and bursts out the door, following her siblings.

The crowd lets out another resounding laugh, but Jazz fades into an intense longing. The people, the dancers, the waitresses, Jimmy, and even Teezy exist in one world, but, for Jazz, something has just changed in his stratosphere. A piece he never knew was there has suddenly been found and lost in the same glimpse. And in the aftermath, he feels that pang, that stretch of the human soul, his heart skipping, whatever one may call it—he cares, and he knows that he cares. He actually feels for someone other than himself; he actually cares about something other than music, though he wonders if her love for his love has altered the scenario. They share a mutual talent for rhythm and blues. He has seen the same passion, sadness, and longing in her that also exists within himself, but now, she is gone.

Moments like these make life worth living, when decisions determine what the world will become. The powerful prophecy in music is that the search for harmony, cohesion, and beauty drive the spirit to create art—the actualization of those precious dreams into reality. Life mimics the artist's determination; humans play their hearts like violins that strum to the daily tune and change tonality ever so slightly with each passing person in the world's orchestra.

Hope relies mostly on the ignorant who chase dreams in a crazy fantasy while believing life is more than suffering, more than hardship, and more than confusion; but, music makes the dream real. Music makes moments like these possible when a decision can change the very fabric of one's existence. Jazz downs the rest of his whiskey without hesitation, swallowing it all in one voluminous gulp and placing the partially-empty glass next to the other on the countertop—two almost-hollow companions with melting ice within. He digs into his right pocket for some fresh bills, roughly pulls the entire wad from his pants, and plops a five dollar bill onto the table. Lucy encourages tactful spending; she helps him manage his money, but he also doesn't realize the value of money beyond booze and food. He's only focused on his goals and his world begins to move in frames as he formulates the plan: that blonde singer, with a voice from a place that she has probably never been, is a necessity for him to find the next level of his career. Jazz's true aspirations rest in her voice and her skin.

He has specific ideas about his self-image; Jazz doesn't want to be Chuck Berry nor Jelly Roll Morton and he doesn't want an executive stealing his sound to make millions. Exploited musicians and two-timed band managers litter New Orleans with stories of how they lost it all because they trusted the wrong person. How could he risk another person exploiting his art by profiting from it without providing him with just compensation? He demands that his sales are the product of his intellectual suffering, not the contractual agreements of advances and back-end deals.

Lucy believes that he should insist on owning his material, and although Jazz wants to sell his music to the masses, he agrees with his big sister. She has shown him that it's possible to accomplish his goals without compromising his soul. And after Ray Charles signed with ABC-Paramount Records in 1959, every musician believes he can make it to the big time and sign a lucrative contract, but even they know, the hierarchy in Scapetown is clear. Jazz has the most talent, but unbeknownst to some, he has the most fear. Yet and still, he knows, for better or worse, he's given his soul to music because he could never be happy working on a farm in Winniper County.

Yes, June is a necessity.

His feet fumble underneath him and his arms balance his weight against the service bar while he rises and steps to the side, feeling the rush of inebriation. He shoves his stool under the counter and glances around to see if anyone is approaching him. He takes a step toward the door and meets a barrage of handshakes, hellos, and how-ya-doins that keep him farther from the exit than if he had remained in his seat. A feline figure twinkles in the corner of Jazz's eye, and the Creole waitress hustles toward him in a hurried huff, breaking through the huddled masses with her hips swishing right to left like a deadly hazard sign. These New Orleans women always have something enticing for his eyes to feast on.

"You leaving, hun?" she asks cutely, her lips puckered eagerly; she's curious whether he will actually turn her down, again. Jazz feels his eyebrows arch, and he tries to mask his amusement of her ample features, again. She's proving harder to ignore than he first thought, but still, another need occupies his attention.

"No, I'll be right back. I'm just stepping outside for a smoke." Jazz lies, sidestepping and shuffling past her, and then smiling wickedly over his shoulder. He often lies to avoid conflict; it's an amiable agreement with the world to ignore their mutual hypocrisies. The waitress refuses to let him leave so easily; she must have heard he is close to signing a record deal, one of many constant rumors.

"Teezy said you can smoke in the back if you want." She nimbly grabs the left sleeve of his dress shirt, stopping his escape. Her fingertips massage the fabric over his wrist in a way that only a woman can express so much while doing so little. She moves in closer, although Jazz is sure at least a few have heard her advances; she has no shame at this point and their lips pulse merely a whisker apart. "I can take you back there if you want. It's very private."

"I just need some air. We will go, when I get back," Jazz asserts sternly, clenching his jaw and softly placing his hand on her arm and lifting her grip from his sleeve. He looks her deeply in the eyes, to show her that he genuinely cares for her and he does not want to embarrass her. He feels the only way to deal with the desires of a woman is with authoritative compassion. After moving to New Orleans, Jazz has seen many women break the will of their men, especially the female managers. The alpha women hold dominion over their sad clown husbands while happily cuckolding their men's lost masculinity—these imps are dwarves of their bachelor selves.

Though Jazz is not against marriage or relationships, he is against vanity, and it seems to him that many sexual conquests are merely vain attempts at self-validation. It's easy for a shy virtuoso to drown himself in his art without cause for escape; he is a king in his world so why would he ever leave. He chooses to focus on his musical pursuits and delve into the roots of his true nature: enjoying the search for harmony.

"Promise you'll come back for me, baby," the waitress begs pathetically, overlapping Jazz's hand with her own, staring intently into his eyes, and hoping to see some returned affection, some shared attraction. Lucy has warned him constantly that the Scapetown women will become harder to shake the longer he remains locally available. She has begged him to accept a record deal and move to New York or Los Angeles; though he would be far from her, she knows that he is safer where these kinds of women and these kinds of people cannot readily approach him. She already sees her baby brother as a celebrity because he has the potential to become one. If only he could wield that potential with confidence, he wouldn't need to lie to waitresses in the middle of a dank dive bar.

"I promise. I'll be right back and you can have me all to yourself." Jazz lies with his words and his eyes, placing a feigned filter over his pupils to create a loving illusion. The waitress falls for both, mesmerized by what she believes is a melting sincerity. She has broken through the cold artist's heart; she plans to tell the other waitresses to prepare a baby carriage as she releases him softly. He glances around to see several male patrons smile and watch the waitress give him a lasting wink before walking away. Their gawking eyes give Jazz a moment to sneak through the crowd and exit through the front door like a thief who didn't steal anything.

The outside air is humid and filled with the commotion of Scapetown, New Orleans. Jazz smells the evaporated perspiration and musk from the Creole dancers in Sennet Square. Although they perform on Sundays, their sweat lingers through Wednesday evenings in a thick haze that hangs over the outside pavilion like a moldy blanket.

Jazz raises his head over the fedora hats and quaff fronts, searching as far into the distance as possible, aiming his sight for a blonde. She's probably the only clean blonde he's ever seen in Scapetown; of course, there are some white women who frequent the area, but sadly, most are either hookers or addicts. In either case, each is a different version of the same shadowy white girl hiding from daddy, strung out on rock with no role—no place in life to call her own.

But this girl, June, is different from the usual strumpets and everybody else.

∞

From the first time he saw her singing onstage, she stuck out to him, maybe because she looked just as odd singing the blues as he does playing it.

∞

Her voice and appearance separate her from the average to above average talent that Jazz normally sees in Scapetown; she is originally gifted, elegant, yet unrefined, and consequently, she seems both comfortable in her own skin and out-of-place in her environment like a beautiful princess hidden amidst the common folk. Maybe she doesn't know her value and no one has shown her but, he will, if he has the chance. Jazz strains his neck left, right, and then back left, stretching to broaden his search, tilting his head, and squinting his eyelids so that his eyes don't dry in the hot air. She's nowhere in sight.

"Hey." Her voice wafts from behind him. Jazz spins around, and June grins, leaning against the concrete wall. Promotional flyers cover the area next to the bar's entrance. There's a fleeting instant when she looks like the missing piece to a puzzle—crookedly misplaced, ajar from her fit within this New Orleans backdrop. She requires a helpful hand to place her in the correct position.

"Hi." Jazz's voice does that soft filter modulation; he can feel the muscles tense in his throat, clenching the sound and diffusing the bass in his tone. The words barely escape his lips with any force. "What are…uh…*you* still doing here?"

"My sister and brother left me. The next rail back to our hotel doesn't come for another half hour so…I'm waiting…" June replies coyly and checks an invisible watch. Her eyes narrow in the evening sunset and she parts her lips so that a sliver of her tongue peaks through. That killer tease throws a dagger directly at Jazz's heart, but it bounces off his frozen center. Her demeanor has a sharp edge made for this kill, and, so early in their encounter, she has already pierced his surface and left a small, unseen crack where love may drill its way through.

"Um…I can't stand the monorail." Jazz mentions uneasily, as if they don't have more pressing topics to discuss. His words hang in the air from the same nooses that women use to hang many men's advances. He regroups quickly and returns to his stage persona—standoffish and challenging. "You could wait at the rail station. So what are you really doing *here?*"

His implying inquisition, a tactic he often employs when disinclined to admit his interest, but she returns his question with a coy laugh and another smile. Maybe she sees through his technique, or, maybe, he has struck a nerve with her as much as she has secretly intrigued him. Now is the time for justification on both accounts; he leaves for her and she waits for him, but will they admit that these actions were for each other?

For Jazz, implications and tone mean more than the words themselves; *how* one says the words is more important than *what* is actually said. While looking into June's eyes, and seeing her as a beautiful blonde obscenity, grinning shyly amidst the wall signs for Teezy's "Friday Night Firepit", Jazz can't help but return her smile with his own—it's their first genuine moment of joy since birth.

"Well, I *was* going to wait at the station, but I was hoping...you would come outside." Again, June hits Jazz with another toothy chuckle and those funny feelings continue smoldering somewhere deep within his chest. His iceberg heart pulses and skips a beat; he's off rhythm. His angst causes an excess of heat that slowly, slowly, slowly begins to thaw his inner cool.

Jazz catches himself caring, or feeling, or whatever one calls it when one loves without self-concern. He retaliates against the notion, tightens his lips, and says nothing. Again, he glances to the left and then to the right, surveying the streets for prying eyes that watch the white girl and the brown boy in the black neighborhood—Jezebel and the Devil meeting in the darkness. His silence creates an uncomfortable pause between them that forms a bridge to nowhere that breaks before being built—flawed planning and no execution.

"Maybe I *should* wait at the station..." June murmurs with a sigh, lifting her back from the wall and beginning to turn away. Her eyes roam away from his gaze and she studies their surroundings in the middle of the bustling black concrete jungle—heaven to some and hell to others. All the Scapetown musicians struggle to stand out from the black and Creole crowd just enough to make a living without drawing too much attention from the crime syndicates that finance the underground enterprises.

Even outside of Scapetown, most of the New Orleans bars and record labels receive capital and muscle from the purveyors of illegal gambling halls, red light hotel rooms, and dope houses.

∞

Though the suburbs enjoyed a protected and privileged surplus of income and luxury during the 50s, America's cities enjoyed the modernization of national crime syndicates and the profits of sin became as institutional as Congress itself. Jazz surrendered to the depravity long ago. He chose to hold onto his music in hopes of getting away from America as if it were only a larger and equally exclusive Winniper County; yet after a year of performing in Scapetown and seeing the vultures willing to ensnare his soul in a crooked contract, he has realized that he cannot escape alone and unscathed.

∞

He is still not strong enough to leave Winniper County behind; he still can't beat his feelings of being worthless in a world of such power.

"No…uh…*June*, I'm glad you stayed." Jazz tries to relax his muscles and let his voice peek through, but he wonders how much the whiskey has begun to affect his judgement. He can sing in public and ignore an attractive waitress, but this small, thin blonde has completely disturbed his confidence. "I…uh…I'm…Jazz…uh, you know, uh, I was actually looking for you, too."

His honesty evokes a rare purity in his heart and their smiles return quickly, as does the connection; they share a brief understanding until a burly black male, puffing a cigar, passes between them and bumps Jazz roughly. He grumbles under his breath and Jazz quickly realizes that he is in new territory.

His Sioux skin already makes him an oddity, that's a potential commodity in New Orleans, but, with June, he could become a pariah in the Deep South. Alone, he is protected by his talent and his connections, but in 1961, no colored man in America is safe while in the company of a white girl. Jazz understands Teezy balking at the mere disturbance in his bar; angry whites bring more heat than a gunfight. Although New Orleans is a melting pot, it is still unsettled, boiling over amidst the turmoil of segregation.

"Yes, *Jazz*, I do know you. I'm glad you came outside, I don't think Teezy will let me back in." June frowns while shrugging her shoulders and lowering her head apologetically. "I made a fool of myself in there."

"He'll be okay. Give him a few weeks," Jazz reassures her in a comforting tone while stepping closer to June and removing himself from the sidewalk traffic.

"I don't have a few weeks; I finally got my chance!" June pouts, returning to that childish voice from her spat with her siblings; Jazz can tell that she likes getting her way and he laughs to himself. "I need Teezy to let me sing on Friday."

"What do you mean?"

"Big Charles is supposed to see me perform this Friday!" June announces happily, loud enough for several people to hear and stop. "I heard he's going to be there."

"Big Charles gon' be at the Firepit?" A passerby stops in between them, and pushes Jazz to the side. He bumps into other onlookers and the accusing eyes become more blatant. "That's one dangerous Injun. I heard he killed a man up North."

"Yep, I heard he's locked into the recording game, too!" Another passerby adds as she stops in front of June. "If he likes ya music, he'll give you a big recording deal!"

A small crowd begins to form around them, grumbling back and forth and eyeing the couple with curiosity. Some know him and none know her.

"Your brotha got you on dem peckerwoods now, Jazz? Colored girls not good enough, huh?"

"Uh...she's...uh, just a singer...who, uh..." Jazz stammers nervously and steps closer to June, thinking to protect her while whispering, "...maybe we should leave."

"Is there another piano around here?" she asks softly, looking into his eyes and hoping the murmurs around them dissipate. "I want to hear some of your music while I wait for the rail."

"Um, yea...sure," Jazz replies awkwardly as he stares into her curious features; she reminds him so much of *himself*; direct and off-putting, shy and strong, a complicated self. He points down the corner, but his apartment is actually a right and left away, though he is very familiar with the monorail. "My place is over there."

"Your place? Do you have a piano?"

"Yes."

"Oh…great, then you can help me write a song!" June explains thankfully, ignoring the crowd, stepping around Jazz, and strolling merrily through the remnants of their momentary fan club. She is a white tiger prowling confidently through the jungle, undisturbed and unnerved by her surroundings. "I need something new for the Firepit!"

"*Something new?*" Jazz calls from behind, playing catch up as his feet shuffle quickly over the city sidewalk and he reaches out to her right shoulder. "Do you think I just write songs out of nowhere?'

"Yep! You just did!" June smiles over her shoulder, continuing to walk through the crowd and working her way toward the corner. "And we can figure out how to get me back onstage Friday!"

There's a moment where her smile widens enough to reveal all her teeth, big, bright, and wonderfully white. She discovers a joy that she has never known; that angry child is gone, and her smile makes Jazz buzz instantly. He can't help but match her enthusiasm, although he's trying to hide it. When he joins her side, a kinetic connection pulses between them while they glance back and forth at one another, and he feels a sense of oneness like the harmonies in his songs. He hears the perfect composition of sounds sweetly caressing each other, making the movement consonant, peaceful, and predetermined in the even flow of circumstances.

"My place is just over there." Jazz motions across the street and to his right and he waits for her to move in front of him. She instinctually reaches for his arm, but a passerby walks between them and separates them further. They pause while staring at one another fearfully, unwilling to acknowledge any negativity and hoping to ignore the implications of their pairing.

Simultaneously, June and Jazz realize that they exist in mutual isolation from the world around them; the blonde singer and the Sioux pianist finally seeing the answer to each other's worries and only now do they feel the potential thrill of true companionship. Jazz is the first to smirk and June mirrors his affectionate grin; he points to his right and tilts his head calmly.

"Let's go. We'll be able to hear the rail when it comes." He takes the first step and moves across the road, maneuvering through the crowded street as June follows carefully. He can't tell if she's skipping over the cracks in the pavement or merely stepping clumsily behind him.

"Can you slow down?" she pleads desperately with the high-pitch inflection women use to express their discontent. Jazz recognizes her tone immediately like an off-pitch in a choir.

"Sure." Jazz stops at the edge of Bourbon Street and waits for June; he grabs her hand when she joins his side. He's already obedient to her whim, willing to protect her, and he wonders...*why?* Usually, he becomes coldhearted and disconnected when faced with any affection, but June seems equally engaged. She's normally a difficult and stubborn rock, but, with him, she's a delicate rose. Though, in her own way, she still has thorns filled with venom; she's a woman who was wounded when she was too young to understand...*why?*

∞

When Jazz first heard her sing a couple weeks ago, she crooned "Cruel Blues" at *The Voice Restaurant* on 9th street. Unlike tonight, she didn't have her siblings for encouragement. She was all alone in a packed Scapetown bar, singing a cappella until her throat tensed against all odds or reason.

She had stood onstage proudly belting her soul, the only non-colored person in the entire room, wailing, unrelenting, and recklessly free as if no one else mattered. Jazz saw then that June has the confidence that he lacks; but while she howled and yowled in her best Mae Watters bravado, her eyes never locked onto one thing. She squinted and only opened her eyes to gaze around aimlessly; she remained disconnected just like he does while playing the piano. Immediately after hearing her voice, he knew there could be a special sound between them, if only they could collaborate and connect with the crowd. Her voice, his piano: his sixth sense began to dream of a harmony that could be…groundbreaking.

∞

"I saw you play at *The Voice* recently," June comments after apparently reading his thoughts. "Everyone loved you."

She leans slightly into Jazz's right shoulder, and he veers left to turn the corner, squeezing between June and the wall with a subtle grunt.

"The crowd *don't* know me. They could never love me if they did," Jazz responds with a mild chuckle, stretching his neck and glaring ahead toward his apartment building. A few loiters and lowlifes meander around the front stoop, gambling away their change, smoking dope, and flapping their gums about a prior conviction or the latest trivial detail in their criminal lives.

"They *do* love you. You see how they dance to your music. They respond to you. I wish people treated me like that…they treat me like a fish in a bowl." June looks back and forth between him and the apartment building, noticing the concern in Jazz's pensive expression. "What's wrong?"

"Um…uh, nothing," he stammers and turns to her hastily. "Listen, maybe you should go back. These hoods up here are trouble sometimes…and I don't…I don't want anything to happen to you."

His words convey genuine concern, and June remains silent. He dives into her eyes, trying to dig for an idea and devise a plan to get past the riffraff on the front stoop.

"We'll be okay. I...I trust you. I don't know why, but I do." She mutters in slight confusion before her face contorts as though she remembers something her grandfather told her about men. "But don't try anything funny."

"I won't, but...these *gentlemen* might." Jazz explains calmly while nodding his head toward the buffoons perched on the front stoop of a 1930s art deco apartment building. Gothic sculptures adorn the terrace of each stainless steel balcony. Unfortunately, Jazz doesn't enjoy much of a view from his basement unit underneath the New Orleans street traffic.

∞

Jazz found his studio apartment after being expelled from the music reformatory for frequent transgressions against the school's strict code of conduct. Jazz heard from a former classmate that Dr. Frankford threw a small party; his brief mentor gloated and guffawed that the heathen Sioux jazz player could no longer corrupt his student body. Initially, when Jazz arrived at the reformatory, he was more into bebop and hard style than classical or even contemporary jazz. He refused to study Mozart and, instead, he obsessed over Thelonious Monk and Charlie Parker because he knew he wanted to experiment with the experience of sound. He wanted to create a continual consciousness with small pieces of space where people can dance. Back then, Jazz believed that he would enjoy thrilling the crowd, but, after meeting the crowd, he has realized that performance art can be a sadistic relationship.

∞

Now, Jazz feels as though the audience needs to escape more than he needs to perform. They feed off his music and move their hips to forget their daily misery. He has become a bar night cliché; the owners hire him to make the girls dance so that the fellas buy more drinks. Jazz is good for business. He doesn't know how Berthine's Christian upbringing can protect him from the fratricide and hedonism that he sees in the streets, especially the streets near his front stoop.

He nudges June forward and as they walk closer to his apartment building, Jazz sees Jermaine Jermaine, the main instigator who always leads his crew of simple-minded crooks into a foolish prank. Jermaine Jermaine is known for organizing an unsolved crime or two, but his arrest record actually validates the police by listing *their* accomplishments. Jazz doesn't know why Jermaine Jermaine has the same first and last name; he never explains and becomes very rude if questioned about his parents, his family, or his past. Jermaine Jermaine sits along the bottom step, undoubtedly hurting his back against the concrete though he thinks he's too cool to show discomfort. He slowly puffs a Newport 100, his red eyes darting from here to there while chatting through exhales.

Next to him, Nelson Mumps leans against the stoop's steel side-railing; he is the tallest and skinniest bass player in Scapetown. Nelson likes to rhyme his last name during conversation, which is a weird tactic that he has found oddly successful with women. Nelson starts rhyming Mumps with bumps, moving from bumps and jumps to beds and pumps—it works more than it should.

Nelson once told Jazz that his mack is like the pied piper playing a tune—the simpler the rhyme, the more the ladies follow. His words may have influenced Jazz more than Jazz would like to admit because Jazz's lyrics have grown increasingly simplistic. His choruses and verses are easy to repeat but they're not easy to forget because the catchy melody embeds the music into the listener's mind like the rhymes in Nelson's courtship.

On the stoop, Nelson continuously clasps his fist into his palm like a catcher at home plate, squeezing his mitts within one another while rolling his wrists—often a sign of a coming fight. Jazz hopes the goons are planning to find someone specific, already intent on a desired prey. Usually the mutts on the front stoop still desire another altercation *after* a fight; no matter with whom, the wolves remain hungry after the feast.

A local legend named Stubs lounges at the top of the apartment's front steps. Even though a grenade cost him his right arm and leg in the Korean War, he refuses to use a wheelchair. Instead, he hobbles through life with one crutch tucked under his left shoulder. Supposedly, Stubs became desperately suicidal after returning from duty with half his body gone. His alcoholism and crippled misery combined with his post-traumatic stress, but the apartment's landlady took mercy upon the veteran.

A quiet, rarely seen widow, Mrs. Margaret Shanahan hired Stubs as a watchman and gave him free room and board. He resides on the first floor, which is a welcome deterrent; Jazz presumes that if any of the outside vagabonds attempt to rob the apartment building, they'll make a stop at Stubs's apartment first and then make their way upstairs, completely overlooking Jazz's apartment in the basement.

"What do we do?" June whispers softly as they approach the front stoop. She leans in and tilts her head up to Jazz; again, he can't help but feel whatever men must decide when they protect the women they love.

"Just…uh, act like you're sick…" He mumbles from the corner of his mouth, wraps his right arm over her shoulder, and motions for June to lean closer into his body. For a moment, she loses herself in his light brown eyes; she smiles uncontrollably, and then rests her head on his chest. June rolls her eyes and falls further into his upper body and he wraps his other arm around her and holds her carefully. She can hear his heart beating fast. He whispers reassuringly into her hair as they stagger ahead and move close enough to hear the conversation on the front stoop. "Okay…I got you, June. I'll handle the rest."

"Dey ain't never gonna be a better boxer than Suga' Ray!" Jermaine Jermaine proclaims noisily, yelling toward the street, daring anyone to disagree. "I don't care dat-dat-dat-dat white boy beat ol' Suga'! Suga' still da best boxa' dat ever lived!"

"I heard dere's a kid outta Kentucky." Nelson Mumps bellows noisily while extending his lanky arms and shadow boxing with an invisible foe. "I heard he's a contender!"

"You talkin' bout dat boy, Clay?" Stubs asks from atop the stoop. "He won da gold last year! Dat boy can fight!"

"Dat boy ain't *nut-tin*! He ain't ever gon' be champ!" Jermaine Jermaine continues to yell defiantly. "Ain't ever gon' be no better boxa' dan Sugar Ray! End of da story!"

June and Jazz reach the bottom of the steps and Jazz gives her one last look. Her eyes remain glazed and her cheeks puff and twist in a sickly grimace. She groans in exaggeration and Jazz briefly chuckles before tilting his head to survey the three jokers on the front stoop.

"Hey, fellas," Jazz greets them casually and adjusts June's weight in his arms, gripping gently around her hips.

"*Hey,* y'self!" Jermaine Jermaine howls excitedly as he stands from the bottom step to glare over June. "What you got here?"

"Look like a new fan," Nelson Mumps adds with a modest round of hand claps, patting his palms together and chortling in a low, throaty gargle. "You got one for me, Jazz?"

"Uh no, Mumps, she's just…uh…yea, just a fan." Jazz smiles awkwardly, lifting June past Jermaine Jermaine's prying eyes and overhanging jaw. Jazz cradles her as he lifts her frame up the first step. She groans noisily and murmurs indiscernible incantations through her pouting lips.

"Look like you need some help," Jermaine Jermaine proclaims, walking up the steps alongside June, clenching his hands in preparation to touch…

"Don't! I mean, no, thanks. We're fine." Jazz declares defensively, creating a barrier between his hand and Jermaine Jermaine. He also quells his male aggression, fearing that his boldness might agitate a known knife-carrier. His shoulders begin to tire as June's body leans into him, and he wonders if she's enjoying this ruse. She can feel his heart pumping and his muscles tiring, and she knows that he must keep up the act. They have no choice but to fully commit; not doing so could result in an explosive exchange.

"Okay fine, Sittin' Bull! I was just bein' polite! You're lucky I know your brotha'." Jermaine Jermaine responds jokingly and takes a satisfying peek at June's rump. He steps aside and allows them to move up toward Mumps with both men still staring at June's curves. "Don't be shamed to invite me in when she still…*unsatisfied.* You know dem Injuns can't slang it like the brothas!"

He laughs at his joke as Jazz and June continue ignoring the stares and ascending the stairs where Nelson Mumps leans sideways against the rail. Nelson maneuvers his slim body and tilts his head, trying to get a glimpse of June's face.

Her eyes are completely closed with wisps of blonde hair draped over her serene face. Jazz would believe she has fallen asleep if he didn't feel her body pulsing and twisting slightly in his arms—undeniable signs that her previous malcontent was an act. She feels too good to be so reckless, an angel that acts like she can't go back to heaven. Her skin betrays her affection and her attraction to his touch and her heavy breathing reveals the wheels turning in rhythm with his heart. Jazz can feel her blood pumping speedily, her nerves turning inside her stomach. He squeezes even tighter around her waist as he guides her up the steps. Nelson narrows his eyes sharply and lifts up the brim of his hat.

"Hey! I know her!" Nelson Mumps announces assuredly and repeatedly points his right index finger at June. "I seen her before!"

"Impossible. She real," Jermaine Jermaine retorts with a hearty laugh. He hoots and hollers at his joke again, a frequent remedy for his cricket humor; he learned to be his only fan. "You don' know no real girls, just dem girls in dose magazines!"

"I know plenty of females! Ask y'mammy 'bout me!" Nelson Mumps retaliates, a sure-fire spark to ignite more banter, maybe even a distracting, fireworks-like, fist fight, if Jazz is lucky. "It was her idea not to call you Nelson Junior!"

"Hey, fool!" Jermaine Jermaine hops up the steps quickly and reaches into the pockets of his dirty slacks, presumably digging for a knife or some other small weapon. "Don't talk 'bout my Mama!"

"Dat's no way to talk to yo' father, son." Nelson Mumps throws up his hands and leans back calmly against the side rail. "You should learn to respect me, 'specially...when Papa brought you a gift."

Nelson pulls a long joint from between his hat and his ear and hands it to Jermaine Jermaine, a peace offering between addicts and a mutual distraction from life on the stoop. Jermaine Jermaine grabs the joint and stares sternly at Mumps, determining his next action while Jazz continues to trudge up the last two steps with June in his arms.

"Boy, you lucky Jesus saved me yesterday," Jermaine Jermaine muses while placing the joint in his mouth and removing a book of matches from his slacks. "I can only do the Savior's work now!"

"But...we just beat up Davis earlier today." Mumps reminds Jermaine Jermaine.

"And you two robbed Mrs. Mathers," Stubs adds adroitly from above, while simultaneously eyeing June and Jazz. "You still owe me my cut or…"

"Hey, God told me to do all dat!" Jermaine Jermaine strikes a match and ignites the edge of the joint with a deep inhale. Much like when he smokes his Newport cigarettes, he begins to speak during his exhale, blowing thick clouds and coughing throughout his diatribe. "Davis is a thief {cough} like most of dese lowlifes {cough} and *Mrs. Mathers* had it comin'! {cough} Leavin' all those pills in the window, {cough} she know dat's temptation! {cough} The Bible says dat's a sin!"

Any other time, Jazz would defend his Christian values and honor all the life lessons that Berthine has taught him, but, today, he's too busy with un-Christian-like behavior. He has chosen to follow his heart and ignore the words of his mother, his country, and his faith. After reaching the top of the front steps, Jazz stands upright and pauses at the threshold of his apartment building, holding a cumbersome, blonde in the middle of Jim Crow's South. The paradox seems to dawn upon Stubs at the same time, and the half-limbed veteran grumbles threateningly at Jazz while still leaning on his crutch, posted against the wall to the right of the door.

"Hey Stubs," Jazz utters sheepishly. "How you been?"

"Don't want no snow birds in hea, young blood." Stubs growls sternly, repositioning his left shoulder over his crutch and taking more weight off his right side. "Dat's how I been."

"Stubs, I pay rent here. I'll bring whoever I want inside," Jazz counters with an equally intent tone. The only way to deal with these military-minded men is to bring them back to boot camp with direct orders of law. "I signed a lease, you know, a contract?"

"Contract don't say you can break da law!" Stubs answers toughly, bouncing off the wall with his crutch snuggly under his left shoulder. He makes a couple exasperated hops but stops after only traveling a short distance, breathing deeply from just a few moments of movement. His exhaustion and powerlessness infuriate him even more and he glares coldly at Jazz. "We still follow Jim Crow 'round hea!"

Jazz stares back at Stubs, but remains silent and he moves toward the door with June in his arms; her feet stumble along the top step and he catches her swiftly. Her entire weight falls into his grasp, and he feels a quick fantasy, holding her closely, very closely, in a hotel room or on a cloud. They lie together in their future nirvana, ever so briefly, sharing the peace and comfort of their mutual happiness with only the strands of her hair to pass the time. He breaks from his trance long enough to regain their balance, remove his keys from his left pocket, and unlock the front door. He twists the knob before turning his head back to Stubs.

"Call the police if you want," Jazz challenges while clumsily gathering June in his arms, his keys clanging in his left hand, "and when they come, I'll make sure *everyone* knows who turned on the heat."

He fumbles with June and staggers through the doorway as they leave Stubs grumbling, irritated, and defeated. Jermaine Jermaine and Nelson Mumps laugh behind him, appreciating the rare spectacle of Stubs's silence. Believing his role as the building's watchdog, Stubs loves to terrorize the tenants about their comings and goings, using his veteran service and suicidal tendencies as a hybrid excuse-reason for his verbal interrogations. He expects the tenants to pass the gate of his insanity in order to enter their homes, yet, his scrambled consciousness leads to a predictable outcome once his prey applies escapable logic.

∞

The military equipped him to survive the Korean War but left him unable to survive what the war made him become.

∞

Jazz guides June through the first floor hallway until he reaches the basement steps. He looks over her tranquil face; she's still acting sick or unconscious, and, for another flash fantasy, those feelings arise in his fingertips as he holds her frame. Electric sparks scatter throughout his hands, arms, and chest, resting in his head and feet. He begins to tell her that all is clear, but he doesn't want the feeling to end, so he continues to play the game.

"We're almost in the clear, just have to head down these steps," Jazz confides softly, edging June's feet toward the steps leading to his basement apartment. "I've still got you."

"Okay." June replies in a whisper, dipping her head back into his chest and continuing to listen to his heartbeat. He considers the scene's sinister connotations and glances back down the first floor hallway, searching for any prying eyes. Seeing nothing and no one out of the ordinary, he snickers under his breath and continues to guide June down the stairs, stepping before her and caring for her frame so that neither a hair nor a toe ruffles during their descent. Slowly, but surely, slowly but surely, they move down the steps. When they reach the basement floor, Jazz cradles her body lovingly and lifts her so that they stand side-by-side outside his apartment door.

"We're here," Jazz announces with a deep inhale, gasping for breath, but he tries to hide his exasperation. June straightens her body and shakes off her false ruse with a glowing smile.

"That was fun!" June muses cheerfully and shakes her hair back into place, or out-of-place, however it may seem. "Do you think they bought it?"

"Yea, you did great," Jazz comments, rubbing his shoulders. He stretches his arms with his keys in left hand. "Stubs started a little adlib but..."

"*Add what?*" she responds quickly, staring at him with wide eyes like she has seen a squirrel for the first time.

"Never mind..." Jazz scoffs softly, assuming she doesn't know what the word means. He turns toward the door, but then spins back to June. "One more thing, uh, my apartment...it's a mess."

He returns to the door, inserts his key, and tries to push forward, but the door frame only budges slightly. A large obstruction blocks the doorway and Jazz surmises that his piano has slid across the studio, *again*—a consequence of living under a New Orleans street that is so close to the rail station. His apartment turns into a disaster zone when the monorails pass nearby, and even his piano slides around the room. He thrusts his shoulder into the wooden door, nudging the plank inward and establishing a sliver of space for June to scoot through. The piano leans against the heavy slab and Jazz pushes back toughly, gaining more leverage.

"Need some help?" June asks with a smirk while watching him squirm. Only minutes before, he wheezed heavily after helping her down the steps; and now, he struggles to hold the door open long enough for her to move past. She takes her time playfully, slowly sauntering between Jazz and the doorway. "Looks like you're having a tough time."

"Nope...I got it. This happens all the time! I think...the...St. Charles just passed." Jazz pants and pushes the door with his back, continuing to explain through heaves. "Those monorails...shake the...street so much it...moves my...piano...all over the apartment."

∞

When he moved into the building about a year ago, he refused to complain about the surrounding traffic. The fact that Mrs. Shanahan had a piano in the basement apartment made the hidden studio perfect for Jazz. He didn't want to ask Lucy for anymore favors in order to transport a piano to his new home. Truthfully, he was fuming during his first night when the St. Charles monorail rolled by and caused all his newly shelved dishes to shatter on the floor. But over the past few months, the cramped apartment has become his isolated home, a musical oasis away from the crowds and critics.

∞

Jazz continues to push against the door as June slowly slips into the apartment. She turns back and reaches for his hand, squeezing his palm and pulling him through the opening and into his apartment. Inside, the already confined studio is like a war trench recently rocked by a grenade, completely disheveled with no survivors. Whiskey bottles, music sheets and composition books lie on the loose grey carpet among his dirtiest set of dishes; the leftover spaghetti once within the dishes covers the carpet in a slightly moldy mosaic.

His red cushioned couch in the right corner remains virtually unscathed, but his dinner table, a square folding contraption, is upside-down near his kitchen area. Continuing to inspect the routine damage, Jazz looks over his plastered kitchen counter where noodle boxes, cooking pots, rotten tomatoes, used and unused dinner plates, molded beef, frying pans, and old newspapers mingle around the empty sink, refrigerator, and trash can. He takes a moment to absorb the image and its absurdity; his demolished and disordered studio is a true portrayal of his mind.

"Well, uh, welcome to my home!" Jazz welcomes her blushingly while fanning his left arm over the disaster and trying to stave off the butterflies of embarrassment; the critters begin to flutter in his stomach. He's self-conscious, but there is no stage; it's just her and he wants to make a good impression. "Would you like something to drink?"

"No, thank you. Your place smells like whiskey." June replies curtly, raising her nose and smelling the damp, musk in the apartment with a grim frown. Noticing her disapproval, he springs into action and begins to push the piano back into place, moving the massive instrument to the right of the door. Jazz opens a closet next to the piano, places his coat inside, and then turns to June with his hand out.

"It's okay," June murmurs and clenches her jacket. Her tone makes Jazz wary that his home actually misrepresents his character: a dirty apartment for a dirty Sioux from South Dakota; he's heard these remarks before. Self-conscious to the core, he knowingly fears how people perceive his people, his actions, and his home. Lucy often criticizes his attitude, his studio, and his overall life decisions; he still lacks the confidence to believe he is worth more. Now, he refuses to let Lucy visit because she constantly nags him to move closer to her and her husband.

∞

Last year, Lucy married her beau and business partner, Creole trader-exporter, Marcus Cashmen. Since the marriage, she has stopped bothering her brothers so much and left to tend to their vices in Scapetown. The fragments of Berthine's chains finally dissipated as Charles and Jazz battled their New Orleans demons in the form of women, alcohol, drugs, and pride. While Lucy willingly dove headfirst into love and domesticity, Charles established his lowly criminal enterprise and gained a reputation for violent debt-settling. As his older siblings chose their paths, Jazz has remained somewhat stagnant, unwilling to advance his career or his cause beyond his comfort zone; his basement studio has become his sanctuary. His underground piano is free from the expectations of the world, his siblings, or his foster mother, and although he maintains a fairly disemboweled living space that forbids long-term visitors, he welcomes short-term distractions, especially from young women.

∞

"Have a seat while I clean up a bit," Jazz implores gushingly, hurrying around the apartment and grabbing every morsel of spaghetti and sheet music into his hands. "Piano's over there."

"You don't have to clean, really it's fine. It's just that...my father drank a lot...so I noticed the smell." June reassures Jazz by holding out her palm and moving closer to him in the middle of the room, but he still flutters around frantically, hoping that she doesn't leave before he can pick up the mess. He finds his aluminum trash can near the table and tosses two empty Jack Daniels bottles inside before placing the can back in the kitchen. He then retrieves three dirty dinner plates from the kitchen floor and throws them into the sink, hoping they don't shatter while waiting for the crash. There is none—cheap plastic.

"I usually keep it clean!" He lies. "It's just the St. Charles. I...had no idea...when I moved!"

Out of breath, Jazz pauses for a few deep inhales while holding a handful of spaghetti noodles and meatballs in his right hand and a handful of sheet music in his left. Some of the noodles slips through his fingers and fall to the floor, but he seems more concerned with looking over the notes in his left hand.

Each sheet contains scribbles and scrawls of new songs that remain unfinished. He never completes his work on paper; he's paranoid that someone might break-in to his humble abode just to steal his genius. The sheets are more like notepads for his fingers to improve upon during a performance, but still, his forethought and planning cannot ease his anxiety onstage. Jazz always fears that whatever he plays will never be good enough...*for him.* He sees how the crowd dances to his music, but he doesn't believe them; he doesn't trust their judgment any more than he trusts his own. He folds the sheet music around the sinking noodles and meatballs and throws the wad away in the kitchen trash can.

"Wait! What are you doing?" June questions frantically with her eyebrows arching in confusion. She steps closer to the kitchen, planning further protest, holding her hand out, and hoping to save the music. "You're throwing your songs away!"

"No, I'm not. I'll remember what I need. It's like the sounds are trapped in my head." Jazz laughs at her concern while fumbling over more discarded papers and clearing his bed of any unsightly garments. He moves back quickly to June, grabs a foldable seat next to his toppled dinner table, and places the chair at her feet so that she faces the piano. He senses a fight or flight moment, when a pause could doom him to an awkward silence; and still, he only wants to impress her. "We have infinite memory, you know. Humans can see the future and even change it. It's just like when we write a song and change it to make it better. Here, have a seat."

"I stopped writing songs…I haven't played the guitar in a few weeks." June admits sadly as she sits down, staring up to Jazz and wondering if she should filter her honesty. "It's been harder than I thought it'd be. No one likes *my music,* so I just started singing old blues tunes that I learned as a kid. I guess I'm not that creative."

She shrugs in her chair and her posture becomes awkwardly self-conscious. Her toes point inward, her knees touch at the knobs, her chest leans forward in the chair, and her shoulders slump over her waist. Jazz walks toward the edge of the kitchen area, flips the dinner table onto its legs, and continues to arrange his apartment.

"You can always pick up the guitar again. I bet you're very creative." Jazz encourages her out of courtesy, unconcerned with honesty or subjectivity. He has a plan to execute, and his compliment seems to appease her inner need for acceptance. "You have a great voice, though; it's very unique."

"You think so?" She places her elbows on her knees and relaxes her shoulders as he washes his hands in the kitchen.

"Yea, I do. You caught my attention the first time I heard you." Jazz dries his hands speedily on a worn washrag before bounding across the studio and sitting on a leather cushioned piano bench near his weapon of choice. He turns to June and raises his hand, pressing his forefingers against his thumb. "You have the voice of an angel."

"Where is that quote from?"

"What?"

"Is that from a movie or is *that* how you talk?" June looks away and leans back in her chair again, almost dismissively, but she returns to him with a glowering scowl and throws a well-aimed dagger. "All that infinite memory and humans seeing the future stuff, what does it really mean?"

Jazz pauses, shocked by the challenge. *What does it really mean? What does it really mean?* He repeats the question in his mind over and over again; his ego begs him to mount a defense but, he remains vulnerable in the moment. A little white girl questions his common sense, undermining the eternal understandings of his Sioux heritage; no, he can't allow this harlot to breed self-doubt within him.

"Maybe, you should go," Jazz growls, rising from the piano bench and standing above June, "I'm sorry. I don't want to confuse..."

"No...I'm sorry. Sometimes I get...*defensive*. It's just...how I grew up. You saw how I am with my siblings. I'm just...not that good with people." She leans forward quickly and places her hand on his arm; her cream fingertips contrast with his wheat complexion, sliding against his skin like tiny feathers. Her touch is lighter than the air itself and the thought crosses his mind that her fingertips are the softest material ever made: June tips. He freezes under her spell, forgetting his getaway and looking from her fingers to her eyes while both massage his ego. She pouts by poking out her bottom lip, lowering her head, and staring at the floor in doubt and disillusion. Her Midwestern accent twangs the word "*defensive*" and Jazz sits back down on the piano bench while contemplating the familiar feel of her voice. "My sister and brother are going to leave me here, so I don't have much time left before...I might have to go back home. Everyone's always thought that they knew what was best for me. So I don't trust anyone."

"Yea, your sister said your grandfather is Papa Winniper."

"Oh, God, let's *not* talk about him!" June reacts roughly, removing her hand from his arm and leaning back into her chair. Jazz scoots his bench toward the piano, raising his eyebrows and assuring her that he will not stop prodding for an answer.

"No, tell me. It's your accent...it sounds so familiar." Jazz quips sharply and rubs his hand under his chin while staring curiously at June. "Only people from South Dakota talk like that."

"Is that so?" she asks in a dismissive trill and inspects Jazz's face with the same inquisitive look. "What do you know about South Dakota?"

"I grew up *near* the Winnipers, in Winniper County. I even knew one, I think." Jazz admits unsurely, proud and ashamed to have grown up so close to June; he's sad that he could never truly call the town his home. "I lived there 'til I was sixteen. I think your grandmother use to visit my family."

"*Oh...small world*," she murmurs uncaringly, trying to avoid any further discussion on the subject, but another awkward pause falls between them. Jazz refuses to speak and she huffs while crossing her arms. She inhales deeply and prepares for a long explanation. "I lived there for a while, too...but we left when I was fourteen and we've been traveling ever since. We went to Chicago and then we were supposed to come here but we spent some time in California, getting lawyers to secure our trust funds from Papa. We've only been in New Orleans about two months, staying at the Monteleone, but, as you heard, Christina and Duke want to leave. They think the hotel is haunted. My sister says she saw a ghost. One of Duke's friends came to see us about a week ago, Papa wants Duke to come back home, Christina likes his friend, but, I'd kill myself before I ever went back home."

"I feel the same way. Your sister seemed mean, no offense. And why didn't your brother say anything?"

"None taken. My brother hasn't spoken in years and Christina has always been bossy, even when we were young. Between her and my grandfather..." She exhales in desperation while uncrossing her arms; a worried wrinkle forms over her forehead.

"My sister didn't speak for years either. I think we got along better back then," Jazz declares sympathetically, hoping to lighten June's mood, and she darts her eyes toward him with a quick smirk. He feels a need to kindle her joy. "We should just runaway together. Family is overrated."

"Ha, *'overrated'*?" she repeats with a giggle, goading him to explain himself.

"Yep...you and I are a lot alike, you know. We don't get along well with people and we both don't really like our families. *Family is completely overrated.*" Jazz leans toward June, placing his hands between his knees while preparing a convincing argument. "Think about it: some people have parents, some people don't. Kids with parents don't want them, kids without parents don't have to grow up and take care of two people leeching off them 'til they die. Maybe you and I had a messed up childhood so that we could have a better adulthood."

"That's an interesting viewpoint." June pauses while considering his logic, leaning closer and placing her hands between her knees so that she mimics Jazz. "Did you ever meet your parents?"

"No." Jazz responds shortly, afraid the conversation has become too real. "My mother...uh...she's not my real mother...um, I think she adopted us...but we don't really know. I just know she's not my real mother."

"Maybe that's best. My mother died in a car accident and my father went crazy." June explains sadly but an inner truth abandons her usual shyness and forces more honesty to come forth. "My father said I have a brother that I don't even know. He said my family is filled with secrets. I barely remember my Mom before she died...I was only four. I don't remember much except her funeral."

"You're right, we're probably better off," Jazz interrupts with an uncomfortable chuckle. "Our parents were probably psychopaths. They could have been murderers. You never know."

He twirls his right index finger around his right ear and swipes his left index across his neck—a simultaneous pantomime. June returns his antics with a fading grin.

"Knowing me, both my parents were probably insane." June asserts cautiously, almost ashamed at the possibility that her words are true. "They should've been clowns in a circus instead of having me."

"And now, *we're* the clowns. We're both fools for even being here, *together*." Jazz surmises their situation and the stereotypes and stigmas of Jim Crow creep through a crack in the door, bringing them back to reality. The lily-white princess and the colored jazzman were strangers only moments ago and now they sit alone in his basement apartment. "We could get in a lot of trouble...if Stubs or someone else calls the fuzz. What are we doing here, really?"

"I told you, I need some new music for Friday. I can't keep singing old blues songs and no one responds to what I write." June scoots her chair even closer to Jazz and clenches her hands together before peeling them apart, asking for an offering of sorts. "You said that you like my voice, right? You heard something in me and I see something in you, so, maybe we could work together. What was on some of those sheets you threw away?"

"Just some...uh...*business*. Teezy says he wants to record a radio spot for the bar's rib special. I'm supposed to write a *jingle* for him." Jazz sticks his chest out proudly but he quickly deflates as June begins to giggle lightly. She covers her mouth to protect his ego, but her eyes water while she laughs.

"A rib commercial?"

"Hey, I don't like it. Teezy always asks me to write his commercials." Jazz explains, as all sell-outs do, while not revealing that a 15-second commercial pays enough to buy recording time for his personal projects. One hand washes the other, so to speak. "A man has to do what a man…"

"How does the jingle go?" she prods, still chuckling under her breath. "I want to hear it!"

"I'm not going to play it if you're already laughing!" Jazz retorts, twisting back to the piano, instinctually revealing himself as a musician who is always willing to display his art for an attentive ear.

"Oh, hush! You know you want to! So go ahead!" She orders excitedly, clapping her hands happily, smiling brightly, and digging into his ego. He places his fingers on the piano and begins to play his latest attempt at a masterpiece.

"Okay…well…since you asked, *so nicely*. This is the opening and then I transition into the chorus," Jazz continues as if he is leading one of Dr. Frankford's lectures; he imagines himself as the distinguished professor, until June interrupts his pompous musing.

"Uh, I need to hear the lyrics please!" She waves her arms in the air, egging him on. "I want the whole rib experience."

She laughs heartily, and he can tell that she already loves the game they play—his fingers with her voice; it is nirvana for both. They make each other forget where they have been and all the expectations and restraints from the past; they create and share a dual reality that allows them to experience the early stages of their long-awaited dreams.

"Okay…" Jazz concedes with a deep breath, willing to make a fool of himself for her, because…she's a fool herself. He looks over his shoulder and stares into the mirrors inside her eyes; still playing the chorus, he surrenders any fleeting concerns of his ego with one caveat. "You better enjoy this…here we go…"

Teezy's Bar got ribs, soft like a baby's crib.
Barbeque hot, they deliver fast wherever you live.
Ribs in the morning, ribs at night, ribs better after every bite,
Teezy's Bar got ribs, they deliver fast wherever you live!

Jazz finishes climactically, forgiving his uninspired lyrics and ascending to a high cadence that he learned from Dr. Frankford. June claps enthusiastically, but she refuses to hold her laughter and bursts out loudly between breaths.

"*Soft like a baby's crib*...that's genius work!" she bellows boisterously and slaps her knee. "I can't believe...*you* made that! You're so serious onstage but then...you're singing about barbeque!"

"Say what you want..." Jazz points his finger at June, hoping to quell her joking tone. "...every musician has to pay his dues."

"Or *her* dues..." June responds quickly and points her finger back at Jazz; again, they mirror one another as they sit merely a foot apart. "...but you...you have no excuse. I see how the scouts look at you. You could get a deal anytime you want. Why are you wasting your time with rib commercials?"

"It's not about the money. I want...I want...something more." He asserts his soul honestly, shocking himself with the truth that he seldom reveals to anyone. "I want to change how people think. I want to change how we treat each other. I want people to feel something more than their hormones after they hear my songs or dance to my music."

"I'd be happy if they feel anything." June blushes and relaxes back in her chair. She crosses her arms again, a reflex that Jazz associates with her discontent. "I'm just a white girl to them. The coloreds will never see past my skin."

"I could say the same thing, but my name is Jazz, so I have to play their music. You, you could do something else. Why do you sing the blues?" Jazz questions her decisions while turning back to his piano and fluttering his fingers over the keys between blues chords and traditional major tones. "You could make a good career singing country music."

"You mean because I'm white?" June counters angrily and folds her arms even tighter in defiance. She looks away from him and glowers over his cluttered studio. "I don't share much with my mother and grandmother, but they loved the blues, too. It's in my blood. You're just as bad as the rest. All you see is skin color."

"No...I didn't mean..." He stammers as he tries to backpedal from his unintended insult. He's usually so busy feeling persecuted that he never considered that he could also be an offender. "I'm sorry. It's hard to avoid..."

"What do you mean?"

"I mean, you can go freely wherever you like, but me and those blacks at *Teezy's*, we don't spend much time with white people. You stick out and so do I, but…I was raised not to. I only knew one white woman when I was growing up and I haven't seen her in years. These Jim Crow laws force us to be different when we get older…and…I know everyone doesn't fall into…you know, types. I know you're different."

"Well, I'm glad you *know* I am different. I probably have just as much *soul* in me as you do. My mother loved the blues and jazz music." June explains her passion, turning her head and looking back toward him with a sad smile. "She had a New Orleans jazz band play at her funeral and I wanted to come here ever since. That music made me happy during the saddest moment of my life. I knew right then that I'd wind up in New Orleans."

"I'm the same way. Of all the cities in the country, I dreamed of playing music here." Jazz admits with a slight smile, still moving his fingers over the keys at random. He remembers his youthful fantasies of attending Mardi Gras. "Now that I'm here, it's not everything I dreamed it would be."

"*Agreed*. But things could always change." She empathizes and pauses as she contemplates her next words. She leans in and wobbles her head jokingly. "At least, you don't look at me like I've grown a second head."

"If you grow a second head, I'll grab an axe!" Jazz jokes, raising his hands over his head and pantomiming an axe in his grip.

"But what if my second voice can harmonize?" June rubs her throat playfully, massaging her skin with her fingers. "We might have a great circus act!"

"Back to the circus, huh? You're right, though…we could make millions…or at least buy some ribs!"

They laugh together and that sense of play returns between them; both are happy for the first time in a long time, maybe for the first time ever. They each enjoy the company of a stranger while oddly reminding one another of home. Still within the genesis of their first meeting, they find comfort in their exchange and they forget the despair that they experienced during their respective childhoods in Winniper County. June relaxes a little more; her shoulders rest back against her chair and she looks over the untidy apartment, glancing from an old acoustic guitar on the bed to the piano.

"I was so young when I heard that jazz band. I've been singing blues ever since. It's all I've ever wanted to do."

"Uh huh, but your brother and sister don't seem too supportive. How will you convince Teezy to let you back in the bar after that catfight?"

"Worse than that, how can I afford to stay if my siblings leave me here?" June asks discouragingly. She tenses her shoulders and feels a chill of reality trickle down her neck so she arches her eyebrows emphatically. "They handle all our money. I don't think Papa would give me any to stay here alone. He just assumes I'll return with Duke and Christina; but, besides, didn't you say you were going to take care of Teezy for me?"

"Uh…no, I didn't. I don't even think I offered to help," Jazz states matter-of-factly while roaming over the piano keys and teasing June with a display of his technical prowess. "We both need to take a class on how to handle money. Winniper or not, talented or not, if we can't make our own money *and keep it,* then what's the point?"

He looks over his shoulder, nods knowingly, and shrugs as he continues to work his fingers through a playful B-flat melody. Songwriters hold a certain power over vocalists and other musicians. The performers must march to the writer's beat, follow the conductor's lead, sing the lyricist's words, and play the composer's notes. Performing as the creator desires, the muse facilitates the receptive energy between design and implementation.

Jazz uses these chains in the creative process to hold musicians and performers accountable during renditions of his music. In response, many colleagues within the New Orleans music scene view Jazz as a band pariah. Minus Lenny Vargas, the other virtuosos and lesser-talented contemporaries label him a tyrant, destined to struggle as an unrelenting solo artist. Now, he looks at this songstress as a mutual outcast, knowing that he must renounce his old ego in order to find new opportunities.

"Well, then, will you help me, *please?*" she begs tenderly and her eyes fill with diamonds that would make any man submit; Jazz wonders if she learned that look on her own or if another woman taught her how to tilt her head to the side and widen her pupils so that a man may stare into them forever and become transfixed upon a selfless fantasy of pleasing her every need. "I have to get onstage Friday. This may be my last shot."

"Okay, okay...I'll help you, June. Just don't start crying." He surrenders completely and becomes a fool from now until forever, feeling the willpower to do whatever is necessary to see her smile. "I'll talk to Teezy...but you should start recording. It'll take you farther than performing in Scapetown."

"But I barely have money to survive. I can't afford to record." June replies and lowers her head to the floor, admitting a nonexistent flaw, though Jazz can see through her ruse.

"Papa Winniper's granddaughter has no money? What about your trust fund from all those oil profits?" Jazz quips teasingly as he leans one arm against the piano and stares at June. He sees her as a quintessential Winniper County princess, but something or someone transformed her into a fallen angel, who ran away from home after she wasn't allowed to fly. Now, her volatile siblings will probably drag her back to South Dakota. They have indulged their misfit sister while suffering in the underground slums of America; now, they are begging her to return to the comforts of their grandfather's wealth. "I know about your family. We lived near your oil refinery. I bet your family owns half the world by now."

"Maybe, but...I told you, I left home years ago, because...well, it doesn't matter." June stumbles over her words and stares at the carpet as if she plans to escape through the shabby, frayed fabric. "My family...my father...he left us and skipped town...I tried to find him, but..."

"What happened?"

"It doesn't matter. I'm not going back home. I don't care if I starve to death. Christina thinks Papa may let her go to school, but...he never will. He won't let us do anything; it's like we're trapped. I don't know what I'm going to do, but..." June pauses and nervously nibbles her left thumb. "Maybe I'll join a convent."

"You mean become a nun?" Jazz coughs at the thought and his hand accidentally slips on the piano keys. He looks at her with a stern face, unwilling to give her musings any life. "I don't think they let nuns sing the blues."

"All musicians have to pay their dues, right? At least nuns can sing on Sundays." June tilts her head back and rubs her hand over her throat, presumably remembering the raspy feeling of learning to sing the blues. "I just don't know how long I'll have this voice, and I sure don't have my grandfather's money."

"I told you, money isn't everything, though," He reminds her, while pausing his play and leaning toward her. "You have a gift, you should use it."

"I do, you just saw me onstage. I'm doing the best I can!" June waves her hand, dismissing Jazz and his comments. He laughs at her quirky behavior; her mannerisms are South Dakota-born and she continues to remind him of home. "You say I should record, but I don't have the money. And I damn sure don't have the songs!"

"I didn't say it would cost you money." Jazz smiles and scoots closer to June. "We can work something out…"

His words turn the moment cold and June's face twists in that familiar grimace, crinkling her nose and wrinkling her forehead. She leans back, crosses her arms tightly, and looks toward the door.

"What do you mean by *'work something out'*?" She asks timidly, "I've had *those* kinds of offers before."

"Well…" Jazz reads her inflection and realizes the implications of his word choice. "No! Sorry, I didn't mean…*that*!"

He quickly blurts out his apology and throws his hands into the air, almost losing his balance and falling off his piano bench.

"Then, what did you mean?"

"I meant that we can work together, like you mentioned. I want to record with you."

"Hmm…" She pouts and turns her head back toward him, a slight smile stirring in the corner of her mouth. "Keep talking."

"Well, you've heard me play and I've heard you sing. I didn't walk outside the bar for nothing tonight. I want us to record together. I just didn't know how to ask, but, it seems like we're already on the same page."

"So you want to record, *together*?" June repeats his words and her eyes fall to floor again. "I've never recorded before."

"*Never*? Recording is the only way to make any real money!" Jazz stands from his piano seat and wipes his hand over his piano. "One day, musicians will earn more from recordings than performances!"

"That'll never happen! What about the costs?" June asks as she leans back in her chair and glances up to a large crack in the apartment's ceiling. "Maybe you should save your money and fix this ceiling."

"June, just think about it," Jazz begins, ignoring her jests and stepping closer to her with his hands up and palms open. "Where would a brown piano player and a white singer be able to perform together? Where would Jim Crow allow that?"

"Teezy would let us!" she replies confidently. Jazz knows that she's right, but he also knows that she does not see the grander consequence.

"Yea, he would, and he'd be closed down before we finished! And then, what would we do?" Jazz rants, pausing for a moment as he hears the St. Charles whistle in the distance. He begins to wave his arms around as he works himself into a fuss. "If we record, we could ship our music all over the world and people wouldn't even know what race we are. But if we stick to performing, we'll never go anywhere. Do you want to go back home?"

"No! *I told you*, I never want to see Winniper County again."

"Me neither, but we can't perform in these dirty bars, either. Recording is our only chance to do something else...I don't know exactly what, but...we could go far. Do you..."

"I already told you...I trust you. At least, I think I do." June interrupts quickly, and they confirm their union with mirrored smiles as the noisy monorail rattles through the streets above. The St. Charles barrels over the ceiling and the entire apartment shakes in an engineered earthquake. Sometimes, Jazz wonders which came first: the basement apartment or the nearby monorail. From the floor to the ceiling, the underground studio rumbles violently, and the dinner table topples over into the kitchen. The piano begins to scoot through the apartment, moving past Jazz and heading towards June. She panics and reaches for Jazz's left hand as she rises to her feet and he pulls her close.

She wraps her arms around his back as the apartment continues to quake thunderously. The dishes dislodge from the sink, pans drop from the kitchen shelves, and all the kitchen utensils scatter across the counter and floor. After about thirty seconds, the noise and calamity subside as the monorail passes on its way to the rail station near the French Quarter and Sennet Square. The daily disaster has left June and Jazz in the middle of a re-demolished apartment, standing still in each other's arms.

"We're safe," He whispers softly into her hair; they break apart slightly and stare into one another's eyes. "I'm sorry. I tried to tell you…the St. Charles always shakes the place up. You have about five minutes until it leaves the station."

"I'm okay. I was just *surprised*," June whimpers with a low chuckle and Jazz feels her body relax. Her spine eases its tension; her fear evaporates and exposes her honest core. She is comfortable with him, but her mind still holds her back. "Maybe I should get going. I don't want to miss the train."

There's a knock at the door, and June tilts her head, questioning whether Jazz has set her up, but again, they mirror each other. Similar looks of confusion cross their faces.

"Are you expecting anyone?" he asks in a low whisper while hunching closely over her head.

"I just met you, remember? I have to catch that train," June whispers back as another series of knocks wrap at the door. "I bet it's that waitress you were flirting with at *Teezy's*?"

"No! What waitress?"

"Jazz!" a woman yells from the other side of the door. "Open up!"

"*It is* that waitress!" June exclaims in disgust while leaning away from him and pointing an accusing finger between his eyes. "Is she your *girlfriend*?"

"No, I…well…wait, were you watching me?" Jazz wonders out loud as another round of knocks rattle the apartment and he decides that he'd rather address the knocks at the door than the angry bird in his face. "Who is that? Who's there?"

"It's Lucy!" his sister screams from the hallway, "I need help!"

"Oh!" Jazz reacts quickly, releasing June, rearranging his dinner table, throwing papers aside, and quickly piling his dishes and utensils back into the sink. He takes one moment to glance at June and exhale before he moves toward the door. "Just relax, and everything will be just fine."

"What are you talking about? Who is it?" June asks, left idle amidst the still disheveled apartment. Jazz's attempts to clean the studio simply rearranged the chaos into corners and pockets, but the trash and overall sense of clutter still remain. June stands within the melee, hoping to offer help, but she also wonders about the woman's identity. Jazz ignores her questions and continues to walk toward his displaced piano, which once again blocks the door, but June takes a step toward him as he notices her angst. "Jazz, tell me, who is that at the door?"

"It's...my...sister! Her...name...is...Lucy." Jazz explains through grunts while pushing his wayward piano away from the door. He finishes with a long sigh and wildly opens the door, almost swinging the wooden slab off the hinges. His sister Lucy leans against the wall, nine months pregnant and breathing heavily. She heaves her weight upon him and his knees buckle as he takes her into his arms. "Sis, are you okay?"

"No, I...I was on the monorail! My water broke!" Lucy stammers weakly, and her legs crumple under her bulbous belly. "I...I think the babies are coming."

"*What?* Where's your husband?" Jazz asks harshly as he pulls his sister into his apartment and kicks the door closed behind him. June stands in bewilderment, wondering what to do. He sees her confusion and considers a plan of action while struggling to tow Lucy through his unkempt studio. "June, can you clear the couch while I hold her? I'll get you some water, Lucy and you'll be just fine. There's got to be a clean glass in there somewhere."

He motions toward the red couch and June pauses briefly, staring at the mess before springing into action and clearing papers and clothes from his couch in the right corner of his apartment. After paving a space for Jazz to place Lucy on the couch, June rushes into his war-torn kitchen and begins to search the sink, shelves, and counter for a clean glass.

"Marcus went to...to meet Charlie," Lucy wheezes as Jazz gently lays her pregnant frame on his couch's red, cotton cushions, a love seat for his love nest.

∞

Charles helped him carry it down the steps when he moved in; it fit against the wall farthest from the kitchen.

∞

302

For Jazz, the couch has become a great pit stop for female company; he entertains a new damsel before canoodling in the love seat or crashing in his thin, twin-sized bed tucked in the corner. In his cramped studio, he is always steps away from paradise, so he thinks; but, while looking at Lucy's protruding frame as she sweats and smolders over his drab crimson cushions, he realizes that his sister may soon defile his tiny love cabana in a way he can never forget.

Behind him, June turns on the faucet, presumably after finding a clean glass, and Lucy wipes her hand over her soaked forehead, continuing to breathe deeply. Her eyes glance frantically around Jazz's dirty apartment. Even as a silent older sister, she was always mothering him and, even after speaking for over eleven years, Jazz thinks she has never learned how to communicate correctly or choose her words wisely.

"I was on that...that...*damn* monorail...I had to come here. I think the train station was cleaner. This place is still a dump!"

"*Of course, it is, sis!* We had an agreement. You're not supposed to be here at all. What were you thinking when you came here?" Jazz asks in frustration, obviously perturbed by her intrusion. He loves his sister, it's true, but he values his solitude above any relationship. "You need to go to a hospital, Lucy! You and Charles agreed that you wouldn't stop by unannounced anymore! No one's allowed down here!"

"It doesn't look like no one's allowed here," Lucy snaps and folds her arms over her swollen belly as June returns from the kitchen with a clean glass of water and a thin, torn, and faded violet towel.

"Oh...uh, Lucy...uh, this is...uh, June, she's a singer. She was performing at *Teezy's* tonight." Jazz explains while feeling those eyes from outside Teezy's bar, yet, the ocular accusations come from his sister. He steps away from Lucy and makes room for June to hand Lucy the glass of water and the towel. "We're thinking about working on some music...*together.*"

"Oh, she's a singer, huh?" Lucy coos as she grasps the glass and towel from June and scans around the dismantled apartment. She grimaces after feeling a sharp pain pass through her stomach, but she maintains her momentum. "And you two were here *rehearsing*...in this mess, huh?"

"It wasn't like that."

"Sure, Jazz! Half the bar owners have told me stories about you, baby bro'!" Lucy begins to scream as her stomach pulses with contractions. "You've dated and dumped half the waitresses in this town…and you know what Mama said about white girls!"

"Maybe I should leave?" June concedes, taking a step back from both Jazz and Lucy. Her face spoils and the opening to her heart begins to close. She turns away and walks through the apartment, dejected, rejected, and hurt. "I still have to catch the rail home…"

"No, wait! June!" Jazz yells as he runs speedily to stop her exit; he reaches the door before her and places his back against the oak, standing in front of her and forcing a pause between them. He slowly points to Lucy, laying on the couch and panting desperately. "There's no way you're leaving me here…*with her*!"

"Ah!" Lucy screams in pain, and Jazz can't decide whether to tend to June or his sister—ignorant of the irony. He steps beside June, still looking at Lucy and pointing his finger back and forth.

"Listen, Lucy, it's not what you think. June and I just met tonight. She's a damn good singer and…I could probably use her help. And you…you definitely need my help."

"What's your point?" Lucy growls and glares threateningly at Jazz. His once silent sister has become a tyrannical tigress.

∞

As she developed her speech and gained social confidence, Lucy began to demand submission from all the men who remained in her habitat.

∞

She is nobody's fool; in fact, she's a savage when she smells a rat.

"Are you trying to bargain with me? We're family."

"There is no bargain, sis. You can't come in here offending my guest. June is…" Jazz pauses, wanting to call her a friend but knowing better. "We were just talking about music and you barge in ready to explode *and* you're being rude. What are we supposed to do?"

"Can't *you* just take me to the hospital?"

"Lucy, I don't even know how you waddled down here," Jazz explains with his palms pressed together, pleading and hoping that she understands her situation. "It was hard enough for me to get you to the couch, but it would take a forklift to get you back up those steps."

"But...I...I don't know where Marcus is. I...I'm just scared, Jazz." Lucy confesses softly, a betrayal of sorts for the newly crowned queen of the New Orleans music scene. She looks over to June and twists her lips into a worried grin. "I'm sorry if I offended your friend. I wanted to go to the market before Marcus came home and then it happened. I didn't know what to do, so I came here."

"I don't know what to do either, Lucy," Jazz empathizes as he walks toward her, grabs the towel from her hand, and wipes his sister's face. "Why is Marcus meeting with Charles anyway? Charlie's always into some trouble."

"He's our brother, Jazz. Don't you care about him at all?"

"Uh, well, I don't know for sure, but..." Jazz stammers before looking to June as an ample distraction. "Hey, Lucy, guess what? June is from Winniper County."

"*Really?*" Lucy muses sarcastically and smiles too widely; her disinterest is evident. "She looks like it."

"Your brother said the same thing," June adds plainly as she walks closer to Lucy and stands next to Jazz. Although she may seem like an outsider, she's quick to counter in the exchange with her own brand of sarcasm that drowns Lucy's attitude in her privileged and overly embellished South Dakota twang. "I was born in Winniper County and raised there 'til I was fourteen."

"I'm surprised we never met." Lucy jests and a sliver of her initial disdain seeps into her tone until she screams from the pain. She hands the glass of water back to June as the tattered towel falls on her shoulder. "Oh Marcus, where are you? Jazz, please help me!"

"Calm down, sis." Jazz places his hands above his sister's belly, hovering over her as she writhes on his couch. He tries to reassure himself while calming her, hoping to erase his fear through positive projection. "Maybe it's just a false alarm, Lucy. I bet this will pass, just relax."

"Jazz..." Lucy begins and struggles to speak through pants and contractions. "...I'm...having twins."

"I know…I got the letter. I just didn't think you'd be having them here. We agreed that no one would come here." Jazz speaks hardheartedly, but he gently takes his sister's hand. He understands how cold his words must sound, not only to her, but also to June, and he employs a little acting, though the moment provides him with all the motivation he needs for candor. "I'm sorry I've been so distant. I'm just trying to work through some things, but…we're going to get through this."

More booming knocks pound against the door and Jazz stares at Lucy and June. He's filled with a sense of fear, frustration, and relief. Too many people have already infiltrated his creative lair, but he's proven that he is totally outmatched by each. He needs help with more than Lucy's pregnancy because he still has so much to discuss with June.

"Jazz!" A man screams from outside. "Are you in there?"

"It's Marcus! Open the door, quick!" Lucy cheers happily and props her body up on her elbows, wiping her face and primping herself as best she can. "He found me!"

"Oh, thank God!" Jazz screams and moves swiftly toward the door, tiptoeing over fallen papers and stepping around his piano bench. He looks back at June, who stands in the middle of the apartment, oddly out-of-place where she once seemed so comfortable. When he reaches the door, he quickly opens it and sees his brother Charles and his brother-in-law Marcus. Both men stand sullenly, covered in oil, breathless and hunching against the door hinges. Once Marcus lays eyes upon his wife, he rushes by Jazz without a word of consideration.

"Lucy! I'm so sorry, honey!" Marcus shouts and maneuvers through Jazz's messy studio like a running back eluding practice obstacles. He tracks oil through the apartment and leaves a trail along the carpet. "Your mother called and said you were in trouble."

"What happened to you? Is that oil?" Lucy asks in repulsion, staring at her oil-drenched husband and folding her arms over her belly again in a contrived, yet consistent huff. She looks at her husband dripping from head-to-toe in black gold and she smells the stench in the air. "*It is oil.* Jazz, we know that smell from that damn village. Marcus, what's going on?"

"Uh...yes, dear, it is oil, but..." Marcus hesitates and turns back to Charles, who still stands at the door, sizing up Jazz. Marcus senses the coming exchange and chooses a sacrifice. "Your brother...it's all his fault, he really did it this time, Lucy."

"Hey, it was business...these oil mongers are teaming up with the mobsters. They think they can come down to Scapetown and play tough. I had to teach those Rizattos a lesson!" Charles explains, pushing past Jazz with similar inconsideration, though he is careful not to touch his baby brother while entering the apartment as if he is the lord of the manor. Like Marcus, Charles drips oil during his steps and leaves a trail through the already messy room. "Jazz, is *this* why we're payin' your rent? This place is a pigsty."

"The St. Charles came by...and I thought we had an *agreement* that no one would come here. You said I could have this space for myself." Jazz explains tersely, closing the door behind his brother and glancing toward June, still conscious of his personal goals and he wonders how she perceives his new guests. "And you don't pay my rent anymore, remember?"

"Uh huh...well, it's about time you became a man. What are you now? Not even twenty, right?" Charles sidesteps Jazz's piano bench and begins to ogle June curiously. He looks back over his shoulder at Jazz and grins devilishly, jumping to Lucy's earlier conclusion. "And where did you find Lana Turner, here? Mama's gon' love meetin' her."

"Um...this is June, she's a singer." Jazz informs his brother and passes between Charles and June, dreading the coming introduction and fearing the consequences. Charles and Jazz have always competed for everything, and Jazz worries that Charles will view June as just another guitar. "June, this is my brother, Charlie."

"*Big* Charles...Big Charles Lancaster." Charles corrects his brother sharply and steps closer to June with a smile and an outstretched, oily hand. "Everybody who's anybody in this town call me Big Charles or Big Charlie; it's nice of you to meet me, darling. I'm sure you've heard of me."

"Yes...um...likewise. I have heard of you." June repeats and her eyes grow wide again. She shakes his hand gently without caring about the oil. Jazz becomes jealous in an instant, seeing her react with the same excitement as when she mentioned his brother earlier. "I heard that you have helped some musicians make it in New Orleans."

"Well, I do have certain connections…but, to get my talent you have to have talent, baby." Charles presents himself confidently, and he releases her hand to raise his oily arms in the air, spraying oil droplets around the apartment. "I am a big deal in this town, darling. And I could change your life."

"Well, that's what I'm hoping for, sir. I heard you'll be at *Teezy's* on Friday. I'm supposed to sing." June beams excitedly and turns to Jazz, but he sees her as an imposter who has betrayed his loyalty. She suddenly views him with the same mistrust and her eyes narrow with curiosity. "Why didn't you tell me Big Charles is your brother?"

"Because we don't need…"

"Jean, baby bro has always been jealous! I'm the big brother, the alpha male. Me and Lucy have the juice in this town and…he's a head case!" Charles booms loudly over the room while sauntering around the piano, pressing an off key here and there, and leaving a smudge of oil with each press. He turns his head and leers over June's frame, gazing from head-to-toes before looking to Jazz with a wicked smile. "He couldn't help you even if he tried, but me, well, I don't see why we should wait until Friday. I may not even show up to *Teezy's*; I have a lot of numbers to tend to. You can audition now, though. You do seem to have some…*talent*."

"Excuse me! I'm going into labor!" Lucy interrupts angrily with Marcus crouched by her side. She's often allowed Charles and Jazz to go back and forth with their macho games, but, in the throes of labor, she has very little patience. "I'm giving birth…to twins…right now! I'd appreciate a little more attention, please!"

"Come on, sis, just hold on. It'll only take a minute." Charles pleads as he casually raises his palms, hoping to convince Lucy to let her little brothers play a little while longer. "She can start singin' right now, I can offer some uh…uh…*performance tips*, and you can have those babies later."

"No! Absolutely not!"

"But what if she can really blow? She's got the hips for it."

"Charlie, I don't care if she's the white Ella Fitzgerald!" Lucy bellows heatedly, balling her fists and stretching her neck. The tigress begins to emerge in her eyes and both Jazz and Charles know that her wrath is near. When a woman finds her voice, no matter the time in life, she unleashes a torrent of pent-up frustration that breaks through any constructed dam within her. The truth, as she sees it, has no choice but to break down her barriers and run free from her mouth. "My babies are not coming into this world with you two idiots sleazing over some white girl!"

"Calm down, honey," Marcus whispers softly and wipes his hand over his wife's forehead. He looks back at June apologetically; always a pacifier, he tries to neutralize his wife's rant. "She's just excited. We're having twins."

"You're not doing anything! I'm the one in pain! Get me to a hospital, Marcus!" Lucy howls nervously, holding her stomach and tensing all the muscles in her face. "I have to get these kids out of me!"

"Stay strong, Lucy. Your mother told us to meet here. I'm so sorry, we have to wait." Marcus apologizes and turns his head. "Jazz, do you have some water?"

"Yes, we already..." Jazz begins to answer while he glances around the apartment. "Wait, what'd you say about Mama?"

"I have it," June interrupts, walking toward Marcus with the glass of water in her non-oily hand after using the other to make acquaintances with Charles. Marcus ignores Jazz's question and stares at June while she moves closer. He quietly takes the glass from her, mindful of his wife who observes the exchange, paying extra attention to their hands.

"Thank you, uh, June," Marcus mumbles before turning back to Lucy and kneeling by her side. He takes the violet towel from her shoulder and pats her forehead. "Lucy, I need you and those twins to make it through this. Okay?"

"I'm...I'm scared, Marcus. Please, take me...to the hospital." Lucy stammers tiredly, though her tone does little to reassure anyone in the room. Looking from Jazz, to June, to Charles, and then to Marcus, she rests her eyes on her husband's gentle face, searching for comfort. "My water broke...on the train...and I was in the back...I don't think anyone saw...but it was embarrassing, you know."

"Don't think about it, sweetheart...just...just take your time," Marcus whispers in his wife's ear and kisses her forehead twice, once for each child. "We'll all be here with you, and we'll just take it easy until your mother gets here and-"

"Wait, Mama's in town?" Jazz interrupts, stepping closer to Marcus and Lucy, but they don't acknowledge his question. "She's definitely not allowed down here! Y'all have to go!"

"Guess we'll do that audition another time," Charles chirps over June's shoulder, still leering over her body. He continues to walk around her like a leopard stalking his prey. "Your name is June, huh? That's a pretty name."

"Charles! Leave that girl alone!" Lucy roars from the couch, but she secretly enjoys her brother's antics. At the very least, Charles's pre-occupation provides another distraction from the pain; he is another target for her venom and anger. "New Orleans has turned you into an animal."

"I'm sorry, sis, I can't help it. I'm just being *friendly*," Charles apologizes half-heartedly and strolls closer to the couch so that he stands next to Jazz while Marcus kneels over Lucy, carefully wiping her cheeks and forehead. Charles nudges Jazz with his left elbow and raises his eyebrows. "Ladies love the Injun blood right? I find the black birds really dig it but some of the snow birds in Scapetown will do..."

"Dammit, Charlie, I'm giving birth! Can't you shut up for once? Does it always have to be about you and Jazz? You two ignored me enough when we were kids!" Lucy blasts, clenching her fists at her sides. This is the dragon that her birthday wish released. She stares back and forth between her brothers, breathing fire and seeing the same two selfish siblings from Berthine's cabin. After more than eleven years since that fateful day, her brothers still haven't changed. "You two drove me and Mama crazy in that cabin and I couldn't say anything about it for years. You two fought and yelled about anything and everything and still, I couldn't say anything until the day I made that wish. And even after I could speak, you two still don't listen to me! You use me and rely on me more than I have ever relied on you! Charlie, Jazz, if there's ever a time when you two should worry about me, focus on me, and help me, then it's now! Can you at least give me that?"

"Sure Lucy, fine. Geez, there's no need to rant." Charles relents quickly, throwing up his hands without much resistance. Again, he nudges Jazz with his elbow, pushing his baby brother off balance. "She was so much nicer before she could talk. Remember those days?"

There are three slow, deliberate knocks at the door and the group remains silent. Jazz stands still amidst the nonsense, unsure if he can handle much more family time. He takes a moment to stare at June, remembering their connection before all the intrusions. He sees their bond as an oasis that he's trying to recreate as soon as possible.

"Get the door, Jazz," Marcus commands roughly, inspired by his wife's fury, while taking her hands and unclenching her fists. He places their palms together and smiles reassuringly. "That's probably your mother, dear. Everything's going to be alright."

"I told you, we had an agreement. None of you are supposed to be here except June!" Jazz asserts without averting his eyes from the door, sensing the monster that lurks on the other side. Three more ominous knocks pound against the door. "I'm not letting her in!"

"Hello?" a woman calls from outside the door.

"It's Mama!" Lucy recognizes Berthine's voice and her eyes widen hopefully while both Charles and Jazz recoil in fear. "Hurry! Open the door for her, Jazz!"

"Wait, I'm with baby bro on this one." Charles announces, looking to Jazz and the brothers nod together, instinctually reverting back to insolent toddlers, temporarily banding together against a mutual foe.

"What is she doin' down here?" Jazz whispers angrily while creeping closer to Lucy and Marcus. "I moved here to get away from her!"

"She's been staying with us for a few weeks," Lucy explains between heavy breaths. "My contractions...they've been getting worse."

"That doesn't answer the question," Jazz continues to whisper, looking to June and smiling before turning back and crouching over Marcus and Lucy. "What is Mama doin' down *here*?"

"Why don't you open the door and find out?" Berthine calls from outside the hallway. Jazz imagines her stern Sioux expression, a seventy-year-old Sioux woman with no bend and no budge. "That apartment must be really little. I can hear everything you're saying!"

"Get the door, Charles," Jazz orders, backing away toward Marcus and Lucy while pointing his big brother toward the door. "You're closer."

"No, little bro, you pay the rent now, remember?" Charles banters as he walks toward Jazz, leaving June in the middle of the apartment. She stands closest to the door but she stands alone, mostly unnoticed. Charles looks at his brother and raises his hands in the air. "Get your girlfriend to open the door."

"*Someone* better open this door before I break it down! God made me from strong clay!" Berthine barks in her overbearing tone and both Jazz and Charles cringe, reverting back to their childhood. "You boys are not too old for a whooping!"

"Relax, Mama. I'll get the door!" Jazz calls obediently, rushing through the apartment, shrugging again as he passes June and opens the door with a false smile. As expected, Berthine stands with her hands on her hips, wearing a flower hat, an old maid's shall, and wool overcoat which is incredibly out-of-season during the New Orleans springtime. Nothing about her resembles her Sioux heritage except her beaded moccasins patterned in the colors of the old Sioux village—green for the earth, yellow for the sun, red for the fire, and black for the night. She tugs a bulging, brown leather purse over her left shoulder and smiles cheerfully at the sight of her adopted son.

"My baby boy…" she beams before slapping him on the cheek and chuckling as he absorbs the blow. She coos softly and keeps her hand on his face, rubbing the pain away. "Don't ever make your mother wait like that!"

"Sorry, Mama," Jazz apologizes wincingly and moves aside as Berthine strolls into his jumbled apartment.

"Lawd, have mercy! My child became a pig!" Berthine clutches her purse while wrinkling her nose in disgust and, for a moment, her face reminds him of June's grimace, but the notion quickly fades. She ignores the blonde in the middle of the room and, instead, notices Lucy wheezing on the couch with Marcus by her side. Berthine turns up her nose, passes June with only a dismissive glance over her shoulder, and quickly moves toward the couch. "Oh Lucy, you're practically ready to bust!"

"Hi Mama!" Charles interrupts from Berthine's right, and she glares at him contritely before turning back to Lucy. Charles puffs his cheeks in frustration and takes a threatening step toward Berthine. "Well, ain't you gon' say hello to me, too! I am your oldest son!"

"*My son* would not behave like you! And why are you covered in oil? You got Lucy's husband involved in your mess. They fixin' to be parents!" Berthine chastises him harshly, almost pushing Marcus aside to aim her disappointment at Charles. "You moved down here and became a criminal! You disgrace us, son. No good Christian would do…"

"*Good Christian?* Listen to you, Mama. There's no such thing! You're not even good." Charles responds tersely, walking away from the couch and almost stumbling over the piano bench. He catches his balance and leans against the chair near June. "We didn't ask questions when we were young but we're adults now. We don't have to respect you! We know you're not really…"

"Charles, don't!" Lucy calls out to her brother and raises her arms to beckon him closer, but he backs away, moving closer to June in the middle of the room. Jazz closes the door amidst the drama, happily excluded, and he plots a sensible exit. He figures that if his family won't leave his apartment, then maybe he and June could leave them here, but where could they go without Jim Crow?

"Sorry, sis." Charles continues to move past June while staring at Berthine in contempt. Jazz steps in front of his brother and looks back and forth between Charles, their adoptive mother, and June, who quietly watches the family reunion. As Charles reaches Jazz at the door, he stares at his brother with a sullen skulk over his oil-covered face. Charles turns toward the room and waves his sleeves so that the slick liquid drips over the carpet just at June's feet. "I would stay, but there's one too many chefs in the kitchen."

"Charles, wait, don't leave Lucy like this!" Jazz speaks up in a rare moment of confidence around his family. He steps toward Charles and stands close enough to whisper, though, he knows the others still hear him and they listen intently. "Seriously, don't' leave me here with her. I know we've grown apart, but we've always looked out for each other. Mama's half crazy."

"I'm sorry, lil' bro," Charles replies coldly as he turns and opens the door with a slippery hand. "Don't count on me anymore. I'm the bad guy now."

"Charles, come back!" Lucy calls after her brother and again reaches her arms out, holding her hands in the air in hopes that Charles will return.

"Let him go, darling," Berthine advises as she gently grabs Lucy's hands. "It's best for your children if…"

"Yes, Lucy, Mama knows best! Mama knows the secrets! Mama knows why we had to stay in that cabin all the time!" Charles yells from the doorway and slaps the apartment wall loudly. "Jazz, Lucy, you two can keep listening to this old bat if you want, but I'm done!"

He pounds the wall one last time, slams the door behind him thunderously, and stomps noisily up the steps. Another pause falls over the room, a common sound during all Lancaster family gatherings. Berthine scans over the group and rests her eyes upon June, planning to expel all unnecessary parts.

"And who might you be, blondie?"

"Um, Mama, this is June," Jazz answers with a quick introduction while stepping between his adoptive mother and June. Briefly, he notices a fleeting look of recognition that runs across Berthine's face, but she quickly changes her expression and resumes her accusatory glare. She then rolls her eyes and prepares to throw a skeptical dagger toward June. Jazz holds out his right hand like a shield, trying to ward off her plan of attack. "She's a singer, Ma'. We were just rehearsing when Lucy came here."

"Uh huh, *just rehearsing*…*here*? Seems like my Sioux son really knows how to pick 'em." Berthine practically repeats Lucy's earlier complaints while glancing around the shambled apartment until her eyes once again rest upon June. "Is this how respectable young women *'rehearse'* nowadays?"

"I'm a good girl, ma'am," June defends herself, and Jazz can see her shoulders tense nervously, instinctually becoming protective as she braces for a fight. "I assure you that nothing inappropriate happened."

"And your parents don't mind you breaking the law, visiting colored boys at night?"

"Both my parents are dead, ma'am." June sulks on cue, trained to spill her sorrow in order to elicit pity and empathy. "And I try not to see race."

"Hmm, *you try?* Well, I guess that's a start, right?" Berthine laughs and pats Lucy's wrist. "But my daughter is due to give birth any minute. I believe it's time for you to leave, uh…what you say your name was? I'm getting old…*Daisy*."

"It's June," June corrects her softly, but she understands Berthine's dismissive tone. June obeys sadly and lowers her head. She looks up to Jazz for help as she turns toward the door and begins to walk away from the family.

"Hey, wait, June! You can't leave now. There won't be another train headin' uptown for at least an hour." Jazz holds out his hand and steps between June and the door; they've done this dance before. He looks past her shoulder toward the couch where Marcus and Berthine whisper to Lucy. "Mama, it's not safe for her to be outside this late. And…and you can't kick people out of my apartment!"

"Excuse you, son. I would have never talked to my mother that way! A good Sioux woman, she was, and so am I! Good mothers don't deserve that tone!" Berthine derides him while shaking her head from side-to-side and wagging her finger. "And I'm sorry that I'm more concerned for your sister! You have no idea what's about to happen here! Daisy needs to go and don't question me, boy!"

"Ma, I'm not…but you don't have to be so rude. She told you her name is June." Jazz paces back and forth between June and Berthine, pleading his case like an attorney at trial. He is still unwilling to relent, knowing that he may never catch up with June again. He envisions her leaving his apartment and leaving town shortly after while he's stuck fending off his family's accusations. "Ma', she's not goin' outside this late by herself. So if she goes, I'm going with her. And before Marcus and Charlie got here, she was helping me with Lucy. And…and…Lucy actually wanted her to stay!"

"What?" Lucy interrupts dazedly from the couch, still holding Berthine's hands and regretting the man that she has allowed Charles to become. They are all so distance when they were once so close. "I didn't…"

"Yes, *you did*, Lucy, remember?" Jazz growls at his sister, but he immediately stops when he sees Marcus glaring at him intently, taking Lucy's hands from Berthine and asserting himself into the fray. Jazz backs away and stares at his sister and brother-in-law. "Lucy said she wanted June to stay and you're all in *my apartment*, and I want June to stay, too…at least until the next train comes."

"Um…maybe it's best…" June pauses, unknowing what to say before looking to Lucy who remains frightened from the pain and distraught over Charles. Her mother's ghost flashes before June's eyes while she looks at Lucy in labor. Teresa wears a sky blue sundress and stares over Lucy with grave concern before looking at June with a nervous grin. The ghost quickly vanishes and June freezes, though no one notices her shock. Her demeanor changes and she can't help but feel a connection to Lucy; she imagines a duty to see the labor through. "I'll stay if Lucy wants me to. And…um, I'm sorry Charles left."

"Uh…thank you…pay Charlie no mind. It's…it's fine with me if you stay." Lucy utters her consent while looking at her near empty glass of water. "Jazz seems to like you, so…I like you, too, for now. And I may need some water soon."

"Lucy," Jazz fusses tiredly, exhausted as he continues to extinguish his family's ire toward June. "Be nice…or…at least, be nicer than Mama if you can manage."

"I was just kidding. I'm sorry, June. Charlie just gets me so mad…I really hate him sometimes."

"Lucy, don't say that." Marcus whispers to his wife as she winces from contractions. He then looks over his shoulder to June, again playing the peacemaker. "I promise…she's not usually like this. She's a really sweet person. It's just the twins, she's really…uh, *stressed.*"

"It's okay, I understand." June forgives and walks toward the couch. "I just want to help, if I can."

"See that, Ma!" Jazz jibes while arching his eyebrows and tilting his head toward June. "She's helpful."

"Uh huh," Berthine grumbles, rolling her neck and pointing toward the kitchen. "Just find some clean towels in this mess and keep your eyes off Daisy."

"June. Her name is June, Ma."

"Well, at least you know that much about her." Berthine waves her hand dismissively and turns back to Lucy. "Child, I don't know how you survived down here with your brothers. They two of the most inconsiderate…"

"You raised us…" Jazz utters under his breath while walking away to retrieve towels.

"Say what?" Berthine snarls sharply, daring Jazz to admit his insolence.

"Nothing," Jazz mutters and grabs a handful of towels from a drawer in the kitchen. June joins him and looks for another clean glass; they share another moment, together, vibing amidst the banter. He looks past her shoulder toward the couch and Berthine stares back at him impatiently. "I found some towels, Ma."

"Good, now bring them here!" Berthine instructs, positioning herself at the edge of the couch. Jazz walks toward her and hands her the towels; she roughly places them beneath Lucy's thighs and over her cocked knees. "We need to make a landing spot."

"Wait," Jazz interrupts, "you're not going to…not on my couch! I mean, what about the hospital?"

"We can't go to the hospital, Jazz!" Berthine bats the idea away with her hand. "These New Orleans hospitals are filthy!"

"Lucy needs to be comfortable, Jazz." Marcus adds calmly, caressing Lucy's hands and wiping her face. "We didn't plan on being in your apartment, but…I guess it's meant to be this way."

"But what about my couch?" Jazz asks and stares over his cuddle couch. "It's…kind of special to me."

"You didn't even buy it," Lucy counters angrily and groans through the pangs of labor. "Charles paid for it!"

"Well, you don't have to broadcast that, Lucy," Jazz whispers quietly while June returns to his side with a glass of water. He raises his head and steps away from the couch. "It's fine, whatever you need, sis. We're here to help."

"That's a better tone, baby brother. And thank you, June," Lucy remarks sarcastically as Marcus takes the glass of water from June. He places the glass over his wife's forehead and she exhales slowly. "Whew, I feel so warm."

"Do you want some ice from the fridge?" June asks, still standing next to Lucy and Marcus. "On hot days, I cover myself in ice cubes."

"*Lil' hussy*," Berthine murmurs under her breath. "White women are so *perverse.*"

"Ma!" Jazz gripes and glances between June and Berthine. "Don't be rude!"

"Well, it's true! We are good Christians, children of God, descendants from the Ghost Dance tribe from South Dakota!" Berthine complains in a huff, ruffling the towels underneath Lucy and jostling back and forth on the couch. "We don't want to hear about Daisy *covering* herself in *ice cubes*…that's not appropriate, Daisy!"

"I'm sorry, ma'am."

"*Ma*, her name is June." Jazz continues to play peacemaker, trying to calm Berthine enough to appease her motherly smothering. "I know you're doing that on purpose."

"Doing what? You know I'm old son; just turned seventy, I reckon, but I'm not sure. I have a hard time remembering my own name." Berthine grins knowingly; she enjoys playing the senile, old maid, oblivious to her insufficient charms. "I'm sorry for telling the truth! I raised you better than to be around anyone talkin' like that."

"I said I'm sorry, ma'am," June apologizes and lowers her head to the floor again; it's an involuntary concession that Jazz has begun to notice. He reads her sad eyes and surmises that she has trained herself to never risk crying again. She has his scars. Her lower lip quivers as she retreats to a safe haven deep within her psyche and summons the confidence to defend herself once more. "I was just trying to be helpful."

"Well, I think you've done enough. I still think you should leave. I'm sure the streets are perfectly safe." Berthine chastises June before looking to Jazz, who glares back at his mother, begging her to find common ground and hoping that she will stop embarrassing him. "But…since my son and daughter want you here…I…uh…uh…I guess…uh, you…it was nice…"

"I think she's trying to thank you," Jazz interprets, looking curiously at his infrequently flummoxed mother. Though she plays senile, he's never actually seen her so rattled. He can only remember his Sioux family being around one other white woman and Olivia is far removed from *his* life. Lucy suddenly screams and the family's attention turns to the couch.

"They're coming!" Lucy's face stretches, pain stricken, and Marcus hovers close to her.

"You can do this, baby," Marcus cheers softly as he holds her hands and squeezes her palms. "Just push."

"Wait! Don't push yet!" Berthine holds out her hand before reaching under the towels and inspecting between her daughter's legs. Jazz steps away from the couch so that he stands next to June near the kitchen, close enough to see the action, but far enough to miss the blood. Both musicians watch as Berthine checks under the hood. "We have to take our time, okay?"

"What? Why…not?" Lucy questions while wheezing in exasperation. "Mama, I can feel them! They want out now!"

"Sure they do!" Berthine agrees with a chuckle. "But you've got two on the way. Let them take their time! These babies need to come out just right!"

"Mama, please! I'm ready to push! I want them out now!"

"Just breathe, child," Berthine coaches gently in a calm, maternal tenor that makes the anxiety seem less intense. "Marcus, give her some water, dear."

"Huh? Oh, yes ma'am…uh…here you go, Lucy." Marcus replies with confusion; he's shocked that Berthine has included him in her instructions. He leans toward Lucy and places the glass of water to her lips; she sips slowly and when she's done, he wipes her mouth tenderly and grips her left hand, pressing his fingers into her palm and encouraging her with his touch. "Let's do as your mother says, darling. Just breathe with me."

"I…I…c-c-can't…d-do…th-th-this!" Lucy whines while trying to mimic Marcus's breathing pattern, but they inhale and exhale in different rhythms. Marcus's oil-covered chest caves inward and expands voluminously, steadily deflating and exaggerating his posture as Lucy's pregnant breasts pulse up and down, frantically, exasperating her efforts to remain calm and pull air into her lungs. Her vulnerable fear and painful expectations seem to crowd her consciousness, and she begins to panic in a coughing fit.
"What…if…I'm not…a good…mother? What if…they…don't…like me?"

"They'll love you, Lucy, just like I do." Marcus kisses his wife's forehead sweetly and leaves an oily imprint over her eyebrows. "Oops, um…sorry, honey."

"Ugh! You're getting me dirty! That's what you do, Marcus. All you men, you dirty us. I was a virgin before I met you, you, *man*." Lucy pouts and clenches Marcus's hand tightly. She uses this opportunity to voice her innermost grudges, a chance that a former mute would never miss. "You men just walk around sticking your privates into things! And we women get stuck like *this*!"

"That's improper conversation, Lucy," Jazz adds from the sidelines, mocking Berthine's voice and smiling at June before he catches his sister's frown alongside a mutual scowl from Berthine.

"Shut up, Jazz! Don't get me started on you!" Lucy fires at her brother, howling through the pain. She's gained her air and her confidence back; her brothers tend to bring out her best and worst. "Damn near twenty years on this earth and you still don't have your life together!"

"Lucy, calm down." Marcus tries to console his frantic wife. "Just…"

"No! I can say what I want! Mama said 'wait'! Both you and Jazz, both of you, all men, you're all fools! If I had a…a…AH!" Lucy shrieks wildly and releases Marcus's hands to clutch her belly with her left palm and wipe sweat from her forehead with her right wrist. She then glares at Jazz; she would attack him if she could rise from the couch. Instead of heeding her husband, she prepares to shoot a few rounds of truth at her baby brother. "Jazz, you think you're *so smart* and you have all this talent but you waste it…*and why?* 'Cause you're too arrogant! You were too arrogant to stay in school, too arrogant to work with any other musicians, and too arrogant to admit that you're scared and you need help!"

"You're not even supposed to be down here," Jazz responds quietly and lowers his head, walking away from the couch and staring longingly toward his piano before looking back over his shoulder. In his mind, he has a great comeback for his sister; though, he's never said it, he's always wanted to blurt out, "*I wish you stayed a mute*", or shout a quip that's equally hurtful, but, as he glances over his sister's hysterical expression, he softens his demeanor because he doesn't want to cause her more pain. Charles has done enough and the twins may finish her off.

"It's just the pain talking," Berthine remarks confidently, reading his thoughts from the edge of the couch before taking another peek between Lucy's legs. "You're almost ready, Lucy."

"She doesn't mean what she's saying," Marcus persuades himself and Jazz, trying to resolve what every father must wonder—why do we hurt the ones we love?

"Yes, I do! I mean every word!" Lucy asserts angrily. "Charles is lucky he left! I'd tell him a thing or two…too!"

"Lucy, do us a favor and reverse that wish you made. I liked you better when you couldn't speak." Jazz unleashes a small sliver of venom, unable to hold back a variation of his one-liner. He backs away from the family so that he stands in front of his piano and he reaches for a fallen cigarette under one of the legs of his piano bench. He feels his blood burning within his veins, roasting from the gall and intrusion of it all. His family believes that they can be anywhere and anything to him, come into his life whenever they choose with impositions and judgments.

"Put that cigarette away, son!" Berthine commands abruptly as she removes her arm from between Lucy's legs and raises her hand high. "This is a Christian home when I'm in here."

"What's that got to do with anything?" Jazz asks curiously, reaching for a lighter, daring to disregard Berthine's command. "Christians can smoke."

"Son, the body is a temple! You're disrespecting yourself and the Lord Savior Jesus Christ!" Berthine preaches and throws her head back, staring up to the ceiling. "Oh Jesus, where did I go wrong with these boys? I thought they moved down here to make something of themselves!"

"I am something," Jazz squeaks, flicking the cigarette under his piano and glancing sullenly at June while he sits on his bench, facing away from the family. Seeing his embarrassment and angst, June instinctually wants to console him so she walks slowly toward the bench and sits closely beside him, facing toward the family. They stare silently in opposite directions, huddled on the closest piece of furniture besides Jazz's twin bed, a destination for many but none tonight. Jazz leans toward June, almost placing his chin on her shoulder, as they share the leather cushion of his piano bench. "I told you family is overrated."

"Say what?" Berthine barks sharply and raises her head from the towels that cover Lucy's legs, daring Jazz to respond in any way.

"Nothing," Jazz replies meekly and another long pause descends upon the apartment as he leans away from June and disregards his family; still the irony saturates the room, each mind locked in a respective reality. Marcus and Lucy pray over her bulging stomach, Berthine makes frequent estimates of Lucy's diaphragm, Jazz stares longingly at the piano keys, and June observes and absorbs the entire scene, seeing and soaking in all the similarities between her family and the Lancasters.

"You know, Mrs. Lancaster, your son is a very talented piano player." June remarks while turning her head and smiling toward Jazz, but he continues to gaze at the piano keys, still lost in an unheard melody. "I was hoping to sing one of his songs."

"Uh huh, so you're going to hell, too, eh?" Berthine declares strongly and wipes her hands on the towels over Lucy's legs. "I shoulda known that boy would grow up and make that Devil music."

"Um, 'devil music'? What do you mean?" June asks and looks to Jazz for help; he returns her look with indignation, questioning why she made the remark and wondering if their partnership is a big mistake. She notices his ire and leans away from him, ignorant that she has opened Pandora's box of judgmental Christian values.

"The boy was raised in a good Christian home! I use to read the Bible to them every day, all day sometimes. Let them have one radio and look what happened!" Berthine explains and presses her lips together in disgust before shaking her head and continuing her zealous rant. "And he just got hooked…fixated…yes, *fixated* on blues from *New Orleans*! Olivia telling him about us as children…I could barely stop him from playin' that devil music in the cabin! Now, he travelled miles away from home so he can lose his soul! He just wants to make all the people gyrate and act a damn fool!"

"Mama…" Jazz pleads for Berthine to diminish her ever-present criticism; he views her as a constant obstacle to his growth. "It's not devil music."

"Well, that's exactly what the devil would say!" Berthine continues to chide Jazz, unable to forgive his descent into blues bars and speakeasies. "You were a good boy when your brother left. You can always stop this sinning and come back home."

"I'll never go back to that cabin. I'll never stop playing my music."

"Then you know where you'll end up!" Berthine proclaims confidently and points her finger to the floor, indicating that the fires of hell await him. "That music is poison and you feed it to people. How can Jesus save you if you don't stop, Jazz?"

"Maybe, I don't want to be saved, Ma."

"Ah!" Lucy yells and grabs Marcus's forearms in her hands, trying to bring the attention back to her swollen belly. "Mama, please let me push!"

"Not yet, honey," Berthine answers pleasantly, before looking angrily at Jazz and raising her right hand at her son. "I've tried and tried with you, boy. The Good Lawd knows I did my best, but my best was obviously not good enough! You had to find yourself here, in this place, with this... *Daisy!*"

"June, Ma. Her name is June." Jazz continues to correct his adoptive mother, tiptoeing on a line he has often avoided, but his patience is wearing thin. "And you don't know a thing about *me* or *her.*"

"Is that so?" Berthine questions his response with wide eyes, preparing to knock her son down a few notches and prove her continued matriarchal superiority. "So I don't know that *you* wet the bed 'til you were twelve? And I don't know that your sister and brother paid your rent 'til you started singing in them clubs? Should I mention *what else* I *don't* know?"

"No, Mama," Jazz mumbles as he turns back to the piano and stares at the keys in silence.

"I thought not," Berthine scolds abruptly, pleased with her dominion over Jazz, while disregarding the fact that she's in his home. She chuckles to herself and checks between Lucy's legs. "Child, you're about to pop! Do you feel ready to push?"

"Yes! Get these babies out of me!" Lucy shouts and grabs Marcus's arms even tighter, preparing to push with all her might. "Of all places, why did it have to be here?"

"Okay, just hold onto Marcus," Berthine coaches and peeks at Jazz as he sits next to June on his piano stool. They squeeze closely together, conferring away from the family.

"Are you okay?" June whispers to him softly. "We can still work on our music another time."

"What about your family?" Jazz responds quietly, taking a quick look over his shoulder to see if Berthine is listening—she is. His heart flutters a little at June's mention of *"our music"*, so he turns back to her and leans closer.

"I don't want you to go back to South Dakota. Don't let the last person you meet in New Orleans be my mother."

"*You really don't like her, huh?* She's not that bad." June giggles gently and leans closer to Jazz. "I can tell she loves you, in her own way, you know?"

"You don't know her."

"I know her type," June continues, placing her right hand on Jazz's right shoulder. "Mothers, grandmothers, grandfathers, they're all the same. They all think they know what's best."

"Maybe, but that doesn't mean..."

"Uh, excuse me, uh, Daisy...can you get Lucy some more water, please?" Berthine calls, pointing to Marcus as he holds the glass of water to Lucy's lips, guiding the last sips into her mouth. "And Jazz, come over here and comfort your sister."

"Yes ma'am," Jazz and June respond in unison, looking strangely at each other before splitting from the piano bench and attending to their respective duties. June retrieves the glass from Marcus while Jazz walks around the couch to hover over Lucy as she clutches her husband's arms tightly.

"How are you hanging in, sis?"

"How does it look, Jazz?" Lucy responds sarcastically, struggling to push and stay conscious. "I just...don't understand why...we can't go to the hospital."

"Darling, I wish I could explain, but Olivia...uh...I mean, someone told me, I mean...well, *it's just safer at home.* If we have problems, God forbid, we can call a doctor." Berthine informs Lucy while peaking back and forth between her legs. "You just have to keep pushing, Lucy. The first one's starting to crown."

"You're doing it, baby," Marcus continues to encourage his wife as June returns with a full glass of water. Marcus takes the glass and nods in appreciation, before turning back to his wife. "Just keep pushing, Lucy."

"Ah!" Lucy screams while clutching her stomach again. Her face winces in pain and she exhales with a long wheeze. "Our doctor...didn't say...it would hurt this much!"

"*Doctor?*" Berthine repeats quickly and lifts her head from the towels over Lucy's legs. "You went to a doctor?"

"Um..." Lucy stammers, looking to Marcus to fend off Berthine. "It was just once, Mama, before I called you."

"Lucy didn't feel the babies move for a day or so," Marcus adds with a shrug, his broad shoulders crowding his neck. "We got scared."

"You shouldn't have done that! You could've called me sooner!" Berthine woofs like a dog left outside, and nervous wrinkles form over her forehead, creating waves of concerns around her face. "Lucy, I told you: *'no doctors'.*"

"But why? I haven't seen Olivia since Charles and I left. Why did you even tell her I was pregnant?" Lucy asks between short breaths. She continues clenching her bulbous stomach, grimacing through the increased pressure as the babies move through her cervix. "And how'd you know we'd have twins? Did Olivia tell you that something is wrong with me?"

"No, baby, I...I, uh...I just guessed after you called me. You sounded like you were in a lot of pain." Berthine explains reluctantly with a quick glance away from Lucy; she looks blankly toward nothing and no one and Jazz thinks that she's hiding something. As he previously noted, his adoptive mother rarely has an awkward moment when the words don't spill or shoot from her mouth; yet, here she is struggling to communicate. Every time she wavers or dawdles, Jazz assumes that she can't think of a lie quick enough. "I don't know everything that's going on, but Olivia Winniper has never steered this family wrong."

"*Olivia?*" June repeats after Berthine mentions her family. "Do you mean my grand-"

"Oh, Lawd, it can't be!" Berthine exclaims while crouching between Lucy's legs at the edge of Jazz's crammed couch. "The first one is coming! I bet it's a boy!"

"Mama, pull him out!" Lucy screams while pushing and straining and wheezing and clenching; her world turns without stop. "Please, it hurts!"

"No, no, no! He's got to do some more work, Lucy!" Berthine yells and maneuvers her hands on the edge of the couch for a quick catch. "Just keep pushing!"

"Come on, baby," Marcus cheers whiles Lucy continues to scream and Jazz stands beside June, both watching in amazement as Lucy gives birth; they are two introverts caught in a real moment with other people.

"Thanks for staying," Jazz whispers through the side of his mouth. "I couldn't handle this alone."

"Jazz, get some more towels!" Berthine yaps as she reaches between Lucy's legs. A baby's cries fill the apartment, and her face tightens in astonishment. "I've got a...*slippery* grandson!"

"You did it, Lucy!" Marcus celebrates, moving his right arm behind her back and placing the glass of water to her forehead, calming her furrowed brow. He cradles her weight and Lucy breathes deeply, wincing in pain as if every movement hurts her to the core. The couple stares at Berthine as she gently lifts a Sioux baby boy from beneath the towels while reaching into her purse to remove a pair of forceps and cut the umbilical cord. Marcus prays over his wife and massages her temples. "Thank you, God. I…I'm so proud of you, Lucy. You brought me a son."

"I think I'm going to die, Marcus," Lucy pants drowsily, and her eyes roll involuntarily, looking aimlessly around the apartment. Her spine begins to tense and she envisions a red-haired woman, passing away in a similar predicament, pregnant beyond her willpower. "My body feels…cold…*and* my back hurts…*and* I-I-I'm seeing things. I'm really…tired."

"Here, have some water," Marcus advises softly and places the glass of water to her lips, lifting her back and willing Lucy to tilt her head and sip until several drops spill down her neck. He lays her back against the couch and fans her forehead with his right hand. "Try to rest, sweetheart. We have another one on the way."

"*These* are all the only towels I have left!" Jazz announces as he returns from his kitchen with more tattered towels. He stands near the couch as Marcus worries over his wife, proud and fearful, and Berthine coos over the Sioux newborn before looking up at Jazz contemptuously and taking the towels. Suddenly, Lucy's Sioux newborn has taken his place. Jazz is no longer the baby in the family, and Berthine sees Jazz for the twenty-year-old drunk that he has become.

"Just look at these towels. They smell like liquor. I don't even want to know when you washed 'em last. Jazz, you couldn't help a fly find dung," Berthine nags while cradling the whimpering baby boy and chuckling happily over his tiny nose. "No, he couldn't, could he? Your uncle is a fool, isn't he? This might be the cutest baby boy I've ever seen."

Berthine guffs and begrudgingly wraps the babe in more towels. She then softly hands him to his anxious, yet exhausted mother. Lucy grins excitedly, unable to contain her joy amidst her pain as she retrieves her son and holds him tenderly in front of Marcus.

"He has your nose," Lucy beams breathlessly over her baby boy and kisses his forehead, blessing him as only a mother can. "He's so handsome. Look at his eyes; he's looking right at us."

"What will we name him?"

"He's your *firstborn son*, Marcus," Lucy boasts proudly, hoisting the boy a little higher on her chest, showing a renewed sense of strength. "We should name him after you."

"No, I...I mean, I know...usually a man wants to name his first son after himself. I'm named after my father." Marcus answers quickly, but he rambles while remembering his reasoning and recollecting past sorrow. "I don't want our son to feel like has to be me or live up to my name..."

"Then what will it be?" Jazz interrupts, hoping to lighten the mood as he moves over Marcus's shoulder, angling to have a closer look at his nephew. "The kid can't go nameless, right?"

"Well, I had a little brother...he passed away when I was ten. Pops couldn't take it after that." Marcus admits quietly and lowers his head for a moment before raising his eyes to Lucy. "I told you about my brother, a long time..."

"*Darrel.*" Lucy remembers clearly, still smiling radiantly over her baby boy. She only looks up to Marcus briefly, before returning her eyes to her son. "You don't talk about him much. He liked baseball, right?"

"Yes," Marcus answers softly, leaning closely to his wife and joining her as they smile over their newborn son. He's caught between joy and despair, wishing his family could be here to see this moment with him, but knowing that the Lancasters are the only family that he has left.

"How'd he die?" Jazz asks without sensitivity, more curious than sympathetic.

"Polio. It took my mother a month earlier. We come from Haiti to try and save him. He was only six."

"Then, it's settled. We'll name him Darrell, after your brother." Lucy decides quickly and swaddles her baby boy under his father; she's still the leader that he needs during troubling times. Marcus knows what he wants, but he needed a strong woman like Lucy to help him find it, and she needed a self-assured man like Marcus to let her lead him to this...a family. "Darrel...Darrel Cashmen."

"Maybe he'll like baseball, too." Marcus hopes, but the fantasy is short-lived as Lucy's face changes from a beaming new mother to a grimacing woman, who is halfway through labor with twins. She passes Darrel to Marcus and clutches her stomach in pain.

"Ah! My God it hurts! I think the other one's coming!" Lucy shrieks as Berthine checks between her legs. "This one hurts more!"

"Oh lord, I…" Berthine stammers and looks under the towels, but she immediately raises her head with a flustered expression on her face. "I don't know what…I'm seeing…"

"What do you mean?" Lucy asks in agony, beginning to panic, but she resists a rush of anxiety from within while glancing at her baby boy in Marcus's arms. She takes a deep breath and exhales as she turns her head back to Berthine. "Mama, what's wrong?"

"Nothing's *wrong*, Lucy." Berthine musters a response, waving her left hand and continuing to probe between her daughter's legs with her right arm under the towels. "The baby is crowning. You…uh…you need to push. Take it slowly but surely and uh…don't worry about a thing. Mama's here."

"But it really hurts."

"I told you, Lucy. Olivia and Mama talked, I'm prepared for this…I just…it's different than I expected…but just trust me."

"What are you talking about? Marcus, help me."

"Do as your mother says, Lucy," Marcus implores, while carefully handing his son to Jazz and taking his wife's hands from atop her belly. "Stay strong."

"This baby is heavy!" Jazz announces while cradling his Sioux nephew. He turns to June and the two coo over baby Darrel while glancing at one another with quick and silent smiles. They remember a moment before anyone arrived at the apartment and they wonder if they would trade that moment for this one as they beam over this unexpected interruption.

"It hurts, Marcus! I…feel….like…I can't…breathe. I'm…I'm passing out…" Lucy wheezes feverishly and clutches her husband's arms. Sweat covers her forehead and she struggles to maintain eye contact with him. Her eyes move around his shoulders and dart up to the ceiling as they roll uncontrollably and begin to close. "I just…want…to sleep."

"You can't sleep, darling. Not yet." Marcus consoles his wife and wipes her forehead with his oily hand, causing more slick black oil to smear over her eyebrows. He almost tosses the remaining water on her face, but he pauses, knowing that his wife will not likely forgive or forget such an action. He opts to rub her shoulders tenderly until her eyes open completely and she stares at him silently; both remember their vows and know that this is the life that they have chosen. "Come on, Lucy. Stay with me, we still have a little more work to do."

"Keep pushing!" Berthine orders and Lucy grunts in response, fighting exhaustion and pushing with all her might.

"Ah! Why did I have to have twins?"

"He's so cute." June swoons over Darrel and forgets her hardened shell. In truth, she and Jazz have forgotten their egos and each has become mesmerized by the Sioux baby boy discovering the world. His little head bobs gingerly in Jazz's arms, and his eyes dart back and forth, trying to figure out the shapes and sounds. June continues to delight at the sight of his tiny limbs and she places her index finger against his left hand. "Look at his little hands."

"Yep, he's going to be a piano player." Jazz predicts happily and glances back to his mother before leaning to June. "A *blues* piano player."

"*Maybe.*" June chuckles with Jazz and little Darrel whimpers softly. "He might be a singer too."

"Jazz, you and Daisy, bring that boy over here!" Berthine orders as she remains on the couch with Lucy. "We need to keep him safe."

"Aw, Mama, lay off. Focus on Lucy." Jazz responds boldly, caught in the euphoria of holding his nephew. "Lil Darrel is fine with his *crazy* uncle for now. Lucy needs your help."

Lucy screams morbidly, accentuating Jazz's point. Berthine huffs at Jazz's refusal, but she quickly turns back to Lucy's legs and tends to the coming child.

"It's going to be okay, Lucy. You just need to stay strong. We Sioux are a fighting people. We never give up."

"I can't, Mama." Lucy gasps and rubs her hands over her forehead, smearing more of the oil. "I'm struggling to stay awake…I feel like I'm dying."

"Here, hold still." Marcus quickly grabs the glass of water and splashes it into Lucy's face, acting upon his earlier inclination and washing some of the oil from her forehead. "Feel better?"

"Marcus!" Lucy yelps and pushes her husband away from the couch. She growls threateningly and wipes the water and oil from her face with the back of her hands. "When I get back on my feet, I'm going to..."

"The baby's crowning!" Berthine announces, but suddenly her cheeks fall and her jaw drops in a look of pure confusion. Her eyebrows burrow together and her head tilts to the side, awkwardly cocked; she's unable to verbalize her thoughts. "I...uh...it's...uh..."

"What is it, Mama? Is it a boy or a girl?" Lucy asks, trying to lift her upper body with her weakened arms.

"Be careful, Lucy." Marcus places his hand at her back, gently supports her weight, and leans her forward slightly.

"Uh..." Berthine continues to stare frozenly between Lucy's legs. "Jazz, get some more towels!"

"But I told you these are all I have," Jazz admits while still holding Darrel and standing next to June. He and June are still more concerned with him than the new-newborn. "You all should have brought your own towels if you were going to turn my apartment into a...uh...*birthing* room!"

"Listen to the mouth on this boy! This child can't do nothing!" Berthine proclaims and shakes her fist at Jazz. "Your sister has another child coming! Get a shirt or something! And hurry!"

"Yes Mama." Jazz concedes quickly and softly places Darrell in June's arms while Berthine and Marcus tend to his sister. Berthine eyes June for a moment before returning her ire to Jazz.

"Hurry up!" Berthine demands while reaching between Lucy's legs. "This baby's almost out!"

"Wh-wh-what..." Lucy gasps exhaustedly and her cheeks tense from the pain. She grabs Marcus's arms and continues to push both the baby and her words through. "What...is...it?"

"It's uh...a...uh, *girl*." Berthine stutters to find an explanation as Jazz walks toward the couch with a balled-up shirt in his hands. "But she's..."

"Here, I found a shirt!" Jazz announces proudly, holding what looks like a crumpled black cotton rag. "It's clean...*mostly* clean."

Berthine reaches with both hands and delicately grabs the garment with her fingertips; she holds up the tattered black t-shirt and reveals a picture of Chuck Berry on the front.

"Who is that?" Berthine asks, pointing to the guitarist doing the duck walk.

"That's the king, the *real* king," Jazz explains with a smile. "It's Chuck Berry."

"*Who?*"

"Mama, you know Chuck Berry. You wouldn't let me listen to his music but I told you about him. He was always in the news for this or that." Jazz continues to prod Berthine, hoping they have at least one shared memory. "He played with Muddy Waters, the Wolfman…"

"I only remember the gospel music, son. The rest was you letting the devil inside." Berthine openly mocks Jazz and places the shirt under Lucy's legs without care for his feelings. "It's sad that you find a way to disappoint with the simplest tasks, especially during the most important moments."

"You're welcome, Mama." Jazz responds without a smile and walks away quickly, again retreating from the couch and his family. "I'm done trying…"

"*What?*"

"I said, 'I'm sorry, Mama'," Jazz apologizes while he resumes standing beside June, who still cradles baby Darrel. Jazz leans over his nephew and tickles Darrel's stomach. "I'm sorry for you, little guy. Your family's crazy."

"Ah! This is torture!" Lucy shrieks from the couch and balls her fists in Marcus's oily sleeves. "Is she out yet?"

"Almost, darling. Here we go." Berthine advises and slowly pulls the child from within. "She's just…"

"What, Mama? Why…are you acting….so weird?" Lucy questions, beginning to panic, no longer feeling any need to remain calm with the twins out of her body. "Tell me what's wrong! And let me see my child!"

"There's nothing…*wrong*, okay? I told you…that this…uh…it's just…uh…she's…Olivia said…it's just hard to believe…" Berthine grabs the pair of forceps and cuts the umbilical cord. She pauses and wraps the baby girl in the Chuck Berry t-shirt, covering her softly and smiling at the baby's cream hands. "She's just…*somewhat*…uh, lighter skinned."

"Huh? '*Lighter skinned*'?" Marcus and Lucy repeat together and Lucy stretches her arms out to her mother, wanting to hold her newborn baby girl.

"I don't know how to explain this to you." Berthine hesitates and stares at the blonde baby girl before passing the child to Lucy. "Uh, maybe it's Marcus's Creole blood."

"What about my blood?" Marcus wonders as he and Lucy look over their daughter. The baby girl stares at them with bright blue eyes. Thin strands of wavy, blonde hair glow against her ivory skin. The couple looks at their baby girl in shock as June and Jazz step closer. June still holds baby Darrel in her arms and the contrast seems unavoidable amongst the astonishment.

"That baby is not *Creole*, Mama!" Jazz remarks sharply and looks around to Marcus and Lucy as if he notices something they don't. "That baby is white! She looks like June!"

"But…" Marcus pauses, unable to bring words to his mouth.

"I…I don't understand, Mama." Lucy stammers, staring over their newborn baby girl. She looks to June and grows mildly angry, trying to rise from the couch. "June, give me my son!"

"Now hold still, Lucy!" Berthine interjects, holding her arm out to stop Lucy from moving. "A woman needs to rest after giving birth, especially to twins."

"Marcus…" Lucy cries sadly, holding her baby girl away from her chest and struggling to make sense of her brown and white twins. "Marcus, get Darrel, please."

Lucy points toward June and Marcus hops to his feet. June places the babe into his father's arms and steps away from the couch. She walks toward Jazz's piano and gives the family space to confer amongst themselves. Berthine tends to Lucy's afterbirth and cleans as much of the blood off the couch as possible with the used towels. Marcus kneels by Lucy's side and the parents look over their twins, one boy, one girl, one Sioux, one…well, *not Sioux*. The entire family remains quiet, all wondering the same question.

"How is this possible?" Lucy asks in shock. "Mama, tell me the truth. Did you know this would happen?"

"Of course she knew." Jazz blurts out, not giving Berthine a chance to dismiss Lucy's question. He begins to recollect a forgotten tidbit, a casual piece of conversation that he has intended to use. "That's why Olivia told her not to go to the hospital. They both knew."

"What does it matter?" Marcus broods toughly, clenching his arms protectively over his son. Berthine remains silent, tending to Lucy, using her care as a distraction to avoid any unpleasant answers. Marcus studies his brown son and his white daughter, filling with more questions and concern. "Nothing can explain this, Jazz, unless…"

"Unless what, Marcus? Lucy would never be unfaithful to you so what is the only other explanation?" Jazz counters, stepping closer to Marcus and Lucy. "I hate to say it, but Charles was right. Mama has lied to us before and now…all of this…your Creole blood and our Sioux blood mix together and poof! You have one Sioux boy and one white girl and Mama conveniently comes to town and makes sure you stay away from hospitals— this after getting advice from some woman we haven't seen in years! Isn't that crazy? When none of us believe that she is our real-"

"Jazz! You're still not making any sense! Why do I have a white baby girl in my arms?" Lucy snarls momentarily, but she doesn't want to disturb her children. She stares at her quiet, blonde baby girl with fear and love, knowing what she feels for her daughter, but she questions how long these feelings could last. "It's just impossible. She's white."

"Maybe it's a miracle," June adds sympathetically, wrinkling her lips, knowing she may have spoken out of turn. "I mean, if it's impossible, then…it must be a miracle, right?"

"Now that might be the only sensible thing this girl's said all night!" Berthine cheers and smiles brightly at June before looking to Lucy. Given a way to avoid a hefty explanation, Berthine is overcome with joy and inertia; she forgets to fear her son associating with a strange white girl. Like the rest of the family, Berthine wants to make sense of something she has feared for years; and it seems that June, of all people, has found the ray of light that they needed. "Daisy, I believe you're right. None of us know exactly what happened…or why it's happened, but…*it happened.* The Good Lawd has blessed this family tonight! We've witnessed a miracle! Miracle twins!"

"But…"

"Marcus, no buts, but the butts I'm going to kick if you two don't raise these children right! Both of them, you'll love and raise both of them! No matter what happens! You hear me?"

"Yes ma'am," Marcus concedes with a jubilant smile, rocking his son in his arms and nudging Lucy. His loving eyes encourage her to comply. "What do you say dear?"

"Ha…not much I can say…but…we will, Mama. Of course, we will. I promise." Lucy agrees happily and exhales her frustration and fear. "Marcus, I want to go home."

"We will, darling," Marcus assures his wife, kissing her forehead and leaving another oil imprint over her eyebrows. "You've done enough work tonight."

"Hey!" Jazz interrupts quickly, raising his arms in the air. "What are you going to name her?"

"Um…I don't know…" Lucy answers, looking down at her daughter, perching her eyebrows and turning her head to Marcus. "I don't know any white names. Maybe, *Stephanie?* What do you think, Marcus?"

"I already named Darrel, honey," Marcus whispers and softly bounces his son in his arms. "You should name her. She can have any name you want."

"Well, I'm not creative. Jazz is the artist in the family." Lucy admits with a smirk before raising her head to her brother. "I want him to name her."

"Oh Lawd, Lucy don't let him do that. That boy ain't got no sense…"

"Yes, he does Mama. You're just too hard on him…we all are." Lucy beams while nodding toward her shocked brother. "Go ahead, baby bro'. Give your niece a good name."

"Are you sure, sis? Maybe you should…"

"Please, Jazz," Lucy implores and giggles over her baby girl. The newborn yawns peacefully while being held near her twin brother, both in the loving arms of their parents—a first for any Winniper offspring. "Name her anything you want, but make it nice…*for me.* Maybe something that goes well with *Darrel.*"

"Got it, *something nice…'goes well with Darrel'.*" Jazz repeats the request, looking at Berthine, Marcus, Darrel, Lucy, her baby girl, and then June, who still stands away from the family, giving them space to work through their dilemma. Suddenly, Jazz grins cunningly as a clever idea crosses his mind like when he hears a new melody that completes his harmony. "I just thought of the *perfect* name. Actually, Mama thought of it."

"Lawd, have mercy. The boy is already blaming it on me! I'm not the reason for all your problems, son." Berthine snaps impatiently and Jazz continues to widen his smile in anticipation, staring at his overly demonstrative adoptive mother. She uses her over protection as a reason to break him down and dismiss his efforts, but he sees now that she is only afraid of a world that she does not fully understand. June scares her because Berthine has only known one kind white woman; but now, Lucy has given birth to a blonde baby girl, and June no longer seems so out-of-place amongst the Lancaster family. Berthine tilts her head again, exaggerating her impatience and accentuating her lack of faith in Jazz's ability to choose a proper name. "Okay, c'mon son, what is it? What's my granddaughter's name going to be? Make it good."

"Ha...well, it's a name...that at least you can remember, Mama." He laughs while looking at June and dreaming of a future filled with bright lights. "We'll call her...*Daisy.*"

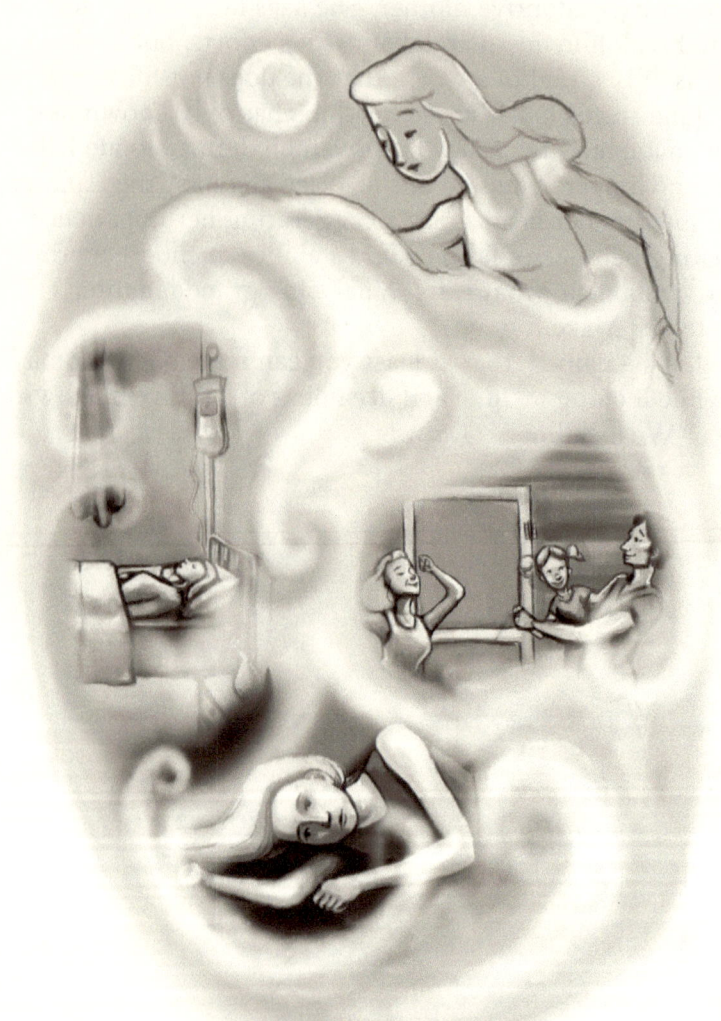

Love in the Summers

JUNE 1963

Sunday	Monday	Tuesday	Wednesday	Thursday	Friday	Saturday
						1
2	3	4	5	6	7	8
9	10	11	12	13	14	15
16 	17	18	19	20	21	22
23	24	25	26	27	28	29
30						

Sunday, June 16, 1963
June Bethune

There's something in the air in Brazil,
A chill that stops the heart still.
With only one last breath,
She screams with all that's left;
Yes,
There's something in the air in Brazil,
A krill unable to be killed,
Telling the world of discoveries
That made life worth the thrill.
There's something in the air in Brazil,
A mill with only love to till.
Sacred ceremonies between lonely phonies
Fail to compare to the one and only.
Yes,
There's something in the air in Brazil,
A will to feel love fulfilled,
The only air that tastes so fair,
The dangerous dare to spill in great Brazil.

June Bethune has millions of stars in her eyes tonight. She paces back and forth in her hotel room, glancing to the door and awaiting the knock that is sure to come.

It doesn't.

She sits on the bed, slides a Chesterfield King from the pack, and lights the end with her steel lighter—a part of the custom-made merchandise from the *Jazz and June World Tour*.

She takes the longest, fullest drag that her lungs can endure; these moments of internal escape have become her most prized possession. Her inner walls shake inside her body and she feels that itch, that chill from the Brazilian air that makes her feel dirty and clean, filthy but pure. She wishes that she knew how to sin; she imagines that she never learned to behave so that she can be innocently obscene in her pleasure-driven pursuits. How could she have known a love affair would arise between them? Or is it only in her head?

June begins to reminisce upon scenes of their music collaborations, trips to secluded vocal booths and studio bathrooms. She pleasured herself in solitude, thinking of him, her partner and friend. Although their physical encounters have remained artistic while they tend to the paint and canvas of their music, their relationship has matured into much more than art, at least to her.

She cannot understand the connection; he admits that he feels it too, but, he is much more reluctant to discuss or act upon their feelings and suspicions. Once defensive and meek, June has become an alpha female, aggressive, demanding, and always willing to defy convention. Now at age twenty-two, she and Jazz have shared so much more than their June birthdays. She celebrates on the 9th and he hides from the media on the 10th, both hoping to recapture some normalcy from the days and nights when it was just them, during their beginning two long years ago.

June finds it funny how the world can change in such a little time and she loves him more than anyone she has ever known. She has all but forgotten her family. Though she remains in contact with her siblings, the rest of Winniper County is a far away nightmare that she somehow escaped. Maybe Jazz saved her. She remembers how he became protective over her when they first met outside Teezy's bar.

∞

Surrounded by blacks and blues scanning them with their eyes and questioning their morality, he moved closer to her and shielded her before she suggested finding a nearby piano. But even then, it was always about the music.

∞

Love and passion have emerged from their efforts and their sound has quickly constructed a musical empire that rivals the Winniper Family Estate. Due to his talent, his gender, or his relation to their managers, Jazz receives top-billing; and "Jazz and June" have become a fast-moving sensation. People dig their rhythm; the press and listening public consider their sound to be "transcendent" and "pure". The duo provides a blend of Northern folk and Southern rhythm-n-blues, and their individual talents complement one another. In truth, both musicians feel neglected by the same society and their shared perspective has produced two chart-topping hits, "Traveling Minstrel" and "Bananas on Sundays".

∞

The blonde singer and Sioux pianist began in New Orleans and quickly blossomed to the American coastal cities of L.A., New York, San Francisco, and Miami. They performed "Traveling Minstrel" live on national television twice and booked a globe tour before their third live appearance, which aired on *The Tonight Show.* As their initial co-manager, Charles orchestrated a grand announcement for their worldwide tour by requesting that Jack Parr deliver the news to the nation just before he signed off.

∞

For their roles as co-managers, Charles and Lucy haven't prevented June and Jazz from spreading their creative wings; Jazz has received top-billing due to his gender, relation, or talent, but the artists have always had each other to lean upon and they have experienced the highs and lows together. After enduring a flash flood of mainstream success, they have discovered people with and without bigoted hatred. There are homes throughout America and the world where their love could last—she hopes.

∞

But as June sculpted with Jean Dubuffet in Paris and Jazz skied with Crown Prince Akihito in Japan, the two performers shared more than words, but less than romance.

∞

They have grown cold towards each other, forming walls to save their hearts from feelings they don't want to admit are there. They refuse to ask any lingering questions from the night Lucy gave birth to Daisy and Darrel; they rarely mention their respective families. Their public personas present an acceptable fusion of modern cultures; but, if this Sioux pianist and blonde vocalist act upon the true desires for their relationship and publicize their immoral copulation, they may never attain the success that they ultimately dream possible.

Neither June nor Jazz will ever betray their childhood ambitions, especially when they have worked so hard to achieve everything that they each set out to accomplish. Even a potential romance between them cannot derail their worldwide success. They have been unstoppable; for two years, they have worked tirelessly, and they only took a break when June became ill in April—and then, clarity came to both musicians.

∞

June struggled through a show in Sydney, Australia; the heat down under had squelched her skin and her insides. She became dehydrated and collapsed behind the curtain while walking off stage. Jazz carried her to a nearby bench, screaming for help, but June refused any medical attention. She dazedly demanded a wheelchair from the paramedics at the venue and the duo still satisfied the audience by returning to the stage shortly afterwards and valiantly completing their show with one of their famed encores. After the curtain reopened, Jazz wheeled her to center stage and sat beside her at his piano as they performed their true finale. Their encores have become a customary goodbye after the fans chant *"Encore! Encore!"*, while they wait for the two stars to appear one last time. She sang sadly from her wheelchair, holding her acoustic guitar in her lap with paramedics standing close by.

Usually June's voice weakens by the end of a show, but, that night, her voice never faltered because her body had already broken down completely. Her fragile throat and lungs had shattered, leaving her voice free to roam and play in a heavenly inertia. Her mind wondered what truly makes the human body succumb to suffering—is pain a symptom of reality or is it a nuance of perception? Wading through that conundrum, it all seemed so clear; the spotlights were God's awareness shining upon her and showing her exactly what is worth and worthless in this world.

Her sluggish, sullen eyes tilted to Jazz as he watched her carefully, softly playing blues chords on a black baby grand piano while smoking his cigarette in a billowing haze. She completely abandoned her accompanying guitar chords and she crooned a simple melody as her mind disengaged from her physical exhaustion. June travelled to an observant reality in another dimension, where she watched herself and Jazz from outside the bubble. She saw what their managers, agents, and publicists wanted the world to see, she felt what the crowd wanted them to be, and she instantly realized what she and Jazz have always been—in love, without context or fame.

Yes, she loved him, a Sioux boy from the indigenous people of Winniper County. He was one of the *others* that her grandfather had told her to avoid, yet her life decisions have led her to find an *other* who made her feel like more than just another.

∞

Jazz has made her feel at home and at peace. Over the past two years, they've shared the blues and constructed a harmony that they struggle to understand or describe fully. It's as if they are the only inhabitants in their musical world built for two. They have the creative impulses of God's prophets, but they can't see their past and they have remained distant from one another in spirit, reluctant to discuss their desires and fears.

∞

After the concert in Sydney, June lay in the Prince of Wales Hospital with Jazz at her side; he remained moodily quiet, huffing and sighing without words.

∞

Jazz, without a piano, is an awkwardly dreadful relic; he becomes a man without a purpose, a builder with no tool in sight.

∞

June looked into his eyes and saw piano keys, his mind filling with rhythms, patterns, and sounds that couldn't escape. Trapped with her in that Australian hospital room, he couldn't leave or even walk the hospital hallways without being accosted by guards, nurses, reporters, doctors, and clamoring fans.

As armed officers stood outside the hospital room, the room itself became a sanctuary where the truth waited to run free from either musician; but, June and Jazz simply stared at each other in silence, for days it seemed. He puffed on kings and tried to angle the smoke towards the window, often glancing back to June and narrowing his eyes as he took another drag. No doubt, he wondered incessantly when she would be well enough to leave.

Truthfully, she began to feel better after a few hours, but she was in no rush to continue the hustle and bustle. The tour, the agents, and the managers had all come into their lives so quickly; the music world had waited months for Jazz to choose a direction, and June came along for the ride. As their handlers fluttered around the hospital, mixing amongst the various medical staff, June remembered how she was never asked to meet or approve any of the people who work for her.

∞

Jazz probably doesn't know many of their names, either; they're both locked within their music, but at what cost? Strangers surround them and they are both so far from their families. The distance doesn't seem to bother him, and her opinion is rarely given consideration.

∞

No, preferring a hospital bed to a tour bus, June was in no rush to resume their profitable puppetry. In those few days inside the hospital, she and Jazz were actually human and they remembered what made them friends. They spoke in private for the first time since the beginning of their whirlwind, worldwide tour. While smiling, laughing, and recalling the birth of Lucy's twins, they reignited their early connection and they began to drift away from the handlers who have turned their art into a commodity. It was then that June decided to confess her love, immediately following her decision to start smoking.

"Pass me a fag." She grinned wryly. After she watched the London girls approach potential boytoys with this clever line, she relished the thought of using it herself. Their Manchester roadie Hank Christford told her that the girls ask for a cigarette because the boys know *if she smokes, she pokes*.

An ode to the promiscuous female, June never intended to become an exhibitionist, but the blues spoke for her in a way that she could never express in plain speech. She saw too many morals and standards in the world, but in response, she learned how to run from the spotlight at a very young age.

After her father left her and her siblings in Papa's care, she quickly adopted a code of sorrow and silence and she spent most of her first few months at the estate crying in her bedroom. During her paternal grandmother's visits to the estate, Tilly tried her best to assure June that Kenny would return, but June knew her father was gone. He wasn't dead like her mother, but he was missed just the same, and she blamed Papa.

While watching the old man praise Duke for being the family's youngest male heir, June realized her assigned role as a Winniper woman meant that her life had little value beyond producing another Winniper male heir, who could help fortify the family's legacy. Papa prohibited Christina and June from attending school once they arrived at the Winniper Family Estate; he said there was no reason for education since they would marry as soon as they were of legal age. He still somehow blamed them for their mother's sins; Teresa's ghost haunted the family, but Papa chose to treat Christina and June harshly and without preference.

∞

Though June loves her sister, she is happy that she followed her dreams, unlike Christina. Their temperaments have always been decidedly different.

∞

When they arrived at the family's colossal mansion, the sisters separated and chose to seclude themselves within their respective bedrooms instead of bonding together to form a united front against their grandfather's authority. June would have gladly helped her older sister put up a fight, but Christina lost herself in a teenage crush for Duke's friend, Earl, and she quickly dropped her dreams of becoming an archeologist and traveling to Pompeii. Then, June and her dreams of singing in New Orleans became Papa's primary domestic focus. Although their grandfather had given Teresa the freedom to travel, he refused to give the same leeway to her offspring, still fearing similar results down the road—Winniper mothers that he could not control.

So while Papa encouraged Duke to travel the world, sow his wild oats, return to Winniper County, and enroll in college, Papa confined Christina and June to the Winniper Family Estate. The family operated with the understanding that soon enough Duke would usurp the Winniper throne from their Uncle Thomas and Christina and June would enter proper marriages.

Papa had executed his plan perfectly and his dynasty seemed set in stone, until Duke suddenly lost the ability to speak on his eighteenth birthday. Papa spared no expense trying to help Duke regain his speech, but the longer Duke remained a mute, the more Papa became unraveled. He thumped around the house, blaming God for giving him two, weak male heirs. Usually, he ensured that both Duke and Thomas III were within hearing distance. Papa's paranoia broadened when he began to suspect that Kenny's soup had somehow cast this cruel spell upon his grandson, irrespective of the lack of similar effects on Christina and June.

After receiving extortion threats from Kenny, Christina even helped Sheriff Cobb, Jr. track down her stepfather in Chicago, but Kenny survived an ill-fated attack. Then, when June overheard Papa Winniper give the sheriff an order to hunt down her father again and "finish him off", she felt an instinctive need to protect the man who had abandoned her. She begged Christina and Duke for their help and, for the first time, Teresa's children left Winniper County in April 1956 and Duke drove his sisters to Chicago.

After failing to convince Kenny to leave his deathbed, the feeling of freedom became overwhelming and the siblings embarked on a journey that took them through the Midwest. Their chaotic trip involved an extensive elopement in California, and June's pleading eventually brought them to New Orleans. Ignoring their grandfather's instructions to return seemed worthwhile once she met Jazz. By then, she had mastered her mother's guile and she persuaded the Lancaster family to accept her and support her work with Jazz. Lucy and Charles helped the duo promote a live show in Scapetown, and their musical pursuits have reaped incredible rewards and profits ever since.

∞

She doesn't think she or Jazz could have envisioned their success happening so quickly, yet, over the last 25 months, the vast sums of money have become less and less fulfilling for the two artists.

∞

Inside the Prince of Wales Hospital, June continued to smile while Jazz shot her a look of inquisition, questioning her request for a cigarette. As she raised her hand weakly, the hospital bed's rusted metal creaked under her shaky, frail frame. June only hoped that Sydney maintained healthy prescription outlets; surely, the doctors could recommend a sufficient narcotic to stabilize her nerves and help her sleep at night. She wasn't simply dehydrated, but she was also exhausted as a result of a lifestyle lived on the brink of a shotgun. Feeling forced, she had to survive show business as the frilly white girl performing black music.

His experience was different from her ordeal, and she could barely explain her plight. He was at least Sioux, but her skin made her something that his skin did not make him. She had become a puppet, or at least she felt that way at times. Then at other times, she felt as though her life couldn't have happened any other way because she met Jazz and they make beautiful music that connects with people. June glanced at him with the doll eyes that she had learned to give to the crowd and reporters.

Their marketing consultants taught her how a blonde's eyes can mesmerize the public and make the populous incapable of objective judgment; their American fans could only wonder and the international press could only adore instead of criticize the sweet and innocent, *June Bethune*. She was the media's darling, a genetic gem from two of the most powerful families in the most powerful nation of the world. For Jazz, the music was the tool for his soul's expression, but for June, the music was the place where her soul still searched for a home. One artist had found what the other still desired. Amidst the swirl of the stage, the recording sessions, and the success, she found him as he had found her—the answer to everything. She finally realized that Jazz is the most important in a world filled with the unimportant. Though, she didn't have this revelation until she lay in a hospital bed, dipped in a tired haze.

"Get some rest, June." He dismissed her waiting hand and softly pushed her palm away. He looked out the window, blew smoke through the window's small opening, and stared desperately as if he hoped the smoke would carry him away to freedom.

"Give me a cigarette, *please.*" June pouted in shambles, her hand still dangling over the edge of the hospital bed. Jazz turned away from the window and observed her as if he was God himself, peering over her face for signs of her conviction. She gazed into his eyes; they were cold and endless. She could see the music flickering in his retinas, swirling around in his pupils after receiving a spark of inspiration. His perception ignited the harmonies that men rarely find in life, but she could always hear his soul, and she believed he could always hear hers, too. Two tortured doves from the same cage that flew away together only to find themselves still in chains, they learned society traps all. Jazz knelt beside the bed, grabbed the cigarette from his lips, and leaned closely to her face.

"June, we've got to get out of here," he whispered while placing the filter at the edge of her lips. Without thinking, June inhaled briefly and began to cough. Jazz held the cigarette away from her mouth, and her eyes grew wide from the sensation filling her lungs; he watched her amateurish nicotine exhibition without amusement or applause.

"Why are you doing this?" He asked softly, still questioning her intent.

"I love you, Jazz," June admitted impulsively, no longer able to withhold the truth, but unable to soften the blunt reality with any opening gravitas. She had tried buffer conversations, small innuendos, and light kisses upon his cheek, but nothing seemed to express the fact as plainly as the words themselves. She grabbed the king's stem from his fingertips with her index and middle finger, lingering for a moment to gently touch his hand with her thumb and ring finger.

∞

While in public, they mostly communicate through these light exchanges and brief embraces before, during, or after a performance or appearance. They are two sad musicians locked behind glass walls while hearing and feeling every move the other makes. They are usually in close proximity, yet their hearts have recently turned in opposite directions. He seems like he could play forever, but she knows that the end is near. If these past two years foreshadow what life will be like for them, she thinks it would be better to go back to her grandfather than to continue at this pace.

June and Jazz, the brown and white showcase, have become pop icons of the 60s' social revolution, yet they are still slaves to the old world order. Jim Crow has not changed one bit since their first meeting in 1961 and they are prisoners wherever they go in the United States and beyond. Only behind a closed and guarded hospital door in Sydney, Australia, could they share moments away from cameras flashing and reporters asking those same old questions about their beliefs and their relationship.

∞

"I love you too, June." He repeated her sentiment with a smile, but he kept his lips tight, closing them completely after the words escaped. His crocodile smile looked more like a verbal clamp to prevent any further exchange.

∞

June now realizes that most of Jazz's smiles are meaningless. She's seen him smile in a room filled with mainstream reporters asking him how he feels about being a colored man performing in places where colored people aren't allowed. She's seen him smile while his brother Charles slammed new contracts onto his piano, refusing to help them if they did not sign with Lancaster Records. She's seen him smile when he found out his mother had breast cancer, shortly after they began the tour. He continued as if nothing happened. To this day, he has not spoken a word about any of his family, except when they were inside the hospital room; and, in truth, she hasn't spoken about hers, either. Yes, she's seen Jazz's smile hide many tears, and she knows that deep down he only wants what he has always wanted: to stay far away from his family and play his music in peace.

∞

"I know you want to leave, Jazz." June sympathized while taking the cigarette and lifting it away from her face. "I'll be better soon."

"I hope so…I'm dying here." He turned away from her and removed another Chesterfield from the pack; he paused as he looked out of the window again before inhaling a long drag, unable to feel any sincerity. "I told you to take better care of yourself when we got to Australia. We still have to go to finish Europe in May and South America in June."

He held the smoke within his lungs and continued to stare out the window as the sunlight danced on his face, worried wrinkles decorating his concerned countenance. She knew that he hoped for her speedy recovery more than anyone else; he definitely wanted to leave more than she did, but she wanted to stay inside those hospital walls, if only for the moments of honesty, moments that June and Jazz had rarely shared until then. The days spent within that hospital room gave June time to rest and think about their future. Maybe, she dreamed too hard, but their seclusion unlocked the flood gates of her emotions and she became resolved to get well and act upon her feelings without fear of the consequences.

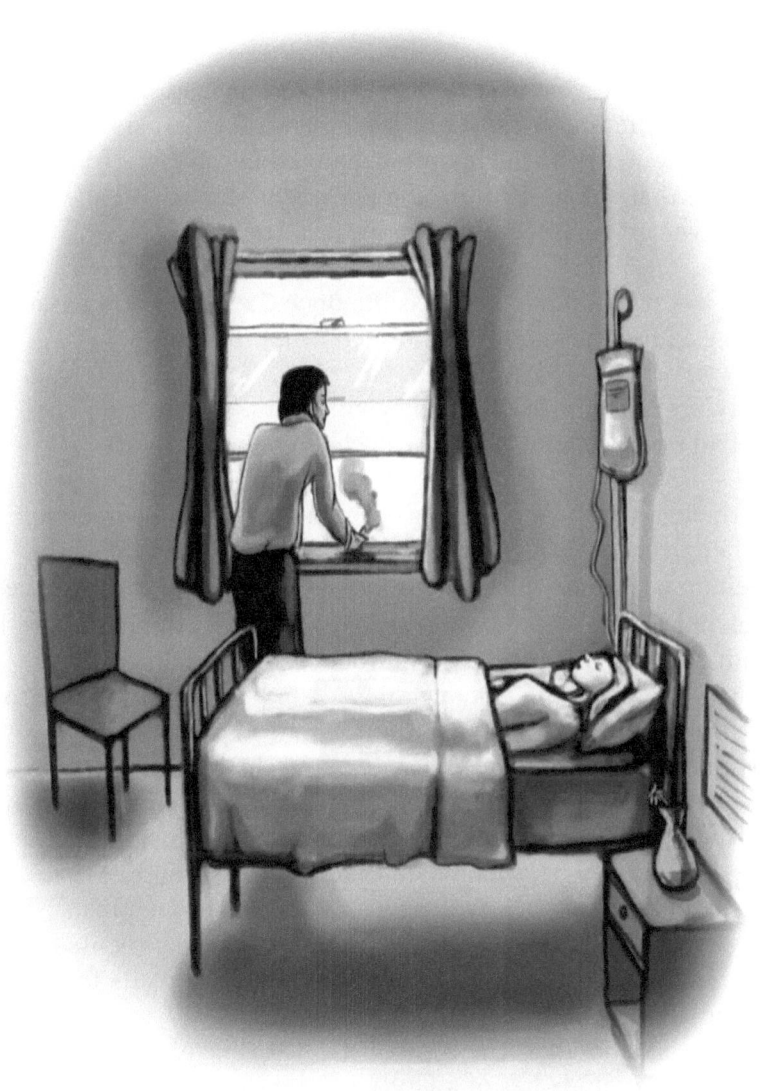

∞

Now, almost two months later, June paces back and forth within her hotel suite at the Copacabana Palace in Rio de Janeiro while wading in those emotions that broke through the levees she built around her heart years ago.

∞

She planned to never love, to only sing and protect herself from pain, abandonment, and legacy; but her bout with exhaustion and those honest moments in the hospital changed her forever. When she first told Jazz that she loved him, she knew it was true and she knew she could never go back to being ignorant of the truth.

∞

Love is a certain kind of submission; once the confession passes through one's lips, one can no longer deny that it exists.

∞

After lying in the hospital for fifty-six hours, she realized how futile life had been without someone special to share it with.

∞

Over the last two years, Jazz has become her special someone, closer to her than any of her family; and she knows that she is the closest person to him because he barely likes any of his family, except for Darrel and Daisy— *"the miracle twins"*, as he calls them, though he still cannot connect the dots between their origin and his own.

June has her suspicions about how Jazz and his siblings came to Berthine's cabin, but, because Jazz refuses to discuss his family beyond short sentences, June can easily avoid the topic for similar reasons. They find joy in their music, that oasis that spawned when they first met; yet, June is willing to risk her happy illusion for the real thing. She paces with such haste that her feet sting; her tips, soles, toes, and heels prickle over pins and needles in the plush, purple Peruvian rug at the foot of the bed. Her minor ailments beg her to rest and quiet the tension in her body. She still waits for the knock at the door, hoping he will come soon.

She finally sits down at the edge of the bed. The expansive suite's luxurious décor reminds her of a Hollywood movie; the white marble floor accents the lilac rug and the overhead lights brighten the room. She feels like she is on the set for one of their commercial endorsements, but she knows that this moment is, indeed, happening in real life without scripts or stand-ins.

Mostly, life has become a game, within which, she and Jazz sell their music to corporations, who eagerly pawn their sound to customers. The brown boy and white girl from South Dakota have grown into international stars in such a short time that it all seems predestined. Jazz has become world-renowned for his musical ability, the fusion between old blues and new rhythm, while June has become admired worldwide for her sweet, American pride and feminine vulnerability. She is the white rose, pretty in pink, but able to wear white. She would never discuss sex publicly; instead, she conceals any suggestion that a virgin still has erotic feelings and sordid desires.

They are everything that everyone wants them to be. They have played their roles to perfection: Jazz as the quiet genius and June as the delicate libertine, though they never meant to commercialize and divide their art for mass consumption to the degree that Charles and Lucy have managed.

∞

As his first duty, Charles played rough with the locals in Scapetown, but, once the duo moved to the coasts and beyond, Charles lost himself and left June and Jazz to Lucy, who was too busy with her family to handle an up-and-coming megahit by herself so she arranged for the managerial duties to become the responsibility of several industry handlers, who served the duo to more industry know-hows, who fed Jazz and June to the program directors, the crowds, and the press, who all gushed when they heard the music and learned the story of the two South Dakota stars who met in a blues bar.

At least in the beginning, when they were inside his apartment, their dream was pure, but they succeeded so fast that the dream quickly became an uncontrollable nightmare. She began to seriously question their path after Australia and her doubts have grown with each performance. They started their duet as two entities searching for self-expression and they hoped their music could speak for their pain while bringing people together; but, little did they know that once people come together, they kill each other.

"Segregation be damned," June thinks. *"A man could never divide himself from his self-destruction."* She grabs a fading Chesterfield from a glass ashtray on the nightstand to the right of the bed, takes three excruciating drags, and holds her breath tightly without coughing; now, she even smokes like Jazz. She dreams that they could fit very nicely into a domestic lifestyle if they collect their tour money, pack their luggage, move into a starter home, and remember to smoke outside. A knock at the door interrupts her brief fantasy and she hesitates a second too long and begins to cough loudly.

"June? Are you okay? Open the door!" Jazz yells from outside. She tries to speak, but the smoke clogs her lungs and she continues to cough. From the outside, she probably sounds as though she is choking. He bangs on the door again and June hears a murmured *"Ow!"*

She musters the strength to stand, wiggle her toes with a large inhale, and look in a nearby mirror that stretches from the floor to the ceiling. She grimaces at her running mascara; her eyes are puffing, blotchy, and glazed.

"One second!" she calls toward the door, patting her hair and positioning her curves inside her teal sundress. She reminds herself of her mother and she plans to do something dangerous. June stretches her arms wide and her skin still feels the sting of an ill-fitted costume change. Their elaborate stage show has become a complete circus filled with trained animals from countries where most of the citizens can't even afford the high-priced tickets to the *Jazz and June World Tour.* In every lavish nuance of their traveling sideshow, June sees another hypocritical acquiescence. The usher vests for their Bahamian chimps or the fake cigars on the Panamanian flamingos have begun to make her sick to her stomach. She has heard of artists who lost their way, but she never thought she would become one.

She knows that she and Jazz lack the same motivation and drive from two years ago; they both miss the innocence to believe that art can be more than profits. While checking her face in the mirror, she can see the exhaustion around her eyes and she hopes to convince Jazz that they can have a life together beyond music and the stage. She wonders if that's the only reason he spoke to her in the beginning; he needed a singer, maybe he saw the circus act even then.

No, he's a fool a like her; they both believed…they *still do* believe. She collects her confidence and prepares for the inevitable showdown, sauntering to the opaque door and stretching her arms into the air with one, elongated, labored inhale. She exhales deeply and shakes away her nerves as she reaches for the door with both hands, twists the knob in her palms, and pulls the door open across her body. Jazz stands in the doorway with a confused look on his face, wondering what she is up to.

"Hi," she whimpers in a girlish tone as if they are unfamiliar and their meeting is happenstance. She pretends that they haven't spent the past two years side-by-side, practicing, recording, and rehearsing a sound that is unique to them both. They never helped Lucy give birth inside a dirty, shaky apartment in New Orleans, and they are not traveling around the world, spreading the sound that they both created. When she sings and he plays, she knows their partnership is fated, but they pretend that they don't share an intimate harmony and they ignore the pasts that led them to each other.

She again tries to shake herself from her usual personal boundaries, so that she can break down her walls and calm her insecurities. She hopes to allow herself to actually become vulnerable; she prays that she can forget the father who drugged and abandoned her, the grandfather who disregarded her, and the siblings who left her stranded in New Orleans. Fortunately, she found Jazz just in time, and in her new life, she wants to forgive the people who taught her to never be strong, never reveal her secrets, and never trust anyone, especially family.

"Can I come in?" he asks with his right hand extended, his slim wrist poking through his baby blue button-down. She loves him in light colors, often admiring the contrast between his clothes and his skin. Whether under a spotlight or the lights of a hotel hallway, Jazz's caramel skin glows wonderfully, and he usually chooses the best wardrobe to accent his features.

∞

After meeting Ed Sullivan and seeing the tailored suits that filled his wardrobe room, Jazz refused to wear anything but expensive tailored garments. Once an anti-establishment anarchist, he essentially began to crave what he once abhorred. For two weeks, he would repeat, *"I have to get some suits like Ed"* or just sigh and release a dreamy, *"Ed's suits…"* while looking away longingly. Finally, an executive from CBS shipped forty designer suits to Charles's studio and Charles forwarded the suits to Jazz during the West Coast leg of their tour.

∞

Now, Jazz keeps most of these stylish suits in storage while traveling overseas with a few gems in his luggage; sometimes, he even wears one of the jackets to sleep.

"We got back from the show almost four hours ago. What took you so long?" June questions, stepping aside and watching Jazz enter cautiously; she only moves enough so that their shoulders rub slightly as she squeezes behind him and closes the door.

"I was tired, June," he mumbles over his shoulder, rubbing his back to accent his exhaustion. "We were crazy to let Charles and Lucy and *all these* leeches book *all these* shows. Our first world tour and I feel like we really went all around the world. My back, my fingers: everything's sore."

"Well, you wanted to be big stars, remember? You can relax here, if you want." She motions broadly over the spacious suite, indicating that he may choose the bed, the chair, or the floor—a move she practiced when scoping the suite before their show. Jazz stands awkwardly and glances between the edge of the bed and the nearby chair. She waits patiently; preparing for all the potential outcomes was a delicate point of emphasis in her plan's precision. She is a spider anticipating every move the fly might make.

Jazz chooses the least invasive option—the wool-cushioned chair between the bed and the door. He probably feels more comfortable remaining close to the exit. He steps toward the cushioned chair and allows June to pass by him. Again, their shoulders rub together and she lingers under his nose, hoping that he soaks her in. She knows that he can smell her hair as she slides under his chin, another move she practiced during two years of silenced affection. She is adept at expressing herself in playful gestures while passing through stage doors, press rooms, and vocal booths.

Though she had never spoken of her love for Jazz until her hospital stay in Australia, she now hopes that they can admit they have frequently communicated their fondness for one another. She understands that they can't dare to explore their emotions in public, but they have taken risks, secretly nudging, poking, and caressing each other when deemed publicly appropriate or privately acceptable. Jazz chuckles above her blonde locks and she feels his breath tickle her ear as she continues to pass. She peeks back and looks into his eyes and he smiles blushingly; she wonders if this smirk means contentment or contempt.

Again, she remembers that she has heard that chuckle after he makes a great song and she has seen that wry smile after he feels an interviewer has crossed a line. Their handlers have trained them not to respond when reporters begin to ask too many questions about their past or their relationship.

∞

Their creative marketing team crafted a story about a destined duet that met and began in New Orleans, the mecca of jazz and soul. Their origin provided enough *"street cred"* for the masses to believe in Jazz and June, especially after the people heard their music; but, their profile's platonic ad line limited the musicians' relationship with each other.

∞

Though the tabloids and general public have suspicions and rumors of a scandalous, secret romance; their handlers have convinced the mainstream that the duo is strictly in love with the music. They are freedom fighters, not miscegenists. In public, June and Jazz can never be 100% genuine. She fears their falsehoods have seeped into their personal relationship and they can no longer be open and honest and vulnerable with one another. Such an arrangement would never fulfill June.

A selfish diplomat at heart, Jazz only wants the peace to play his music, but June hopes to use his heartstrings to keep their song in tune because she can already hear the coming dissonance. Her exhaustion in Australia was a warning that they cannot continue to lie forever. She wants to convince him to be true to their love, even if they have to leave their newfound success and search for a difficult harmony in a simple life. June believes that if they see their love through, they will become the mother and father of the happy home that she lost years ago.

"I asked you to come by tonight so we could talk." June sits down on the edge of the bed with their knees merely inches away from each other. Her dress hangs just above her kneecaps, *a Brazilian dream*, as many Rio men have already explained to her during their brief stay. "I…I think we should…you know, *talk*."

"June, we had a seven hour flight from Buenos Aires, we came here to drop our bags, and then we rode into town for a two-hour show…" Jazz begins, slapping his hands together. He begins his joke with a wink and a slight twinge of angst, while leaning back in his chair and retrieving an identical novelty lighter and two Chesterfield Kings from his shirt pocket. "You couldn't talk to me at any point during all that?"

Intuitively, June reaches for the glass ashtray on the nightstand, and places the ashtray on the marble floor between them. She's unsure whether he enjoys her smoking, but she knows that he also doesn't mind a partner; company makes Jazz comfortable with himself.

∞

Maybe their insecurities helped spark their collaboration; they each felt like they needed a partner for the journey. Before they met, they each would stand or sit onstage alone, lonely, and incomplete, disconnected from the crowd. It wasn't until they joined forces that their sound became special, unique, and representative of a spirit that now spreads across the globe.

Who knew that these two were just as mixed up as the rest of the world?

∞

President Kennedy has promised a new era of peace, but it seems like America is on the brink of a full-scale war in Vietnam. The 60s is becoming a volatile time in America and their music, their controversial live show, and their budding relationship challenge everything that America once stood for, or maybe, they represent everything that America should have always been. They highlight hypocrisy in the land of the free, but, are they making a mockery of themselves in the process?

Secretly, June knows that she and Jazz fear going back to the United States. While being adored overseas, they have experienced a world beyond Jim Crow. They have seen people living lives that American society wouldn't allow, but, still, they won't address those fears because they can't even admit their problems. Jazz and June afraid to express their love for each other, not only because they deny the feelings, but also because they know that once they don't deny the feelings, the repercussions will most likely be disastrous to their careers, their families, and their personal lives.

Jazz lights the two cigarettes at the same time and hands one to June. She takes it and holds the stem to her nose playfully, smelling his lips on the tip, nothing sensed really, but she imagines the musk of dry martinis and potato fries. Placing the filter to her lips, a familiar inhale calms her nerves, and the two tired artists share a brief instance of awkward clarity, knowing the next moment is both contrived and spontaneous.

"I know...we're together...a lot...but, I wanted...I mean, I want...to talk...*alone.*" She gives him the look that she learned in the mirror after their first publicist told her she could double their sales on military bases.

∞

"The pouty lips make the boys go crazy," he'd say. Charles eventually fired him for selling pictures of June sleeping in a nightgown to the *National Enquirer.*

∞

Jazz notices June's learned look and raises a curious eyebrow, returning her look with a question attached. He leans back in the chair, perching the cigarette to his lips for a long drag.

"Okay...so...we're...*alone.* What...do you...want...to *talk* about?" He blows the smoke out from his lungs while pausing between words. June knows he wants to imply that they must *only* talk, reinforcing a constant barrier to any physical interaction. He consistently avoids any connection to anyone. It seems their roles, though subtle and unknown to the public, have reversed from the natural norm. June is the male chauvinist, brash, confident and unashamed, and she chases Jazz, the female damsel, quiet, shy, and unsure. She leans forward and stares directly into his eyes, the predator to the prey.

"I know it's hard…but we have to talk about…*us*." She tries to place her hand on his knee, but he recoils quickly, readjusting his legs in the creaking, cushioned chair. The wooden joints crackle against the marble floor and the moment turns sour.

"What about us?" Jazz prods defensively, taking another long drag and blowing the smoke between them. June leans back from the edge of the bed, fortifying her walls to absorb the exchange.

"Fine, I'm not afraid to say it…we both know there's more than music between us, Jazz. There always has been." She states her words forcefully, still leaning back against her arms, tilting away from Jazz. "We've been playing this game for the managers, the fans, and for what? We've damn near done everything we ever dreamed we would do, faster than either of us thought we could, but it's not as good as we thought it would be!"

"Speak for yourself," Jazz responds coldly with another low chuckle, and she still cannot tell whether he is truly content or if he feels contempt for their discussion. Or maybe, he is afraid that June is right.

"Be honest, Jazz. You're not happy and I know it." She leans forward, ashes swiftly, and places her hands between her knees. "You almost killed that reporter from *Rolling Stone* last week! You choked him half to death!"

"He deserved it! You heard what he said!" Jazz throws his left arm in the air, bringing his right hand to his lips for a long drag and exhaling with a scornful glare. "He asked me if I like being the Sitting Bull of Blues!"

"It…" June pauses to hide her giggle. "It was a joke."

"There are certain things we Natives don't joke about, June. I thought we could get away from all that when we performed overseas but the press keeps following us. They treat me different than they treat you. I keep telling you that but you don't understand." Jazz leans forward, ashes once, leans back, and glances away, trying to stare out of a curtain covered window across the suite, along the wall farthest from the door. He takes another drag and exhales the smoke, savoring the momentary escape from the world; they are safe from the press and the public's prying eyes, at least for tonight.

"I do understand, Jazz. I've always felt out-of-place, all my life." June takes a short drag and narrows her eyes as the smoke from Jazz's exhale billows across her face. She exhales her tension into the cloudy mix and stares down at the floor, remembering when she sat in Jazz's apartment, ashamed of her family's money. "Remember, I know what it's like to be misunderstood."

"No, you don't June. You're the rich white girl from Winniper County. The press treats you like a princess and they treat me like...like your pimp. They make it seem like the colored boy corrupted their *sweet angel.*" Jazz blasts sharply, looking around the hotel suite for any exits that he may have missed. "You think it was fate that we met but it wasn't. I found you and made you into a star."

"Wait, that's a lie and you know it! I performed in Scapetown by myself!" June begins to raise her voice; the lioness angers at her prey's vanity. "I begged those bar owners to let me sing before I even met you so don't try to take credit! You didn't make me!"

She points her cigarette at Jazz to get his attention; he turns his head back to her and his bright eyes investigate her intentions. They still have that connection, where they know that they know what they know. June remains at the edge of the bed, still remaining far enough from his contact barrier so that she cannot touch him without his approval.

"I'm not trying to take credit, June. You know I've always believed in your voice, but..." Jazz hesitates, pondering his words with his cigarette dying in his fingers. "They use me to sell you. You'll never know what it's like to be Sioux and I'll never know what it's like to be white. We come from two different places."

He surmises his plight so emotionlessly that his words push June back a little; she knows that he places his defenses so stiffly around him that no one knows who he is inside. His pride blocks his deeper sensitivity and his music is a Front Street façade for a very cold and sad soul.

"Say what you want, Jazz, but I see how you look at me, when we're onstage and even when we're not." She glares intently into his lying eyes, embracing his harshness with a similar candor and aiming her attack at his calculated resistance. "I told you how I feel in Australia. And you knew what I meant when I said it. It's become more than just music...for both of us."

"You're my muse, June, nothing else. Your voice inspires me, I could write songs for you forever, but…we could never be more than that. Think about how people would react!" Jazz throws his arms in the air, signifying that he has had enough of their honesty. The game is over and they must obey the rules of American society even when they are not in America. "Everything we've worked for would come crashing down. We survive because we're a novelty in the 60s, like a sign of the times. But, if people thought…we were…*together*…as *lovers*…they'd lose it. We'd either be killed or thrown in jail. Even me being here is dangerous."

"We're in Rio! No one cares here!" June makes another attempt at contact and catches his right knee in her left palm before he can stand. She tries to look into his eyes, but the moment escapes frantically as he tilts his head away and brushes her hand from his knee.

"Stop, June." Jazz stands swiftly, scrunching his nose like he smells a freshly cut onion. The tension within their conversation has soiled the air and he places his spent cigarette in the ashtray on the floor. "I have to go."

A common Jazz improvisation when faced with a tempo too fast: he bails on the rhythm completely. During a performance, he will abandon the entire melody that she's singing and create a transition toward a new movement or even a new song. Adept at following his spontaneous desertions, June rises to join him as he stands, and she places her hands on his forearms, trying to balance herself and anchor his feet.

"Please don't leave. Let's talk this through. I'm not like your family. You can't just shut me out." She gazes into his eyes, still trying to reignite that connection from the past when they could both be completely honest while sitting on the floor in his dingy basement apartment.

∞

As they molded their sound, they sang their songs at half speed so that they could learn their tempo and perform their live set with synched perfection. Their instant dedication evolved into a high level of mutual dependency and trust and she has patiently waited for him to acknowledge their bond, but she can't wait forever.

∞

Life is too short. Australia taught her that.

"Jazz, I don't want to keep making the same mistake, do you? We both have practically abandoned our families for this dream. We barely talk about home, and now, we can't even talk about us. How long are we going to lie to each other?"

"June, I'm sorry, but..." His words hide his impulses, the nerves trying to break from his instinct while his arms still remain in her grasp. She feels his fingertips lightly caress her skin in those sly touches that reveal his inner desire, but he continues his stoic struggle between good and acceptable. "We can't do this. I...I don't want to lose you. It'll ruin everything."

"No, it won't...and you won't lose me, as long as you're honest with me. We're special, Jazz. We can do whatever we want!" June gives him that cutesy smile that she practiced in the mirror for their private audience with JFK. The president loved the leaked photos that captured his eyes when June laughed at his jokes; famed photographer Lyle Hutchins caught the Commander-in-Chief looking down her blouse. Remembering her escapades, Jazz recognizes her guile and wrinkles his lips. He knows her looks all too well, but she hopes a joke will add levity to his concerns. "We don't have to hide...*from anyone.* We're not in your dirty apartment anymore."

"Hey, my apartment wasn't that dirty." He smiles finally, relaxing for a moment and tipping his head to the side. "It was all I could afford...*back then.*"

"And what could you afford now?" She asks knowingly, prodding him to dream just a little; she knows how to stroke his ego.

"*Now?* Now, I could buy that entire, crummy apartment building from Mrs. Shanahan." Jazz replies, "I could blow it up and build a movie theater on the land."

"You're right, you *could do* that. You *could do* anything you want." June continues to stroke. "But, why don't you do what you want? Why are you so happy being unhappy, when what makes us happy is right here, right now?"

Her questions pounce on his ego and his rationale at the same time. She has executed a last desperate assault to seduce the only person who understands her, knowing that such a seduction could bring the downfall of their careers and even endanger their lives.

"If we…it's just…it would ruin everything, June. I don't want to lose you and…everything we worked for. I've had enough relationship problems." Jazz confesses, pleading with June while she moves closer within his arms and leans into his chest without opposition. "My family doesn't even speak, because we have too many secrets. Do you understand? This would just be another secret and…we'd be in more danger than we already are. Why can't we just keep *'us'* in the music?"

"I told you, it's bigger than music," she coos softly, still moving in ever so slightly, so that she doesn't scare her skittish prey. "And we're special. We don't have to keep secrets from one another."

"But they'll never let us go back home, June. Not that we want to go back, but still. Our families, the whole country would turn against us. What about our fans? What about my mother? What about your grandparents? Everything about everyone will change. Maybe if we were in a different time…" he replies in a progressively gentler tone, and the moment becomes more intimate. A faint heat develops between their bodies, pulsing in mutual attraction. She senses the energy that emerges when she anticipates his intuition while they improvise through a bridge in a song and she knows where the inevitable harmony will lead them. She remembers when they first sang together in his apartment; it was like they were uniquely bonded.

∞

Their voices formed a spontaneous yet planned harmony that sprang from a deep consciousness. She could sing his thoughts while he accompanied her voice with his piano. Two souls seemingly intertwined, and for them to deny their connection would be even worse than death.

∞

"I can't imagine how our families would react, June; but I don't think it would be good. We still don't understand why your grandmother never told you about visiting us as kids. Berthine, she acts like she never knew your family, but, I swear I recognized you when she first saw you."

"It's like you said back in your apartment…" June lifts up her head to look into his eyes and they lock in that trance when their onstage, and the music takes over, and they don't even feel their physical bodies. They simply glance at one another, and then stare out to the crowd, and only sound and perfection sink into their cognition as their love flows with a feeling of heaven falling all around them. "Family is overrated…especially if they don't support you doing what you love or being with someone who makes you happy. Our families barely support us now. Only your sister Lucy has really tried. Charles just wanted to get rich and my family abandoned me before I even left Scapetown. We don't owe them anything, because we're in love. Everyone can get over it or not but it's just that simple."

"What if…" Jazz tries to question but June raises her index finger to his lips.

"If you don't love me, then leave. If you don't feel what I feel, you can call me crazy and go," June demands assertively, steering their conversation toward an impasse where he must decide their fate. She's not willing to walk out on their tour if he spurns her, but they will both know that their time together is coming to an end. "But if you *do* love me, then just shut up and kiss me. I'm tired of waiting."

She speaks her words powerfully, remembering the instructions her grandfather gave Duke before he became a mute: *"Speak confidently, and demand what you want and you will never look weak."*

June has found that the madman's lessons are effective during most applications, yet Papa never intended for his advice to help his granddaughter succeed in business or true love. June looks Jazz squarely in the eyes as if they are gunfighters preparing to draw, and in a sense, they are. She only hopes that he shoots her first.

There is a long pause that feels like a small eternity as the hum of the air-cooling fan purrs through the hotel suite. June believes the climactic moment is finally here, but his eyes still resist lingering upon her features for too long.

"I can't, June. I mean…*we can't.* I do…I do care about you…*a lot*…and I may feel…*something*, you know…like what you say you feel, but…" Jazz stumbles over his words and his feet as he breaks their embrace and twists his body away from her. He almost loses his balance on his heels so he leans against the chair and sidesteps toward the door. "It's…I mean, I…I…uh…it's just not worth it if we lose everything."

Jazz trips slightly at the door, but he quickly recovers, turns the knob, and steps out of the suite before stopping and turning back with a sad, but relieved face. A wry smile graces his lips and the worried wrinkles in his forehead vanish from over his eyebrows.

"I'm sorry." he whispers without force, truly vexed while he carefully closes the door as delicately as he apologized, leaving June incomplete in the middle of her hotel suite. She stands barefooted and unsatisfied in her undersized sundress. She knew of no other way to court the uncourtable man, chasing the unchaseable dream. Jazz remains unyieldingly committed to never being committed to anyone.

After a few moments, there is another knock at the door and June's heart skips a beat as she eagerly races to open the door, yet she hears a low grunt as she does.

"June! Don't op..." Jazz yells from outside as June opens the door; Jazz tumbles into the room, bleeding from his head. Two masked gunmen follow him and they push June onto the marble floor. She falls with a hard thud as one of the gunmen searches Jazz's denim pockets before joining his partner and ransacking the hotel suite. The frightened stars are receiving a proper welcome to Rio.

"Jazz! Jazz, wake up!" June screams hysterically, turning her head to him and watching his eyes flutter in a haze. His pupils roll around uncontrollably and she fears that he may lose consciousness. The gunmen pilfer the suite feverishly, speaking frantic Portuguese while raiding June's luggage on the opposite side of the bed. She travels light, rarely carrying any money or jewels, except for her grandmother's pearls.

∞

The day after she and her siblings arrived at their family's mansion, Olivia gave June the pearls as a part of a promise that they both could never keep. Her grandmother begged her to forgive her grandfather and enjoy her life in Winniper County, and Olivia promised to protect June and Christina, something she said she could not do for Teresa.

∞

Though June hopes that one day she can forgive her grandfather for his many offenses, she will never enjoy his company. She could never live happily under his watchful eye, not after what happened to Kenny.

So, because she was unable to keep her side of the bargain, June rarely wears her grandmother's luxurious pearls unless she's onstage. The jewels shine wonderfully in the stage lights, and when she wears them during television appearances, she hopes that her grandmother sees her and knows that June still loves her. June also sends pictures and magazines to Duke, hoping to console her big brother, whom she once admired but has now replaced. He, Christina, and Earl left her in Scapetown; he chose his side of the fence and they must play on. To June, Duke has become "Papa in-waiting", and the closer her brother has become to their grandfather, the farther he has removed himself from June's heart.

Much like Teresa, June views Olivia as a blameless victim; the family's matriarch is a woman caught within whatever circumstances the family still refuses to share. All that money and wealth still cannot buy their freedom, but June still wears her grandmother's necklace so that when her family still sees her, they realize that she still thinks of them. She hopes they understand that her distance is only intended to protect herself from Papa, though she knows that his reach is both far and wide. She knows what her grandfather is capable of doing to those who don't obey.

Carelessly, she has left the pearls around her neck, keeping them on after tonight's show, dreaming of a special occasion. Jazz sometimes speaks of Olivia fondly, though she and Berthine have lost his trust. June prays that all their coincidental connections will help him believe that their union could be a blessing for both their families. She had hoped to make all these special points tonight, but, undeniably, tonight has become special for all the wrong reasons.

"Turn! Turn!" one of the gunmen shouts over June, flipping her onto her back roughly. She stares into two, coal-black eyes with furrowed eyelids that peer menacingly through a dusky grey ski mask.

Surprisingly, this is not June and Jazz's first time being robbed.

∞

They were the victims of several French pickpockets and London surcharges during the first European leg of their tour.

∞

Some artists think the Europeans are polite, but June thinks they're just nice enough to stealthily rob a bloke without pushes to the ground or guns to the face. The Europeans simply empty pockets and leave nothing but a dumbfounded look on their marks' faces. June wonders if the European thieves even look back. Are they proud of their craft or remorseful for their crime? Are they still disinclined to see the despair they've caused? Does a con artist take time to appreciate the finished product?

"It's best to avoid eye contact," June thinks, *"But the South Americans have more machismo than the Europeans."* The thieves in Rio will rob a nun face-to-face and stare into her eyes so that she knows who she really belongs to.

In this domineering fashion, the masked gunman hunches over June and places his entire weight on top of her so that his jean-covered genitals press against her thigh. She must have given him a contemptuous look that incited his anger because he growls at her and reaches for her neck roughly. "You don' like?"

"No! Don't!" June cries into his ear as he rips the pearl necklace from her neckline and lifts her grandmother's gift in his right hand, taunting her. June can see a devilish smile crease his lips and she looks to Jazz, who is still unconscious and unresponsive, as the armed bandit points his gun at her right eye.

"Please, no! Jazz, wake up!" She pleads desperately and keeps her eyes focused on Jazz.

"You, June? He, Jazz, right?" The aggressive thief tucks his gun under her chin, turning her head back towards him so that he has her undivided attention. "I like you guys, *'Bananas on Sundays, oh-oh, Bananas on Sundays'*, ha ha!"

"We thought you have more cash," the other gunman adds with a laugh as he tugs on his partner's right arm. The necklace thief rises from June's frame and motions for his partner to open the door before waving Olivia's necklace over June. The two exit and leave June and Jazz lying on the floor in the defiled hotel suite. She reaches over to Jazz and places her hand against his face, but he remains unconscious on top of the Peruvian rug near the foot of the bed. She rises to her knees and crawls to him until she kneels over his bruised and bloodied head, trying to figure out what to do. She doesn't want to call security; she instantly imagines the scandal, but what if he needs medical attention?

"Jazz! Jazz, wake up! Wake up, please!" June softly lifts Jazz's head into her lap and she runs her hand over his forehead gently, causing his eyes to blink. His body begins to stir and he opens his right eye, wincing from the pain of his wounds. June smiles to see him awake, but she still worries over the bruises on his head. "Are you okay? Should I call a doctor? Should we go to the hospital?"

"No...no...don't...I'm okay...I'm okay...I...I told you...after Australia...I'm never going...to a hospital...again." He slurs his words, filled with pain and pride while stammering in confusion. Jazz continues to blink his eyes as if he is seeing the world for the first time, like a newborn child. He raises his hand to June's face, mesmerized by a new light, before glancing dazedly at the open door. "Can you...lock the door? I still...need a second."

"Okay. Here...just take it easy." June lifts his head, reaches for a pillow from the bed, and slowly slides it under his head. She then rushes to the door, closes it, locks it, and slides the chain latch into place. Jazz tenderly lifts himself up on his elbows and begins to lean against the pillow and bed as June rushes back to his side. She kneels next to him and stares at a bloody gash over his right eyebrow.

"How bad it is?" she asks worriedly, seeing a large bump already beginning to form.

"I don't think I'll be doing any photo shoots for a while," Jazz jokes, patting the blood from the wound and taking a taste. "Hm, strawberry."

"We could put makeup over it once it heals."

"May I have a wet towel for now?" Jazz asks with discomfort in his voice; his tone has a tightness that a mother can hear, knowing her child is in pain.

"Okay...just a second." June rises from her knees, walks to the sink next to the bathroom, turns on the faucet, and grabs a towel. She hasn't processed everything that has just happened and her mind flashes to her memories of Lucy's labor, when they bustled around Jazz's apartment retrieving towels and glasses of water. She comes back to the present and rinses the towel hurriedly before turning off the faucet and wringing the towel in the sink. When she walks back to Jazz, she kneels next to him and dabs his wound lightly.

"Ouch!" He grimaces, narrowing his eyes and curling his eyebrows. His hands instinctively grab her arms, and he carefully tries to guide her as if they are learning a new song. "Take it easy."

"Don't be a baby. Let me do it," June orders as she throws one leg over Jazz's hips and leans in closer, straddling him, putting more of her weight on his waist, and pinning him into submission. She continues dabbing his forehead with the damp towel and wiping away the blood caked around his right eye. The wound over his eyebrow is deep within his skin, but the blow did not break the bone of his skull. June gently presses the towel onto his wound and soaks up the blood inside the gash.

"Ah!" Jazz yelps sharply, grabbing her arms again and pulling her closer to him. "June, you could never be a nurse!"

"Be nice…" She smiles while cocking her head to the side. "I just saved our lives."

"They weren't going to kill us. They just wanted money."

"Apparently they were fans, too."

"What do you mean?" Jazz replies unknowingly, forgetting that he was completely unconscious during the robbery.

"One of them sang 'Bananas on Sundays'." June answers and there is an awkward pause between the two before Jazz bursts into laughter. "He sang our song while robbing us."

"'Bananas on Sundays'? 'He sang our song while robbing us'?" Jazz repeats as he impulsively takes June into his arms and begins to playfully roll around with her on the Peruvian rug. "I remember the first night we sang that song in *Teezy's*…I knew we had something special!"

"Well, I'm just glad we didn't sing that rib song!"

"You didn't like my rib song? How did it go? Uh… 'Teezy's bar's got ribs'…uh…I don't remember the rest."

"Good, I like *our* music! I'm glad you stopped writing those stupid jingles." June coos softly as they play until she rests on top of Jazz and lightly pats his drying wound. He winces with a smile; the two now lay together on the soft rug, no longer prone for a robbery, but still prone. "I'm even glad they robbed us…at least they brought you back here."

"Wow, that's a horrible way to look at this, June. Ow, shouldn't we call someone, Hank, our security?" Jazz wonders and feels to the top of his head with June still leaning into him. He rests his head against the pillow at the foot of the bed and her face remains close to his lips while she still pats the wound over his eye, every so often. Her close care gives her a reason to keep him in this position.

"I asked everyone to stay away tonight for a reason. I knew the risks; I bet someone in our security team tipped them off, but this is what we asked for remember?" June leans in closer, their lips merely a hair apart. "You have to take the good and the bad."

"Yes, I remember...I just never thought it would be like this. June, you can't tell me that you imagined everything happening this fast, I mean...I knew we had something, but..." he pauses cautiously and glances toward the door, but he then returns his eyes to her. There is another long break in the conversation as they communicate with their eyes. They're back onstage, consorting over an improvised melody and resolving the tonality so that they can return to the chorus and bring the harmony home.

"Jazz...I just had to tell you...earlier, I'm just tired of lying to myself. And I don't care what anyone thinks. I don't care if we lose everything we worked for. Right now, I only care about you." June confides delicately, while dabbing his wound with the towel in her left hand and holding his left check in her right palm. "I'm afraid, too. I don't want to ruin things, but..."

"Life is short," Jazz completes her sentence, still staring into her eyes, seeing through her pupils, and resting deeply within her soul—a place only he can find.

"Yes, it's too short. Since Australia, I've..." she tries to finish her sentence, but he kisses her swiftly, taking her by happy surprise. All those wonderful feelings come to fruition. Their kiss unleashes a rare, humanistic honesty, locked safely behind a latched door in a foreign hotel. Far away from Winniper County and Scapetown, their kiss creates a spiritual bridge built for two. Their tongues walk together, side by side, crossing social boundaries as their lips meet over and over. They release repressed passion that has existed since the first time they met two years ago in May.

A sweet kiss, she hopes it is their final surrender. At twenty-two, June has no interest in returning to America if it means that she is not free to love him, free to connect openly with the person who makes her the happiest. When June and Jazz met, they knew their connection was special, and they saw their relationship evolve into a musical destiny; they are two pieces to the same soul, sharing one unspeakable bond.

She could never completely explain their attraction even with an infinite amount of words, but she knows their love is real and eternal. She would lay within his arms forever if the Copacabana Palace could drift into heaven. Their kiss, long, slow, and soft, seals their truth. They part briefly and there is a hesitation like tip toes edging against a cliff. They tenuously tremble in the finality, bodies shaking in unison, knowing that once they cross this threshold, their world will never again feel the same balance. The cliff will be gone and the rules of gravity will take hold in an endless free fall with unknown damage to their careers and maybe even their lives. The danger can't be overstated.

Could this moment be the best of it all? Are they now on a fated path to fall? Will they fail at love and forever know that this kiss was a blessing and a curse? She feels a quick twinge of vulnerability and she timidly touches her neck. It's a nervous reflex that he recognizes; she likes to feel her grandmother's pearl necklace before she performs onstage, thinking that the pearls are her only connection to anything of value.

"Where's Olivia's necklace?" Jazz asks abruptly, recalling the necklace from his own past, when the mysterious white lady would come pay charity to his family. June pats her neck, momentarily missing her pearls while remembering how she would clutch them out of habit.

∞

She often hoped that male callers and catty women would see the luxurious peals as evidence of her wealth and esteem; and consequently, they would treat her accordingly, with proper taste and respect.

∞

Now, those admiring faces are gone. and the vainest parts of her identity have left with them.

"They stole it. It was probably the only thing of value in here." June admits softly and Jazz's face changes to sorrow. He seems more upset than her and slams his fist into the plush rug.

"I should've killed those animals...it...it just happened so fast..." he stammers sadly and touches his finger to his wound, shaking his head in disappointment. "I'm sorry, June. I'll get them back for you. I know they meant a lot."

"But you mean more." She laughs tenderly and leans into him again, holding Jazz's chin in her hand as he stares affectionately into her eyes. "I don't need that necklace."

"No, it's not about the necklace. That was Olivia's. I remember her wearing it. It's special." Jazz retorts instinctively, and she can see a burgeoning masculinity, a call to duty that he has never expressed. "I should've been able to protect you, June. How can I protect us in America if…"

His words and worries make June smile without concern; she sees the world differently and the melting of a cold heart is all the evidence that she needs to believe in a better future. She didn't know how much she wanted to hear the famously insolent Sioux boy confess that he cares for her. Her joy somewhat scares her because she never wanted protection, until now.

"Is this really every little girl's dream?" June thinks. *"Do we all want someone to love? Or am I somehow becoming a cliché?"* She doesn't know the answers, but her instinctual reaction to his words betrays any feminist mantra of a 60s rabble-rouser. Her militant attitude eases toward all the social mores and all the walls that protect her heart begin to crumble.

"If you want to protect me, Jazz, then all you have to do is stay here," she whispers, leaning in closely to his face so that their noses touch at the tips. "And promise not to leave me."

"June…you know I'm not going anywhere. I…I promise," Jazz sighs, giving up his fight and relinquishing his fear of the future consequences. His worries fade as he begins to enjoy their present truth. "I love you…it's true. I always have. I just…"

"Don't say it if you don't mean it," June demands firmly to assure his sincerity. "This is not about music or business. This is about *us*…June Bethune…and…Jazz Lancaster. Who are we going to be from now on?"

Their lips touch slightly as she speaks, feeling the edges of their noses rub together and their breathing matches in rhythm.

"I promise. I love you, June. I hate that it took a bump on the head for me to admit it, but…you're right. Life is too short." He seals his words with a kiss that equally seals their future success and demise. In the back of their minds, they both wonder if they should ever return to America's Jim Crow society. How can they live in a divided country? How can they enjoy their love with their families, their communities, and their country at war?

June and Jazz forgets their apprehensions like loving drug addicts sharing a needle through their kiss. They appease each other's senses, knowing that the high can never last and the effects will dim with each touch, because nothing ever compares to the first time.

Happily satisfied and spiritually satiated, they dip into a cool confusion, kisses and caresses they can't mention outside of her hotel suite in Brazil. They have found a quiet, temporary oasis; the poor, Sioux boy and the wealthy, white girl roll through the suite, locked in one another's arms while the world sleeps. Far away, their fans and families rest, unknowing that a new, controversial love barrels toward American society on a collision course that no one can stop. She leans into his ear and touches her lips to his lobes.

"I don't fear the cage 'cause only you can trap me," June croons with a giggle. "We're fools 'cause we waited too long to be happy."

JULY 1965

Sunday	Monday	Tuesday	Wednesday	Thursday	Friday	Saturday
				1	2	3
4 	5	6	7	8	9	10
11	12	13	14	15	16	17
18	19	20	21	22	23	24
25	26	27	28	29	30	31

Sunday, July 4, 1965

Lucy Lancaster Cashmen

Fear for her children,
Raised in a world of hate,
Hoping for love
And a place of escape.
Dreams within dreams,
Fantasies achieved
While reality creates the chains
Where love can be cleaved,
Chopped and deceived,
Corrupted and believed
The fairytale that love
Is all they need to succeed.
Still as a force
With the strength to avoid a slaughter
And save the father,
The mother,
Their Sioux son,
And their white daughter.

Lucy Lancaster Cashmen quietly waters the vegetable garden outside her mountain home in Spokane, Washington. She planted squash seeds two weeks ago, and she's already seeing the seedlings sprout from the ground. She leans back, draped in rare sunlight, and inhales the fresh air, remembering the hot New Orleans humidity.

∞

After her children were born, Lucy no longer liked living in Scapetown, and she never considered returning to Winniper County.

∞

Now, at age thirty-three, Lucy still remembers the desolate Sioux village as a place of poverty, fear, and haunting silence.

∞

When she was a child, she often walked to the edges of her village, near the Winniper family's oil rigs, and she would stare into the forest, wondering what lay beyond. Berthine told Lucy, Charles, and Jazz that Olivia and her family lived on the other side of the forest, but Berthine forbade the children from meeting the rest of the Winnipers, *"times as they are"*, she'd say.

Although Lucy was mute until her eighteenth birthday, after she found her voice, she also discovered her confidence. A few years later, emboldened with newfound poise and some savings from Berthine, Lucy moved to New Orleans with Charles and established herself as a helpful sidekick to her brother's treachery. Almost immediately after their arrival, the siblings diverted from one another, delving into ventures that represented their respective identities.

While Lucy immersed herself in the culture and music that Jazz had always cherished from inside their cabin, Charles followed his ego and became a surly, dominating force in Scapetown's underground. As a Sioux playboy and hustler, he could pass for Creole or black and his ruthless ambition quickly made him a town favorite. "Big Charles" financed pool halls, sponsored racketeering, and hired jazz musicians that purchased Lucy's imported instruments, or else they couldn't play in Scapetown, not safely, that is. He made it a point to exploit anyone and everyone he could while living some previously conceived fantasy.

Even as children, growing up in Berthine's cabin, Charles often thought of himself as *the man of the house*, and due to her early speech impediment, Lucy never mounted much resistance. She played the role of the submissive older sister, the nurturing pseudo-maternal figure that counterbalanced Berthine's domineering ways. Lucy never had much ambition until she began to speak. It was like her words gave her the power to interact with the world in a more complete way. When potential clients showed interest in her eye for uniquely crafted instruments that she found tucked away in Scapetown's many music shops and culture boutiques, she saw an opportunity to spread her wings, but she still felt reluctant to do so.

Lucy only developed notions of becoming a serious entrepreneur because Charles became increasingly reckless and borrowed more money for gambling and alcohol binges. While he began to waste money in Scapetown blues bars, Lucy created a music supply service and ordered custom instruments for New Orleans' most gifted and wealthy residents. Her niche catalog eventually became a hit and Lucy's high-class clientele rewarded her business with access to a world that she never imagined. She instantly surpassed Charles in name and stature. He waded through the underworld, squeezing profit from crooks and addicts like himself, and Lucy built a modest music empire based on legal transactions and her love for a life and culture that she had only heard Jazz dream about while they lived in South Dakota.

No longer a quiet mouse, Lucy attracted the attention of the musical elite in New Orleans; their deep, Southern pockets found a fashionable appreciation for her novelty instruments purchased throughout the city or imported from abroad. One very appreciative trader, Marcus Cashmen, a Creole business man with familial ties to the Rockefellers and Standard Oil, created a notable partnership between Lancaster Instruments and the East Atlantic Trade Commission. His fruitful negotiations led to the import and export of more custom-built pianos, horns, and string instruments to and from the New Orleans docks. With Lucy's exceptional eye and Marcus's access to unlimited supplies, they facilitated large-scale cargo shipments of branded instruments to every shipyard along America's Eastern Seaboard.

How could life be any better? Lucy had become a successful colored woman in the South and the fruits of her labor doubled when she and Marcus fell in love. They enjoyed a simple wedding at the courthouse chapel; Charles sobered himself enough to give away the bride and Jazz forgave Charles long enough to play a black, timber piano during the ceremony. Their marriage created a powerful union between a Sioux woman and a Creole man who shared the same vision of their future. United against the odds, Lucy and Marcus happily turned their modest success into middle-class wealth, yet their money could not protect their ideal future after Lucy gave birth to Daisy and Darrel.

To the gawking eyes in Scapetown, little Daisy was a white girl being raised by colored parents during the tumultuous last stand of Jim Crow. The family did not fit the mold or the social norm. While no one bothered to question their Sioux son Darrel, people walking by and police officers often stopped the family and asked what they were doing with a white child. During their first year as a family, Lucy became increasingly fearful whenever she was with Daisy in public. As Lucy ran her errands and tended to business, she couldn't leave Daisy at home because whenever the twins were apart, they would wail and cry incessantly. Even if she hired a nanny, she still dreaded the evenings and weekends, frightened to hold her child in front of the wrong bigot.

Suddenly, Lucy felt the need to avoid the New Orleans streets that she once loved. As a single entrepreneur, backed by her wild brother, she could roam around Scapetown searching for new novelties, but, after her children were born, Lucy became a cautious mother, concerned only with protecting her children and her family above all else. They became her highest priorities. Though she enjoyed helping Jazz and June promote their stage performances, she didn't have the time or energy to balance her readjusted concerns. She also grew tired of watching over Charles, as if he were another child with a completely different set of problems. He tried to control the family's success by forming a record label, but she saw him as a train wreck waiting to happen; and when Jazz and June began to tour across the coasts, Lucy knew it was time for her and her family to leave New Orleans.

In the fall of 1962, unhindered by money or means, Lucy and Marcus packed all their belongings into a moving truck and drove as far northwest as they could. They visited towns and suburbs across Oregon, the Dakotas, Montana, Nevada, and Idaho before traveling to Washington where they immediately felt safe within the mountains and open plains.

Lucy found a hilltop farm for sale on the outskirts of Spokane; and when Marcus saw the sprawling lake at the edge of the property, the Cashmen family settled into a new home with new hopes for peace and tranquility.

∞

Going on three years as of the coming fall, Lucy has basked in a level of comfort that she has never known.

∞

At first, it was hard for her to release the stress of living such a secluded life in Berthine's cabin and looking after her younger brothers for all those years. Compounded with the anxiety of raising a white daughter in New Orleans, Lucy was grateful that her family left the city, though she still had questions that remained unanswered.

Suffering from speech loss had affected the early years of her life more than she initially understood, and even after gaining her voice and finding success, she still struggled with her unknown past. Her means and resources allowed her to ensure Berthine had the best care in Winniper County; and, after Berthine survived her cancer scare, Olivia Winniper came to visit her longtime friend in the hospital. Lucy had travelled to Winniper County, alone, so she had a chance to speak with Olivia for the first time since becoming a mother. Lucy asked Olivia whether she knew Lucy would have twins *like Darrel and Daisy*, but Olivia said she didn't. Olivia even denied remembering any conversations with Berthine about Lucy's pregnancy.

While she was a child, Lucy saw Olivia deliver both Jazz and Charles to Berthine's cabin during the night. Over the years, Olivia visited Berthine's cabin for birthdays and special occasions, yet Lucy knew so little about Olivia and the Winniper family. Berthine told her tidbits about the Winnipers' oil wealth and the rig churning in the distance, but Olivia's connection to the Lancasters always seemed…secretive and mysterious. As the children aged inside her cabin, Berthine never confessed that Olivia had delivered Jazz and Charles, and Lucy could never ask questions before she could speak. Once she could communicate, she told her brothers what she knew, but, in truth, she no longer wanted to know. Though she feared that Jazz and Charles may not be her brothers, she avoided pressing Berthine any further; and once Lucy gave birth to Daisy and Darrel, she had more immediate concerns.

∞

Life has taught her that ignorance is bliss; Lucy has attained success, established financial independence, and built a family of her own that is now safely tucked away in the mountains.

∞

She didn't want to ask any questions or, worse, discover any answers that might disrupt her world any further. She left all the drama behind in New Orleans and she chose to accept that Berthine was her adoptive mother and there was no need to know the identities of her or her brothers' biological parents. She concluded that their parents were simply unwilling, unimportant, and/or dead.

Still ignorant to the fact that she is the eldest Sioux child of the late Teresa Winniper, Lucy became content to care for her adoptive mother as penance for lessons learned. In Berthine's household, Lucy had felt more like a mother figure than a child. She supervised her younger brothers and cared for the family as Berthine said a daughter should; in fact, her childhood had prepared her for motherhood. Lucy never questioned her responsibilities and even after she could speak, she still tried her best to care for her brothers.

While stumbling into their teenage years, as Jazz and Charles grew under her nose, she could already see her brothers begin to veer toward diverging paths. Jazz went the way of the wayward artist, trapped in his mind, always trying to find himself, while Charles went the way of a willful warrior, trapped in his pride, and always trying to prove himself.

Lucy remained in the middle, trying to help them as best she could. After traveling to New Orleans and seeing her spontaneous success, Charles implemented his plan to fully infiltrate the Scapetown underground and she did her best to keep him alive. He robbed gambling spots and conned poker games, manipulating the players to mistrust one another; he created the conflict to engineer fast allies and, in truth, Big Charles was born long before he arrived in Scapetown.

Lucy had listened to his plan during the trip down south, but she never believed Charles would fulfill his gangster goals. He had witnessed Jazz grow up with talent, and Charles realized that he had none. While Jazz listened and emulated the blues bands that they heard on the radio, Charles listened and emulated the crooks and con-artists from the crime blotters. When he and Lucy left town, he reluctantly gave his guitar to Jazz, and, in New Orleans, he tried to make his own way.

One night, when he arrived at their shared apartment with his hands filled with bloody money and his palms literally covered in dry red splotches, she knew that he had gone too far. She also realized that he would self-destruct and possibly take her with him, unless she helped minimize the damage. Much like back in South Dakota, Lucy became a sister, a mother, and a friend. Several times during their first year in New Orleans, she bailed her brother out of jail and helped him skip town when the heat got too close, even at the risk of her business and her budding relationship with Marcus.

During that time, Charles and Lucy developed a sacred kinship that Jazz couldn't understand, nor did he try. Lucy was willing to dirty her hands to keep Charles relatively clean, but Jazz never required such sacrifice because he resented the idea that he needed any help. Left in Winniper County while Charles and Lucy ran the streets of New Orleans, Jazz was already the odd boy out; but, as Charles and Lucy increased their monetary allowances that they sent home to Berthine, they encouraged their brother to pursue his art and they tried to care for him as they cared for each other.

When Jazz moved to New Orleans for music school, Charles and Lucy helped pay for his trip. They had prepared to slowly introduce their baby brother to Scapetown, but they couldn't predict that he would be kicked out of school within his first year. Initially, Lucy allowed Jazz to stay in her apartment until he drove her nuts, and then she found him a boarding house until he drove the den mother nuts, and then Charles found Jazz a basement apartment with a piano inside—the former tenant was a nosey musician who reneged on a bet with "Big Charles".

Before Jazz moved into the basement floor of Mrs. Shanahan's apartment building, he never knew about the raucous monorails that rattled the underground apartment. As those noisy trains entered the nearby station, the frequent, passing commotion became the most unique feature of Jazz's basement experience. He complained constantly, and Lucy and Charles laughed about his complaints just like when they were children in Berthine's cabin. Their baby brother added a color balance to their life in New Orleans; and, when he left with June, Lucy and Charles had only memories and new problems.

∞

Today, Lucy grins and chuckles sweetly while remembering the night she gave birth to Daisy and Darrel. She believes the birth of her Sioux and white babies was a fortunate occurrence for Jazz and June to experience.

∞

Two musicians turned to lovers after witnessing a miracle, though they refused to admit it until years later. Lucy knew from the moment she met June that Jazz loved her; but, it was only a matter of when he would submit to the idea that yes, he may always need her because she makes him happy.

∞

Now, Lucy prays that her baby brother is happy with June and his career, because Lucy understands how love and money can change a person for better or worse. Loving her children with all her heart, Lucy believes her Sioux son and white daughter are gifts from God. She glances at the four-year-olds through an open window while they play and laugh together in the living room. She believes that Darrel and Daisy will always be happy as long as they have each other. She can't help but laugh as she hears their loud rants from within the two-story cottage home.

One of them raises the volume of the television so that a rerun of *Superman* blares throughout the first floor.

∞

Against her wishes, Marcus installed a satellite receiver and bought an RCA color television for the children. He explained that the family needed to stay somewhat connected to the rest of the world, in case of an emergency. He also wanted Darrel and Daisy to see their Uncle Jazz's televised performances; but, in reality, Marcus wanted what all parents want: peace and quiet, for as long possible, yet, that is often the opposite of what a television actually accomplishes inside the home.

∞

"Superman is a weirdo!" Daisy screams from inside the living room. "I love Wonder Woman!"

"Wonder Woman is the worst!" Darrel barrels, hopping on the couch and jumping up and down on the cushions. "Superman can fly and see through walls!"

"Mama can see through walls, too!" Lucy yells from outside, peering through the window and staring sternly at her little munchkins. Darrel stands on the edge of the couch, preparing to fly, while Daisy sits inches away from the television. "Darrel, get off that couch! And Daisy, move away from the TV!"

"Sorry, Mama," Daisy murmurs politely, scooting back toward her brother as he jumps from the couch and bunny hops toward the window.

"Hey, Mama, what's for dinner?"

"I'm not sure, my little wabbit." Lucy admits casually, removing her gardening glove and running her hand over Darrel's forehead. She then places her hand on the side of his face and tugs his left ear. "My, how big your ears have grown."

"Aw, Mom, stop!"

"How come you don't cook like the moms on TV?" Daisy asks, joining her brother as they talk to their mother through the open window.

"Yea, Donna Stone cooks every night," Darrel adds, playfully pushing his mother's hand away from his face. "She bakes cookies and cakes…"

"Well, all of that baking and cooking is a lot of work, son."

"But you don't have a job anymore."

"You and Daddy quit," Daisy explains, giggling into her hand.

381

"We didn't *quit*, we retired," Lucy explains to her children. "Which means we didn't want to work anymore, and that includes *cooking* and *cleaning* and…"

"Is that why you hired Maria?" Darrel interrupts; he moves his hands over an imaginary broom and imitates the Cashmen family's live-in maid. Normally, Maria hums around the cottage, seeing to any household duty; but, right now, she's out running some special errands for the family's Fourth of July celebration.

"Yes, that's exactly why we hired her. Don't you like her?"

"Oh yes, she's lovely," Daisy confesses happily and places her hands against her cheeks.

"She's teaching us…uh, *es-span-nyol*," Darrel pronounces his Spanish delicately.

"Muy bien," Lucy responds with an encouraging round of applause, clapping her open palm against her gloved hand. "Now, you two keep quiet in there, and wait for Maria while I finish my gardening."

"Okay," the twins answer in unison, returning to sit in front of the television, one a little closer than the other.

"Daisy…"

"Sorry, Mama," Daisy mutters as she scoots away from the television. Lucy continues to tend to her squash sprouts until she hears the family's 1965 Mazda Familia Coupe pull into their uphill, gravel driveway. Marcus honks the horn while accelerating and coasting toward the home. He stops the car next to the garden, turns off the ignition with a broad smile, opens the driver's side door, and hops out excitedly.

"Hey, honey!" Marcus strides to her and playfully grabs her waist as she rises to meet him. He pulls Lucy in close and kisses her on the cheek. "You smell nice. Has Maria come home yet?"

"No, not yet…" Lucy frowns, wishing he would concern himself more with her, though she also feels the inside of her stomach growl. She can't tell whether her insides churn from hunger or nervousness.

"Oh, ok. I hope she hurries up. I'm hungry." Marcus pouts briefly before tugging Lucy's shoulders so that she leans back and looks him in the eyes. He gives her a sly wink and their plan remains in motion after a tactical illusion to hide a surprise from their inquisitive children.

"Happy *Independence* Day to you, too," Lucy jokes in a false huff, a Sioux woman jesting at the holiday's notions, but she still hopes for more attention from her husband. Marcus leans over her and wipes her hair from her face.

"Oh, right. I'm sorry, dear." He kisses her forehead twice and leans even closer as he wraps his arms completely around her and gently lays her down amongst her daisies; they share a serene moment, while submerged in their youthful garden like new plants finding their resting plot. "Happy 4th, Lucy. I'm happy we're having *company*, today…at least for the kids."

"Me, too."

"What are the rascals up to?" Marcus asks, raising his upper body and peering into the home through the window. Daisy and Darrel continue watching Superman fly through the air while they mimic the hero's arms in flight. Their father happily spies on them before speaking loudly enough that his children can hear him. "Where are my superheroes?

"Dad!" They holler and begin to scamper, turning to the window and running toward their father.

"Oh, they are extremely *super*, today," Lucy begins, as she rises beside her husband and leans her head into his shoulder, savoring the lasting moments of quiet before the munchkins take over. "They've been debating superheroes all afternoon. I told you not to get that television."

"Sheesh, Lucy, you're just as strict as your mother. They'll be fine," Marcus chuckles casually as he stands and opens his arms to scoop Daisy from the window.

"Daddy, where were you all day?"

"Well, I had to pick up a few things, Daisy," Marcus teases with another wink towards Lucy. "We had to get ready for the celebration!"

"What'd you get?" Darrel asks, sitting eagerly in the window seal.

"Nothing that concerns you, little man," Marcus jests, holding Daisy in his left arm while reaching out with his right index and poking Darrel in the nose. "Except for a couple surprises, maybe we'll see some fireworks!"

"*Fireworks!*" Darrel exclaims elatedly, leaning on the window's edge. "Oh, this is going to be great."

"Watch yourself, Darrel! Don't fall!" Lucy warns her son as she stands within the garden and places her hands against Darrel's waist. "Last thing we need is to call the doctor on a holiday."

"We could go to the hospital in town!" Darrel suggests quickly, and Lucy can tell her son has started to yearn to spend more time around people, whether in town or on television.

"Son, you've never been to a hospital. Neither of you have." Marcus explains frankly and rocks Daisy in his arms. "Your mother may be right; maybe you're watching too much TV."

"Hey, I read, too!"

"Baseball cards don't count!" Daisy adds with another giggle.

"Good one, Daisy." Marcus laughs with his daughter as he lifts her above his head. "Speaking of reading, did you two do your homework?"

"But Dad, it's a holiday!" Darrel pouts while repositioning himself in the window seal and mounting his rebuttal. "All the public school kids have off! You can check our homework tomorrow."

"I can also check it tonight, son."

"But..."

"No buts, but the butts I'm going to kick if that homework's not done before dinner!" Marcus muses, remembering Berthine's one-liner and patting his daughter's behind. "You two turn that TV off and get to work! Maria will be here any minute!"

"Aw, c'mon!"

"Do as your father says, Darrel," Lucy commands, smiling at her husband and enjoying his sternness. She loves when he takes charge because his leadership allows her to play sidekick. The children sulk as Marcus lifts Daisy back through the window. Darrel runs to turn off the TV and Daisy follows with a swift kick to his behind.

"Ow!" Darrel squeals as Daisy runs away.

"Hey, you two!" Lucy shouts through the window. "Stop horsing around!"

"Sorry, Mama," the two apologize and trounce slowly up the stairs, grudgingly looking back and forth to their parents before disappearing to their rooms upstairs.

"Do you think we're too hard on them?" Marcus wonders softly, moving closer to his wife and wrapping his left arm around her waist.

"We treat them better than *the world* will," Lucy answers coldly, remembering their first year in New Orleans. "We have to prepare them to handle being different."

"But times are changing, Lucy." Marcus dreams a little while standing over her, clenching her closely to him. "I think people will accept them as brother and sister. Jim Crow will be completely abolished soon. At least, maybe we could move into town someday."

"I don't think so," Lucy counters quickly and avoids further eye contact by removing his arm from her waist and kneeling down into the garden. She acts as if she is resuming her diligent soil bedding, but she really just wants to ignore Marcus's fantasies. Her struggling garden provides a useful and frustrating distraction.

∞

Last year, Lucy spent the entire fall preparing to plant flowers and vegetables for their spring harvest, only to have some of the sprouting plants ruined by the mountain's many scurrying creatures.

∞

"We would have rows of fresh carrots if it weren't for those meddling raccoons!"

"Honey…" Marcus begins his appeal as he kneels next to Lucy. He is her perfect match; he knows when she wants to avoid a subject, and he knows how to turn his voice into a gentle lather that soothes her worries. "Daisy and Darrel are going to grow up and leave home someday. They can't stay up here hidden forever."

"*Why not?* My mother kept me and my brothers inside a cabin in the woods for years." Lucy challenges tersely, waving her arms over her garden and refusing to look Marcus in the eyes. "We have everything they need: fresh food, fresh water, and fresh air."

"What about friends? What about family?" Marcus volleys as he places his hand under her chin, tilts her head toward him, and waits until she looks into his eyes. "The kids don't have anyone to talk to except themselves, that TV, and us. And, I'm never bored, but…"

"*But what?*" Lucy impatiently asks her husband, turning her head away from him and lowering her head amongst her plants. "What are you trying to say, *Mark?*"

"I'm not trying…I'm saying you're too wound up, sweetheart." Marcus asserts himself, placing his arms around her again and laying her body down within the garden. She looks up to him and remembers the man she fell in love with. She needed a general who refused to back down, a leader who is strong, confident, and persuasive. "You've been on edge ever since…*you know who* arrived."

"I'm just worried, Marcus. He's always in trouble, just like in New Orleans. We can't afford mistakes. And now, we're having more visitors today..."

"Hon', we retired for a reason. What's money for if we can't enjoy ourselves and our family?"

"We can't be careless with our children's lives, Marcus," Lucy declares firmly, grabbing her garden pick and slamming it back into the soil. "We need *Charles* to leave, soon."

"Darling, I know that's your plan, but is that really best?" Marcus questions her without being skeptical; his tone drips with real concern. "Charles will never go *with them* and...I don't think Jazz will help."

"He has to," Lucy proclaims, wiping her forehead in a huff. The couple turns in unison as Maria drives the family's Ford wagon into the driveway. They begin to lift themselves from within the garden and dust off the soil and grass from each other's clothes. "Regardless of what happened with Charles's record label, we're still family."

"Hola!" Maria calls from the station wagon's window. The Cashmen family's maid only leaves the property to drive to the market for groceries or visit her cousins in Oregon. Maria has been with the Cashmens since shortly after they arrived in Washington; Lucy found her ad in the *The Spokesman-Review* classifieds.

∞

At the time, Maria was only seeking a part-time nanny job. Having recently separated from her American husband, she needed proof of employment to receive a work visa within the states. A lot of immigration reform occurred in the early 1960s, but the system still left Maria in a difficult situation. Lucy and Marcus offered a solution to her problems and she appreciated the opportunity to get away from the close-knit towns in Washington, whose inhabitants usually harbored prejudicial stereotypes of working immigrants.

Maria never questioned the Cashmens, primarily because they welcomed her into their lives and they never mistreated her. While living in a guest house next to the main cottage, she instantly became a part of the family, caring for the rambunctious twins as if they were her children. Oddly enough, when Charles came to stay with the family, he moved into the guest house, and Maria moved into a spare bedroom on the first floor in the family's cottage.

∞

"Hola, Maria!" Marcus yells happily while standing and waving toward her. "Qué pasa?"

"Nada, Señor Cashmen." Maria answers cheerfully as she exits the car and walks around the back where she opens the car trunk and removes several grocery bags. "I got the groceries for tonight!"

"Great, swell," Marcus remarks and raises his head with an inquiry. "But did you happen to…"

"Si, señor!" Maria shouts excitedly, carrying the bags from the car. "But, they had a car and a driver already. They should be here any minute!"

"A driver?"

"I told Jazz to let Maria drive them!" Lucy frowns, feeling as though both her brothers still disregard her wishes. "I don't want anyone else to know how to find our home! They always have so many press and paparazzi around them! Who knows who could have…oh no."

Just then, a loud horn blares and a white limousine pulls up their driveway.

"Honey, just try to relax, please. No one's following them. Sheesh, I didn't even need to buy fireworks, I'm sure we'll see plenty when Jazz gets a hold of Charles!" Marcus jokes cheerfully as he walks closer to the stretched luxury car while it creeps toward their home. "Would you look at this limo? I didn't even know they had limos in town?"

"Leave it to my baby brother to find one! Those two have had more success than they know what to do with. I bet they're just throwing money away by the barrels." Lucy boasts proudly, walking away from her garden and joining her husband. They stare at the limo as the chrome wheels come to a complete stop. The driver opens the door and hops from his seat, anxiously checking his watch and straightening his hat. When he opens the door, June and Jazz lay in one another's arms, kissing and cooing tenderly in the backseat.

"Excuse me, sir," the driver intrudes, coughing conspicuously. "Ma'am, um, we're here."

He continues to clear his throat as the lip locked lovers break from their backseat cuddle fest.

"Why are you stopping?" June asks Jazz teasingly, placing her hand on his chest.

"The man said we're here," he replies, looking up to see the driver, his sister, and his brother-in-law. "Hey, sis! How you been?"

"Not good enough it appears!" Lucy laughs and raises a motherly eyebrow as her brother and June tumble out of the limo. Jazz pinches June's bottom lightly, and she jumps into Marcus's arms with a scream.

"Ow! Sorry!" June exclaims while Marcus places her feet on the ground. June turns to hit Jazz in the shoulder. "Jazz, that was not funny!"

"Sorry babe." Jazz smiles brightly, a new habit, and he hands the driver several bills from a wad of cash in his pocket while never letting his eyes leave June. "I can't keep my hands off you."

"Thank you, sir!" The driver cries happily, overjoyed at the amount of money in his hands. "And might I say, I'm a big fan of your music!"

"Yes, thank you," Jazz utters dismissively, walking his fingers along the air to insinuate the driver's exit.

"You can leave now," June adds, waving her right hand at the driver. "Jazz, did you tip him?"

"Yes, I did sweetheart," Jazz answers calmly, moving closer to June and placing his arm around her waist. His mannerisms remind Lucy of Marcus and she leans closer to her husband, hoping he takes the hint. "I gave him a big tip, didn't even look at the amount."

"Then why is he still here?"

"He said he's a fan."

"I know, but he already said that," June continues to prod jokingly, poking Jazz's chest. "So why is he still here?"

"You're right babe, I don't know." Jazz plays along with a sly look, turning his head toward the driver who still stands amidst the family. "Why are you still here?"

"I-I, uh…" the driver stammers. "I just wanted to say, I'm a fan."

"But you already said that!" June repeats noisily, stepping toward the driver. "So why are you still here? Are you from the press? Are you paparazzi? I bet he has a camera!"

June begins to frisk the driver up and down his slacks, circling around him like a hyena checking her kill.

"Wait! Stop!" The driver protests, stumbling toward the limo's front door. "I'm sorry!"

"Why are you sorry? What'd you do wrong?" Jazz questions as he follows the driver with June in tow. "Are you running off to tell the National Enquirer that you picked us up at the airport? Huh?"

"He's got a guilty conscience, Jazz! Look at him shaking!" June screams as she continues to poke and prod the driver who struggles to open the front door.

"You better keep your mouth shut about where you drove us!" Jazz orders threateningly, glancing back to Lucy with a wink. "Lucy, release the hounds!"

"Arrgh! Arrgh!" June barks spiritedly and the driver finally opens the door and hurries into the limo, quickly locking himself inside. June makes funny faces in the tinted window, while laughing childishly. "Write about that, paparazzi!"

"Care to explain, baby bro'?" Lucy asks curiously as she walks toward Jazz and places her hand on his forearm. "What's that about?"

"Just a lil' fun, sis. You said you don't like people coming up here. We want to respect your privacy, but, we also wanted to ride in style." Jazz answers happily and his face glows with a joy that Lucy has never seen in him. The family watches the limo reverse speedily down the driveway with June chasing mightily, pumping her legs and arms through the air. Jazz turns his head to his sister and smiles brightly. "We're just happy to be here."

"Ah!" June howls and runs around the Cashmens' front yard like a child released early from school. She dances wildly, swaying her arms around in rhythm. "Look at all this open space and those mountains over there!"

"We haven't been outside in a while…" Jazz admits with a guilty chuckle. "We've been uh…*working*…on a new album."

"It's been amazing!" June continues to roar loudly as she marches closer to Lucy and Marcus. "Cashmens! I'm so happy to see you! Lucy and Marcus, still together and still going strong! Where are the kids?"

"They're upstairs, finishing their homework." Marcus affirms sternly. "Or at least they better be if they know what's good for them."

"Oh, you're tough!" June points at Marcus before turning back to Jazz and leaning softly into his chest. "Jazz, promise we'll be like them when we have kids."

"We'll be *better*," Jazz proclaims snidely, stepping away from Lucy's side while grabbing June by the hips and waltzing with her around the lawn. "We won't have to hide in the mountains, either."

"Say what?" Lucy questions Jazz's jibe, trying to step closer to her baby brother with her head held high, but he and June continue to move away from her. "What do you mean by that?"

"Well, we won't live in a shack on a hill," Jazz jokes, still in mid-waltz, but he also releases some pent-up frustration.

∞

Lucy knew that Jazz felt betrayed when she and Marcus left New Orleans and moved into isolation, but he had already left with June. When he and June left, he created a void between himself, Lucy, and Charles. Once so close, gangsters, handlers, managers, and public relations reps became their go-between connections.

∞

In truth, this is the first time that Lucy has even seen Jazz in almost three years. So even though they share a mutual frustration toward Charles, Jazz, as usual, spares no time before discussing his sister's faults.

"I would never make *my sibling* catch three flights from three airports just to visit! It's a miracle we even got here! This place is far away from...*everything*."

"Hey, you asked to come visit, remember?" Lucy responds sharply, knowing that if it weren't for Daisy and Darrel, Jazz may have never come at all. "Do you know how crazy these kids are going to behave when they see you? We couldn't even tell them you were coming."

"Kids!" June shrieks deafeningly into the mountains, stopping her dance with Jazz and running toward the home. "Daisy! Darrel! It's Aunt June!"

"Uh, *'Aunt June'*?" Marcus repeats, turning to Jazz with open palms. "Do you have something to tell us, Jazz?"

"Well, she will be soon," Jazz confirms with another smile and begins to follow June toward the house.

"What do you mean?" Lucy reaches out and grabs Jazz's arm, hoping to slow his steps toward the home long enough to receive an explanation.

"We're thinking about getting married some time next year, you know, after our *final* tour. June wants to tell you about it later." Jazz delightedly enlightens them and continues walking away toward the house, pulling Lucy along with him. "She wants to wait until we're *all* together."

"Like I said, *fireworks*." Marcus whispers with a soft chuckle, trying to comfort his perplexed and worried wife while Lucy wonders what plan her little brother has concocted now.

∞

Jazz was always a trouble maker, a natural-born fire starter. When they were children, though he played the artistic innocent, he knew how to push buttons and ruffle feathers. Despite being younger than Charles, Lucy considered Jazz the natural winner between the two. He was always the intellectual and moral superior, yet both her brothers were equally capable of destroying a family gathering.

∞

"Ah! It's June!" the twins shriek from within the doorway and rush to meet June at the front porch. They embrace her excitedly, both climbing on June's legs and laughing with their uncle as he bounds toward them. "Uncle Jazz is here, too!"

"Here we go," Lucy muses as she walks toward the home with Marcus by her side.

"When should we bring up Charles?" Marcus whispers, leaning into Lucy's ear.

"Let's see if they mention him first," Lucy responds quietly, her eyes darting to June wrestling with the twins on the porch as Jazz joins the bedlam. "If not...then I'll say something."

"Mama, why didn't you tell us they were coming?" Daisy exclaims while jumping into Jazz's arms.

"We had no idea!" Lucy jokes, but her nose begins to twitch oddly. "It was a complete surprise!"

"She's lying!" Darrel points at his mother. "Her nose is twitching again! Mama's lying!"

"You taught them that?" Jazz chuckles, remembering how he could always tell Lucy was lying if her nose started to twitch. "I thought you would stop doing that when you got older, especially once you started talking!"

"Old habits die hard."

"Mama, we figured it out all by ourselves!" Daisy boasts proudly to Jazz as Darrel dances with June on the porch. "Mama said that Santa Claus brought our presents, but I saw her nose twitching and Darrel saw Daddy put them under the tree!"

"You're such a smart pair," June croons happily, rubbing Darrel's curly scalp and brushing a few strands of Daisy's blonde hair from her face. "You two have grown so much!"

"We talk about the night you two were born all the time…" Jazz begins to reminisce, placing Daisy down gently on the porch. He removes a Chesterfield cigarette and a custom lighter from his coat pocket and glances at his sister for approval to light up—she gives none, but he sparks his cigarette anyway. "I was so scared that night…you know, for you, sis."

"I think we were all scared," Marcus admits, finally wrapping his arm around Lucy and pulling her snuggly under his shoulder. They join the family on the porch and look happily over Daisy and Darrel, delighting in their children's joy while they dance with their uncle and June. "We didn't know what to expect…what with twins."

"But look at them now! Jazz, they look like us!" June grins cheerfully and looks to Jazz with a curious stare. "A Sioux boy and a white girl…they're absolutely beautiful."

"You're beautiful too, June," Daisy interjects with a toothy smile, and her rosy cheeks look as though they might burst.

"Why, thank you, Daisy! That's nice of you to say!" June twangs in a slight Dakota accent as the faint whispers of Winniper County creep through. "I just can't get over how big you two are now!"

"They eat enough for four," Marcus jokes with a hearty chuckle and Lucy tugs playfully on his shirt; he is every bit the man of the house. "It takes two trips to the market ever week to feed them!"

"How far away is that market?" Jazz questions while stealing a sharp glance toward Lucy.

"About an hour," Marcus answers quickly, sensing a coming feud between his wife and brother-in-law. "It's not bad without traffic."

"You drive an hour away, twice a week? June, do you hear that? Seems like a lot just for groceries."

"It's not bad; we have Maria to do the shopping in town." Lucy explains, beginning to feel the fast approaching pangs of aggravation within her body. She remembers the constant stomach cramps that occurred whenever she would try to diffuse an argument between her brothers, especially during their childhood. Even now, she avoids any altercation with either of them because they aggravate her more than the discussion is worth. "Maria has been a godsend, really. She's a maid, a nanny, a cook…"

"So what do *you* do?" Jazz interrupts sharply, nodding his head toward Lucy and taking a drag from his cigarette.

"I do…uh…*nothing*, Jazz! And I earned that right!" Lucy declares heatedly, but she resumes leaning against Marcus. He is her crutch in moments of turmoil and angst. "Don't you remember how hard Marcus and I worked in Scapetown? All those bar owners, musicians, meetings, and shipments? We've earned our retirement."

"That must be nice!" June remarks unabashedly, sitting on the porch and bouncing Daisy on her knee. "We're going to retire, too, after our next tour."

"Can we come see you two perform?" Darrel asks intuitively, sensing the opportune time to strike. He's aware that they live in seclusion, and he's started to hone in on any chance to visit modern society. Darrel reminds Lucy of Jazz as a child, and she worries that her son's curiosity will lead him astray. "We know all your songs!"

"Well…" June hesitates and looks up to Lucy and Marcus. "I…uh…I'm not sure. It's up to your parents."

"Sure, they can come!" Jazz intervenes with a wide hand wave, passing his cigarette across his body and pointing his fingers to Lucy. "You can't keep my niece and nephew locked away up here forever!"

"They're not locked…" Lucy starts to protest, but Marcus tugs her arm discreetly. He can hear the fire beginning to burn from within his wife, and he knows that she could incinerate the entire evening with one scorching rant.

"Honey…" Marcus whispers softly. "Stay calm."

"I'm calm, Marcus…I'm perfectly calm." Lucy eases her tension by folding her arms quietly. At times, she wishes that she still didn't have her voice. She remembers feeling a sense of freedom when her family didn't expect a response; she has never liked to explain herself to ears that did not and still do not care to listen. "I'm sorry, if…"

"No, you're right to be upset," June interrupts, rising from the children and walking closer to Jazz and his sister. "Jazz, we're guests here. This is *their* home, and they can raise their children how they want, right? Don't you want that for us?"

"Yes…of course," Jazz answers delicately, blowing another cloud of smoke into the air. June is to him, as Marcus is to Lucy, a careful consciousness who can ease the most tumultuous times. He turns toward Lucy and Marcus, but he keeps his eyes to the ground. "I'm sorry, sis. I just want my niece and nephew to come see a show, y' know? They've never seen us live and we won't have many more shows. We're both getting sick of the road and the flights and *the press*. It'd be nice if you all could come see us before…we leave it all behind and settle down together."

"Well, we can discuss that…" Lucy concedes softly but she can't help snickering a little, imagining her wayward brother as a domesticated dad. Lucy can't remember Jazz ever cooking for himself, let alone caring for anyone other than himself. To hear him even mention the idea of settling down, fills her heart with empathy. She knows that he is trying to change so she tells herself to remain patient. "We can talk about *everything* at dinner. Please, come inside."

"Great, I'm starving!" June shouts, kissing Lucy on the cheek and raising her hands to the sky. She turns to the twins before stepping toward the front door. "Let's eat!"

"Just make your way to the dining room. I'm sure Maria has some snacks prepared by now." Marcus instructs, ushering everyone inside their home. "The bathroom's on the left."

"Wait, where's your luggage?"

"Don't need any, sis," Jazz answers contritely, flicking his Chesterfield stub over the side of the porch and following the group through the door. "We chartered a flight for midnight. Figure you want to drive us back to the airport but we can have the limo come back to pick us up. I know you want your *privacy*."

"But…I thought you'd be able to stay for a couple days," Lucy stammers, perplexed, and she approaches Jazz, trying to understand her brother's sudden coldness. "You could spend time with the kids."

"We'd love to stay, sis…" Jazz murmurs half-heartedly, moving past his sister at the front door. "But we have a new album, new tour…y' know? We're *not* retired…*yet.*"

"But we will be soon!" June announces gleefully as she rushes through the foyer with the twins.

"Right, June…*soon*," Jazz agrees with a sly smile and Lucy wonders what his true intentions are for the short- and long-term. It seems her youngest brother has mastered being mysterious and aloof while appearing genuine. He glances to Lucy and Marcus as he makes his way into their foyer. He eyes the inside décor, the glass menagerie, the custom piano up ahead in the living room, and the Persian rugs on freshly polished, hardwood floors. "Soon, June and I will retire like you and Marcus, but until then, we have to get back to work, and time is money."

"My brother finally became a capitalist."

"Hey, I'm sure Marcus understands," Jazz asserts frankly, scanning over the family's hanging portraits and scattered keepsakes as they enter the living room—a knick-knack here, a Bible there. "A family man thinks differently than a bachelor. I want to build a future for June like Marcus did for you."

"But you already have all the money you could ever need, Jazz," Lucy explicates, walking with Marcus and trying to catch a glimpse of her brother's face as he strolls through her place. "Between your music and your endorsements, what more do you need? Marcus and I have less than you and we have everything we need…"

"If you have everything, then why do you hide in the mountains?" Jazz responds callously and turns back to Lucy and Marcus. His face is completely stoic, expressionless, and stern. "It's not that you left New Orleans. It's that you disappeared with my niece and nephew and we didn't even know where you were. Come to find out, you left because you're afraid. You think money can't buy equality. So you retired too soon to find out."

"Then what do you think *you* can do about it? What's the point of making a new album and going on another tour? Do you think you can buy people's acceptance?" Lucy challenges her brother, hoping deep down that he has a magical solution. She often prays that one day she will walk alongside her children without eliciting stares and gawks. Secretly, she believes Jazz is strong enough to change the world, but she can't allow herself to feel any optimism. "Do you think you can play some song and end racism?"

"I do," Jazz confirms his naiveté, "but not just one song, and not by myself but June and I…*we're different*. We've played songs all over the world. And people love us, some hate us, too, but we're building consciousness, Lucy. People are starting to change for the better."

"No, Jazz...you're just selling overpriced tickets for a social gimmick. You're supposed to some symbol of social equality. You're a model for something that doesn't exist. You should see how that new record label is advertising your shows." Lucy begins forcefully, forgetting her quaint nuances and remembering the tiger that emerged when she found her voice. "I wish we could've helped you more because...the people you're working with now, they sell you like a jungle fever duo playing stage tricks. You have giraffes and animals in your shows; it might as well be a racist circus coming to town. You're the monkey and June is the clown."

"Lucy," Marcus grimaces at her remark, as he notices the children watching from the dining room. "You're going too far. Think about the kids."

"Listen to your husband, Lucy. *'Think about the kids'.*" Jazz circles around Lucy and Marcus as they stand in their living room. "Marcus is smart. He doesn't want your big mouth to ruin your only chance to get *Charles* away from here."

"What? Um...h-how...how do you know he's here?"

"I'm not just your little brother anymore, sis. I'm a monkey with a lot of power." Jazz growls in a firm tone and pushes his words throughout the living room so they are truly felt in every corner. "I have minions at ABC that bring me information from all over. They tell me things I don't even care about; I know who *really* killed JFK!"

"But wait." Marcus raises his hand, pondering Jazz's logic and preparing to pose a question. "If you knew Charles would be here, then why'd you ask to visit? I thought you hated him."

"Hm...see Lucy, I told you he's smart." Jazz stands tall, staring back and forth between Lucy and Marcus before smiling brightly and walking toward the dining room. He chuckles to himself. "Whew, I'm famished! Let's eat!"

"Wait, Jazz!" Lucy calls after her brother, but he continues to stroll away with an extra pep in his step.

"I told you, I told you...*fireworks.*" Marcus speaks through the side of his mouth, continuing his running joke as he and Lucy walk behind Jazz toward the dining room. Red, white, and blue streamers adorn the oak walls of the two-level cottage and decorate the home for the 4th of July.

∞

Settlers built the oak cottage and a small secondary house during the final push of America's Westward Expansion and it became a hideout for many outlaws and their families. Lucy chose the cottage for its seclusion, and because the oak frame reminds her of Berthine's cabin. Hidden in the foothills of Mount Spokane, one must know the way in order to find their family's home.

∞

"We have no chance, Marcus. Jazz is crazy and June, well, she's just as looney for loving with him." Lucy mopes sullenly and leans into her husband as they enter their dining room. June follows Darrel and Daisy's dance moves as the toddlers give instructions, imitating their guests' most recently televised performance. Lucy worries that her children will be as happy and conflicted as their uncle and aunt-to-be. While watching her children dancing, she laughs and whispers to Marcus, "Daisy and Darrel *really do* look a lot like June and Jazz."

"I just hope they're not as crazy, Lucy. Your whole family is nuts, but...they're better than having no family at all." Marcus laughs quietly and dreamgazes at the dance fest in his dining room; he sees how sweet life can be. "And we do need their help, Lucy. Think about Charles."

Marcus raises his eyebrows and tilts his head toward the guest house at the side of the family's cottage. Lucy can tell that more than anything, Marcus wants Charles to leave the property so that he may have her full attention.

∞

He's not a jealous man, but Lucy knew from the moment they met that Marcus needed her to need him. She loved his diligence and his ambition during their business negotiations; his ideas and follow-through made her life so much easier. He introduced her to the New Orleans elite; but, after they married and amassed even more money in their mutual bank accounts, their union produced two beautiful children who required extraordinary consideration. The stress became too much to bear, even for a man of Marcus's caliber.

Whether it was the stakes in business or the steaks that Marcus regularly ate, his first heart attack before forty provided a rude awakening. Lucy realized their lives had to change. She didn't want to continue agonizing about how to raise a Sioux boy and a white girl in a city and country that would not accept them as a family. Although Marcus felt a need to protect them, Lucy never completely relied on her husband. Knowing his weak heart and his strong ambition, she knew their family could not last in the southern heat. The pressure began to mount with the looming prospect of school and the accruing success of the Cashmen family's profile. They wanted the best for their children, but the South could not reciprocate.

∞

"Where'd these two learn to dance like this?" June asks, mirroring Daisy and wiggling her hips from side-to-side. Jazz and Darrel play a similar game while pausing simultaneously in robotic movements.

"They learned from watching you two!" Lucy answers from the dining room doorway. "They watch you every time you're on TV."

"But they're better than us! This is why I told the label I only want to play piano." Jazz laughs with a short twist that must feel as awkward as it looks. "I still can't dance."

"That doesn't stop you from trying though."

"Nothing…ever stopped me, sis," Jazz wheezes, forgetting that he recently smoked a cigarette. He continues to dance alongside Darrel and both have worked up a sweat.

"Kids, go wash your hands and faces." Lucy orders soundly, taking her motherly tone from Berthine. "Let's get ready for supper."

"Ha, '*supper*'? You sound like Mama." Jazz scoffs at Lucy and stops his dance, happy to have a reasonable distraction while June and Daisy continue to groove together. "Why is it called '*supper*'?"

"It's French, babe!" June answers over her shoulder, pumping her fists up and down as Darrell and Daisy dance around her. "It comes from soup!"

"Go on, kids!" Marcus roars with a hearty laugh; he is a content father who is unable to feel overly upset with his dancing children. "We'll be waiting when you get back."

"Okay!" The kids concede in a huff, stopping their dance moves and walking toward the bathroom as Maria passes them and enters the dining room with a smile.

"Hola, Señor Jazz y Miss June!" She eagerly greets the well-known stars using her most gleeful Spanglish and hugs them each tightly. "I told Mister Cashmen you'd make it. Are you two hungry?"

"I'm starving!" June rolls her hips, rubs her stomach, and slumps her shoulders over her waist. She's filled with life in every move and shake.

"Oh, bueno!" Maria exclaims while clapping her hands together. She looks to Lucy and Marcus, remembering the holiday and their plans for a celebration. "I'm preparing the hot dogs and hamburgers for the American tradition, fourth of July bar-bee-cue. Es la verdad?"

"Si, Maria," Lucy confirms with a nod, delighting at Maria's jovial attitude. "Do you have any snacks we could eat in the meantime?"

"Yes, of course, señora! Please, have a seat!" Maria implores the family, motioning for Jazz and June to sit at the dining table as she exits the room and calls back over her shoulder. "I'll be right back with some papas fritas and fresh lemonade!"

"Maria makes the best lemonade," Marcus adds casually, placing his fingers to his lips. He always finds the best ways to accent a conversation.

"Can you put any uh…*spirit* into it?"

"We don't have liquor in the house, Jazz."

"Oh, sorry to hear that, sis." Jazz looks disappointed as he sighs deeply and raises his eyebrows. "I just assumed with your recent company…"

"Charles is clean now, Jazz." Lucy explains, trying to defend their alcoholic brother and minimize any ounce of antagonism that Jazz may have planned for his visit. "He hasn't had a drop since he's been here."

"Yeah, sure, he's staying in the guest house, right?" Jazz inquires, walking to a nearby window and pointing toward the family's dimly guest house. All the lights inside are off. "I bet he's got a distillery under his bed."

"You have to forgive him, Jazz. He's sick. He needs help."

"I don't care, Lucy! You know he took advantage of us from the very beginning! He helped himself to *our* money!" Jazz counters toughly, refusing to lower his voice and Lucy wonders if he will be able to keep a lid on his emotions long enough to enjoy dinner. "Do you know how many people he stole from? Do you know what kind of people are after him?"

"We know, Jazz. We do," Marcus chimes in, looking down at Lucy and holding her closer. "Please, try to keep your voice down."

"Can't you see that's why I'm so scared?" Lucy asks, fighting tears and wrapping her arms around Marcus's weight. He is her anchor, holding her steady when her worries rock her world. "What if someone comes here looking for him? Think about our kids, Jazz."

"What are you saying?" Jazz questions curiously, eyeing Lucy with newfound suspicion as he tries to see deeper into her intentions. "What do you want *me* to do about it?"

"We're done!" The kids return to the dining room, bouncing happily and showing their hands still glistening with soap and water.

"Your hands are still wet! Come here, you two!" June laughs, walking to the twins and wiping their hands on her sundress. Lucy can tell that she is eager to play a mother's role.

"Oh, June," Lucy tries to interject, but the damage is done; her dress is wet with little hand prints. "You didn't have to do that. Darrel and Daisy need to learn how to use towels instead of being so excited."

"I don't mind." June shrugs and tosses her hair to the side. She wipes her own hands on her dress, patting the wrinkles from her backseat romp with Jazz. "We don't pay for clothes anymore."

"Oh, well, it must be nice." Lucy assumes, turning towards Jazz, but she is unsure if they should continue their conversation with the children around. She pauses before mentioning Charles again, and, instead, she chooses to question Jazz's *Bozo Brand Car Warsh* t-shirt, brown slacks, and black Converse kicks. "Free clothes, huh?"

"Hey, you know me, sis, I just go with the flow. I like to keep it simple, so whatever they send, I usually wear. Like June said, '*I don't mind*'." Jazz affirms, mimicking June, shrugging his shoulders, and wiping his hands on his shirt. "So many businesses, designers, and outlets know our sizes now that we get clothes from all over the world. And what do people always ask when we see them? '*How do you like the clothes?*' '*Are you wearing the clothes at your shows?*'"

"'*How come I haven't seen you in any magazines with the clothes?*'" June adds in a low grumble while prancing around the room like she's floating on air. Daisy begins to follow her around the table, imitating her actions.

"We've completely sold out, sis. Maybe you were right." Jazz announces sadly, running his hand over Darrel's face and remembering a time when life was much simpler. Lucy sees that her baby brother has surrendered himself in some ways while becoming stronger and more independent in others. He is an odd duck, indeed. She and Marcus watch silently as Jazz leaves Darrel's side and saunters around the dining room until he meets June and gently grabs her waist. Still in tow, Daisy and Darrel stand nearest to the couple, watching the lovers from below. "Lucy called you a clown, June. She said our ads make us look like a circus. Remember, when you said your parents should've been clowns instead of having you and then I said we were clowns for being together. See, I was right and you were right. We have become what your parents should've been. We were fated to become what we are now."

"So true, my love. We're clowns in our own circus. We get paid in popcorn." June laughs and throws her arms around Jazz's shoulders, kissing him softly while the twins giggle beneath them. The two music stars stop smooching, but they stay locked within their embrace, staring into one another's eyes. "Sometimes I feel like we only have each other."

"Lemonade!" Maria announces as she enters the room, holding a tray with seven glasses of lemonade and a large plate of potato fries.

"Yay!" The children bounce merrily as Maria places the lemonade tray on the dining room table. The twins take their seats, grab their glasses in both hands, and begin to sip eagerly, sighing with satisfaction after each taste.

"Please, help yourself." Marcus implores Jazz and June, following the plan to have a little bite before the bark.

"Maria makes the best lemonade," Darrel mimics his father, wiping his mouth and smiling brightly at Jazz.

"So we've heard." Jazz chuckles, seeing the son imitate his father. He then stares back at June, holding on to her hips in their embrace. "Can you get a glass, babe? My hands are full."

"Sure, don't move." June happily leans across the table and retrieves a glass from the tray. She holds it in front Jazz's mouth while he keeps his hands firmly on her waist. Before tipping the glass toward his lips, she pauses and turns her head to Lucy and Marcus. "How about a toast? What do you think Marcus?"

"No, I'm fine, June." Marcus responds quickly, always content to remain in the shadows. Lucy loves him because he doesn't need or want the spotlight. He takes two glasses from the tray and then nods his head toward Maria, encouraging her to join them. "But, please, you go right ahead. It'd be my honor."

"Well, thank you," June accepts jovially, raising the glass toward Lucy and Marcus. She takes another moment to kiss Jazz before beginning her toast. "Um, this is to the Cashmen family and the Lancaster family. May we all live together in peace and love each other...*forever.*"

"Here, here." Jazz cheers before June raises the glass to his lips. He takes a sip and then she follows as they swoon in a starry-eyed trance. He holds her a little closer, feeling her waist twitch in his palms. "Aw, that was beautiful, babe. I love it when you're romantic."

"Honey, you're...embarrassing me," June giggles girlishly, imitating the twins while looking over to Daisy and Darrel. "Not in front of kids."

"We don't mind!" Daisy assuages before developing a question in her mind and turning to her mother quickly. "Hey Mama, how come you and Daddy don't kiss like that?"

"Uh, well..." Lucy stammers and looks away, searching for an answer; her inquisitive child's question is not the problem, but her inability to answer is deeply perplexing.

"We kiss like that all the time," Marcus interjects, grabbing Lucy's waist strongly. She instantly feels a calm wave pass over her body; her knight has saved her again. Marcus hoots devilishly and winks at her before looking back at Daisy. "We usually wait 'til you two are asleep, but if you want to see..."

"No!" The kids scream in horror, covering their eyes with their hands and lemonade glasses. The children never plan their unison movements; they instinctually react with a shared intuition.

"Exactly, I thought not. That's why we lock the door during Mommy-Daddy time."

"Marcus, stop!" Lucy gasps unaffectedly, hitting her husband's broad right shoulder. She loves him even more when he protects her, and she enjoys her natural physical attraction to his masculinity. She breaks from her momentary embrace and notices Jazz and June still within their dreamy lull, feeding one another papas fritas. Lucy turns to Maria who watches the movie stars with a gooey-eyed grin. "Maria, how long do we have before dinner's ready?"

"Ah, señora, the bar-bee-cue will be ready in about twenty minutes." Maria explains and waves her hand over the piping papas fritas on the dinner tray. "I have some more appetizers, those winged buffalos and carne asada."

"Great, please bring the those for the kids." Lucy continues, pointing to the munchkins as they sit at the table, devouring the rest of the papas fritas. Lucy nods her head away from Jazz and June and walks toward the back door that leads to the guest house. "Twenty minutes should be enough time for the adults to talk."

"Are you going to see Uncle Charlie?" Darrel asks anxiously, never allowing his parents to make one solitary move without his knowledge. He is a devious rascal during Christmas and birthdays. "He's been here almost two weeks and we only saw him once."

"Uh…" Lucy stops in her tracks, staring at her son as if he were a burglar in his own home, a traitor to the cause. "Yes, but…"

"Can we come?" Daisy quickly joins her brother's inquiry, always willing to be his partner in any investigation or adventure.

"No," Marcus answers sternly, leaning across the dinner table and softly pinching Daisy's nose. "You two rapscallions are going to stay here, munch on some snacks, and wait for dinner."

"We never get to see him. It's not fair, he's our uncle."

"But you know he's sick, Darrel," Lucy confides, trying to empathize with her son and remove any doubt in Jazz's mind that her children are well-adjusted. They don't hide in the mountains, secluded from human interaction. "We can't risk you or Daisy getting sick."

"Then why do Uncle Jazz and Aunt June get to go?" Darrel replies, flailing his arms and bouncing up and down in his seat. Again, his angst reminds Lucy of his uncles when they were kids. Jazz and Charles would bop all over Berthine's cabin, each angling to get his way, especially at the other's expense. "What if they get sick and can't perform? They're more important than us!"

"No, we're not! We're too old," June corrects Darrel, hobbling toward him, leaning over his shoulder, and squeezing his cheeks. "You still have a lot of living to do and life is all that's important."

"Twenty-four, and our birthdays keep getting better and better though." Jazz coos, raising his eyebrows to June while walking behind her and resting his hand on her back. "I thank God for letting us be so happy. I just hope it'll last."

"Oh, I hope so, too! Darrel, I don't want them to get sick, either!" Daisy whines to Darrel, putting a potato fry back on the tray and turning her head to Lucy for help. "Mama, can Uncle Charles make Uncle Jazz and Aunt June sick, too?"

"No, Daisy! Your uncle and June are going to be just fine! They're going to live a long, long..." Lucy freezes; for some reason, she focuses all her attention on keeping her nose still—and she feels a chill slide down her spine. "Jazz, please stop scaring my children."

"Sorry, sis. You know I'm not accustomed to being around company. I hope we all live forever, except that rat out th-"

"Uh, listen, kids, how about some more TV?" Marcus interrupts Jazz's coming tirade and walks around the table so that he stands over Daisy and Darrel. "Take the tray in the living room and watch some TV 'til we get back, okay? If you're lucky, we'll talk about you two going to see your uncle and June perform."

"*Really?*" They light up together and begin to clamor over the leftover lemonade glasses and papas fritas. They are twins who are linked in heart and mind. June takes a moment to grab a handful of papas fritas for herself as the children rise from the table. Jazz promptly snags one of the snacks from her hands with a wink. The twins laugh and the paradox seems clear, yet, the revelation remains unnoticed as the kids begin dancing toward the living room. "We're gonna see 'Jazz and June'! We're gonna to see 'Jazz and June'!"

"*Maybe*, and don't push your luck!" Marcus cautions firmly, wagging his finger at his kids. "You two better behave while we're gone!"

"Did you have to encourage them to watch *more* television? They could've eaten at the table." Lucy snarls at her husband, taking out her anxiety over the coming drama on the most pliable target. "You'll turn them into zombies!"

"Lucy, we want them to behave while we're gone, right? Well, mission accomplished." Marcus replies with a convincing smirk, pointing to the children as they quietly watch a cartoon and munch on the potato fries. "Let's hurry up and get this over with before the food's ready."

"Fine...lead the way." Lucy sighs and opens the back door. Marcus walks past her with another wink and she timidly follows her husband out of the dining room before looking back to Jazz and June. "We don't have to do this now. We can wait until after dinner."

"I just hope he's sober. I want him to feel this." Jazz grits his teeth and grinds his fist into his palm. He then turns to June, grabs her hand, and begins to walk through the dining room and out the back door. Their feet creak over the wooden deck and descend down the steps toward a short cobblestone pathway with Buxus green gem shrubs along both sides. A low-hanging canopy covers the rear deck veranda and the setting sun beams down upon them as it dips behind the mountainside. Jazz gazes admiringly over the picturesque view and he smiles when he notices the array of yard accessories. He thinks about his meticulous sister spending her time crafting this image and he decides to throw her a much-deserved compliment.

"Nice landscaping, sis."

"Um…thanks, Jazz." Lucy beams, happy to have a guest recognize her outdoor décor. She and Marcus have spent countless hours detailing the family's property, but, given their seclusion, they rarely receive any praise for their home's panoramic ambiance. The family continues to walk toward the guest house in the evening light and the sun slowly sets over the mountain range while a beautiful orange fog mingles within the cream clouds above. Lucy wishes they could take some time to enjoy the scene and maybe she could soak up more appreciation, but she knows they must take care of business before dinner, or else, even the most savory barbecue will taste bitter when buttered with trepidation.

"It took Lucy almost a year to get these shrubs to bloom," Marcus informs Jazz proudly, pointing to the plants aligning the walkway. "My baby never gives up."

"She was the same back home." Jazz laughs and pokes Lucy on her shoulder. "Lucy spent two years trying to plant a garden outside Berthine's cabin. Mama said Thomas Winniper, Sr. gave her father the worst land in Winniper County! Lucy, you can thank June's great-grandpa for those two years trying to get that oil soil to sprout seedlings!."

"Hey!" June pouts loudly and grabs Jazz's right arm, stopping their trek through the backyard. "He's still my family, Jazz! You don't have to be so…so…*disrespectful*."

"Sorry, babe, but he was a jerk! He murdered our people and took their land. We saw the records for ourselves. He didn't own that village before the so called 'Ghost Dance War'. He stole that land and the oil, and your grandpa, your grandma, your parents, your siblings, and even you, all of you have blood on your hands, too." Jazz states surely, squeezing June's hand to console her, but his words only incite more anger. Lucy and Marcus glance toward one another, unsure how to react; should they intercede or let the couple be? They only freeze and watch the fray. "For years, we didn't even know who Olivia *really* was. And now, we know why they're so secretive, why they're so ashamed. She was saving some poor Sioux orphans, giving them a home with her privileged Sioux friend who could never have children of her own. You know I love you, but…"

"But what? You're talking about *my family*, Jazz."

"So, when was the last time you even saw them? Four years ago, back in New Orleans? All that money and they haven't even come to a show. They're ashamed that you perform with a Sioux from the same tribe *your family* murdered to become wealthy…excuse me, *more* wealthy."

"I still love them, Jazz. And if you love me, then you should love them, too?"

"Of course not," Jazz dismisses her logic gruffly, raising his hand to the night air and pointing to an unknown target. Somewhere to the east, the Winniper oil refinery still pumps over the bones of his ancestors. "Your family's the reason this country is so messed up! They massacred the Natives so they could build that an *empire!*"

"But it's not my grandparents' fault, Jazz. It's not my parents' fault, or my siblings, or me. We inherited the family business. We're not *all* bad."

"I know a lot of dead Sioux who would disagree," Jazz counters sharply, but June readjusts her grip and tugs his arm firmly, pulling him closer to her.

"Take it back, Jazz!" She squeezes his arm and glares deeply into his eyes, but he remains silent and stoic, refusing to apologize. Lucy steps toward them and reaches out her hand to protest, but she pauses and stands idly next to the suddenly unhappy couple.

"Guys, we don't have much time," Lucy interjects, stepping closer to them and trying to nudge June, but the little blonde, born of privilege, won't budge.

"Tell him take it back, Lucy! I love your family, even your mother! And she *still* calls me Daisy!" June shouts, stomping her foot and continuing to look directly into Jazz's eyes. "How can you hate my family when I love yours so much?"

Tears begin to form in June's eyes as she wails wildly; she is a wiry woman who has truly become untamed. Lucy remains quiet, still unwilling to discuss how Olivia delivered Jazz and Charles to Berthine's cabin. She fears where further revelations could take the evening, so she leaves Jazz to fend for himself, while recognizing the look within June's eyes and knowing that June won't relent until Jazz apologizes...*sincerely*.

Lucy witnessed her brother change the night he met June; she is still the only woman for whom he has no defense. While he has always stood up to Lucy and Berthine, June has always slipped through his walls and sacked his heart. Even now, amidst the setting sun, Lucy watches her brother squirm within June's grip and she realizes that June is the only person in the world who completely understands Jazz. The two stare into one another, searching their souls, and Lucy sees the connection still burning from the night they first met—and Jazz is still unable keep her away from his heart.

"I-I...oh gosh, June. Don't cry about it...okay? Okay? I'm sorry, June. Don't cry." Jazz apologizes, gently removing her grip from his arms, wiping the tears from her face, and taking her hands into his palms. "I...uh...maybe, I...I know we said we wanted to know the truth and once we found it...we'd move past it, but....it's just hard, knowing what happened to my tribe...and still not knowing where we came from, my parents, how we survived. We still have so many questions and we said we'd never go back home. Remember, we..."

"Well, maybe *we will* go back home soon...sometime next year, right after the tour. Your mouth just got you in trouble, mister." June vows strongly, walking forward with Jazz in tow, pulling him toward the guest house. Lucy and Marcus resume walking with the couple until they reach the guest house door. June still chastise Jazz. "I know we said we'd leave it all behind and never go back, but...it's time for us to grow up. If we're going to be a family, then we need to be *with* our family."

"Just to let you know..." Marcus prepares to enter, stepping toward the front door. "It smells. I mean, *he* smells. It's one of the reasons he couldn't stay in the house."

With that, Marcus opens the door to the guest house, but it is completely dark inside. He steps forward into the foyer and stubs his toe on a cardboard box. "Ow!"

"Honey, be careful!" Lucy cautions as she walks closer to the open door. Marcus stumbles toward a light switch and illuminates the living room, noticing a bulky moving box still sitting in the middle of the foyer.

"He still hasn't put his things away. Maybe that's a good thing." Marcus wonders, lifting the box and placing it alongside an adjacent wall. He steps farther into the guest house and studies the messy living room; discarded leftovers, clothes, blankets, and pillows lie all over the floor. "Oh God, look at this mess. I thought Maria came in here every other day to clean up."

"He stopped letting her come inside, Marcus. She's scared of him now." Lucy explains quickly, following her husband and scrunching her nose as she enters the guest house; Jazz and June follow cautiously and step through the doorway.

"I can't believe how filthy it's gotten in here," Marcus scoffs and continues walking further into the living room while noticing scattered vinyl records and empty bags of luggage.

"Where is he?" Jazz asks as he steps over dishes and spoons. "This place looks like my old apartment."

His words remind Lucy of the days in Scapetown when *Big Charles* was in control and Jazz was in shambles.

∞

Charles ran the streets while Jazz hid in his basement apartment or performed at the same cramped bars, afraid to spread his wings.

∞

Now, the roles have changed: Jazz has travelled the world and experienced more than any of his family, and Charles is hiding away in a dark guest house within the mountain. Maybe both feel as though they deserved this turnaround, given how Charles mishandled Jazz and June's early career efforts, but Lucy did her best to right the wrongs. She now questions how honest and compassionate her brothers will be toward one another. Will Jazz play the Savior after being Charles's sacrifice?

"He's just through that door, that's the bedroom." Lucy points ahead toward a single door next to a disarrayed kitchen. Mold-crusted dinner plates and abandoned concoctions drape the shelves and kitchen counter. Marcus approaches the bedroom door and looks back at Lucy, who waves her hand impatiently, thinking about her rambunctious children in the main house. "Well, go on, Marcus. We don't have all night."

Her husband slowly twists the knob and opens the door quietly, delicately pushing his way through and peeking into the bedroom. He steps through the doorway, but turns his head to Lucy, placing a finger to his lips.

"Sh...he's sleeping," he whispers as Lucy follows him into the dark room; she turns on an overhead light and leaves the door open behind her.

"Jazz..." June pauses and turns to Jazz, holding his hand tightly and looking up to him with those bright, blue eyes. "Are you sure? Do you want to do this now?"

"It may be our only chance, June. He may be dead soon." Jazz reasons sternly and clenches his fists, thinking about the money his brother stole and the years of sibling rivalry; but, he freezes on the precipice of confrontation.

"Are you coming?" Lucy asks from the doorway, staring at her baby brother as if they are back in the village. She waits for him to follow her to the edge of the forest that separates their home from the Winniper Family Estate, daring him to show that he is not afraid.

Though Jazz has matured to become a mythical enigma in many fans' eyes, Lucy still sees the part of her brother that will always be a scared, little boy. There is an immovable sliver of insecurity that prevents him from making sense of the world around him. Amidst his wealth, his fame, and the fleeting remnants of Jim Crow, he still does not understand why he is not free.

While Lucy and Charles accept American society as an exclusive hierarchy that will never accept their kind, Jazz refuses to accept such an assumed fact. A surviving Sioux dreamer, he drowns himself in his music and art and he never confronts his inability to deal with the past or present. His reality relies upon questions he has not answered. Truth scares him more than anything. Lucy continues to stare at her timid brother while he stands silently near the bedroom door.

"Jazz, are you coming?"

"What?"

"*Are you coming inside to talk to Charlie?*"

"Um…" Jazz continues to hesitate and June squeezes his hand softly, shocking his senses into action. He takes a deep breath and steps closer to the doorway. "Yes. We're coming."

He walks toward Lucy and enters the guest bedroom with June by his side—Lucy notices how quickly Jazz and June turn from turmoil to teammates. The bedroom resembles the living room; the floor, dresser, and bed lie in complete disarray. The shambled scene looks like the St. Charles monorail travelled from Scapetown to Spokane and barreled directly through the bedroom. A nearby timber desk leans on its side next to an inkwell dripping on the floor. Drying ink covers torn papers, dirty clothes, and Charles's old acoustic guitar, reclaimed after Jazz left Scapetown. Both the boys have abandoned the childhood toy they once coveted. The family scans over the dark figure in the bed, shrouded in blankets and pillows.

"How long did the kids say he's been here?" June asks, looking over the carnage and leaning closer to Jazz. Her cheek rubs against his shoulder and her touch comforts them both.

"About two weeks," Lucy answers curtly, walking around the bed until she stands next to Marcus. "He just said he needed a place to hide."

"He was worse when he got here." Marcus adds, placing his hand over his nose. "We hired a nurse, but she started asking questions about Daisy."

"That's why we can't keep him here." Lucy whispers over her shoulder as Jazz stalks around the room with June beside him, both eyeing the still object under the covers. "He needs help, Jazz."

"No one can help him," Jazz sneers bluntly, shaking his head in disbelief. "He owes money all over the country…probably all over the world, too."

"Then why are you here, Jazz? You haven't spoken to him in years. He knows you hate him. Why'd you ask to come if you knew he'd be here?" Lucy ponders honestly and places her hand on Marcus's shoulder. "We could've stayed in the house with the kids if you don't want to help."

"I just…" Jazz stops, glancing to June before releasing her hand and stepping closer to the bed. "I just have a few things that I want to say to him."

He points angrily at the mass on the bed, while walking past Lucy and Marcus and peering over the blankets and pillows. He moves toward the headboard, lifts the large crimson comforter, and uncovers two gangly, brown feet with overgrown toenails. Jazz grimaces in disgust before dropping the comforter; he walks back to the foot of the bed, pulls the comforter off completely, and reveals his sickly, skinny, and smelly older brother. Charles's eyes remain closed; crumbs and lint cover his unkempt beard.

"He wouldn't let us shave him, Jazz." Lucy explains, waving her hands over their shambled brother. "He's a mess."

"What happened to his eye?" June inquires as she leans forward, examining a bulging bruise over Charles's right eye. His worn face has become wrinkled from years of drinking Scapetown whiskey and smoking Chesterfield cigarettes—fortunately, Jazz quit the former (no more dark liquor).

"Some *thugs* caught up to him in Denver before he called us," Lucy winces at the thought of her brother being beaten by criminals.

∞

While she was in Scapetown, she saved Charles from himself, helped him avoid the police and his ego, and she even aided him as a fugitive when he ran from the law on occasion. So when he called and begged for a safe place to hide, she knew he had no other option and she felt those same maternal instincts from long ago. Lucy reacted as Berthine had instructed; she performed the role of a mother, sister, and savior, but now, Lucy has her own children with special needs and specific eccentricities.

∞

She must choose how long she can protect her brother without endangering Daisy and Darrel. Probably sensing his wife's worries weighing upon her drooping shoulders, Marcus wraps his arms around Lucy's midsection and leans her weight into him. She sighs deeply, exhaling her concern and staring at Jazz.

"Charles is in real trouble, baby bro'."

"He didn't explain much," Marcus expounds while holding Lucy close to his chest. "He just said that some bad people are after him."

"Charlie…" Jazz whispers, placing his hand on Charles's shoulder. Charles wrinkles his eyebrows and groans, reluctant to rouse from his sleep. "Charlie, wake up."

"He can hear you, but he don' wanna listen." Lucy chastises like an impatient mother, waking her child in the morning for school. "Come on, Charles, wake up! He's one of the heaviest sleepers I've ever known."

"Charlie, wake up! Charlie!" Jazz bellows raucously while placing his hands over his mouth and leaning over Charles's head. "The Rizatto brothers are here!"

"*The Rizattos?*" Charles sits up quickly and rubs his eyes with his palms. His family takes a big whiff and collectively gags from the odor of an alcoholic man who is two weeks removed from a bath and his last drink. He reeks of body sweat and dead funk. Charles continues to search around the room. "Where are they? I've got to hide!"

"Calm down, Charlie." Jazz raises his hands defensively, looking into his brother's eyes, but Charles stares back blankly as if he doesn't recognize Jazz or, at least, he behaves as if he is afraid to confront the past. "It's just me, *your brother*, remember?"

"*Jazz?*" Charles rubs his eyes again and runs his scraggly hands through his mangled black hair. He is a Sioux warrior straight from the ancient battlefield, beaten, mangled, and disappointed. "Is that you? I'm so tired…I can't tell."

"Save it, Charlie!" Jazz points a finger at his brother before lunging forward and grabbing Charles's throat within his palms. "I don't care about the money! I don't care that you booked me and June for all those shows and then stole the profits by the time we got off tour! But don't act like you don't know your own brother!"

"Jazz, don't!" Lucy screams, rushing around the bed and placing her hands on Jazz's forearms, but she is unable to loosen his grip. "Marcus, stop him!"

"He embezzled over four million dollars that should've been ours! And you let him do it, Lucy! You should've stayed in Scapetown!" Jazz shouts while choking Charlie to death, squeezing even tighter around Charles's neck. "We came back from South America damn near broke! We were going to buy a home!"

"*Four million dollars?*" Marcus repeats in shock, taking a moment to calculate how he would invest that amount of money. "Listen, Jazz, you know we had our own problems. We didn't even know you were actually making that kind of money…"

"Well, we do when our managers don't steal from us! Jazz found us a nice mansion in Bev Hills," June adds steadily, speaking in her Dakota twang and smiling as she remembers their would-be home. "It was real plush, right next to Paul Newman and Joanne Woodward."

"Jazz, please stop! You're killing him!" Lucy pleads frantically, straining to relax Jazz's grip. "Marcus, help!"

"Okay, Jazz. C'mon, he's your brother!" Marcus joins his wife and grabs Jazz's arms, trying to release his grip around his brother's throat. "Just let go, Jazz!"

"I have two years of anger built up! If you two would've stayed, this would have never happened!" Jazz grunts, holding firmly around Charles's throat and twisting his body away from Marcus and Lucy's attempts. "We came back from Brazil with only the money in our pockets! He's the reason we had to sign with our new label! He made us new slaves!"

"You release that anger, baby!" June cheers, hovering behind Jazz's back and pumping her fists into the air. "Remember how Master Lee taught you to apply pressure!"

She reenacts the movement, pinching an invisible artery and watching her victim die. Lucy watches June in horror and amusement, always unable to understand how the shy blonde could be so dramatic in one moment and then so playful in another. In so many ways, June and Jazz mirror one another; they are the same person. Indeed, since they met, Lucy has felt that the two complete one another; but, while one of her brothers chokes the other, Lucy wonders if any of their relationships will last.

"Jazz, please don't do this," Lucy cries, willing faux tears, conjured from frantic fights in Berthine's cabin. She hopes to pull at her brothers' heartstrings. "What would I tell Mama? You're going to kill him, Jazz!"

"Better me than someone else." Jazz continues to choke Charles; and for his part, Charles is wide awake now. He worriedly wheezes under Jazz's force and he pathetically paws at Jazz's hands, trying to loosen his baby brother's grip.

"Look, he's trying to apologize!" Lucy assumes, but Marcus resigns himself to let the brothers resolve their differences. "Marcus, do something!"

"I can't loosen his grip! He's strong for a piano player!" Marcus concedes half-heartedly, unwilling to battle anymore with the insane Lancaster clan. "Just let them work it out, Lucy."

"It's too late for that!" Jazz continues to squeeze his brother's neck as Charles points to his mouth and tries to speak. "Save it for St. Peter, bro! Maybe Jesus will forgive you, but I won't!"

"Jazz, stop!" Lucy wails and glances to Marcus and June for help, but neither move to Charles's aid. Still programmed to avoid serious confrontation, remembering Berthine's advice on a lady's conduct, Lucy retreats from further physical intervention. She releases Jazz's forearms and stands at the edge of the bed, watching Cain kill Abel. "At least think of the kids. Is this how you want them to remember today? They're going to know…"

"Ah, you always use the kids…but you don't know…what we've been through." Jazz momentarily relaxes his grip, but he remembers the feeling of betrayal when they returned from being overseas and he resumes choking Charles. "He stole from us, Lucy! His own brother! He put us on tour for two years and somehow we came back with nothing! Turns out he was funneling the money from our records and our shows into his own cash accounts. This moron was breaking so many laws that even the mob turned on him. And for what? Look at him. Me and June had plans…"

"Did you say 'plans'? Marcus and I had plans, too!" Lucy interrupts, once again placing her hand on Jazz's wrist and feeling the tension ease in his skin. She takes the opportunity to continue appealing to her baby brother. "I'm sorry about what happened, Jazz, and I wish could've been there for you and Charles, but I have kids now that I have to protect and we moved up here to keep them safe! But I'm afraid, Jazz. Charles showed up half dead and the other half drunk! I don't know what to do. Every damn second, I worry that whoever's after him will come here! "

"C'mon, Jazz…look at your brother's face." Marcus implores, detecting a need to reassert himself as he moves beside his wife. He points to Charles's morbid expression, sullen and defeated; his brown skin swells in a purplish hue while he struggles for air to fill this shell of his former self. He is now weak and infantile and Jazz is strong and domineering. Jazz stares at his brother and becomes sick to his stomach at the sight; he releases his grip and backs away as if he has seen a ghost.

"What..." Charles gasps hoarsely, his lungs violently pulling air through his raspy throat. "What the...hell, Jazz?"

"Oh, now you remember me," Jazz points to Lucy. "You see? He's always been a liar!"

"You..." Charles continues to gasp, "...you...almost...killed me!"

"I can try again!" Jazz rushes toward his brother, but Marcus stops him before he reaches a radius where he is close enough to choke Charles.

"Take it easy, Jazz," Marcus sighs calmly, gently pushing Jazz away from the bed. "Let's try to work this out."

"There's nothing to work out! I just wanted to come see the bastard on his deathbed!"

"I wanted to see the kids," June admits happily, turning to Lucy. "And you and Marcus, of course. You're all one big, *happy* family, just like us Winnipers."

June's sarcasm is not lost on Lucy, who absorbs the remark and the sting, yet, Lucy continues to move closer to Jazz and Charles, focusing on one confrontation at a time.

"Listen, both of you," Lucy begins softly, raising her palms between them. "Charles, you can't stay here anymore. And Jazz, you can't hate your brother forever."

"Oh, I don't hate him, not anymore. He's already dead to me," Jazz growls in a tone that reminds Lucy of when her brothers would argue over Charles's guitar. The childhood trophy that now lays drenched in spilled ink didn't mean anything back then, but who could hold it meant everything. Jazz wipes his mouth and looks away from his brother, glaring at the old guitar and laughing to himself. "I don't have a brother anymore. I hear the Rizattos want to make him an example."

"That's fine, baby bro', feed me to the wolves." Charles concedes, wiping his frothy, exasperated mouth and combing his beard with his fingers. He falls back onto the bed and places his hands over his face. "Get to the back of the line and pick up the scraps when the feds and the Rizattos are done!"

"No, we're here now; pay us the money you stole! You had no right and you still spent it all anyways!" Jazz demands with his hand out, stepping closer to the bed, but Marcus raises his hand between them. Jazz halts his next assault, though he threateningly points his index finger at Charles. "We want that four million from the tour sales. I know you stashed some bread before the feds came."

"You don't know what I been through, either. I didn't stash anything, Jazz," Charles admits sadly, looking his brother in the eyes for the first time. "I got a waitress from '*Teezy's*' pregnant after you all left Scapetown. She had twins just like Lucy's...I tried to...they were beautiful. But I couldn't change. I couldn't stay away from the streets and now they're gone!"

"How dare you! You're still lying!" Jazz yells aggressively, charging into another assault, but Charles raises his hands in fear as he laments over his past.

"Wait, it's the truth, Jazz! They killed them, my whole family, just a few weeks ago! They almost got me, too!" Charles protests, breathing deeply and wiping his hands over his face. "Do you know how hard it was keeping the heat off me with a lily-white baby? You two performed all over the country and overseas, and you never had any problems. Why do you think that is? I put my life on the line for you! I spent that money protecting you two and now my *real* family's dead. You and June owe me!"

"What do you mean, '*owe you*'? How much money did we put into *your* pocket? Don't act like you did it for nothing!" Jazz scoffs at his brother and tries to rush toward Charles again, but Marcus and Lucy stop him, holding their arms out to prevent him from getting too close to the bed. "You used our money to put your hands in every illegal hustle you could! You just couldn't get enough and now it's backfired! You left Lucy in charge, and when she was too busy to care anymore, we ended up on tour for two years!"

"It was a great two years, babe," June coos softly, stepping beside Jazz and taking his left hand into her palms. "Remember in Brazil, when we..."

"Honey," Jazz straightens his back and stands tall over June. "I'm trying to talk business."

"Oh, sorry," June replies quietly, releasing his hand and returning her glare to Charles. "Get him, babe."

"Listen, you two..."

"No, *you* listen, Charles." Lucy interrupts, growing tired of the tedious back and forth while thinking of her children and knowing that only one solution will suffice. "Jazz, you can keep blaming me all you want, but I'm sick of you two talking about money and the past! Do you remember where we came from? Our family has more now than we could have ever dreamed and you two are missing the point! You're putting *my babies* in danger! And we're not leaving! Charles, I let you stay here, but it's been far too long!"

"We're safe here, Lucy." Charles explains, waving his arms over the bed. "I'm honestly proud of you for finding such a secluded home. No one knows I'm here!"

"Jazz knew you were here," Lucy counters, feeling fed up; the tigress within her spirit begins to rouse because she fears for her cubs and their safety. "So someone does know you're here."

"What? How'd you find out, Jazz?" Charles asks fearfully and props up his body with his arms, but Jazz remains silent, smiling sadistically. "C'mon, little bro, tell me! I took every precaution to make sure no one followed me. How'd you know I was here?"

"ABC-Paramount, they have investigators all over the country, probably all over the world." Jazz pulls on his shirt collar. "We're with the same record label as Ray Charles, now. Didn't you hear?"

"No, I've been busy...*staying alive.*"

"Well, even after your *label* went bankrupt and we lost *all* of our masters, we had a lot of offers."

"We signed to the biggest record label in the world! They gave us eight figures and lots of perks!" June boasts pseudo-sternly, imitating Jazz's tough tone and placing her hands on her hips. "Our deal made that four million dollars look like peanuts!"

"And at ABC, we get chauffeurs, private jets, VIP treatment, whatever we need, whenever we need it." Jazz continues to gloat, ignoring June's mimicry and trying to temper his anger toward Charles. "Even though you kicked us down big bro', we still got back up and now, we're richer and better than you'll ever be. We got all your files, I know every shady thing you've ever done and I know how much you owe the feds and the Rizattos and everyone else. There's no way you get that kind of cash, so it's just a matter of time."

"But how'd you find me?"

"I guess you were a little sloppy, *Charlie*. Rats always leave a trail of crumbs," Jazz insults his brother bluntly, seeming to take pleasure in Charles's descent from whatever *greatness* he once had to this lowly, life inside a moral subterfuge. "It won't be long before someone finds you, Charlie, and they'll make you pay. Either the feds or…who knows. You owe money to a lot of dangerous people."

"Rotten feds. They shut me down all over some taxes; and those damn Rizattos, I know they were in on it, too!"

"Apparently, last week, wiretaps captured Jimmy Rizatto saying he was coming west to find you."

"And he's on the way here?"

"No…at least, not yet. Lucy's done a great job at wiping her family off the map. They don't even use credit cards and the maid does most of their shopping." Jazz glances over his shoulder to Lucy, nodding his head in a salute to his sister. "But we found you."

"How?" Lucy asks quickly, sensing a deeper conspiracy.

"Never mind that," Jazz mutters, evading her concern. "It's…not important."

"No, I think it is important, Jazz!" Lucy begins to raise her voice, a privilege that she never takes for granted. The tigress will roar when she feels a potential threat. "Tell us exactly how you found out he was here?"

"I…uh…listen, I told you…ABC…" Jazz pauses and darts his eyes around the room before landing on June. She smiles and instantly transmits a burst of confidence into his lungs. "Listen, Lucy…June and I worry about you and kids. People may try to hurt you to get to me and June, who knows? We know Mama is fine back home; she'll probably outlive us all. We just want to make sure that you are perfectly safe up here, too."

"Jazz…" Lucy steps closer to her brother. "How did you find out?"

"I…well, like I said, it's a part of the perks of our new contract…" Jazz reveals, still eyeing June oddly and soaking up her reassurances. "We have whatever we need, and…*sometimes*…that includes…*surveillance on our families.*"

"The FBI told us Elvis used wiretaps for his girlfriends!" June divulges cheerfully, posing in a karate stance and delivering short, quick chops to the air.

"What are you saying?" Marcus probes as both he and Lucy try to understand Jazz's intrusion. "Are we being watched?"

"No…of course not…not *all* the time," Jazz finally confesses, turning his head and raising his eyes to meet with Lucy's searing glare. "We're pretty important now, sis, and it's a pretty scary time in America. President Johnson called us personally and said that we're national treasures, *'a symbol of progression'*. They have to keep an eye on us and we wanted to keep an eye on you. Just to make sure you're safe, too."

"Jazz, is someone watching us now?" Lucy questions suspiciously, walking toward the bedroom's window and peering into the night.

"No, not right now," Jazz clarifies, nervously wiping his mouth as he struggles to explain. "Um, I'm not sure about the range. June, do you know?"

"I think the Colonel said about a hundred yards around the property line." June stretches her arms wide and stands on her toes.

"So they know where we live?" Lucy angrily steps toward Jazz and balls her fists in a rare display of anger; the tigress prepares to strike. Recognizing that his wife is about to explode, Marcus instinctively grabs her waist and pulls her away from Jazz.

"Take it easy, honey." Marcus spins Lucy around and steps between her and Jazz, but he wisely turns to Jazz, aiming his ire at his wife's true target instead of taking his place. "Jazz, who is the Colonel?"

"Listen, Marcus, don't worry. You're both safe and your kids are safe. Isn't that what's important?" Jazz raises his palms and tries to diffuse the rising tension in the room. Suddenly, his sister and his brother-in-law have begun to turn him into the villain of the evening. "There are good people in our government watching over us and they help me and June out when we ask them. Like the President said, *'we're national treasures'*!"

"What's happened to you, Jazz?" Lucy asks her brother, looking at him like a monster that could destroy her quiet home life. "How could you have us under surveillance without telling us?"

"I told you, I worry about you, sis, we both do. We've always gotten death threats, but…it's worse since we came back from tour and announced our…*relationship*." Jazz admits, wiping his hand over his forehead and walking toward June. "We've stayed away, you know. We haven't seen you in three years. You left Scapetown and moved into the mountains. Mama told me over the phone that you visited her when she was at her worst, but you never came to see us once!"

"It's not like you saw us before, Jazz! You and June left New Orleans way before we did!" Lucy retorts, raising her voice and feeling a fleeting fear that somehow her speech will fail her again. It is an inner anxiety that constantly plagues her; long ago, she was given a gift that she fears will one day be taken back. "You don't know what it was like trying to raise Daisy and Darrel in the South! They could've taken Daisy from us! Especially, after Charles kept causin' such a fuss!"

"I did my best," Charles grumbles, still lying sleepily in bed and pointing his index finger in the air before aiming at both June and Jazz. "I made you both what you are today."

"You put us all in danger, Charlie! And you're still doing it! Neither of you have changed a bit! You're both still the most selfish people I know!" Lucy moves past Marcus and chides her brothers, remembering all the times they've both hurt her. She imagines a continuous movie reel that replays her life—the once mute sister who now tries to speak sense to her deaf brothers. "You both have always been at odds, but our family has been torn apart since you stole that money, Charles. And Jazz won't forgive you until you stop denying it! Jazz, he's doing this to himself because he feels like he let you down! He's too stubborn to apologize so he's going to kill himself with his guilt, or let someone else do it for him!"

"Let *me* down?" Jazz points to his chest and widens his eyes in faux surprise. "How could you say that? You just said how selfish he is! He doesn't care about anyone but himself!"

"That's a lie and you know it!" Lucy states boldly, stepping between her brothers, refusing to accept any other outcome for the evening than the one she has planned all along. "When you came to Scapetown, Charles was the one that *protected* you. I couldn't do it alone! He was why you had it so easy at those clubs!"

"Pardon me, maybe I'm still jetlagged. I could've sworn that you just said, I…'had it so easy'?" Jazz repeats in shock, pointing to himself and shaking his head in disbelief. He steps closer to the bed, but this time his anger aims squarely at Lucy and she prepares for the full force of his rant. "I never had anything easy! You two left me at home with Mama and I had to get a music scholarship just to get out of that cabin. And when I got to New Orleans, I made it on my own!"

"Oh, you did? Did you forget that you lived at *our* apartment? And who paid your rent when we found you a place? Do you remember that it was Charles who got you that apartment? Charles may not be right, but he's not all wrong, either." Lucy widens her eyes to match her Jazz's glare and she tilts her head as she questions his memory and his mission. They share contempt for each other's inflexibility. Their stubborn Sioux nature resonates in their firm stances. Neither is willing to accept that a family in shambles needs one another to remain stable. "Do you think Teezy bought that piano 'cause *you* asked him or because *Charles* forced him? Charles was already promoting you before and after you met June. The whole time, he was just waiting on you to…you know, *step out of your shell.*"

"That's a lie, Jazz! Remember, when I gave you my guitar?" Charles waxes whimsically, weakly raising his hand in protest. He hopes to take Lucy's attention away from her truthful attack. "You always had the talent! I was just being a big brother."

"He was more than just your brother, Jazz! Charles was your financier, your manager, and your muscle in the early days and when you went on tour. He helped you more than you know back then. Yes, he made some mistakes once you and June became stars, but…he was always reckless. Your success enabled him, but you would have never been a success without him." Lucy continues to rant, but she begins to lower her voice, feeling a raspy itch form in her throat that threatens her resolve. The thunderous pitch bellowing through her voice eases into a low rumble and she looks into her baby brother's eyes and throws a few well-placed darts of truth. "Whatever you think, you do owe him, Jazz. He looked out for you in the beginning. He helped you become *more confident.* And if it weren't for him, you probably would have never met June and you probably would have never gotten out of Scapetown alive."

"Lucy, don't. What's done is done. Look at what our little brother has become." Charles speaks soberly and rises to sit up in the bed. His eyes groggily meet with his siblings and the three simultaneously remember their many arguments inside Berthine's cabin. These memories now have a new beginning, but much of their childish play is gone. They are adults now, with adult problems and concerns, none more pressing than the safety of the two children in Lucy's home. Realizing these factors, Charles surrenders whatever ego he once had and falls back onto the bed, his arms flailing above his head. "It's not worth it to fight anymore. I was born a loser and I'll die a loser..."

"No, you're not going to die, Charlie...at least, not tonight." June giggles affectionately as she leans over the bed and rubs Charles's bearded face. "We're going to help you."

"Excuse me, *we are what?*" Jazz asks testily, filled with utter confusion and feeling a tinge of betrayal; he contorts his face to express his disgust.

"Yep..." June affirms, smiling mischievously and looking to Jazz and Lucy. "On two conditions..."

"Anything, he'll do them!" Lucy agrees emphatically and points to Charles. "You better not mess this up!"

"Well, the first condition is up to you, Lucy...and Marcus." June continues to chuckle as the devil inside forms a plan in her mind. "I want the kids to come to one of our shows. They should see us perform before *we* retire."

"But..." Lucy hesitates and glances up to Marcus for help. "I know what we told them in the house but I don't know..."

"*Honey,* I think we should make an exception...at least once." Marcus whispers with a smile; Lucy absorbs his calm demeanor and she feels at ease. She knows that Marcus has been angling for the children to experience the world sooner than later; attending Jazz and June's show is a perfect opportunity. "We have to let the twins get comfortable being around other people."

"Marcus...I'm just worried." Lucy pauses and contemplates her predicament; she looks over Charles's pathetic frame decaying in her guest bedroom, and she realizes that he could be gone in a few hours if she agrees to June's request. "I don't want to draw any attention. I don't want anyone to know we're family. We'll go and sit in the nosebleeds..."

"But you won't come backstage, sis? The kids should see the new production!"

"Jazz, I just don't want the hassle!" Lucy argues, reenacting her business negotiations from years past when she haggled alongside Marcus and utilized her feminine charm for financial gain. "I know how it is backstage. Those paparazzi are murderous. Just one photographer finds out I'm your sister, and we'll be all over the tabloids!"

"Oh, and we wouldn't want that," Jazz muses sarcastically and rolls his eyes, considering Lucy's concern as a mere drop in the bucket of greater publicity problems. "We already have enough gossip, right June?"

"We were aliens and robots in the same issue of Esquire."

"So then we have a deal on the first condition?" Lucy asks, anticipating a finalized agreement. "We'll bring the kids to a show in Seattle and–"

"We're not playing in Seattle," Jazz interjects, wiping his fingers on his shirt collar and searching aimlessly around the room.

"Then where?"

"Well, sis, the closest place to *Seattle*..." Jazz begins while walking around the bed. "...would be Tokyo."

"'*Tokyo*?'" Marcus and Lucy exclaim in unison, mimicking their children. Lucy feels another chill move up her spine as she remembers her brother's devious ways and she acknowledges that June has only provided an extra catalyst to his antics. The two lovebirds smile like cats plotting against a canary in a cage, their eyes darting back and forth between each other, trying to hide their laughter. Lucy steps away from Marcus and stares at her brother as if he has played another prank.

"Aren't you performing in America?"

"No, sis'! We're making a socio-cultural statement!" June responds joyously, throwing her fist into the air before draping her arms over Jazz. "I told the President that we'll come back when Jim Crow is dead in all fifty states! They're going to have to enforce that Civil Rights Act and when they do, when there's finally equality in America, we'll come back and perform at the celebration! We'll make a big show of it!"

"We don't want to perform where it's still illegal for a colored man to marry a white woman or a colored woman to marry a white man or..."

"But June, interracial marriage *is* legal in *most* parts of the country," Marcus explains, glancing at his watch and looking to Lucy who also understands the need for expediency. They both imagine their antsy children, bopping around the living room, jumping off the couch, and making it difficult for Maria to focus on the preparing dinner. A proud, Creole man, Marcus steps beside his Sioux wife, forming a united front, as they stand toe-to-toe with Jazz and June. "Believe me, I've travelled around the world, too. America is by far the most accommodating."

"That's not the point, Marcus! It's about principle…and profits!" Jazz declares, raising his index finger into the air. "ABC says we generate more revenue when we make a political statement!"

"We're calling the tour, 'Jazz and June Stand Up For Human Rights'!" June throws her fist into the air and falls over Jazz, pushing him onto the bed and almost landing on Charles. "And we're going to Brazil, again! I want us to find a home in the countryside."

"Sh…sweetheart, remember they can't come visit us there. We said we'd keep our…uh…*plans*…a secret." Jazz purrs softly over June before lifting her from the funky bed. They wipe themselves off as they stand and look at Marcus and Lucy. "So you and the kids will have to fly to Tokyo to see us perform."

"We'll pay for expenses, of course," June confirms while recalling a past exploit or two that causes a warm trickle to sprinkle down her shoulders. A noticeable shiver spreads throughout her body. "Oh, Jazz, maybe we can hit the slopes again with Prince Akihito!"

"Sure, it'll be fun! Come on, sis! No one will bother the kids in Tokyo!" Jazz cheers convincingly, staring at Lucy and imploring her consent. "We're done after this tour; I want my niece and nephew to see us perform before it's too late."

"Alright, alright, good God, Jazz. Fine, we'll come to Tokyo." Lucy concedes while looking at Charles, who still rots in the bed; she feels a heated rush, an over-arching need to *not* see him in her home anymore. "I think we could use the vacation. Now, what's the second condition?"

"Well, the second condition is for Charlie!" June begins, eagerly pointing to Charles and placing her knee on the edge of the bed. "We're going to pay off your debts and make sure no one comes after you, but…you're leaving with us *tonight*, mister! You're going to get out of bed, come eat dinner with your family, and then we're leaving!"

"Really? You'll pay my debts?" Charles repeats hopefully, beginning to rise from the bed. "Why would you do that after I..."

"We're family, Charlie. We have the money and I don't want you to die." June looks back to Jazz and smiles toothily so that he knows he has no other choice but to agree with her. "And I know we said we'd never go home, but I think it's time we go back to Winniper County. We'll take it slow with your mother and my siblings and grandparents, but...it's long past time for us all to meet."

"No!" Charles protests and falls back into the bed. "There's no way I'm going back there!"

"You have no choice!" Jazz responds roughly, raising his voice and his chest while hovering over the bed, daring his brother to complain. "You'll do as you're told, big bro'."

"I'm not goin' back to Mama and that cabin!" Charles pouts childishly, slamming his fists into the mattress. "That woman is the reason I'm so messed up now!"

"Listen, Charlie. Your mother's been in and out of cancer treatment for a while now, and Lucy's the only one who has gone home to see her." June begins as she places her hand on Charles's shoulder. "It may do you both some good to talk to Berthine and have some kind of...*closure*. I wish every day that I could still talk to my mother."

"But..." Charles stammers, trying to figure a way out of this compromise, but his circumstances are clear: death or self-defeat.

"You don't have a choice, Charles! We're not going to pay your debts!" Lucy assures him, seeing the wheels moving inside Charles's mind. "If Jazz and June are offering to pay off the feds, the Rizattos, and whoever else is after you, then you have to leave tonight! And Winniper County is your safest option!"

"But what about *their* safest option? Do you really think the government will protect them from her grandfather?" Charles asks, pointing to June and evoking the angst from the music duo's confrontation outside the guest house. "You think people only wanted you dead after you became a couple; the people in Winniper County have always hated what you two represent, especially *her grandfather*."

"That's not true!" June shouts angrily; his comments have rekindled her earlier frustrations with Jazz and she struggles to contain her emotions. She removes her hand from Charles's shoulder and backs away from the bed. "I spoke to my sister last month! She said my grandfather loves our music! He had the school board name the Winniper High auditorium after me!"

"*Your sister* says that, huh? Her name's Christina, right?" Charles jests as he raises his bushy eyebrows. "Yeah, I had some spies, too. She's the one you were fighting in the bar when Jazz met you, right? When was the last time-"

"And you're a saint, Charlie? Everyone has faults!" June defends her family with a cocked fist and Jazz holds her arm back, though he secretly loves her feisty temper. "I know my grandfather has done some dirt. I know more than I want to know about it, but you can't hold the past against your family! You can judge other people, but you help family, Charles. And I want our families to come together and live happily ever after."

"But this isn't a fairytale, June. You don't know your family. Everything about that Sioux war is a lie. Your great-grandfather killed our people and took their land." Charles explains intently and points to his brother. "Jazz forgives you and treats you like gold, but...your family has done some evil things..."

"Listen, *bro'*...you don't know who I forgive or how I feel." Jazz moves past June and leans over Charles, feeling both the urge to kill and console. "We don't know everything about the past, but what I do know is...you're getting out of this bed and *we*...yes, *we* are going home! If for no other reason than because June says so...and I love her. We're leaving tonight."

"I agree, Charles. It's time for you to get up." Marcus steps closer to the bed, flexing his arms as he stands beside Jazz. "Now, I can help you out...or I can throw you out!"

"I hope you throw! I think this window opens!" June jokes and cracks her knuckles while narrowing her eyes at Charles. She may pay his debts, but she won't soon forgive his slick tongue.

"Well, then it seems *everyone* is in agreement!" Charles concedes and rises from the bed, placing his mangled feet on the floor. "But I'm not responsible for what happens! I warned you both! I warned all of you!"

"Just hurry up!" Lucy scolds her brother and a rush of excitement moves through her abdomen while she watches Charles as he prepares to leave. She's so happy to see him go that she has to consciously hide her smile. "I'm sure dinner's ready by now!"

"Take my arms, please. I'm too weak." Charles pleads, holding his arms out as Marcus and Jazz move under his shoulders and balance his weight.

"God, you smell like old shoes."

"Sorry, baby bro'. Maybe I should take a bath before dinner."

"Don't worry, Charles! The kids already know you stink." Lucy softly pushes Charles's back and he rises from the bed. Jazz and Marcus slowly guide him toward the bedroom door and Charles tries to gain his footing underneath him.

"Can we please just hurry?" Marcus complains, shuffling with Jazz and taking a full whiff of Charles's rank armpits. He scrunches his nostrils and closes his eyes as a sharp sting burns his retinas. "He smells so bad my eyes are starting to burn! I think I'm seeing stars!"

"Don't complain now, *Mister* Cashmen!" Lucy guffaws as she winks at June and delivers a swat to Marcus's behind. The two women giggle, happy to see their men grumble and stumble toward the door. "Remember, you wanted to see *fireworks*!"

AUGUST 1966

Sunday	Monday	Tuesday	Wednesday	Thursday	Friday	Saturday
	1	2	3	4	5	6
7	8	9	10	11	12	13
14	15	16	17	18 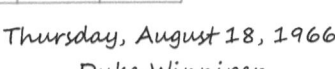	19	20
21	22	23	24	25	26	27
28	29	30	31			

Thursday, August 18, 1966

<u>Duke Winniper</u>

He hears the rain,
But will he ever speak again?
Quiet in his disdain,
Seeking truth instead of pain,
Duke, once a neglected stain,
Now a silent heir to the Winniper throne,
Never ambitious
Until shattered and delivered
To the Winnipers' home—
A handsome ransom
Turned his father and stepfathers into capitalists,
Escape artists who left,
Without completing the paternal performance.
So, though, Duke may soon control
Black Winniper gold,
As the plot unfolds,
His voice is dead and cold,
Covered in anger and sold,
His alibi will remain untold.

Duke Winniper drives his grandfather's crimson 1953 Aston Martin Spyder through the infamous Winding Winniper Way with Christina, and Earl Bethune sitting beside him. Whenever he whips around a violent turn, Christina screams just for show, bouncing on Earl's knee and begging her brother to press his foot harder on the acceleration.

His newly acquired driving goggles clench tightly against his cheeks and his confidence soars through the street as he forgets any memories of abandonment and loss. Now at the ripe age of thirty-four, Duke has finally gotten serious about his future as a Winniper tycoon. He has begun to leisurely attend courses at the local college and, in return, Papa Winniper has rewarded his grandson's ambition by replenishing his trust fund to a balance over 4.1 million dollars—a little less than .01% of the Winniper family's 4.6 billion dollar empire.

Papa Winniper has also treated his only *acceptable* grandson to trips, riches, and expensive cars, and Duke wishes that he could thank his grandfather with words, but he hasn't spoken in over *sixteen years.*

∞

If he had grown up with his twin Sioux sister Lucy, he would know that he lost his ability to speak to her after she made a fateful birthday wish—his sacrifice resulted in her gain. Stricken with Lucy's speechlessness on their eighteenth birthday, Duke became a mute who bottled his anger until the pain condensed into delusional ambition.

∞

His early thirties have evoked a desperate cry to cement his legacy, any legacy, within the Winniper lore. Suddenly, the boy, who never cared about anything, has become a willful man who has begun to feel the need to prove himself beyond his affliction. Undaunted, Papa Winniper has shielded Duke from any public scrutiny by enrolling his grandson into the family funded Winniper County College. Papa's protection proves that the middle-aged mute still rests comfortably within the Winniper family's arms—shielded by name and rank.

Duke looks at Christina and she laughs ecstatically, forming her hands into circles over her eyes and mimicking his eye goggles. Although she is twenty-eight, she still acts as if they are children playing in the second floor hallway of their late mother's suburban home. Duke narrows his eyes and clenches his mouth, refusing to laugh and expose the gap between his teeth.

∞

He lost two buck fronts in New Orleans, casualties of a bar brawl with June—his baby sister packs a mean punch.

∞

He's not exactly sure why, but, ever since he lost his speech, he's become far more irritable, more inflexible, and more violent.

∞

Absent the luxury of verbal communication, he began to feel the compulsive need to physically assert himself amongst friends and family. Immediately after becoming a mute, Duke felt like the bully who suddenly had become the bullied. Public perception portrayed him as another weak Winniper male—a clownish role that he now shares with his Uncle Thomas III.

∞

The insecure mute has joined the ranks of the county's often ridiculed prince, the mayor of the farmer's market. Both begotten sons have become the laughing-stocks of the oil town's elite. Playing the silent fool is a role that Duke has grown accustomed to as an unworthy Winniper male.

∞

During his escapades in California and New Orleans with June and Christina, Duke fell headfirst into the doldrums of his family's wealth, wasting his twenties on alcohol, fast cars, and disingenuous relationships.

∞

Since his return, Duke has developed an interest in attending college with the hope of redeeming his self-esteem and learning enough to usurp his uncle's claim to the Winniper throne. His ambition has earned a modicum of respect from his grandfather, who has started to welcome his grandson into the inner circle of the Winniper fold or, at least, that's Duke's impression.

His driving goggles continue to cling tightly to his head; the straps and plastic edges constrict against his skin, turning his cheeks into cherry red blossoms. The gap between his teeth has grown since June knocked out his two fronts; time and alcohol loosen the gums, and though he remembers their frequent tussles as children, teens, and young adults, Duke truly misses the moments that he shared with Christina and June.

Now, he's often left wishing his baby sister would leave her traveling minstrel show, but she still refuses to settle down in Winniper County beyond her recent, short visits. She leaves quickly without spending much time with her siblings; June still chooses her music over their family's oil wealth.

∞

Last, year, she returned home for the first time since she left, but she only remained long enough to drop Jazz's brother off at his mother's cabin. Duke barely saw her and, since, she has only returned twice and stayed briefly without visiting their grandparents. Christina told Duke that June wanted their grandparents to meet Jazz, but she was still afraid to ask them. So, instead, she left hastily during all her visits as if she never cared to spend any valuable time in Winniper County—too busy travelling the world, performing with a colored boy that she professes to love more than anyone else.

While growing up, June gave Duke a lot of confidence because she looked up to him as her big brother, but, over time, her admiration faded and her success outside of Winniper County has now become another point of ridicule for the powerful family who let one of their fair sheep flock to a forbidden wolf.

∞

Papa says that every time June and *"that Sioux boy"* perform onstage, she disgraces the family. His main concern has become their relationship behind closed doors. Even worse than performing, she has fallen in love with a Sioux native, a son from the ashes upon which the Winnipers have built their empire. The contradiction sickens the old man, weakens his heart, and strengthens his resolve to prevent the family members that remain at the estate from enjoying any unapproved freedom. Although they are respectively grown adults, Papa confines Christina and Duke to the Winniper family's mansion as much as possible, hoping to avoid any further embarrassment from Teresa's offspring.

Duke continues to drive wildly down the winding road and the Aston Martin handles the curves snuggly. Roaring through Winding Winniper Way feels like an erratic Sunday drive and Duke realizes how their Great-Great-Uncle Christopher lost control of his Motorwagen in 1888.

∞

A legend in Winniper family folklore, their Great-Great-Uncle Christopher Winniper, Jr. survived his car crash and often bragged about how he had destroyed a rare, patented Karl Benz Motorwagen. Sadly, Christopher, Jr. was killed during the Sioux uprising on New Year's Eve, December 31, 1890. The next day, his younger brother, Thomas, Sr., established the Winniper County municipality and began building the family's immense wealth from the Winnipers' newly-acquired oil strike. Duke became inspired by his ancestors when he read an old newspaper that detailed how his Great-Great-Uncle Christopher, Jr. and his Great-Grandfather Thomas, Sr. had raced the earliest model cars, vehicles that were barely equipped to eclipse speeds of thirty miles per hour. Somehow, they still crashed.

∞

Being reckless has always been a trait of a successful Winniper man.

∞

According to old news clippings and historical documents in the Winniper County College Library, Winding Winniper Way became a well-known derby track in South Dakota's racing circuit. Papa, who gained his nickname as a testament to his family's paternal patronage, explained that the passion for cars runs deep within the Winniper men's blood. In his time, Papa raced his blue Spoister all throughout Winniper County, recklessly steering his sports car wherever he pleased—the entire county has always been his kingdom.

When Thomas III refused to show any interest in anything besides the produce harvest and the market's supply, Papa felt that his son lacked the necessary intangibles of masculinity, the manly maniacal essence that he expected from his male successor. Papa had lost hope until Duke expressed a love for fast cars when he was a teenager; in response, Papa began to concoct a new plan to ensure his family's future prominence.

In fact, delivering Duke to the Winniper family's mansion was the main reason that Papa paid Kenny to abandon Teresa's children. Papa wanted his grandson under his roof, but he knew that he needed to allow the boy to become a man; and, it wasn't until after Duke returned from New Orleans that he had exhausted his options for self-pity. Five years ago, when Duke, Earl, and Christina returned to the estate, Duke immediately showed a greater interest in usurping his uncle and Papa rewarded his grandson by giving Duke access to fast cars, foreign money, and free courses at the local college.

∞

Now, Duke intends to make his mark on his family's legacy, but his ambitious plans rely upon Papa continuing to shower his grandson with the fruits of the Winniper family's fortune. For Duke, wealth and power provide ample incentives to overcome the ridicule heaped upon him for being a mute. He fears that if he is unable to take over the Winniper family's dynasty, then he will be cast aside forever like his uncle—left in a market or a public square as the object of the town's mockery. Still scraping more and more gravel and dirt under his foreign grip wheels, Duke begins to drift slightly from side-to-side, taking delight in Christina's pleas.

"Duke, slow down! You're going to kill us!" She yells hysterically, turning her body away from him and clinging to Earl's shoulders. "Earl, darling, tell him we don't have to rush!"

"Sure we do!" Earl shouts while shifting Christina's weight on his knee so that he can cradle her like a baby in the passenger seat. "Your grandfather called my Aunt Tilly and she called us at *Arnold's!* A man like that doesn't call anyone unless it's important! And my aunt...well...she's a peach!"

"Do you think it's about June?"

"Of course! The old man probably had a heart attack when she told him. Aunt Tilly said the national press knows, too. They got photographers followin' 'em around town 'n everything!" Earl answers Christina loudly, while also speaking to Duke, who focuses more on the road than the conversation. He pats Duke's right shoulder while Duke speeds around the last turn and cascades down a long hill that leads to the edge of the Winniper Family Estate. "June really crossed the line getting engaged to that Sioux boy! She didn't even ask my aunt or Papa for their blessing! They are powerful people! They don't like to be embarrassed!"

Duke turns into the front gates of the estate and drifts down the lengthy driveway, smelling every nuance of home and comfort. The Winnipers' landscapers constantly manicure the estate's well-trimmed grass, hedges, bushes, and trees. Duke continues to drive past the front of the family's famed mansion, heading toward the garage, but he slows down as he notices Sheriff Cobb, Jr.'s patrol car parked at the foot of the steps to the mansion. The yard workers tramp around the home's expansive lawn, doing this job or that, keeping their heads down long enough to earn a meager salary and a sharecropper's shack in the nearby village.

Though Duke has never trekked into the forest outside of the estate nor seen the sharecroppers' village, he has heard enough to justify his disinterest. Apparently, the Negroes, natives, and even some immigrants live together in an old tribal village near the Winniper family's oil refinery.

∞

The tribal village was the site of the Sioux uprising that threatened the Winniper family's bread harvest. Duke's great-grandfather defended his land and defeated the Natives' attack. Papa told Duke that the few surviving, servile Natives moved into the remaining available land, became sharecroppers, and joined their poor, minority counterparts amongst the ranks of Winniper family's workers. His grandfather said it's a veritable congregation of coloreds living off the white man's good fortune and God has always willed it so. Duke never needed further explanation.

∞

Frequently, Papa Winniper tells his grandson that the family's landscapers, sharecroppers, and oil rig workers are quite disorderly when left alone— *"violent drinking"* and *"improper music"*. Duke has always believed his grandfather's every word, but Papa has very rarely said a nice word about his employees or anyone else for that matter. Whether the domineering patriarch understands his hypocrisy or not, Duke realizes that Papa needs both the workers and his family to assert his authority. They are all subservient slaves to the Winniper family's wealth because power can only exist with subjects and servants to command.

Money allows the purposeful to instill or inflict an impulse upon the purposeless, yet, as Duke has learned in college, if money's purpose is merely to make more money and finance more power, then pursuing wealth can be very fulfilling. He still can't decide his true interests outside of driving fast and controlling the Winniper family's fortune. Filled with these superficial desires, he experiences a rush of confidence while imagining the moment that he fulfills his birthright and ascends to the throne. He observes his castle grounds as he rolls the Aston Martin by the estate's plush courtyard decorated with Civil War statues, stone bird feeders, and a small chestnut pond for their grandmother's ducks.

The interests of respective Winnipers cover the property; Duke glances to a sculpture of his Great-Grandmother Ruby Winniper in the west lawn veranda—a commissioned memorial constructed under the orders of his Great-Grandfather, Thomas Winniper, Sr. Duke coasts into the family's garage, passing unique model cars, motorbikes, and other scrap heap innovations from his grandfather and great-grandfather.

∞

Thomas Winniper, Sr. shared his love for automobiles and power with his only son, Thomas, Jr., who idolized his father throughout his life; and after Thomas, Sr. passed away and Thomas, Jr. matured into "Papa" Winniper, Papa behaved according to his father's wishes. He became a cynical man who achieved undeniable success while being incredibly cruel to family and foes alike. Marrying Olivia and raising two children were merely circumstantial chores for the Winniper patriarch who needed to continue his family's legacy. Sadly, when the time arrived for his son, Thomas III, to assume a similarly poisoned prominence within the Winniper male lineage, the *would-be heir* wilted under the pressure.

∞

Absent the traits of a proper successor, Papa Winniper has turned Thomas III into a weak and privileged pawn, who is culpable, yet incapable. The third generation inheritor has become increasingly dependent upon the family's wealth and protection, while he still avoids the associated expectations placed upon privileged male heirs. Thomas III's inability to ascend into the proper rank of a powerful prince has left a void that Duke now attempts to fill after years of silent self-pity. He fears that he wasted the opportunities of his youth.

∞

After being drugged and abandoned by Kenny, Duke became the second son that Papa never had. In February 1948, when Kenny delivered Teresa's children to the mansion, he actually delivered a potential heir and two bargaining chips for future corporate-family mergers. Papa quickly changed Duke's name from "Duke Townsend", after Teresa's first husband, to "Duke Winniper"; this change ensured that his grandson and his grandon's offspring could carry on the family name. Papa allowed June and Christina to keep the respective last names of their forgotten fathers; in truth, he planned to marry them off quickly so they would lose their surnames anyway. Papa made this decision following Teresa's betrayal; even back then, he was thinking of these times.

Because Thomas III had not conceived a male child and Teresa refused to associate her children with the Winnipers' wealth, the family was absent a bona fide male heir. Teresa's death and Kenny's failure to play both mother and father to three mourning children gave Papa Winniper the opportunity to pay Kenny to deliver Teresa's children back into the Winniper fold. In his end, Kenny learned to never deal with a snake; Papa Winniper was, and still is, a prairie rattler. He not only eats vermin and weaker morsels, he also eats other snakes.

After arriving at the Winniper family's mansion, Duke's sisters were cast off to their new bedrooms in the cold east wing and, at age fifteen, Duke began his west wing apprenticeship under Papa's close supervision. Papa began immediately preparing Duke, who was still capable of speech at the time, to command the Winniper oil empire when he became of age or if Papa passed away. Having taken the reins himself at the age of fifteen, Papa expected his grandson to be able to follow suit in order to prove himself. For Duke, his grandfather's attention was a welcomed distraction from his father's absence, his mother's death, and Kenny's betrayal.

Over the next four years, both Duke and Papa hoped to fulfill one another's missing parts—the son without a father and the father without a worthy son. While racing to a pool party with Earl and his friends, primed to celebrate his ascension into manhood, Duke lost his speech in the afternoon of his eighteenth birthday, and he eventually lost his grandfather's support.

The old man believed his male seeds were somehow cursed, mainly because Thomas III still had not conceived a child, much less a male heir, and his grandson was suddenly stricken with silence. Neither of his potential successors was fit to lead the family, but Papa Winniper remained patient with Duke because, even in silence, his grandson could still drive fast and Duke still presented more of the masculine qualities that Thomas III lacked. Duke was stronger, more impressionable, and angrier due to his affliction, which were qualities that Papa trusted more than Thomas III's submissiveness. Thomas III followed orders because he had no other option; Duke followed orders because he needed a father figure to love him in spite of his faults.

Papa's confidence shifted further from his son to his grandson after Duke asked about attending business courses at the local college. Papa began to develop so many goals for his mute grandson that when Thomas III actually conceived a child with Terry Sue, a Winniper Market cashier girl, Papa no longer cared about his son's attempts to prove his manhood. Thomas III impregnated a former high school cheerleader of ill-repute, who gave birth to a white daughter and another cursed Sioux baby.

In 1962, when Nancy Winniper was born and her young mother lay dying in the Winniper family's mansion, Duke understood why his grandfather made the women and the workers leave the estate. Papa said he wouldn't allow any more mistakes. Duke witnessed the birth of twins and one was a Sioux baby boy, the same color as the surviving sharecroppers. The ambitious heir saw the Winniper male's true birthright.

Papa cradled Nancy as her mother died and he ordered Thomas III to dispose of her brown-skinned brother. That night, Duke watched his uncle tearfully burn and bury a living, breathing baby in the barn beside the mansion, but Duke never asked questions, not that he could anyways. He accepted that his grandfather knew what was best for the family, and if Thomas III was willing to execute one of his children under Papa's orders, then Duke, too, must be willing to do the same if he is ever asked.

∞

"Here we go," Christina grumbles, as Duke parks the Aston next to their mother's old, blue Spoister. Christina rolls her eyes and quickly hops up from Earl's lap, climbing over the passenger side door. "Grandpa is probably in a bad mood!"

"Don't worry, honey, that's why I'm here. Your grandfather loves me." Earl encourages her confidently, envisioning himself as the man in charge and opening the door so that it pushes Christina away from the car.

"Hey, watch it!" Christina scoffs, affectionately sliding beside Earl as he climbs out of the car. She throws her arms around his neck, ignoring Duke, while he turns off the ignition and exits the car. He leaves the keys in the ignition and tucks away his goggles behind the driver's seat. Walking behind, he moves through the garage alone as Earl pulls Christina along with him, wrapping his arm around her waist. "What did your aunt say on the phone?"

"I couldn't hear so good at *Arnold's*. The guys kept fussin' over darts. Aunt Tilly just said that your sister and that toma…" Earl pauses when he sees Clyde Thompson, one of the groundskeepers, walking into the garage.

"Excuse me, sirs…ma'am, don't mean to intrude." Clyde apologizes and shuffles toward a nearby tool rack. He grabs a garden hoe and smiles a toothless grin that makes Duke worry that he may one day look like Clyde. Duke runs his tongue along the inside of his mouth and feels the gap of his missing front teeth. Clyde walks toward the garage door, holding the garden hoe above his head. "The grounds always need more hoeing."

"Aunt Tilly just said that your grandpa wanted us to get here fast." Earl continues, whispering while watching Clyde exit the garage and march away toward the Winnipers' barn. "I reckon that dinner didn't go so well last night."

"I still don't know why granddaddy wouldn't let us stay! We haven't seen June in months!" Christina exclaims, playfully hitting Earl on the shoulder while they continue strolling through the garage. "But…*I am* glad your aunt let us spend the night at her house."

Christina leans closer to Earl, pushing him away from Duke as they exit the garage and walk through the courtyard. Duke tries to catch up to the two and stares at Earl, trying to elicit more information from him about his conversation with his aunt, but Christina occupies Earl's attention. The two lovebirds gawk at the surrounding statues, entranced by art they do not understand.

∞

After Kenny left Teresa's children on the steps of the estate, Christina's only time away from the mansion was when she, June, and Duke travelled to Chicago. The siblings were unable to save Kenny, and then they absconded to Los Angeles, and, ultimately, they journeyed to New Orleans to help June follow her dreams. In the end, their tryst became a disappointing and invaluable venture for both Christina and Duke. Teresa's two eldest children returned to Winniper County while June remained with Jazz and became an international superstar. Duke and Christina were left in the shadow of their little sister amidst the gossip and grandeur of their family's wealth.

∞

"I hate that we missed dinner too, babe. I bet your grandfather wanted to kill June right then and there! Plus, your chefs are so much better than the ones at my Aunt's mansion." Earl emphasizes his remarks by rubbing his stomach and reading Duke's facial expression, a required skill for a mute's best friend. Over the years, Earl has mastered the art so well that he has become Duke's voice; he helps his friend to communicate when necessary and he hopes his talent will prove financially and socially beneficial. Everyone has a dream. "Duke, stop glaring at me. Aunt Tilly didn't tell me anything about the dinner. She just said your grandfather wants us to 'come back home' quick. Those were her words, directly from him, 'come back home'. So we're here, we'll know what's going on soon. I said, stop lookin' at me like that! I told you everything! Christina, have you talked to your grandmother?"

"Nope, not since last night, but…I got a call from June the day before yesterday. If they talked about what she said…well…I told her I wouldn't tell, but…" Christina pauses and crouches between Earl and Duke, playfully pulling their necks into her arms. "It's true! He proposed and she said yes! They're engaged! June's getting married!"

"Really? 'Married'? She's really getting married to that Injun?" Earl repeats in shock, shaking his head and releasing himself from Christina's grip. He pushes her away from him and steps toward the freshly manicured front lawn for a somber moment of reflection. "Women these days don't know how to hide their shame. Your grandfather…you know, he won't stand for this…"

"Well, I told her something was bound to happen. She spends more time with him than any of us." Christina mumbles, sneaking a peek at Earl and Duke. A shell of her former self, she shivers while making her point. She is no longer the strong-minded dreamer from her childhood; Kenny's abandonment and Papa's restrictions have eliminated her confidence. "They seem happy. It's not such a bad-"

"Keep talkin' like that and you're gon' get a smack." Earl turns and steps toward her aggressively. He raises his hand to slap Christina, but Duke grabs his friend's wrist. Duke is always willing to intervene to protect his sister, but his willpower will soon be tested.

"I was just joking," Christina mutters even more quietly; her words dissolve under her breath and she sulks away from striking range while they walk by Sheriff Cobb, Jr.'s patrol car and begin to ascend the front steps of the Winniper family's mansion. "I just wonder why Papa called us here, that's all."

"Me, too, we were having such a good time," Earl agrees with a sly smile, running up the steps and wrapping his left arm around Christina, but he quickly releases her hips as he sees another Winniper servant exiting the mansion. The obedient servant hustles down the steps and passes the three privileged peons without raising his head. Earl waits until reaching the top step of the front porch to pinch Christina's side. "Gosh, you can't get any privacy around here!"

"Granddaddy likes to keep the workers busy."

"I guess that includes us, too, huh? I'm joining the Winniper payroll soon, and then I can stop asking Aunt Tilly for cash. Maybe I could build us a proper mansion." Earl grins while filling his mind with dreams and returning his hands to Christina's waist. Duke can feel them forget his presence, but he has grown accustomed to fading into the background. "You know, your grandpa probably owns the whole country by now. Winniper oil pumps all over the globe; he could be president if he wanted."

"I think he'd rather *buy* the president," Christina corrects Earl and pokes his nose teasingly. "Papa always says politicians should be bought, not believed."

"That's right, my dear!" Papa Winniper calls from a rocking chair on the right side of the front porch. Thomas III stands quietly next to him, holding his four-year-old, Nancy, in his arms. He stares into the distance, dreaming of being anywhere but home. Papa chuckles throatily and strokes his grey beard, observing his grandchildren with narrowed eyes. "I'm glad someone's been listening to me around here!"

"Granddaddy, you scared me!" Christina exclaims elatedly, rushing to hug her grandfather as he rocks in his char. Even at twenty-eight, she is still a little girl, unmarried and unworthy of further consideration. Duke recognizes her falsehood toward their grandfather, yet he knows the hug is a pleasure for both—his money and her appreciation flow freely. "You're pretty sneaky, Papa!"

"Well, I'm sorry, darling! You know in business, a man has to know how to be quiet." Papa Winniper apologizes in his gruff South Dakota twang and he takes a quick glance at the back of Thomas III's neck, sending chills up his son's spine. Papa mockingly taps Christina on her nose with the tip of his index finger and begins to stand from his rocking chair. "I'm just happy to hear someone appreciating my wisdom for a change. Lately, I feel my *instructions* haven't been heeded."

"Oh, let me help you, Papa." Christina holds her grandfather's right arm and helps him rise from his rocking chair. The seventy-five-year-old man's hefty frame creaks as he rises to his feet, trembling over his weak knees before steadying himself on the porch.

"Thank you, sweetheart! I'm not as young as I once was!" Papa sighs fortunately, thinking of the lives lost in the meantime and wiping his white blazer sleeves with his palms. "Your grandmother keeps telling me to exercise, but she doesn't understand that I have a business to run, right Thomas?"

"Yes, sir," Thomas III whispers without turning his head or shoulders; he remains entranced in dreams of escape while cradling his daughter. He wishes he could take Nancy away from the Winnipers' world, but he knows he couldn't get too far without turning back. His sins are sown too deeply within Winniper County; he could run away forever and still never be free.

"Is Grandma home? That looks like Sheriff Cobb's car down there, is he around?"

"Uh…well, yes, Christina. The sheriff is out back, waiting on the boys and I. But your grandmother's sick in bed. We had a horrible shock last night and she has a bit of a tummy ache. Your sister has really dropped a bomb on this family."

"Is June still here? Can I see her?"

"No, June is long gone, probably on her way to the airport with *that Sioux boy*! No, you and June, er, uh, Nancy can stay in the east wing for now or, better yet, enjoy some lemonade here on the porch! We don't want your grandmother to get you sick, too!" Papa Winniper bellows with a laugh and raises his hand to emphasize his decision. He is a man who decides before the discussion; his will is the culmination of predetermined calculations. He knows what is best for the family, and all other considerations fall to the side. "I have a whole team of nurses upstairs tending to your grandmother's every need and a whole security team looking out for young June's safety in our fair county. There's nothing to worry about, okay, sweetheart?"

"Okay," Christina concedes, lowering her head in submission. Duke watches and remembers the girl who once fought for every inch of respect.

∞

As a child, Christina was always the leader. She protected her siblings until Kenny destroyed any lasting sense of security when he dropped them into the waiting clutches of a patriarchal maniac.

∞

Now, Christina has relinquished every ounce of her free will in order to live within the comfort, luxury, and privilege of the Winniper Family Estate.

"Now, you sit down here." Papa Winniper commands, moving aside and grabbing Christina's wrists. He pulls her toward the rocking chair until she sits down obediently. "I'll have Bessie bring you and Nancy two glasses of fresh lemonade while the men folk talk over some business."

"But…" Christina begins to protest and Duke thinks she may remember her former self.

"No buts but the butt sitting in this rocking chair, you hear?" Her grandfather demands with a country smile, repeating his favorite joke from the Winnipers' deceased field hand, Johnnie Robinson. Papa Winniper remembers Mr. Robinson fondly; when Papa was a child, he helped Johnnie remodel his cabin in the woods near the estate. Papa wonders if somehow those early associations softened his heart to Johnnie's daughter, Berthine. He worries that somehow his own weakness is to blame for the Winniper family's current calamity.

Papa quickly disregards these notions, turns his back to Christina, and taps Thomas III on his shoulder. Thomas III cradles Nancy a little closer, ignoring his father, but he can feel Papa's disappointment. Papa huffs and mumbles something under his breath, ashamed of the son who couldn't produce a single, suitable male heir. He places his right hand on his son's shoulder and points toward Nancy. "Leave *her* here, son. It's time for us to talk to the boys."

"Yes, Pa," Thomas III agrees quietly, lowering his shoulders and gently placing Nancy at his feet. He briefly brushes his hand over her cream dress and black dress shoes. In a fleeting flash, she reminds him of June, walking out of the house alone on the day of Teresa's funeral. Seeing through Thomas III's eyes, Papa scoffs at the memory and turns away while Thomas III kneels down to speak to his daughter eye-to-eye. "Nancy, stay here with your Cousin Christina. I'll…uh, I'll be back real soon, okay?"

"Okay, Daddy. Come back soon." Nancy answers softly, hugging her father. He breaks her embrace and nudges her toward Christina's lap, knowing that she will likely learn her place before she learns the alphabet. Duke and Earl observe each character as Papa scowls at the Winniper girls, revealing his true feelings toward these potential fiascos. At best, Nancy and Christina can submit to powerful family mergers. Their marriages offer more protection if managed correctly, using the secretive offspring as a bonding force of mutual culpability. No one wants to face prosecution for killing babies and no one wants to face the shame of raising the Sioux children. And, as the worst possible outcome, Nancy and Christina may become casualties of the cruel curse that has created regrettable victims like Ruby, Teresa, Kenny, and Terry Sue.

Papa believes the Winniper women have caused mostly headaches and heart pains.

Having lost his mother, Ruby, during his birth, Papa never knew her touch so he can't associate a woman with the maternal moments that he missed. Although he grew up with his Uncle Christopher's widow, Rita, helping around the Winniper family's mansion, Papa never learned to trust women or appreciate their softer sensibilities.

Unlike Papa, Duke lost Teresa at the age of thirteen, and her memory brings him both joy and sadness; but, over the years, Duke has forgotten the feeling of his mother's touch. As a child, he ignored and resented her for divorcing his father and marrying other men.

∞

He has since removed those early frustrations and filled her place in his heart with his grandfather's orders. Papa controls Duke just like he controls Thomas III, Christina, Nancy, Mrs. Winniper, Winniper County, and, as some may say, America and the world at large. Amidst Papa's vast power, June is the only Winniper who acts with autonomy; but, Papa is a man who demands that his expectations be met completely. He steps toward the center of the porch and raises his right eyebrow toward his grandson, observing the second candidate for the honor to bear the family's concerns. Papa wishes he could trust his son or grandson enough to transfer his power to either of them soon. Duke can tell that his grandfather has become tired of his responsibilities.

"Come along, grandson…Earl…we've got work to attend to." Papa Winniper pivots slowly and walks toward the top step of the porch with Thomas III following behind, demoted to third in line behind a mute and a family friend.

"Yes, sir, we're right behind you, sir. I appreciate you bringing me aboard!" Earl responds eagerly, nudging Duke as they step down the front porch with Papa. Earl takes a moment to look back at Christina, who holds Nancy in her lap, rocking back and forth on the porch. In a vision, Earl sees Christina as his wife, cradling their child on their porch and, suddenly, the Winniper family's mansion, the estate, and the oil business are all his. He smiles to himself before quickly covering his fantasy in a deep scowl, making sure neither Papa nor Duke have noticed his inner ambitions.

The group descends from the final steps and walks together at Papa Winniper's slow, labored pace. They troop steadily around the left side of the Winniper family's mansion and pass Clyde hoisting the garden hoe over his shoulder and pushing a wheelbarrow filled with soil.

"Clyde, tell Bessie to bring my granddaughters some lemonade!" Papa orders in stride, but he doesn't stop. He continues to pass Clyde while calling over his shoulder and only turning his head slightly. His actions show Duke and Earl whom they should respect with words and actions. "And I want you and Bessie to share a glass! It's an early wedding present!"

"Oh, why thank you, Mista Winniper, sir," Clyde replies brightly, putting a hop in his step and turning the wheelbarrow toward the front of the Winnipers' mansion. "I'll get Bessie on that lemonade real quick!"

"He's a good boy, that one," Papa remarks proudly, loudly enough that Clyde can still hear him. Knowing his content servant has heard his compliment, Papa turns his head and continues to walk toward the rear of the mansion. "I just hope their children work as hard. I want to keep this property in pristine shape, into perpetuity."

The old man continues to lead the group around the back of the mansion until they reach the garden veranda at the edge of the patio in the backyard. Sheriff Cobb, Jr. sits silently in one of the wrought iron lawn chairs, carefully placed around a marble table on the cobblestone deck. At ninety years old, the sheriff is over a decade older than Papa. His wiry white hair peaks through the bottom of his pale brown felt sheriff's hat. The gold-plated star on the front shines in the sun, matching the badge on the left pocket of his crisp Winniper County Police uniform.

The sheriff remains seated as they approach him; he watches each member of the group with a curious stare while they enter the patio area. The Winnipers' backyard overlooks the southern edge of the estate, giving the king a masterful visual of his kingdom. Sprawling trees and pampered shrubs stand in rows and columns along endless acres under the South Dakota horizon. The Winnipers' land feels all-encompassing when staring south of the estate; the entire world rests beneath their feet. In the distance, they can see the oil refinery with the forgotten Sioux warriors buried underneath. Somewhere within lay the secrets of the Winniper family's wealth.

"This is what it's all about, boys. I can hear our oil refinery pumping beyond the horizon. I can feel our stocks doubling in New York and our trade partners smiling in China," Papa Winniper boasts unapologetically and waves his arm over his portrait of plush American real estate. Though he has all the wealth he could ever need, he still doesn't seem happy. He leans toward Duke and places his hand on his grandson's shoulder. "Duke, I don't think you know *everything* about how your great-grandfather discovered our oil, but when the time comes…you'll find out more than you did when Nancy was born. But, at the very least, you've learned that Winniper men must *always* do what's best for the family. That's our duty as men. Do you understand, Duke?"

"Yes, sir." Earl responds quickly, answering on Duke's behalf. Duke nods along silently, listening to his grandfather, though he rarely understands Papa's deeper intentions. He simply nods and feigns comprehension, because he knows that, for now, he's merely a pawn in his grandfather's game. Duke hasn't proven himself beyond his affliction; therefore, he remains obedient so that Papa may find it easier to use him.

"Thomas? Have you learned what men must do?" Mr. Winniper asks, while sitting down next to Sheriff Cobb, Jr. and opening his hand to invite Thomas III to sit to his right. "I know I've asked a lot of you, and haven't you proven yourself twice?"

"Yes, I have…*twice.*" Thomas III replies softly, sitting to the right of his father and turning his head away from the stench of his answer. He stares into the horizon, searching for another place of escape. Duke watches his uncle and notices the same look of desperation that he frequently sees in the mirror. Although his uncle is now fifty-three, almost twenty years older than Duke, Thomas III is still a boy under his father's thumb.

"Yes, your obedience has made me proud, son. You took care of Teresa and I rewarded you with my grandfather's revolver. That weapon is a symbol of our manhood and our honor. My grandfather gave my father that revolver as a reward for his service in the great Injun wars defending this here land—the land you and Duke will one day inherit. Our forefathers have always done what they needed to do in order to survive, and we must follow in their footsteps."

Papa Winniper pauses for a moment, giving Duke and Earl a chance to take their seats amongst the king's knights. Papa eyes Duke curiously, wondering if his grandson still does not realize that his uncle murdered his mother years ago. His grandfather smirks and continues to praise Thomas III, yet his words still reek with a scolding tone.

"My son, you have acted nobly. Whenever these *women* have produced a problem, we have moved quickly and decisively to protect the family name. The question is, are we ready to protect our family again, son?"

"I..." Thomas III hesitates before rethinking his tone. He swallows a large gulp of gumption and tucks his tail between his legs. "I'm here, aren't I?"

"That's hardly enough. You don't even sound enthused," Papa Winniper jokes and prods his son with his finger, poking him in the chest. "Duke and Earl need to know that you support what they're going to do, today. We are the men of the family and we need to be strong. Can we count on you, son?"

"Y-Yes..." Thomas III stammers, flinching under his father's consistent pokes. He caves his chest inward and shrinks to the size of an ant crawling on the estate lawn. Duke stares at his uncle, who finally looks up to meet his eyes. *I support you, Duke. And you, too, Earl, just do what Papa says and everything will be fine.*

"Good. That's the spirit." Papa glares at his son and tries to detect any ounce of coming betrayal. He finishes his survey of his son's face with an abrupt grunt and turns his attention to Earl and Duke. "Now, Earl, I've given you special access to the Winniper inner circle, haven't I? You brought my grandchildren back from New Orleans and I'm still grateful for that. You've been friends with my grandson since childhood and our families have an extensive history together."

"Yes, sir, and I thank you for letting me come around so much." Earl sits upright alongside Duke, taking his elbows off the table and placing his hands in his lap. Papa continues to eye Earl suspiciously while he waits at attention, expecting instructions for their special task.

"You seem fond of my granddaughter, and since you brought her back from New Orleans, I've seen her become...much more...*obedient*. For that, I'm also grateful."

"Yes, sir, I mean, uh, thank you, sir? I mean, I only did what any man should, sir, but yes, I'm very fond of Christina."

"Now, I've spoken with Tilly, and we both agree that another Bethune-Winniper marriage would not be bad for business, despite our dealings with Teresa and Kenneth, Jr."

"I never liked Cousin Kenny, sir. Aunt Tilly was heartbroken when he skipped town them years back." Earl states honestly, balling his fists and narrowing his eyes. He has always been envious of the admiration and benefits that the townspeople and the Winnipers heaped upon his late cousin. Earl finds some solace in the fact that Kenny's misplaced trust led to his ultimate downfall. "If I had a chance, I'd stomp his heart for what he did to both our families! He left Duke here like garbage! He's a traitor!"

"Well, I agree with you, son, but your aunt and I dealt with 'Cousin Kenny' a long time ago." Papa chuckles deviously and smiles while thinking of his late son-in-law. Duke tries to remember a time when he's seen his grandfather smile without thinking about money or a deposed enemy. Papa rarely takes pleasure in much else. "I like your attitude, Earl, but for today's work, you must use your best discretion. As a member of our family, you will learn many important secrets, secrets which must be kept *within* the family and our trusted friends like the sheriff. And anyone or anything that threatens to expose these secrets must be eliminated. Do you understand?"

"Yes, sir. I'm with you. *'Secrets must be eliminated'.*" Earl answers, agrees, and sloppily repeats the creed while placing his right hand over his heart. "I'll do whatever you tell me to do, sir."

"That's very wise, very wise indeed. We already have enough betrayal to deal with today." Papa squints and surveys Earl's conviction before returning his glare to Duke and Thomas III. "As you may know, June has chosen to become engaged to that...*Sioux native.*"

"Yes, I...uh, I have heard rumors, but I couldn't believe it, sir."

"Earl, you know I've tried for years to dissuade that girl from her wild ways, just like her mother. I sent you down to New Orleans to bring them back but she has always been hell-bent on being...*difficult.* Now, her actions are downright destructive. She could ruin everything our family has built." Papa Winniper wipes his forehead with a handkerchief and glances at Thomas III, continuing to survey his son and judge his commitment. "Thomas, I believe she's still dealing with losing her mother at such a young age."

"Please, Papa…" Thomas III mutters, still trying to forget his past sins, but his sister's ghost still haunts his dreams and forces him to remember how he drove her off the road on her way home from his market. Duke continues to watch his flustered uncle and he finally realizes that Thomas III is the weakest amongst the Winniper men. They sit outside the Winniper family's mansion, overlooking the Winniper land and the one who fits oddly is the heir most entitled to the family's fortune. Duke recognizes that the time is at hand; he can use today's task as his chance to stake his claim as the rightful heir to the Winniper Empire.

"You still haven't faced your demons, Thomas." Papa shrugs his shoulders and stares away into the distance, searching for whatever his son hopes to find in his aimless daydreams. "Teresa was going to betray us and you did what was necessary. Now Duke will have the honor of protecting our family's name, and I'm sure he will not disappoint."

"Papa, isn't there another way?"

"We don't have time, son! June and *that Sioux boy* are leaving on the next flight back to California! I had to close the airport this morning just to give us time!" Papa shouts roughly, raising his hand, but he stops before striking his middle-aged son. Papa regains his composure, places both hands into his jacket pockets, leans back in his lawn chair, and removes two long stem cigars and a gold, custom lighter with a "*W*" imprinted on one side. He casually hands Sheriff Cobb, Jr. one of the cigars and then turns his head toward his son. "Do you know one of them Sioux killed my Uncle Christopher? The night of the uprising, one of them Injuns shot our kin right in the neck. Those people have always been savages!"

"What do you want us to do, sir?" Earl inquires excitedly, and Duke feels the familiar impetus of their many pranks and hijinks. Although Duke and Earl have been close since childhood, their friendship truly eclipsed Duke's other relationships when he arrived at the estate.

∞

Never one to choose his companions based upon moral standards, Duke's erratic ambitions connected with Earl's brash confidence and the two became best friends, almost like brothers. They quickly bonded during visits between Papa and Earl's Aunt Tilly; the boys spent most of their time dabbling with boyhood mischief and dreaming about one day controlling their respective dynasties.

∞

Known as a reckless elitist like his Cousin Kenny, Earl has enjoyed a life filled with pranks and small crimes that ranged from juvenile delinquency to larceny. Always the agitator, Earl has often gushed over his plans while concocting a new gag or goof, his voice trembling anxiously and his eyes gleaming brightly just as they do now; but, in this moment, Duke sees his friend as a smooth tactician, massaging Papa's concerns while ensuring his place in the family fold. Earl is a minor prankster who is now willing to commit whatever crime Papa commands and Earl believes that he is ready because the rewards fit his ego.

"I need you two to stop her. Stop both of them. I have agents watching them now. They left their hotel about a half hour ago; they've stopped at the coffee shop on Main and Swift Creek. They're waiting for a flight out this afternoon." Papa Winniper explains while lighting the sheriff's cigar and waiting for the sheriff to nod appreciatively. Papa then places his cigar at the edge of his lips, lights the end, and takes a few puffs before leaning toward Earl. Papa carefully returns his custom lighter back to his pocket, but he never takes his eyes off the unremarkable, once forgettable Bethune. The attention that Papa gives to Earl shows both Duke and Thomas III who is the real alpha male amongst his potential heirs. "Earl, I need you and Duke to go to the shop and make sure they never reach the airport. They want to get married as soon as they land, but this wedding can never happen."

"I agree, sir. That wedding is a horrible idea, but, we go to the shop and then what?"

"Well…Earl, do I need to really spell it out? Our family honor is at stake. I should've never let it come to this. June…she…uh…she is…" Papa stammers, unsure how to continue. He glances at Thomas III, but his son simply stares at the table's intricate marble design. Thomas III is unwilling to offer any support for his father's explanation. "June is a disgrace! She plans to marry *that Sioux boy* and infect our Winniper bloodline! They think they can get married and live out there in Hollywood for the whole world to see! They want to shame us and live happily-ever-after, but it won't be that easy! Our honor demands obedience!"

"Papa, please, we can work something out with her. Why does it have to be this way?" Thomas III pleads sorrowfully, trying desperately to finally assert his voice. "She can get married in secret...and maybe *they can* have a quiet life. She said they're going to retire, right? They could-"

"I asked her to live here on the property, but she wouldn't listen! That's the only acceptable arrangement but that girl is so stubborn! She's just like her mother! She still won't learn her place!" Papa booms as he becomes more irate, disgusted by Thomas III's suggestion. His thunderous words cause the table to shake and the ashes from his cigar fall on the cobblestone deck. "Duke, she's just like your mother! We can't have...*another disgrace*...these *abominations* could ruin the family! Can you imagine if they have a wedding for all the press to see? What about if they have children? I should've never let Olivia save those children! Now, we have a real mess to clean up! I just hope we don't have to torch that cabin..."

"I-I understand, sir, *I think*. Aunt Tilly would never let me marry Christina if her sister marries that Injun. I don't want to imagine them having a family. Even if she is a Winniper, a white girl can't be respected after lying down with a colored." Earl chooses his words carefully and lifts his head up like a soldier at arms. Again, his demeanor and behavior are both a ruse to calm Papa's worries and solidify Earl's rank among the Winniper men. "I know what you want us to do, sir. And I think June deserves whatever she gets...*Papa*."

"Well, that's mighty noble of you, Earl. I thank God for sending my granddaughter such a fine gentleman. Duke, do you understand what must be done?" Papa relaxes slightly, consoled by Earl's concession. The sheriff and Papa puff their cigars ominously; and Papa blows his smoke toward his grandson. Duke shakes his head from side-to-side, stuck within denial and genuine ignorance. He remembers the sight of his uncle burning his newborn, Sioux son, and he wonders if he could spare June from a similar fate. Imagining her as the baby and envisioning himself as her executioner, he rips his mind into chaos. A solitary tear forms in the corner of his right eye, but he wipes his eyelid with his index finger and dries his inner anguish. Earl leans toward his friend's ear like a snake sliding toward a rosy apple.

"Your sister…she's disrespecting your family. All those nights we spent talking about someday being like your grandfather. This is our chance, but it could all be gone if we wait. People are already talkin'," Earl divulges the truth of their circumstances as he glances back to Papa, making sure his assertions are correct. Papa continues to smoke his cigar, while turning his head toward Sheriff Cobb, Jr. and flashing a knowing smile. The weary Winniper king is happy to finally have a younger tyrant who is willing to get his hands dirty. "If June starts running around as that arrowhead's wife, what will happen to your family's name? The Bethunes are just as much at risk as the Winnipers if June shames us *in this way*. What about our future? Decent whites have no business being with any coloreds, least of all savages that killed your kin! We have a duty!"

"Papa, let someone else go for them," Thomas III suggests in a falsely heroic tone, a soldier too weak to carry his own rifle, let alone lead the charge. He knows that his suggestion is impractical. Papa wants all their secrets to stay within the family, so the Winniper men must always complete the most dastardly deeds with the upmost discretion, in order to protect their legacy and the secrets which could tear that legacy to shreds. "Sheriff Cobb can send some of his men. Or why not pay the feds more? Duke and Earl will be recognized…"

"It doesn't matter if they're *recognized*, Thomas! The sheriff's men will take care of any…*clean up*, shall we say. We own the agents, the press, the police, the judges, and everyone else. The whole world could see and my boys will always be protected by our power! We are bigger than the government, itself, and that's the point, my boy, that's the reason we value our power over everything else. And we will not allow June to shame us! Our power makes everything possible, but you, you are still too weak to wield it."

Papa dismisses his son with the wave of his hand, swatting away an invisible fly and leaning back in his chair. He continues to puff his cigar and periodically peek toward the sheriff in order to make sure his most loyal servant instinctually understands his role. For his part, the sheriff simply nods knowingly; years of deception and training have shown him how to survive in Papa's regime. Both men confirm their characters without words as they blow clouds of smoke above the marble table. Papa exhales deeply into the air, darts his eyes toward his grandson, and speaks to the group.

"This is Duke's responsibility now. I've been grooming him since I knew Tommy boy couldn't cut it. Duke's been taking *business* courses at the college and today, he will have a different kind of exam. If he performs well, he and Earl will protect the family name from now on and that 4.2 million in his trust fund will look like pennies compared to what's in his account tomorrow."

"Yes, sir!" Earl answers happily, showing more joy and respect than Duke has ever seen his friend display. Papa's words have sealed their destiny as Winniper heirs; Duke and Earl imagine themselves as kings sitting atop the Winniper oil wealth. The path they take to the throne suddenly seems irrelevant, even if their steps become soaked in June's blood. "Sir, we may need help. Even in town, your granddaughter and that Injun are still big stars. They always have press and people around them."

"I know, Earl. I have plenty of people *around them* myself. You see the sheriff is here to support us, and I have an entire local government at my disposal. Just get the job done and you'll be fine, but…if you're *uncomfortable*…maybe…"

Papa Winniper ponders a reasonable obstacle, still staring at Earl inquisitively while masking his calculations within an apparent lack of forethought. Two men in their thirties may be enough to break through a crowd and destroy a dream, but a few more hunters couldn't hurt the execution.

"You know, Earl, you're the only friend I've seen Duke associate with. You were naturally the first person I thought of to help my grandson. Do you have anyone who can help you boys?"

"Well, sir, like you said, I just want to make sure we *'get the job done'*. We left two buddies over at *Arnold's*. Loyal friends, of course, they'd love to help…as long as they haven't gotten too liquored up, with all due respect, sir."

"No problem at all. Your respect and ambition are refreshing, Earl. I only wish my son was more like you, but at least my grandson has you for a friend. You can't have enough ambition at a young age. Invite your friends, but don't tell them anymore than they need to know. The facts are raw enough without being cooked. *Just get the job done.*"

Papa Winniper places the almost spent cigar into a glass ashtray on the table, reaches into his jacket pocket, removes a large money clip filled with cash, and holds the small fortune in front of Earl instead of Duke or Thomas III. Maybe he now believes Earl is more than a pawn; maybe Earl can become a donor to produce another grandson with Christina—a father to a new male heir.

Earl's worth within murder and marriage is apparent to Duke and Thomas III, who both wallow in their shortcomings, both respectively lacking in speech and manhood. Papa rests his back against his chair and his eyes scan over his two disappointing heirs while placing the wad of the table and whispering to Earl.

"Make me proud, son. Make sure he's in good spirits and there will be more for you and my granddaughter; but remember...*don't let them get to that airport. You uphold our honor and I'll make you a very wealthy man.*"

"Yes, sir, and thank you, sir, I won't disappoint you. Me and Duke are gon' make you proud! We want you to know we can handle the business! We'll follow your orders to the tee!" Earl declares confidently, taking the money from the table without any hesitation. He was born to swipe and grab, to take and claim without care or consideration. A large grin emerges over his face as he removes the money clip and shuffles through the dollar bills, imagining all his future expenses. He has first world problems in a bloody market; he has truly found a home in Papa's nest. "June won't be a problem anymore. You can trust me...*Papa.*"

"Good, *son.* I think you'll prove yourself to be a very valuable asset!" Papa smiles sneakily; he is a wolf sending roosters to kill a hen. "Now, you and Duke get going. Get your friends and get to that coffee shop quick! And don't worry about the crowd; remember, I have eyes everywhere in this town."

"Yes, sir! Come on, Duke!" Earl stands eagerly, salutes Papa with his right hand to his forehead, and places the money into *his* pocket with his left hand. His actions show no consideration for Duke until Earl tugs his friend's arm, pulling him up from his chair. Without any time to resist or make any speechless murmurs, Duke submits to the task at hand. Earl pulls him from the table and the two stumble away from the patio.

Duke still struggles to digest his grandfather's orders, but he understands enough to realize that there was no discussion of when or whether the attack would occur.

∞

They had already determined who would carry out the deed.

∞

Once again, he remembers the night when Papa ordered his uncle to bury his newborn son, and he replays Papa's confession about Thomas III "taking care" of Teresa: murder is a just method to protect their wealth. Duke has never wept for his mother, because he's unsure if he ever really loved her, but June...she's an innocent, or, maybe, she's not. Earl continues to lead Duke away from the veranda and Duke looks back at his uncle, but Thomas III averts his eyes and looks away, resuming his search through the horizon for any hope of escaping with Nancy. Papa coughs anxiously, removes two more cigars from his jacket, and passes one to Sheriff Cobb, Jr. The sheriff promptly places the roach of his first cigar into the ashtray and takes the new, unlit cigar into his right hand. He obediently waits for Papa to light it.

"Just like old times, right, Sheriff Cobb? That girl *was* a dreamer just like her mother, huh? Thinking she could get married to *that Sioux boy*. Tommy, if you had given me a proper male heir, I could've killed all of them right after Teresa. Almost would've been worth it to have a suitable male heir, but June won't stay here! We have no other choice!" Papa broods carefully so that only the sheriff and Thomas III can hear his complaints. He doesn't qualify his statement to show any real respect for Duke, but Papa turns his head toward the next generation of henchmen and smiles mightily, watching his plan unfold as Duke and Earl walk toward the side of the mansion. Papa raises his cigar in the air and yells from the veranda so that his words echo over the estate's backyard. "When you boys finish, we'll talk about you owning some land, too! Earl, I have forty acres of prime Winniper County real estate for you and my granddaughter!"

"Oh, well...wow, yes, sir! I mean, uh...thank you, sir! We'll be done in a flash!" Earl calls back excitedly and punches Duke in his shoulder. Earl beams joyfully over his friend and sighs in contentment, dreaming of all the money and property that will soon belong to him. "You hear that, Duke? Things are really lookin' up for ol' Earl! Me and your sister will probably be getting' married soon! I'll be your brother for real!"

Duke grins sheepishly at the thought; finally he will have a brother, but at what cost? He remains sullen; his mind caught in a conflict, confused about the mission, and wondering why he should live in a world where his grandfather asks him to harm his baby sister. Is this really the solution? *And for what?* Is a Sioux brother-in-law really such a *disgrace* to the family? Are colored babies so bad? Jazz is a successful musician; maybe the family could accept him...somehow.

∞

When Duke lost his voice, June was the only family member who didn't treat him differently; in fact, she remained obedient in her subservient role within the Winniper family, until she overheard their grandfather's plot to have Sheriff Cobb, Jr. travel back to Chicago and finish Kenny off. Christina had helped with the first attempt, a mere warning, but June convinced her siblings to leave Winniper County and help her reach Kenny before Papa's minions visited him. Teresa's children hated Kenny for abandoning them, but he was still June's father and she tried to save him.

Papa had already decided that June and Christina would only be used for promissory marriages. He never entertained nor indulged any of their dreams once they arrived at the estate. After his eighteenth birthday, Duke's silence made him a marginal man in Papa's eyes, but June and Christina had always been an afterthought to their grandfather. Upon their arrival to the estate, they stopped attending school and their grandmother began preparing them to assume the duties of a Winniper woman—no cooking and cleaning, just a mannequin's silence so that they resemble good girls who are suitable for marriage. Under their grandparents' rule, each girl found their respective escapes; for June, her salvation lied in music, but, for Christina, who was a teenager in a world of opportunity, boys, namely Earl, became a natural distraction.

Over the years, while Christina drowned in her affection for Earl during his visits to the estate, June and Duke bonded during the off times when Duke wasn't with Earl and Papa didn't demand that his grandson observe a meeting or contract signing. Papa had made it clear that he hoped to mold a new, potential heir. June and Duke enjoyed the disproportionate treatment that they received from their grandfather. Duke indulged in his need for a father figure and June simmered in her disgust for the very idea of fatherhood.

Duke and June had a mutual disdain for male authority and that disdain fueled their escape from Winniper County; but, while June remained in New Orleans with Jazz, Duke returned and began to crave his grandfather's *approval* because he no longer had that sense of appreciation—no one looked up to him, no one had any high regard for the mute. Christina continued to swoon over Earl; she practically fell into his arms when he came to retrieve them from New Orleans, so, when he, Christina, and Earl returned to Winniper County, Duke was left alone. Ostracized and confined to the Winniper family's mansion at Papa's request, Duke pined for his grandfather's attention. Appeasing Papa became Duke's only ambition despite the ample affection that he received from his grandmother and uncle. In an effort to further align himself with Papa, Duke began to ignore Olivia and Thomas III; he disregarded their input and opinions as he matured into a Winniper man. He valued them less and less.

Restricted to the mansion upon his return, Duke submitted himself to his grandfather's will. Papa insisted on having complete control over his youngest male heir. By that time, he had finally given up on the prospect of Thomas III becoming a proper successor.

Duke couldn't speak and he had a slight alcohol addiction, but, left to cower under Papa's whims, Duke's life became Papa's sole source of patriarchal validation. Papa's orders, requests, and commands became Duke's gospel, even more so than when he was a child. Duke sought to impress his grandfather as he never had before, and Duke's desire for appreciation grew into a need to one day be crowned the Winniper family's king. So, Duke began to obey Papa's instructions throughout his late twenties and early thirties, hoping to claw his way into the old man's cold heart. Although Duke never thought that his grandfather would order him to commit murder, once Duke saw his uncle fulfill the honor, he knew this day would come eventually.

∞

"Duke, what's wrong with you?" Earl interrupts Duke's reminiscent thoughts as they walk around the side of the massive mansion, turning the corner and making their way toward the front of the house. "Listen, you won't have to lift a finger. I'll call the guys, and we'll '*get the job done*'. Just come along and show the ol' man that he can trust you. You heard what he said; he's going to give us the keys to the castle. All of this will be ours!"

"Hey! Where are you two going?" Christina shouts from the porch, still reclining in Papa Winniper's rocking chair and sipping a tall glass of lemonade. Next to her, Nancy sits on the porch with the edges of her dress draped flat over her knees. She holds a small cup of lemonade to her lips and stares down at Duke with open, curious eyes, though she is well-trained to only speak when spoken to and, even then, she knows to never voice her concerns.

"Papa gave us a job to do! And I got a bunch of cash for us to spend tonight, babe! You and me are goin' dancin' later!" Earl explains proudly and sticks out his chest. Duke tries to plead to Christina with his eyes, desperate to convey the exact details of their coming business. He struggles and strains, pushing his throat and trying to force a sound, but his vocal chords haven't worked in years. Inexplicably stricken mute, he feels as though God cursed him on his eighteenth birthday. He doesn't realize that he simply traded gifts with his long-lost twin sister, Lucy, and, sadly, his voice may never return.

"Hey! Duke, what's the matter?" Christina questions boorishly, emboldened by Papa's absence. She places her lemonade glass on the porch and rises from the rocking chair. She runs to the edge of the front steps, but she doesn't dare to descend, just in case Papa is behind them. "I can tell something's wrong, Earl! Tell me what y'all are doing! What did Papa say about June?"

"Everything's fine! Just stay here and look after your cousin like Papa said. Come meet us in a little and I'll tell you all about it!" Earl reassures her confidently and hangs his right arm over Duke's shoulders, pulling him away from the bottom steps. Earl throws his left hand into the air and waves to Christina and Nancy as he and Duke continue to pass the porch and make their way toward the garage.

"What are you two up to?" Christina calls behind them, resembling a worried mother who watches her child leave home with the neighborhood bully. Duke turns his head and stares blankly at Christina, meeting her eyes and sharing a sense of mutual desperation, but they remain in their roles. She stands at the edge of the porch, wishing she could assert herself, but she's only able to bark like a bitch on a leash. "You better not get him into any trouble, Earl!"

"Don't worry, babe! We're just... *following orders!* Behave yourself and I might pick up an engagement ring on the way!" Earl declares over his shoulder as he and Duke walk into the garage. Even though Earl often boasts about his control over Christina and his privilege to speak on Duke's behalf, he's wise enough to leverage the siblings against one another. Earl refuses to tell Christina that he and her brother are on their way to attack her sister at their grandfather's behest. Perhaps, it's an innocuous detail: orders are orders, even if he told her, how would that change the outcome? She would only complain more and Earl doesn't need the hassle. He leans toward Duke, whispering their secret plans as they move through the garage. "I'll call the guys from a payphone. You never know who could be listenin'."

He playfully slaps the side of the Aston Martin and hops over the passenger door. Duke remains outside the car, hesitating and fearing the inevitable trap of inheritance and expectations, when a man must act to prove his manhood in a cruel world. Duke has dreamed of becoming Winniper County's king, and now that he has the opportunity to usurp his uncle, he is afraid of the kind of man that he must become in order to do so. Earl slides across the front seat and opens the door so that it hits Duke's thigh roughly, causing him to stumble back on his heels.

"Come on, buddy! Get in!" Earl encourages his friend with a pat on the driver's seat. "I don't want to tell your grandfather that you were scared!"

He pauses and allows his words to sink into Duke's ego, still buried deep within his silent frame. Earl always knows how to irritate Duke's insecurities while also evoking his evolved sense of entitlement. Earl loves to challenge his friend's manhood and question Duke's place in Winniper lore.

Duke weighs his concerns on a balance beam of self-doubt; whether fight or flight, his actions will cause enough personal turmoil to ruin his life and his family. Either way, he can't win. He will disappoint and hurt someone he loves no matter how today plays out, so he commits to a certain betrayal with one step forward. He slowly slides into the front seat, slams the door shut, and turns the key in the ignition. Duke revs the engine; the Aston roars. Earl beams wickedly and pats Duke on his right shoulder. Excited for their future, he watches his best friend reverse gears and back out of the open garage.

They both ignore Christina and the family's workers. Duke hurriedly maneuvers through the driveway and speeds out the estate's front gates without a glance back to the porch or the house. Duke forgets about his life before Papa ordered him to attack his sister, when innocence still existed in his heart. His hands are still clean, but he feels the coming blood, knowing that he must fulfill his grandfather's wishes in order to gain the old man's rewards. Duke and Earl sit in silence as Duke drives back through Winding Winniper Way. Both contemplate their separate aims until Earl glances over to Duke's crimson visage; his face is mad red from self-hate.

"I know how you must feel, Duke!" Earl states empathetically, leaning across the front seat and tapping Duke on the shoulder. Duke turns his head to his friend, but he continues driving wildly through the street with the wind whipping all around them. He forgot to grab his driving goggles from behind his seat, but he doesn't care. He's thirty-four years old, he still lives off his family's wealth, and his grandfather just asked/ordered him to hurt his sister badly enough that she can't leave town and marry a colored man. Nothing seems to matter at this point.

"You don't have to worry! Your best bud Earl will take care of everything! You know, even after all these years of you being a mute, it's still hard to tell what you're thinking!" Earl shouts, staring at Duke while sticking out his tongue and scrunching his cheeks to make a childish facial expression. Earl balls his fists and rubs them over his eyes, but Duke remains sullen and stoic. Duke refuses to acknowledge Earl's attempts at humor.

"Stop being so mopey! You heard what your grandfather said! June went too far! She didn't ask for his blessing because she knew he would say no! Now, she's elopin' with that Injun for the world to see! It's embarrassing and it would ruin my relationship with your sister! Your family would be shamed!" Earl emphasizes his words by throwing his hands into the air, but Duke simply stares at Earl without watching the winding road ahead. Having memorized much of the Winniper streets, Duke momentarily questions his mental aptitude because he hopes for a crash. What use are all those business classes when Papa still asks him to pass this kind of test? Earl slams his hand over the dashboard, trying to rouse Duke's attention.

"Papa is right, June has always been reckless! She knocked out your two front teeth, remember? She's always been selfish! She chose that feather neck over you and your sister! Now, she could ruin everything! Think about *our* family! All that oil money, the land, none of it will matter because every decent white person in the whole world will know the Winnipers are mixing their blood with a savage."

Duke shakes his head from side-to-side while gliding along the road without looking ahead. His tongue lightly touches the space between his teeth and he feels the sting from when June dislodged two of his pearly whites during that bar fight in New Orleans. Although some of her actions have been *reckless* and *indefensible*, Duke still feels a need to protect her while he plans to administer her punishment.

"What do you mean 'no'?" Earl readjusts his hips in the passenger seat so that he turns his entire upper body toward Duke. "You think your sister should marry that Injun?"

Duke shakes his head from side-to-side again, still maneuvering the Aston through the winding road.

"No, of course not! Race mingling may be fine for them niggers in the cities, but not for us in Winniper County. Think about what people will say; think about what they're already saying! We have to stop this before it goes any further! We have to protect our family, right?"

Again, Earl playfully hits Duke on the shoulder, a constant show of his dominance because Duke never protests. He is never able to voice his frustrations. Earl sighs dramatically, jokingly wipes his forehead, and leans back into his seat.

"Whew, I thought you turned into some kind of sympathizer. Hey, pull over to that phone booth on Turner Street! I'll call *Arnold's* and see if the guys are still there!" Earl points ahead to a nearby phone booth. Duke turns quickly and drifts his sports car onto Turner Street, stopping abruptly alongside the payphone. Earl raises his palm in front of Duke like a child waiting for milk money, neglecting the fact that he has a wad of cash in his possession. Duke rolls his eyes, retrieves several coins from his pocket, and places them into Earl's palm. Earl folds his fingers over the change and punches Duke in the shoulder again.

"That's for pulling that driving without looking stunt! Now, don't forget who's *really* running this show!" Earl yells sternly while hopping out of the car and running to the phone booth. He continues talking to Duke as he dials, stuck between his concern for his friend and his commitment to the task at hand. "You're not going to cost me my chance to have my own mansion! Papa doesn't just give out land in this here county!"

Duke watches his friend throughout his phone conversation, but he can't hear the words clearly. He once hoped that when he lost his speech, he would sharpen his other senses, but, that never happened. Over the years, his childhood hopes of becoming a painter or a race car driver dissipated into thin air. There has never truly been enough room for Duke's dreams to come true within Papa's world. Duke has always had a role to play in some form, whether he accepted that role or not; the part has always been there for him to fill—the good Winniper stooge, always obeying every one of his grandfather's orders. Earl hoots happily, hangs up the phone, and runs back to the car, his worn black boots kicking up dust and dirt.

"The guys are in!" Earl proclaims joyously while hopping back into the car. "They're a little lit, but they'll come through. We just have to wait here."

He removes a Wayfield cigarette from his shirt pocket and lights the end, offering another tobacco stick to Duke. Duke pushes Earl's hand away and continues to look ahead, still trapped within his conflict, yet he knows the deed has already been done.

"You'll see, boy, I got everything figured out. The guys are…uh, *bringing some tools.*" Earl speaks surely and looks over Duke's concerned face, trying to help his friend see the light. "We won't hurt her too bad, Duke; your grandfather just wants to stop the wedding. We'll give that colored boy a once over, too, just to make sure he don't get in the way."

Duke turns to Earl with anguish burning in his eyes, but he can't decide the best course of action in a world that has suddenly turned too complex. Always understanding the benefits of wealth, he has never encountered any real responsibility, nor any real risk or downside.

∞

Even when he lived away from the estate with Teresa and his stepfathers, Duke was always within wealth's blessed arms, cradled closely to Papa's bosom. He always knew he was special, but, as a child, his grandfather never asked much from him.

Papa only wanted Duke to present some semblance of masculinity and worthiness as a Winniper male heir. He judged Duke against Thomas III, who was, and still is, a constant source of disappointment; but, Duke's uncle balanced his lack of gumption with his responsibilities at the Winniper Market. Uncle Thomas III performed a community service while Duke transformed into a thirty-something, muted leech without a job or prospect—a known dependent, reliant upon the Winniper Family Estate.

∞

He has enrolled in a few credit courses in order to gain some form of self-respect and public approval, but he still doesn't have a genuine career path beyond following Papa's orders. In all honesty, he has never really had a genuine life path outside of driving fast and following enough orders to stay under the money tree.

"Hey, cheer up before the guys get here, Duke!" Earl grumbles as he takes a long puff from his cigarette. "They'll think you're soft like your uncle! They'll say you're no better than a nigger lover like your sister! She might as well marry Marty the King Joonya!"

Earl's insults cut Duke deeply, and the friends stare at each other while questioning each other's resolve. Duke thinks his friend may have lost any real notion of friendship, given Papa's recent promises. As long as he completes the task, Earl assumes that his dutiful obedience will reap all the rewards that Papa suggested, with or without Duke's assistance. Earl does not care that June is Duke's sister; Earl only cares about the money, the power, and the respect. He urges Duke to willfully enjoy their traitorous treachery, but he speaks from a place of political reasoning.

"I don't mean to hurt you, Duke. You're my friend, my *best* friend, but you need to face the facts. Your grandfather knows best; he's a very wealthy and powerful man." Earl casually explains his viewpoint as he puffs his cigarette, leaning back in the passenger seat. "Do you know what I could do with 40 acres of land? What about Christina and the guys, too? You can't mess this up for us! Me and Christina could be married in a couple of months, and then we'll be brothers. June could ruin all of that!"

Earl points a finger at Duke, but the Winniper heir only stares back blankly at his friend, wondering where these moments will lead. His friend is now just another monster.

∞

Like June, Earl once seemed innocent; he was a fallen pearl from the Bethune clam. He barely respected his Aunt Tilly and he loathed his Cousin Kenny, Jr. Earl Bethune is the only son of Reginald Bethune, who was Kenneth Sr. and Tilly's half-brother and one of William Bethune's many illegitimate sons. Initially believing that he would have very little claim to the Bethune family's fortune, Earl became a known petty thief. His antics earned him a reputation as a bad boy, yet, as he aged into a teenager, he became most prominently known as Duke's friend and the apple of Christina's eye. Given his family's close-knit relationship with the Winnipers, Christina's affection only helped Earl assimilate into the corners of high society.

When Christina, Duke, and June left Winniper County and ended up in New Orleans, Papa enlisted Earl to retrieve them, in part because Papa trusted that Earl's hooligan nature would help him wade through the muddy waters of Scapetown and emerge clean after retrieving Papa's grandchildren from the muck. Once June teamed up with Jazz, choosing him over her family, Earl easily convinced Christina and Duke to travel back to Winniper County. All along, Earl remembered Papa's instructions— *"Don't return without my grandson. You can leave the others, but Duke must come home."*

For Earl, maintaining his romantic relationship with Christina was always a financially motivated affair, so returning to Winniper County with her and Duke was always his plan and his success was a major accomplishment. He had done well for himself. He never particularly liked June and leaving her in New Orleans was his preferred course of action. He thought she would be strung out and/or fed to the wolves, but her success made him despise her even more.

∞

Duke does not know whether Earl has since become more loyal to their friendship or Papa Winniper, but Duke does understand Earl's fixation with the economic value of profitable partnerships.

∞

Earl was something of an outcast in his family, but his triumphant return with the prodigal son proved his reliability. His efforts earned him a room at his Aunt Tilly's mansion on the Bethune estate; Earl's father had passed away years ago, which helped to eliminate the remnant stench of his illegitimacy. Absent Kenny, Jr., Tilly used Earl to resume her motherly maneuvering, and Earl's long-term motives became prevalent topics of discussion, which Duke has never allowed to corrupt his friendship with Earl.

∞

Throughout their childhood and adulthood, they have still remained best friends, joined with mutual ambitions. Earl has the voice and the bravado, and Duke has the name and the birthright; together, they can accomplish whatever Papa Winniper desires of them.

"You need to understand how much this means to us, Duke. Your grandfather doesn't trust many people and finally, here's our chance. You should be excited!" Earl implores his friend to come aboard while placing his hand on Duke's right shoulder. "We're going to be a big deal in this town. Hell, we'll be a big deal all over the world! We'll be more famous than your sister and that Injun! You're going to own the entire empire one day!"

Earl shakes Duke's shoulder and boasts joyously, continuing his attempts to convince Duke to follow Papa's orders, but Duke sits stiffly in the driver's seat, struggling to resolve the moral implications. His programming begins to falter as he questions his path and he begins to look for a way out.

"Here they are now!" Earl interrupts Duke's thoughts of escape when he sees a red Lincoln, four-door convertible with a black soft-top whirl wildly around the corner and turn onto Turner Street. Earl nudges Duke and chuckles sinisterly as the convertible shifts across the traffic lanes and comes to a stop beside Duke's Aston. Earl leans toward Duke one last time and points at him sternly. "Don't embarrass our families. We're the kings, now. Just follow my lead."

"We heard you boys plannin' a lynchin'!" Guy 1 hollers drunkenly from the driver's seat.

"Yea buddy!" Earl screams, turning excitedly and hopping out of the Aston. "Duke, get out! We'll take their car!"

"Yea, that there Aston is a purrrtty car!" Guy 2 adds sloppily, taking a swig from a Burgermeister beer can and eyeing Duke's sports car from the convertible's passenger seat. "You don't want to scuff your grandfather's wheels!"

"No, this here is Duke's car now! We got enough money to buy two, ain't that right, Duke?" Earl protects his friend while walking around the Aston and opening the driver's side door. He pats Duke on the back and tugs his collar until he exits the vehicle. "You listen here, guys. Duke and me are two men that you boys better respect! We're the kings 'round here, starting today!"

"Then what does that make us?" Guy 1 inquires quickly, instinctively thinking of himself while snatching an open beer from behind his seat and taking a sloppy swig. Most of the beverage drips over his shirt and over the front seat of the Lincoln. He wipes his mouth and places the beer can between his knees. "Are we some kind of drunk servants to the kings?"

"No, boys, and take it easy on that stuff! We got work to do!" Earl answers crossly, pointing at the beers tucked all around the car and piled up behind the front seats. "You boys are the kings' right hands. Whatever we order you to do, you boys will do and we'll reward you, handsomely!"

"*Well, how's Duke gon' give orders when he can't talk?* I guess we'll be doing a lot o' nothin'!" Guy 1 jokes from his driver seat and takes another long, slovenly swig from his beer can. The two guys laugh from the front seats of the convertible as Duke balls his fists and steps angrily toward the driver. Earl grabs Duke's right arm and calms his friend with a reassuring nod, stopping Duke from defending his disability.

"Hold it there, Duke. That's what I'm here for." Earl consoles his friend and smiles childishly before turning to Guy 1 and punching him in the mouth. Guy 1 rocks back in the driver's seat, spills the rest of his beer over his pants, and clutches his face in shock. Earl pulls the wad of cash from his pocket, places his hand into the convertible, and waves the money in front of his friends' faces. "Now, I told you two, you better respect us, but you better especially respect Duke here! His grandfather's going to make us all rich and I'm going to marry his sister! Me and him is practically brothers already, so any remark you make about him, you better be ready to deal with me!"

"I'm sorry, Earl!" Guy 1 moans, wiping his lips, checking his nose, and staring at the wad of cash over his face.

"He was only kidding, Earl. We're sorry. We're *really* sorry." Guy 2 apologizes profusely, equally entranced by the money that dances in front of his eyes.

"Apologize to *him!*" Earl points to Duke, while still displaying the money. The cash has also mesmerized Duke and he reminds himself that when duty calls, men must sometimes act with drastic means in order to solve dire problems. Suddenly, the guys' slick talk and Earl's right cross have galvanized Duke's inner ambitions to become a king who will one day crush all jesters and jokesters. "You know, it was Duke's idea to bring you boys in on this. We didn't have to call you at *Arnold's*. We could've let you two get drunk and stay poor all your lives, living off mommy and daddy's money. I'd rather split this cash between me and him anyways! We can go back and tell Papa that we can handle this all by ourselves!"

"No, Earl, now come on! No need to get sore. I'm sorry, Duke, it's just the beers talking, I promise! I appreciate you thinking of us, and uh, whatever you need, we'll take care of it." Guy 1 vows sincerely and raises his right hand to his chest. "I didn't mean you no harm. I have…uh, a lot of respect for you and your family, everybody knows that. There wouldn't be a Winniper County without the Winnipers. Here, hey, do you want to drive my car?"

"No, kings have chauffeurs!" Earl interjects toughly and pulls Duke towards the backseat. "Now, hurry up and drive us to the coffee shop on Main! And you better hope they haven't left."

"How d'you know they're going to be there in the first place?" Guy 2 asks suspiciously as Earl opens the backseat and pushes the six-packs and car magazines out of the way, making room for Duke. Earl steps aside and ushers Duke inside with his hand out, waiting for Duke to enter the car first. When he moves into the doorway, Earl pushes him into the backseat and promptly follows his future co-king into the chariot.

"I know because the old man told us so. Now, stop askin' questions like you're second guessin' me! The old man has people watching them, right now! They're all waiting on us to get over there and stop those two freedom riders from getting to the airport!" Earl explains the plan assertively, adjusting his weight and pushing Duke even further into the car so that Duke's right shoulder presses against the opposite door. Earl leans forward over the driver's right shoulder and whispers carefully. "Did you bring them *tools?*"

"Yea, everything's in the trunk!" Guy 1 announces while accelerating away from Duke's car and driving into the street. "Arnold gave us a few bats and some pipes, enough to hit a home run or do some plumbing!"

"Great! We just have to move fast! We'll be rich in no time, boys!" Earl cheers eagerly and pats Guy 1 on the shoulders. He leans over toward Guy 2 in the passenger seat and snatches the beer from his hand, taking a quick swig before throwing the beer can out of the window. "Let's get focused, boys! I have to admit...I'm a little excited! The old man said he has some land for-"

"But what if these two are over at that new coffee chain further down on Main Street?" Guy 2 interrupts, raising his eyebrows in concern, while looking through the rear windshield and watching his beer can rattle in the street behind them. "You know that new donut place?"

"Well, Papa said he's got people watchin'...there's people...high up types...supportin' us!" Earl reassures his cohorts and places his fist in his palm. "What did I just tell you, boy? This is a family matter! I got the inside scoop 'cause I'm destined to be a Winniper man! No more borrowing from Tilly!"

"But it's the middle of the day! What if someone sees?" Guy 1 wonders fretfully, speeding through the freshly paved roads of Winniper County. He turns sharply onto Main Street and the tires barely make a sound. Plush sports cars, suspended pickups, and oil-filled eighteen wheelers barrel through the heavily trafficked street and Duke considers how all these mundane events can surround such a devious plan. Guy 1 continues to question the plot, turning his head from the road while dodging between traffic. "The town is too busy right now! Someone will see, won't they?"

"Boy, keep your eyes on the road! I swear if you ask me one more question, I'm gon' sock you into tomorrow. And tomorrow, me and Duke will be rich as thieves and you two idiots will still be driving your mama's Lincoln! You still haven't figured out how to put this top down! And listen here, the whole town could see us, and it won't matter!" Earl proclaims cockily, stretching his arms inside the convertible top and pushing Duke further against the backseat. "Papa controls the police, the D.A., and the courts! He told us it don't matter who sees, the press won't do a thing! You think Papa would let Duke go to jail? No, this here is about honor! It's a privilege for you two-"

"There's the coffee shop!" Guy 2 announces and points ahead. He tilts his head around the windshield and squints his eyes, hoping to see farther into the shop. "I can't see if they're inside though!"

"Pull into the parking lot across the street!" Earl commands as he also strains his neck to look inside the coffee shop. He leans into Duke and pushes him down against the door. Duke's head nearly submerges under the side of the backseat and he lays face-to-face with several fresh, frosty six packs, still dripping with condensation, presumably snagged from *Arnold's*. "Duke, keep your head down in case June is in there!"

"I see 'em!" Guy 2 proclaims, as the convertible veers away from the coffee shop and drifts into the parking lot of the Winniper Bowling Alley. "They're right there in the window, *together*! Just the sight of 'em makes me sick!"

"Well, boys, that's why we're here! These coloreds need to learn to stay away from *our women*!" Earl repeatedly smashes his fist into his palm as Guy 1 slows and stops his convertible inside an open parking space. "I hope you boys aren't too liquored up to get the job done! We're here to do God's work! We have orders straight from Papa, himself! We've got to stop them before they leave town!"

"Earl, we ain't ever too liquored up to give a beatin'! Just let me get one of those bats! You remember I played in high school!" Guy 1 exclaims raucously, turning off the ignition and opening his door quickly. The rest of the group exits the sports car as Guy 1 pops his trunk, revealing an arsenal of spontaneous artillery. He happily grabs a baseball bat, steps away from the trunk, and takes a few practice swings while surveying his surroundings. The street traffic continues to move along as usual and there's an eager contingent of fans, reporters, and photographers camped outside the coffee shop.

"We need to hurry up!" Guy 2 worries, walking around the Lincoln, but he never removes his eyes from June and Jazz. He watches anxiously as they rise from their table inside the coffee shop and make their way toward the door. "I think they're leaving!"

"No, they're not! No one's getting in the way of me and that land! They'll never see that airport!" Earl growls and leers as he repeats his promise to Papa Winniper and takes a thick, lead pipe from the trunk. He looks at Duke who stands frozen on a moral precipice, reluctant to grab a weapon, though his presence has already sealed his fate. Duke thinks about his grandfather's instructions and he imagines Papa's disappointment if he heard that his grandson got cold feet. Tasked with the duty to uphold his powerful family's honor, Duke doesn't want to recede back into the abyss with Thomas III. No, he's been the black sheep of a royal, American family and, now, he can become the next king. Earl observes Duke with a disgraced sneer, while witnessing his longtime friend waver back-and-forth between his destiny and his defeat. "You don't have to grab one, Duke. You don't have to lift a finger. You're the king, now. Me and the guys will take care of everythin'."

Duke stands still, glancing beyond Earl's shoulder and noticing June through the coffee shop's glass window. Her smile sickens him and her joy exudes an inner glow that infuriates his insecure nature. She stops to sign autographs for some of the employees, laughing cheerfully with Jazz at her side. He throws his right arm around her shoulders, leans in closely, and whispers a joke that makes her chuckle. Duke feels a burning rage surge through his body. She is no longer his innocent sister; she is no longer the sad, little girl who went to their mother's funeral alone. She is a colored boy's whore, an unapologetic traitor to the powerful family that has always protected her from the demons she inevitably chose herself. She is the villain who has caused her own demise.

Guy 2 pushes Earl aside and seizes two ominous objects into his hands: another baseball bat and a jagged metal cylinder from a washing machine. Holding the lead pipe in his left hand, Earl takes a moment to reach out and run his right palm over the cylinder's sharp edges. He begins to laugh.

"I like your ambition, boy. Ol' Arnold really gave us some fine weaponry." Earl continues to chuckle as he steps beside Guy 1. They both pause and assess the street traffic, onlookers, and paparazzi. The commotion builds around June and Jazz as they continue to work their way toward the door. The media frenzy surrounding their pending nuptials has increased the public's interest in their activities. Speculation over their retirement runs rampant. The headlines describe how the two stars turned lovebirds are finally planning to settle down and make a nest somewhere in the American melting pot. While clustering and fussing around the duo, the photogs and faithful fans fawn over the international superstars who have returned home to share the joyous news with their families...wading amidst the controversy of their fame and social status.

"Look at all these parasites..." Earl grumbles as he molds with his weapon, becoming the steel of the lead pipe, cold, hard, and deadly when held in the wrong hands. He continues to scowl at the amassing crowd outside the coffee shop while the fans and press yell for June and Jazz to come outside. Earl turns to the guys, preparing for war without mercy. "We've got to get them fast! I'm going to personally knock that Sioux boy's block off! Smash those cameras if you can, but don't bother too much. We got Papa's protection on this one and no one's going to stop us in his town. Soon, it'll all belong to me and Duke. We're the-"

"Okay, enough talk! Lead the way, Earl!" Guy 1 goads Earl enthusiastically, waving his bat forward. Earl pauses and narrows his eyes, unhappy that he was interrupted, but, he steps forward, nods his head, and leads the group across the street. They move through oncoming traffic and push past the people gathering on the sidewalk. There are no agents or professional guards in sight. The couple trusted someone too much; they walk side-by-side, unprotected and vulnerable. All along, the henchmen continue to watch June and Jazz as they exit the coffee shop. The tension boils in the hunters' veins as a cold wind brushes against their skin, sending shivers down their shins; **and, still, only a silent few know that June and Jazz are kin, cursed twins born in a world of sin.**

Duke hears a soft whisper that he cannot completely understand. His Great-Great-Grandfather Christopher Winniper, Sr. speaks through the wind, begging Duke to stop his forsaken steps. He says he once failed to convince his son to choose peace on a cold night in December. The airy voice pleads for Duke to turn around and save himself, but Duke does not listen. He has chosen the beaten path of the Winniper men; he damns himself to repeat the sins of his ancestors and the cycle of violent birthright will continue through 1966, over seventy years after it began in 1890.

June and Jazz finally meander through the crowd at the doorway and they successfully exit the coffee shop. They stroll slowly amidst the paparazzi's flashing cameras, casually attempting to escape down the sidewalk. They don't see the pack of wolves following them; their love blinds them to any possible harm. Consumed with jealousy and ambition, the guys can only see a Sioux boy and a white girl who act as if God will not punish them for their sins. Duke concedes to the coming malice and abandons his loyalty to his baby sister while he remembers Papa's words—"land", "honor", "duty". His grandfather must have implanted a piece of planned programming that activates in this moment of reckoning. An upgraded definition of loyalty installs into Duke's body and a deeper purpose courses through his blood—he is the future Winniper patriarch and he must protect his family's reputation.

Duke suddenly looks at his wayward sister with a dismissive disdain for her betrayal. June left him, so now, he leaves her. She never cared that he returned from New Orleans and entered the extreme tutelage of their grandfather, so it's only fitting that she reaps the repercussions of his lessons learned.

∞

She remained in the arms of a colored boy while her family missed her and begged her to return. She chose a Sioux native whose ancestors probably murdered more Americans than Duke could count—yes, she deserves this pain.

∞

A quiet hatred continues to pump through his blood, mixing with a vengeful adrenaline that allows him to become complicit in the crime. The guys conceal their weapons under their arms as they worm through the crowd. Duke follows slowly, watching June lean into Jazz's chest with his arm draped over her back. Their affection increases the killers' fury and Duke thinks that he may be able to enjoy the carnage as long as he focuses his disgust upon the cause of all the coming violence: Jazz.

The Sioux pianist calmly lights a cigarette, while cradling June under his shoulder and daring the outside world to challenge him. His confidence is so cool that his energy escapes his form and transfers to June as she leans further into him and wraps her arms around his waist. Duke can see her face beaming brightly when she turns her hips and their genuine joy, their visible glow, and their positive aura are palpable and infuriating. Fans and casual citizens join a growing mass that continues to descend upon the stars with the killers in their midst.

Duke feels deceived as he deceives, staring at June and Jazz through salutary goodbyes, congratulatory handshakes, and obsessive camera flashes. He observes a power in their bond that he has never shared with June, though he once thought his relationship with his baby sister was special.

∞

He once protected her, or at least, he tried, but she abandoned her family for *her dreams*. The morning after she met Jazz at that bar, Duke saw her change. She refused to leave with him and Christina; she felt she no longer needed their protection.

∞

Duke still does not know what convinced her to trust Jazz and join him onstage, nor does Duke understand how she could be so confident and so blasphemous while performing with a colored man, knowing that her actions would tarnish her family's name and jeopardize their privilege.

∞

In her youth, Papa implored June to understand social graces and the consequences of attracting the public eye. Maybe hope was something June always had in excess, but, when she refused to return from New Orleans, she also ignored Duke's plight as Winniper County's heir apparent. She never imagined that he would become Papa after returning home with Christina and Earl. She escaped, but sadly, the fact that she never cared to save *her brother*, has now delivered her fate into his hands.

∞

It's ironic how selfishness always leads to self-destruction.

∞

When they were younger, Duke loved his sister's music. He loved to hear her within her room, strumming her guitar or singing a tune. She could capture a feeling that he had also experienced—the inner pain of the blues. His sorrow became her melody, and, when she performed, she could sing their pain to the crowd. Yet, when Jazz arrived and swept her off her feet, she forgot to take Duke or her sister along.

The brown and white duo maneuvered through the ranks so speedily that neither the Winniper family nor the world could defend themselves. Their music and their love forced the world to confront its hypocrisy: how can one world have one God when so many differences divide the people and conquer their hearts? Their records appealed to the masses in over twenty countries, courtesy of the now defunct Charles Lancaster Records and their new label, ABC-Paramount. Even on the cusp of retirement, their faces will still be worldwide symbols of equality—a misnomer for many of Winniper County residents who now beg the superstars for their autographs.

June once told Duke that Charles Lancaster promised that they would travel the world, and he delivered on every word of his vow. Over time, June became perfectly content with sharing less and less about her success with the Winniper family, but, last year, she tried to re-engage her communications with Papa. Still a dreamer with too much hope, June thought she could reconcile with her family as she formed a family of her own. Sadly, it seemed that their grandfather and June were lost in different aims: art and fame, greed and claim.

∞

The two musicians have become dark shadows that escaped from the Winniper family's deadly closet; they are ghosts that need an invisible hand wrapped around their throats, choking them in the afterlife so they can haunt no more. June and Jazz have developed a relationship that Papa can no longer allow to flourish. Papa had planned to have their lights snuffed out eventually, but the threat of a Hollywood elopement has made the issue more pressing. June has knowingly entered her grandfather's clutches and the Winniper name has once again become a mercenary's tool, a wartime reason to destroy anything that threatens the family's legacy.

∞

Touring, touring, and touring until they often forgot where they were, Winniper County, South Dakota became Paris, France and London, England became Spokane, Washington.

∞

Over the past year, during their final world tour, June and Jazz have covered all their classic hits from the past five years. They have also added a few unreleased originals to their live show. The duet has crooned for hours onstage, and after each show, they have returned to the stage and improvised an encore filled with raw, real emotions, hoping to give the crowd their best show before their retirement.

Their show has become a traveling exhibition for the Winniper secret; but, only Berthine, Olivia, and Papa know how to explain their connection. Jazz, June, Lucy, Duke, Charles, and Christina have no knowledge about the process by which the Winnipers have disposed of their dead Sioux babies. Even after Duke witnessed Nancy's birth and her Sioux brother's execution, he still has not drawn any connections to himself or Jazz and June. He forgoes any deeper understandings in order to secure a more prominent role for himself as the future lord of his family.

June has told Duke that she can't explain her relationship with Jazz, but she has always known how important he is to her. He is someone who she has always been destined to meet. She said that her love for Jazz is *something pure*, and, even though she hasn't said so specifically, she has never held Duke in the same regard. She has replaced her brother and her family with a colored imposter, but Duke's silence and her busy schedule have prevented him from expressing any real anger, until now.

∞

For Papa, Jazz and June's tours have evoked complex, moral questions and offered few answers. The exchanges between Olivia and Papa have changed from a mature delight to a measured concern. The moral paradigm of their dainty white rose singing the blues with a hard brown soul has tainted every dollar the family wealth has been built upon. What is the need for privilege and prestige when they allow their sins to perform on stages around the world? They are a mockery that has torn the king and queen apart. Papa regrets his silent consent, which allowed Olivia to keep Teresa's Sioux children with Berthine. He believes a sinister Shakespearean tragedy has developed beneath his feet and he has become determined to act before the playwright ends the story with a dramatic, public sacrifice.

Can June and Jazz be any more opposite or any more the same? Both fragile and both divine, June told Duke that she and Jazz have transcended physical forms. They love through music, but the public, the press, and Papa Winniper are not rushing to progress toward harmony. American society has always been reluctant to address its intolerant ideals.

Though Papa can't publicly rebuke his granddaughter, not with millions in stock options annually at stake and public opinion on civil rights shifting with every new political leader, he has privately planned her execution without questioning his tact. His objective is as clear as it has always been: protect the Winniper family as any good son should. He remembers his father's teachings and broils in the shame while death threats have joined the well wishes for June and the Winniper family. Papa imagines his father's disappointment at his son's weakness and he has silently manufactured a death scheme to tie up all loose ends.

With all these considerations, Jazz and June's triumphant return to announce their engagement in Winniper County seems fated for disaster. God's daylight shines upon their shoulders and the children of South Dakota sing sweetly in the distance. *"Traveling minstrel…traveling minstrel…dancin' in the street!"*

The couple continues to stroll down the sidewalk, locked in their love, unaware, and unconcerned, showing no signs of worry. They only hope to end a lovely morning with the first flight to their new home where they will start a new life with a newfound freedom to express their love and raise their growing family in peace. Is that not the idea of heaven on Earth?

And love, as peaceful as it once seemed on any street in America, has become as unimportant as the next patch of owned land. Earl and the guys sneak through the last shreds of press and fans while undocking their weapons from underneath their shoulders. As they push toward the unsuspecting couple, Duke questions the worth of his inherited estate, when bloody expectations and corrupted arrogance still dominate the human heart.

The two fated musicians, who thought a life filled with love could be so sweet, only flinch when the wolves attack. Duke hears screams fill the air as the crowd scatters in chaos and his baby sister disappears within the melee. Having been sent by a master manipulator and a cold-hearted grandfather, Earl and the guys find their prey surrounded yet unprotected by paparazzi and pariahs. Within this sovereign quaint county, the perfect vision of Americana, the murderers unleash a fast flurry of violence, flogging Jazz and June's flesh without mercy or shame.

Duke walks through the ruckus to look over the carnage as it unfolds; he wishes he could run to her, but he's stuck in the circumstances while his baby sister drowns in flashes of battery and blue light bulbs. Her attackers beat her body to a pulp, and Duke sees his once, darling sister, as she was then, and as she is now. She's four-years-old, a wide-eyed sprout dreaming of the world as love; and she's twenty-five, a dying damsel covered in her own blood and tears.

Somewhere within her cracked skull, she believes that somehow, someone will save them; yet, in her tragic, tearful last breath, June finally realizes her naivety. She believed too openly in the American Dream, and now, a future filled with so much promise is gone forever. Several paparazzi still snap pictures, but some remain too long. The guys rush the remaining photogs and smash their cameras before they can escape; a few men in plain, black suits stand around the corners and across the street, whispering into their palms.

Once a loving brother, now a complicit executioner, Duke numbs himself, preventing himself from absorbing the entirety of the viciousness—the mission is to make his grandfather proud and restore their family's honor. He must complete the task with valor as any good heir should. Duke can see Jazz, broken, battered, and bloodied, still trying to gather the strength to reach her and shield her, hoping to protect his dead fiancée, but Duke recognizes the sense of helplessness, the inability to protect those he loves. Dark moments such as these leave no future options of moral absolution; the fate of his family becomes entwined within this horror, a bloody beating that shatters two lives who hoped to become one. Their murders are malicious, brutal, and unforgivable. In the final blows, battered backs break at the ends of two wooden bats, a lead pipe severs a kneecap, and two broken skulls endure a few short prods to see if they're still alive.

Jazz shakes and seizes and his twitching frame reminds Duke of a dying chicken on the Winnipers' farm—they have served this songbird rare. Earl strikes the soon-to-be-corpse through the head with the lead pipe, before scrunching his face and spitting tobacco on Jazz's blood-coated face. The once bright, blue sky becomes a lethal red, massacred bodies and dreams, ripped inside and out. The pair's previously star-filled eyes are now empty and dead. Some of the crowd still screams and gawks from afar, but no one approaches to help and there are no sirens to be heard—the true colors of Winniper County flow along this bloody sidewalk.

June, once a darling child and a beautiful blonde, is now a motionless corpse, a victim of her grandfather's vengeance. Papa Winniper warned her, much like Teresa, and she lies still in her punishment. All along, Papa has prepared his grandson to murder his baby sister with purpose, the only purpose a Winniper man should have in mind—protecting the family's empire, protecting the family's legacy, protecting the family's reputation.

Tragically, Duke does not understand the true nature of his treachery. He still doesn't know that Jazz is also his brother, and he still doesn't realize that June and Jazz fell deeply in love because of a curse that also affects him, though he has never met his twin. He has never known unconditional love and his actions have only made his family's pain worse. June told Duke that her chance meeting with Jazz was fate bringing them together, but her corpse tells a different lie. The truth is a wretched rag doll, crimson covered with every wisp of her blonde hair stained with blood, tears, and ripped flesh. Earl and the guys have mangled her face so that she is unrecognizable to her own brother; her skull and chest cave inward from the force of repeated blows. There is no possibility of life inside her body.

Earl and the guys smile demonically at one another and look over June and Jazz, plastered against the sidewalk beneath them. They are artists observing their work with culminating amusement while photographers and citizens continue to clamor around the melee, some fleeing, and some crowding, and still none make a move to stop the assailants. Shock and awe have gripped the entire scene; secretly, some have always wished for this end.

The guys take another moment to appreciate the greatness that they have achieved or the chaos that they have helped avert—either may seem correct. More cries emerge from the people gathering around the dead superstars and the reality sets in and begins to interrupt the guys' parade of laughter. The murderers deter their elephant egos because the shouts suddenly convince them to run away.

Earl grabs Duke's arm and tugs him along roughly, but Duke pauses, while staring at his sister's bloody frame. He is still lost within the morbidity, seeing the little girl who once played her guitar alone in her room.

∞

They both had fathers who abandoned them, but while Duke, as a male heir, could appease their grandfather, June could only rebel or submit. She followed her heart and now she lies in a pool of her own blood as it mixes with the blood of the only man she has ever loved. So, was her life always a trap? She never asked to become a Winniper, neither of them did, yet, their lives have come to this climax and they will never be the same.

∞

History's thinnest tears form at the corners of Duke's eyes and he re-emerges from his sudden sorrow, trying to remember Papa's convincing argument. It all made so much sense when balanced against money and power, but, looking at them now, lying still on the ground, knowing they will never marry, knowing they will never experience the joy that they dreamed of all these years, knowing they will never sing together again...Duke realizes that hell is a place filled with these mistakes.

No one deserves this end, and those who bring such misery upon others must surely face their sins in this life or the next. Earl and the guys have just beaten and killed the rarest angel to ever emerge from Winniper County and God will never forgive them. Earl continues to pull Duke's arm and Duke feels the conflict ripping his spirit in two. He stares at his baby sister's corpse, but his soul jerks away from her famous body, crumpled on the sidewalk, while more people run to the scene and more cameras join the flash frenzy. Waking from his guilty trance, Duke begins to flee and his legs rapidly patter through the street, desperate to keep up with Earl and the guys. Their hasty getaway is an all-consuming blur, but Duke's mind cannot connect to his escape and his head turns back toward June.

Duke sees her as the center of her final masterpiece. More people gather at the scene, while more and more aghast onlookers gawk at the bloodbath and some point to the killers in their escape, but none pursue. Winniper County is a town that is bought and sold upon civility. The police are nowhere in sight as a bundle of limbs rest amongst the crowd, dangling along the curb.

June and Jazz are invisibly dead; no one can see them anymore. Their lights bear no resemblance to the once brightly burning candles that lit up stages around the world. Their dreams are lost inside numb minds that will think no more and love no more. Their grandfather will rest easier, knowing that the Winniper family's secret rests with their bones. Duke has once again sealed the family legacy in cold blood. All that really matters is that he has eliminated the threat of disgrace by overseeing a deadly beating. The two stars are convenient casualties, vengeful kills for another Winniper usurper who chose honor over family, in the name of family, itself.

Earl and the guys pile back into the convertible and throw their blood-soaked weapons into the backseat just as Duke reaches the door. He stares at the deadly tools and notices bits of flesh and hair caked against the bats and lead pipe. The washing machine cylinder has considerable chunks of brain clinging to its sharp edges. Duke's eyes grow wide with disgust, but he has to sit down quickly and his ego refuses to let the guys see him flinch. He wipes his face with his hands and pushes the tools onto the floor behind the front seat. Guy 1 fires up the ignition and speeds out of the bowling alley parking lot as the celebration riot begins in earnest. The guys' voices spike with adrenaline and merciless success.

"You see how I popped that Sioux boy!"

"Damn near knocked him back to the reservation!"

"He was easy! Blondie gave a real fight, er, uh, sorry Duke…"

"What's done is done, and Duke knows that, boys!" Earl shouts happily, removing the money from his pocket and throwing it around the car. "Let's get laid! We just got made! We're going to run this whole damn town! Duke, hand the guys some beers!"

Unconsciously obedient, unable to communicate any defiance, Duke shuffles through the weapons and slowly retrieves a Burgermeister six-pack from under the seat in front of him. His movements are merely a mechanical instinct. The mute is only good for fetching, hauling, and culpability. He can't express himself, but he's big enough to use for tasks involving a heavy hand or fast capital. His last name gives him a value that most mutes cannot enjoy, and he finds fleeting comfort in his fortune while dreaming of what his life would be like if he were not a Winniper. He falsely realizes that he would have no life at all.

The guys laugh at his disability, but little do they consider and little does he reveal that his mind still ticks rapidly. He does have free will, though his complacency, especially while witnessing murders, challenges any notion of his intelligence or morality. He has done what he needed to do to survive as a Winniper man and the farther the car drifts away from the scene, the more his mind reconciles with his betrayal.

Duke hands Earl and the guys their beers before grabbing one, popping the top, and lifting the aluminum can to his lips. The guys continue to snatch the fallen cash throughout the car; Guy 1 swerves back and forth over the traffic lanes, caught between a getaway and a come up. Earl steals the beer can from Duke's hand, sharply taps, taps, taps the top, takes the first swig, and hands it back to Duke.

"I had to take the poison out, your Highness! You're a king now! You need an official taste tester!" He scrunches his mouth before opening his beer can and taking a long sip. In a curious way, he lets Duke think that his disrespect is camaraderie, but Duke wouldn't care either way. Earl is his only friend; the only person who has stayed with him when others abandoned him like June, Teresa, Kenny, Christina, and his father. Earl is the brother that he never had, and, soon, Earl will marry Christina and become Duke's brother-in-law and his second-in-command. As two Winniper men, Earl and Duke will rule the Winniper Family Holding Company and travel all over the world to places where their sins may never haunt them. They can start a new chapter for the Winniper family, a new family all together and, well, family comes first—a principle that June forgot.

∞

She chose to travel the world without Papa's approval, perform black music with a Sioux boy, and embarrass the family with their exploits. She chose Jazz and she dared to return to Winniper County, right under the nose of the man who ordered their mother's murder. Her mistakes brought about her demise. *"Just like your mother"*, as Papa said.

∞

What Duke believes is inconsequential in comparison to his grandfather's will. Duke is a mute with no voice to voice; Earl and his grandfather speak for him, and he knows that they must continue to do so if he expects to have the power he so desperately craves. That power is the mitigating compensation for his disability. Yes, the mute has earned his throne today.

He realizes that he needs his family's support if he plans to represent the Winniper name and forge any real legacy, but he still turns his head back to the rear window, beer in hand, hoping to see his sister still standing, still living through the fog of the unearthed gravel from the escaping road. The evergreen trees and manicured bushes whizz by the car as the coffee shop fades into the distance. Duke continues to stare out of the rear window until Earl quickly strikes his shoulder and grabs Duke's face in his hand. He glares at Duke until their eyes meet and then he squeezes Duke's cheeks within his grip, narrowing his eyes intently.

"You know I'm all you have now, right? Papa doesn't really care about you, Christina loves me more than you, and your grandmother and uncle are too weak. I'm doing all your talking from now on." Earl explains harshly, growling with a devilish smile and laughing as if this was always a part of his plan.

Much like Papa, Earl has always wanted to eliminate any competition for Duke's companionship. He is now the voice of the future king; for him, the reward for murder is an empire. Duke finally realizes that they have only earned hell. Earl continues to grill Duke, assuring that his friend understands and submits to the new world order.

"You need me, Duke! You need me now more than ever! You need me way more than she ever needed you! So stop lookin' out that damn window…

June…is…dead!"

An Empire Falls

SEPTEMBER 1968

Sunday	Monday	Tuesday	Wednesday	Thursday	Friday	Saturday
1	2	3	4	5	6	7
8	9	10	11	12	13	14
15	16 	17	18	19	20	21
22	23	24	25	26	27	28
29	30					

Monday, September 16, 1968
<u>Thomas Christopher Winniper, III</u>

Imagination dies here.
Confining morality in a phase,
Losing days in this rainy malaise,
Paving pathways through decaying haze,
The crowd looked on.
Dreaming who might he be,
Believing the King cares for them
As much as they care for him.
It's a sin.
Forgiving as ever to weather the pleasure,
Desiring their leader's solace
In order for them to sleep,
The crowd still looked on.
Investing a collective consciousness,
Bargaining the many for the few,
Accruing stress for his success.

Thomas Winniper III knows that his nephew, Duke, may soon burn in an execution chair or swing from the lynching tree outside the courthouse. He imagines his nephew simmering, his arms and torso tensing and his legs twitching while he roasts; and he envisions his nephew hanging, his morbid limbs entangling within the branches—stiffened and stretched in mimicry, the oak prophetically pantomimes Duke's dead corpse. Thomas III flashes back from his visions of the future; he is a fifty-five-year-old child, daydreaming in despair as he continues to walk with his parents toward the Winniper County Courthouse.

He remembers that he never knew shame until he killed his sister Teresa. Now, his family, their business team, lawyers, and associates tread toward the courthouse, surrounded by reporters and camera crews, and the shame is a comfort to him. Finally, the long arm of the law has revealed the Winniper family's secrets. At least that's how the media has billed Duke's murder trial. A Winniper heir helped assassinate his superstar sister—surely the court system will uncover his motive. Thomas III hopes *a willing witness* will slip through Papa's web and expose the Winnipers' crimes.

Thomas III believes the world may empathize with his wealthy family, understanding that Sioux-and-white twins present a certain dilemma for any family, especially an affluent one. The Winniper men have made difficult decisions under unnatural circumstances. Cradling oil money and privilege in the right hand and crushing their women and their Sioux babies in the left, the men have shown their true loyalty and concealed their true plight.

∞

"The Winniper honor is worth far more than any one of us!" Papa once yelled, upset after learning Teresa planned to leave town with Kenny and all her children. Suddenly, Papa had to confront the fact that his wife and daughter had hidden Teresa's Sioux children at Berthine's cabin. He immediately feared that Teresa would try to contact her children, or, worse, she would escape from Winniper County and live elsewhere, as if the Winniper name did not travel beyond the county lines.

As Papa stewed over these revelations, heard through the thin grapevines in Winniper County, Olivia sat in her lame corner chair, knitting, sewing, tinkering, and toddling, doing enough of whatever to seem disinterested when Papa gave Thomas III the orders to take care of Teresa. Though she had deceived her husband, she was still his wife and she had delivered a son for him—for that, Olivia earned Papa's eternal gratitude, but his sympathies for his wife have never extended to their wayward daughter. For Thomas III, his mother has always been a doe in the woods, who couldn't offer protection or assistance, even while Papa gave their son the orders to "take care" of their daughter and *"protect the family name."*

Thomas III worried for days, with razors churning deep within his stomach, knowing what he must do while he waited for the moment when Teresa would arrive at the market. Papa had Sheriff Cobb, Jr. wait near the market, too, just in case Thomas III didn't have the stomach to complete the task. Finally, when Teresa didn't come to the market soon enough, the conspirators enlisted Kenny's help to give Teresa a reason to come by the market. She had to retrieve a forgotten loaf of bread for a picnic and swim at the country club.

She had planned to leave Winniper County with her Sioux children, so taking care of her probably saved their lives. Thomas III acted as both savior and executioner, at his father's behest.

∞

He imagines that Duke felt the same dreadful responsibility when Papa told him to *"take care"* of June. The Winniper men have been too weak to resist these notions of family legacy and honor. Programmed to protect that which feels larger than life itself, they cling to a false idolatry. Thomas III has realized that man dooms himself when he only realizes his mistakes after the weight of the world crashes down upon his head. Dead men never learn.

∞

Papa always told his only son that every great man must mastermind a great plan, but instead, Thomas III planned to escape from his father's lessons as soon as he could. Traveling alone to boarding school wasn't enough. When they were young adults, Thomas III begged Teresa to explore the world with him. They found far away destinations where they could drown themselves in available inebriants, but they never found peace. When they returned to Winniper County, Teresa began trysts with bachelor after bachelor while Thomas III lived in the Winniper family's mansion, trapped in dissolution and chastised in his childhood bedroom.

Although Thomas III was his only viable male heir, Papa Winniper worried that his son may never mature into a man who could run the family's international oil business and their considerably profitable portfolio. Papa diminished his son's access to the inner workings of the Winniper oil empire and he found a sadistic joy in helping his son establish the Winniper Market.

Thomas III became a willing clown in the middle of his family's county. A prince turned to a pauper, Papa rarely invited his son to attend dinner in their home unless there was a social gathering.

∞

The two men have lived under the same roof, but they engage in dissimilar lifestyles. Their paths have only merged out of a mutual need. One needs compliance, the other needs acceptance, but both have only a scarce affection toward each other unless a problem arises. Papa Winniper has occupied his pride with his plans for more global import-export while Thomas III has lost himself within his market and the young women under his employment. He has exorcised his insecurities by enjoying the perks of being a middle-aged prince.

∞

Teresa once told Thomas III that Papa wanted them to defend the kingdom, but he never gave them the keys to the castle. Their father spent too much time wheeling-and-dealing, instead of hearing-and-understanding.

Papa's neglect left Teresa searching for their father within her marriages while Thomas III distracted himself with the market and the women therein. Always willing to spend his inheritance on a cheap skirt, he remained on the sidelines while Papa and Teresa argued over her scantily clad outfits. Beginning in her teenage years, she dressed like a posh, New York socialite, unabashed about her attraction to wayward men. Given the challenge she presented for their father, Thomas III remained an unnoticeable, second fiddle to his reckless, older sister.

Initially, Papa indulged Teresa's rebelliousness because he felt she was a product of her fiery nature. He secretly enjoyed her willpower to demand her autonomy at any cost; yes, willpower is an excusable offense, a masculine moniker, and a respectable trait for a Winniper man, but not for a Winniper woman, nor any woman from a good, moral upbringing. Within these sentiments, imagine Papa encouraging his only son to be more like his sister. He chastised his only male heir for being less masculine than a girl: Thomas III never recovered his self-confidence and his lust for vulnerable, female conquests derived largely from these early conflicts.

∞

Though Thomas III never met his grandfather, most people in town agree that Papa became the embodiment of everything the Winniper County founder believed a man should be. Papa adored his father and he tried to pass along the old man's tutelage to Thomas III. Most people in town also agree that neither Duke nor Thomas III will ever eclipse Papa and Thomas, Sr. Winniper County's fond admiration for the Winniper men has ended with the third and fourth male heirs. Duke and Thomas III are the weak links in the Winniper lineage.

∞

According to Papa Winniper, he realized that Thomas III could never lead the corporation when Thomas III was only a toddler. His doe-eyed son followed his older sister like a lost pup, so much so that Papa never envisioned his son as a leader. Thomas III wouldn't be able to concoct an international marketing plan; he could barely organize the deliveries to the Winniper Market without a costly mishap. Papa surrounded Thomas III with accountants, lawyers, and a few old family side hands like Mr. Potter, who all helped Thomas III keep the fresh produce market as a symbol of the family's charity and love for the community. The Winniper Market was a quaint consolation prize between a father and son; Thomas III was simply incapable of becoming a man who could transcend his deficiencies. He couldn't do anything that would bring him closer to his father; he also soon realized that he would never control the Winniper family's conglomerate.

Floating mellifluously within the Winniper Family Estate and stretching his imagination only far enough to deceive his parents, Thomas III transformed into a pet within a cage. He became a main attraction in a zoo built by his grandfather's cruelty and his father's ambition. There's so much power in a name that the *Winnipers* required murder to protect the public's perception of their value and valor—the hypocrisy has proven fatal. Papa believes as his father believed; their actions defend the family's principles, maybe, but still, the Winniper men have cared more for the family than the people in it. They have sacrificed the few for the many and shed no tears when the ids lost sight of their egos.

Thomas III awoke this morning, anxious after barely sleeping the night before. He mostly tossed and turned, seeing Teresa in his nightmares and fretting over Duke's trial. The night before, Papa instructed Thomas III to bring the family's lucky revolver to the courthouse, "just in case". The old man had become increasingly suspicious, fearing any potential threat to his family's legacy.

Since receiving the Colt 1851 revolver, Thomas III has only fired the weapon once; he had been drinking Bourbon in the south end of the family's estate. Nervously loading six bullets into the chamber, he didn't expect the old revolver to fire, but it did. Last night, Papa ordered Clyde to bring a jacket holster to Thomas III during a mandatory family dinner, an unavoidable commiseration before Duke's trial. When Papa suggested that Thomas III bring the revolver to the trial, Thomas III tried to protest; he explained to his father that he may be searched, but Papa heard none of his son's objections. After all this time, Papa still believes that his son will never mature into the correct version of a Winniper man.

After waking this morning, Thomas III groaned at the sight of his closet, knowing the steel revolver slept inside. He dreaded the descent down the mansion's front steps. Every movement brought him closer to the trembling thought of wading through the courthouse with the press hounds, the police officers, and the public surrounding the family.

∞

At least, his tailored, black cashmere Stein-Bloch jacket conceals the holstered revolver. The understated jacket accents the family's mournful visage while they ascend the courthouse steps. The clamoring media salivates over the scandal—the young Winniper rose, June Bethune, plucked from the earth too soon by the callous hands of her jealous brother and his greedy henchmen. Once considered a recluse like her mother, Teresa, June has become a postmortem hometown hero. Beloved and revered, the public frenzy surrounding her murder and the trials of her accused have hid the true horror behind a family secret that still haunts the Winnipers. Only Papa, Olivia, Thomas III, and Duke know about the Winnipers' two-toned-twins, but Duke cannot speak in his defense, he has no one that he can trust, and Thomas III fears that his father has plans to eliminate all loose ends.

Walking through the cameras, microphones, and questions with his mother and father on his left and right, respectively, Thomas III wonders if a similar trial awaits him one day. He's curious, but not worried. The Winniper name buys judges, juries, politicians, and even freedom. Still clinging to a prayer that Papa Winniper has pulled the appropriate strings, Thomas III hopes Duke's trial will end before lunchtime. Papa has organized a number of inexplicable dismissals and hung juries.

Power pays for itself, especially when concentrated within a small town and exerted forcefully upon the proper pressure points. Weakening social and moral resolve, true power achieves the necessary acquiescence, from enemies and associates alike, in order to gain more influence and enforce more compliance. This is a never-ending cycle; power feeds itself and never tires of the process. It is only the humans—the rats on the wheel, the hands turning the dials, the perpetuators of power—who are weak. Thomas III remembers Papa Winniper's early attempts to groom him for the grind of his oil inheritance.

∞

After hours of childhood preparation, Papa bounced his son from his knee and dropped him into Eton College, one of the finest boarding schools in the United Kingdom, if not the world. At age thirteen, Thomas III experienced his first escape from his father's ever-present dominance. Thomas III would often write to Teresa, telling her about his day trips through the East London countryside and the Southend Pier. On weekends, he'd take a ferry to France or Germany; in fall 1930, he even flew to Rome as the co-pilot in a Fiat Cr.1 fighter plane with an Italian classmate, who had enlisted in Italy's Royal Air Force.

Teresa implored Thomas III to describe all his companions and their trips in great detail, hoping to aid her imagination. Papa Winniper would not allow his only daughter to travel during her childhood; he would often remark that a woman's only vacation should be from the kitchen to the bedroom. Thomas III believes these words somehow ingrained in Teresa's mind, not as truth, but as flawed scruples within a purposefully placed paradigm. She vowed to smash, maim, and eviscerate her father's ideals and she found the most effective weapon in the shake of her hips.

Over the years, Teresa treated luxury and men like items on a menu and she learned how to enjoy whatever her father served. Sadly, self-destruction was often her dessert of choice. While contemplating their mutual need for masochism, Thomas III wondered if each Winniper has a switch that activates the devil inside. Do all humans have an anti-self within the spirit that wants the whole to fail, fall short of expectations, and wallow in self-pity?

∞

While looking at June's battered body, plastered in the newspaper, and comparing magazine images with crime scene photos of bloody pearls, Thomas III could think of only one word: *shame.* Despite Papa's best intentions to remain discreet, his hasty redemption has created an unavoidable fiasco. The entire Winniper family now endures immense shame and scrutiny while walking through the same international media that made June and Jazz famous. The monster that transformed their secret into a worldwide commercial commodity now surrounds them, suffocating the family's business stronghold while prying into their private lives. They are no longer protected within the quiet world of Winniper County.

Most of their skeletons remain burned and buried inside the barn. The others remain hidden within the mansion's many closets, but their victims' bones rattle around the estate. The ghosts feel the tension and the warmth from the light of investigation. The more questions asked, the more cameras flashed, the harder it becomes for the family to conceal the truth. In fact, the need for truthful absolution has slowly begun to build within a forgotten heir's soul. Thomas III knows enough to expose the family's murderous past, but he would also expose himself and submit his loved ones, his daughter, and their future to the mercy of the courts and public opinion. Of course, the business would not survive. Their oil refinery and their land would probably be confiscated for their crimes, but even beyond those damages, the family would still have very little to salvage. For too long, they have been a family in name only. Thomas III can't imagine how the Winnipers would function as just a family without mergers, accolades, and legacies to protect.

As Thomas III, his parents, and their liaisons bowl through the crowd, the press snaps photos with the same cameras that captured June's dead body while ignoring any signs of life from Jazz. Thomas III raises his elbows and pushes through the masses, helping to clear a path for his mother and father. Papa Winniper believes the family was lucky that Jazz survived the massacre—one murder is cheaper to cover-up than two.

∞

In the days, weeks, and months after the attack, Papa Winniper paid every notable doctor and specialist in the country to visit Jazz in the hospital. The old conspirator squeezed out every ounce of credentialed expertise within the region in order to ensure the survival of the famous Sioux songwriter. Papa spared no expense, hoping to prove his compassion to the public in the wake of allegations that his own grandson had been involved in June's murder. The announcement of first-degree murder charges against Duke and three other males caused an international outpouring of sympathy and outrage; and when the press reports, newsreels, lawn interviews, and home invasions continued to increase in frequency, Papa Winniper begged, pleaded, and prayed to God that Jazz would live, just long enough to ease the news coverage.

The Winniper patriarch had created a media monster that even he could not control with all the power of his wealth. He began to grow distressed with all the attention aimed at his family; he feared that the Winnipers' secrets would all come to light if the international press continued to sniff around their exclusive county, digging into every detail of the Winniper family's history. He had a wayward daughter who died unexpectedly in a mysterious car crash, and, most recently, his famously insolent granddaughter died after being attacked in broad daylight. Despite his approval of the final results, Papa just wished the scandals, the press, and the aggravation would all disappear so that he could resume focusing on his businesses and accumulating an astronomical amount of wealth.

The earlier Winniper murders were much easier to conceal: babies burned and buried inside the barn. The unthinkable horror, shielded by the family's silence and secrecy, became an easy oversight for the public eye. No one in Winniper County could imagine that the founding family had chosen such a heartless solution to their perceived problem. Even Teresa's death caused only a mild fuss; she had fallen asleep and drove off the road. Doctor Morten, Jr. performed a high-priced autopsy, a foregone farce, and Papa Winniper organized a quick cremation and a fast funeral. He had an empty casket lowered into the ground; yet, Teresa and the evidence of her murder had already vanished from the world, at least, in the physical sense.

∞

Thomas III has never mentioned the apparitions to his father, but, for years, Teresa's ghost has appeared before his eyes, standing in her blue sundress as if she were still in the market on the day she died, laughing over bread loaves. During his waking moments, she haunts his morning; during the nights, she disturbs his sleep. Her presence keeps them both trapped within the toilings of this life. Her spirit saddens her brother; she constantly forces him to experience her sorrow, and they are both unable to change the events which led him to murder her. Thomas III feels that Teresa blames him for perpetuating the circumstances which led Duke to murder June. Her children have become sacrificial lambs to ensure the Winniper blessings, but he feels the torment of a dead mother watching her children join her too soon. He hasn't seen June, but he wonders when she will visit.

∞

Thomas III begged his father to order some minions take care of June; he hoped to save his nephew from the sins historically bestowed upon a Winniper male, but Thomas III knew all along that salvation never mattered to Papa.

∞

The family name has always meant everything to the Winniper men. The inherited legacy is a measurable value that Thomas, Sr. taught Papa; Thomas III's inefficient ambitions proved that he was unfit to fill his inherited shoes. Much like Duke, he has become a useful pawn for the family, a willing protector without the responsibilities of the throne. He hates himself for killing to protect his birthright. It is as if Thomas III's weakness has emboldened his father's treachery and forced Papa to act more heinously towards the Winniper women. Papa feels the burden of holding the Winniper throne longer than expected and he validates Teresa and June's murders by highlighting the lack of an alternative path that equally protects the Winniper family's lineage. Papa is still their leader, for better or worse.

∞

Long ago, the Winnipers received a blessing and a curse filled with wealth and heartache. Still, none of them—fathers, mothers, daughters, or sons—understands the mysterious two-toned twins: one Sioux, one white, one boy, one girl. Papa Winniper only knows that he was the first to have a Sioux sister, whom his father promptly killed. When he became a father, he complied with the orders that Thomas, Sr. had given him, defined clearly for every Winniper male that followed. Bloodshed would be part of their birthright: a Winniper heir must murder when necessary.

A bulldozer with an inherited plan, Papa Winniper steamrolled over anything determined to jeopardize the family's wealth and legacy—*the definition of a Winniper man's duty,* Papa Winniper would often tell Thomas III. Yet, even after pushing Teresa's car into a tree, Thomas III could never accept his duty and he's still unsure if he ever can become a Winniper heir, regardless of his blood. As a teenager, he completely ignored Papa's lessons after years of abuse. By adulthood, Thomas III lost all interest in trying to be a part of the Winniper male hierarchy. He committed the murder to remain within his father's golden halo, dazed in the haze of their wealth. Even at the cost of his sister, Thomas III knew that he never wanted to stray from his father's good graces.

∞

Now, jaded from luxury and convenience, Thomas III embraces his only true motivations: the financial benefits, the co-operative tax funds, and the unessential essentials that separate the *haves* from the *have more than they ever could want.* The price for instant satisfaction is self-respect, and Thomas III gladly pays the bill.

Duke and his lawyers huddle outside the courthouse; several well-armed officers surround the youngest Winniper male, keeping an angry mob away from striking range. Tilly Bethune stands alone near the doorway, watching the procession while still grieving for her granddaughter. She loved from afar, but refused to interfere, remembering how Papa had handled Kenny and knowing Papa's temperament towards women. Tilly wears a black satin dress and black velvet gloves; she wishes she could blink and open her eyes to the end of the trial.

As the Winniper family joins Duke, his lawyers, and the officers assigned to protect the accused, Tilly falls amongst the ranks and the group marches inside the courthouse. Thomas III feels his feet sinking into the linoleum floor of the main hallway and he steps away from his parents so that he can walk next to his silent nephew. The darkness of coming doom descends upon his spirit; a few fleeting breaths leak from his lips and he learns in that moment what fear truly is—*death is near and mortals can never escape.* Once they reach the courtroom's oak doors, Thomas III, Olivia, and Papa Winniper gather around Duke, shielding his shackled wrists and ankles from the public eye while his lawyers and the officers clamor to keep the cameramen at bay.

"I can't believe they've got him in chains, Thomas!" Olivia whimpers, leaning into her husband and crying on Papa's shoulder. Thomas III watches his mother's face flood with meaningless anguish. These tears know their way down her face, consistently traveling paths laid by tragic opportunities that have tracked grief down her cheeks for years. The chance to change their trajectory is long gone. Olivia dabs her eyes lightly with a cream handkerchief, staring at Duke's wrists with shame and pity. Thomas III walks beside one of the officers while tugging his jacket snugly around his waist to ensure that the revolver stays concealed. He then glances between his mother's eyes and his nephew's handcuffs.

"Are the cuffs necessary, officer?" Thomas III asks stoically, his grim voice rolling through the nuanced procedure, but, the officer remains motionless without acknowledging his presence. Papa moves away from his wife, flanked by two business associates, and he distinguishes himself from his son by nudging the officer's shoulder.

"Now I know I'm getting old, and I've started to forget a few things, but I still have quite a bit of pull in this here town, son," Papa begins, speaking to the officer and not to his actual son. "Can you at least remove the handcuffs *before* we enter the courtroom? We don't want to prejudice the jury."

Papa pleads affectionately, allowing his low South Dakota drawl to course through his clotted throat. Thomas III learned to mimic his father well enough, but his voice never dove to Papa's timbre. Thomas III hasn't smoked enough cigars or drank enough brandy. Papa leans forward toward the county officer with a wink.

"You know, I always take care of anyone who takes care of my family."

"Sir, our orders from the sheriff are to keep Mr. Winniper in shackles for *'his protection'*." The officer whimpers like Olivia; both are filled with the same pitiful platitude. "Sir, I'm sorry. I wish I could. I don't have no qualms with your family."

He desperately wants to appease Papa, knowing how one of the most powerful business men in America rewards a favor, yet, the rules of the ordained hierarchy stitched into his uniform remain intertwined in his consciousness, sown even deeper within his moral fabric than his ambitions for monetary salvation.

"Oh yes, the orders, I remember now…I'm getting old, son. You don't need to apologize; I know you're only following orders. Young men should always follow orders, it builds character." Papa Winniper gestures to the rest of the officers before removing a fistful of Franklins from his jacket pocket. "Now, I want you boys to take good care of my grandson with all these people around. Don't forget he's a Winniper, okay? We founded this county."

"Yes, sir!" The officers reply amiably as Papa Winniper separates the money in his pale, wrinkly hands and slides several bills into each officer's front jacket pocket. They are bred dogs being given a reward for their obedience.

"Now, you boys buy something nice for your wives and girlfriends. Women love shiny things!" Papa Winniper pats one of the officers on his shoulder, smiling to the others and hiding a shaft within his tip. His advice never comes without recompense. A man with such power would never ask the help for permission to unlock his grandson; Papa Winniper commands *their superiors*. The sheriff, the medical examiner, and the D.A. have orders to deliver magnificent performances in order to gain their apportioned parcels of his power. Ninety-two-year-old Sheriff Cobb, Jr., having taken part in the Sioux massacre years ago as a teenage boy, has followed the Winniper family's orders throughout all of his life. He now administers the prerequisite course study in Winniper County, examining the depths of the residents' social submission.

Thomas III remembers the conversation when Sheriff Cobb, Jr. ate dinner at the Winniper's mansion last week. Surely Papa could have dictated whatever nuance or permission he desired for today's legal showcase, but still, Papa *chose* to have Duke displayed outside the courthouse in handcuffs and leg shackles. He *chose* to allow the press to stalk the courthouse steps and snap pictures throughout the family's arrival. He *chose* to have the family ascend the steps before meeting Duke and his lawyers and entering the courthouse together, as one. Papa still sees himself as the ringleader of a corporate circus worth all the sorrow and stocks in the world.

∞

The grieving Winnipers marched into the courthouse amidst the media flurry of the trial's first day, seemingly broken after losing one child, hoping to save another.

∞

How could anyone feel anything but pity for the poor Winnipers? True, they are wealthy beyond their billions, but they look poor in their memorial visage, while still lacking in mere morality. Duke remains quiet and emotionless, as usual, standing still, sullenly stuck in his status, not knowing who to trust. The family, more specifically his grandfather, put him in this perilous position—prods and promises from a patriarch to his pseudo-heir. Papa has the exclusive power to free his grandson from a fate that their family's history has engineered. Long ago, Thomas, Sr. made a decision to massacre the Ghost Dance Sioux and he chose a course of action that his heirs now follow.

Another circumstance that Thomas III and Duke share is that they are both beholden to the social constructs of their genes—the importance of the male heir. Thomas III's personal suffering from the expectations associated with being a male heir has resulted in a lifelong fear of conception and, rather unexpectedly, he has conceived only one child—his daughter, Nancy.

Born in 1962, Nancy is now six years old. She is her father's pride and joy and heaven and earth and moon and sun and all those cheesy monikers that apply to daddy's baby girl. For Thomas III, there is nothing like being a father, and he is happiest when he is with his daughter; but, he also refuses to conceive another child because he fears what will happen if he serves another Winniper male heir to Papa. Thomas III dreads the moment when Nancy falls in love or lust and bears children who are cursed with the Winnipers' blood.

Thomas III secretly believes it is the Winniper men who perpetuate *the curse*, producing a Sioux child and white child as punishment for past sins. The men could act differently, behave more compassionately toward their family, but they don't because they're weaker than the society they claim to control. Thomas III plans to absolve himself by raising his daughter to break the mold or, at least, challenge the family's patriarchy like Teresa. Maybe then, his sister's ghost will take pity upon him after seeing his redemption in Nancy's salvation. When Nancy saves herself and her children from Papa's orders, she will earn a victory that has eluded every other woman in their family—a failed feat that sealed Teresa's fate.

Every day, Thomas III feels the weight of protecting Nancy from his father. He teaches his daughter the hardest lessons without a true companion or a wife of his own. Her mother, a cashier, pseudo-prostitute, and extortionist, passed during childbirth, or maybe shortly thereafter. To date, Nancy's mother and Ruby Winniper are the only Winniper women to die during childbirth, but that body count is equal to the number of Winniper women who have died at the hands of Winniper men.

∞

During their final moments, Teresa and June became victims of a crime far worse than murder-homicide: the betrayal infected their souls. They finally understood their worth as life seeped from their senses, their spirits screaming in anguish, desperation, and confusion.

Papa Winniper accepted his deeds as displays of a powerful man's prerequisite talents, but Thomas III drowned within the guilt of his actions.

∞

Now that he faces the prospect of raising his daughter to become a Winniper woman, he fears the consequences of his sins. How can he raise Nancy right when he has committed such horrible wrongs? Thomas III tries not to worry as the family finally walks through the oak doorway and enters the courtroom.

∞

During the days leading up to Duke's trial date, Thomas III pondered the possibility of facing his crimes in court and he began to fear a retributive trial within the invisible future where he would one day confess his most heinous sins—*the hit-and-run murder of his sister, burning his newborn son, and his silence while Papa planned June's murder.*

∞

His conscience pleads for solace, begging him to drop the boulder of lies that weighs down his mind. His soul yearns for the moment when he will finally tell the truth...to his family, his town, and himself. He doesn't know whose murder haunts him the most—his whimpering newborn, June, or Teresa.

Sadly, the same prideful malice that approved the murders now surrounds his daughter as she grows up in the Winniper family's mansion. Papa already treats Nancy like a future problem; he often scoffs at her, squinting and grimacing because he knows she poses another threat to the family's legacy. Thomas III hopes that Nancy has Teresa and June's fearlessness, but he quietly dreams of escaping Winniper County and finding a place where he and Nancy can be free from both the expectations of their wealth and the curse of their bloodline. He finally understands why Teresa wanted to leave so desperately; he remembers his sister's anguish that day in the market, knowing all along that he had orders to fulfill.

Still, the conflict has always rested equally between his hypocrisy and his father's duplicity. Every day, he regrets following Papa's orders, remaining ineffectual during June's murder, burning his newborn, and running Teresa off the road. Thomas III knows that if Nancy ever disgraces the Winniper name, forsaking lessons learned from the stewards of high society, then Papa will remove her from this world just as quickly as he removed June and Teresa. The consequence of success is that it must be maintained, with any and all necessary means, or else, success becomes failure without pretext—'tis tragic and true. No one cares about a loser's back-story.

Struggling to consider any reality in which the truth could place him in the hands of a judge and jury, Thomas III begrudgingly quiets the jittery nerves in his body, silences any free will, and submits in order to ensure his survival—the necessity of self-preservation. Tilly and the Winniper family hunker together as they wade through the court gallery, passing anxious members of the press, inquisitive onlookers, and colloquial constituents. The entire community is loyal to the Winniper oil empire that has made the town a wealthy oasis within the American Midwest.

Surrounded by financial thugs, accountants, lawyers, and investigators, the respective subordinates receive orders that Papa whispers to Freidrich Potter, the family's business manager. Freidrich frequently leans in to hear Papa's commands and then turns his head to instruct the proper minion. The family's corporate operatives spread money across the world and buy influence in international courtrooms, creating a home-field advantage wherever their money plays.

The Winnipers reach the front row and file into position, sitting strategically close to the defense table so that Papa is nearest the aisle and the defense counsel. Olivia sits to his left, then Thomas III, and Tilly, all positioned stoically statuesque, the pitiful image of family sorrow. Thomas III adjusts his upper torso to accommodate for the long-necked revolver poking into his left side. Glancing around, no one is the wiser and he smiles to himself, believing that as long as he remains still, no one will know that he has a concealed weapon. He reminds himself that he only has to use the revolver in order to protect his family in the worst case scenarios.

Freidrich and Papa's business leeches crowd the old man's shoulders, even pushing nonentities from their second row seats near the king's ears. Tilly Bethune turns and scours over the suits and screw faces before turning back and nudging Thomas III with her right elbow. She knows the front row well; she has become very familiar with the courtroom in these past months.

∞

She attended Earl's trial diligently, and wept openly; another Bethune male lost his soul for Winniper gold.

∞

Tilly dabs her eyes with a crimson handkerchief in her left hand and places her right hand gently on Thomas III's shoulder. She leans her head softly against his suit jacket so that her right cheek rests on the inline cushion. The weight of her worries transfers into his body; he can feel her nervous vibrations, but sadly, he cannot calm her. He has his own neurotic rhythm causing chaos in his harmony. There is no comfort between them.

Tilly lifts her head and looks up to him knowingly before leaning away and searching quickly for more prying eyes. The courtroom buzzes with anticipation while wondering when the judicial illusion will commence. Privileged members of the press clamor in the back row with pens noting the family's every movement. Several radio reporters dictate the action and describe the mood while the officers lead Duke and his lawyers through the galley. The stenographer fiddles with her typewriter as she awaits the bailiff's call and the jurors remain seated in two rows of six. They are the least important people in the room, the carefully propositioned peons.

"All rise! In the presence of the flag of our country, the emblem of our constitution, and remembering the principles for which they stand, the Winniper County Superior Court is now in session! The Honorable Judge Donald K. Rupert is presiding." The County's newly-hired black bailiff bellows over the courtroom while facing a large American flag in the opposite corner. The eager onlookers stand at attention as the entire courtroom stares at the flag. Papa Winniper handpicked the bailiff from a shallow pool of two non-white officers (one black, one Sioux, both males) in the Winniper County police force—all to show the national and international press that Winniper County is, in fact, diverse.

Thomas III places his arm under his mother's wrist so that she can balance herself as she rises to her feet. Olivia's right hand reaches for Papa, but he moves his arm away. The old man hisses from the corner of his mouth; he stands alone and quietly leaves those he loves without his help—the family man's public persona is a façade.

Judge Donald K. Rupert enters the courtroom slowly. He is an elderly, wrinkled curmudgeon with white wisps of hair still clinging for life to his scalp. Holding a brown paper bag in his left hand and clutching a worn black briefcase under his right arm, he tangles his belongings within the sleeves of his cloak. He tilts his head forward to adjust his glasses and stumbles into his raised, tan leather seat. The courtroom pauses while the judge collects himself and stares over their heads, a judiciously keen father blessing his children. There is no love like this moment; the world anticipates a reckoning that only exists in the reflection of a broken mirror—the shattered illusion reveals untouched joy and overindulged misery.

"You may be seated," Judge Rupert mumbles into his bench with a somber tone; he understands the trouble that he has inherited. A favor for Papa carries benevolent benefits and moral-shifting responsibilities. "Bailiff, please read the case file."

The members of the court sit silently within their rows; the nuances and intangibles of the proceedings must be apparent to them: the slain damsel, the assaulted musical icons, and one of the most powerful families in America—the Winnipers are the industrial age's preeminent monarchy.

Truly, the spectacle will pay for itself; the press alone will spawn an infinite collection of books, movies, and albums to sell the trial's story. For generations, eyes and ears will savor every image seen and every word spoken during the trial—the *final* trial for the murderers of June Bethune.

"Case 64206, the People of Winniper County vs. Duke Townsend Winniper!" The bailiff roars over the courtroom. Thomas III turns his head toward Papa and his father flashes a fearful look to display a brief moment of vulnerability. Papa senses the undetermined reality within which all the family secrets may be revealed, yet, his money may still be enough to keep those bloody skeletons hidden.

Thomas III distinctly remembers that Judge Rupert arrived late to a recent closed-door meeting at the estate. Also in attendance: the county sheriff, Cornell Cobb, Jr., the county attorney, Mr. John Allen, and the county medical examiner, Doc Morten, Jr. In fact, many of the most important men in South Dakota have recently paid their respects to the family at the forefront of the state's bustling oil industry. They have journeyed to Winniper County to kiss the hand of the legendary man who accomplished the professional exploits that have given South Dakota its largest economic surplus of any state in American history.

∞

Any motions to remove the trial from Winniper County were weightless when balanced against Papa's wishes and the Winniper family's wealth.

∞

Having the Winniper name attached to any crime in their county may seem disastrous to an outsider, but these matters only require swift, calculated justice to clean the bone, sever the joint, and eliminate any lasting connections which could lead to the truth within the family's cursed marrow. Sacrificial lies can even break the bond between father and son, or grandfather and grandson, just to ensure the survival of the Winniper Family Holding Company. Every murder has fortified their familiar American myth: all is white in the world, Christopher Columbus discovered America, and anything dark is God's mistake.

"Members of the jury, you've received your instructions at length during the selection process. I trust you and everyone here will behave accordingly." Judge Rupert moseys through his words out of sheer formality, yet his stubborn mule delivery makes his instructions feel like a chastisement. He points his gavel at the jury box before swinging the large mallet to his right and holding it toward the courtroom audience.

"Members of the media, family, friends, and the public at large, allow me to bestow the kindest advice that I will give you during the duration of this trial: *don't try my patience.* One peep and you will be escorted out of my courtroom and held for a night in the county jail, no questions asked! I've been told Sheriff Cornell Cobb, Jr. is waiting near the cells, hoping that I send him a few of the reporters that stood around and watched and took photographs during the uh...*the incident.*" The judge's slow, labored soliloquy exhausts the enthusiasm from the courtroom and the anticipation diminishes under his tender, elderly tone. The courtroom hinges upon every unhurried idiom of his inflection; interspersed between his bumbling, his bulbous cheeks inflate so that he looks like a spoiled chipmunk. Thomas III begins to question time itself, a life sentence in a South Dakota prison seems like a fairytale when compared to enduring Judge Rupert's molasses-like speech.

"The jury has a grave task here, to assign innocence or guilt to the charges of first degree murder and attempted murder. I will not have any member of the public interfering with their ability to do so. Counselors, the accused has entered pleas of not guilty to the charge of first degree murder and not guilty to the charge of attempted murder. At this time, the court will hear opening statements, beginning with the prosecution. Mister Allen, if you please."

Once the judge's diatribe ends, the common metronome resumes a livelier pace, building back to the awaited moment, yet the judge's puffed cheeks still bother Thomas III. That stuffed chipmunk sits on his high throne, speaking of fairness and the public good, knowing who lines his pockets and fills his cheeks with all the honor, pride, and attention he can handle.

Such a small nuance as a facial feature or a force of habit can reveal so much about the personality behind it. As the county attorney, John Allen, rises from his seat and walks toward the middle of the courtroom. He keeps his head bowed deep in thought, his fingers tensing while he squeezes his palms together.

"There is, uh, but one question that needs to be answered here today...and that question is... *'Who killed June Bethune?'*" Mr. Allen's thick South Dakota twang collapses every word under a dense slang. The courtroom becomes a good ol' boy establishment, and the jury prepares for a helping of Mama Allen's grits and scrambled eggs. "Now, many of you knew my Mama, and I declare if she were here, God rest her soul, she would weep and wail in shock...anger...and sadness for the loss of Winniper County's dearest and most famous daughter—the talented, sweet, and innocent June Bethune."

Several Amens resound throughout the courtroom.

"Like many of us, Mama loved June and the entire Winniper family. We are all familiar with the Winniper family's contribution to our great county and state. Their generosity has built schools, businesses, and even this very town. We feel for the family as much as we feel for June, herself. Despite her, uh, *promiscuous ways* during her later years, June Bethune was a beloved child of Winniper County who most of us remember as a little girl, playing in the pool at the country club. She went on to accomplish more in her short life than some accomplish with twice as much time. She was special. She did not deserve to die. Though she was not all good and she was not an angel, the good that she did possess, came from being raised in our little town."

John Allen steps closer to the jurors and peers over each face, emotionally communicating his genuine concern while strategizing how to manipulate each juror's life history. The county attorney has enjoyed tremendous success in Winniper County, mainly due to *his* family name.

∞

Mr. Allen's father, Robert, gained national recognition after becoming Papa's legal guardian after Thomas, Sr. passed in 1905. Even in its infancy, Papa's reign took on a tumultuous tone; Robert Allen was the guard dog who could not keep the young heir on a leash for long.

At the time, managing the fifteen-year-old Winniper king's legal tiffs gave the Allen family access to the crème-de-la-crème of Winniper County's financial frosting. All the elite members of the community employed Robert Allen's firm, in order to get close to the young king. While growing up within this delicious destiny, John Allen sought to prove that he could continue his father's legacy and service. Like Doc, Jr. and Cornell, Jr., Johnnie boy always believed that he would be more valuable to the Winniper family than his father—another prince desperate to stake his claim. He wanted to surpass the other Winniper County leeches and stand above the townspeople. After law school, he even planned to hover amongst the elite clients of a private practice, but power was always his aim. Eventually, the county attorney channeled his ambition into his work as a vaunted and valiant public prosecutor with eyes on becoming a Winniper-approved politician.

∞

Now, as a third-term, incumbent, County Attorney John Allen is the people's champion for all the aesthetic and aristocratic reasons. His privileged name and doe-eyed face have made him electable enough to become the county attorney, and now, he has greater ambitions. He sees himself as mayor, possibly even governor, but, that precise political end consumes John Allen's ambition and jeopardizes any semblance of a noble nature. Mr. Allen knows that Papa would never allow his grandson's executioner to become a political figure in South Dakota. Forget any presidential plans, too; the kingmaker holds immense sway throughout the entire lower 48. The old oil desperado's dominance is a known fact, accepted and congratulated by the each citizen of Winniper County, especially the taxpayers in the jury box.

The courtroom watches John Allen as he observes his handpicked jury, each man selected under Papa's supervision.

∞

Thomas III attended several nightly meetings between the prosecution and the defense, many without the judge present. Papa made sure the get-togethers produced a multicultural, all-male jury.

The jurors are all Christian pragmatists who care little for the artistic or the agnostic. Seven white labor workers from the oil refinery, two black business-coons imported from Atlanta, and one brown field hand from the Winnipers' estate—they sit in their appropriate stereotypes, preparing for a public submission. The prosecution and defense secretly agreed that they couldn't find twelve citizens who did not work for or gain profit from the Winniper family's businesses and holdings, so they didn't even try to hide any notion of conflict. The whole town expects the twelve gentiles to filter the details of a colored boy's dead mistress through considerations for the oil wealth at stake—enough said to perform with a puppet's precision and fulfill the master's wishes.

Chosen for the purpose of their purposelessness, the jurors lean awkwardly in their seats, shifting side-to-side or hunching their shoulders forward. Each man, one after another, places his hand nervously to a chin or cheek. They are all caricatures of modern, patient brutes, willing to listen though they have already concluded their ruling.

Much like the jury, courtroom, and town, the outside world also knows the fix is in. The box score is irrelevant in Winniper County. Capitalism builds islands within America that can't be touched by the media or the federal government; and the people within a jurisdiction of power submit to the kingdom of whichever corporation provides their livelihood. The only inevitability in this public charade is the verdict. Duke Winniper's release is guaranteed because the Winniper family's interests are teetering in the balance.

Freidrich projected that the family's portfolio will take at least a .002% hit every day the trial lingers on, giving the media surefire headlines. The conversation about a speedy trial included another easy consensus between the prosecution, the defense, and Papa; only Mr. Allen conceded that he needed time to deliver a good enough effort to convince the voters. The sullen men sitting in the jury box remain unconcerned with the amount of sincerity in John Allen's tone. The county attorney is beyond reproach, especially within the climate of the town's hierarchy. How could these men judge him? They still listen without listening, but rather, they wonder how far the county attorney will push these high-profile proceedings in order to save his credibility and ensure his defeat?

"So I ask again, '*Who killed June Bethune?*' The Good State of South Dakota has already convicted and sentenced three men for the crime, but...*someone else*...killed June Bethune. *Someone else* watched while his friends beat her with weapons. *Someone else* stood by while they stomped her head into the sidewalk and spit on her dead body. *Someone else* planned this crime with his friends and committed it inside our dear county, in broad daylight, no less, with cameras flashing on the street. We, as a community, have suffered a terrible loss, and we have endured sadness and shame from this tragedy.

"June's murder was a brazen act of violence for which the public has demanded and received *some* justice for the victim and her family. But we cannot stop until all the perpetrators are brought to justice, even if the truth brings more pain to the family. As God is my witness, if there were 100 men involved in June's murder, I would prosecute every single one of them and ask the judge for 100 death sentences!" John Allen raises his index finger to the sky to further project his sincerity, while continually disregarding Jazz as a victim. Having already prosecuted three murder trials, Mr. Allen has decided that neither the jury nor the courtroom cares about Jazz outside of his testimony. He is one of the unmentionables from Winniper County's history, yet, his time to speak will come. The county attorney continues his opening statements with a renewed gusto; he turns sharply and points his index finger toward Duke and his lawyers.

"I had the duty to prosecute Mr. Winniper's friends, and the three death sentences speak for themselves. Duke Winniper, Earl Bethune, and *their two cronies* wanted to impress their elders. They thought, in some sick, twisted way, that they were saving June from a life of living with a colored...but they stole her life and her future. They murdered an honored and celebrated daughter of our dear town. June was a modern princess, a descendant from the closest family that we have to royalty here in the great United States of America. Her murder must be treated like an assassination, a crime against the people. There's no excuse for the violence June experienced...and for what—pride, honor, and jealousy? *It's all so senseless.*"

Mr. Allen takes a breath to look up to the ceiling and ask God, "*why?*" Hearing nothing, he lowers his head, says a solemn prayer, and then raises his eyes to the jury.

"Gentlemen, the defense will spin stories from any fairytale that's convenient. They'll try to use misdirection to convince you that the facts are not facts and that there is *reasonable doubt,* but remember the one question that we need to answer today. We've answered this question in the previous trials and I believe today will be our last time asking, because we have our final co-conspirator, *the ringleader,* the victim's own brother. So I ask you gentlemen, who has the real motive to plan such an attack? Who could be so hateful and so unkind to stand by, in plain sight of witnesses, while his sister was murdered in front of him, beaten to death in front of him, breathing her last breath...*right there in front of him*...no more than a few feet away. His youngest sister dying *at his feet*...and not only did he do nothing, but he actually planned the entire attack with Earl Bethune. So, gentlemen of the jury...you are tasked with adding the most important name to the list of June's murderers. No matter how difficult it is for the family, we must have justice. There is one more name that answers the question, *'Who killed June Bethune?'*"

John Allen pauses in front of the jury, staring deeply into each juror's soul and seeking access to imprint ideas into their consciousness. We all must follow orders and the county attorney really is a good guy; the hanging tree and the electrocution chair are not *just for show.* Often, silence has its own sound, and the jury, the judge, and the people within the courtroom are all deafeningly short of breath, contemplating the answer with an indoctrinated curiosity— *"Who killed June Bethune?"*

Are the pictures true? Did Duke Winniper plan to kill his sister, or was it all Earl's idea? Could Papa Winniper or Tilly Bethune be co-conspirators in the plot? How could they not? Maybe it was a tragic case of jealous sororicide, as the county attorney, the county sheriff, and the medical examiner claim. Winniper County's officials all agree that June's murder was an unvirtuous attempt to gain favor, a secretly noble, yet publicly disgraceful sacrifice to save the Winniper family's honor.

The town and country have divided into two equal factions. One side silently whispers their support for the violence that is necessary to secure an empire. They hope for swift justice, swept under a plush rug via a dismissal or mistrial paid-for-in-full by oil profits in order to protect more oil profits. The other side cries that the suspicious Winniper family has so many skeletons in their mansion's closets that the town can hear the bones rattling at night.

While one side plans the fall of an empire, the other celebrates an American son taking matters into his own hands and preventing a mixed race baby from entering his pure-white family. The Winnipers represent the best of South Dakota and American enterprise; for their bloodline to be tainted by colored blood would symbolize not only the infiltration of some Sioux boy into one of the country's most powerful families, but also the *immigration* of colored people into America, itself—or so the liberal media said. Some talking heads use June's murder as just another advertisement for the American melting pot. No matter the understanding of these proceedings, the intrigue continues to build in every mind. Mr. Allen steps away from the jury box, raising his eyebrows and returning to his seat. His hand strokes his chin, as if he is in deep thought while still pondering the question—"*Who killed June Bethune?*"

"Thank you, Mr. Allen. Uh...now, the...uh...court will hear...from the defense," Judge Rupert bellows from his dark oak bench, halfway between sleep and boredom. The ritual is all too familiar, a plug-n-play operation from case to case. He motions for a nearby assistant to refill his coffee, pointing down to his empty grey mug with his index finger.

Dennis Erickson, the lead defense counsel, stands amidst the teams of lawyers surrounding Duke at the defense table. Mr. Erickson is a wild stallion, a second-generation Italian, only in his bloodline, yet not in his mind, because he has few, if any, ties to his Sicilian heritage.

∞

After finishing law school at the age of twenty-four, he left the *Erillio* family's 2-story townhouse in Long Island, changed his surname to Erickson, and moved to a country cabin with two day laborers in Winniper County. His entire motivation behind pursuing a career practicing corporate and criminal law was to live the life of his clients. He wanted to wine and dine with the Winniper family and share their particularly powerful and secluded lifestyle.

He married a Protestant and bore unequivocally Christian-American children, knowing Papa has always trusted Christian family men because they have more to lose for their failure. Mr. Erickson used his moxie and competitiveness to secure a legal stronghold on the Winniper Family Estate's business litigations around the world. Whenever the Winniper Family Holding Company loaned a developing country equipment or performed contract work overseas for a third party, Mr. Erickson's growing firm negotiated terms and supplied the legal means to accomplish Papa's desired ends.

Dennis Erickson literally wrote the book on economic genocide and criminal creativity. He called it *"A Guide to Profiteering"*, but he published the work in a 642 page anthology under a pen name with no reputation. With discretion, Mr. Erickson knows that he has waded through Papa's muck for too long; neither could shine publicly for their deeds. They deserve shame, not acclaim, but, because of their proven ability to calculate, manipulate, and execute, Papa felt Dennis Erickson's presence would be necessary during Duke's trial; the possibilities, or rather, the risks, are still too great.

∞

"Your Honor, we have elected to consolidate our opening arguments into one united statement…if it pleases the court." Mr. Erickson's smug nature seems to annoy Judge Rupert. The beleaguered judiciary raises his hand limply, nods, and turns to his assistant to retrieve a refilled mug of coffee. Rupert smiles over his elixir, a happy moment for an elderly, caffeine addict; his face beams brightly before he glances back to Mr. Erickson and raises his mug, beckoning for the defense to proceed. Mr. Erickson takes his cue and promptly sits back down in his seat. He whispers amidst his team of lawyers while the only female within the group stands and adjusts her business suit over her petite curves.

Papa personally selected Ms. Robin Shields; she is another legacy child, who is also an attractive and confident criminal defense guru from Atlanta. Her appearance today gives her access to a much grander public profile. She has the burgeoning bravado to search for social relevance—the first female justice of the Supreme Court is her ideal accomplishment. Ms. Robin Shields is a feisty feminine specimen with all sorts of grand ambitions, but, most importantly, she knows the value of a nice paycheck.

∞

Immediately after graduating from the University of Georgia, Ms. Shields' father brought her aboard his Atlanta-based legal team at Shields & Webster. Mr. Shields was a strong partner throughout the legal community in the lower 48, specifically the South, and his interstate negotiations facilitated a personal and professional bond with Papa that involved secret trading and corporate espionage.

Thomas III watched Mr. Shields converse with his father as equals, observing the vastness of their connection, which was always astounding. Mr. Shields assured Papa that any Winniper man could become president if he so wished—the family had enough wealth to buy the country; but, Papa never desired the public eye.

∞

Thomas III imagines how business negotiations would collapse if the world knew the family's secret, the biracial twins, the murders, and the conspiracy to keep it all quiet and contained within Winniper County. If their enemies ever learn the truth…no, that could never happen. These musings create space for Thomas III to deviate from the court proceedings; he often feels his imagination soar during anxious situations where his stress rises above his ability to understand the circumstances.

∞

Papa often tried to coach his son to become a better public speaker; he hoped Thomas III could master enough to conduct simple boardroom meetings, but Thomas III never appreciated these lessons and he never implemented any new understanding into his performance. The rightful heir to the Winniper family's throne only wanted to learn how to escape from the kingdom. He desperately yearned to continue life outside the Winniper family's sphere of influence, but he also clung to the same sphere for protection, sustenance, and cheap thrills.

Little boy Tommy turned into a whimsical man who watched weakly while his family's empire stretched around the world and smothered the globe in South Dakota oil. For Thomas III, his family's wealth never felt real; people who were poor might endure the rigors of hardship, but the Winniper family could never find peace or happiness, especially within their world of elitists who would shun the family if they only knew the truth.

∞

The same citizens who revere the Winnipers would never treat the family's cursed Sioux children with equal respect.

515

∞

When Papa first told Thomas III of the family's curse, he explained how he was born with a Sioux sister. Thomas, Sr. returned home to his pregnant wife after defeating the Sioux uprising on the edge of the Winniper family's land. Ruby died giving birth to Papa and Doc Morten, Sr. pulled the Sioux baby from their mother's carcass. Upon seeing the child, Thomas, Sr. ordered one of the family's servants to burn and bury the crying infant inside the barn. Thomas, Sr. believed it was necessary to conceal the curse, and he subsequently amassed his fortune over the graves of the fallen Ghost Dance Sioux. He never fathered another child. He remained content to torture and train his only son until the boy became the perfect heir to his fortune. And when Papa assumed control of the family's estate, he followed Thomas, Sr.'s orders and eliminated the cursed Winnipers with brutal means when deemed necessary.

Like his father, Papa ordered the burning and burial of Teresa and Thomas III's respective twins. Papa and Olivia only chose to have another child after Teresa because the family needed a male heir, and only a male heir, to inherit the Winnipers' business empire. They could only envision a man having the gumption and gall to lead a monarchy in the oil industry.

∞

A clean-cut tyrant is a staple of America's global economic dominance.

∞

Thomas III grew into a skittish man who learned of the Winnipers' biracial curse and, subsequently, refused to marry or maintain a consistent relationship throughout most of his life. Yet, Teresa, a fated idealist, married and conceived three times, believing each time would make her happy. Thomas III helped his wayward sister as best he could; but, when Papa finally confronted the fact that Olivia and Teresa had hid her Sioux babies at Berthine's cabin and Teresa had plans to leave town with Kenny and all her children, Thomas III could not ease his father's wrath. Olivia begged Papa to spare the Sioux children, and in return, Olivia fed Thomas III to his father—a willing sacrifice. Papa forced Thomas III to choose between his sister and his family. Teresa's betrayal had led to her downfall; she had committed a sin that Papa would not forgive—she shamed him by threatening to take his control.

The retributive attack had to come from a male heir, as Papa explained. He told Thomas III that on the Day of Judgment, God will hold the Winniper men accountable for the murders of Sioux newborns, after considering the responsibilities and the burdens placed upon the family. The men tasked with disposing of the family's trash, knowing their forefathers did the same when confronted with the curse; thus, the duty to kill Teresa fell to Thomas III. It all seemed mathematical.

Thomas III completed his duty by running Teresa's car into a tree, killing her on impact, and he was relieved when Papa failed to conjure the malice to order the murders of Berthine and Teresa's Sioux children. The delay between the original orders and Teresa's murder gave Olivia enough time to work her wifely magic and compel Papa to choose a more peaceful path than complete elimination. At the behest of his wife, Papa absolved the sheriff and Thomas III from any further obligation to restore the family's honor. Papa decided to allow Jazz, Lucy, Charles, and Berthine to remain isolated in their cabin, as long as Teresa's Sioux children never knew they were a part of the Winniper family.

Inevitable, and, still unimaginable, Teresa's murder created an avalanche of tragic circumstances that descended upon Christina, Duke, and June. After Kenny drugged and abandoned them at the Winniper family's mansion, Thomas III watched Teresa's grieving, dejected children mope around the estate that their mother once despised. They grew to loathe the Winnipers' wealth in their own ways and for their own reasons—more innocent victims of the family's blood curse.

∞

Thomas III imagines Teresa rolling in her grave, knowing that her brother forced her car into that thick oak tree. She must writhe every time she thinks about how he only stayed long enough to know she was dead.

∞

He watched her body transition into a corpse. In her driver's seat, she slumped against the wheel, her mangled blue mineral sundress, as bloodied as the pictures of June. Thomas III silently reflects upon these tragedies: a father and his mercenary male heirs murder a mother and daughter in order to protect the family's honor.

The Winniper County Courthouse usually functions as a tantalizing ploy, a faux house of justice where Papa executes his true will. He is the master of proceedings and appeals, all while sitting patiently in the front row, casually observing the farce. His go-to hired hand, Mr. Erickson, is a nationally-distinguished defense counsel and the increasingly-familiar, Ms. Shields, is a thinly-framed courtroom specialist. On the surface, Duke's defense team is a formidable foe for the county attorney's office. Papa has shown a modicum of respect for due process, or at least the appearance of it. With such a high profile case and Freidrich's projected revenue losses, the rewards for all the actors are available in ample supply from a communal trough. Papa has made it clear that he's paying top dollar for compliance.

"Gentlemen of the jury, I ask that you forgive me. I'm from down South and I don't know how things are done up here in South Dakota. I'm just a simple Georgia peach, you see," Ms. Shields begins her opening statement while sauntering past the prosecution table and swishing her pint-sized hips in front of the jury and judge. "But I believe in a *good, Christian union,* and in a *good, Christian union,* there's never a wrong time…to pray. Please, *good Christians*…if I may…please join me in prayer. Bow your heads and close your eyes."

Ms. Shields looks over the jurors' eyes, waiting for each man to lower his head and close his eyes. They quickly comply, and she turns to the gallery, tilting her head up, particularly acknowledging the press in the back rows. Thomas III lowers his head, but he can see Papa keep his head raised. The old man's eyes focus on Ms. Shields and a shy, unnoticed smirk creases his lips while he takes in her girlish frame.

"Papa, ain't you gon' pray?" Thomas III whispers, and his father turns his head slightly before burrowing his eyebrows and glaring at his son.

"Mind your mother and Tilly…and *keep quiet.*" Papa growls sternly, and Thomas III remembers his place, far removed from his father's love, if any exists. Thomas III has never gained his father's affection; he has only garnered curt disappointment. Papa has been deeply saddened that his only son has not lived up to the Winniper men's legacy.

Thomas III has performed multiple murderous honor killings, but his inability to conceive a son and his unwillingness to attempt another conception has placed the entire family in jeopardy. Papa has feared that the lack of a suitable male heir would create a power vacuum in his empire; and a mutual disdain and codependence has developed between father and son. The boy has become a man according to everyone except his father, and the father receives perfect obedience from everyone except his only son.

Confusing their purpose and duty, the father and son stare at one another while Olivia weeps softly between them and Tilly Bethune leans gloomily against Thomas III's left shoulder. The women are weary mothers and grandmothers of the deceased. Christina and Nancy remained at the Winniper Family Estate, one looking after the other while a staff of maids, landscapers, and armed security forces march around the property, assuming their servile roles in a still vibrant hierarchy. The scandal hasn't changed the estate much, besides the extra guards to ward off prying paparazzi and reporters. Sadly, the family's mansion has become more like a fortress. Teresa's despair consumed Christina at a young age, and Thomas III can already see the same angst creeping into Nancy.

The Winniper women have few options and Olivia continues to cry with squelched anguish, knowing what she will never speak in public. She will never shame herself or her family. All along, her husband, son, and grandson are murderers sitting within a courtroom, fulfilling their respective roles, while awaiting justice. Olivia bows her head derisively, tearfully sobbing, mumbling the Lord's Prayer, and stealing a moment to whisper into God's ear before Ms. Shields begins her prayer.

"Lord and Savior Jesus Christ," Ms. Shields prays solemnly, clasping her freshly manicured hands together. "It is your humble servant, Robin. I know my father sometimes calls me, 'Bob'...he wanted a boy, but...you gave him me and I got the best father in the world. So I thank you, Lord. And Lord, I thank you, because all of my life, you've led me where I am most needed...and, I want to thank you for bringing me to Winniper County. Lord, I see that I am needed here because a young man has been wrongly accused of a crime he did not commit. Lord, I pray that you show your mercy through...*justice*, and I pray that we may see your love when this young man is back with his beloved family...freed from these false accusations in the name of the Messiah, our Lord and Savior, Jesus Christ. *Amen.*"

Like a warm blanket that only covers the head or the toes, a slight reverence falls over the courtroom as another round of *Amen* echoes amongst the rows. Ms. Shields smiles sheepishly while breathing in her sense of control. She does an unnoticeable shimmy, shaking her hips and spirit before strolling closer to the jury and taking long, lingered strides all the way across the eyes of each man. Someone in the gallery whistles and a burst of laughter fills the room.

"Order! Order!" The judge bangs his gavel abruptly, reacting quickly, shocked at the disrespect. Such a damsel deserves better. "We'll have none of that! The gentlemen will respect the courtroom and everyone within it! Proceed, Ms. Shields."

"Thank you, Your Honor. I seem to have a few fans." Ms. Shields giggles over her shoulder toward the gallery and promptly turns back to the jury, leaving everyone to question whether her comment referred to the judge, the jurors, the laughs, or the whistler—each notion encourages a scandalously, salacious suggestion. "Gentlemen of the jury, the county attorney was right when he spoke about a question. And he was even right about the question, you fine, South Dakota gentlemen must answer today: *'Who killed June Bethune?'*"

She nods toward the prosecutor before changing her facial expression to a grave frown.

"Gentlemen, you have the task of sifting through testimony, evidence, and rational thought to answer that question, *'Who killed June Bethune?'* It would be too easy, too naïve, too incomplete to close your eyes, ask *'Who killed June Bethune?'*, and then open your eyes and point the finger at the first person you see—but that's not justice, that's a lynching! Don't let the ambitious county attorney execute a son of Winniper County for a crime he did not commit!

"And yes, we grieve because a woman has been viciously murdered in this fair, good county, but, don't kill an innocent person as revenge. The county attorney has quite a case, and he's batting three for three; the county has already convicted three men for this same crime. Three grown men with families and friends are now on death row awaiting their final moment in the execution chair, but it's not enough for the county attorney! The truth isn't enough! He needs more scandal, more headlines to advance his career, I regretfully suppose.

"So, while I agree that during this trial, we should answer the question *'Who killed June Bethune?'*, I also believe we already have answered it, three times over. All of Ms. Bethune's killers have been brought to justice and *that's the truth.* Duke Winniper did not kill his sister. We concede that he was present during the crime, but he was merely there to see his sister. He had no idea what Earl Bethune had planned for his Cousin June. We challenge the county attorney to produce a single, *credible* witness to identify our client as one of the attackers. There are no such witnesses. We are only wasting Winniper County tax dollars to build the public profile of a reckless county attorney. Gentlemen of the jury, I just hope *Mr. Allen* doesn't waste too much of *your* time. Our client is not guilty of any crime. He's as innocent now as he was the day God brought him into this world."

Ms. Shields lightly pats the oak frame of the juror's box with her manicured left hand. She lightly grazes the polished wood with her fingertips before she twists those thin, edgy hips and walks slowly back to the defense table. Her co-counsel beams while chatting amongst themselves, feeling the momentum in the room slide in their favor. Prying eyes question the county attorney's motives—all according to plan.

"That was grand. We're moving along swiftly." Judge Rupert grumbles into his coffee mug, moving through the motions as mechanically as a rigged slot machine, clanking and jerking into a programmed position. "If the prosecution is ready, you may call your first witness."

"We're ready, Your Honor." Mr. Allen hops from his seat and nods toward his three assistants; he is eager to defend his honor. "My office values the court's time as well as the jurors' service."

"Proceed." The judge replies, equally eager to disengage from the proceedings.

"For its first witness, the prosecution would like to call Lyle Hutchins to the stand."

Lyle Hutchins, the Hollywood parasite, is a freelance photographer who attained infamy after snapping pictures of the attack.

∞

A deceitful, self-aggrandizing professional, Lyle tended to his craft, along with the rest of the parasitic paparazzi, while June and Jazz lay dying. The media hounds had followed the forsaken duo throughout their hometown visit, but no one intervened to help the music idols during the mauling. The public's callousness became a sad travesty within the tragedy, an additional layer of moral decay added to the scandal.

∞

The courtroom's wide oak doors open and two officers usher Lyle Hutchins through the center aisle. The air rushes from the room as the doors close behind him, confining him within the finality. The case is real, we are here, and the world will soon know the truth.

"You pig!" A woman in the gallery lashes out at Lyle, but the nearest officer grabs her hands and pulls her to the floor. The courtroom erupts as several officers rush to help subdue the woman while she kicks and screams. "He killed June! He should've helped her! She was an angel and he killed her!"

"Order! Order! Officers, remove that woman!" Judge Rupert pounds his gavel against his bench and the commotion begins to ease as the officers gag the woman and carry her squirming body from the courtroom. Even with her mouth covered, she continues to wail into the officer's hand, her eyes still virulent. June's death has affected many lives. "Damn it all, I knew this trial would be a headache. Bailiff, bring the witness forward!"

Judge Rupert points to Mr. Hutchins, and the obedient black bailiff leads the photographer to the witness stand, retrieves the Bible from a compartment within, holds the book to Lyle's chest, and waits for him to place his frail, pale hand on the word of God.

"Need you to put ya' hand on this here book and swear fo' God."

"How can I swear *fo'* nothin'?" Lyle Hutchins replies loudly, searching for kicks and giggles as another ripple of laughter rolls through the courtroom.

"Order! Order!" Judge Rupert bellows and then points down toward Lyle. "Watch yourself, son. I'm not only old and cranky, but I'm…I'm a Christian—a *very good Christian!*"

"I'm sorry, Your Honor, but I don't believe in God!" Lyle Hutchins announces boldly, waving his arms over his head, presenting himself in all his grandeur. "So how can I say I swear to tell the truth, 'so help me God', if I don't believe God exists? It's a contradiction for me. It would make me a hypocrite and a liar."

"Listen here, Mister…*Hutchins*, your personal salvation is not my concern today." The judge begins, raising his gavel across the witness stand and placing it at the tip of Lyle's nose. "Whether or not you rot in damnation is your prerogative, but if you want to testify and do all your prime time interviews and print all your pictures, you will take the oath and say, '*so help you God*'!"

Judge Rupert gut-checks the weak-minded photographer, reminding Mr. Hutchins of *his* bottom-line; it seems to Thomas III that we all have them. Lyle stares sternly at the judge and tentatively places his hand to his pointy chin while he ponders his prospective options. The ambitiously immoral photographer dramatically raises his right hand in the air and delicately descends until his fingertips lightly touch the cross on the Holy Bible.

"You swear tell the truth, whole truth, nothin' but the truth, so help you God?"

"I do…so help me…*Allah*, I mean God, I mean Shira, I mean Mickey Mouse, I mean…"

"Bailiff…"

"Wait, judge! I do, *so help me God!*" Lyle Hutchins proclaims over the courtroom, turning to the judge and throwing his hands up frantically. "Sorry, Your Honor, I have seen the light. There were just so many gods; I forgot which one to swear to!"

Lyle sits down in the witness chair, hunching his shoulders sheepishly and placing his finger over his lips. Judge Rupert huffs from his bench and shakes his head in disappointment; he thinks today's youth leave little hope for the future.

"Mr. Allen, please proceed." The judge waves his hand toward the prosecution and tilts his head over his cup of Joe, inhaling the only thing that soothes him. John Allen rises with a scoff, while ruffling his suit and patting any creases. He's upset that his first witness is not making a great first impression with the judge or jury. His case is not off to the best start after Ms. Shields all but accused him of bloodlust. He worries that each citizen in the gallery may already have a pitchfork. One of the county attorney's assistants reaches for a manila folder on the prosecution table and holds it up for Mr. Allen until he takes it in his right hand and strolls around the table as if mesmerized by the folder's tan color.

"Thank you, Your Honor. If it pleases the court, I would like to enter into evidence, Exhibit A1001." John Allen proclaims with a sordid scowl forming on his face. He continues his perplexed steps without any real momentum; he moseys toward the center of the foreground.

"So noted, Exhibit A1001." Judge Rupert responds, pointing to the stenographer, who sits typing away at a school desk next to the jury. Several other school desks huddle in a corner behind her right shoulder, delicately positioned to occupy the least amount of space in the packed courtroom. The Winniper County Courthouse often hosts law classes for Winniper County College, all funded and poisoned, of course, by the Winniper family's wealth.

"Mr. Hutchins, I have in my hand a folder containing the photos you took on the day of the murder." John Allen finally aims his steps and launches towards his witness, hastily placing the folder on the stand in front of Mr. Hutchins. "Would you open the folder, please?"

"Sure, I'm my biggest fan," Lyle replies arrogantly and quickly opens the folder with a gasp; he's been preparing these reactions for months. "Whoa! I forgot it was that bad! They really gave it to that broad…"

"Objection!" Robin Shields jumps from her seat at the defense table. "Your Honor, I ask for an immediate mistrial! The witness is insinuating that our client…"

"Overruled!" The judge interrupts in stride. He can already smell her intention, chomping at the bit for any chance at a dismissal.

"But, Your Honor…" Ms. Shields pleads, balling her fists instinctively and clenching her eyes tightly, a look she mastered to sway her father.

"I said, you are overruled, counsel! Now, sit down!" Judge Rupert barks like daddy chastising his disobedient daughter. "And Mr. Hutchins, just answer the questions. Keep the side comments to yourself."

"Yes, sir, Your Honor. Sorry about that." Lyle glances back to the pictures and grimaces with gritted teeth. "It was just…*spectacular violence.*"

He continues to admire his work, changing his horrified facial expressions as he flips through the pictures in the folder. John Allen strolls around the witness stand, trying to shield the courtroom from the sight while Lyle continues to scoff at the pictures.

"Mr. Hutchins, please try to conceal the pictures. We do not want to shock the courtroom. The jurors will have their chance to view them in detail during deliberation."

"Sorry, boss. I just can't help admire my work."

"Um, uh, hm…okay, Mr. Hutchins, now, uh, so you do remember taking these pictures?"

"Of course, I'll never forget that day," Lyle Hutchins confirms proudly, leaning back in his chair and adjusting his waistline. "I paid my alimony with these snaps. I'm free, Dorothy!"

"*That's touching.* Can you describe what's happening in these pictures?" John Allen hunches over Lyle's shoulder, continuing to conceal any clear view for the jurors and courtroom. His maneuvering builds tension within the autumn air trickling through the courtroom's open window; nature itself is eager to experience the drama.

"Yes, sir, I can describe *exactly* what's going on. A group of us…"

"*Us?*"

"Yeah, you know…*photographers,* who specialize in capturing the lives of celebrities."

"Mr. Hutchins…isn't the increasingly used term, *'paparazzi'?*"

"Well, sure, if labels are your thing, doc. We're artists, too, and a group of us had been tailing Jazz and June for a few weeks. Those two…they were always cash cows, but…when rumors started up that they were engaged and planning a wedding, well…a group of us dropped everything and followed them everywhere. It would've been the scoop of the year, maybe the decade—that first public post-engagement kiss. The money would've flowed like…*oil*."

"Mr. Hutchins, please stick to the events…"

"Okay, okay. I'm just providing a bit o' context. So that morning some national papers picked up the engagement story, but they still hadn't gone public, still no kiss. There I was, with a group of the guys, I mean, *artists*, snapping pics of the two of them drinking tea or coffee at that little café down on Winniper Road…or Winniper Drive…or Winniper Street? I mean, everything in this town is Winniper something, right? They own the whole county!"

"It's called the *American Café*, Mr. Hutchins," Mr. Allen corrects the witness hurriedly, but he can't prevent a few chuckles from filtering throughout the courtroom, imploring Lyle to continue his antics. Mr. Allen now feels that he is in a fight to salvage his witness's credibility. "Please, *continue*."

"Okay, okay. So they get up, they're leaving, I'm snapping pictures, someone is asking June about their engagement, the wedding preparations, you know? There were rumors they were planning a small service in Beverly Hills, but no one knew for sure." Lyle laughs to himself and massages his chin, still dreaming of dollars lost, without regard for the millions he's reaped from his role, or lack thereof, in June's murder. "Wedding photos sell through the roof! I could've made two fortunes."

"Yes, we have a witness who will testify that Jazz Lancaster and June Bethune became engaged shortly before their tragic visit to Winniper County and they did, in fact, have plans to marry after departing." John Allen wipes his left eye with his index finger in an exaggerated swipe. He turns over his shoulder to the jury box, searching for each man's eyes and hoping to emote his empathy. "She was a bride-to-be, slain in cold blood. Please continue with your testimony, Mr. Hutchins. Tell us what you saw."

"Yeah, it's all...*very sad*...so out of nowhere, these hoodlums rush through the crowd with weapons and start beating on them. It happened so fast, I honestly wondered why there was no security. I don't know...it is Winniper County, what really ever happens here? I'm surprised they have a police force at all, but...these guys just really went to town, real home run stuff.

"You can see what they did in the pictures. I got it all, blow-by-blow. I really felt like I was capturing a moment in history, the slaying of Caesar, the burning of Joan of Arc, the crucifixion, if you're into that, judge. Scouts honor, I thought they were both dead instantly, so I kept snapping pictures."

"And you never feared for your life?"

"Nope, there was a big crowd. Those guys wanted nothing to do with anyone else but those two. It was a hit-job, an assassination, plain as day. They didn't care about the cameras until the deed was done. Then they roughed up a couple of my buddies, got scared as more people came to the scene, and they ran away."

"And did you get a good look at these men?"

"Of course, anyone who has seen my pictures got great looks of the other three! That Earl Bethune was all over the place."

"Well, some of the pictures are slightly blurry," Mr. Allen prods and tilts his head over the open manila folder, pointing to several points in one photograph. "No doubt you are a competent photographer."

"*Competent?* Excuse me, sir, but I'm much more than *competent!*" Lyle defends himself with girlish gusto, folding his arms over his stomach and huffing in his seat. "Those pictures are legendary. I've gotten covers on TIME, Life Magazine, you name it."

"But there are portions where it seems like it was difficult for you to focus. Some of the faces are distorted."

"No, it just...it just happened so fast! I couldn't get *all* the attackers...you've used these same pictures in the other trials. I didn't know they'd be used in court, at the time, I just knew June would be the real story. So I stayed with her, because..."

"*Because what?*"

"Because...editors always paid more for pictures of her...she's always been the story with those two. She was the rebel. I thought they were both dead, I couldn't do anything to help them, but June...she was the fallen angel. She was the meal ticket. Her dead body paid for my future."

"Mr. Hutchins, a little respect, please."

"I'm sorry, Mr. Allen. You said stick to the facts."

"But, *in fact*, Jazz was still alive, and he survived the attack. And you didn't help."

"Well, he could've fooled me. It's been over two years and no one's seen or heard from him since it happened. I know people, who know people…and no one's gotten so much as a Polaroid." Lyle pouts and hands the folder of photos to Mr. Allen, done with whatever façade his testimony now amounts to. He's still unsure which team his testimony represents; all he knows is that he's been given the green-light to spill the beans on what he witnessed during the attack.

"Mr. Hutchins, again, may I remind you to please, have some respect for the *victims* of this attack?"

"I'm sorry. It was a tough day for me, too! I'm…uh, kind of an indirect victim. I told you, those two were all the rage. Kids couldn't get enough of 'em. The country was going crazy over an Injun and white celebrity couple! They were going to be a boon for our industry."

"Mr. Hutchins, please, try to focus. Did you see the men who killed June Bethune?"

"Yes, sir. I did."

"Do you see any of these men in the courtroom?" John Allen leans over the witness stand, glancing between Duke and Lyle, while the eyebrows of the courtroom arch with intrigue.

"Well, it's hard to say." Lyle Hutchins strains his neck comically, glancing over the entire court gallery and even scowling over the judge, inspecting his gavel and coffee mug. Lyle places his hand over his forehead and searches the courtroom, again. "I see a few pretty girls…and even a few pretty boys."

The liberal minority within the courtroom begin to chuckle and murmur sycophantic musings about morals while the courtroom's conservative majority finally concludes Lyle Hutchins is, indeed, a spawn of Satan. He is a homosexual demon sent to uproot everything good and holy within Winniper County. Their South Dakota ethics collide violently with Mr. Hutchins's brazen promiscuity.

∞

He once photographed nude males for an ill-advised art magazine based in Brooklyn which had some scattered national distribution. These lurid photos never reached Winniper County because Papa paid the shippers and shop owners to destroy the magazine issues before they appeared in stores throughout South Dakota and the Midwest.

∞

Even though Papa's hands are anything but clean, he believes his motives are pure. Papa views himself as a constant protector, a patriarch who carries a sword and shield. On the surface, in small social circles, he promotes the highest moral standard, but within the pit of his stomach, where his ambitions fester, Papa craves to control any and every facet of information surrounding his family's immense wealth. As their estate grows, his greedy attention and his ambitious grasp consume more of the world.

Thomas III remembers his father having loud, verbal fits over Lyle's magazine, languishing over American boys traipsing around without clothes.

∞

Papa found it all lewd and lascivious, and he instigated a national uproar that fueled a feverish debate amongst the liberals and conservatives. Under-paid and over-clothed clamor-mouths argued over a new scandal that fed the media like never before... *until now.* Even Lyle believed he would never gain more notoriety than being known for his controversial nude-issues, but, after capturing the clearest photos of June's murder, the photographer has received more reprints, interviews, and book offers than he could ever accept.

∞

Today's testimony is his climax, the apex of his cultural relevance and the performance that will feed him forever. Thomas III can see a gleam in Lyle's eyes that soaks up the spotlight and prays the publicity will never end—please, may someone always care. He acts out like a neglected child in class, hoping to steal any available attention from his peers or the authority figure, who, in this judicial classroom, is a grumpy, over-the-hill, and possibly diabetic judge. Seeming to lose patience, Judge Rupert bangs the gavel twice and leans over toward the wanton, wayward witness.

"Now listen here, Mr. Hutchins, I've had just about enough of your antics," Judge Rupert rumbles over the witness and grits his teeth, trying to maintain his judicial composure. "You won't turn my courtroom into some exposé, no sir. You will answer the counsel's questions directly and stop sputtering your liberal drivel. Do you understand?"

"Why, sure, *Your Honor*. I don't mean nothing by it," Lyle explains, placing one hand over his heart and raising the other with a bright smile. The mockery continues within the courtroom. "It's all these questions, I'm just a little nervous, you see. I apologize, honest. I'm doing my best, nothing but the truth."

"Counsel, proceed." Judge Rupert anxiously waves his hand toward John Allen, dismissing the witness and the process. He refuses to bend his personal disposition and initiate any true order. John Allen takes his cue and steps closer to the witness stand, tucking the tan folder with Lyle's notorious pictures under his left shoulder and staring toward the defense table.

"Now, Mr. Hutchins, think back to that day," John Allen begins cautiously, remembering his instructions from Papa. "Do you see any of the men who killed the sweet and innocent June Bethune? Are any of those…*cowards*…in the courtroom?"

While asking the question, Mr. Allen steps away from the witness stand and walks directly toward the defense table, waving the folder over Duke and his lawyers with evident appeal and aplomb. For his part in the play, Lyle peruses over the defense table before resting his eyes soberly on Duke.

"Well, Mr. Allen. I believe I do see…*one of them*." Lyle narrows his eyes sharply, arches his back, and stretches his neck from side-to-side. "My eyesight hasn't been the same since I retired, but, yep, I see one, sure do."

"Uh huh…um, can you please identify whom you recognize?" John Allen bellows from across the courtroom, still standing near the defense table, eyeing Duke and his lawyers with meaningful intent. Mr. Erickson and Ms. Shields glare back at Mr. Allen, knowing his intention and calculating two respective counterattacks. Each lead counsel confers with a nearby associate. Both militant defenders protect a farce. Papa choreographed these moves months ago and he watches from the front row without awe or much intrigue.

"Yes, sir, I recognize him…the main perpetrator, right over there in the end!" Lyle shouts as he strains his neck enthusiastically and points excitedly at Duke, exposing his eagerness to snitch. "I saw Duke Winniper do it! He gave the orders for them others to kill his own sister! He was the main perpetrator, the leader of the whole thing!"

Gasps fill the courtroom and the shockwaves freeze the entire county; whether false or candid, the effect is pure and felt throughout the world. Thomas III glances to Papa, but the old man does not flinch. Papa has supreme confidence in his manipulative moves, his contrived coordination, and his appreciation of the art in this courtroom choreography.

Lyle Hutchins would need Papa's permission to identify Duke; even a lowlife photographer knows the penalty for defying a king, but Thomas III still does not understand his father's strategy. Thomas III still wilts under the pressure surrounding the throne; he is unable to assume the strategic responsibility of a Winniper heir. He wonders what decision his father has made. If the judge, the lawyers, and the jury are all playing their respective roles, then what script has Lyle Hutchins received?

"Mr. Hutchins, you're sure that Duke Winniper helped kill his own sister? You saw him among the other three convicted murderers who slayed young June Bethune in broad daylight, on that tragic Thursday afternoon?"

"Yes, sir! He killed her, practically led the whole mob! Saw it with my own three eyes!" Lyle Hutchins flashes a fake camera in his hands and smiles happily before remembering the seriousness of his testimony. His face tenses and he stares back toward Duke, remembering his lines. "Duke Winniper was the *main instigator*! He was jealous of June because he's a mute. He's a disgrace to the Winniper family!"

"Uh, Mr. Hutchins, please try to confine your answers." John Allen begins, hesitating for a moment, almost anticipating an objection from the defense, but his opponents remain silent. Both Mr. Erickson and Ms. Shields have consented to a certain measured approach, Thomas III thinks. The county attorney spins on his heels and grins as he feels the green light to continue leading the march toward his fourth murder conviction. June's death may make him governor one day. "Now, Mr. Hutchins, although we can't discuss your testimony in prior cases, can you explain why you feel Mr. Winniper was the leader, the *main instigator*, as you say, in June's murder?"

"He practically forced the others along! Ordered 'em to push the crowd aside and…attack *'sweet and innocent June'*…" Lyle pauses, contemplating whether he should add to the rumors about the town's beloved daughter; could he spice up his future features? He decides against that move, glancing once at Papa before looking over to Duke again and aiming his testimony toward the approved target. "Duke Winniper was the only one without a weapon. He was like a master with a pack of wolves. He turned them boys on his own kin, but he's the dog. He killed his sister and you can see what he done to her in my pictures!"

The courtroom experiences another wave of shock and vitriol. Broiling murmurs bubble throughout the gallery, ignited by the indifference, cooked by the callousness, and fired-up by the frivolousness of this photographer with the gall and guts to testify against Duke Winniper—the youngest male heir to one of the largest fortunes in the world. Is the mute a scapegoat for a crime that could have only been committed with Papa's approval, or is he a jealous renegade who convinced his friends to commit murder?

Papa leans back in the front row; a faux wave of concern passes through the wrinkles in the forehead, but he does not flinch. Thomas III inspects his father, watching for any signs of weakness—there are none. The old man is as in control as he has always been. The only change is that there is a new Winniper whose life hangs in the balance while the family's secrets continue to dance within the world's theater. For Papa, his wealth and family have become a sport without real consequences. His revenue continues to increase and his power grows in proportion.

John Allen takes a moment to turn toward Papa, his body language asking the old man if he desires any further testimony on the record. Papa nods ever-so-slightly; his gesture is barely noticeable to anyone other than his observant son. Thomas III has lived in his father's home for over fifty years now. He has watched the man closely, always seeing his father as a giant. Thomas III fears that his father will never be brought down to size. Papa truly is a king governing his American empire, and the sight of John Allen's submissive grin reminds Thomas III of his own submission to the Winniper flag. It is as if the entire county is stuck in the middle ages, a monarchy transferring power through the first-born male heir, but if the county folk only knew truth…would they treat Papa like a king, a murderer, or, even worse, a freak whose white family produces non-white babies.

Thomas III sympathizes with Papa's predicament, but he also regrets his father's decision-making. Even now, within this theater, there are dangerous consequences for what seems to be another public sacrifice. If Duke is convicted, he will be sentenced to death; and he cannot produce another male heir if he's dead; thus, the responsibility will once again fall upon Thomas III to provide for the family's future. These considerations continue to wheel around in Thomas III's mind, but, he looks over his father's calm face and he wonders what the old man truly has sanctioned here today.

John Allen has accepted his place within the defined, colloquial hierarchy, but, he still hopes to climb a few rungs higher. The ambitious county attorney turns back toward the judge and the witness, resigning himself to a job well-done. He walks toward Lyle and places the manila folder on the banister of the witness stand.

"Thank you, Mr. Hutchins. Your testimony has been very…uh, *valuable.* Your Honor, I yield the floor to the defense." John Allen explains confidently before stealing a quick glance toward the jury as he turns and strolls back to his table. His assistants clamor to congratulate him on a strong opening testimony, but he only acknowledges their praise with a subtle hand wave. Mr. Allen sits, leans back in his chair, and stares over to the defense, trying to decipher their strategy. An unsteady hush falls over the courtroom while the defense team chats amongst themselves, whispering between Mr. Erickson and Ms. Shields and discussing their next move.

"Does the defense intend to question the witness?" Judge Rupert asks impatiently, scrunching his nose while looking to his left and eyeing the courtroom clock on the wall. It reads 10:26 a.m. He double-checks the watch on his wrist and the judge wonders if he can survive this charade until lunchtime.

"Uh, yes, Your Honor. I believe we would like to ask Mr. Hutchins to clarify a few statements from his testimony." Mr. Erickson raises his hand as if he is answering a question in class. He stands slowly, arching his back to show his age, diligence, and contrition while he prepares to present an annotated soliloquy from Shakespeare's *Macbeth*. He briefly turns his head over his left shoulder and looks back to Papa, confirming the procedure that will deliver his client to a cell on death row.

The entire county knows that the Winniper family's wealth has paid for one of the highest-priced defense teams ever assembled—only the best for the best. The fact that Duke is the family's youngest male heir adds undeniable value to his trial. The stakes are extremely high. His acquittal maintains the status quo; his conviction jeopardizes the family's empire and the county's future. Whispers within the town's barbershops and salons cannot stop gossiping about how the three convicted accomplices should meet their respective ends—hanging, electrocution, a firing squad, maybe all three, at the same time. No execution seems violent enough to satisfy the people of Winniper County, but Duke's conviction is an impossibility.

True, June's murder has evoked the town's bloodlust. Earl and the guys are three expendable henchmen who deserve to die, but Papa's mute grandson is the town's only hope for a somewhat, suitable successor, given Thomas III's inadequacy. Although a typical middle-aged man would feel disrespected if his family and community considered his younger, disabled nephew to be a better leader, Thomas III rarely flinches when the townsfolk denounce his prince hood. He ignores these insults to his claim and his masculinity; he allows the peasants to ridicule him. They act as if they forget that he is a Winniper man, but, while they act, Thomas III dreams of the reality when he is truly no longer a Winniper man. In his dreams, he would just like to be a man…and a father; yet, while quietly dreaming about achieving an escape that is similar to Teresa's plot, Thomas III remains under his father's watchful eye. Despite his inability to ascend to the throne and unburden his father from the responsibilities of being a Winniper patriarch, Thomas III still has the principal paternal claim to the mega fortune that floods an entire community with oil drilling profits. Despite his faults, he could still become the gatekeeper that provides all their associates and business partners with wealth, privilege, and means.

But, amidst the Winniper family's enterprise, Thomas III is a missing link that no one remembers to include in any meaningful consideration. His father's negligence has turned him into a victim with a victim's mentality. Thomas III sees himself as a rightful heir who was both passed over and forgotten in the lineage, but happily so. He plays his role, the devoted son, the grieving uncle, and the noble father, but, in truth, he has always fallen short of any, and every, expectation. He has never reached his full potential.

Nancy has become the only bright light in his dark life, and he intends to protect her from the sinister shadows lurking around their family's mansion. She is still innocent, naïve to the Winniper curse, and Thomas III often wonders if he'll tell his daughter about the family's bloodline. How much should she know? These thoughts send spine-scraping thumbtacks up his back, causing his body to jilt against the back of his row. He feels the steel revolver digging into his left side and he winces as the barrel pokes his ribs. Tilly's head adjusts to his movements and she leans against his left shoulder, still sobbing silently into her handkerchief. He worries that his baby girl will one day cry similar tears and he vows to somehow save her from such sorrow.

These fleeting desires leave little hope for the inevitable, a fact that Mr. Erickson also considers as he steps away from the defense table and walks across the courtroom in silence. He slowly contemplates his method of attack along with the physical accessories. He plans the contrived movements that will establish the necessary culpability and remove any doubt that Papa and Duke's defense team have adequately responded to Lyle's testimony. The accusing stench still remains in the courtroom, the confusion whether Papa has calculated his grandson's demise—it seems impossible, yet, quiet rumors abound that the town's patriarch has committed similar betrayals in the past.

Why would Lyle Hutchins identify Duke? The public thinks the mute is the only one whose hands are reasonably clean. At worst, he is a powerful puppet who stood by while his friends attacked June and Jazz.

∞

During his trial, Earl happily took the stand and explained how Duke remained behind the photographers while the guys put on a show. Earl smiled while recounting their fury. He confessed that he knowingly killed June and he admitted that he and the guys were not financially compensated. They committed the crime *"to protect the honor of their hometown"*.

Even after being found guilty, as they wait for the governor to decide whether they will die suffocating from a hangman's noose or sizzling in an electrocution chair, many people believe that the three murderers captured on camera were convinced to kill for money or some secret agenda. Duke was merely a twisted pawn, too simple and too ineffectual to mastermind a celebrity assassination. No, he couldn't, and still, jealousy is a ghostly motive.

Maybe the murderers had girlfriends and bastards who received large payments for death sentences. Maybe Papa wanted to extinguish a sudden spark of unwanted attention before it became a forest fire of uncontained intrigue.

∞

The viewing public has demanded its pound of flesh and Papa has been more than willing to provide several entrées, but his very survival demands that certain sections of the family's all-you-can-eat buffet must remain closed. Thomas III wonders what money *can't* buy and who money *can't* satisfy; yet, now he asks today's truly critical question, and then he thinks about the possible answers and their implications.

Who killed June Bethune? Would Papa set up his mute grandson, prevent the accused from communicating with genuine representation, and then serve him to the public in order to conceal the family's secrets? Thomas III's stomach turns while he looks around the courtroom, hoping no one notices his discomfort. Papa has always taught him the rules of war; their manhood has always been a bond that men share—the responsibility and the privilege. For Papa to sacrifice Duke, is he breaking that bond or upholding his responsibility? Thomas III believes his father is a man trapped on a balance beam that is destined to break; the force placed upon the successful American man is unbearable even for a giant.

Deep down, Papa only wants to save his family, but every decision he makes consequently places those he loves in greater danger. Still, he is a man unnerved by the dilemma of his hypocritical malice. The victims of the Winnipers' curse mourn all around him, and he refuses to relent from his chosen path. Thomas, Sr. ingrained a merciless self-understanding into his son, and so, Papa judges himself by using the standards of a man who slaughtered an entire village. Papa watches the trial without a care on his face. His eyes remain still while he casually observes the courtroom's freshly clean, oak and pine scenery as if he is an elderly man at the park.

The preening goose, Lyle Hutchins, ruffles his feathers inside the witness stand and prepares to squawk for more morsels. Mr. Erickson continues to stride confidently toward the anxious photographer, seeing this first witness as a pivotal role player in the trial's outcome. Papa's favorite legal henchman is a sly fox during cross-examinations and a maverick during legally ambiguous debates. He relishes the craft of courtroom litigation; it is the theater at its highest stakes.

"Now, uh listen, Mr. Lyle Hutchins, *you say* you were taking pictures...*you say*...you were at the *America Café*...you say..." Mr. Erickson tiptoes over his words and the cedar pine flooring beneath his polished Oxford shoes. He fears that he may trip on a misplaced splinter, crack the courtroom's foundation, and disrupt the judge and the jury's sensibilities. "*You say*...you were taking pictures at the *American Café* on the day of the...uh, *incident*, correct?"

"Yes."

"And were you the only photographer taking pictures that day?" Mr. Erickson steps closer to the witness, inching nearer to his point. He knows his main tactic is to turn the entire trial into an entertaining show, filled with twists and unanswered plot holes. Doubt is simply another step toward salvation.

"No, of course not. There was a whole swarm of us, *as usual.* Jazz and June are...er, I mean, uh, they *were* big news." Lyle rolls his eyes as he corrects himself with a fleeting frown. The finality of June's murder hits him mid-sentence, and he hides his genuine sorrow while remembering her loss.

∞

Lyle Hutchins had followed the performers since their buzz started in New Orleans. He helped pump the angle that they were symbols of American freedom. During their tours, he and a growing group of photographers chased the duo around the world and back. Lyle saw Jazz Lancaster as a silent outcast and June Bethune was a "good girl gone blues". Together, they were cultural icons, and Lyle exploited their tragedy and milked the horror capture in his pictures like a cash cow. As his salacious acclaim rose to rival the incident's infamy, Lyle secretly developed a morbid conscience because he began seeing June's bloodied corpse in his nightmares and having hallucinations of her crushed skull during the day.

∞

"So, why did *Mister Allen* choose you to be the prosecution's *first* witness?" Mr. Erickson throws his question toward Lyle before taking a quick look at the prosecutor. The defense counselor's accusatory tone attempts to elicit an objection from John Allen, but none comes. Mr. Erickson decides to turn up the heat a little. "And, before you answer, can you also explain why the prosecution has used *your testimony* to convict three other men? It would seem you've become Mr. Allen's hired gun."

"Objection!" John Allen calls from his seat, leaning forward and raising his index finger. "Your honor, Mr. Erickson is completely out of line. His comments should be–"

"I'm sorry, Your Honor!" Mr. Erickson interrupts before the judge may decide. "Please allow me to rephrase the question!"

"Ugh, boys just stop bickering and proceed." Judge Rupert grumbles into his coffee mug again, mildly irritated that he has become such a useless necessity in these proceedings.

"Mr. Hutchins, why *do you think* the prosecution chose you to be their very first witness, today?" Mr. Erickson asks delicately, glancing back toward the prosecution table, daring John Allen to object to his carefully worded question.

"Well, I don't know…could be my good looks. The jurors are all men." Lyle remarks with a smirk and a nod toward the jury box before turning his head to Judge Rupert, who scowls virulently at the witness. "I mean, I don't know why. Maybe, I'm just special."

"*'You don't know why. Maybe, you're just special.'*" Mr. Erickson repeats while reaching for the manila folder on the banister of the witness stand. He opens the file containing the famously bloody photos of June and Jazz and flips through the dreadfulness. From musicians to mush, the murder and gore depicted in these photos has been painfully plastered on every major press outlet in the world. "What about *your pictures*? Do you think *your pictures* are special, too?"

"I do, sir. They're *quite* special. Maybe the other paps didn't snap such good flicks. Mine just happened to appear in most of the papers."

"Incredible. They *'just happened to appear'*?" Mr. Erickson continues to repeat Lyle's words, but in a slow, deliberate cadence. He rhythmically questions every nuance of Lyle's statement while beating a critical drum over every syllable. "Is it true you were the only photographer that kept taking pictures during *and* after the attack?"

"No, that's incorrect! The other guys were there, too! It just so happened that I was the closest to June! And I didn't get my camera smashed!"

"Is it true, then, that you were the only one with the stomach to take pictures while a young woman died in front of your camera? And you didn't even help her…"

"How dare you..." Lyle leans back into the witness stand defensively. His hands grasp the arms of his chair and his forehead wrinkles in waves over his eyebrows. "This is a rough business. We capture the moment, we don't alter it! I took pictures in Korea and 'nam! I've seen burned mothers and maimed children! It's just a job to me!"

"You take photographs of burned children and you say *that* is *'just a job'*? I pray that none of the good people of Winniper County have to endure such horror for a paycheck." Mr. Erickson holds the manila folder up in the air, threatening to open the folder, but he is truly unwilling to show the jurors any more gore from the murder of poor June Bethune. He fears he may further implicate his client and arouse the jurors' collective malice. Several news outlets ran the story that Duke can be seen in one of the photos. Mr. Erickson doesn't want to give Lyle or his treasure trophies any more of the spotlight. His only aim is to destroy Lyle's credibility or, at least, give the appearance of a genuine effort to do so. "And how much money have you made in connection with the incident? Not just from the pictures, but all the interviews as a result of testifying in three murder trials. How much have you made from your involvement in June's murder?"

"Objection! Your Honor, the witness is not on trial!" John Allen yells from the prosecution table, rising to his feet and straightening his suit jacket. "The revenue that Mr. Hutchins has received is irrelevant!"

"I disagree, Your Honor," Mr. Erickson retorts and steps to the middle of the courtroom, turning his arms wide to the jury and then staring out to the gallery. He prepares to make his point to the masses rather than to the judge, who yawns through the attorney's obvious theatrics. Presumably preparing to speak to the judge, yet, mainly facing the audience of the court, Mr. Erickson inhales the anticipation and exhales his explanation. "The money gained from these pictures speaks directly to the witness's state of mind and his motivations for giving his testimony, today. If the witness has already earned substantial revenue from his testimony in other trials and the photos he took of the incident, then the court should know whether or not the witness plans to earn even more revenue from June's death after appearing *again* as a *witness* in *another* murder trial. Mind you, Your Honor, and, with respect, I'm not suggesting the witness is exploiting the victim's death for his own personal gain, but rather, I'm merely asking the court to consider all the possible motivations for the witness giving his testimony here, today!"

"Well...you are right, Mr. Erickson. The witness admits that he has profited from his photos of the incident, thus his motivations for further involvement in *any potentially profitable proceeding pertaining* to the incident, whether personal, financial, or professional in nature, yes, these motivations and proceedings are, in fact, pertinent to *this trial.*" The judge explains his reasoning swiftly and nods his head; he had already made his decision, but he wanted to take the time to articulate his lengthy ruling so that both the prosecution and defense realize that he, too, understands the mechanical irrelevance of their maneuvering. He stiffly turns his grim, wrinkled face toward Lyle and leans closer to the witness stand, emphasizing his seriousness. "The witness will answer Mr. Erickson's question. To date, how much money have you made from your pictures of the incident, the interviews, and anything else associated with the crimes of this trial here, today?"

"Uh, well it's hard to say how much money I've made, especially from these *particular* pictures." Lyle replies and rests his hands on his chest as he leans back in his chair. He is still proud, although he is growing more defensive the longer he spends in the spotlight. He knows the bright heat of intense scrutiny is coming too close to his center. A promiscuous man of his persuasion always has secrets to protect. "*These pictures* have appeared in numerous magazines, newspapers, and even some prime time television. I'm still collectin' royalties!"

"Again, very impressive, Mr. Hutchins, *'even some prime time television'*, you say? And you're still earning payments; that sounds very lucrative, indeed," Mr. Erickson muses, swiftly re-seizing the reigns of control from the judge and the witness. The skilled defender turns away from the courtroom audience, strolls toward the witness stand, and continues to circle his prey. He takes a moment just to stare intently at Lyle, acting as if he's calculating the appropriate number of moves to an efficient checkmate. "Can you give the court a rough estimate? How much do you charge a newspaper or magazine to run one picture in one article, roughly?"

"Well, *'roughly'*, my usual fee is $2,000, but for *these* pictures...especially the ones of June..." Lyle opens his eyes wide and arches his eyebrows, mentally adding up to a number appropriately close to the truth. He chooses soft words to leaven the harsh reality of a carnivore's livelihood. "I'm a working man like anyone else. When the opportunity presented itself, I took it. On average, I have received at least $20,000...per print...for each of June's pictures."

Lyle hunches his shoulders as he mumbles his asking price. He's *almost* ashamed at the implications of how lucrative his pictures of June's murder have become. A whistle travels over the courtroom along with the realization that any fool with a camera could have become a millionaire with a few quick snaps of a midday massacre.

"Wow, $20,000 per print. That's a very lofty charge, ten times your usual price." Mr. Erickson continues to stroll confidently through the courtroom, walking toward the jury box and glancing from juror to juror. His suspicious glare convinces them that the real heel is the pariah in the witness stand—the advantageous artist. "And your folder has over twenty photos of the incident. So it's safe to say that you've profited a great deal from just these photos, let alone your involvement in June's murder?"

"*My involvement*? I wasn't involved, sir." Lyle bristles nervously, straightening his back and sitting up in his chair. His hands clutch the chair's arms and he visibly clenches his teeth—the good times are over. "I just happened to be there. I didn't do anything wrong. I just did my job, it was them...eh, I mean *him*!"

"*Them*? *Him*? Was it them or him? You seem confused, Mr. Hutchins," Mr. Erickson has suddenly become a chiding serpent, slithering back and forth to accentuate the witness's indecision. "At first, you identified my client as a murderer and *now*, you say *them*. Were you referring to the three other men, as them, the ones who are really responsible for June's murder? Are you and the county attorney just greedy for another guilty conviction, more headlines, and more payoffs?"

Mr. Erickson continues to glance between the jurors, breaking their trust in Mr. Allen's chief witness. As an accomplished architect of reasonable doubt, his words depict the paparazzi as wet silk. Lyle is disgusting to their touch; his presence is unnatural and callous.

"No, sir, I misspoke, I meant Duke. He was there, too. He was the leader!" Lyle points enthusiastically at the defense table where the youngest Winniper heir sits aloof while in the center of a sacrifice. Lyle's intense assertion shoots through his index tip and hits Duke square on the forehead; though, the mute remains silent as he has been since his eighteenth birthday. Within his mind, he knows that he is the new martyr of the Winniper curse; he has accepted his fate because the morbid images of June's dead body haunt him, too. Lyle continues to point at Duke, bending his arm back and forth so that his finger scolds Duke like a disappointed father.

"He was the main one and the other guys were just following *his orders*. He was the ringleader! I saw him!" The finality in his certainty accentuates the conundrum. The witness, who must be on Papa's payroll, acts in accordance with Papa's plan, but the plan no longer seems conventional. Duke's trial and the surrounding spectacle expose the fact that the Winnipers' patriarch is now reckless and homicidal.

"I see, '*misspoke*', you say. Are you aware that my client can't speak? He's been a mute since his late teens. So how could he give these convicted murders any *orders* at all?"

"Uh...um..."

"And before you answer, consider this: you saw my client lead three men to kill his sister, and you didn't snap one clear picture of him even at the scene!" Mr. Erickson boasts jokingly, again grabbing the manila folder from the witness stand and holding it above his head like a well-earned trophy. "But you expect these good, honest Americans to believe that the only defendant *not seen* in these pictures is actually the *ringleader* of the entire crime! That sounds incredibly far-fetched, Mr. Hutchins. How do we know that you did not kill June?"

"Objection!" John Allen yells from his seat, finally hearing enough to warrant some form of reaction, though he's careful to mind his place while Papa's hired gun performs his duty-bound charade. "Your Honor, the defense counsel is being highly argumentative! And, personally, I don't care for his tactics."

"I withdraw the question, Your Honor. My apologies to the court." Mr. Erickson raises his hands sorrowfully and places his right hand over his heart. "I only have one more question for the witness."

Judge Rupert shakes his hand, motioning for Mr. Erickson to proceed quickly, but the defense counsel pauses and allows the tension to build. The jury and court gallery run through a myriad of possible questions, wondering what will be the finale to the first witness's testimony.

"Well, go on." Lyle barks impatiently, anxious to exit the courtroom and run into whatever bar or bath house he can find first. "What is your question?"

"Oh, I'm sorry, Mr. Hutchins." Mr. Erickson apologizes with a smirk, knowing his prey has fallen into a well-placed trap. "I don't want to keep you from *another payday.*"

"Keep the commentary to yourself, counsel." Judge Rupert commands sternly, finally finding a moment to become relevant. Mr. Erickson's bountiful Southern charm is beginning to weigh on the judge's stalwart nerves, but the defense attorney apologetically raises his right hand as if he is still in a classroom, asking for the teacher's indulgence.

"Pardon me, Your Honor. I will not delay any further." Mr. Erickson steps closer to the witness stand, still smiling over his subtle ploy. "Now, listen, Mr. Hutchins, my question for you is actually quite simple…and I'd like for you to take a moment and answer as honestly as you've answered every question, today. Mr. Hutchins…do you have any remorse?"

The air rushes from the room again and another pause falls over the court as the jurors and citizens experience an uncomfortable reengagement with the moral toll once forgotten. The dead corpse in the ground transforms into the lovely musical spirit that once was and never will be again. Surely, the witness will show some contrition for his role, or lack thereof, during the demise of June's mortal form.

"*R-r-remorse?*" Lyle stammers, reverting to Mr. Erickson's own repetitive tricks, yet, in this use, the stutters only invoke more suspicion. Within these crucial moments, the jury begins to assume the witness's falsehood, taking note of his continual inability to face his true emotions. He won't admit the nightmares and confront the anguish he feels after witnessing the murder of June Bethune. "Remorse, for what? I told you, I didn't do anything!"

"That's precisely the point, Mr. Hutchins, *you didn't do anything!*" Mr. Erickson bellows while repeatedly slamming his fist on the witness stand. "Do you feel any remorse for doing nothing except snap pictures while two people were attacked right in front of you? Do you feel any remorse for profiting from murder?"

Several women in the gallery gasp at Mr. Erickson's directness, shocked at the defense attorney's candor within the quaint town of Winniper County. His antagonistic tone points the insatiable lynch mob toward a new neck. Lyle's remorselessness makes him a potential substitute for the town's ire; their attention turns completely from Duke to the man in the witness stand. Lyle Hutchins is the true criminal, the real provocateur, the prosecution's *suspicious, star witness.* Feeling this new wave of inquisition, Lyle pauses, contemplating what may be his last words before being condemned in the court of public opinion. He soberly questions himself and his profession, forms his resolve, and digs his heels deep into his conscious decisions while accepting their consequences.

"I just did my job. *I don't feel a thing for the people or places I photograph.*"

"*Nothing?*" Mr. Erickson continues to prod, stepping aside to reveal the witness to the jury with a wave of his hand. He is a matador unveiling the bull to the crowd. The jury now sees a broken circle of trust where the photographer's indifference creates a reasonable doubt of his credibility, his morality, and even his salvation. Knowing his Christian Dakota surroundings, Mr. Erickson doesn't miss a gospel triplet; he is in-step with the choir. "You know, Mr. Hutchins, the Good Book says that any man can be forgiven if he is truly remorseful. So if the court will indulge me, I will ask you one more time. Not for me, but for you, to give you once more chance to redeem yourself. Do you really feel any remorse, any responsibility for June's death?"

"*No...none...at...all.*" Lyle answers deliberately, matter-of-factly, and in a wry tone that excludes exception. He chose his words carefully; for the first time in a long time, Lyle is being honest. Another damp pause falls over the courtroom and several minds wish the lynching could happen right now; but, they no longer measure a noose for Duke Winniper at the defense table. Rather, the most malicious members of the town's revenge-seekers measure the dimensions to hang the cruel character in the witness stand. Lyle Hutchins has completed his transformation into a known villain; he is the one who could have stopped the tragedy, but instead, he chose to fulfill a self-defeating paradox—he is the photographer who took such infamous pictures that he made himself famous.

"I told you, I don't feel any responsibility. I did nothing wrong."

"And may God forgive you, Mr. Hutchins, even when you don't deserve it. No further questions, Your Honor." Mr. Erickson shakes his head, steps away from Lyle, and exhales while wiping his brow. He acts as if he is relieved to distance himself from the devil in the witness chair and he marches back toward the defense table like a triumphant warrior. His cohorts on the defense team silently salute their hero for purging the courtroom of this demon—Lyle is the ambivalent exploiter.

"Does the prosecution wish to rebut?" Judge Rupert asks impatiently from atop his bench, motioning his fingers toward the county attorney. His tone singes with indignation; the old man is already growing weary of this formality.

"No, not at this time," John Allen mumbles weakly, allowing the judge's mood to cloud the fact that the county's first eyewitness testimony has been reduced to sewer scum. He glances toward Mr. Erickson as the defense attorney rejoins his team and pats Duke on the shoulder with a bright smile. Thomas III observes the moving parts and he wonders exactly how these pieces will fit together; John Allen and Dennis Erickson seem genuinely engaged in their respective roles, but their acting feels disjointed, disconnected, and distant from the normal, acceptable performances within a Winniper County courtroom.

In normal Winniper County court proceedings, the Winniper-backed side wins every objection, motion, and decision, but, Duke's trial feels oddly competitive. Thomas III questions the limits of this formidable façade. Is the prosecution actually seeking to convict his nephew? Are the motives of the court somehow pure in a decidedly impure environment?

"The witness may step down." Judge Rupert dismisses Mr. Hutchins with the swipe of his hand. "Try to stay away from the press until the trial is over."

Lyle Hutchins rises to his feet, scrunches his nose coyly, and sulks away from the witness stand. He looks over to the jurors and his eyes meet a mutual hatred, the coldness he felt watching June die, the knowing indifference.

∞

She saw death in sight and found no compassion in its finality. How could he take pictures while watching the angel die? He asked himself this question once, and now it's the only question the jury really cares about.

∞

They have forgotten to wonder who killed June Bethune. Her death is a side note, a circumstance of this wretched man's villainy. As Lyle sifts through the center aisle, he cautiously glances around the courtroom for any lone attackers. Their eyes throw daggers into his body; the Winniper County upper crest crowd believes he is more dangerous than Duke. If the fourth generation prince is found guilty, Lyle Hutchins will still suffer more in life than if he were hanged outside, today. To the Winniper County citizens who continue to grieve over June while sufficiently aggrandizing her scandalous, yet beloved nature, the pariah who snapped the final pictures of a life snuffed too soon must suffer until his last breath. And even beyond, they pray that he has an especially fiery reservation in the afterlife.

"The prosecution may call its next witness," Judge Rupert instructs, weakly waving his hand to push the process along. No doubt, he is dreaming of lunch; the disgruntled grump's stomach growls under his black cotton robe.

"The prosecution calls…um…J-Jazz…Jazz Lancaster." John Allen stutters in the moment; murmurs begin to fill the courtroom as the doors open with a loud creak. The tension releases through the hinges and old oak, crackling fragilely and echoing throughout the gallery as the back row press mongers clamor with more and more intrigue. The prosecution spared no expense for this morning's drama; the Winniper County police officers form a copper and white fleet that enters the courtroom and positions armed lawmen throughout the main aisle and the gallery rows. Somewhere nearby, Sheriff Cobb, Jr. listens to the proceedings on a police radio and gives directions to his subordinates. He, of course, follows Papa's orders. As a new consideration, Winniper County's widely publicized witness protection efforts must help absolve every county official from the guilt and liability surrounding the original attack.

∞

Duke, Earl, and the guys had their chance to kill him, but they didn't succeed.

∞

So now, Jazz must live, in order to pacify the public outrage. A Catawba nurse, petite in form and purpose, emerges through the doorway and pushes a wheelchair-bound man down the aisle with several officers in tow. Berthine and Charles follow Jazz closely, but Thomas III struggles to see them clearly through the armed guards' highly orchestrated entrance. The sheriff's most trusted henchmen shield Jazz from any possible ambush, although the damage has already been done. The twenty-seven-year-old musician is a shell of his former self.

White gauze covers his still brittle limbs; his casted right leg extends over a perched lift that stretches his leg in front of him. Even more bandages cover his left arm from his shoulder to his elbow. A dead man who was brought back to life with nothing to live for, his limbs remain motionless from his toes to his head. He's cold and the uncovered parts of his skin tremble unnoticeably as the crisp September air bristles into the courtroom through the open window near the defense table.

Thomas III stares at Berthine and his other nephews, who still do not know their bloodline or their entire family; yet, even with battered eyes, bruised skin, casted legs, and bandaged arms, Jazz still resembles Teresa. Thomas III wonders how June and Jazz never noticed their similarities; maybe, they also could not see past their skin, or, maybe, they only saw deeper.

∞

After Kenny abandoned Teresa's white children, Thomas III visited Charles, Jazz, and Lucy at Berthine's cabin while living with Christina, June, and Duke at the Winniper family's mansion. Even though they have different shades of skin, all Teresa's children have always looked, and often acted, like their mother.

∞

Teresa still haunts Thomas III through her children and her ghost always appears during times of anxiety. When Thomas III sees Teresa's ghost, she looks as though she hasn't aged since her death. Her face, skin, and clothes remain within the moment he ran her blue Spoister off the road and pushed it into a tree. That look of confusion and betrayal, she stabs him through his heart every time and his very soul wishes that he could have died for her.

∞

She left him in a world where they weren't able to be siblings; duty called and questioned their devotion.

∞

Through the years, Thomas III has noticed his skin loosen, his forehead has become wrinkled, and his hair has grayed with age, but, Teresa's ghost still wears the turquoise sundress from the day she visited him at the market.

∞

Papa made sure that she would show up for free food sooner or later; the orders were clear at every level.

∞

Even as a ghost, she has tormented her brother and begged him to compensate for the years she never lived. She wants him to feel the horror of watching her family mourn, suffer, and implode without her.

Her crystal eyes constantly question and beg Thomas III to explain, confess, and wipe his soul of all the misery he has caused in the name of a name. The Winniper family's oil, power, and wealth will never be enough to rest her soul. Years ago, Thomas III realized that he can't escape Teresa or his deeds. Whether through her ghost or her children, her eyes will always watch him and wonder why. And those big, blue, Winniper eyes have remarkably intuitive vision that can see into anyone and send Teresa's daggers directly to his soul.

He will die a thousand spiritual deaths before his corpse ever feels the inside of a coffin. Every time he sees a family member, even his own daughter, those eyes will accuse him and wonder why. They'll carve out every nuance of his lies, seeking an inherited depth from their bloodline. The Winniper family has survived and thrived on the ability to see what *it is* for what *it is not*.

∞

The Native American nurse continues to push Jazz down the aisle, flanked by officers. A young, white debutante near the back row screams, "I love you, Jazz!" The crowd erupts into cheers and jeers as Judge Rupert bangs his gavel and points toward several teenage men. They hoot and clap for their fallen icon. Jazz is a brown bird with a broken heart; his beak works fine, yet he can no longer sing.

"Officers, please remove those gentlemen and that young woman!" Judge Rupert orders contemptuously, angered by the repeated outbursts. The county officers hustle to muffle another loud scream and the audience wonders what will happen to these raucous fans. If Sheriff Cobb, Jr. is in a good mood, he may allow the miscreants to listen to the proceedings outside, while they wait for another chance to re-enter the melee. If the sheriff is in a foul mood, he may personally lock these *agitators* into concrete and iron holding cells within the police headquarters. Sheriff Cobb, Jr. could wait a day or two just to file charges and beyond that, the judge could deny bail and these outspoken citizens may not see the light of day until some far away court date in the unknown future.

"Please, God, let the judge call for a recess, soon. I need a bathroom break." Thomas III prays quietly and pinches his thighs together while squirming in his seat and feeling Tilly's head tilt on his shoulder. She listens silently and looks ahead toward the judge, refusing to acknowledge the Sioux grandson she has never known. Like many, Tilly blames Jazz for June's demise; he lured her from Winniper County and corrupted her morals for the world to see.

Dr. Morten, Jr. is the only living soul outside of the Winniper family who knows the truth, but the entire world feels as though they do. Thomas III can sense Tilly's sadness and angst as she leans meekly into his side, passing her despair through his jacket until it reaches the revolver still holstered within. She reacts to the touch, but relaxes momentarily as Thomas III pats her hand and whispers under his breath. "

Sorry, Papa asked me to bring it for protection." He hopes a recess can alleviate some of the tension in the courtroom. Jazz's testimony has become the most anticipated event in the country and possibly the most publicized event in the history of Winniper County. Since his name appeared on the witness list, the media has hyped and chronicled every potent aspect of the potential plot twists. Even now, Papa grumbles into Olivia's ear, no doubt complaining to his wife about how the media still fawns over Jazz.

∞

The old man had to pay costly overtime wages for the officers and security teams who guarded *the Sioux boy* while he recovered in the hospital; and, in the meantime, the press turned June into a modern Joan of Arc. Kept at the gates of Winniper County Central Hospital, the reporters and word weavers knitted a quilt with June's image among the martyrs of women's rights and social equality. Sojourner Truth, Fanny Mendelssohn, Cleopatra, Harriett Tubman, Bette Davis, Helen of Troy, Queen Elizabeth, and June Bethune stood together in heaven and the media burned their names in effigy for all to see.

Papa often niggled around the mansion, griping over every rumor and gagging on headline after headline. Slowly, he became less concerned with the family's international oil conglomerate. He lamented the fact that, even after her death, June continued to shame him and disgrace the family. The secrets were becoming too much for him to contain; he looked to his heirs and felt only disdain.

∞

Maybe, in her own way, June is haunting Papa while Teresa haunts Thomas III. A security officer opens the pit entrance and ushers the witness and nurse through, while motioning for a few of the other officers to stop Berthine and Charles. As the officers halt her silent coddling, Berthine gasps in audible displeasure, but several officers quickly usher her and Charles into a reserved space within the front row, again, another calculated maneuver. Berthine and Charles wear their Sunday's best, purchased and provided by Lucy and Marcus. The Cashmens still refuse to join the rest of society, especially after the attack. Instead, they have remained within the safety and solitude of Mount Spokane, leaving Berthine and Charles to tend to Jazz without driving each other crazy.

Papa may know Berthine Lancaster better than anyone else in Winniper County. They played together as children. He knows she's liable to tear the entire courtroom down by the walls if she's not given direct access to see "her baby", the youngest of Teresa's Sioux children.

Amidst these secrets and understandings, known and unknown, Papa has given every minion clear instructions about how to proceed during this crucial testimony. Is it far-fetched to assume that one of Papa's little birds flew to Berthine's cabin prior to the trial and tweeted a message into her ear? Why did Mr. Allen save Jazz's testimony for Duke's trial? Without hesitation, the indifferent nurse continues to wheel Jazz forward and she turns his wheelchair so that he sits in front of the witness stand, facing the prosecution table and courtroom audience in the background.

She pats his shoulders softly and whispers into his ear before stepping ever-so-slightly to the side so that she still hovers over his left shoulder. Jazz remains sullen; his face, without emotion or expression, rests still while he prepares to speak his first words to the world since losing his fiancée and abandoning his music. The black bailiff steps forward and presents the Bible under Jazz's right hand. Jazz stares at the book silently for a moment, and then he stretches his fingers weakly and lays them over the cross.

"Do you swear to tell the truth, the whole truth, so help you God?" There is a pause; in which, a hero dies.

"I do," Jazz whispers with a smooth serenity, and softer words have never been spoken; his tone is frail at best. Thomas III doubts his Sioux nephew will survive his testimony. Still on cue, John Allen rises from his seat behind the prosecution table and walks directly toward Jazz.

"Now, uh, good morning, Jazz…"

"*Mister* Lancaster," Jazz interrupts forcefully; an anxious bass emerges within his tone.

"Um, excuse me, *Mister Lancaster*…" John Allen fumbles slightly, dwarfed in the spotlight of an enigmatic celebrity, a well-known heart-throb. Although Jazz is an accomplished artist, he has fallen so far from his social pedestal that he is almost unrecognizable. A king without a throne isn't much of a king at all. Even as a colored musician, most of the public still respected Jazz for his talents; but now, as a crippled hermit, losing two years of his life recovering inside a hospital room, his presence only inspires remorse, guilt, and sadness.

As the courtroom absorbs the intensity of the moment, the ambitious county attorney struggles to maintain his confidence. Mr. Allen feels like a sheepish fan who may need to be escorted from the courtroom, but he inhales deeply and regains his composure. He raises his palms in order to reset his balance and he hangs his head as if he is trying to transmit his sympathy through gestures.

"I apologize for my candor, Mister Lancaster, but I must ask, how are you feeling?"

"Objection!" Ms. Shields shouts from her seat and holds a felt-tipped pen in the air. She hopes to steal some more of the attention for herself. "What is the relevance?"

"Boo! Let Jazz speak!" A press hound calls from the back of the courtroom. A round of cheers, sneers, and hoots follow the outburst.

"Order! Order! Officer!" Judge Rupert bangs his gavel thunderously and motions toward the reporters gathered in the back row. Another shriek echoes over the crowd as more hysteria spreads throughout the courtroom. Several officers descend upon a few scapegoats and throw several pieces of talkative trash out of the judicial dumpster. A few onlookers wonder if the outcasts will wait in a line again tomorrow for another chance to come back. Judge Rupert adjusts his position within his high seat and stares vengefully over the courtroom. "And let me warn every member of the court, *again*: do not disrupt these proceedings. These *loudmouths* are going to jail! Sheriff Cobb, Jr. is waiting across the street at the police headquarters...and he has lots of South Dakota justice for anyone who disturbs my courtroom!"

Ah, the end of a mystery: those who cannot contain their excitement will fill the jail cells in the Winniper County Police Station, a dreadful concrete relic from the early 1900s.

"Your Honor, the county attorney is pandering to the court, almost inciting a riot. The witness's well-being has no relevance!" Ms. Shields reclaims the court's attention while standing from her seat in her business suit and heels, jutting her hips to the right, and reminding the male jurors to make *her* happy. "The prosecution is trying to prejudice the jury!"

"Your Honor, I was merely asking a compassionate question as a concerned citizen of Winniper County," John Allen begins emphatically; he walks closer to Jazz and waves his hand over the crumpled musician on display. "This man was, and still is, a guest in our beloved town and he was hurt here. I believe many of the Winniper County citizenry share my sentiments when we wish this tragedy had never happened. *We* genuinely care about Mr. Lancaster's well-being like any good Christian should."

"Hang the three others! Duke, too! Justice for June!" Another ruckus erupts in the courtroom and Judge Rupert slams his gavel apathetically. The routine has begun to set within his bones; he's dreaming of lunch and his evening tea. He longs to be alone in his study with his centennial wife devotedly tending to her duties at home.

John Allen soaks up his moment of religious self-righteousness. A few citizens whisper *"Amen"* and quiet murmurs trickle through the rows. The holy exhalations add small slivers of light and force to John Allen's cause. The town's support feels slightly more forgiving; maybe Winniper County is more open-minded than its history may portray. A surviving Sioux native sits before the witness stand, testifying about the murder of his white bride-to-be, and the people express remorse, vitriol, and embarrassment at the crime and the spectacle. Sometimes, fate and circumstances and a few bad apples bring the entire world to the smallest, most remote places. Maybe, indubitably, no community deserves to see its children murdered in the streets.

"Your concern is noted, Mr. Allen, along with the objection from Ms. Shields. And I think most of the people here today agree with Mr. Allen's sentiment," Judge Rupert dribbles proudly, while tucking his gavel under his arm and leaning back in his chair. "Defense Counsel Shields, it is not legally unethical to ask a witness how he or she is feeling, nor is it prejudicial. In my opinion, it is just good ol' fashioned Christian upbringing. Mama Allen should be proud. Ms. Shields, you're overruled!"

"But..."

"Overruled, Ms. Shields! Your Pa' knew when he was licked!" Judge Rupert bellows and swipes his hand as if swatting a fly. Ms. Shields stamps her foot tersely like a pouting child; she hastily pleats her dress and sits amongst her colleagues without further protest. Her light dims ever-so-slightly. All along, Jazz has remained apoplectic within his wheelchair, wrapped in his bandages. Over two years after the attack, his body remains shattered and he is still in constant pain without steady morphine drips.

The prosecution required that he give his testimony under completely lucid circumstances, so he stares ahead, silently agonizing through soreness and dreaming of returning to his hospital bed. His mind desires distance from this reality. Thomas III watches his nephew and, for the first time, he feels empathy for a boy with so much sorrow in his eyes. Jazz suffers for a crime that he did not commit and he languishes inside a life that he did not choose.

"Thank you, Your Honor." John Allen regains the floor, by waltzing across the courtroom and standing next to Jazz. The county attorney makes a show of his concern, lightly patting the top of Jazz's right hand. The musician's weak, thin wrists peek through his arm bandages, exposing his once magical hands.

∞

A lead pipe broke his forearms, according to the papers and the nightly news. One of the perpetrators used the same weapon to shatter Jazz's kneecaps, as well. June fell under the punishment of a bat and an unidentified object. Mr. Allen argued that the respective weapons indicated that multiple attackers targeted Jazz and June separately. The extent of June's injuries supported the prosecution's theory, but, as Dr. Morten, Jr. explained to the Winniper News Gazette, the blunt force trauma from the assorted weaponry began to look similar after repeated blows. The jagged flesh wounds from the laundry cylinder made the only distinct marks; the serrated weapon ripped pieces of June's skin from her back. An animated simulation portrayed the attack on the national news and showed both musicians' wounds developing like a landscape painting. June's skull looked like breaking glass. Her bones cracked in small fractures before crumbling under remorseless blows.

Because the medical examiner announced June's passing while Jazz still teetered upon the brink, her death photos became fair game for instant ratings. Some primetime news outlets chose to blur Lyle's more graphic, postmortem photos, but they all ran some version of the expose: the starlet with a head wound spilling open in the street. Amongst the photos in the court folder, the most lurid originals show the back of June's skull as a brain matter casserole. Her bones, membranes, and blood appear in all shades of red, white, black, and blue. In one fatal instance, Lyle Hutchins captured the new American flag. June became a symbol of morbid freedom in a death-or-equality state.

Jazz lay next to her, coma-bound with his eyes wide open, watching June die while remembering a moment when he told her that he would protect her, and he knew, then, the reality that he had failed.

∞

These considerations collide with the present day trial and Thomas III feels another chill run up his spine, sensing Teresa's ghost is near, watching her sons from nearby. There's a brief flash in his cognition and he sees his sister's ghost weeping in a corner of the courtroom, crying tears for her sons that they don't know enough to cry for themselves. All silent, Charles, Duke, and Jazz remain equally detached. They stare ahead of themselves, avoiding any eye contact. They mirror one another, in a way, yet, Thomas III feels he is the only one who notices the resemblance. He understands why Jazz and June never realized their twinship; who would ever believe they were even related? Still relishing the spotlight of the young man's celebrity, John Allen leans down to look into Jazz's sullen, brown eyes.

"Now...um, Mr. Lancaster, I ask, again, and sincerely, as any good Christian American should, how...how are you feeling?" Mr. Allen asks sweetly as he delicately grabs the top of Jazz's exposed right hand. He feels Jazz's tendons tense under his grasp and the prosecutor fears that the young artist may shatter from unseen fissures—maybe the medical advisors and reconstructive surgeons that Papa publicly hired and privately chartered from around the country did not piece the delicate icon back together completely.

"How do I look like I'm feeling?" Jazz retorts sarcastically, biting into John Allen's public and transparent concern. "And I want to correct you again, sir..."

"Excuse me?"

"You said *'I was, and still am, a guest in Winniper County'*. But, I'm not a guest at all. I was born and raised here, in the old sharecroppers' village with all the other poor people you love to forget about. We're not guests. The Sioux your people slaughtered weren't guests. My family was born here even before June's family. We're the real citizens. If she's your town's daughter, then I must also be a son. And how could a son ever be a guest in his own home?"

"I-uh...I understand, I-uh...*Mister* Lancaster. I apologize, again. I misspoke...and, uh...I'm sorry." Mr. Allen concedes contritely as he stands upright and adjusts his crimson necktie. Once again, he feels minimized by this celebrity witness. Usually, he can operate as the star and main attraction; but here, in the midst of this historic testimony, John Allen struggles to keep his footing. The county attorney takes his time and turns slightly to Dennis Erickson at the defense table; the two nod and acknowledge the futility in their performances. Again, they have their orders. Mr. Allen then raises his head toward the courtroom audience and looks over Papa and the masses packed into the dimly lit courtroom. "And I apologize to the court, Your Honor. I just can't help feeling remorseful...I just want to express my sincerest condolences on behalf of the people of Winniper..."

"You don't speak for me! I wish they'd have killed that Redskin!" a Dakota rebel squeals from within the rows and several aghast heads turn to search for him.

"Order! Order! Officer!" Judge Rupert shouts tepidly, pointing again for the man's removal. The process is noticeably beginning to wear on the judge's beleaguered face. He is a broken record who speaks from memory and collects scratches with each turn. "One more outburst and I will clear the courtroom! We'll drag this testimony out all week!"

The judge's voice booms authoritatively and his throat clogs from the force within his tenor. He begins to cough and an inner excitement rises in Thomas III's stomach. He imagines a door that Judge Rupert might unlock. His mind dreams of a possible mistrial, a fast dismissal, and the Winniper family could return to their quaint and powerful lives. Duke could regain his position as the future heir, and Thomas III could leave Winniper County with his daughter. Unfortunately, reality begins to set in as the judge catches his breath and sips a healthy gulp from his lukewarm coffee. Thomas III ends his hopeful daydream, but even a short recess would give him time to ask Papa why Lyle Hutchins identified Duke as June's killer. If the fix is in, then why does the plan seem broken?

"Your Honor, please do not clear the court," John Allen pleads, raising his palms defensively and scanning the jurors' faces. "I don't want Jazz to bear a lengthy recess. I promised him only a few questions. God forbid, he would have to leave his hospital bed to testify more than once."

Mr. Allen calmly explains his courtesy while conveniently forgetting to mention the heavy expenses incurred by the parade of police officers assigned to protect Jazz. The heavily armed guards still line the walls and the main aisle of the courtroom gallery, prepared for anything more than a shouting fool. John Allen feigns his compassionate consideration in order to hide the hurtful indignation of his politically minded motivations. He's spent the trial's budget for a show. He never intended to expend any resources on substantive justice, because that would cost him more than any amount of money can buy.

"I agree, counsel." Judge Rupert nods his head and clears his throat, still recovering from his louder outburst. "I dare say that it would be a further injustice to have the witness removed from his care any longer than necessary. I would hope, for his sake, that we can continue without further interruption."

The judge scans the courtroom, awaiting an antagonistic sentiment from anyone in the gallery. Most sit quietly, continuing to salivate over the trial's spectacle. They awe over Jazz's appearance and whisper about Papa's facial expressions, all without any personal investment in Duke's fate. Sadly, very few actually care what happens to him, personally.

"I'd also like to add," Mr. Erickson begins as he rises from his seat at the defense table, "it is also the defense's profound hope that we may continue without interruption. We have already agreed to limit our questioning of this witness, due to his physical condition. I believe the good people in attendance should pay homage to the memory of dear June Bethune by allowing her loved one to testify. I…"

"Mr. Erickson, do you have any objection?" Judge Rupert interrupts the lead defense counsel, raising his wrinkly hand with his palm open as if he expects Mr. Erickson to pay him for wasting the court's time.

"Uh," Mr. Erickson hesitates queasily, and he turns to his co-counsel, arching his eyebrows. "No, I don't, Your Honor. I just…"

"Then sit down so we may continue with the testimony. Officers, please continue to remove and arrest anyone who disturbs these proceedings." Judge Rupert delivers his orders brashly and wags his finger over the courtroom like a disappointed grandfather. He realizes the caricature that he has become and shakes his head in diminution. "Mr. Allen, please proceed."

"Thank you, Your Honor." John Allen turns on his heels and opens his arms widely. All the eyes in the courtroom fall upon the county attorney while he positions himself between Jazz and the jury box. Mr. Allen takes a step toward Jazz and kneels next to his wheelchair. The county attorney's mannerisms continue to portray his sympathy for the forsaken star caught within the media's eyes. The boy fell in love, watched his love die and, now, he must recount the horror for a courtroom audience. Mr. Allen leans closer, but he whispers loudly enough for the jurors and judge to hear. "Are you okay, Ja-uh, Mr. Lancaster? Can you still testify?"

"Let's get this over with," Jazz growls, staring back at John Allen like he's holding a magnifying glass and aiming the sun at an ant. He hopes he can burn a hole through the attorney's center. Mr. Allen backs away from Jazz slightly, and gives the artist and the coming questions space to breathe.

"Uh…right. Well, Jazz, can you tell the jury what happened on the morning of August 18, 1966?" John Allen asks and gestures toward the jury, preparing the children for a bedtime story.

"Four animals tried to kill me and my fiancée," Jazz answers in a simple, monotone decree and the courtroom curdles in response to his bluntness. How the truth hurts in cold blood, the harshness; how matter-of-factly the victim recalls his nightmare in one statement. His eyes dart directly toward Duke and another murder takes place. The courtroom watches Jazz imagine a dagger slicing across Duke's throat. His aggression is real and the audience watches the fantastical violence, but no one even cries for help. "They're animals because I can't even call them men for what they did. June is…she *was* an angel. I want these animals to hang or burn or whatever you do in this godforsaken town…all of them, including Duke, deserve to die."

Ms. Shields raises her hand to begin an objection, but Dennis Erickson reaches out to stop her with his left hand and places his right index finger over his lips. He then taps the top of his Monte Blanc watch and smiles before looking back to Judge Rupert, who also checks the clock against the adjacent wall. Mr. Erickson, like the judge, has a strict snack schedule; and as the old man becomes hungrier, he also becomes prejudicially irritable. Mr. Erickson assumes that Judge Rupert will begin to hold a grudge for poorly timed objections in a farce trial.

"I-I-I'm truly sorry for your pain, Mr. Lancaster. I…" John Allen pauses and takes a moment to appear affected by Jazz's tone. The uncultured savage's brutish delivery must fluster the delicately crafted morals of Mama Allen's baby boy. "And at this point, I'm even sorry for repeating how sorry I am, but again, I-I just need you to be more specific about the events. Can you please describe what happened, as best you can, for the jury?"

Again, Mr. Allen waves to Jazz's most important fans in the jury box and their eager ears perk up in anticipation of an unpublished piece of tabloid dirt. Oh, how badly they desire a morsel that has not already been feltched by the press.

"Yes, please, allow me to…*be more specific*," Jazz begins grouchily. He glares between the prosecutor, the jury, and the faces in the courtroom. He detests the public forum; the stage is long gone and June is never coming back. "June and I were grabbin' some tea at the AC. June said she went there as a kid. I never went there because they didn't allow any coloreds when I was young. We were visitin' home because June wanted to tell her grandparents about the wedding. She said it'd be different, but I knew how they would treat us…"

Jazz stares intently at Papa and allows his indignation to sink in. The boy despises the air of South Dakota; he feels sickened by the hypocritical humidity that smothers his senses. Winniper County is both cold and warm, offering disproportionate perceptions of race, society, and finance. Even with so much hate for Winniper County, Jazz still does not know his complete connection to the land or his family. His investigators told him how the Winnipers killed the Sioux and he read about the Ghost Dance War in a history book, but he still doesn't know what happened. Thomas III ponders how Teresa's youngest son would react if he learned that his mother was white and June was actually his twin sister.

"I understand your frustration, Jazz, uh, excuse me, *Mister* Lancaster." Mr. Allen empathizes while moving away from the musician, so that the jurors may focus on the surviving victim. His testimony offers an exclusive, close-up examination of one of the most interesting and provocative figures of the American 60s. Papa and Mr. Allen want to ensure the jurors have no reason to complain about the show, so that they will decide accordingly, without pause or cause. "Mr. Lancaster, you seem to have had ill feelings about Winniper County even before this incident. Can you explain why?"

"There's no why because it's everything…everything about this place makes me sick. *My home*, we stayed in my mother's cabin for years, afraid to come into town. Now, I see what my mother warned me about. Winniper County feels so *evil* to me, all the anger and hatred," Jazz explains his emotions in more depth than ever. He stares blankly toward the ground just ahead of his feet, still disconnected from the judgmental world around him. "We left for a reason. It just so happens that we met like we were drawn to each other. I wanted to leave as soon as we got here, but June…she wanted to tell her grandparents about the wedding, so we went to see them."

"And did you visit June's grandparents?"

"Yes, we saw them the night before. We went to the family's *castle* for dinner." Jazz glances toward the Winnipers and, for the first time, his eyes connect with Thomas III and Olivia.

Ostensibly, he has no ill-will toward them. He remembers them both visiting his family at Berthine's cabin, but, he sees them as silent co-conspirators, quiet confidants in the plan to destroy his happiness. Forgoing these questions, Jazz aims his eyes and ire back toward Papa and the vengeance in his stare is so potent that the old man is noticeably rattled. Papa adjusts his position and mumbles under his breath. Teresa's ghost paces across the courtroom and scowls at Papa before appearing at Jazz's side. Thomas III can see their sadness and pity; they endure heartache that they are unable to understand, yet they believe Papa could have saved them, their family, and himself.

Still, Thomas III considers how Jazz would react if he learned that the same blood that runs through Papa Winniper also courses through his veins. While forgetting the murder trial, Thomas III softly chuckles at the silliness of their relationships. Jazz and Papa hate each other because neither has been what the other expected him to be; and, neither has ever given the other a chance to be anything but a source of disappointment in his life.

Papa knows about Jazz; he has no excuse except the creed that he learned from his father.

∞

Jazz didn't meet Papa until the night before June's attack, but Jazz hated Papa long before then. If the public learned the whole truth, more people may consider Jazz a victim, some may condemn him as an incestuous pervert, but mostly everyone would crucify Papa and the Winniper family.

∞

"Old Man Winniper's castle is pretty close to my mother's cabin. Me and June grew up about a mile apart, but we had to go all the way to Scapetown to meet. I told June things would never change around here, but she…" Jazz stops speaking and just lingers on his words, refusing to share anymore. He continues to stare at Papa with ill-intentions, fighting back tears through his still eyes. He knows he has answered sufficiently.

"I see…" John Allen walks toward the center of the courtroom while placing his thumb on his chin and contemplating his next, *very important* question. "And who attended the dinner at the Winnipers' home?"

"Just June, her grandparents and me," Jazz responds tepidly, his voice trailing, tightening, and choking during his testimony. "A few servants were there to tend to her grandparents' orders."

"Well, the Winnipers are known for their lavish events. I know personally that they are very hospitable guests. They host many charitable gatherings at their home, but it seems, by your description, that this was a very intimate dinner." John Allen gestures over to the Winnipers and Papa smiles wryly. His lips clench as if wires are pulling his cheeks and forcing him to be the Winniper family's symbol of power and dominance. Thomas III watches his father from the corner of his eye, studying the gestures and trying to mimic the mannerisms that he could never perfect as Mr. Allen continues along his delicate line of questioning. "You and June were two of the most popular figures in American entertainment and you were having a double date with her grandparents, the patriarch and matriarch of one of the wealthiest families in the world. It must have been a *very* special occasion, right?"

"You would think that, when you put it that way, but her family didn't treat us like anythin' special." Jazz counters tersely, causing more commotion in the gallery. His overall attitude elicits angry yells. More disrupters enjoy spontaneous exits with rough police escorts. Jazz lifts his head over the fervor and continues to testify. "I felt like they were ashamed! After all that June accomplished, *without them*, and they still…they still acted like we were some kind of freaks!"

"And tell us, what happened at the dinner?"

"Objection, Your Honor!" Ms. Shields exclaims, speedily rising from her seat without giving Mr. Erickson a chance to grab her leash. "I thought we agreed to limit our questions for *this witness*. What does the dinner have to do with the facts of this trial?"

"It goes to motive, Your Honor! The defendant was not invited to this dinner!" Mr. Allen interrupts, pointing his index finger in the air. "I have witnesses who will testify that Mr. Winniper was so upset after learning about June's engagement and being excluded from this dinner that he plotted to murder his own sister! What happened at that dinner is important to establishing why Mr. Winniper was upset enough to commit the crime he is on trial for today!"

John Allen stands triumphantly in the center of the courtroom. Almost Christ-like, he knows his point is valid and he believes his truth will lead his sheep to salvation. The judge pauses and places his gavel under his chin as he reaches the same conclusion and recognizes Winniper County's legal messiah.

"Mr. Allen, I'll allow this line of questioning for the moment," Judge Rupert concedes, lowering his gavel to the bench and wiping his brow with the right sleeve of his robe. His pale hands shake over his forehead as he collects the thoughts rambling in his head. "Ms. Shields, your objection is overruled. I wish you would..."

The judge murmurs something under his breath and motions for Mr. Allen to continue his spiel. Ms. Shields sits down in a huff. She consistently comes up short in this male-dominated courtroom, but she tells herself to remain strong and vigilant; her time will come.

"Thank you, Your Honor." John Allen continues, securing the court's attention and directing his hands toward Jazz. "Now then, Mr. Lancaster, what happened at the dinner?"

"June told her grandparents that we were engaged." Jazz answers softly, still fighting tears and feelings his fragile bones ache inside his bandages. "We planned to get married when we arrived in Los Angeles..."

"Yes, there was quite a scandal brewing the morning of the incident, when the news broke." The county attorney added, raising his eyebrows toward the audience and then nodding his head toward the defense counsel. "Throughout your career, you and June received death threats, didn't you?"

"Objection!" Mr. Erickson bellows from his seat, confident that his voice will be heard. "He's leading the witness!"

"I withdraw the question, Your Honor," John Allen recants casually, turning away from the defense counsel with a clever smirk. He then walks toward Jazz and changes his facial expression to a grim reflection. "So, June told her grandparents that you two were going to be married. And how did her grandparents react?"

"They just sat there...real quiet...they didn't say or do much of anythin'. At first, I thought her grandmother was just happy to see us. I knew Olivia as a kid. She friend's with my mother, but I never knew who she was really." Jazz continues, glancing at Olivia briefly before returning his focus to Papa. The old man stares back at Jazz, knowing that the town's eyes are upon him. The onlookers question their king's resolve, but he refuses to crack under the pressure of Jazz's intense glare. Thomas III watches Papa rub Olivia's wrists, consoling his wife, their hands concealed behind the timber barrier between the pit and the gallery. Inside, Papa does have a heart, and it beats a little faster as he experiences the same confusion and grief that cause his wife's tears, but he is unable to show his pain.

Olivia observes this brown-skinned man and remembers the wide-eyed boy in Berthine's cabin; once, Jazz was filled with innocence. He experienced pure joy within the simplicities of arguing over a guitar with his brother; but now, Jazz stares at the Winnipers with such hatred that Thomas III believes his nephew will never be able to love the people he despises so much.

"June's grandfather wanted us to stay in their mansion. Said he would have to make arrangements and handle the press and things. It was a nice idea, but, we had gigs, interviews, a whole thing planned. We just wanted to tell them, we didn't expect them to even come to the wedding. Our life was such a circus, and even now, it's hard to remember and separate fact from fiction. So much has been said in the media. I try not to watch TV, but that's all I can do in the hospital. I just started gettin' my head right a few months ago, but my body...everything...everything hurts...and I still can't play..."

Jazz lowers his head and looks to the pine floor; his sorrow weighs down his spirit. He feels shame for his inability to access his previous talent and his sadness spills through his words. He is a lost man without vision or purpose.

"Indeed, I can understand wanting to avoid the news, Mr. Lancaster. Your relationship with June has been the subject of much gossip and tabloid fodder over the years." The county attorney steps away from Jazz and pivots so that he can aim his questions toward the jury. He wants to make sure the story continues to captivate their eager ears. "Do you know if June's family members were fans of your music? Did they approve of your *professional* relationship?"

"I-I don't know about all of 'em. I can't remember so well. Olivia showed us a scrapbook with news articles and pictures. She said Duke made it." Jazz darts his eyes toward Duke, who still sits in a daze. Either, he is unwilling or unable to make eye contact with anything, except a wayward fly on the one of the window seals. "I don't know if I believe her; he looks too stupid to make anything. Only beautiful people make beautiful things...and look at him. June was the best thing in his life and he destroyed her."

"Uh huh, but you say, June's grandmother told you that Duke Winniper had made the scrapbook?" John Allen asks a copycat question, deliberately attempting to waste time while he casually walks toward the prosecution table where his minions wait obediently. When he reaches a large, cardboard box positioned symmetrically with the edges of the table, he begins to rummage through the insides, dramatically delaying the magician's final prestige. "Did she mention how he collected the scraps…the uh…*articles* and…*photos?*"

"Yes, she did. She said that June sent him pictures that we took or articles from overseas. June rarely talked about any of them, but… I think she just knew I didn't like her family." Jazz recounts with a brief smile that disappears before its fruition. For a moment, he remembers how well she knew him, and then he realizes that she's gone forever. This is the perpetual sorrow of his life; yet, he must endure, if only to receive *some form* of justice for her. "She'd call them from time to time, but…she didn't feel as close to them anymore. She was never that close with her grandparents or her sister and Duke couldn't talk on the phone. So I think June started sending the clips as another way to communicate with him."

"What do you mean by, *'another way to communicate'?*"

"He's a mute. My sister once was…so I know. It's hard to communicate with someone like that. They can't talk like regular folk. You have to find other ways to communicate like gestures or pictures."

"Oh, yes, I see…" John Allen realizes that his theatrics are beginning to become noticeably evident as he continues to carefully pilfer through the medium-sized cardboard box while barely listening to Jazz's answers. He could have easily delegated this responsibility to one of his assistants, but, in a farcical trial, there's only so much fake glory to share. Finally, Mr. Allen finds the rabbit and pulls a protruding brown-framed binder from the cardboard box. The binder looks like an overstuffed enchilada; newspaper clippings and pictures explode from the pages. Mr. Allen struggles to hold the dense binder; he twists his arms hurriedly and drops the book onto the prosecution table with a deep thud. "Whew…Mr. Lancaster, if you can, is this Duke Winniper's scrapbook?"

"I can't tell," Jazz scoffs and curls his frail fingers into his pale brown palm, motioning for Mr. Allen to bring the binder toward his wheelchair. The county attorney stares at the bursting scrapbook and then glances back to Jazz, surmising his best options—a hernia or a moment of embarrassment for the superstar. Mr. Allen nods surely and hustles toward Jazz while glancing to his right and smiling widely at the jurors. He is a true master of ceremonies.

"If the court will indulge me..." Mr. Allen croons in order to buy time as he nudges the nurse out of the way and grabs the back of Jazz's wheelchair. He pushes the former star toward the prosecution table like they're starting the lamest push-cart race ever. Mr. Allen unmasks his juvenile joviality for a moment too long; he exposes himself as a playful fan. Maybe, he's still not ready to excel within the discipline and decorum of the Winniper County spotlight. When they edge closer, the toes on Jazz's extended right leg touch the oak table, Mr. Allen motions over the binder with a triumphant wave. "Mr. Lancaster, is this Duke's scrapbook?"

"A little closer, please..." Jazz taunts, nodding toward his casted right leg that prevents him from inching closer to the table. Mr. Allen grimaces, feeling his back tense, but he promptly twists and turns the wheelchair to the right, so that Jazz may observe the scrapbook near his left shoulder.

"How's that, Mr. Lancaster?"

"Much better...well...yes...uh huh, it does look like Duke's scrapbook."

"Objection, Your Honor!" Ms. Shields howls, still unwilling to accept her subordinate role within the Winniper County court system. "How could the witness know whether this book belongs to my client? The witness already stated that my client was not present at the dinner! He's never spoken to my client. The two have still never even met!"

"We have met...*indirectly*," Jazz interrupts sharply before looking at Duke and narrowing his eyes. "Do you remember, Duke? You and your sisters started fighting at Teezy's bar in Scapetown. That was the day June and I met and she told me how much she couldn't stand being a part of your family."

"Your Honor, this is all a part of *this witness's* testimony!" John Allen retorts, forgetting Jazz at the prosecution table and sauntering toward the judge's bench. "Mr. Lancaster has taken the oath and sworn to tell the truth! Your Honor, the jury has the responsibility to determine the accuracy and importance of his testimony, but he has the right to answer a question pertaining to motive and cause in as much detail as pleases the court."

"Indeed. The jury may determine the voracity of the testimony, but the witness is also clearly capable of giving his version of the events and the evidence presented here in court." Judge Rupert explains his reasoning flatly, although he is happy to include himself within this meaningless process. He's already on the winning side, whoever that might be. "Once again, Ms. Shields, you're overruled. And Ms. Shields, I would recommend you review your legal training before your next objection."

"But, Your Honor? That's a highly prejudicial comment!" Ms. Shields protests as she becomes more frustrated at the judge's continued abeyance. Usually, her curves and intelligence combine to intoxicate most of the members of a courtroom; but, in this predetermined play, she regrets the size of her confined role. "I move for a mistrial on the grounds..."

"Watch your tone, little lady. There will be no mistrials here, today. Now sit down before you embarrass yourself further." Judge Rupert chastises her emphatically, raising his gavel in an odd, paternal threat. Ms. Shields sees her demanding father in the judge's behavior and she obeys instinctively, cowering into her chair. Her reddening face absorbs the insult of being treated as an obsolete, feminine ornament. Feeling the train begin to skip on the tracks, Judge Rupert points his finger toward John Allen in hopes of resuming the approved protocol. "Without further delay, Mr. Allen."

"Thank you, Your Honor." The county attorney adjusts his suit jacket and regains his rhythm as he walks back to Jazz, points confidently at the scrapbook, and brings the courtroom's focus back to his line of questioning. "Now Jazz...er, uh, excuse me, Mr. Lancaster, can you tell the jury and Counsel Shields *why do you believe* that this scrapbook belonged to Duke Winniper?"

"Um, like I said…June's grandmother showed it to us at dinner. She said he made it and June sent him the clips so, one plus one is still two, right?" Jazz describes his inference while glancing over to Olivia and studying the tearful woman he once believed was just a family friend to Berthine. Although she has aged along with his adoptive mother, he sees that Olivia's spirit has also changed.

Once she was a blessed benefactor, Berthine's welcomed guest who would save them from the doldrums of their isolation within the sharecroppers' village; but now, she's a mysterious, co-conspirator in a web of lies. She's a white racist who no longer speaks to his Sioux mother. The two women completely ignore each other in the courtroom; yet, maybe, they are both just following orders. Olivia remains curiously devoted to her husband, but she weeps pitifully as if she never had any way to prevent this outcome. Jazz continues to stare at her while she sobs softly into Papa's shoulder.

"I don't know what to believe about dear Olivia anymore. Don't even know why my mother was her friend in the first place."

"Uh, well…uh, Mr. Lancaster, I know this is difficult and *very personal* for you given your history with the Winniper family." John Allen empathizes somewhat in order to transition to an approved line of questioning. He's permitted to ask about the scrapbook, but not Mrs. Winniper's relationship with Berthine's family; he tips his head and begins to pull Jazz away from the prosecution table. The Catawba nurse steps to the left side of the witness stand, next to the black bailiff; the two remind Berthine of her parents. The nurse stretches her thin neck to look over Jazz periodically, searching for any signs of stress or pain.

After positioning Jazz in front of the witness stand, Mr. Allen resumes his ringmaster performance in the center of the courtroom. He looks over to the jury and opens his arms wide as if he's going to hug the entire courtroom.

"Now, Mr. Lancaster, please tell the distinguished members of the jury, why, even though Duke Winniper lived at the home, why *do you think* he wasn't present at that dinner?"

"Well, I *think*…her grandparents didn't want to celebrate our engagement. June kept asking about Duke and Christina. We even waited for them to show up, but…I *think* the old man wouldn't let them attend." Jazz responds contritely, refusing to speak Papa Winniper's name. "June's grandfather…he doesn't even trust some of the people in his own family."

"And did you find that odd that June's adult siblings did not attend the dinner?" John Allen expounds in rhythm, ignoring Papa's role, as instructed. He places his index finger to his chin while pondering his question. "Why would June's thirty-five year old brother, a grown man, allow himself to miss this celebration and not make an attempt to see her, if he cared for her so much that he made a scrapbook filled with her accomplishments?"

"Maybe he was jealous. He's just like the rest of them. They never supported us; they wanted us to fail. They always tried to force June to come back here." Jazz answers meanly, but he begins to shake his head in confusion, searching his memory. "I remember…June was so upset. After so many years, she thought her family would be…*different*. But, at that dinner, they still treated her like they were ashamed of her. She couldn't stop crying that night at the hotel. The airport was closed in the morning so we waited. I wish now…that we had taken a train…or gotten a car service. We could have left before…"

Jazz fights back tears and glances desperately toward Papa, who remains unchanged and unfazed. Papa is a powerful man who was raised in the public eye while preparing to overlord a private and evil inheritance. Garnered from stolen land, the oil money permeates his aura; his wrong will always feel right, but he has no other option except to rule with prejudice.

Olivia crumbles into her husband's left arm, sobbing into her handkerchief and holding his wrist. Her weight, dampened with tears, forces Papa to feel the sorrow that he caused. She has lost her resolve, her pride, and her will; she can no longer protect herself from pain that she cannot avoid. Years ago, Mrs. Winniper experienced the grief of losing her firstborn; and after witnessing so many other young family members perish, her only consolation exists in sharing her pain with its lead architect—her husband.

To Olivia, Papa is the craftsman of much of their present tragedy. He has caused more death than his father's massacre of the Ghost Dance Sioux during which the Winniper family secured their oil empire.

∞

Thomas, Sr. instructed his son to kill his family *for his family*, so Olivia never allowed her husband to feel guiltless for following his father's orders. Before he killed Teresa, Olivia tried to prevent Thomas III from following the lessons of his murderous patriarchy; but, after she learned that her son had killed her only surviving daughter, well, she had very few words for Thomas III or Papa. Silence and success consumed the Winniper family's mansion, but since Teresa's murder, Olivia has believed that no amount of repentance can ever justify her men's murderous methods and their maniacal means.

"So what happened once you realized that June's brother and sister were not coming to dinner?" Mr. Allen continues to circle Jazz while taking periodic glances toward the jurors, the judge, and the defense table. He wants to ensure that his questions sufficiently entertain his audience. "You mentioned that you were invited to stay as guests at the estate, correct?"

"Not quite. We were invited to stay *as prisoners*." Jazz responds with malice in his tone, but, again, he begins to blink his eyes slowly while he struggles to recall the facts. "We…uh…didn't stay long…after dinner. I don't even remember what we ate. We went back to the hotel…I saw it on a news clip the other day…I just can't remember the name."

"Yes, that's okay. I believe it was the Marriott on Beacon St. But, more importantly, do you remember *why* you and June didn't stay at the Winnipers' mansion?"

"The way her grandfather…I-I don't know…we didn't feel comfortable. He went from not carin' to wantin' to control everything about our engagement. We just didn't want to be around family anymore…hers or mine." Jazz pauses and stares at Berthine and Charles without a smile or expression. He waits for his mind to catch up to his words and he remembers moments lost in the beating, drowned within the events surrounding the brutal attack. "The next day, we decided to never come back to Winniper County. We were going to get married in Hollywood without any of our family members there. We just wanted to leave…"

His voice clenches tightly, his eyes begin to water, and his chest swells under his bandages, but his heavily wrapped limbs and fragile nerves inhibit any movement throughout most of his body. Scattered throughout the gallery, several fans cry for the musician's plight, believing the bird may never fly again.

"I know it's hard, Mr. Lancaster. I promise this will be over soon…" John Allen stands in the middle of the courtroom and waves toward the jury. "I'm sorry we have to go through these difficult details, but, the jury needs to hear *your testimony*. I only have a few more questions. The following day, you and June were attacked while on your way to the airport. Please, tell us, do you see any of the men who attacked you the day after your dinner with the Winnipers?"

"Yes," Jazz answers knowingly, staring at Duke with hatred and disappointment while imagining the life he could have enjoyed with June. "I see that piece of…"

"Can you point him out?" John Allen interrupts timely, hoping to prevent Jazz from becoming a vulgar villain like Lyle Hutchins. The county attorney sheepishly realizes his blunder when he looks at Jazz's bandaged arms. "I mean, uh, can you *tell us* where he is? Where is the man who attacked you and June?"

"He's over there, sir. Her brother…Duke Winniper. He was there. He planned and watched the whole thing happen." Jazz glares at Duke Winniper and mentally murders his mute brother. He stabs him over and over and dreams of bats, knives, and lead pipes descending upon Duke's head. In Jazz's fantasy, he forces Duke to feel every ounce of the desperation that Jazz felt while the attackers murdered June. That fear, that hopelessness is worse than the beating itself, because that terror still haunts Jazz more than his wounds. "Duke and his gang killed June right in front of me. He murdered his own sister, right here, in *Winniper County*! Our home that was never home…this is the place where *you people* raised those murderers!"

The courtroom gasps collectively as Jazz nods his head toward the Winnipers. The judge contemplates banging his gavel, but he hesitates, fearing that his actions could cause more fervor within his already tense courtroom. He feels the entire gallery absorb Jazz's venom and they pause in awe of the truth and the horror.

"Are you sure you saw Duke Winniper kill Ms. Bethune?" John Allen prods, still hoping to keep Jazz in the most positive light. The perceptive, county attorney can also sense Jazz's darkness begin to emanate through his tone. Jazz remains silent before answering; he gags on his own anger. The tension within his muscles causes his face to twinge and Thomas III can see Teresa's torment within his eyes. Her ghost appears through his painful expression when he winces due to physical pain and emotional sorrow. The wounded bird attempts to force himself to sing. Seeing his struggle, Mr. Allen steps closer to Jazz's wheelchair and glances nervously toward the nurse; he worries that his celebrity witness may fold before he can pin the crime on the final donkey. "Mr. Lancaster, are you okay? Can you answer the question? Are you sure you saw Duke Winniper kill his sister?"

"Yes, I'm fine. And yes, I-I'm sure of what I saw. Duke Winniper was with them and they all killed…they…man, they killed June." Jazz confirms with a shiver down his spine and tears cascade down his cheeks as his eyes tremble in rage. "I hope they all fry forever. They deserve to burn in hell."

"Uh, yes, I…uh…I agree wholeheartedly, Mr. Lancaster. And uh…I thank you for your testimony." Mr. Allen stammers silkily, trying to make a smooth exit. He bows his head toward Jazz, quickly surveys the jurors' stunned faces, and smiles toward Judge Rupert. Mr. Allen knows that he has succeeded in delivering a riveting performance that will surely appease the most scandal-hungry members of Winniper County. "Your Honor, the prosecution yields the floor."

Mr. Allen turns and strides back confidently toward the prosecution table, happily satisfied that he will soon send another culprit to death row. Four young men will die in gratifying executions; the sound of a neck breaking during a lynching or the sight of sparks flying during an electrocution often satisfies the public's bloodlust.

As the county attorney takes his seat, the courtroom exhales in unison, but the anticipation remains in the air as the people's eyes dart back and forth, searching for a momentary scandal in this brief intermission between Jazz's candid testimony. Thomas III can feel hot ants crawling across the back of his neck, and he wonders how many of the burning stares actually care about his family or the victimized musician testifying in their midst.

Once a mecca for South Dakota business negotiations, only a few privileged citizens have visited the Winniper Family Estate since June's murder. Outside the estate, several *former* business partners have told Papa that they're afraid of the ghosts. Secretly, Papa worries that he's losing his powerful grip on the community, but he will never show his fears publicly. He would rather die than confess his sins or admit his mistakes; yet, the ghost stories that circulate around the town force the surviving Winnipers to confront their demons.

A few brave visitors to the Winnipers' mansion have shared rumors from frightened citizens who claim to have seen June or Teresa in town. Several citizens have relayed stories of June's ghost playing her guitar in the street, her hair still bloodied from her fatal wounds. Over the past year, the folklore has become truth; the entire town has gorged upon its own gossip while scaring each other with tales of ghosts and scandal.

Winniper County's citizens have witnessed their founding family's deceased kin running wild through their town. Teresa raided a jewelry store, and June appeared amongst a choir during a Nativity rehearsal; suspicion, hysteria, and grief have mixed within the town's water supply. Now, every citizen questions the power structure that allowed June's murder to occur in Winniper County.

The turning tide of public opinion has decreased the financial returns throughout the Winniper family's local holdings, but that's been the case since Teresa's death.

∞

The coincidence and circumstances surrounding her car accident caused a cold skepticism to spread throughout the entire community. The growing national media in the late 40s ran several reports about Teresa's final moments, especially her stop at the Winniper Market. The bread aisle where she last spoke with her brother became something of a memorial. Many remarked how she and Thomas III argued in plain sight. Each version of the story made him look weaker and more inefficient.

Most Winniper County citizens and local reporters respected Teresa for her reckless abandon and her rogue, overseas adventures, forgetting that Thomas III had joined her on these voyages. The town admired her moxie and courage under Papa's oppressive personality. She was a difficult child to discipline because she would never accept the Winniper name as a public burden, although her father treated it as such. But, as much as the town transformed the narrative of her life and death into a tragic legacy, the Winniper County community disregarded her brother as the worm in the family's apple.

Some had their quiet suspicions about his involvement in her death, but Dr. Morten, Jr. claimed the incident was a narcoleptic accident, caused by sleeplessness and, maybe, depression. Tilly and the Winniper family's business partners remained loyal while Thomas III continued to slug through his fortunate, yet inconsequential life.

∞

He is without determination or status. Over the years, following Teresa's death, Papa has refused to either embrace or exile his disappointing son. Thomas III is still a child as much as any other privileged youth. He is the grandson of the county's founder and the son of one of America's foremost proprietors.

And now, another Winniper brother implicated in the death of another Winniper sister, the questions have slowly turned to quiet outrage. The local and national media have increased their microscopes' dimensions. They constantly observe the Winnipers, hawking the family inside and out of their estate.

∞

While peeling through their history, specifically Thomas III's lackluster performance in school and business, the reporters and pundits and analysts built the narrative that the more Papa had implored his son to blossom and protect the family's legacy, the more Thomas III had allowed that legacy to slip through his fingers. The town members told any reporter who would quote an anonymous source that Thomas III was never fit to rule. He held his silver spoon too tightly within his awkward, frail hands. He was too eager to please.

∞

With Duke on trial for murder, the illusion of the Winniper family's honor has now drowned in the Winniper men's murderous sweat and the Winniper women's tormented tears.

"Defense, please proceed," Judge Rupert instructs coarsely, still dreaming of the roasted turkey sandwich his wife packed for his lunch. He contemplates concocting a reason to call for a short adjournment, but, as he watches Ms. Shields shift her hips in her seat, he realizes there may be more pressing entertainment still yet to come.

"Thank you, Your Honor," The defense lawyer rises eagerly, content to have the floor and regain the courtroom's attention. An obvious tactic, Lead Defense Counsel Erickson remains in his chair, leaning back against the gallery rail. His team calculates that the jury will absolve a pretty woman aggressively questioning a weak and wilted witness. Mr. Erickson stares at the jurors and steadies himself so that he is close enough for Papa to whisper into his ear. Ms. Shields slinks around the defense table and prepares to question Jazz. She grins and glares sternly at him, eyeing her prey before placing a drop of feigned compassion in each of her eyes.

"Are you okay, Jazz?" She asks with a mother's sympathetic tone. "Can you continue?"

"You wear a better disguise…*sweetheart*," Jazz whispers as he glances sullenly toward Berthine. "My ma' taught me to respect women, but you're still a lawyer. Let's finish this and call me, *Mister* Lancaster, please."

"Oh, I'm…I'm sorry, *Mister Lancaster*," Ms. Shields apologizes coyly, placing her right hand over her chest while turning toward the jury. "I'm just such a big fan. I guess I'm still a little star struck. I really do love your music."

"You're a *'big fan'*, huh? That's terrific. Where were you when I needed you, huh?" Jazz asks tersely, glaring at the spectators in the gallery as they fidget and mutter amongst themselves. Ms. Shields pauses, taking the temperature of the room and gauging the jury's intrigue before barreling her eyes back toward the broken musician. She remembers his victimhood and she realizes that he is ripe for a good squeeze. This loose screw is already becoming noticeably unhinged.

"What do you mean, Mister Lancaster? Do you hold your fans responsible for what *allegedly* happened to you?"

"Ha…*allegedly*…you're good, *allegedly*." Jazz huffs and rolls his eyes; his hands instinctively tremble, wishing he could press a lit cigarette to his lips and inhale to calm his nerves; but, his bandaged limbs and his internal injuries prevent him from enjoying many of his former pleasures. "I don't blame anyone except those responsible. As for my fans, I don't care about them anymore. I quit caring the day June died. I'll never touch an instrument again."

"I'm sorry to hear that…because I am a *big fan*. And I'm at least happy you don't blame us. And, please allow me to repeat the prosecution's condolences. We are all so very grateful that you survived the incident and that you are able to give your testimony today." Ms. Shields raises her voice in a clear proclamation, moving closer to Jazz and placing her manicured right hand on his raised right leg. She runs her French-tipped fingers along the length of his covered shin. "If my questions become too tough or if you'd like to stop, *at any time,* just let me know and I'll ask the nice judge for a timeout."

"Well, that's mighty white of you," Jazz remarks sarcastically; the courtroom bustles briefly and the judge grumbles and growls over the racial jab, coughing into his hand and silencing the gallery.

"Quiet down, and keep the color commentary to yourself, Mr. Lancaster. This will be over soon. Proceed, Ms. Shields."

"Yes, Your Honor. Please tell the court, Mr. Lancaster, on the morning of the incident, were you and the deceased having coffee at a local diner?"

"No…"

"No?"

"It was tea," Jazz corrects Ms. Shields with a sly smirk, curling his eyebrows and questioning her qualifications. "June never drank caffeine."

"I see…so it was tea…" Ms. Shields glances back to Mr. Erickson with a Cheshire smile of her own, forming a plan to drown the musician in finite details. "And while not drinking coffee, not drinking caffeine, and drinking tea at the café, what were you two talking about?"

"We were…uh, planning to leave." Jazz struggles to think back to the moment when they were sitting in the diner, dealing with the aftermath of their failed attempt to reconcile with her grandfather. "We talked about the future, our music, and building a home out west. June had an offer to act in a movie. I wanted to go back to Hollywood to record. It just made sense."

"So, you two were happy." Ms. Shields states plainly and continues to walk around Jazz in his steel wheelchair, circling her prone prey. He looks like he's been served to her on a silver platter. "Did you and the deceased talk about what happened at dinner the night before?"

"Please, stop saying the deceased. She's…uh…uh…I just don't like it."

"I'm sorry. Can you please answer the question?"

"What was the question?"

"Did you and *the deceased* talk about what happened at dinner the night before?"

"You're doing that on purpose."

"Doing what, Mr. Lancaster?"

"Nothing, *Miss* Shields. Yes, we talked a little about what happened. June was just upset…" Jazz trails off, tilting his head toward the floor and lifting his eyes toward Duke. "Her brother and sister didn't show up and her grandfather…he scared her."

"Hm…you say '*June was just upset*', and that's according to you, from your conversation." Ms. Shields prods, stopping next to the jurors and giving the attentive gentlemen a whiff of her Estée peach perfume. "And you, what about you? Were you upset, too?"

"No."

"Why not?" Ms. Shields asks girlishly, tilting her head to the side and throwing her arms out wide in wonder. Some of the jurors' eyes pop out of their heads as they gawk over her sleek frame, momentarily forgetting the line of questioning. "June was upset about her family, soon-to-be your family, so why weren't you upset?"

"Objection, Your Honor! Ms. Shields' line of questioning is repetitive and inconsequential." John Allen stands slowly from his seat, patting the waistline of his jacket and adjusting his tie. "Mr. Lancaster's feelings about events occurring the night *before* the incident have no bearing in this proceeding. The defense counsel should stick to the facts of this case!"

"To the contrary, Your Honor, the witness's state of mind has a direct bearing on the credibility of his testimony!" Ms. Shields reels off her prepared rebuttal, memorized and delivered with perfect precision. She straightens her back confidently and steps away from the jury with a swish in her hips while Judge Rupert places his hand under his chin and ponders her point and her curves.

"Overruled, Mr. Allen." Judge Rupert grouses reluctantly; his derisive tone reveals an inner will to deny the female counsel any consent, yet he knows her argument is valid. Appeal cases turn on such errors, and even if the fix is in, he has a judicial obligation to at least maintain the appearance of impartiality. Ms. Shields gives Judge Rupert a small gesture of appreciation in the form of a head nod and a fleeting smirk. John Allen sits down in a huff and rolls *his* eyes toward the jury, hoping to gain some favor with the deciding members who no longer care about the formality. Some of the men are noticeably captivated by Ms. Shields' *presence* and they stare at her like lions in a zoo during feeding time.

"Thank you, Your Honor." Ms. Shields turns her attention back to Jazz and she steps toward the wilting witness; her early faux compassion begins to sharpen several potent daggers. "Now Jazz, excuse me, Mr. Lancaster, given the deceased's reaction to what you say was an unpleasant experience with your would-be in-laws, why weren't you equally as upset as her?"

"June and I never agreed on much except music." Jazz smiles and feels his lost love while remembering their many quarrels; she's there in his spirit, if only for a moment. "She saw the world one way and I saw it another."

"How so?"

"She always thought the best of people...and...I always thought the worst," Jazz explains coldly, losing his smile as he looks over to the Winnipers. He questions their existence; their faces remind him of June and it hurts to see her in them, especially Papa. Jazz stares into the old man's eyes and he speaks June's truth. "June expected her grandfather to forget how she left town, forget that she stayed away when the others came home. She thought they could forgive each other and he would open his arms to us and...we could be...a family. Ha, imagine that."

"And you?" Ms. Shields inquires, continuing to poke and prod her prey, wondering how long it would take him to fully expose himself to her kill shot. "What did you expect from the wealthy Winniper family?"

"I expected exactly what we got. They treated us…like we disgusted them." Jazz's glare darts from Papa to Mrs. Winniper and then to Thomas III. "I just want them to know they disgust me, too."

"I see, that's pretty strong language, yet, you weren't upset? June was upset and you were not, but, the next morning, you both wanted to leave," Ms. Shields surmises his testimony, taking a moment to lean against the jury box and place her hand under her chin. "But, maybe you can help me understand, if you weren't upset, then why did you also want to leave so soon? You still have family here, a mother and a brother of your own."

"My mother's old, cranky, and senile. And my brother isn't much better." He croons plainly, looking at Berthine and Charles sitting together in the gallery. They stare back at him through the crowd; their dazed faces mix within the gawkers, scoffing at Jazz's vitriolic tone and salivating over the superstar's testimony. He continues to appease the masses, as they savor his every word. "They spend all day arguing in her cabin, ignoring how people in Winniper County have always treated people like us."

"And who are these *'people in Winniper County'*, specifically?"

"There is no specific. There's only one kind of people that matters here. The Winnipers and their…*family friends…the elites…*they control everything. Everyone else is a second-class citizen. I've heard the stories how the Winniper family stole land from my people. All these years later, and Winniper County is still spilling my blood." Jazz growls, tensing his weary muscles. He wishes he could rise from his wheelchair and tear down the walls of the courtroom. His angst must be permeating through his facial expression because an anxious presshound, who is unable to resist capturing the moment, snaps a flash photo and tries to hop over the backrow but several county officers quickly grab him. They confiscate his camera and hoist him through the main courtroom doors. Ms. Shields remains slightly stunned; for a brief moment, she is incapable of maneuvering through her mischief, caught in a glimpse of sympathy while her famous prey squirms in his bandages.

"So you never…uh, you…you never enjoyed living in Winniper County? It is your home, correct?"

"Winniper County has never been my home, ma'am." Jazz replies sharply, scowling at the thought of his cabin. "I just lived here."

∞

Growing up, he hated feeling like an *'other'*, born into a family of Sioux natives, forgotten inside a ghost village. They lived on the edge of the Winnipers' opulence, but they were never included, never invited inside.

∞

"My mother raised us by herself. We may have been inside the county line, but we weren't a part of Winniper County."

"And do you still feel hatred toward the people of Winniper County?"

"I don't hate anyone...except the demons that killed June."

"Did you say *'demons'*?" Ms. Shields repeats, raising her eyes and scoffing in front of the jury; her mannerisms challenge Jazz's sanity. "Are you referring to the perpetrators of this crime as *'demons'*?"

"Yes. That's what they are."

"Are you involved in some kind of holy war?"

"No. I'm no saint."

"But you identified my client as one of the perpetrators, so, is it safe to assume that you consider him a demon?"

"Y-yes. He is. One of many here, today."

"I see...but when the county attorney asked you earlier to identify my client... my colleagues and I noticed a slight hesitation" Ms. Shields walks to the front of the foreground, before turning sharply, stepping toward Jazz, and closing in on her kill. She smells his weakness, his senses beginning to crumble. "Were you confused when identifying him? Are you sure my client was one of the perpetrators of this crime?"

"No...I wasn't confused," Jazz defends himself, feeling the skin on his forearms tightening. "I'm just tired. I've only left the hospital twice in two years."

"But Jazz, Mr. Lancaster, you've already admitted to being upset about the night before the incident. And then you were attacked and almost beaten to death. You were in a coma for days and incapacitated, well, even now, so how can you be so sure that you saw my client take part in the incident? No one would fault you for being mistaken...especially since you claim there were *'demons'*. It's common to have trouble accepting reality after experiencing trauma."

582

"I'm not mistaken, ma'am. I saw Duke. I remember him and the three others, but he was definitely there. I see him vividly…he's in all my nightmares."

"Yes, he's one of the demons, as you say. But, answer this, please, do you see his friends as vividly? Are they *'demons'* in your nightmares, too?" Ms. Shields asks mockingly, poking his resolve and hoping he breaks down further; now would be the perfect time for a psychotic episode. Jazz pauses, seeing her lascivious intent, but he closes his eyes and tries to recall a visual of the other murderers at the scene.

"I don't remember them as clearly. That's why I wouldn't testify…until now." Jazz protests, scrunching his eyebrows together and narrowing his eyes as if he is trying to see through the present and look into the past. "I saw Duke…and I think June thought…for a second…I think she saw him…"

"Yes, you think, you thought, but you don't actually remember my client as vividly as the other, previously convicted, criminals?" Ms. Shields asks quickly, hoping to confuse Jazz; he freezes, his eyes open wide, and he remembers too much, too fast. A polished, overly sultry defense lawyer, Ms. Shields notices him skip a beat and she finally steps to him defiantly and pounces upon her prey. "Your Honor, can you please instruct the witness to answer the question? Do you actually remember seeing my client during the incident?"

"The witness will answer the defense counsel," Judge Rupert orders sternly as Jazz remains silent, staring just ahead of his lifted leg. A long pause falls over the courtroom and he continues to search his mind for any answer that makes sense. His lapse becomes noticeable to everyone, and the judge leans slightly over his bench, stretching to interject himself between Jazz and Ms. Shields. "I don't know, counselor. The boy might've had enough for today."

"Your Honor…please, allow me to repeat the question," Ms. Shields implores sweetly, turning cutely between Jazz and the judge. "I only have a few more issues and then he can go back to the excellent care of the doctors and nurses at the county hospital if you will allow me a moment."

"Proceed." The judge relents, willed by the petite princess's perky disposition. The image of his turkey sandwich dances through his daydreams and his mouth waters. He thinks of the thinly cured slices smothered in Honey Dijon. He hopes this testimony won't last much longer.

"Now Jazz, excuse me, Mr. Lancaster, truthfully, given the violent attack, the extent of your physical and mental trauma, and your troubled state of mind from the night prior, can you say with absolute certainty that you saw Duke Winniper during the incident? Are you *absolutely certain*?"

"No. How could I be? You said yourself I was knocked unconscious. But I believe-"

"You'd like a jury to convict a man of murder based on a *belief*, a belief in demons." Ms. Shields pauses, twisting his words, spinning on her heels, and allowing her conclusion to sink into the courtroom's collective consciousness. The realization sends subtle strikes through their dammed confidence, once reinforced by the star's testimony. "But since you can't remember my client actually being present during the incident then, why is our client the only perpetrator you've attempted to identify from the incident? Why did you really choose to testify here, today?"

"I...I...I had to. I...I owed it to June." Jazz concedes, nodding his head in confirmation. All the circumstances seem to hit him at once. Thomas III wonders why Ms. Shields is concentrating upon Jazz's mental state; she's manipulating her line of questioning in order to confuse him. Thomas III turns his head toward his father; Papa glows with a mastermind's rosy-cheeked gleam like when a chess master plays against a novice and a powerful plan comes to fruition.

"Your Honor, I move that the witness's previous statements identifying my client at the scene of the crime be stricken from the record." Ms. Shields states confidently, folding her arms and cocking her hips to the side. "The witness just admitted that he didn't come here to tell the truth. The jury should not consider his statements against my client because the witness just admitted that he has no vivid recollection of my client being present during the incident. He has contradicted himself in front of the entire courtroom."

"So noted, the jury will disregard the witness's statements identifying the accused at the scene." Judge Rupert confirms, pointing again to the stenographer and glancing over the brim of his glasses. He eyes the adjacent wall clock and compares his watch (11:45am) to the clock (11:50am), his watch, the clock, his watch...

"Thank you, Your Honor." Ms. Shields walks away from Jazz before looking over her shoulder at his devoured carcass. She has shredded his credibility without care. "The defense yields the floor."

She smiles slyly, walks to her colleagues, and resumes her seat at the defense table. Mr. Erickson pats both of her shoulders like a proud father congratulating his daughter at a spelling bee or dance recital. He's satisfied to cheer as his legal protégé hones her craft.

"In light of the witness's physical condition," the judge mumbles, internally considering whether to add more Honey Dijon onto his turkey sandwich, "and if the prosecution has no more questions, I would like to take a brief recess before the next testimony."

"No objection, Your Honor, the prosecution does not need Mr. Lancaster anymore and we thank the court for hearing his most important testimony." Mr. Allen lampoons toward the jurors as he stands from his seat at the prosecution table. Jazz remains in his wheelchair, the butt of everyone's joke. "I believe we could all use a lengthy break, Your Honor."

"That's grand, Mr. Allen. Let's resume in about one hour. We will reconvene at 1:00pm. Bailiff, please release the jury." Judge Rupert orders hurriedly, but he muffs his exit as he glances back and forth before finding his gavel under his nose. He promptly slams the gavel against his bench one time and the bailiff quickly steps forward, waving his hand to usher the foreperson to lead the jury out an adjacent door.

"All rise!" He booms over the courtroom, and the people in the gallery instinctually follow his command. This is the only arena where the elite will obey the orders of a colored man, but, in truth, he is still their boy.

The judge rises feebly from his bench and lumbers toward a timber-trimmed door leading to his private chambers. He doesn't look at Jazz, the jury, or any of the other distractions. He exits solemnly and several press agents scramble toward the main courtroom doors, presumably hurrying to grab a limited amount of phones. In the lobby, the reporters frantically deliver updates to their anxious editors and ad-hungry executives, who sit in newsrooms, decide angles, and spin the reports into gold headlines for the masses.

Jazz's nurse beckons the officers to clear the courtroom's main aisle while she moves past the bailiff, walks to Jazz's side, and whispers in his left ear. Thomas III stares at Jazz, still seeing his sister in her son's face. His nephew seems so different from his bright, childhood self—the happy boy from Berthine's cabin who conquered the world. He is now spiritually disheveled—the trauma, tragedy, and testimonies have wiped that cool *Rolling Stone* cover look from his face. He can no longer maintain the media's manufactured façade; his aura is gone and both of his heroes are dead. One blonde corpse lies encased in a wood coffin, and the other, the musical man he once saw in the mirror, withers away slowly. He is trapped in a lonesome, public persona.

With one glance at Jazz's sullen face, Thomas III can see why his nephew left Winniper County before he turned eighteen.

∞

Lucy and Charles travelled to New Orleans and Jazz was left alone with Berthine. Outside of her cabin, the confined community silently excluded anyone of color. Jazz realized his second-class citizenship at an early age, but, if he knew the truth, he may think even worse of himself.

∞

The lasting Sioux workers in Winniper County have always been treated like the walking dead. Even now, the crisp fall climate complements the county's cold culture and corrupts his entire essence. Jazz was once a wide-eyed boy, fighting for his brother's guitar and dreaming of stages and fame, but, reality has stolen much of who he built himself to be. Here and now, within this courtroom, he is no longer Jazz; he is no longer an international rock star. Jazz is a twenty-seven-year-old crippled survivor, just another grieving, American veteran whose life has been destroyed in a war that he has never completely understood.

Papa continues to hold Olivia under his left arm as he raises his right hand to brush her cheek softly. He's hopeful that the recess will give his shoulder a break; the old man's bones feel even wearier today. Looking toward Papa, Thomas III notices that his father's eyes are undeniably empty, completely impartial to the court proceedings. The Winniper patriarch has a general disregard for the judicial system as a whole because he has used his money to influence countless verdicts. Today's theatrical performance is simply a formality; they all fill their roles out of necessity. Most, like Papa, do so while being devoid of a sincere interest in justice.

Jazz's nurse leans forward and begins to push his wheelchair toward the open courtroom aisle. She wheels him slowly through the aisle, flanked by police officers and emerging press. The cameramen angle eagerly for a clear shot, emboldened by the lax courtroom procedure during the recess. Two officers help Berthine and Charles walk through their row and join Jazz and his nurse. Several cameramen jostle for space while snapping pictures of the family like rabid dogs feasting on a live kill. Their deadlines demand urgency; the greedy ghouls grin and salivate as if they can already feel their pockets bulging with their respective paydays.

The prosecution and defense huddle around their respective tables. Duke still sits stoically at the defense table, though he is now surrounded by security officers. He stares statuesquely at the courtroom window, dreaming of another reality, but he remains within this dimension, without any escape from space or time. The respective camps finish preparing their post-recess protocol, and they each break their huddles with rounds of applause and audible congratulations for their morning arguments.

Mr. Erickson turns over his right shoulder and gives Papa a short wink before walking toward a side door that leads to the west wing of the courthouse. Most of his gang follows in tow as Ms. Shields and her select cohorts collect papers from the defense table—Duke continues to stare out the window, ignored and unimportant. From the front row, Papa observes these courtroom maneuvers with the grin of a calculated genius. He marvels at the chessboard and mentally moves his pawns into sacrificial positions. Thomas III watches his father stealthily, still not understanding the plan; but, he remains steadfast within his role as a *good, noble son*. He still sits between his mother and Tilly as they sob silently into their handkerchiefs.

Diligently performing his public role, John Allen ends his exchanges with his associates, turns toward the gallery, and approaches Mr. and Mrs. Winniper with his right palm extended like he is walking through the desert, begging for a handful of water. His face contorts and mourns over the circumstances; his bottom lip protrudes like a mounted fish. The county attorney walks until he stands just in front of the wooden barrier separating the foreground from the gallery. Many audience members continue to wander in and out of the courtroom, side-eyeing every interaction between the important players. John Allen raises his cupped palm over the barrier so that it rests just under Papa's eye level. Mr. Allen's hand hangs in suspense, awaiting the old man's validation while the ambitious, yet self-conscious, county attorney glances around the courtroom, inspecting the faces of potential voters. He hopes they will soon see the king bless his grandson's executioner. The county attorney plans to follow orders and reap the benefits of doing so—it's a truth that the Winniper County citizens understand, yet, one wonders, if the citizens learn the truth about corrupt officials, will they still allow their officials to accept the benefits of being corrupt?

"I just want to say that we are doing everything…*absolutely everything* you've asked us to do, Papa. We're going to get justice for June." John Allen proclaims both proudly and somberly, trying his best to tap-dance between mourning and message while his hand still waits for acceptance. He galvanizes his courage to deliver another pitch. "I hope we can expedite the process to make things as easy for you…I mean, uh…as easy for *the family*…as possible."

"We appreciate that," Papa responds roughly, his gruff voice scraping through his cigar chafed throat. He glances at Mr. Allen's hand skeptically. "I didn't think we needed much of a rebuttal. I'm glad you let that Injun go back to the hospital."

"I-I, uh, well, thank you. In Winniper County, we're raised to care for people." Mr. Allen rumbles headfirst into a campaign speech, momentarily forgetting his place; there are still too many moving parts for him to become nonchalant. His hand still hangs in front of Papa, desperate for support, still hoping for a life raft to save him and show him that he still matters. His extended arm begins to tremble slightly and he uses his left hand to support his right wrist. "I-uh, I'm planning to call Doctor Morten, Jr. to the stand next. We should be able to wrap his testimony by the end of the day."

"Good...quite good. I'm sure he'll be a very convincing witness. He's been present at practically every birth in Winniper County for the past fifty years. Everyone in the courtroom probably saw him or his father before they even saw their own mothers." Papa smiles brightly, extending his bulbous right paw to grab Mr. Allen's quivering hand. When the old man grips the prosecutor's mitt, Mr. Allen experiences a jolt of exuberance. His spirit climbs upon Papa's life raft and the county attorney feels all the comforts and rapture of being close to the messiah. The frog submits to the snake and another pawn slides into another sacrificial position. "You're doing very well, young man. The lights of this stage are not too bright for you. You could be very successful, maybe even Mayor, if you continue to perform well. Never lose sight of the big picture."

John Allen smiles and sticks his chest out so far that Thomas III thinks the prosecutor might burst. Mr. Allen holds Papa's hand firmly and smiles for the stragglers still in the courtroom. He nods while affirming that there are enough Winniper County voters bearing witness to his anointing; the news will spread like a wildfire. He can hear the gossip mills cranking up to churn conversation into campaign contributions for the future Mayor of Winniper County, South Dakota. In the distant corners of his foresight, he envisions the American flag flying high as a local school band plays the "The Star-Spangled Banner".

"Thank you, sir. I appreciate your confidence and I will not let you down." Mr. Allen returns his attention to Papa and bows his head submissively, attempting to hide his bursting smile. When he raises his eyes, Papa nods his head surely, retracts his hand, and pats the top of Olivia's head, reassuring her that he is still in control.

There is a lingering, spacious pause as Papa waits for Mr. Allen to walk away; the family has more pressing business to attend to during the recess. The county attorney finally notices his irrelevance and he sighs heartily before scuttling away, searching for Dr. Morten, Jr. Mr. Allen's associates rush to follow his exit while he continuously looks at his right palm as if to check and confirm that he did just shake the king's hand. Still sitting in the front row and ignoring Duke at the defense table, Papa Winniper looks to his left, past his wife, and he glares glibly at Thomas III. Papa's head tilts sharply and his cold blue eyes burn a hole through his son, yet Thomas III returns his father's scowl with only distance and disrespect. A son and father looking into a mirror, and they only see a slight resemblance.

"Let's get some fresh air," Papa orders quickly, leaning back and using his left arm to lift Olivia's frail frame to her feet before attempting to rise himself. His back creaks and his joints rattle, but he finally stands beside her, unaided and still deadly. Mimicking his father's timing and motion, Thomas III leans back and helps Tilly to her feet while she sobs into her handkerchief. Her tears have nearly soaked the white linen, though Thomas III wonders which murder evokes her sorrow. He stands next to her and looks down at the family's old friend, thinking, *"Does she mourn for her granddaughter, her son, or is she merely playing a role, too? Are we all marching to Papa's orders?"*

Freidrich "Fred" Potter and the rest of the family's entourage rise and crowd around Tilly and the Winnipers; each member of their inner circle has been trained to obey Papa's commands. They are obedient servants, chess pieces that he is more than willing to sacrifice. Fred organizes and chastises the Winnipers' aides, attendants, attorneys, accountants, and agents. They discuss personal and professional strategies, assessing how the Winnipers' conduct during the trial will affect the family's billion dollar portfolio. Their main focus is damage control; prevent losses and rebuild the Winniper Family brand. In truth, the family's oil land ensures a nation's financial prosperity. As long as the Winnipers' own the land, the elite will never starve; but, power…unbridled power is still Papa's true passion.

At this point in his aged life, he's absolutely drunk with the need to dominate.

∞

When Thomas, Sr. settled the land, established the oil company, and founded Winniper County, he made his mark upon the world. Papa inherited his father's business and transformed the domestic juggernaut into an international stronghold, fortified by powerful alliances and elitist connections in every inhabited region of the globe.

∞

The Winniper family's oil ships throughout the world like kinetic pulses moving along the nervous system. The exchange of energy is clear; Papa provides life and industry and his resources demand consideration. His hand stretches across the world and he grabs ahold of whatever he desires; yet, although, at age fifteen, Papa inherited his father's spoils, he still does not have a trustworthy heir to bestow his power upon. He fears rolling around in his grave, tormented in the afterlife, nervously fretting about his family's future.

For Papa, yesterday's power may be lost today; and, for this reason, Thomas III assumed that Papa would insist upon a speedy mistrial and spring Duke from the jaws of public outrage. Thomas III hopes that his father can somehow resume grooming Duke to usurp the throne, but, the trial's beginning troubles Thomas III. He watches his father, accepting handshakes and pardons; the center of the courtroom circus, the white-haired oil merchant plays the role of a persevering, patriarchal ringmaster. Papa seems as though he is supporting his wayward grandson and grieving for his deceased granddaughter, yet, underneath his pale blue eyes, he considers the variables of an unseen equation. Papa has found a mysterious solution that has eased his concerns about his family's future; but, he must double-check his work after each step, in order to ensure that he has not made a careless mistake.

As the leeches gather around him, he protects himself and pulls Olivia alongside him. The two slink through the front row and enter the main aisle, followed by Thomas III and Tilly. Olivia is the only one who looks back momentarily to gaze at Duke through a crease in the cronies. Papa doesn't even care enough to turn his head; his mind focuses on his minions' discussion of the estate's plans for a new bicoastal pipeline—the road back home to prominence and prosperity through unprecedented endeavors. The family will capitalize upon the drama of the trial and baptize the Winniper Family brand in a purifying lake of American justice. The enterprising possibilities are endless—3,000 miles of uninterrupted oil distribution. Papa could pump oil into any town in America. A Hollywood movie or, at least, a primetime special seems inevitable—a propaganda piece highlighting the legacy of the Winniper family and the ingenuity of American industry.

One of the estate's publicists has scheduled a series of post-trial interviews for Papa and Olivia. The family's handlers believe the grieving grandparents can help garner public sympathy and lay the foundation for the estate's next promotion: The Winniper Family Comeback. Thomas III hasn't been included in any plans for interviews or public appearances. After the trial, he will return to the Winniper family's mansion and remain on the property with Nancy and Christina, indefinitely—one of Papa's decrees. Because he is no longer working at the market, Thomas III has been relegated to the role of a Winniper woman. He is only brought out when the family needs to present the appearance of a family. This may be his only chance to see or speak to anyone outside of the Winniper Family Estate for a long time.

While Papa leads Olivia through the main aisle and Thomas III escorts Tilly behind them, the family's supporters continue to flow around them, exiting the courtroom in a whispering exodus. The flock leaves Duke alone at the defense table with the armed officers pacing around the courtroom entrance and aisle. The black bailiff stands guard in front of the judge's chambers. The Winnipers migrate through the courtroom amongst a professional beehive, amassing more business partners and constituents from around the world. One aged, accountant catches shivers while thinking about all the billions of dollars that are hinging upon the outcome of this trial. Guilty or not guilty, either verdict will send a clear statement about the amount of power that the Winniper family is willing to yield to protect its own.

Several cameramen nudge through the outer ranks and stretch out their arms so that they can flash their cameras close enough to capture brief moments of the family's genuine grief. Tilly, Thomas III, and Olivia bear solemn expressions that pay true justice to their roles as mourning, bereaved, and tested Christians, but, Papa remains detached. He is a callous conniver, consumed in his casual conversations, hearing hedge bets and sharing inside information. While he continues to march out of the courtroom, he leads his family through the flashes and fanfare like a symbol of the modern, Christian patriarch—immersed in a false light filled with fake praise and full-blown hypocrisy. The sheep believe their shepherd is both benevolently beautiful and boyishly brave, but he is really buoyantly bad-intentioned and boldly brutal.

Thomas III has never seen his father cry or show remorse for the murders that have occurred within his reign. Papa has transformed his cruelty into a powerful statement, a supremacist standard that Thomas III could never meet.

∞

Born as a Winniper prince, with all the lies and confusion attached to his claim, Thomas III cried more often than the average boy and much more often than his sister. Frightened by the weight of his family's oil kingdom, his life became more tears than smiles. The would-be heir to the Winniper family's throne, he often wept under the burden of his anticipated inheritance. He cried tears and carried his fears into his adulthood, until he finally realized and conceded that he could never fill his father's shoes. After Thomas III continued to disappoint and underperform, Papa accepted his son's resignation—they silently agreed that Thomas III will never lead the family.

∞

Thomas III has always worn his heart on his sleeve; he never had Papa's talent for deception and margin calls. Long ago, the forsaken heir understood that he gained his sensitivity and impishness from his mother; for decades, Olivia has cried constantly, tucked away in the master bedroom where so much pain has been conceived. Her grief has never waned while mourning for the lost members of their family. Like Thomas III, her sorrow has been authentic, omnipresent, and all-consuming.

∞

When Olivia stopped visiting Teresa's children in Berthine's cabin, that sadness turned inward and her white guilt gave her soul a black eye.

∞

Because Papa has never cried for his victims, he continues to deny the villainy in his deeds and his conscience remains hidden, quiet, and ignored. The only dark force that drives Papa is the fear that somehow he could lose his oil empire. Even as he wades through the comfortable fervor of the courthouse, his heart constricts with secretive tension. He is unable to share how much he fears losing it all.

The Winniper family marches through the crowded courthouse lobby and moves down a white marble-floored hallway toward an expansive oak-wall boardroom that provides refuge from prying public eyes. Papa affectionately calls the luxury office suit "The War Room"; the oak interior is the embryo from which he spawns strategies to defeat his foes and conquer the world.

Several onlookers continue to watch and the cameramen continue to exploit the hoopla while Papa's procession passes through the boardroom's eight feet tall oak door. Inside the bunker, red velvet-lined oak chairs surround a long, well-polished oak conference table; oak sofas with red velvet upholstery sit against each wall. Papa's courthouse war room is a world-renowned treasure trove for million dollar settlements and soul-breaking agreements. Whether a distributor that has skimmed some of the oil profits or a shipping company that has lost a few containers, Papa usually turns his enemies into his prey and he brings them here before the feast. The Winniper Family Holding Company loves to play on its home turf; yet, in any American jurisdiction, the judge, jury, and jurisdiction often follow the wishes of the patriarch of Winniper County.

Because he is a self-sustaining multi-billion dollar man, beholden only to self-aggrandizement, Papa's wealth is mostly liquid and he continues to equip his estate with accruing assets—trade agreements, foreign land, and exclusive contracts. For his ambition and exploits, the Winnipers' oil has more global influence than the Savior Jesus Christ.

Several federal and international lawsuits, mostly from would-be competitors, have attempted to restrict the Winniper Family Holding Company's oil exports, especially during the early days when Thomas Winniper, Sr. established the family's oil business.

∞

Their once parched land burst with so much black gold that Thomas, Sr. could have flooded the entire international market within a year. He could've become the wealthiest man in the world in less than two years; and the threats and antagonism that he received as a result of his powerful potential forced him to limit his ambition—a regret that he often shared with his son.

Winniper County's founder chose to ship solely through New Orleans, avoiding the Atlantic to Pacific railways by hiring Mississippi River truck companies to transport his oil exclusively through the South. Despite his extra expenses, he created a prosperous Dakota company and he enjoyed a prominent lifestyle that endowed each Winniper offspring with separate trust funds filled with cash accounts, stock portfolios, and businesses within businesses.

Still, he restricted his success, but he encouraged Thomas, Jr. to pursue greater accomplishments. When Thomas, Jr. became Papa, he took his father's tutelage and molded the Winniper Family Holding Company into an international conglomerate that is now more powerful than any government in the world. Forfeiting the fruits of family for the promise of power, Papa entangled the Winnipers within a toxic web of weddings, widows, and innocent victims.

∞

Yes, sadly, since the Winniper family acquired their oil land, any woman who has conceived a Winniper child has been cursed with extreme pain and a Sioux newborn. The first cursed mother died during labor. Papa has never spoken publicly about his mother, Ruby, even when someone mentions her in conversation.

∞

He had a collection of stories recanted by his father, but he barely felt a connection to her because she died during his birth. Though his father never told him the full story, Papa learned bits and pieces from Sheriff Cobb, Jr. and Dr. Morten, Jr. A "voodoo Injun woman" cursed the Winniper family's blood and the Sioux twin became the family's shameful secret.

And when Jazz and June decided to announce their incestuous engagement, their pending nuptials posed another threat to the great and noble Winniper Empire. The secret was always lurking in their midst, even within their blood. Hardly a polite topic, the most hopeless became the targets and Papa employed the cruelty that he learned from his father. The Winniper women and their Sioux babies have become casualties of the family's legacy and these murders have entwined success with tragedy. Through the years of torment, Teresa was the only Winniper woman who saved her Sioux children.

Thomas III wonders if his sister was simply too brave. When they travelled around the world, searching for answers, she would hop from their RV and chase the wild animals. She thought it was funny to throw her hands in the air and growl madly. During her childhood, Papa would chastise her free-spiritedness and punish her with ballet lessons. Teresa never cared for the typical girl's distractions; she always wanted to be rebellious and *independent*.

A few years ago, while watching June and Jazz perform on *The Ed Sullivan Show,* Thomas III saw Teresa's untamed antics in June's dance moves. June was growling and raising her arms onstage like a Wacchu tribal woman in the jungle; Teresa was still living through June, still chasing the animals away. Seeing a ghost inside an angel, Thomas III watched his niece prancing around on the bright stage, and he saw his sister's ghost enter his living room through the television.

Alive and dead, she stood before him, staring at the brother who killed her. These images still haunt Thomas III, yet, long ago, he relinquished any hope of being free.

∞

The guilt and ghosts continue to follow him while he is asleep and awake. And, after seeing Duke staring aloofly in the courtroom, Thomas III worries that his nephew faces the same demons.

∞

Papa forced Duke to kill his sister, too. Or, were Duke and Thomas III both willing mercenaries in the cycle to conceal the family secret? Maybe, for just a moment too long, dreams of power consumed the two men and convinced them to do the unthinkable.

∞

Regardless, Thomas III cannot allow another Winniper ghost to haunt him. Given the tenor of this morning's testimony, if the jury finds Duke guilty, he will likely go to death row with Earl and their accomplices. Thomas III fears that Duke may join Teresa and June. Thinking of himself, he imagines a tormented future, surrounded by the ghosts of slain and sacrificed family members. His skin crawls when he considers Jazz; his Sioux nephew may not last long either. The Winniper closet is quickly collecting more skeletons; the secret pushes anxiously against the walls and threatens to smash open the door within Thomas III's conscience.

Papa helps Olivia sit within the center of a crimson sofa, positioned against the wall to the left of the boardroom's oak door. He walks away from his wife until he reaches the far right corner of the boardroom; Papa then stands upright and raises his right index finger in the air as if he has just had a brilliant idea. He promptly waves his right hand and gathers his team around him.

Still mimicking his father, Thomas III helps Tilly sit next to his mother and then, he moves quietly through the crowd of constituents, hoping to find his place next to Papa. The son searches for his father at the circus; he nudges his way through a few envious clowns and several legal lions until he finds the ringleader's shoulder. Thomas III tugs on his father's tailored cream cashmere jacket and leans under Papa's left ear so that even those closest to them cannot hear his words.

"What's going on in there, Pa'?" Thomas III whispers cuttingly; there's newfound venom in his tone, filled with anxiety over his father's pending answer. Realizing his candor, Thomas III quickly adjusts his tie and his tone and glances around to Fred and a few onlookers. "I mean…excuse me, sir but…Johnny boy is burying Duke. And you shook his hand in front of everyone."

"Your nephew is fine, Thomas." Papa dismisses his son by calling him *"Thomas"* or *"boy"* in public. He refuses to publicly acknowledge his middle-aged prince, who, in the father's eyes, is still too small to lead the kingdom. Even so, Papa turns his head slightly and glares at Thomas III with an all-too-familiar look of displeasure. Thomas III remembers the lesson that accompanies that look—questioning your father is blasphemous. "I think you're forgetting your place, again, boy. Everyone is where they need to be, doing what they need to do, except you. County Attorney Allen is doing exactly what he's been elected to do by the good people of Winniper County. He's an elected official and you, what are you? What are you doing?"

"What am I, Pa'? I'm…uh…I'm your son."

"Don't embarrass yourself, boy. My empire overwhelms you and my son wouldn't be overshadowed by anything. And you wonder why you will never lead this company. My colleagues…these accomplished professionals, would never respect you." Papa growls as he clutches his weary chest tenderly. He laughs quickly to avert attention from his tensing heart, but Thomas III can sense something is wrong with his father.

The surrounding suck-ups continue to huck-yuck at Thomas III's expense, hoping that they may gain favor with the king by validating his strength and devaluing his unfit heir. The old man removes his hand from his chest, narrows his eyebrows, and turns fully to his left so that he stands toe-to-toe with his third-born, and least favorite, child.

"You know…I remember you and John boy were in school together as kids. What did his mother do for him that I didn't do for you? Look at how he turned out. And you…you're… nothing like me. Your blood makes you the heir…to the company…but you could never…be me, not even…after I die. You'll…never…be…me."

"Papa, are you okay?"

"I'm fine, boy." Papa sighs heavily, returning his hand to his chest and glancing around the closest observers to inspect who has noticed his discomfort. The old man, well-versed in exploiting weakness, knows what happens when corporate sharks smell blood in the water. Feeling a moment of trepidation, Papa takes a deep breath and scans the entire room nonchalantly, scoping for new fins in his pond. "It's all about respect, boy. Respectable people don't respect you, because you don't respect yourself. Hell, you don't even respect your own father."

"Papa, you know that I respect you," Thomas III pleads, patting his father's left arm. The son lowers his head and returns to his sad childhood. His reflexes recall this familiar recoil: a whimpered concession and a few tugs on his father's arm will usually result in a gratuitous reward. Gaining Papa's affection once seemed like a carnival game that Thomas III never agreed to play. Papa bargained with the devil for his son's life without his son's consent.

Papa has always been his son's magical genie, presenting a spinning wheel of expensive prizes—each more costly than the next. Papa eventually shattered every fantastical dream that Thomas III once had, and the boy grew into a man who lost every slithering notion that he could be free from his father. His boyhood notions of becoming noble and good died after he crashed his sister's car into that tree and watched her take her last breath on the side of the road. At that moment, Thomas III learned who he really was; he abandoned his true nature and he became the monster his father taught him to be.

"I'm just worried, Pa'. Jazz and Lyle Hutchins identified Duke as a murderer, and Mr. Erickson isn't putting up much of a fight. I was there when you told him-"

"Everyone is doing exactly what they've been told, *Thomas*—everyone except you." Papa gripes, raising his hand and interrupting his son's diatribe. He ruffles his feathers so that his staff, partners, and cronies can hear his condemnation of his son. He is still a king staking claim to this throne. "Must you always disappoint me, boy? You're over fifty years old and you're still sniveling like a child. You still lack the courage to be a man."

"Papa, please..." Thomas III stares at his father intently, squeaking through his objection and searching for some sense of connection. "This wasn't the *strategy* that we discussed. Johnny and Erickson look like they're about to bury Duke and..."

"Keep quiet! You whine like a woman!" Papa clenches his fists and admonishes his son quickly. The old man steps forward and pushes Thomas III back so that the two may speak in a private, 2-foot radius space next to the oak door of Papa's white opal bathroom. Taught to communicate discreetly, the Winniper men usually pass secrets in close whispers; their words are so quiet that the air overtakes them.

"Sometimes I wish you were a mute like Duke. You have no tact! Every time you speak, I feel betrayed. You overreact like a woman. You would rather see our entire family fail because you are too weak to be our leader."

"That's not true, Papa. I'm sorry for interrupting, but..."

"You're always sorry...but nothing ever changes, does it? You're in your fifties and you're still unable to lead our family. And I'm stuck here, in my old age, fending off lawyers and the press, while you do what? Raise your *daughter*? You couldn't even keep Nancy's mother alive. Everything you have is because of me."

"Papa, I'll never..." Thomas stops speaking, realizing his tone. He takes a breath and leans closer to his father, hoping that the closest confidents cannot hear him. Surrounding ears continue to pry into their conversation, a consequence of the family's control over so many lives and futures. Most notable among the listeners is Freidrich Potter, the son of Carl Potter, the Winniper family's old German messenger boy.

∞

Carl made his bones with the family on the night he rode his horse into the Sioux uprising to bring Thomas Winniper, Sr. back home when Ruby Winniper went into labor. Until the day he died, Carl was a loyal and valued servant. Following in his father's footsteps, as is accustomed in Winniper County, Fred has become Papa's most trusted slave.

∞

Fred is Papa's proverbial right hand, *"The Hand of the King"*, some say. As an official title, he is the Winniper Family Estate's business manager who separates the Winniper Family Holding Company's expenses and taxes from the family's land licenses and investment returns. Fred has a keen mind for disaster control, risk management, and insurance coverage; he spends his life predicting the rise and fall of the Winniper family's assets and liabilities. His only charge is to protect the family, by any means necessary.

Thomas III glances between Fred and Papa and realizes that the family's bottom line is still paramount. As usual, the honorable and prestigious Winniper name is at stake; and, with the family on both sides of the courtroom as the victim and the accused, Papa must spearhead the most appropriate strategy that will ensure his family's continued prosperity with absolute certainty. No tactic is too taboo, even if his strategy employs a callous, yet perfectly executed ruse.

The horrid stench from June's murder still lingers around Winniper County and the ominously vapid air warrants a thorough decontamination. The county, state, nation, and even the world must collectively exonerate the Winniper family in order to whitewash the brand, cool the international markets, and return the Winniper Family Holding Company to prominent stability. Papa envisions himself standing atop the highest mountain and never coming down among the peasants unless more damning secrets require him to distract the public eye with pomp and circumstance, court theatrics, and assumed justice. Thomas III stares up to his father, feeling the weight of those damning secrets and trying to steady himself against the steepness of Papa's mountain. He climbs as high as his spirit will allow him, and he hopes his father may finally hear him.

"I just need to know that Duke is still okay, Pa'. You said we'd have a mistrial by lunchtime."

"I was speaking in jest, son. We must provide the people with a good show. Duke will be fine." Papa waves his hand between them and brushes away his son's concern. The old tyrant steps back and sticks out his chest while placing his hands on his hips and looking Thomas III up and down. "I really wish I had not named you after me and my father. Had I known...but, alas, you needn't worry yourself, boy. *These* are high level matters. You're only of use to me if you can have a son who can become what you never could."

"Please, Papa, tell me honestly," Thomas III pleads, stepping forward and grabbing his father's right arm; the cream cashmere sleeve crumples within his hand and he can feel his father's tender muscles tense within his grip. "I deserve to know. I'm your–"

"Unhand me, boy, before I show you your place in front of all these fine gentlemen." Papa rebukes his son and pushes him away strongly. The father steps away from the son and raises his voice a little louder so that Fred and a few onlookers may hear him. "Do you really think you *'deserve'* anything? I made you what little you are, and I pray God will forgive me for that. I even financed that produce market of yours, gave you crops from our farmland, and let you put the Winniper name on it, and it still loses…how much, Fred?"

"A little over $10,200 a year, sir," Fred chimes in with a smug smirk; his skinny, sickly face tightens as he calculates the expenses for an unprofitable market. He straightens his back as he adds up the figures. "Plus, you pay taxes on the property, merchant licenses, permits…"

"See, you cost me over $10,200 a year even after you quit working there. I've only kept it open because the townspeople would have a fit if I closed it. All your life, I've taken care of you. You and your daughter sleep in my house and you eat my food. Everything you have, you have because of me…"

Papa complains gruffly while furrowing his eyebrows and calculating additional fees for his son's excessive mooching.

"Some nerve you got, comin' to me when I have real business matters at hand. Today, of all days, you cause me more trouble when I make your life so simple that a trained monkey could be you without any further instruction!"

"Papa…please, lower your voice." Thomas III begs, placing his hands in his pockets and dipping his head between his shoulders in total dejection. A slither of pride remains within his chest and he tries to muster a few remaining specs of confidence. "I never asked for your money, and I tried to be a good son, but now…you're…you're goin' to let Duke be executed."

"Hold your tongue, boy. '*Executed*'? That's a big word for an idiot," Papa berates his son and narrows his right eye like a marksman aiming for the kill. Once again, he steps closer to Thomas III, lifts his chest over his son, and stares judgingly at him. While looking down upon his son, Papa can see the shiny steel from his father's Colt revolver, peaking through the holster inside Thomas III's jacket. "You don't even deserve to have my father's revolver. You continually remind me that I failed you in ways he never failed me and he died when I was fifteen. Did I teach you anything? Do you still remember what a real man does to protect his family?"

"Yes, sir, I still remember."

"Tell me."

"*A real man does everything he can, Papa…he does everything he can to protect his family.*" Thomas III repeats an old lesson learned years ago when Papa cared to place his son upon his knee and force his supposed heir to memorize certain edicts and mantras. Still remembering his father's intonation, Thomas III tries his best to mimic his father's tone, but, his inability to do so clarifies their respective roles.

He recognizes his father's common debate tactic when defending his viewpoint and softening his victim to his perspective as the tormentor. Papa often deflects and claims that there is a misunderstanding that his lessons can resolve. He is the family's patriarchal savior, free from persecution in this life; Papa often uses this quintessential deflection to gain ground within any discussion, negotiation, or confrontation. Whether at home or inside the war room's walls, Papa has a bag of clever tricks to capitalize upon the weakness of others.

Papa haggles with lenders and leverages his allies in order to secure his sense of success. His partners, investors, assistants, and employees perform his bidding throughout court hearings, lawsuits, and motions for arbitration. Sadly, today, Papa maneuvers his minions into formation to perform a grand prolicide.

Thomas III can see the frozen ice in his father's lake blue eyes; the men around him snarl with equal intent, ready to wage a murderous smear campaign against Duke. Pending a guilty verdict, the publicists, lawyers, and handlers are eager to begin the press manipulations to absolve the family from the depressed actions of one member. These concessions would no doubt exonerate the company from any liability, but, could the family ever repair itself after another betrayal?

Although they have killed newborns, hunted down a crippled in-law, and murdered their women, the Winniper men have always supported one another. Now, with these actions—Papa sacrificing Duke for the family's absolution—such betrayal may save their wealth, but it will dismantle the only unbroken bond within the family. Finally, after four generations of deceit and murder, the Winniper men will war among each other, forcing Thomas III to watch Duke's execution at the hands of their patriarch.

A twinge of disgust stirs within Thomas III's stomach and he becomes nauseous; the implications collide within his spirit. He remembers Teresa and the guilt is all too real. He remembers how he once wanted to be a hero, but he has never saved anyone in his life.

Faced with a moral conundrum, he envisions a way to save his nephew, a way to save himself. Thomas III begins to think that if he confesses to his role in June's murder, he may be able to save Duke from conviction by incriminating Papa as the mastermind of the crime. His mind continues to churn and he can't foresee delivering himself to the fate from which he hopes to save Duke. A full confession seems counterintuitive, and how could he reveal his sins without unleashing all the skeletons and ghosts in the Winniper family's closet? Could his mother be convicted for her role? What about Christina? What will happen to Nancy if the entire family is sent to prison? Are any of the Winnipers innocent? Thomas III looks deeply into his father, staring eye-to-eye and feeling uneasy, like he's racing a runabout on the open seas.

"Papa, I just want to protect Duke. Think about Teresa. I just want to do what's right."

"As do I, Thomas. One day you'll understand, maybe if you ever have your own son. You know, if you really want to do what's right, you still have time to give the family another heir. I would try myself if your mother wasn't…well, there are plenty of women in town who would put up with you to get close to our money. And you would really prove your worth to the family." Papa steps away and retrieves a cigar within the inside pocket of his suit jacket. "Maybe, just maybe, God will bless you with a son who can become what you never could. Until then, I suggest you comfort your mother and Ms. Tilly. Don't worry about these greater matters. Fred and I have it all under control."

Papa lights his cigar and dismisses his son with a wave of his hand. Freidrich and the business leeches close ranks around him, creating layers of tailored suits between the patriarch and the fallen heir. The sea of three-piece suits creases and parts just enough for Thomas III to pass through the waves before they collapse upon any hope for a father-son bond.

In his mind, Thomas III closes the book filled with the meaningful aspects of his relationship with his father, a relationship that never blossomed for either man. The father and the son equally disappoint each other. Papa lifts his head above the ranks and glances toward Thomas III, watching his son sulk and walk toward his mother. Papa chuckles as he remembers his son as a youth, making the same pitiful trek to his mother after disappointing his father. Even then, Thomas III showed signs of the weakness that has manifested itself in his adult life. Papa's chuckles turn into a grimaced snarl and he exhales a cloud of disgust and cigar smoke. He raises his cigar above his troops and prepares to salute his son.

"Thank you for your input, Thomas! You're a valued member of my company!" Papa howls loudly and his closest cronies cackle in appreciation and aberrance as he returns his focus them, searching through business partners for another traitor. He is the center of the collapsed sea and he drowns in their adoration, avarice, and ambition. These are the wolves who will secure the family's success, post-trial and after the sacrificial execution.

A recent law school graduate quickly presents notes about how the Winniper Family brand will rebuild its image through a few well-publicized interviews, a little tax-deductible philanthropy, and a corporate recruitment plan to hire more women and minorities at their firms around the world. A 10% increase in non-white male employees should be enough to claim corporate diversity and the Winniper Family Holding Company's stock will soar once again because the land will never stop pumping oil. Papa only needs public support and political influence to exploit his oil to its maximum profitability. He may truly own the world very soon.

Following his father's orders, Thomas III treads slowly toward his mother and Tilly and sits between them on the sofa. He raises his right arm and takes Olivia under his right shoulder, mimicking his father's courtroom mannerism in a farcical impersonation. He is the boy who could never be the man; and his attempts at imitation are embarrassingly blatant. Mrs. Winniper sits somberly, continuing to weep while wiping her eyes with her worn handkerchief. To Thomas III's left, Tilly mirrors Olivia's sadness and both women stare blankly ahead, hoping to catch a glimpse of Papa within the waves of business suits.

"Pa' says Duke will be fine," Thomas III confides softly, trying to convince himself, but his mother doesn't respond. "D'you hear me, Mama?"

"Don't believe him, son." Olivia whimpers, wiping her eyes with her handkerchief and reminding Thomas III of all the tears she has cried over the years. Her grief quickly diffuses his illusion. Her voice is even softer than his resolve; they are both weak pawns, positioned at the behest of their king. She continues to sob quietly, hiding a deeper sorrow that she is unable to share.

She knows that Papa ordered June's murder to occur in such a reckless, public spectacle, because he has always been willing to sacrifice any or all of Teresa's children. Teresa's supposed plan to leave town with Kenny and her children still draws Papa's ire. Her murder helped him to avoid a scandal, but her death did not assuage his feelings of betrayal. A man must be respected, or else.

∞

Long ago, Olivia accepted the cycle of tragedy. She submitted to the fact that her husband was, and still is, a wealthy murderer.

∞

Her tears fall in memorial for his past victims and in vain for his future victims who will join them soon.

"What do you mean, *'don't believe him'*, Mama?" Thomas III asks sheepishly, still stuck within his childish naivety, but his tone exposes his understanding. He sees the plot to sacrifice Duke along with Earl and the others; yet, unlike his mother, Thomas III refuses to completely accept his father's treachery. He continues to croon for clarification. "Papa was just telling me how everything's under control. Everyone is following orders. He told me…"

"He'll never change, son. Don't you see that?" She turns her head to her left and stares at Thomas III, wishing her son would finally admit his own guilt. He enjoys the view from inside the Winnipers' extravagant cage because he is afraid and hopelessly mediocre. Thomas III is stuck within a powerless paradigm, straddling his duties as an emasculated son and a freeloading father. He can no more provide for his daughter, Nancy, than he can appease his father or assure his mother.

After being uninformed and misled for procreation's sake, Olivia has survived decades of Papa's deception.

∞

At times, she begged him to spare the lives of some of his victims, most notably Teresa's Sioux children.

∞

Jazz, Lucy, and Charles exist today because of her actions, yet, Duke now lies within Papa's claws and, maybe, Olivia is too tired to fight another Winniper family sacrifice. Maybe, she blames herself in some way. Had she not saved Jazz, he would have never met June and, maybe, June would still be alive. With so many babies beaten, bruised, burned, and/or buried, laboring over past mistakes seems trivial.

"Thomas, we are…a family…but…we are a corporation, first. And we belong to your father." Olivia continues to sob into her handkerchief and she raises her head to see if anyone is close enough to hear her words. She leans into Thomas III's shoulder and whispers into his chest. "He'll always do exactly what he wants, anything to protect his business, but he'll always say it's for the family. And he'll never change."

"No, no...*it is* for the family, Ma'. He...he may be hard on me...and the girls...but, he...Pa' still loves us. Everything he done...is for the family. How...how can you say different?" Thomas III stammers, lowering his voice so that he doesn't attract attention from Papa's jovial huddle. The crowd around the old man laughs over an inside joke that remains inaudible to the three seated on the sofa. A few wallflowers remain against the oak walls of the war room, writing notes and calculating new figures based upon the conversation, just in case Fred or Papa asks for up-to-date data. Thomas III watches the in-crowd, still wishing he could be included. "Ma', look at how they adore him. They are employees, but, you're his wife, I'm his son, and Nancy, Christina, *and* Duke are his grandchildren. We're a family first, even Tilly."

"But, what about June? What about my boy, Kenny, and Earl?" Tilly asks tersely, interjecting at the mention of her name. She grieves for her granddaughter and son. Both were victims of Papa's paranoia, but, like Olivia, Tilly shares some of the blame for the bloodshed because she not only accepted Papa's treachery, but she also helped him act out his cleanup plans in order to protect her interests in the famed Winniper Family Holding Company. Although she does not know about the Winniper family's cursed babies, the Bethune family continues to reap the benefits for their role in defeating the Sioux uprising and securing the oil land for Thomas Winniper, Sr. As her family's sole survivor, Tilly has followed Papa's lead, trying her best to be a strong matriarch after losing her only child. "My Kenny boy been dead for over fifteen years now. Sheriff and them boys tore him to bits but your father still wouldn't let him go. I don't know what else I coulda done. We know how Tommy handles betrayal. Your father is going to let your nephew fry."

"No, he won't. Both of you are overreacting, like typical females." Thomas III chastises the women, remembering his father's earlier quip and projecting his own uselessness upon them. He dismisses Tilly's interruption by patting her knee softly and smiling confidently to reassure her that all is well in the fairytale life of Winniper County. He then squeezes his mother gently under his right arm and rubs her left shoulder gently. "You'll see, crazy ladies, Duke will be back at the mansion by Thanksgiving. We'll be eating dinner and enjoying the holidays like a happy, normal family worth $15 billion."

"You are so naive, Thomas. You have too much of me in you. But now, Tilly and I are too old to believe your father's lies anymore. And you, I don't know if you'll ever grow up." Olivia grimly describes their defeat and her words cut deeply into Thomas III's heart like only a mother's judgment can. Tilly turns her head and nods politely, agreeing with Olivia's brashness and her summation. In his mind, Thomas III retreats to the wooden playhouse at the Winniper Family Estate.

∞

He remembers how he and Teresa would use the old shed as a fortress where nothing could hurt them. They would play games for hours and there was always a happy ending. Papa would never walk across the estate just to interact with his children, so they both felt safe inside their playhouse. As he aged into adolescence, Thomas III realized that avoiding the pain that comes from criticism can cause a tension that explodes spontaneously from within. He tried to confront Papa's disappointment, but he soon understood that Papa would never accept his son as long as Thomas III could not lead the family through the blood and secrecy. Succumbing to his own weakness, Thomas III abandoned any ounce of self-respect so that he could desensitize himself to his father's abuse. He submitted his neural control to his fear of rejection and he lost his nerve in order to gain security.

∞

Now, he only fears criticism that could wound him so deep, that he could never heal.

"Your words hurt, Ma'," Thomas III admits candidly after a long pause, twisting his head toward the closed oak door leading to the courtroom lobby. "I wish I could get out of here."

"We're all grieving, Thomas. We've all lost people we care about, but you, you have the opportunity to save her…" Olivia pats her son's hand, instinctively comforting her child after consciously wounding his pride—this is the paradox of their relationship. His mother would fill the role of nurturer if she felt her son needed more care, but in fact, his problem is that he has received too much. He is not self-reliant; and, at the age of fifty-five, he still doesn't have a sense of direction, yet, she still tries to help him find his way. "You should take Nancy and go far away, Thomas. Get her away from your father."

"She's only three, Ma'. I…uh…where would we go? I…she's only ever known life at the mansion. I…we couldn't survive…without the money. What about when she's older?" Thomas III lowers his head again, trying to shut off his mind and avoid thinking about the inevitable implications in his daughter's life. Faced with the possibility of having to make more murderous decisions, Thomas III fears his future responsibilities—the father of a daughter who gives birth to a brown child. Because he is already an indecisive leech, he trembles between the lessons of his father and the moral compass in his spirit; and his daughter's life hangs in the balance. "I don't know what I'm going to do."

"Go home, pack your bags, and leave with Nancy. Do what Teresa couldn't. Take what you need and don't ever let him find you."

"Papa would look all over for me. I'm his son."

"He killed my son. And I helped him do it." Tilly confesses casually, protected by the war room's secretive acoustics. She stares into the mass of business suits surrounding Papa; but, her eyes burn with a newfound hatred. "We're sadistic people, Tommy boy. We justify everything with money."

"Well, we do have so much of it. Papa would find me no matter where I went, so, there's really no sense in running off in the first place."

"But, what about when Nancy becomes old enough for marriage, Thomas?" Olivia challenges her son, refusing to relinquish the subject while they whisper back and forth on the sofa. "If your father is still alive, he will do anything to protect our se-uh…our family. Think about that. Right now, Papa has Nancy and Christina under lock-and-key in that mansion and he will never let them go."

Olivia smiles wryly as she considers all the implications of being a Winniper woman; she recalls how the circumstances have changed over time, the unknown has become known throughout marriage, conception, and childbirth.

Whether they were born within the Winniper family's bloodline or they coupled with a Winniper male, the Winniper women have endured unbearable pain during and after giving birth to white and Sioux twins. Most Winniper mothers have experienced an unrelenting, emotional trauma after conceiving twins and being separated from one. They have been cursed to live within a patriarchal edict that dictates that only the white twin can survive.

Thomas III has come to believe that such sadness and torment would have destroyed a weak soul. His mother has always represented the strength necessary to survive the Winnipers' twin births, but she quietly praises Teresa for being the Winniper family's Madonna.

∞

Teresa saved Jazz, Charles, and Lucy, even at the cost of her own life. Although Teresa is still the only white Winniper woman who successfully saved her Sioux babies, she also suffered more than any Winniper woman, even more than June.

∞

Thomas III smiles at his mother in a moment of genuine reflection. He pats her hand gently and hopes the day's testimony will end soon so that he can return home to Nancy. There's no way Papa would let Christina or Nancy attend this public spectacle. Since Earl's conviction, Christina has battled depression and sleeplessness. Papa pays several housemaids to remain on duty overnight, just to comfort/confine Christina in the mansion's east wing. Though she grieves for the loss of her sister and grapples with the conviction of her former lover, she has not stopped seeking male affection and sexual gratification. In fact, a well-trained staff tends to all her wants and needs so that Christina never has a reason to leave home. Her psyche is so out of whack that she actually wanted to remain at the estate because she arranged for a few well-selected, well-built landscapers to service the grounds throughout the day. Thomas III can't recall one moment when Christina has read an article or even inquired about the attack or the trial. She knows her place and she has succumbed to the simple pleasures of her own exploitation.

Papa pretends not to notice Christina's sexual exploits because he is content that she distracts herself and remains confined to the estate. He remembers a lonely, inquisitive girl who posed so many real and potential problems with her science fair projects and her dreams of becoming a chemist. He would rather his granddaughters be dumb whores than smart, independent women—no one asks questions when dumb whores die unexpectedly. With Christina and Nancy under his roof, Papa can control the two female threats to his empire while orchestrating the execution of his youngest heir.

Still holding his mother under his arm, Thomas III glances around to the men surrounding his father, the wallflowers pressed against the oak, Tilly, and then his mother. He feels like each person in their family exists in an isolated, self-appeasing realm where each soul feels the burden of circumstances that none of them control. The Winniper family's blood and wealth intersect with each person's reality and the emerging conflicts construct a cruel game with the rules etched clearly in the stars: murder for power, God, and country, and never live for family, love, or truth.

"You're both right...we've done things that can't be forgiven. Nancy...she's the only innocent one in our family, but Duke...he still doesn't deserve this. He should've known better; he should've been strong, but...he was just like us. If he deserves to fry, then we all do, too." Thomas III finds his resolution, thinking in spite of inspiration. A large part of his soul wants to hide under the plush, red sofa, while a small sliver of self-respect yells a rally cry to galvanize his courage. Olivia feels her son's angst and lifts her head slightly. She stares at Thomas III and dabs her right eye with her handkerchief before grinning faintly. The moment of pride and joy instantly evaporates into the billowing cigar smoke that fogs the war room. Thomas III can see through the tobacco clouds that his mother doubts his resolve, believing that she knows his instincts, but, he raises his chest confidently, mimicking his father and amassing the courage to challenge him. Thomas III lifts his chin high in the air and becomes a superhero, again.

"I'm going to do something."

Thomas III unhooks his arm from around his mother's shoulders and stands like a soldier ready for war. He turns to both women and nods knowingly; he then wipes the creases of his suit jacket, adjusts the fit around his shoulders, and begins walking through the crowd, toward the war room's oak bathroom door. He ignores his father amidst his constituents and he only turns around once to see his mother and Tilly huddled together on the sofa, consoling one another amidst all the tragedy and coming trauma. Thomas III turns back toward the bathroom and grabs the brass doorknob with a hopeful hand. He feels himself disengaging from his temper, searching for the best intentions among those fatherly words that usually manifest moral miracles and justify the most heinous deeds.

He opens the door and steps into the bathroom silently, tears filling his eyes. He knows that his father is forcing the family to live a lie; and this lie is perpetual, without end in space or time. After stepping in front of the white opal bathroom's cream marble faucet and staring at his reflection in a wingspan mirror that stretches from wall-to-wall, Thomas III begins to loosen his tie, but he stops when he notices his forefathers' priceless revolver, still tucked within his jacket holster.

The sight of the gun's butt makes Thomas III think about how he has been the butt of many jokes. His throat croaks and fills with a small spill of vomit. The realization of his father's never-ending treachery and the threat said treachery poses to his daughter's life causes his stomach to twist violently. His insides somersault and turn upside down; Thomas III spins toward the white chrome toilet behind him and prepares for a purge. He crouches over the commode and begins to gag repeatedly, sending red and white chunks into the stool. Flashes of June's funeral procession fill his mind.

∞

The jazz trumpeters and drumline following her crimson casket as it crept down Winding Winniper Way, so similar to Teresa's funeral—both requests made in separate wills. After attending Teresa's funeral as a child, June always wanted to be buried like her mother, but she never thought she would die like her mother, too. Thomas III wondered why Papa fulfilled their requests and arranged such publicly extravagant funerals.

National and international news outlets broadcast June's funeral from beginning to end, and Papa even allowed them to film the family's mournful procession from the mansion to the cemetery. Thomas III assumed that somewhere within, Papa still felt a kinship, a duty to see his victims through to the other side; but, in actuality, during both June and Teresa's respective funerals, Papa only wanted to capitalize upon the spectacle in order to present the image of a grieving patriarch, willing himself to be strong and keep his family together through tragedy. Life played a cruel joke upon him, giving him wealth while forcing him to murder those closest to him in order to protect it.

∞

Thomas III continues to hurl into the toilet as the memories flood his consciousness: he sees June's blood-colored casket descending slowly into her grave.

∞

Cameras flashed, onlookers cried, and news crews recorded and streamed the event around the world. Papa created a jazz procession fit for a South Dakota queen and the international news replayed June's funeral in its entirety several times throughout the following weeks.

Shortly after the funeral, inside a guarded and secluded hospital room, Jazz, Charles, and Berthine watched the reruns and news coverage from a raised television in the corner. Still struggling to emerge fully from his coma, Jazz passed in and out of consciousness, stuck between reality and his dreams. He remained unconscious for days after the attack, and even when he did wake, it took months before he could maintain a consistent level of alertness. Every so often, he would open his eyes wide, stare at the television screen, shed a tear, and quickly dose off. The swelling in his brain, plus the loss of his love, caused him to experience a queasy unbalance like he was continually tossing and turning on top of turbulent waves. Lying in his hospital bed, he felt incapable of finding a solid foundation in the world.

Ironically, Papa was one of the first people who visited Jazz—he and Thomas III were among an exclusive list of permitted guests who were allowed to see Winniper County Central Hospital's most famous patient. Just a few weeks after the attack and only a day or two after June's funeral, Papa and Thomas III arrived at Jazz's heavily-protected hospital room on the top floor of the 12-story building. In anticipation of meeting his long-lost Sioux grandson, Papa quipped that he hoped for the best but expected the worst. Following Papa's orders, Thomas III quickly escorted Berthine and Charles out of the room in order to give the old man a chance to finally come face-to-face with Jazz in the aftermath of June's death. What was said inside those walls is only known by the two men; maybe Papa promised to serve Duke on a platter. Maybe they discussed and planned today's courtroom tactics without Thomas III's knowledge or input. Maybe, just maybe, Thomas III has finally become a complete outcast in a patriarchal family where so few heirs survive.

∞

His last vile thought elicits more fireworks from his gullet and he pukes full force into the round, white toilet. He takes a moment to glance back toward the bathroom door, wondering if someone will hear his projectile revelation. Suddenly, he does not care, a psychotic break with reality overcomes his modesty and he continues to vomit the rest of his morning toast and eggs benedict into the toilet bowl. He continues to heave until undigested bits of last night's steak tartar launch into his throat. He can feel the clumps amalgamating to the tight space and adjusting through his tonsils as they work their way into his mouth. He spits and gags and coughs a mixture of mucus and minced meat into the toilet. He can feel the emptiness within his stomach, the satisfaction of being free. The sight of his evacuated feast makes him laugh as the last exiled contents of his stomach join the party at the bottom of the bowl.

All his sins seem to stare back at him through the reflection of his vomit: Teresa's murder, pushing her car off the road and watching his sister careen into a tree. He keeps replaying the moment when her head bounced so violently off the steering wheel that the force snapped her neck.

∞

He saw through the windshield that she died instantly, and as he rolled his blue Ford T truck next to her, he slowed down just enough to stare at her through his passenger window. The sheriff followed in his patrol car, waiting for Thomas III to flee the scene.

Teresa was a glassy shamble of her vibrant self and he, he no longer was her hero. With her last breath, her last look, Thomas III wonders if she knew; if she understood how she had betrayed him. She planned to leave with her family, and he would've been stuck with Papa—a son who couldn't follow orders and a brother who couldn't control his sister. June may have seen the same demons in Duke during her last moments; the worst tragedies occur when champions lose to weaker foes. And just like Thomas III turned his truck around and drove back to his market, Duke, Earl, and their two friends hopped into their getaway car and drove back to a local bar. In both instances, the soldiers knew they had done their duty, but at what cost?

∞

The toilet now tells a new truth that is so evident: Thomas III is ashamed that he hasn't had the resolve to rebel against his father's lies. The only way their family's misery will cease is if someone tells the truth and shames the devil. Someone must disrupt the status quo. While hunched over the toilet, the revolver's barrel begins to poke his ribs from inside his jacket holster. He adjusts his position over the rim and feels a few lasting remnants galloping through his esophagus.

Thomas III takes a moment to cough and flex and gag before spitting a few remaining chunks, distilled from his anxious revelry. He finally understands his destiny within today's confusion. The son of a king, but he has never been given the chance to succeed; and his father unapologetically compensates for his weakness. Thomas III has always been and will always be the hacking goat, the family joke, the fool who has only behaved as he was told and still receives no respect from those whose orders he follows.

He leans back, quickly removes his Stein-Bloch jacket, and tosses it over the back of the toilet. He's careful not to make too much noise, but he can hear some of the extra bullets clanking against one another within the jacket's pocket. Thomas III then carefully removes the Colt revolver from the jacket holster and gently places it on the floor next to the toilet.

Feeling the leather begin to burn against his white dress shirt, he unhooks the holster from his shoulders and holds it above the toilet in his right hand. The image of the family heirloom makes him more nauseous and he contemplates tossing it into the toilet. The revolver and the jacket holster represent the sins of his forefathers and the disease that has plagued his family for generations—not pregnant women who give birth to biracial twins, but rather, their family's disease is unrestrained greed without moral context. Such greed can never afford peace. It is a morbid virus that infects and destroys anything it comes into contact with because greed without constraints for humanity has the power to destroy humanity itself.

∞

The leather holster and the revolver originally belonged to his great-grandfather, who gave them to his youngest son, Thomas, who then used them to massacre a village and establish the family's oil empire. Thomas, Sr. gave the heirlooms to his only son, who became Papa and manifested his father's dreams into a reality. Thomas III received them after killing Teresa; Papa had hoped to inspire him.

Neither the revolver nor the holster is to blame for the Winniper family's tragedies, but wicked men have used both to bring about wicked ends. Now, detached from his father's teachings, Thomas III rises from the toilet, filled with a sense of reckoning, still holding the holster in his right hand. He stands on the precipice of his absolution and stares into the toilet bowl.

His decision becomes clear, recklessly so; yet, his simpish nature causes a lasting sliver of trepidation to flow through his resolve. Instead of tossing the holster into the toilet or the nearby trash can next to the faucet, Thomas III merely places the leather gun holder behind the toilet, tucked away with the hope that no one will see it before he makes his move for a resolution. He flushes the toilet and watches his purge descend into the drain; he then takes another quick glance toward the bathroom door and listens carefully for any nearby movement—there is none.

Thomas III promptly grabs his black cashmere jacket from the back of the toilet and flattens the wrinkles with his hand. Patting down the creases and waving the jacket through the air like a waspy matador, he lifts the jacket back over his shoulders and pushes his arms through, but he stops suddenly and stares down at the Colt revolver. What to do? With the holster dispatched behind the toilet, he wonders where he could hide the weapon. The death threats aimed at the family are still real, and there's still no telling what may happen when the verbal fireworks truly start. Thomas III plans to scream the truth so that he is loud enough for the entire world to hear.

He plans to make a spectacle so big that his family has no choice but to change. June's death will not be in vain and, maybe, just maybe, the judge and jury will have mercy on Duke because he was not the mastermind behind June's murder. Yes, the revolver is necessary; the weapon must come along for the same reason that most guns become travel companions—Thomas III wants to make sure the townspeople and his father finally hear and respect him.

The forgotten son reaches down and picks up the old steel revolver, holding the weight in his left hand. He gently slips the weapon into the inside pocket of his jacket and he hears those clanking bullets making space within. The butt of the revolver peaks through the top of the pocket and Thomas III turns around toward the faucet and the mirror so that he can decipher whether onlookers will be able to detect the revolver from several angles.

After inspecting himself in the mirror and twisting his upper body into various poses, he decides to fasten the bottom two of the three buttons of his suit jacket, in order to keep appearances without arousing suspicion. The open top button provides the necessary slack and the closed bottom two create a snug fit that both accommodates and conceals the weapon. Thomas III takes a lasting look at himself in the mirror and he notices a glimpse of self-respect that eliminates his trepidation and solidifies his resolve. He feels Teresa's spirit swirling around him; he knows that none of his actions can bring his sister back or repair his broken family, but, at least, for once, his actions will be pure, genuine, and filled with hope that he can somehow still be a hero by saving Duke from an execution. There will be no more unnecessary bloodshed from the Winniper family because Thomas III has decided that he will be the family's last martyr. He exits the bathroom with the stride of a messiah with a cross to bear.

Stepping out of the bathroom, the entire war room is empty. Only waning wafts of cigar smoke remain over the plush chairs and sofas, escaping through the open doorway into the courthouse hallway. Thomas III sees John Allen walk past the doorway of the war room, crooning with his counterparts from the County Attorney's Office. A crowd of minions and admirers join his procession while they all still ruminate over his public anointment via his handshake with Papa.

The noble prosecutor and his brood laugh about filing frivolous motions and following today's leisurely court exhibition with a few rounds of golf. They know their skins play will be their only true competition, today. Thomas III gathers himself and walks through his father's war room. When he reaches the doorway, he looks both ways down the marble-floored hallway, searching for his parents, Tilly, or anyone from their flock. Seeing none, he sighs in relief and turns his attention to his right where Mr. Allen and his crowd now stand in the hallway's corner nearest to the courthouse lobby. Thomas III remembers his resolution and walks directly through Mr. Allen's cohorts without hearing their words or caring about their purpose. They are passing posts, obstacles to be ignored on the path toward betrayal. Within a moment of pure vengeance and unrepentant freedom, Thomas III stands directly in front of John Allen, prepared to meet his maker.

"Johnny boy…" Thomas III speaks slowly, but surely; he squares his shoulders so that his frame parallels Mr. Allen. They are on equal footing, within a small audience. "Call me as a witness."

"What?" John Allen tilts his head to the side and narrows his eyes sharply, wondering if this is somehow a setup, maybe a test. He glances over his shoulders and around the corner, searching for Papa or anyone with a close affiliation. Seeing no one overtly suspicious, he sighs in relief and turns his attention back to Thomas III. "What are you talking about, Tommy boy?"

"I know what's going on here, John," Thomas III asserts his claim toughly, planting a flag on his newfound resolve and attracting more attention from Mr. Allen's closest confidants. Thomas III can feel the miniscule crowd lean in to hear more of the conversation. He moves closer to John Allen and begins to whisper. "I know that Papa is letting Duke take the fall."

"That's an outrageous claim," Mr. Allen responds coyly, lowering his voice, tilting his head, and turning away from the crowd. He uses his right shoulder to shield their conversation from his legal team. "I think you should rethink whatever you're thinking, because…"

"Johnny boy, I won't let you do this to my nephew. I'll confess and take the rap for him before I let Papa feed him to the dogs. Just put me on the stand."

"I can't let you do that, Thomas."

"Duke didn't plan this, he didn't want…"

"Listen, I understand you're upset, but I can't discuss the facts of the case with you. You should really talk to your father." Mr. Allen pauses, hesitant to make any false moves when mentioning the name of the king. Papa still has eyes and ears everywhere. "Did you hear when Papa said I'd make a good mayor, someday? Practically won me the election right there, huh?"

"What kind of campaign can you run with Duke's blood on your hands?" Thomas III asks angrily, nudging his left elbow against his childhood friend's ribs. "You're letting his own grandfather send him to the chair."

"Maybe it's for the best, Tommy boy."

"How could you say that, John? 'For the best'?"

"I-I'm sorry, Thomas. I didn't mean that," Mr. Allen explains nervously, looking over his shoulder and observing the eager ears crowding around their conversation. All three of Mr. Allen's assistants suspect that the fix is in, many of the townsfolk agree, but the potential for mayhem is always intriguing. "It's just that, you know, we all have orders to follow."

"Duke doesn't deserve this," Thomas III insists; his urgency emerges through his tone as he continues to press the county attorney. "Papa...he has us all on puppet strings, especially you, *Johnny boy*."

"You think I don't know that? There's nothing I can do, Thomas. Your old man has all the power in this town. We all practically work for him."

"But I don't," Thomas III announces convincingly. "I'm my own man, now."

"Thomas, you can't. If you incriminate yourself, I would have to charge you..."

"I don't care, not anymore. I just want to save my nephew. Call me as your next witness."

"I can't do that, Tommy. I already have the medical examiner prepped."

"Perfect. Doc Junior probably knows more secrets about my family than I do. He can testify after me."

"Thomas, you're not listening. Your father would-"

"No, *you're* not listening, John. You're going to call me up to the stand, and I'm going to tell the truth. And if you don't, I'll expose every bit of this cover up on the evening news." Thomas III stomps his words down John Allen's throat and he feels the force of his resolve solidly plant a foundation in the county attorney's consciousness. Mr. Allen stares oddly at Thomas III, searching for any schisms in his old friend's firmness; finding none, he thinks of all the possible repercussions.

"Thomas, you wouldn't go mentioning me or your father, now, would you? I'm just a lowly servant trying to climb my way to the top. Even if you tell the truth, your father will still be in power. Do you know what he's capable of doing if we cross him?"

"I'll leave you and him out of it, Tommy. You can say I forced you, put a gun to your head. Just let me confess to helping Earl plan the attack. I'll say Duke was just there, along for the ride, but he didn't kill June. The judge may even grant Duke a mistrial and you can lower the charges, take the death penalty off the table." Thomas III lies through his explanation, leaning even closer and balling his fists. He plans to serve his father's sins on a platter and he can feel an inner angst bubbling within his stomach and coursing through his veins. "But you better call me first, Tommy, or all hell will break loose inside that courtroom."

As Thomas III leans into him, John Allen looks down and notices the butt of the revolver peeking out of the inside pocket of Thomas III's jacket. John Allen quickly turns his shoulders so that he's facing Thomas III, staring at him in pure shock as if he no longer recognizes his childhood friend.

"How'd you get that in here?" He whispers anxiously, looking around to see if anyone else notices the weapon. "Everyone was supposed to be searched outside before being let into the courthouse. Sheriff Cobb would pitch a fit."

"Papa asked me to bring it for protection." Thomas III responds coldly, leaning away from John Allen and adjusting his jacket so that he conceals more of the loaded revolver.

"Why would your father need protection? He has Sheriff Cobb and a whole police force at his disposal. If anything, we need protection from him." John Allen instinctively identifies the greatest threat in the courthouse, but he quickly pauses and realizes his misstep after reading Thomas III's reaction. Both men understand the repercussions of defying the dictator, but, while Thomas III can become the disgruntled trust fund baby, John Allen must play the role of a compliant public servant, honor bound and forcibly compelled. He senses the implications; Sheriff Cobb, Jr.'s cronies march throughout the courthouse, visually probing every strange face. Mr. Allen is like Cinderella; he's trapped under Papa's wicked sorcery, in which, Papa can conjure any spell or calamity. Thomas III does not fear becoming a toad, but John Allen still has dreams of wearing the glass slippers at the mayoral ball.

"Take the jacket off, Tommy, and put *that*…away."

"No, and don't make a scene." Thomas III steps toward Mr. Allen and places his right palm on his old friend's shoulder. "We do this my way, got it?"

"Tommy, I understand this is tough, but…we've known each other since we were kids. Don't do anything stupid."

"All my life, I've been stupid."

"But you've always been protected, Tommy. You blackmail me into bringing you on the stand, and…I'm not sure…"

"Listen…don't worry about me. Just do what you do best and worry about yourself. I know what I'm doing. And unless you want my testimony to involve the meetings between you, the defense team, the judge, and my father, you'll do what's best for you…just like you always do."

"Tommy, take it easy, and lower your voice." John Allen steps even closer to Thomas III, forgoing normal spatial decency because he values his reputation beyond these mere moments of social awkwardness. Will he allow Thomas III to testify, even though Thomas III holds a grenade that is powerful enough to explode and expose the entire town's corruption? Could some of his convictions be overturned? John Allen can only trust that his childhood buddy will spare the innocent from whatever vitriol he has planned. Mr. Allen hopes he can convince Papa that Tommy really did force him at gunpoint, under threat of death and personal exposure. The county attorney sighs deeply and convinces himself that somehow these events will benefit his self-interests. He still views himself as an anointed child of God. "Do what you will, Tommy, but keep me, your father, and the judge out of it. The defense may challenge your right to testify even if…I mean, *when* I do call you. Some of us have careers to protect, Tommy. And you still better put that damn thing away before you take the stand. There's no way Judge Rupert will let you come to the stand with that on you."

"Okay, I will take care of it." Thomas III backs away and eases the tension between the two men. "Just follow through with your part, Johnny boy…*or else.*"

"Hey, take it easy. Okay…okay, Thomas? You want to cross your father, it's your funeral," Mr. Allen mumbles the last part under his breath, stepping back amongst his team, huddling hurriedly, and disseminating new directives. The county attorney promptly points toward the courtroom and leads an all-out charge around the corner and through the courthouse lobby. Thomas III steps around the corner and stands alone against the wall opposite the courtroom doors. He is a dark silhouette against an all-white background. Refusing to return to his concern for Papa's whereabouts, he shuffles toward the courtroom and walk through the doorway just as the bailiff begins to address the meandering crowd.

"All rise! All rise! The Honorable Judge Donald K. Rupert presiding!" The bailiff yells triumphantly; his voice echoes while he conducts traffic and ushers the jury and the gallery to stand from their seats. Thomas III slinks back into the courtroom and walks gingerly through the gallery aisle to await his father and mother and their troops. He fears the coming moment, if he will or will not testify to save his nephew. Duke stands quietly at the defense table, all alone, although several uniformed officers surround him. The door to Judge Rupert's chambers opens eerily like a haunted, squeaky-hinged door in a low-budget horror film. The judge lumbers into the courtroom, noticeably irritated when he looks up to see that yes, in fact, the crowd still remains and the court charade must continue. An expression of elderly disgust graces his face as he ascends the few steps to his bench and sits down with a disappointed exhale.

John Allen and his legal troops rush into the courtroom through a side door and the county attorney shrugs his shoulders toward the judge, begging forgiveness for his tardiness. Mr. Allen then steals a quick glance toward Thomas III and grimaces at the sight of the newfound traitor. Mr. Erickson and his legal crew follow Mr. Allen's brigade and both teams measure their competition as the defense walks by the prosecution.

When Mr. Erickson and his associates join Ms. Shields and her cohorts at the defense table, the defense outnumbers Mr. Allen and his associates three to one. Although Mr. Allen may seem outgunned, both sides have spent a similar amount of money and time on labor, investigation, and pageantry.

∞

Papa wanted to make sure that everyone knew Duke's trial would be fair.

∞

Even so, the town still talks about the injustice surrounding June's murder. The public and the press begin filling the rows, standing in place, and crowding the walls while Judge Rupert adjusts the neckline of his black robe, scratches the brim of his glasses, and secretly dares anyone to sit without his permission.

Thomas III steps toward the front row, but he glances over his shoulder and see his parents, Tilly, and their legions marching toward him down the main aisle. The accountants crunch numbers on small calculators, the business partners write cables for constituents around the world, and Fred delegates responsibilities to the remaining minions after receiving the orders directly from Papa's lips. Leaning over the tycoon's right shoulder, Fred whispers feedback and interprets every action based upon how to achieve desired results. Both he and Papa are always hunting for another dollar to add to the Winniper Family Estate.

The reporters and columnists continue to clamor and stand in front of their seats in the press rows at the back of the courtroom. Some radio jockeys speak softly into recorders and several journalists scratch shorthand notes on small writing pads. Thomas III straightens his back as his parents approach him and pass without a word. He then joins Tilly amongst the convoy as they enter the front row and stand in front their seats nearest the defense table.

Olivia's eyes start to tear up again at the sight of Duke, still standing at the defense table as the officers leave his side to make room for his lawyers. She wants to call to him, but Papa nudges her right shoulder and gently pushes her forward until she stands next to her son.

Quieted with quieter, Thomas III and his mother are two sheep who must now watch another slaughter. Thomas III stands with Tilly at his side and he drops his shoulders, slouching away from the foreground of the courtroom. His mannerisms and body language physically reject the court's authority, although he remains as quiet as a baby mouse sleeping on cheese pillows. He feels like he once did after attending church for the last time; he's preparing to tell his parents that he no longer believes the lies.

"You may be seated. This court is now in session. I hope you all enjoyed your recess." Judge Rupert bangs his gavel and everyone in the courtroom sits down with one exhausted motion, irritated after waiting so long for decorum's sake. "Remembering that some of us have to be home for their afternoon tea time, I hope we can move along pretty briskly and then adjourn around three. Will the prosecution call for a rebuttal of the last witness?"

"No, Your Honor," Mr. Allen grumbles, throwing another frightened look towards the Winniper family. Judge Rupert has clearly forgotten their previous conversation; the aged judiciary is beginning to reveal his issues with memory loss. Mr. Allen chooses to placate the judge, in hopes of setting the scene for what comes next. "Considering Mr. Lancaster's physical condition, we felt it best to recuse him from any further testimony, if Your Honor agrees."

"Yes…" Judge Rupert concurs in response, upset that he was neither consulted nor included in the petty motions of this farce. His forgetfulness combines with his ego into a potentially catastrophic temper. "I wish you or the defense would have consulted with me regarding this issue. It's customary that the sitting judge be informed when…a witness…a young man from our fair county, who has been through so much. Yes, so much indeed that…"

"Yes, Your Honor, uh…*so much*," John Allen interrupts awkwardly and there is a moment of pause while he stalls and avoids any notion of disrespect. "I'm just thankful that Your Honor is the sitting judge for this trial. Your expertise is world renowned."

"I don't care about the world. I just care about our county and our country, the good ole U-S of A. Mr. Allen, please call your next witness." Judge Rupert finishes his rant and boisterously demands compliance, hoping to move the process along. "I'm having tea with my wife at four o'clock and I don't want to have to hear about it if I'm late."

"Uh, yes, Your Honor…neither do I." John Allen laughs nervously and glances over to Thomas III one last time. "Uh, Your Honor, the…uh, the…uh, prosecution calls…Mister…uh…Mister Thomas, uh…Thomas W…Winniper…*the Third.*"

Gasps from around the courtroom suck in all of the air between the four walls. Thomas III hears his name and the words bounce from his ear drums, consume him, and expand throughout the courtroom in a silent wildfire. There's a still moment during which everyone stops and looks toward Thomas III and his family in the front row; and the people within the courtroom breathe slowly, staring in awe and wondering who will light the fireworks that they have been waiting to see. Papa, sitting with his left arm around Olivia's shoulders, also turns his head sharply to his left and burns a hole through Thomas III's skull, melting his brain and incinerating his spine. Thomas III is suddenly paralyzed with fear.

"*What's this?*" Papa asks gruffly, leaning across his wife as the bailiff walks closer to Thomas III. Thomas III remains in his seat, silent, mimicking Duke in mannerism and willpower, but then, he recalls his resolve to be the hero. His fifty-five-year-old legs can't remember how to stand, but he feels his hips begin to stir. His motor cortex becomes active and the voices of his forefathers beg him to speak the truth and save their family. Thomas III begins to rise within the front row while looking around the courtroom and seeing all the wide eyes mirroring his amazement. He watches them while they watch him, and no one says anything, except Papa. Reaching across Olivia with his right hand, Papa grabs his son's right wrist, and he asks menacingly, growling from deep within his throat. "*What are you doin', boy?*"

Thomas III still can't muster a response, and he struggles to maintain his balance under his father's grip. He feels the pressure to relent and sit down. The patriarch's strength is apparent to those watching, and a scandal forms in each onlooker's mind.

As Thomas III continues to rise from his seat, he looks to John Allen for help or a handout, but the county attorney only glances down to his own suit jacket and pats the pocket. Thomas III remembers the Colt revolver tucked within his jacket pocket and he nods knowingly, encouraged by the talisman close to his ribs. He defiantly tugs his right arm away from his father and slowly takes off his suit jacket, carefully folding the gun within the creases without letting the butt be seen. Initially, he leans to his right toward his father, but when he looks into the old man's face, he can only see a snake preparing to strike. In fear, Thomas III then turns back to his left toward Tilly and holds the suit jacket in front of her.

"Can you hold this for me, Ms. Tilly?" He asks tentatively. Tilly looks up to him with watery eyes and raises her weary, gloved hands. She meekly grasps the cashmere jacket and pauses when she feels the weapon within. She looks back up to him with confusion spilling over her face. Thomas III smiles assuredly as he feels her accept the weight of the suit jacket and the revolver. "Thank you, Tilly. I'll be right back."

"Mr. Winniper, please step forward!" Judge Rupert beckons, and Thomas III turns away from Tilly. Thomas III stares at the judge and then looks toward Duke, who has resumed staring out the lone window of the courtroom. Though his nephew's body is present, his mind and spirit are completely absent. Realizing a larger purpose than servitude to his father's lies and obedience to his murderous conscience, Thomas III turns his head toward Papa and serves the serpent an equally venomous stare. He glares intently at the man who terrorized his youth and transformed his adulthood into a mockery of manhood.

Thomas III breaks their stare to look down upon his mother and grin slightly. He then begins to squeeze past his parents, inching through the row until he reaches the aisle and walks toward the courtroom foreground. Thomas III inhales deeply as he crosses the threshold and he exhales when he walks between the defense and prosecution tables. The silence within the courtroom continues to build expectations and the moment bathes in possibility; anything can happen now. Creaks in the floorboard, nervous whispers, and anxious sighs produce a soundtrack to the coming spectacle: a Winniper heir testifies in the murder trial of the century.

Thomas III once again turns his attention toward Duke, who momentarily detaches his eyes from the window and meets his uncle's stare with an equal look of confusion. Thomas III forces his face to make a foolish smile so that he looks like a child who has been caught with his hand in the cookie jar. Duke responds with a similarly sorrowful grin; they are two bloody-handed babies, posing as men in a cold world. Their smiles reveal an inheritance filled with greed and grief.

∞

Thomas Winniper, Sr. taught Papa to never smile, never show pure joy or amusement. Stern, disconnected strength must protect their money and power. When Papa tried to instill these values into Thomas III, in order to develop the necessary fortitude within his son, Papa lost his son's love because the boy was a constant disappointment and Papa had to let him know it. Papa's chastisement, putdowns, and faux male guilt created a rift between father and son that has never mended.

∞

Truthfully, they haven't connected since Thomas III became an adolescent and his masculine shortcomings became apparent.

∞

The son struggled to impress; he seemed incapable of deceiving, threatening, or conquering the world that Papa had created for his son to inherit. When Thomas III could not perform to his father's expectations, he drowned in insults, yet he learned to swim through the pestilence.

∞

So, although Papa's orders and values are mostly violent and callous, Thomas III credits the moments of brash instruction and murder for secrecy as the defining influences to his withdrawal from the Winniper family's sweepstakes. He has grown to despise their wealth, their estate, their oil, their land, their town, their country, their global empire and everything within that reeks of Teresa and June's blood.

"Who knows how many other women have become victims of the Winniper curse," he thinks.

∞

The cashier girl who bore Nancy, hoping to finance her dreams in a shotgun courtship, died without ever holding her daughter. Her absence forced Thomas III to become Nancy's primary guardian and he obediently remained at the Winniper Family Estate because, even at forty-nine as he was at the time, he could not bear the responsibility. He had little money and no means to provide for her; he has lived most of his life at the Winniper Family Estate. His travels with Teresa were not enough to teach him how to survive in the modern jungle.

∞

Since returning to the Winniper Family Estate, due to fear and instinct, he has witnessed his father's treachery become insatiable.

628

∞

Thomas III felt powerless, unable to muster the energy to escape with his daughter or act against his father, until now.

∞

Realizing Papa's plans to sacrifice Duke for the good of the Winniper Family brand, Thomas III has decided that he no longer wants the right to be miserable. He would rather be happy and free, and, if he can't have that for himself, he would at least like his daughter and all of Teresa's surviving children to be free from Papa's treachery. And while Thomas III and his nephew share a fleetingly jovial smirk, they each struggle to see the humor in their predicament. Thomas III is the hopeful emancipator, marching to replace his nephew and save Duke from death row.

∞

"Now, Your Honor, I must object!" Mr. Erickson rises as Thomas III moves through the foreground and walks toward the witness stand. "Mr. Winniper was not listed as a witness. The defense is entitled to a recess…"

"You are right, Mr. Erickson," Judge Rupert complies, puffing his cheeks and exhaling in exhaustion; his turkey sandwich is starting to settle in his stomach. "Would the defense like a recess?"

Mr. Erickson promptly turns to Papa and the entire courtroom waits for the king's approval to proceed. Papa still scowls at his wayward prince, calculating his faithless heir's significance, combined with the public spectacle. Fred leans forward from the second row and whispers something into Papa's right ear.

"Is Fred giving you permission to let me testify, Pa'?" Thomas III asks loudly, pausing in the middle of the courtroom. The question lingers in the air; Thomas III feels a sense of power and he raises his chest proudly. "I thought you still call the shots in Winniper County."

Papa remains silent, while estimating that despite what happens, his managers can still implement their comeback plan to clean up any public backlash. He could have his son dragged to the hospital and diagnosed as a lunatic. He could have Judge Rupert grant a recess or a mistrial; he could have Mr. Allen drop the charges. He could even have the entire testimony concealed so that no one could ever publish his son's statements. Yes, he could choose any of these actions, but Papa has grown into a miserly, stubborn, and prideful relic.

629

He leans back atop his mountain, gazing down upon his subjects in the courtroom, and he realizes that the future will happen as a consequence of his impartiality. In the end, his money will determine his son's worth, and his power will shape the narrative to benefit his prosperity. Papa smirks after finally noticing the fly in his house. He swipes his hand through the air, dismissively relinquishing the defense to proceed so that his chaste son may bury himself alongside his mute grandson.

"No, Your Honor, I think we can handle the witness's testimony," Mr. Erickson announces confidently, turning back to the judge. The bailiff ushers Thomas III into the witness stand and places the Bible in front of him. The traitor pauses before remembering June and Teresa. He then thinks of Nancy and places his hand upon the cross.

"Do you swear to tell the truth, the whole truth, so help you God?"

"I…uh…" Thomas III stutters sheepishly, "…yes…I do." A thousand drums pound in his stomach as he completes his answer. Anxiety increases his pulse and he sits hesitantly within the witness stand. John Allen slowly strolls around the prosecution table, tiptoeing on egg shells while looking between Papa and Thomas III. Between the powerful and the powerless, the prominent and the pathetic, Mr. Allen has no idea how to proceed, but he has an instinctual motive to begin by protecting his own hide.

"Now, Mr. Winniper, moments ago you begged me to let you testify…" Mr. Allen begins, turning back to Papa and hoping to explain his actions by highlighting Thomas III's earlier insistence. "You practically threatened me to bring you on the stand; my associates were there and can also testify to that fact! You said you have vital information for the court, is that correct?"

"Yes, I did…and I do." Thomas III answers plainly and clears his throat as he glances toward his father, but quickly returns his eyes to Mr. Allen.

"And what is this *vital information*? What do you want to share with the court?" John Allen asks condescendingly, still turning back and forth between Papa and Thomas III. Thomas III takes several deep breaths, while he continues to struggle with the finality of his actions. He knows that Johnny boy's political career will end today if they do not tread lightly. Papa may smear everyone involved in the trial, unless Thomas III delivers a testimonial blow so deep that he punctures his father's protective shield.

Imagine a chink in the old man's powerful armor; a mistake or flaw so disastrous that the family's lawyers, advisors, and henchmen can't repair the damage. Thomas III would have to destroy his father's influence, force the company's stock to plummet, and hope that the old man cannot stop the fall of his empire. Thomas III is an ant plotting the downfall of a giant, hoping to find a weakness where none seems available. He knows that in order to expose his father, he must expose himself, and he sits nervously within his chair, on the precipice of a careful confession. Mr. Allen walks closer to the witness stand and comes to terms with his own circumstances. Praying for a miracle filled with wit and tact, he prepares to balance his approach and carefully maneuver between securing his seat at the Winnipers' dinner table and driving the nails through his own coffin.

"Please tell the court, Mr. Winniper. What do you know about the incident?"

"I...uh...I know that...what happened to June...was...it was more than an act of violence. It was planned...by my father." Another wave of gasps washes over the gallery and Thomas III begins to see the magnitude of his words. He looks beyond John Allen and stares at the citizens, the townspeople he spoke to every day at the market. "I know most of you believe differently, but my father is an evil man. Duke didn't plan June's murder. My father ordered him to do it."

"Is that so? You believe your father, the accused's grandfather, ordered the accused to commit the crime for which he is charged here, today?" Mr. Allen prods with an increased sense of urgency. He is appalled at his old friend's candor, but amidst the testimony, he instinctually plays his role, although he still glances back to Papa and obediently checks with his master. The county attorney still wonders how he should proceed from step-to-step, unsure what he will discover around the corner. He decides to continue a slow-roasted line of questioning that covers all his bases and leaves him with as much protection as possible. He plans to exonerate himself from any wrongdoing regardless of how this testimony ends. "Um, what do you mean by, *'ordered him to do it'*? Care to explain?"

"Duke never wanted to hurt June. He was forced to go to that café."

"A grown man was *'forced to go to that café'*? By your grandfather who wasn't even present?" John Allen begins to hammer away, hoping Papa will see that his tone and delivery indicate that he has no intention of validating Thomas III's testimony. His coercion must seem implicit in his performance. Mr. Allen continues to guard his future while turning around and seeing Papa's wide eyes boring holes into his son. The county attorney steps out of the line of fire as Papa stares directly at Thomas III, ignoring Mr. Allen's role in the betrayal. Mr. Allen can see the malice and vengeance in Papa's eyes, and he knows that at worst, he may encounter only a portion of Papa's wrath, but, at best, he may still be able to wear those glass slippers. "You still haven't told much to the court, Mr. Winniper. Please, justify our time, and your reason for *forcing me* to call you testify, today. What do you know?"

"It was…uh…uh…I mean to say…*he* was…" Thomas III stammers, attempting to bring the suppressed truth to his lips after a lifetime of secrecy. He struggles to contain parts of the painful past, the murders, and the burned babies, but he no longer knows where to draw the line. The dam must break. "June's death wasn't accident and it wasn't those boys' idea to do it. Duke and them were ordered…they were ordered to harm June. And…uh…it was me, my father, and the sheriff that told them to do it."

The entire courtroom reacts: women shriek, men howl, reporters clamor in the back row, and cameras begin to snap wildly throughout the gallery. Thomas III imagines that the cameras transform into guns, and his life is now in danger. The firing squad has received the news, and they won't wait for the judge's ruling.

"Order! Order!" Judge Rupert yells grimly, raising his voice out of formality. He, too, becomes enthralled in the testimony's potential, like all the other people within the courtroom. Suddenly, the old man is a participant in the trial, and his reputation and livelihood hinge upon Thomas III's betrayal. The judge secretly hopes the middle-aged boy will destroy the entire Winniper Empire and emancipate the Rupert family from Papa's control.

For his part, Papa continues to glare murderously at Thomas III, trying to feign a guise of apathetic indifference. Papa ponders over his courses of action, many with violent outcomes; but, on the surface of his face, he is unwilling to validate his son's betrayal and he refuses to become a victim to a former pawn. He is a king who still sits proudly upon his throne.

"So, you're saying...your father, one of the most respected and successful businessmen *in the world*, ordered Duke Winniper to assault and murder his own sister?" Mr. Allen asks sheepishly, feeling the sweat from his feet soak through his socks. It's a new sensation; he fears a witness's testimony and he realizes that he doesn't have a script. He must improvise while ensuring his safety and minimizing his culpability. "Why would your father give such an order? Do you have any proof that what you're saying is true?"

"We have a lot of family secrets that Pa' doesn't want the world to know. He's killed people before...and...*so have I.*" Thomas III admits clearly and the truth becomes easier to verbalize. As the courtroom continues to clamor, stewing in the humid September heat that still lingers from a long, hot summer. The tension rises to a high boil.

"They killed June!" a woman screams amidst the commotion.

"Order! Order! Officers, please tend to your duties! Send those disturbers to the sheriff!" Judge Rupert bangs his gavel roughly, pointing for several officers to hunt down the woman, the frantic press agents, and any overly anxious crowd members. "Mr. Allen, please get on with it."

"Yes, sir, Your Honor. Mr. Winniper...Mr. Winniper, please give me, er, uh, the court...please give the court more specifics!" Mr. Allen speaks over the melee, arching his back and clicking the heels of his black Mezlan dress shoes. "Tell us exactly what you know and what is *your role* in this incident, from beginning to end!"

"Okay...uh...well, the night before, Papa made us all leave the estate while June and Jazz visited. I took my daughter and one of our housekeepers to one of our hotels in town. I thought we might run into June, but we didn't. The next morning, Papa called me back home and Sheriff Cobb, Jr. was there." Thomas III frowns intently toward his father. In response, the patriarch grits his teeth and grumbles under his breath. To his left, Olivia's eyes lock on Thomas III, and she grins proudly, for the first time in a while. Thomas III sees a glimmer of hope in her face, yet, she quickly conceals her joy by wiping her cheeks with her soaked handkerchief.

"And, Tommy, I mean, uh, Mr. Winniper, what happened when you returned to the estate?"

"Papa told me that June and Jazz planned to get married. They...they wouldn't listen when he asked them to keep it a secret and stay at the mansion. They were leaving town and they wanted some big, celebrity wedding in Hollywood. She didn't realize...she...couldn't...know, but...I knew as soon as he told me. He and I waited for Duke and Earl and then we all went around back where the sheriff was. Pa' told Duke and Earl not to let June leave town alive."

"Objection, Your Honor!" Ms. Shields rises instantly, flattening her business skirt and reassuring herself that the male jurors remember her many talents. "This is pure speculation! It's hearsay, at best!"

"Again, Miss...uh, *Shields*," Judge Rupert rumbles while still soaking in Thomas III's testimony. The old judge begins to see a new horizon along with the rest of the Winniper County citizens. The chains of the Winniper Empire begin to crack and the town bears witness to the ultimate betrayal as Thomas III jeopardizes his future for the greater good. "Mr. Winniper has taken the oath. He has a right to answer the prosecution's questions to the best of his knowledge and ability, and soon, you will have your turn to cross-examine his testimony. This is how the process works."

"But, Your Honor."

"*Overruled.* Mr. Allen, please proceed."

"Thank you, Your Honor," John Allen bows his head before turning toward the jurors and regaining their attention. He has taken a subtle cue from the judge, and momentarily disregarded his fears of the tyrant's wrath. "Mr. Winniper, please continue."

"Papa didn't want any more blood on our hands. He said I had done enough to prove my loyalty to the family...so he paid Duke and Earl to stop June from leaving town like I stopped their m...I mean...Papa told them it didn't matter if June and Jazz were alive afterwards. And he promised Duke and Earl more money and some land, if they succeeded."

"But why? The accused has a clear motive, filled with jealousy and envy and insecurity, but your father...why would he behave the way you describe?"

"Because…she…she was going to marry…uh…without Papa's consent, without him controlling her." Thomas III hesitates, noticing the confusion that passes over the courtroom. As he looks over the crowd's faces, he fears a collective implosion from the understood truth.

"Why would your father need to *control* June? She was an international icon; surely, he had given her the freedom to become who she was. Why, all of a sudden, would he order an attack to keep her from leaving town and getting married?"

"Um…it's difficult…in our family. Um…it's hard to explain. But Papa was afraid that she would embarrass the family…if she married…Jazz…and if they had children…Papa just needed to control *everything*."

"Mr. Winniper…you have to be more specific. You're saying Papa…excuse me, your father, was afraid that June would embarrass your family, whatever that means. And, this attack was carried out to prevent that from happening and you, your father, and the sheriff of our good county were all conspiring to see this vicious attack succeed? Is that not far-fetched?"

"Well…uh, yes, it is, but it's true. And I didn't conspire, but I was there. And so was the sheriff. You can call him as a witness, too. Papa had the same problems with my sister and he chose the same solution. June was like Teresa. But she was different, too. She was independent, and she wasn't afraid…she was powerful. She was going to leave that morning and because she was so famous, Papa got desperate to make sure she never left town. I asked him to hire professionals, but…he wanted to make sure Duke knew his responsibilities."

"So he paid your nephew and his friends to carry out the murder? And you saw money exchange hands?"

"Yes, I *'saw money exchange hands'*. And Papa said he would give them land if they did a good job. I don't think he cared if they killed her or not, but Papa wanted to make sure June didn't leave with Jazz." Thomas III asserts the truth simply; he's finding it easier to spill his guts through words rather than vomit. The courtroom reacts to every syllable. Several press agents run to the front row and snap photos of Papa before being removed hurriedly from the courtroom.

"I see…and how did Duke and Earl respond to your father's orders…did they agree?"

"Well, uh, Earl agreed immediately. He wanted to marry my niece…so he felt like it was a good step toward joining the family. But Duke…he was reluctant. I…he wanted to say no, but he couldn't. He's…he's more like me than I realized," Thomas III admits sullenly, cracking a thin smile and looking over to his quiet nephew. "Or maybe, I'm more like him."

"I-uh, yes, uh, indeed, uh I see…" John Allen stammers, while standing, stunned, in the middle of the courtroom foreground. He darts his eyes from Papa, to the judge, and then to the jury: all await his next move. The county attorney believes that an obvious play for validation may help his chances of salvaging any semblance of a credible career. "So, to be clear, your father, Thomas Winniper, Jr., known affectionately by many as *'Papa'*, paid his grandson to harm his granddaughter. But, earlier, you said your nephew was *ordered* to commit this crime; and now, you're testifying that your father also compensated him. Wouldn't it be more accurate to say that you *may have* witnessed a proposition that your nephew then accepted?"

"No…it was not a *'proposition'*, counselor. You know as well as I do that my father doesn't *propose* anything. He gets exactly what he wants, and he will kill anyone to do so, even his own flesh and blood." Thomas III smirks timidly after he responds to the county attorney's posturing. Recognizing the indignation spewing from the faces of many in the crowd, Thomas III leans back in his chair and crosses his arms over his chest. He balks at the backlash from the revelation of his father's blatant arrogance and murderous tendencies.

"Mr. Winniper, do you realize that you're smiling, now? Was this alleged murder plot amusing to you? Do you gain entertainment from interjecting yourself into these court proceedings?" Mr. Allen walks closer, irritated by this middle-age brat's intrusion into a perfectly formed plan of sacrifice, deception, and political destiny. "You claim that your father paid your nephew to murder your niece and you just sat by and watched? Why didn't you intervene? Why didn't you tell the authorities? Why have you waited until now?"

"I tried...but...I couldn't stop it."

"Why not? You've implicated some of the most respected men in this town, but what about your alleged role in the crime? You admit to being there when the attack was planned, but you never mentioned this fact, until now. What has compelled you to confess?"

"I've been loyal to my father and my family...all my life, until now..." Thomas III explains simply, glancing between his father and mother and Duke. "But these days, especially today, it's hard to know what my family really is."

"Well..." John Allen continues while pacing back and forth between the jury box and the witness stand. He's noticeably shocked by Thomas III's testimony, the implications, and the sight of his political future crumbling with every question. He teeters between hoping that a fast end to this line of questioning may keep him within Papa's inner circle and realizing that Papa may no longer have an inner circle after his son's testimony. "I have no further questions for you at this time. Uh, thank you, Your Honor."

"Defense, your witness." Judge Rupert grumbles and glances at the courtroom clock and his watch: both read 1:34 p.m. He considers a coy suggestion to help him reach his afternoon tea a little early. "Mr. Erickson, due to the circumstances, we may adjourn until tomorrow if you are unprepared to question this witness."

"Um, thank you, Your Honor," Mr. Erickson replies softly, sensing the judge's disposition toward a lingering cross-examination. "Please, allow us a moment to confer."

Mr. Erickson, Ms. Shields, and their respective associates crowd around the defense table, huddling in a unified purpose, but, Mr. Erickson deliberately turns his shoulders toward Papa. Thomas III can see the lead defense counsel exchange brief remarks with the monarch, and Papa nods his head twice. Mr. Erickson rises from his troops with a wry grin on his face, eyeing Thomas III before dragging one finger across his throat. The savvy defense attorney then crouches amongst his counterparts, whispers a few instructions, and stands delightedly.

"Your Honor, we appreciate your consideration," Mr. Erickson begins as he tightens his tie around his collar and adjusts the cufflinks on his dress shirt. He is a mercenary, checking his uniform, sharpening his artillery, and preparing for a credibility assassination. "We don't want to waste the court's time with more…*tomfoolery*. We think it's best to discredit *this witness* and his so-called testimony, today, so that the prosecution can proceed with their *credible* witnesses tomorrow."

"Be my guest," Judge Rupert waves his hand toward Thomas III like a hostess presenting a buffet; the judge entreats Mr. Erickson to commence feasting without any further delay.

"Thank you, Your Honor." Mr. Erickson raises his fingers to his forehead and tips an imaginary hat. Papa's hired hand walks around the defense table, strolls casually to the center of the foreground, looks over the jurors' faces. "Gentlemen of the jury, I want to apologize to you on behalf of the Winniper family. Now, this apology comes directly from both my client and his noble grandfather. They want to apologize for *this witness*, who has felt the need to make the spotlight all about him, once again. And at their behest, I will not waste the court's time unnecessarily with *family matters*, but, I must ask one question to *this witness*. Mr. Winniper, and remember that you are under oath, please tell the court, why are you testifying, today? Mr. Allen asked you this question only moments ago, and he let you off the hook after your answer seemed, to me, *unclear*. So please, tell the court, why are you testifying, *today?*"

"Because…because it's the right thing to do," Thomas III responds with a heightened tension in his tone. He sees the onslaught approaching fast. Papa's frequent verbal abuse has given him an innate ability to sense hostility. Mr. Erickson's voice rumbles in lower octaves before rising in pitch, velocity, and anger; and Thomas III can hear his father's disappointment.

"I'm sorry, but please indulge me, your Honor, this is what I meant by *unclear*. This witness hasn't stated one coherent thing since taking the stand, but I just need him to clarify what he means by '*the right thing to do*'." Mr. Erickson repeats the hearty statement, while raising his fingers, making air quotes, and chuckling slightly. "And remember, if your story is true, then you are a co-conspirator in your niece's murder. You expect the court to believe that you witnessed your father and my client plot to kill your niece and you didn't say anything until *today*. At the very least, your statement makes you sound like a coward, so why would you humiliate yourself with all the cameras and hoopla surrounding today's testimony? Why would you choose *today* to insert yourself into a serious trial and betray your father, your nephew, and your family? Because '*it's the right thing to do*'?"

"Yes…yes, counselor. And I'm not betraying my nephew or my mother…or June…or my sister. The women in our family have suffered in silence. It's…it's finally time to tell the truth!" Thomas III responds with rising anger, feeling the points of prickly pins prance upon his skin. He stares at his father and mother. Retribution meets its maker while a son empties his soul of his father's sins. "I'm telling the truth, now…because '*it's the right thing to do*'. Duke doesn't deserve to be executed."

"But, and again, please excuse me, your Honor. I'm trying to dispense with this witness as quickly as possible, but I just feel like he still has not answered the question, why *today*?" Mr. Erickson counters, returning his hand to his chin and staring at the ceiling. He suddenly seems to deduce an important point. "Thomas, I know you may think you're doing the right thing, but you still haven't answered the question: why are you testifying, *today*?"

"Um…I did answer the question. It's the right-"

"But, why today? Why today? You never mentioned these allegations before. What changed? Did something upset you? Why are you testifying, today?" Mr. Erickson repeats his knockout question, after throwing a few jabs and taking a moment to make eye contact with several jurors. He casts doubt upon Thomas III's sanity and credibility. The jurors then turn their eyes toward Thomas III and they begin to burn accusatory holes in his testimony. The spaces create gaps in their understanding and these gaps weaken their overall belief. Thomas III can see the doubt in their eyes, and he becomes obstinate, filled with flex, while Mr. Erickson continues to press him. "Thomas, do you need me to repeat the question? Do you want to take back some of your earlier statements?"

"No, I'm telling the truth! I'm testifying today, because I believe my father is going to let *your client* be executed. He hired you and *Ms. Shields* to lead my nephew to the chair." Thomas III states his fears matter-of-factly, leaning on a newfound righteousness without remorse. He believes that he is right; he believes that now is the time to expose his father and free his family. The courtroom responds to his claim with more roars and press row ignites with camera flashes and hot headlines. Seeing the mini-melee as a form of validation for the seriousness of his testimony, Thomas III leans back in his chair, lifts his legs, and places his black Oxford dress shoes on the edge of the witness stand. He's a South Dakota man fixing to bring home the bacon. "I think this whole trial is rigged! The fix is in, folks!"

"Objection! Your Honor, uh, that's hearsay! Uh, highly inflammatory! Defamatory, too! Uh, the witness should stick to answering the questions asked to him!" John Allen exclaims, flustered by Thomas III's growing betrayal. Anticipating further sabotage and still maneuvering to maintain strategic balance amidst the controversy, Mr. Allen feels that he must find the first life raft off this judicial Titanic and sail away before they all drown. The shamed Winniper prince is an iceberg that is capable of sinking Papa's entire fleet and bringing the Winniper Family Empire to the ocean floor. The courtroom watches in awe, subconsciously planning memorials for the victims of this fateful shipwreck. "I move that the witness's testimony be stricken from the record!"

"Order! Order!" Judge Rupert slams his gavel on his bench until the courtroom quiets in anticipation. He leans closer to Thomas III. "You are making some dangerous allegations, Tommy boy."

"I know, Your Honor."

"This is a very public trial. I could take you off the stand right now and have your testimony stricken from the records, but…who knows? The way you're going, you may need a friend in a high place." The judge scowls over the left side of his bench and raises his glasses over his eyebrows. The old legal miser senses a chance to absolve himself of his culpability, enabling him to preserve his image of impartiality. His eyes open fully for the first time in the trial and he stares seriously at Thomas III, daring the witness to try his luck. "I trust you still have respect for the man in the robe."

"I do, Your Honor," Thomas III reassures the judge with a solemn nod, hoping to appease the most senior member of the Winniper County court system. "I just want to save my nephew, if I can…"

"Very well, then. Objection overruled!" Judge Rupert bellows over the courtroom after finding a soft spot for the prince with the guts to challenge the king. Thomas III has discovered a moment of independence within himself, enough to give himself the guts to think and act without consideration for Papa's wishes. "Counsel, please continue."

"Um, thank you, Your Honor." Mr. Erickson corrals his senses as John Allen sits back down at the prosecution table. The defense counselor has taken note of the actions of his contemporaries and he takes a quick look over his shoulder toward Papa before turning back toward the witness stand. "Now, Mr. Winniper, you say these here proceedings are *'rigged'*. That's a hefty charge. Not only have you accused your father of conspiring with my client to commit a murder, but you have now accused this entire courtroom, including the prosecution, the defense, the judge, and the jury, of being, somehow, *staged, faked, 'rigged', and 'fixed'*. I apologize to the jury and to the court, but I must now ask a few more questions in order to defend myself and the members of the court from these inflammatory, unfounded accusations. Your Honor, we may have a charge for perjury by the end of this if-"

"It's all true, counselor." Thomas III interrupts sincerely. No longer waiting for his cues, he stares sadly at his father. Their eyes meet as equals for the first time. The son tears down the father's reputation, so that they can finally see eye-to-eye. "My father has killed several family members and people who got too close. He has a lot of power because he inspires a lot of fear in his enemies, in his allies, and in our family. "

"But...uh, Mr. Winniper, you make these accusations without any proof." Mr. Erickson wipes his forehead, trying to regain his mental footing. "You testify that your father is some kind of 'Wizard of Oz', pulling all the strings around you, but...I hear a scared child, who still can't see anything but his father's shadow. Do you believe that?"

"No, you're wrong. I know what I've seen," Thomas III replies without hesitation. "I know what I've done."

"*You?* Yes, you, you've done so much, right?" Mr. Erickson asks, pointing to Thomas III and walking forward to the witness stand. He is the point man, leading the charge against the infidel and holding his bayonet in preparation to strike. "You make all these false claims about your father, your nephew, and the members of this court; but, were you there when June and Jazz were attacked? Because we maintain that our client was not even present during the attack. So were you there? Are you testifying that you saw the incident?"

"No."

"So even though you claim to have witnessed a meeting between my client, your father, the sheriff, and the previously convicted Earl Bethune, you actually have no idea who attacked and killed June, because you were not present during the attack! Isn't that correct?"

"I was at the estate when Papa met with Duke and Earl." Thomas III battles back, continuing to cut any remaining strands of loyalty to the Winniper Family brand. He feels the devil die inside of him. The unnecessary evil in the world leaves his spirit for good. "I saw Papa give Earl some money to make sure June never made it to the airport."

"Mr. Winniper, I think the only thing you've got right is that Earl Bethune was involved. We contend that Mr. Bethune and his two friends were the only attackers outside of the American Café that day. You say that prior to the attack, you witnessed this meeting, but you admit that you weren't there when the incident actually happened." Mr. Erickson concentrates on a consistent fact, spreading his arms wide and staring at the jury with bugged eyes and an open mouth. He is shocked that the insane asylum has allowed a patient to testify in a murder trial. "And it so happens, that on one hand, we have your father, the sheriff, and your nephew who have never mentioned such a meeting and, on the other hand, we have you and no one else who can confirm your story."

"There is someone. Doc Morten, Jr. is scheduled to testify after me," Thomas III announces combatively, glaring at his father, knowing the county medical examiner's testimony could be damning if steered toward Papa's past indiscretions. Doc Morten, Jr. and his father have helped to conceal a number of secretive Sioux births and though the Mortens have never participated in the murders of the Sioux babies, they may feel guilt for the brown babies who never survived long after their births.

∞

Doc Morten, Jr. once witnessed Olivia carry Teresa's Sioux infants to the family's old Spoister and drive away from his home moments after Teresa gave birth. As an apprentice, the son had learned from his father to remain largely aloof, but intricately informed and well-compensated for his silence and compliance.

∞

He has "doctored" plenty of medical records and he has even lied about the cause of death in his coroner's exams; but, he has never testified without a clear script to follow. One of the most powerful doctors in South Dakota, Doc Morten, Jr. is privy to the most monumental secret in the American economy, but, he is a relatively simple man—lustful and filled with thirst. He may struggle to testify under oath without prepared questions, prepared answers, and predetermined justice. Though his testimony is usually constructed in cooperation with Papa's concerns, Thomas III must at least name the good doctor and try to elicit a meaningful reaction from his father. He knows the old man can only stew for so long before boiling over in his seat.

"Doc Morten, Jr. will testify, under oath. He knows plenty of our family secrets. I think now is the right place, maybe the only place we'll ever get the truth, if he tells what he knows."

"Well, excuse me, Mr. Winniper, it seems you are willing to drag every notable gentleman from this good, God-fearing town into your mess; but, may I remind you that Doc Morten, Jr. is a well-respected medical practitioner within the great state of South Dakota? He's a leader in his field and his record is impeccable. I believe many of the jurors are shocked by how you casually accuse men who are more successful than you....in this...*Oedipal exhibition.*"

Mr. Erickson waves his hand to the jury box and walks away from Thomas III, but he stops, turns back, and performs another impression of Papa.

"I'm honestly disappointed in you, son. You've wasted the court's time here, today. You've embarrassed and shamed your family and yourself. Why should anyone believe you, when you have no proof?"

"I have the truth, counselor. And I do have the facts on my side. I know the reason why Papa didn't want June to marry." Thomas II retorts, trying to contain his frustration. He knows that he must remain calm, at least until he finishes his testimony. "I know why Papa wouldn't let June leave town."

"Well, please, finally, enlighten us and help us all understand," Mr. Erickson caterwauls, raising his arms on an imaginary cross, yet, he is Judas, persecuting and indicting the Savior. The modern Christ sweats in the witness stand, bearing his truth as redemption. Thomas III wipes his forehead hastily, refusing to look at his parents as he is unable to utter the truth in the moment: the Winniper curse curdles in his throat. Mr. Erickson notices the heir's hesitation, but the counselor miscalculates and pounces during a presumed moment of weakness. "Cat got your tongue, Mr. Winniper? Or have your lies run out?"

Another long pause drifts over the courtroom; the audience's ears perk up and their faces tense without remorse or hope. The crowd is here for a show. Thomas III feels the sweat seeping through his skin and coating his body, but he's still unable to speak. He wishes the words would come to his lips, but nothing escapes his clenched vocal chords. Cryogenically paralyzed in an ice casing of righteous foreshadowing, he becomes cold enough that he feels no pain, no hope for the future. He is the frozen silence before the fall.

"June and Jazz…" Thomas III begins but he freezes as quickly as he started, seeing the cliff dive sharply up ahead and fearing the unknown future that lies below.

"Yes, Mr. Winniper, please continue. *'June and Jazz'*… what?"

"Uh…um…I know this will be hard for…uh…*many of you*…uh, to believe…*but*…June…and Jazz…uh…they were…uh…they were…*twins*." Thomas III finally speaks the truth through sustained trembles up his spine. Laughter erupts throughout the pews and whispers of worried disbelief fill the courtroom. Most of the crowd finally accepts that Thomas III is an insane traitor, an embarrassed, shamed, and defamed disappointment. The autumn air breezes into the small opening in the sole window; the room suddenly feels chillier.

All eyes rest upon Thomas III, and all, but three pairs, look at him with complete confusion. His mother, his father, and Duke stare knowingly, while the rest of the perplexed people in the courtroom believe Thomas III has duped them into believing a sensational tale in order to satiate his own boyish need for attention. Transmitting their indignation through their spirits, Thomas III can feel their resentment as they add another Winniper name to the list of fallen idols from their elitist society.

Papa chuckles at his son and cradles his wife under his left arm. He hides any noticeable anxiety after hearing his family's secret spoken in public for the first time. Those shameful Sioux babies, stained with the blood of their massacred ancestors, he dismisses Thomas III and his words. Another cancelled trust fund; now, there's more money to spread among the loyal and obedient.

Mrs. Winniper dips her head and dab her soaked eyes with her damp handkerchief. The frayed lace splits at the edges after being clenched tightly within her thin, frail hands. She has shared more intimacy with her handkerchief than with her husband, as of late. Olivia emotionally detaches herself from her husband, her son, and her nephew because she can feel her life-force fade after crying so many tears. She doesn't look up to Thomas III; she merely keeps her head low, staring at the floor and hoping for nothing at all.

Duke gazes at Thomas III, unsure of whom or what he sees; his expression resembles the overall sentiment inside the courtroom. Tilly also absorbs Thomas III's confession and her body noticeably pulls away from Papa and Olivia. The crowd continues to look blankly, searching the witness and each other for clarification because his statement seems so ridiculous that their minds cannot process its meaning clearly.

"Excuse me, Thomas?" Mr. Erickson speaks warily, walking closer to the witness stand and chuckling with a wry joy. He is unsure if a prank is in play, but, he's excited to find out. "Can you please…uh…repeat that for the court?"

"I said…" Thomas III pauses while inhaling a deep breath. "*'June and Jazz…were twins'.*"

"Ha, yes…uh, I thought that was what you said that." Mr. Erickson laughs loudly and slaps his knee. "I heard it, but I didn't believe it. You can't be serious! Your Honor, do we need any more evidence that the witness is mentally unstable? I move that his entire testimony be stricken from the record!"

"Well…" Judge Rupert begins to answer and his eyes widen as he tries to find his legal footing.

"I assure you, Your Honor, I'm completely fine," Thomas III interrupts calmly, imploring the judge with a confident smirk developed in the moment's honesty. "For the first time in a long time, I'm telling the truth."

"Your Honor, I don't even know what to say." Mr. Erickson gathers his thoughts with another condescending chuckle. "If the witness actually believes that a colored native and a white woman can actually be…uh, *some kind of incestuous siblings*, then, he should at least have a psychiatric evaluation before he's allowed to testify."

"Yes, you do have a valid argument, Mr. Erickson. It seems…*impossible*." The judge replies before pondering Mr. Erickson's logic and the consequences of the circumstances surrounding these proceedings. He knows that a failed psych evaluation could be a good excuse to eliminate Thomas III's testimony from the trial. Judge Rupert immediately calculates that he could issue a ruling that nullifies the testimony's validity in the press and the hearts of the people. He prepares to deliver the nullification but he looks down at Thomas III, seeing an honest doe in the forest, peaking his head out of the den at dawn. Thomas III is exposed, but, at least in this moment, he is pure. "Mr. Winniper, for the sake of the court, can you explain your statement? Otherwise, I think the court has indulged you long enough."

"It's true, Your Honor. *'June and Jazz were twins'*. They were brother and sister, born together from my sister, Teresa. Teresa had six children altogether, three pairs of twins. It's…it's our family secret. We've…we've killed to conceal it. My mother had four, and the mother of my daughter had two. It's something in our blood, that famously powerful Winniper family blood. Just like our oil, pumping life into everything around us…but we're cursed. My…my mother helped hide Teresa's colored children with Berthine. She was here earlier with Jazz and another one, Charlie. She raised them 'til they were old enough to move away…they think she's their mother."

"So you're saying there are more *twins* like June Bethune and Jazz Lancaster, Mr. Winniper?" The judge surmises, looking toward Papa and shrugging his shoulders because he is unsure how he should proceed. He feels he may have bet upon the wrong horse. "If you want the court to continue hearing this testimony, you have to explain yourself completely. If there are more twins like you say, then where are they?"

"I...uh...well like I said, Your Honor, one was here earlier, Charles. His sister, Christina is home with my daughter. I don't...I don't think Charles and Christina...have ever met..." Thomas III stammers, still trying to withhold the dam of words which may send him to death row where a noose or an electrocution chair will be his final friend. "Duke's twin, Lucy, lives out west somewhere. They ain't ever met either. Um...there were others...other colored ones, but...I...uh...we dealt with them."

"Your Honor, the witness continues to deflect! What does he mean by *'dealt with them'*?" Mr. Erickson challenges stridently, trying to find an easy way to eliminate this incoherent testimony. The attack dog begins to foam at the mouth, anxious for a kill bite. "The witness is constantly speaking in code...or innuendo...I mean, Your Honor, how much-"

"Papa forced me..." Thomas III hesitates to incriminate himself, fearing the inevitable. His life slips through his lips and the truth spills over into a new murder trial. "Papa forced me to kill my sister, too."

"See, Your Honor, the witness is concocting lie after lie, each more sensational than the last." Mr. Erickson protests angrily, stomping his left foot on the floor and slamming his left fist into his right hand. "I move that his entire testimony..."

"Pipe down, Mr. Erickson," Judge Rupert barks, raising his gavel at the defense counselor before turning toward Thomas III. "Now explain yourself, Mr. Winniper, in full. Is this a confession or a testimony pertinent to this trial?"

"*Both.*" Thomas III mumbles under his breath, yet he is passively audible; he hopes someone will hear him and submit him to a forced sacrifice.

"Speak up, Mr. Winniper!" Judge Rupert orders impatiently. "We have no more time for games!"

"I'm telling the truth, Your Honor! I killed my sister and I killed my Sioux newborn. Papa said we had to hide the fact that all the Winniper women bear twins, one white and one colored. Doc Morten, Jr. and his father have known all about it. They've delivered the babies for years."

"But you need to come clean, Thomas. Stop beating around the bush. Tell the court, what do you mean when you say that you *'killed your sister, too'?*" Judge Rupert asks curiously, speeding the inquisition along a path of desired destruction. The old codger senses a true reclamation and he slowly remembers a certain knack for influencing a witness's testimony.

"Ever since the first one was born, the Sioux babies have...always been killed...burned, buried in the barn at our estate, and never spoken of again. You'll find the bones there! Papa said it was our duty as men...to do God's work...and protect the family. But my sister, Teresa...she tried to save them, I mean...she *did* save them—Lucy, Charles, and Jazz."

'Your Honor..." Mr. Erickson tries to interrupt, stomping back to his defense team and slamming his hand down on the top of their table.

"Keep quiet, Mr. Erickson!" The judge points his finger at the defense counsel, who promptly composes himself and adjusts his suit jacket around his shoulders. Judge Rupert leans toward Thomas III. "You sure got everyone riled up, boy. Continue with your testimony, *carefully*, Mr. Winniper."

"Yes, Your Honor. Like I said, I'm telling the truth. Nothing I've said up here is a lie! I was like Duke. Papa came to me and told me that Teresa was disrespecting the family and planning to leave town with *all her children.* He said he made a mistake not killing the…the Sioux babies, himself. He had a soft spot for Berthine and her cabin; he didn't want any more blood on his own hands. I think he had planned to let the Sioux kids grow up as long as Teresa stayed away, but when he found out that she had plans to take Kenny and skip town with all her kids…he told me just like he told Duke. Don't let her leave town." Thomas III grimaces, remembering his father's outrage. He recalls the red hues of Papa's disappointed cheeks and he contrasts those fire tones with the crimson fury currently covering his father's face. The old man simmers in the front row, with his left arm still curled around his wife, pretending that all is still within his control. In his mind, he has a self-destruct button which can tear the entire town to the ground; but, in his heart, he is a weak, elderly man who has tired of the burden of being king.

Beginning to feel his kingdom crumble in front of the public eye, Papa sees himself as a giant that grew too large and became too arrogant to notice that his son grew as well. But Thomas III no longer desires to walk amongst his giant forefathers; no, as father and son stare into respective mirrors filled with everything they each despise, Thomas III realizes his purpose in life: he is a giant slayer.

"The day of the '46 parade, after Teresa didn't come to the celebration, Papa had the sheriff come to the market. He told me that Papa wanted Teresa to be taken care of…they had it all planned out. Kenny gave Teresa a reason to come to the market; she needed a loaf of bread. When she left, I followed her in my truck and the sheriff followed me in his patrol car. I ran her car off the road; I stayed long enough to see she was dead. Papa paid Dr. Morten, Jr. to falsify the autopsy and say Teresa fell asleep behind the wheel."

The courtroom erupts and quakes, lava in the form of vitriol begins to spill from the citizens' mouths as they compare stories of that fateful accident and the suspicions surrounding it. They remember quite well. The citizens are becoming unrelentingly restless now and even the judge can feel that he cannot restrain the backlash much longer. Thomas III's testimony has rattled some core values at the foundation of their bedrock. They no longer listen with eager ears, but rather, their country sentiments have overtaken their reason, and their contempt begins to reach a fevered peak.

"And…you are confessing to killing your sister, in order to prove that your father is capable of masterminding both murders?" Judge Rupert asks softly, looking closely at Thomas III, genuinely inspecting the witness's candor, and wondering about the depths of depravity that have developed under his *watchful* eye.

"Papa thinks our damn name is more important than any of our lives. I promise, Your Honor, I'm telling the truth. He coerced us to murder our own kin. And the sheriff and the doc have helped him…" Thomas III avoids the judge's question, and he pauses as he notices Papa's demeanor change. The crimson tides in Papa's cheeks roll in red waves and Papa suddenly closes his left eye and clutches the left side of his chest tightly with his right hand.

"I'm leaning toward Mr. Erickson's suggestion that you be remanded for a psychiatric evaluation. You've interrupted these proceedings under the guise of having testimony pertinent to *this trial* and *this tragedy.*" The judge dictates his logic for the record, hoping to solidify his credibility, although he does not notice Papa reacting to a desperate pain in his heart. Thomas III's betrayal has finally struck too deep, but the self-minded judge continues to exasperate the point in order to facilitate his own salvation. "Now, please, answer these two questions: 1) Are you testifying, under oath, that your father ordered and paid for the murder of June Bethune? 2) Are you confessing to killing your sister after being told to do so by the sheriff under the orders of your father?"

"Well…yes, to the first question. My father did meet with us at our mansion and convince Duke and Earl to attack June. I believe Papa is responsible because he makes people feel powerless, like they have to do what he tells them to do. And I hope the jury takes that into account for Duke's sake. He didn't want to do it…just like I didn't want to…" Thomas III freezes on the precondition of a sealed fate. His eyes dart toward his father gasping for air in the front row and several citizens in the courtroom start to notice their benefactor's distress. "…and…uh…to your second question…yes, I killed my sister by pushing her car into a tree on January first, nineteen forty-six."

Thomas III turns his head to his right and confesses directly to Judge Rupert; he is no longer testifying to the courtroom or the defense. The Winniper County citizens within the gallery rumble in response to his confession and several press correspondents rush frantically out the oak doors toward open phone lines. A new scandal has emerged in a media boom of headlines and news updates. Mr. Erickson remains within the foreground, standing awkwardly between the jury and the legal teams, but he couldn't be any more invisible. It feels like the entire world is listening to Thomas III and believing that he is either a madman or a Godsend. He speaks without care for his future while reliving his past as a lying, murderous boy of privilege. He stares up to the judge, hoping to absolve his sinful soul.

"Do you realize, Thomas…" Judge Rupert pauses, overcome by the drama, and highly disconcerted that a once methodical trial procedure has devolved into a full-blown public spectacle with all the participants receiving more attention than necessary. "…a confession of this kind would warrant a mistrial. We would have to go through this entire process, again. And what about June? When will she get her justice? You've just made life very hard…for a lot of people."

"I'm sorry, Your Honor…but, you know as well as I do, that it's his fault! He's an evil man! We wouldn't be here, none of this would've happened, if it weren't for him!" Thomas III apologizes sincerely and points to his father who still wheezes noticeably in the front row. Always attentive to her husband's needs, Mrs. Winniper forgets her detachment and remembers the directions for *successful* domesticity. She whispers to Papa tenderly and fans her tear-soaked handkerchief over his brow. Seeing his mother react instinctively to his father's distress, Thomas III brims with a continued hatred for the man he could never eclipse. "He's made all our lives *very hard*…he killed my mother's children! He made me kill my son and my sister! All because they were colored! And, *why?* Because that's what his father taught him! He's made us commit unspeakable crimes!"

"It's true! It's all true!" Tilly yells, rising in the front row and still holding Thomas III's jacket in her hands. She turns to her right and scowls at Papa. "When I had Kenny, and the *other one*, you told me it was *my* fault, Tommy! You let me think something was wrong with me!"

"Order! Order!" Judge Rupert thuds his gavel firmly, perplexed by the interruption, but the scene completely mesmerizes him as an old confidant acts out publicly. Tilly Bethune, in most circles, is Papa's loyal counterpart; the Bethune estate has a significant claim to the Winnipers' oil empire and the families have always seemed inseparable.

∞

Thomas, Sr. gave William, Sr. a substantial stake in the company as a reward for helping to defend the Winnipers' land from the Sioux uprising.

∞

Alongside the Winnipers (56%) and the Cobbs (2%), the Bethunes own over 36% of the Winniper Family Holding Company's stock. The three families share a combined 97% of the company, after consolidating the Newton and Winniper shares once Olivia and Papa married. So, from the ashes and charred bones of Sioux natives, the Bethunes and Winnipers reap the bulk of the beautiful bootie that bursts from the land that their forefathers stole for profit.

Amidst their business, personal relationships have also developed; marriages, affairs, and an incestuous tryst between Kenny and Teresa, within which, the wealthy have protected themselves by bedding exclusively among themselves. Their mutual trust would seem compulsory, but, the judge watches in amazement as his old friend, Tilly, interrupts the trial in a fit of rage. He only prays that she protects their mutual interests and speaks only so openly and only so virulently. Tilly is a well-known, wrecking ball, a female giant with the power to chop another giant in half and Judge Rupert hesitates to offend her.

"Now, Mrs. Bethune, please sit back down or..."

"No, Donny! You're going to call a mistrial anyway, so you shut your fat mouth!" Tilly unloads her mounting anger and quiets the judge with a poisonous glare. She adjusts Thomas III's jacket within her hands and then turns toward the people behind her, seeing them for the first time as peers who need to hear the truth. "Tommy boy is telling the truth. Them Winnipers' blood is cursed, they's got Injun in 'em! It happened to me!"

"Officers, please escort..."

"Stand back!" Tilly shouts, clumsily reaching into the inside pocket of Thomas III's jacket pocket and removing the Colt 1851 revolver. A frightened woman in the second row screams as Tilly raises the weapon in her right hand and aims at Papa, who still clutches his chest and takes shallow, short breaths. He looks back at her with wide eyes, filled with fear, shocked by these developments; he recognizes the Colt revolver immediately and realizes the gravity of his mistakes. Stuck between Papa and Tilly, Olivia remains under Papa's left arm, holding her handkerchief in her hand and staring silently at the steel revolver. She looks at the gun's barrel carefully, noticing its grooves and craftsmanship; she's seen it before, but she can't recall further details.

Several people move away from Tilly and others run to the back of the courtroom as a few advancing officers creep toward her. These are not the fireworks that the crowd wanted to see, although the members of the press have already begun to salivate over the fallout and headlines—"*Mad Woman Pulls Gun on Oil King*". Sensing danger in the corner of her eye, Tilly turns her hips, aims the revolver at one of the officers, and squints her right eye.

"Don't anybody move! Most y'all remember my daddy was the best shot in this whole town! And y'all know he taught me to shoot like a man!"

"How did she get a gun in here?" Judge Rupert asks under his breath, unwilling to bring any further attention upon himself, especially with two empires on the verge of warfare and a grieving matriarch holding a loaded revolver. It would be best to play this out, but, an inner duty to maintain decorum within his courtroom emerges in his spirit. He thinks back to being a twenty-four year old law student, dreaming of being where he is now. He sees Tilly as her former self; as kids, he, Papa, Olivia, and Tilly would play together.

∞

Sometimes, they walked through the Winnipers' estate and met up with Berthine, just to listen to the blues parties at the old sharecroppers' village. Sometimes, they danced among the trees of the forest, together, without care or concern for the future. Was today destined even back then?

∞

"Now, please...Tilly, just calm down. Put the gun away."

"No, Donny! You listened to Tommy boy, now you're going to hear me out! I don't need no testimony! My Pa told me, that them Winnipers didn't even own that Sioux land! They stole it! I bet they's cursed for it! It's all true what Tommy boy said…the brown baby…it happened to me with my son, Kenny. Papa and I had an affair…and he got me pregnant! I gave birth to a brown girl and a white boy…and he blamed me! He said I…I slept with a colored! He accused *me*…of layin' with that kind of filth! Said I had to '*take care of it*'. So I drowned her at my family's lake house!"

The courtroom gasps again, rolling in slop, and several press writers dream of hitting the doors and running for the phones outside the courtroom, but they need the full scoop. No doubt, Sheriff Cobb, Jr. has been listening from the police station. Maybe, he's outside the courthouse, mobilizing an attack that will completely erase this unexpected unfolding. Maybe, the officers inside the courtroom will soon receive an order to silence Tilly and Thomas III with extreme prejudice.

Papa leans back against the pine of the front row, awkwardly trying to maintain his dignity while experiencing a new kind of pain. He can feel the changing atmosphere trickling over his neck, and, he twists his head to inspect the onlookers. It's the first time he has even acknowledged their presence. Their faces show their shock and confusion, unsure if he's still their king; and the officers remain in their positions throughout the courtroom, because they still do not know what to do.

Thomas III can see that the tides are beginning to overpower his father like a swimmer stuck in an undertow. Earlier, Papa was happily swimming with the sharks, but, suddenly, the current has become too rough. Tilly turns to point the Colt revolver at his forehead and he absorbs a shock wave of pure dread. Spotting one of the officers reach for his sidearm, Tilly adjusts quickly, fires the Colt, and shoots one bullet directly into the officer's hand.

"I said, don't move!" She growls like a mother hyena; the officer screams in pain, clutching horrifically to his hand. A few aghast onlookers join the officer's morbid shouts and everyone in the courtroom realizes that they are in serious danger of catching a bullet from this elderly sharpshooter. She spins back toward Papa and aims squarely between his eyes. "That boy'll live, but the next one is going right through your skull, Tommy! *You're a coward!* After all that I did for you, all you had to do was tell me! It could've been us all along! None of these problems would even exist…but…but you chose *her!*"

Tilly nods toward Olivia, who still leans against her husband. With his left arm around her, they both cling to each other though neither has a comforting touch. Olivia vacates her emotions entirely; she has resigned herself to the resolution that the Winnipers' sins have finally burned their legacy to the ground. And as Olivia looks into Tilly's eyes, it seems that there are still secrets that they each never knew.

"Tilly, don't do this. Whatever happened between you and my husband, it's not worth this." Olivia pleads, hoping to maintain her sense of social grace. She remembers the quaint dinner parties and haute gatherings of their youth. If their parents and ancestors could see them now, they would be thoroughly disappointed. After building a town of exclusive privilege, all their families' hard work now hangs in the balance of the very Colt revolver used to seal their fate. "We've been friends for too long, Tilly."

"We were never friends, 'liv!" Tilly continues to brood, aiming the revolver at Papa. She begins to sob while speaking to her former rival and remembering all the years of jealousy as they battled for their man's affection and attention. "All along, we've been competing…*for him!* And he chose you for marriage…and me for business…*and* the bedroom! I knew you were being lied to, but…he lied to me, too! I killed both of our children…*Kenny is gone and…and the other…I had a little baby girl…and she's gone, too…*because I believed him! But the worst part is, you didn't have to lie, Tommy! All of this could've been avoided! It should have been me…*it should've been me!*"

Tilly tilts the revolver down and to the right and shoots Olivia through the forehead.

"No!" Papa screams as his wife's skull rears back against his arm. The bullet passes through the back top of her head and spews blood and brain over the rows behind her. The bloody bullet careens into the courtroom ceiling as Olivia's body falls limply into Papa's chest. Blood-curdling shrieks fill the courtroom and Tilly begins to take aim again, but one of the officers in the aisle draws his weapon and shoots a bullet into her left hip. She twists awkwardly and fires her second shot into Papa's right shoulder. His body pushes back against the front row but he still clutches his dead wife in his left arm.

The hole in Olivia's head is so clear that Ms. Shields can see through it from the defense table. Tilly falls on her right knee, places her left hand over the entry wound in her hip, and pulls the trigger in her right hand, hoping to shoot Papa again, but the revolver jams.

"Shoot her!" Papa orders menacingly through pain and agony and Tilly's eyes grow wide as five officers unload a thunderstorm of steel bullets upon her. The onlookers scatter frantically throughout the courtroom. The gallery dissolves into a melee as bullets riddle Tilly and send her to the floor in front of the first row.

Feeling the bullet lodged in his right shoulder, Papa groans and grits his teeth, trying to rally the strength to continue his reign. Compounding the pain from his shoulder wound, he desperately clutches his chest with his right hand and feels his heart spasm but he still tries to cradle Olivia's limp body in his left arm. Unable to maintain his grip on the symbols of the throne, the horror of his mortality overcomes him and he goes into shock. The old man seizes and his eyes roll into the back of his head. At the same time, Thomas III absorbs the tragedy and watches his dead mother with her eyes open wide, yet she is silent and gone. Another Winniper woman has tragically fallen victim to the circumstances of the family's wealth: the chickens have once again come home to roost.

Both the defense and prosecution teams flee from their respective tables, leaving their documents, their evidence, their high-end briefcases, and the accused. Duke sits within oblivion, staring at his shattered grandparents, resoundingly numb to the violence. Judge Rupert remains at his bench, watching the carnage from a vantage point for the powerless. His gavel rests in his hand, but, he is unable to move. He realizes that his inaction has exposed his hubris; he has not received orders for this outcome.

The world spins out of control and Thomas III finally sees his family's decisions coming full circle. His noble actions now seem like the culmination of plot twists; for decades, every murder and mistake has played a part in several well-placed maneuvers that have now brought his life to this frantic apex.

He sees the gaping hole through his mother's head, dead in the arms of his wilting father. Both are blood-soaked. They remain unaided as the officers call for medics and gather around Tilly. The officers are too afraid to address Papa and his dead queen, *especially* after Thomas III's testimony. The balance of power is unclear; and the officers hope their sheriff will arrive soon and dictate their protocol. One officer kneels next to Tilly's bullet-filled corpse and removes the Colt revolver from her pale hand. He checks the chamber, removes the jammed bullet, unloads the remaining three, and holds up the steel weapon for his fellow officers to see.

Suddenly, Sheriff Cobb, Jr. appears in the courtroom doorway with several deputies at his side. The old sheriff's wiry white hair peaks through the bottom of his felt hat and his near-sighted eyes expand in shock as his mind processes the bloodshed. After almost eight decades of serving as a lawman in Winniper County, Sheriff Cobb, Jr. has only seen violence like this once before—the night he helped his father and Thomas Winniper, Sr. massacre the Sioux natives and take their land.

After listening to Thomas III's testimony and remembering these old sins, the sheriff doesn't immediately step inside the courtroom. He just stands in the doorway while his officers look back and forth between him and Papa. The fallen tyrant still clinches his chest and begins convulsing in the first row. Except for his croaks and coughs, the courtroom is eerily silent. The sheriff can hear the commotion of people fleeing the courthouse; an ambulance arrives at the front of the building, but he remains in the doorway, presumably overtaken by the gore.

Papa shakes uncontrollably, drowning in agony, and Olivia's corpse leans into his chest. The judge, Duke, and Thomas III remain still like statues in their respective positions and the sheriff, feeling evil spirits in his midst, still cannot stir his old boots to take one step into the courtroom. Stunned in their circumstances, for any one of these men to move would be to accept that this tragedy is real. Once again, the inner resolve emerges in Thomas III's spirit and the son wants to end this perpetual evil for good.

"Sheriff Cobb...I confessed to killing my sister!" Thomas III calls out through the courtroom, never taking his eyes off his lifeless mother and his dying father. He thinks about his daughter, Nancy, and he wonders how his words and actions will affect her future. He hopes that somehow her life will be better because he has told the truth. "I deserve to die for it. Please, take me to jail."

OCTOBER 1969

Sunday	Monday	Tuesday	Wednesday	Thursday	Friday	Saturday
			1	2	3	4
5	6	7	8	9	10	11
12	13	14	15	16	17	18
19	20	21	22	23	24	25
26	27	28	29 	30	31	

Wednesday, October 29, 1969
Thomas "Papa" Winniper, Jr.

Let me tell you where roses never grow,
Where Winniper women woe and wail.
They know
Sorrow stands still at the doorsteps
Where he waits for their babies' first breaths.
And yet,
Sorrow wears a social disguise,
Lies devised from ignorant eyes,
Where the weak cannot see
A mirror filled with stereotypes.
The cries
Turn life into a walking hell,
The crowd collectively holding the pick axe
Where, without caution until death,
A forgotten man hopes to escape the tax.

Thomas "Papa" Winniper, Jr. is dying. Bed-ridden and tormented, he believes that these are his final moments before hell breaks loose and swallows him whole. His sins will carry him down to a dark dungeon. Soon, the Devil will open the doors to eternal fire and call him home.

"My son, I've been waiting for you." Papa hears the fallen angel now as a faint whisper wafting over a distant stream, begging for his attention while he rots at death's door. After suffering a heart attack and being shot in the right shoulder, neither his heart nor his shoulder has healed; his blood and skin have become infected, turning his skin into a gruesome, green puss machine that repulses even the most experienced doctors. Berthine Lancaster sits next to the former king who has caused her family so much pain. She plans to nurse him through the end, caring for the dying slob inside the master bedroom of his family's forsaken mansion.

Once a bustling pillar of the Winniper County community, only a few surviving family members and a handful of housekeepers remain at the Winniper Family Estate. The landscape and vineyard have deteriorated without upkeep over the past year since Olivia died. Even Thomas III and Teresa's playhouse has crumbled to the ground; negligence has destroyed the bridge between reality and perception.

Berthine has moved into the mansion to look after Nancy, and make sure Christina doesn't drink herself to death. Because she was Olivia's longtime friend and because she raised Teresa's Sioux children, Berthine now feels obligated to make sure their sacrifices were not in vain. Berthine hasn't walked through the woods to visit her cabin since she moved to the mansion. She drives now and she actually enjoys the time away from the estate, visiting Charles, who still refuses to come to the Winnipers' home or meet the "other side" of his family. Berthine has begged him to see Papa before the old man passes, but Charles fears the moment he will meet his twin sister; and Berthine worries that Christina may only embarrass herself in front of new company.

∞

After Berthine moved into the mansion, she left Charles in her cabin, giving him the space to blossom and the seclusion to stay out of trouble.

∞

In reality, Charles is a happy country bumpkin, who is now content with the simple things in life because he has seen how complicated matters can become deadly. His debts have been cleared; his sins washed away...his only goal now is to stay clean. Yes, reality and perception have changed and they continue to evolve, yet Berthine remains steadfast and loyal to her friend and her family.

"Thomas, do you need anything? Some water?"

"No," Papa grumbles, turning his head to Berthine and staring at her with curious eyes.

∞

Although, she was a housemaid at the estate for years, he appreciates her more now than ever. Sadly, he didn't show his appreciation until after Tilly shot him.

∞

"I'm okay, Berthine, thank you."

"Let me fluff your pillow, then," she insists, standing from her chair and leaning toward Papa, but he reaches for her wrist.

"No, leave it...you...don't work...for me, anymore." He gasps and begins to cough roughly. "Besides it's...of no use, now."

"What about some music?" Berthine asks, her eyes searching for reasons to worry and chores to fill her mind. "I could find a record..."

"No...please, Berthine."

"This is hard, Thomas. Why won't you let anyone come visit you?" She holds his hand tenderly and sits on the edge of the bed. "We're all stuck in this house, while you lie here, keeling over in bed. And you won't even let us help you."

"I can't...be helped, Berthine. I can't...be saved," Papa stammers and spits up a mixture of mucus and mushed cabbage, an unbelievable shame for a once proud tycoon. Now, his tone and delivery sabotage his dignity; his once strong, forceful voice scratches and skips, signaling a transition from sickness to death. His stomach struggles to hold anything down; his bowels rock on an uneasy balance and, every so often, he spits up like a baby. He is an old man reduced to infancy. "Leave...me. I'm...happy...to die...alone."

"No, no matter how much you fuss, boy. I'm going to see you through, ya' hear? Olivia wouldn't want you to be alone, Thomas. No matter how guilty you feel, Olivia did love you. I see now who the stronger one really was between you two." Berthine jests, clenching Papa's hand tightly and returning his glare with a shared disdain. The tables and roles have turned; the mighty has fallen and the meek have risen to prosperity, yet the mighty still mires the meek within his muck.

"Rise up, woman," Berthine tells herself, *"Rise up."*

Many reporters and pundits have turned against the Winniper family, claiming Papa, Duke, and Thomas III are modern monsters and sadists. Although the press has vilified him, Berthine still sees Papa as the same foolhardy boy from their youth. He has always been wayward, cocksure, and scared.

∞

Olivia disarmed his ego in a rare, yet, successful love story of wealth and social grooming. From their moments of childhood, she made him forget himself long enough to care about someone else. But after they married, he distanced himself from those romantic emotions, especially once he realized the consequences of lovemaking and childbearing—his father taught him to hide their secrets without remorse.

He learned that the Sioux babies should be treated like a curse. As the Winniper patriarch, he fulfilled his obligation to purge the curse from the family's bloodline. And when Teresa planned to leave town with her Sioux children and June's engagement to Jazz threatened to expose the family's curse, Papa reacted with his father's instructions in mind.

All along, Olivia played the role of the loyal mother and the good wife, silently devoted to mantras of feminine servitude and patriarchal obedience; but, Papa always knew her true allegiances. He was aware that she occasionally visited Teresa's children in Berthine's cabin, and secretly, in a twisted way, he consented in a moment of weakness that inevitably undid his life's work. The reason: he couldn't bear to have any more blood on his hands. He had killed two of his own Sioux children; the thought of killing Berthine and Teresa's Sioux children caused him to avoid the responsibility. When the problem could no longer be ignored, Papa heaped the responsibility upon Thomas III. Using Sheriff Cobb, Jr. to provide stern supervision, Papa forced his son to dirty *his* hands, because Papa could no longer carry the guilt.

The men decayed in misery while the women died for their maternal instincts to protect their children. And this is how an American family destroyed itself, cannibalized from the inside for the entire world to see; yet, here, Papa Winniper, the embodiment of American imperialism, lies on his deathbed, seeing his secret Sioux sister for the first time, though he still does not know her true identity. He remembers those moments within their childhood when he and Berthine played together as equals. He may have loved her once, while they worked with her father to remodel the cabin, but when he ascended to the throne, their childhood bond conflicted with his responsibilities as a wealthy heir, and he turned his affections toward Olivia, who could always make him forget. She always had that effect.

∞

Missing his dearly departed, Papa remembers Berthine's friendship and he begins to feel a bit of joy for the possibilities when he is gone.

`"I know…you are…strong, dear…I know…" Papa Winniper agrees happily, patting Berthine's hand, puffing his cheeks with little tugs on his heart strings, and tensing his face into a weak smile. He fights to understand the feeling, the joy of human defeat, the thrill of resurrection. "…I just…hope…uh…I…just hope…uh…uh…never mind."

"What?" Berthine prods, grabbing Papa's hand gently, but he remains silent and glances around his bedroom. The four corners expand away from him, vertigo makes the Pearl Carpet of Lakota that stretches across the floor seem like an optical illusion—a trippy lake in a Salvador Dali painting. The oak dresser to his right is a family heirloom that his grandfather brought to the mansion when the family moved from Tennessee. The master bedroom has hosted so much tragedy; the décor surrounds the heavily quilted, white goose featherbed inside an oak-frame—the epicenter of the family's secrecy.

Born in this very bed, Papa ignores his end and stares at the dresser, looking over the family photos, medals, and awards that cover the oak top. He recalls some of his business accomplishments and his charitable achievements; and he gleams momentarily while thinking about his few, purely good deeds. Across from the bed hangs a portrait of his mother, Ruby.

∞

Because she died while giving birth to him and his brown sister, she never had a chance to console him or help him understand life's choices.

∞

Every child needs the love of his mother; without, it, he grows into a monster.

∞

After Ruby's death, Thomas, Sr. decided to memorialize his late wife with an oil portrait. He called Doc Morten back to the mansion and paid the good doctor to restore his wife's complexion as best he could. A mortician of sorts, Dr. Morten cleaned and colored her skin to appear alive. As he founded Winniper County, Thomas, Sr. hired two portrait artists to capture his dead wife's likeness; he chose the portrait that he thought best suited her legacy and hung the memorial across from his bed. Sadly stuck between eternal love and eternal heartbreak, he mourned his wife often and he created a Winniper martyr in their son's mind.

Thomas, Jr. grew up not only idolizing his father, but also reinventing his mother in the women around him. His Aunt Rita, widow to his late Uncle Christopher Winniper, Jr., provided a needed substitute, though she and Thomas, Sr. never became romantically involved. As a toddler, Thomas, Jr. thought of Rita as his second mother while she flitted around the estate, ordering servants and maids, callously taking umbrage to demean and disrespect the help whenever she pleased. Papa began to understand that a woman should be the master of the household and the man must be the master of the world. Sadly, Rita passed away while he was still forming his opinions on women and family, and he wonders what his understanding would be like if he had a consistent maternal figure throughout his life.

While defining his son's ideas of manhood, Thomas Winniper, Sr. molded Thomas, Jr. into a capitalist carnivore, who learned how to convert every family asset into long-term revenue. Papa implemented his father's tutelage, developed worldwide partnerships, and received critical acclaim for the Winniper Family Holding Company's global expansion—he established an American empire.

∞

The awards and adornments scattered around the Winnipers' master bedroom symbolize the family's elite enterprise. Born and bred to capitalize upon every advantage, Papa has reveled in every accolade.

Whether the praise came from the family's oil revenues, company contracts, or profitable trades, the money has meant very little.

∞

He lost his family before he ever had one. For Papa, his mother was the prize he could never win, the object he could never buy. Missing her since his birth, he never learned to understand himself, his family, or love; all of his emotions became casualties of an irreparable void.

Prior to their marriage, Papa treated Olivia Newton as a pseudo matriarch; she comforted him and told him everything would be okay. She always trusted Thomas, Jr.; her father was the first investor in Winniper County and he had idolized Thomas, Sr., so, in turn, Olivia viewed the founding father as a god-like figure in his growing town. After he passed away, all of her family's adulation transferred to Thomas, Jr., in hopes that he would marry Olivia.

When Winniper County's prince began to court his would-be wife, they spent hours laying cheek-to-cheek, hiding away near the shed at the west end of the estate. Olivia learned his expectations of her role; and by the time they married, she had memorized her lines and prepared her mind, body, and soul for the task of being a wealthy and powerful man's wife. She developed her biomechanics for childbirth and motherhood, but nothing could have prepared her to give birth to biracial twins...*twice.*

Olivia Winniper was the second Winniper woman to give birth to Sioux and white twins when Teresa and her deceased Sioux brother were born. She allowed Papa to follow his father's edict and he made the same decision that his father once made with his forgotten Sioux sister. Papa took his newborn, Sioux son inside the barn, and he burned and buried the babe next to the bones of what he thought was his sister.

Upon his return to the master bedroom, the couple basked in Teresa's newborn glow; her little light brightened the entire mansion, but, even then, Olivia knew that a daughter would not satisfy her husband. She knew that she would have to conceive a male heir, and Papa Winniper immediately began poking and prodding his wife, hoping she would conceive a son and undergo the ordeal, once again.

Two years later, when Olivia gave birth to Thomas III, Papa Winniper wept openly in their master bedroom, bawling like the babe in his arms. Killing another brown child was easier because he believed it would be his last; he felt unencumbered as he burned and buried another Sioux newborn inside the barn with her forgotten kin.

After losing a second Sioux child, Olivia became deeply depressed, though Teresa and Thomas III occupied much of her time and attention. She vowed to never bear another child. Papa agreed with her decision, after recognizing his own despair in his wife's depression and her dissident sorrow. Their guilt spoiled the marriage because the ghosts of their Sioux infants haunted the mansion and their dreams. The Winnipers became a sterile couple, who loved through words but little touch. Mama raised their children and Papa built a global empire; both were gladly distracted from one another. And while Papa became colder and colder toward his wife, he became increasingly incapable of viewing her purpose beyond managing the estate's staff and monitoring his wayward children. Still, Olivia continued to support and admire her husband; she never stopped seeing the prince who became the king of their once-small town and turned his father's oil business into a global empire.

∞

Berthine smiles softly and places her hand over Papa's eyebrows. He still lies in silent reverence, staring around the bedroom to his mother's portrait, the trinkets, plaques, and medals. He considers that which he has collected and that which he has missed.

"Tell me what you're thinking about, Thomas."

"Nothing," Papa Winniper grunts shortly and turns his head away from Berthine.

"You have too much on your mind, Thomas." She leans closer and places the palm of her tan right hand on his left cheek. "You have to unburden yourself."

"I'm not…ready…to leave, Berthine. I-I'm…scared…*of the other side.*"

"You don't have to be afraid," Berthine speaks softly and Papa Winniper can feel the warmth of her palm against his skin; a memory of sitting with Tilly on a wooden bench floods his conscious. Outside her lake house, children from the elite circle would skip school and neck from the water to the woods, believing they would stay young, and in love, forever. Much older now, Papa wonders where their love has gone: is it here in this deathbed, or, is it still there on that bench by the lake? He hopes for the latter.

"It's heartbreaking…what a man thinks…on his deathbed," Papa explains, holding back the tears pressing against his eyelids. "I've done…some very bad things, Berthine."

"We can all be forgiven..." she tells Papa, partly disbelieving their circumstances; they are twin siblings, one of whom still doesn't see their connection and the other fears the implications. Even after learning the truth from her adoptive parents, Berthine still has her suspicions and she refuses to broach the subject because of her remaining doubts and her prevailing trepidation. The old man can still give orders to a select few, loyal minions within Winniper County. Berthine only feels safe around Papa given his current condition; but, if Papa knew her true identity, he might try to fix his father's original blunder. Despite his dying tears, Papa may kill her so that he will finally complete his father's work and carry favor with his ancestors. Berthine wonders if perpetual murderers and career thieves can achieve salvation, but, she has faith in God's mercy.

"You can ask for forgiveness, Thomas, but first, you must repent."

"I can't..."

"You can try," She begins, hoping to help Papa find peace before his end. "Let your family come see you."

"N-n-no." Papa Winniper stammers, turning his head to his left and closing his eyes; he secretly hopes the moment passes soon. He opens his eyes, turn his head back to his right, and looks at Berthine, sincerely. "I'm...I'm *green*. Look at my skin. I don't want anyone to see me like this."

"Thomas..." She stares at her sickly, emerald brother; her emboldened, brown eyes urge him to lasso the moon, tie it to a horse, and march around the estate, just for her. The twins share a fleeting connection, like a hand reaching out to grab a rope, but its fingers barely graze the fabric. "You don't have much time. Don't leave us like this, with so much pain..."

"No..." he continues, closing his eyes again. "I told you, they can stay here, but I can't see them. They know everything now...I can't, I'm...too...*ashamed*...and I don't want to."

"You sound like a baby!" She yells, standing over Papa and waiting for him to open his eyes. He remains insolent, yet he takes one small peek to see if she's still watching him. "So old and still a sniveling child! You *should* be ashamed of yourself."

"*Well, I am.*"

"I'm tired of this self-pity. I won't let you do this to yourself." She passes her hand over his forehead, turns, and walks away from the bed. "For once, I won't let you get your way! I'm in charge now, and yep, I'm runnin' things as *I* see fit!"

"Berthine…" Papa calls after her, but she continues to walk toward the bedroom door. She opens the door with a quick look back at him before poking her head down the hall. He hears murmurs and footsteps, and soon, Berthine steps aside for his granddaughters, Christina and Nancy.

At age thirty-one, Christina still lives at the Winniper family's mansion, battling frequent bouts of alcoholism and helping to raise seven-year-old Nancy. When Christina is sober, she can remember her mother, how Teresa tried to raise her children. She also remembers June…and all the lessons learned from being a woman in this family. They are Winniper women; for those still living, a new hope exists for their future. They have opportunities that were never plausible in the old Winniper regime.

"Come in…" Berthine leads Papa's granddaughters by each hand. They both glance at their grandfather and wonder if they've done something wrong. Papa knows that his condition is morose; he looks like a carnival act, a Jekyll-ish freak. He also knows that his past conduct strayed from any decent moral code. Here, his innocent victims walk towards him and bear witness to the beast that his sins created.

The Winniper men, noble patriarchs, stained with the blood of their women, face their crimes in life and death, remorse and defeat. Lying at death's door, Papa Winniper watches his would-be executioners approach the master bed, seeking justice for the Winniper women who have fallen under the patriarch's sword while he tried to protect an empire that he needed the women to cultivate. They gave birth to his dreams and his nightmares. The hypocrisy runs wild in his mind. Berthine walks closer and positions his granddaughters to her left and right and they stare at Papa Winniper, with pity and remorse in their eyes.

She continues to nudge Christina and Nancy toward the bed. Papa coughs loudly to scare them, but Christina senses his ploy, looks down to her young cousin, and shakes her head. Christina is noticeably sober and Papa thinks that it must still be morning. Berthine steps away, pulls two red velvet cushioned chairs close to the bed, and pats the seat covers. Her grandnieces sit down timidly and there is a long, labored pause before Berthine takes Papa's weak, wrinkled right hand and massages his palm.

"Say something, Thomas." Berthine encourages, smiling at Papa and looking over Christina and Nancy. "*Anything.*"

"Uh…uh…girls…" Papa begins awkwardly, trying to muster some of his past authority. "How've you been?"

Pause.

"Nancy, Berthine tells me you've been eating everything in the house," he grumbles in his unusual tone. The density of death hangs over his head and he forgets the need for contrition. Nancy drops her eyes to the floor; her head dips sadly. "It's quite alright. Feel free to eat anything you like. Enjoy it while you're young."

Nancy raises her head and smiles for a fleeting moment; her face reminds Papa of Thomas III. Papa sees his son in the crinkles around her eyelids. His son is long gone, yet Thomas III still lives within a concrete cell alongside Earl and two other guys—all suffering for their sins as residents of death row inside the South Dakota State Penitentiary. Despite her desire to visit Earl, Christina has remained with Berthine and Nancy at the Winniper Family Estate, crying for the men locked in prison and grieving over every spilled drop of blood. With Thomas III sentenced to fry and Duke sentenced to life, serving his sentence in the same prison, the surviving Winniper women are somewhat lost within a curse they cannot correct.

∞

Nancy and Christina have settled into their solemn lives at the Winniper Family Estate, but, initially, Christina tried to leave soon after Thomas III's confession and her grandmother's murder. Unwilling to bury her grandmother, see her brother rot, and witness her former love and her uncle executed, Christina packed one burgundy Louis Vuitton suitcase and drove away in Duke's old Aston Martin with Clyde, one of the Winnipers' groundskeepers. At the time, Papa was in such dire straits that he was happy when he was told that she had left. Weakened, distraught, and dispassionate, he battled to survive his first heart attack and the surgery on his gunshot wound. He did not dispatch any minions as he had for June or Kenny—he had learned from past mistakes.

Also, seeming to learn from past mistakes, Christina returned to the Winniper Family Estate within a week of Olivia's murder, without Clyde and without the car. Papa saw this as a sign and he began to allow the legal and public processes to occur naturally around him, refusing to influence or impede in the affairs of Winniper County while he fought to save his life. After his first heart attack in the courtroom, the frequent sharp pains and numbness in his fingertips became a common fear. Complications from his shoulder wound and a blood infection from the steel of the Colt revolver's bullets combined with four heart aneurysms and forced Papa Winniper to remain in bed to this day. His fragile heart and poisoned body have become too unstable to sustain any physical activity.

∞

Slowly, a once-strong Winniper man has whittled to a green shell of his former frame and he has forbid anyone except Berthine to see his froglike complexion as he wastes away inside his loose-fitting crimson Kush robe. He is in a shambled state. Berthine's presence has given him some strength and a small amount of comfort, as she did when they were young. She has remained a present light in a life filled with self-imposed darkness, but now, while looking at his granddaughters, he realizes their importance, too. These surviving Winniper women are his hope that his family may endure.

Christina and Nancy experience a shared terror, looking at their grandfather's sickly skin and remembering his former image as their powerful patriarch. They are the future mothers of a Winniper family with new circumstances surrounding their curse.

"You know, you two girls are really the only heirs that we have left," Papa begins, looking over his granddaughters and forgetting the *others*. At thirty-one, Christina has never married, though she was close to becoming engaged to Earl before June's murder. She suspects that Papa sacrificed her potential fiancé in order to prevent any more *complications*.

Papa remembers her early battles to attend school and go to college; he secretly hoped her escape after Olivia's murder would lead to some form of education. Now he wonders if she ever intends to leave the nest again. Nancy will spend the rest of her life without her grandfather, her grandmother, her mother, or her father. She is the youngest victim of the Winniper family's curse. Papa thinks she's probably the least deserving of the misery because she's probably too young to understand everything that's happened. In fact, he doesn't understand everything either. He wonders how she will remember him and how these moments will affect the woman she becomes. "Nancy, you and Christina have a lot of responsibility to carry on the Winniper name. You know, our oil company…"

"Thomas, don't talk business now," Berthine interrupts, waving her finger at Papa. "They don't care about that and you shouldn't either."

"But they need to care, Berthine!" Papa protests in frustration; his negotiation tactics have no power in this moment of contrition. Redemption requires nothing less than absolution. "Who will run the Winniper Family Holding Company? *The businesses? The negotiations?* One of them will need to bear a son…"

"Dear, you have lawyers and accountants and business partners to handle all of that." Berthine leans away and pulls Papa's frail right hand toward Nancy's left cheek. His granddaughter tilts her head into the old man's avocado-colored palm and smiles at his soft touch. "These are your granddaughters; talk to them. Make amends."

"I…I…" Papa Winniper twists his lips in disgust and stares off into the corner behind his granddaughters before looking back to them. "I…I know you…can't accept…but…I…I did…what I thought…was best. I did…what I…was taught…but that's…no excuse." He pauses, presenting his repentance to his granddaughters and hoping to receive some sort of spiritual reclamation, yet Nancy and Christina return his explanation with apathy. The room fills with another Winniper family moment.

"I am...very sorry...for all the pain I've caused. I tried...to protect our family...like my father taught me to do. Those Sioux babies...my Pa' told me...he got rid of my Sioux sister...and if any woman...in the family...had any more, then...I had to...get rid...of them." Papa Winniper explains through deep wheezes, while shaking his head and glancing toward his mother's portrait. He remembers his old man's many mournful words for his lost love as he recalled the night Ruby died.

∞

Though Thomas, Sr. died before Olivia gave birth to Teresa, the original oil conqueror explained Ruby's death and the blood curse to his son. Thomas, Sr. detailed the battle between their militia and the Ghost Dance Sioux and he recounted the dying sorceress's hex upon the Winniper family's offspring. Out of precaution, Thomas, Sr. entrusted his only son to carry out the necessary discretion to continue the family's success; the shame of Sioux blood intermixed with an American industrialist would cripple their prestige and their legacy. Even if the oil business and offshoots continued to boom, the Winniper Family brand would never be seen with the same luster—no longer bathed in the same pristine white light. And so, Thomas, Sr. instructed, encouraged, and, even after his death, he still oversaw the development of his son from Thomas, Jr. into "Papa", from sole-surviving heir to murderous tycoon.

Papa married and conceived with Olivia, knowing that she would bear twins marked with the sins of his father and the births would need to be shrouded in complete secrecy. The Winnipers' master bedroom became the birthplace for both Teresa and Thomas III. The Winnipers' barn became a sick Sioux cemetery that always required more and more grave plots.

∞

"I know you may not understand how your Great-Grandfather Thomas Winniper, Sr. could teach me...to do that...*to family*...but...those were different times." Papa continues to shake his head as he removes his hand from Nancy's cheek and places his fingers to his forehead. "It's not an excuse, but...I really thought...and he really thought...we were doing what was best...*for our family*. I can't...ask you...to forgive me, but...do you, at least, understand?"

Nancy grins and nods her head quickly; she's a wide-eyed child looking at her grandfather in awe of his old age and freakish appearance. She's too young to feel remorse or regret and he hopes to steal some of her peace for himself. He's desperate for solace. Christina gently grabs his left hand, but she does not respond to his repentance; she simply stares at their palms in silence. Papa joins her inspection and notices the wiry veins in his hand intertwined with his granddaughter's rosy skin. The contrast between life and death is hauntingly evident; he feels his death move closer, and a tingling fear climbs up his back as the need for absolution becomes paramount.

"I know…you may never…forgive me, Christina. You haven't been…the same since…Kenny abandoned you…and your siblings here. I admit…that I haven't…made life easy…for any of you." Papa Winniper tries to atone, knowing that he has been the architect of much of his granddaughter's misery. "Your mother, your father, Kenny, June, Earl, Duke…I can't expect…"

"Grandpa," Christina whispers, removing her hand from his grasp and leaning back into her chair, "Please, stop."

"And I don't want you…to worry about money…either of you." Papa senses Christina's anxiety and he quickly changes the subject; he glances to Berthine, who silently encourages him to continue. He feels like he's seeking permission to distract his granddaughters with gifts. "I can have Fred…release…some of the money…from your trust funds. You both…can stay here…with Berthine, and Christina, if…you ever decide…to go…to college, you…could do that now, too."

"I don't want to go to college anymore, Grandpa." Christina leans forward toward her grandfather, puffing her cheeks as if she's looking out a window on a rainy day and dreaming of finding a place to play. "That ship has sailed."

"Don't limit…yourself, Christina. You're still young. I know…I discouraged your schooling before, but…that was wrong. You once…loved science, I remember that." Papa recalls her passion half-heartedly, still trying to ingratiate himself with his granddaughters. He stretches his mind back to the days when Teresa and Kenny lived on the opposite side of Winniper County and her family enjoyed a few brief years of happiness before the crash. "I remember, Teresa…telling me…about your…science fair project…on Pompeii. You made…a volcano…that caused…quite a stink!"

"That was the neighbor's fault!" Christina laughs with her grandfather, but a knock at the door interrupts the momentary bond. Berthine promptly walks through the room and opens the door slightly. Her eyes widen at the sight and she leans her head into the hallway. Papa can hear her whisper, and then a young, brown man peaks into the room—Charles. His familiar eyes ease Papa's heart, though Papa has only seen the young man twice before now.

Looking at him intensely, Papa can see Teresa in her Sioux son's face. All along, while Papa knew that Berthine raised his Sioux grandchildren, he never dared to visit, though he contemplated additional horrors to avoid any possibility of the family's secret being revealed. Even still, his fears came to fruition when Jazz and June met fortuitously in New Orleans. It was like the ghosts that haunted him had conjured his spirit to allow the circumstances that brought those two together. Papa felt suddenly overwhelmed by their engagement announcement, the pending Hollywood marriage, and the scandalous union of a Sioux brother and a white sister who never knew they shared the same mother and father.

A few weeks after the attack on June, Papa and Thomas III walked into Jazz's hospital room while reruns of June's funeral played on a raised television hanging in the corner. Papa barely acknowledged Berthine or Charles before Thomas III escorted them out of the room. Jazz lay motionless, barely able to maintain consciousness, though his eyes, when open, followed Papa intently. Every time Jazz looked at the old man, his pupils filled with rage and fire. Papa stood closely to his forlorn grandson and smiled out of pity. Papa had caused the twenty-seven-year-old so much pain, but something about Jazz's survival had forced Papa to reconsider his callousness.

Papa had a special feed patched into the hospital room's television and, without so much as a word, Papa grabbed the remote beside Jazz's hand and turned the channel from the rerun of June's jazz funeral procession to a live feed of a comatose woman, heavily bandaged, laying on an operating table in a dark hospital room. A team of nurses and doctors frantically attended to her, swabbing and sewing, pumping and cleaning. She was so badly bloodied and beaten that she looked like a bowl of chewed fruit, completely indistinguishable, but once Jazz looked up to the screen and saw the faint wisps of her blonde hair, he knew, quite clearly, who she was. June was alive.

Papa smiled again, still out of pity, looking back and forth between the television and Jazz and inspecting his eyes to see if Jazz understood the circumstances. There was a bargain to be made, concessions to be discussed, and more secrets to be kept. With Charles, Berthine, and Thomas III outside the room, Papa told Jazz the complete truth and the two reached an agreement that neither has shared with another soul—Jazz exchanged his testimony and his public silence for June's life and a chance at happiness.

The two men agreed that Jazz and June's past, public life could never resume, but the twins could have a very secluded, private life...*together.* June would probably never wake from her coma; and, even if she did, she would need professional care for the rest of her life, but, that was better than nothing, for her and Jazz. So, while wrapped in casts, struggling on his back with little hope for a full recovery, Jazz watched his battered sister and he made a decision to save her—a decision that he couldn't make during the attack.

Papa left Jazz in his hospital room and made the proper arrangements to ensure compliance among the hospital staff and security. Papa had June flown to a remote clinic in Nova Scotia, complete with round the clock care and protection; shortly after his testimony, Jazz chartered a flight to Nova Scotia and arranged for June's transport to another location. The two quickly fell off the grid and no one has heard from either since.

∞

The terms of his agreement with Jazz have remained completely secret, and, even while marching to his deathbed, Papa has fulfilled his end of the deal.

∞

Tilly's attack created such a firestorm and fiasco that Papa thinks Olivia's murder made it easier for Jazz to disappear. Jazz all but vanished from the public eye and, presumably, he took his comatose sister-lover with him to wherever he felt they could be alone and safe from Papa and the public.

∞

Absent his overpowering nature, Papa envisions Jazz and June living in quiet solitude. They are finally free from their former tormentor as the old man dies, clinging to secrets that still inhibit his salvation. While visiting Charles in her cabin and taking care of the Winnipers at the mansion, Berthine has used every fleeting moment of her time with Papa to forge a secret reconciliation amongst the family that remains in Winniper County.

"Everyone…this is Charles…he's um…well he's a part of the family. Charles, this is Christina and Nancy. Um…you met Papa in the hospital before." Berthine runs through an awkward introduction as she closes the door and ushers Charles toward the family crowded around the bed. Charles follows her timidly, barely glancing at Christina.

"Nice to meet you all…" He murmurs and mostly keeps his eyes locked on Papa. Charles shuffles behind Berthine, hoping to disappear in her shadow.

"Nice…uh…yes, nice." Christina manages, stammering through her own reflection. Meanwhile, Nancy moves closer to her grandfather, leans against Christina, and places her tiny hand in Papa's withered palm. He softly grips his youngest granddaughter's hand and, finally, he feels a small smile form across his face, a tepid accommodation. It seems Papa may remember love before death.

Berthine and Charles continue to make their way toward the bed as Papa repositions his back. Charles stops suddenly and remains at the foot of the bed. He sees his twin white sister up close for the first time since they were split at birth. Their eyes grow in unison as they stare at each other. In order to avoid the moment, Christina hops to her feet, fluffs the pillow behind her grandfather's head, and gently nestles his neck back onto the pillow.

"Uh, thank you…Christina." Papa Winniper whispers softly, staring at his granddaughter and also seeing Teresa in her face. "Do you…forgive me, Teresa?"

The misplaced question lingers over the family; Christina sits back down, and her eyes dart between Charles, Berthine, and Nancy, searching for a safety net to catch her or a vaudeville cane to snatch her from the spotlight. Berthine still stands near the corner of the bed, whispering to Charles and waving her hand. She implores Christina to keep the conversation and her grandfather alive.

When Christina looks back to Papa, he continues to stare at her, seeing Teresa's glowing eyes—the fire that often challenged his authority.

∞

She was a fierce warrior who tried to leave town with her husband and her children and she became a victim of her father's malice and her brother's cowardice.

∞

Now, Teresa haunts the murderous father who sacrificed her mother, her brother, her husband, and her children for a lifelong pledge to protect a family that he actually destroyed in the process.

"Yes, I forgive you, Grandpa." Christina nods slowly, yet falsely, telling the old man at death's door exactly what he needs to hear so that he accepts his fate. "We all forgive you."

Her words save her grandfather from more heartache, but he feels, deep within his spirit, it's impossible to forgive what he has done.

∞

He ordered the killings of his daughter and his granddaughter, carried out by their respective brothers whom he felt deserved the duty.

∞

Now, after realizing that he acted without care for karmic consequences, Papa dies knowing that his shattered family may never again be whole. The Winnipers have only two *acceptable* female heirs, neither has reason nor faculty to wade through a gene pool filled with such sorrow.

"I hope…you both…can be happy. You can have…whatever you want." Papa Winniper insists, encouraging his granddaughters and clutching Nancy's hand in his ghoulish palm. "Nancy, you can have…whatever you want. I've…heard you…plucking that guitar…if you ever wanted…to play songs…like your Cousin June…*that'd be fine*. I'm just sorry…you haven't had a chance…to meet her."

His pleas for forgiveness are unfamiliar for all in attendance. The guitar, June's talisman, is the apparatus of the walking dead; Charles, Berthine, Christina, and Nancy remain silent, refusing to discuss the ghost in the room. Because they believe June is dead, no one wants to mention the deceased within the Winniper family's haunted mansion.

∞

Even though he knew she was alive, Papa once saw June looming over Nancy's shoulder, a spirit instructing a child. Afterwards, he rarely mentioned the guitar and he avoided Nancy anytime she strummed the strings around the mansion. Before the trial, Papa turned his focus to appeasing the partners, politicians, and officials who protected the Winniper Family Holding Company and the family's patriarch. For their monetary compliance, the saviors demanded payment and sinners incurred debts. After the trial, the saints mostly vanished and the sinners have begun to circle the coming corpse, planning to pick his bones clean.

∞

Christina reaches out to her grandfather and gently squeezes his right forearm, still sitting alongside Nancy and ignoring Charles. With Berthine over their shoulders, the serene women strike a peaceful pose as Papa's angels, comin' forth to carry him home. In their dutiful eyes, Papa sees the innocence that he lost long ago and he remembers how his choices have created dangerous fates and horrible outcomes for those he sought to protect. Instead of securing his family members, his walls have suffocated them.

Another round of soft knocks tap at the door. Berthine swiftly excuses herself and walks across the bedroom. She opens the door and murmurs something before taking a letter within an open envelope. With one look, she seals the envelope hurriedly, closes the bedroom's heavy oak door, and walks toward the oak dresser next to the bed. She places the sealed envelope on the dresser and turns toward Papa with a comfortable smile; she is a newly crowned Sioux-American queen, sitting proudly on the family's throne and forming a butt print in the cushion. Berthine pats Charles on the shoulder, walks around the room, and resumes her place in Papa's deathbed portrait. She kisses his sweaty forehead and smiles to cover her grief.

"What have you all been talking about?"

"Oh...just family...stuff...I...uh..." Papa mutters and coughs, ignoring Charles before returning Berthine's smile as cheerfully as a dying bigot can. "Who...was at...the door, Berthine?"

"Just Freidrich; he's always talking business. I don't know how you could stand him all these years." She grabs a dry, lavender washcloth from the bedside and pats Papa's forehead tenderly, while looking at him with those reassuring eyes. "I told him that now is not the right time. You're with family now."

"But, what if…it's something important? Doesn't he…want to…say goodbye?"

"He wants to merge the oil stocks in Beredum Financial with the trade partners and their brokerage firm, blah, blah, blah." Berthine waves her hand playfully and smiles toward Nancy. "It's pointless anyway."

"Why?"

"Because, Thomas, we're going to dissolve the oil company and give away the land." Berthine admits confidently, wanting Papa to die knowing the truth while knowing he is too weak for combat. "The land, the business, all of it has to go."

"What…do you mean *'give away'*?" Papa asks angrily, his eyes growing feverishly; his eyebrows tighten with the last of his strength. "What…have you done, woman?"

"Thomas, Violet told me years ago that this family is cursed…and it's because of that land and every dollar you've got from it. We have to get rid of all of it and it's a good time-"

"You can't do that! I can still…change my will, Berthine! Even on…my deathbed! I can…leave you…all…with nothing!" Papa Winniper yells, coughing loudly. "Technically…you're not even authorized…to make those decisions. Christina is my next of kin."

"No, I am, Thomas. But you're still too blind to see that. But fine, change your will. Go back on your word and you'll damn us all!" she screams back. "It's that oil on that Sioux land; it's that greed that you won't give up! It's all cursed! It's got you so messed up that you can't even see that I'm your sister!"

"You're my what? You can't…sell my land. This…is *my* family's land," Papa Winniper retorts without concern for the truth or the moral high ground. He only cares about the betrayal. The woman, who has comforted him and provided warmth in a time when he feels the coming chill of death, now reveals herself as a deceitful and disloyal double agent. "Why…would you…tell me this…now? What…did Fred…hand to you? I saw…a letter!"

"It was his letter of resignation, Thomas. He has a few loose ends to tie up, but beyond that, he doesn't care. So few people actually care about this family beyond its wealth. You should see that now. And I'm telling you all of this so that you know. Hopefully you gain peace from knowing that I survived and that I've been here all along. And now, I'll make sure that your grandchildren survive, too." Berthine vows solemnly, looking between Nancy, Christina, and Charles and smiling confidently. She dreams of their future and she prays that they can finally live together. "We will be a family, *a real family*. With problems and arguments, but we'll also have understanding and forgiveness."

"You planned…this all along, didn't you?" Papa releases Nancy's small hand, points at Berthine, and then nods toward Charles. "You resented me...while you…raised…him…and *his siblings*. You think…I'm the reason…Olivia's dead, and now…you're taking…my legacy. You're selling my empire! Any joy, any peace…I could have…is gone!"

He spurns her with contempt, seeing her actions as cruel, but Berthine endures his wrath lovingly. She wants the best for Papa and their family, but what he and Berthine envision as best are two opposite realities. Papa sought to reinforce the lessons that his old man taught him, but Berthine plans to abandon the conventional logic and find a new social compassion for their family.

Papa glares at Charles and Berthine, but they remain silent, unnerved and impartial to his threats. Christina and Nancy lower their heads, distancing themselves from any confrontation. Maybe they are still indoctrinated as well-mannered Winniper women, salvaging their souls within a middle ground of passive inertia. They are safe in a Domestic Wonderland.

"Thomas, we are here to *give you* peace. Not take it away," Berthine wipes the lavender washcloth over Papa's forehead and left cheek. "We've seen too much bloodshed over money and power. We weren't meant to live this way, Thomas."

"You've resented me…for all these years."

"I don't resent you, Thomas." She leans in and softly pats his cheeks with the washcloth; his sweaty, diseased skin trembles from her touch as death absorbs his energy. "I love you…you are my brother. I remember watching you and *Mister* Robinson work on our cabin. You two spent hours just runnin' your mouths, carryin' on, sayin' nothin' the whole time, but workin' hard. Do you remember?"

"Yes, ha...your father...*Johnnie boy*...he was kind." Papa replies softly, taking Berthine's hand and pushing his cheek into her touch. She drops the washcloth over his shoulder and cradles his cheek in her hand so that he feels the warmth from her palm. "He was...much nicer...than my father."

"He would have walked through fire for you or your father, Thomas. Now, I think walking through fire would have been easier than what you've done. It would've definitely been less painful. But...I'm going to make sure these girls never go through that, and *that* should give you peace."

Her logic challenges his resolve, and Papa lies in his master bed, feeling like God's most submissive servant, enslaved by a greater force.

Berthine has suddenly become the physical and intellectual superior, and Papa wonders if God has intended this ending all along. The wealthy father has fallen so far from pride rock. He knows now that the trajectory of his fate has a downward direction; its arrow points uniquely straight and true.

∞

Blessed with manifest destiny, his father told him not to interfere with the natural order: kill the Sioux babies to preserve the Winniper family's prestige. Consider their class and kind while concealing homicides, but he never knew, until now, that the "curse" was only an aesthetic problem. The biracial babies, spawned from a land conflict, challenged this American family in order to produce one outcome—**unity** or extinction.

∞

"Forgive me, Berthine," Papa apologizes quietly, becoming vulnerable while remembering his wife lying lifelessly in his arms. Her spirit often calls to him; he sees her ghost alongside Teresa and Tilly. "I never...intended..."

"I know..." She rubs Papa's cheek gently, massaging the stubble on his gangly skin. "We'll be okay, Thomas. And the Good Lord will forgive you..."

"No...he won't," Papa counters stubbornly, sensing the darkness that festers within him. His demons wait anxiously to claim his soul. "And I...don't care...anymore. I never had...a chance...at salvation."

"Don't say that, Thomas."

"No, it's true. My father…told me…what to do…just like…I told my son." Papa Winniper stammers, staring at Berthine and his grandchildren, feeling their pain amplified in his own as the strands of life seep from his heart. His right shoulder, his fingertips, and his toes turn cold. "The Bible…says… *'honor thy father'*. I did…that…I did that…and I…became…a monster."

"Thomas, please…" Berthine pleads, grasping the washcloth again and wiping his fearful face. "Try to be strong."

Papa begins to feel death's delirium; consciousness seeps from his mind and the living end approaches in extreme flashes, mixing his reality with nothingness. Tears fall down Berthine's cheeks, and he knows these times never pass quickly enough. Papa starts to see translucent, bright flashes entangled with his vision. Hallucinations, it would seem to any other, but, to a dying man, haunted by familiar ghosts, these visions are the prelude to real horror.

A blonde, small toddler, blurred in disillusionment, draws sketches among stacks of books, flipping back and forth between her drawings. Her mother scoops the babe in her arms and holds her close. They share soft kisses and tender words. Resembling Olivia and Teresa, the mother and daughter embrace happily, and Papa sees the relationship that he destroyed.

Those murdered women, killed without remorse, begin to dance around his deathbed, weaving amongst the surviving members of his family. Papa searches his mind for a boy, a child who would be his heir. He remembers another prince, a son who never matched his treacherous father's potential.

∞

The boy, once innocently sweet, became another monster, molded by a Winniper man's motives. Confronted with the sins of his deeds, Thomas III exposed his father to the world and showed the depths to which Papa had damaged their family.

"Thomas…Thomas…my boy…" Papa calls into the coming darkness, seeing visions of his forsakenly sensitive son. He remembers the boy's shyness; Thomas III was a kind thinker, ill-equipped to handle the pressure of being a Winniper man. "Where's…my son? Where's…Thomas III?"

"Uh…Tommy can't be here…" Berthine raises the washcloth and dabs Papa's glistening forehead.

"Why? Why not?" Papa asks frantically, still searching for his son as his eyes grow weary. "Where…is my son?"

"He's..." Berthine pauses, looking over to Nancy and wondering if the child fully understands her father's circumstances. She knows that Thomas III is in prison, but she still does not grasp that he will soon die. "...uh...he's still in prison..."

"*Prison...*" Papa Winniper repeats Berthine's words, hearing subtle voices from the other side; he struggles to push the darkness aside and maintain his consciousness.

Berthine pauses and drops the washcloth on the bedside. She leans away from Papa, turns to Nancy, and wipes the seven-year-old's hair from her face. Nancy returns Berthine's gesture with an impish giggle, filled with questions that she's unable to answer. She stops laughing when her focus returns to her grandfather; she senses that this is a serious moment.

Although murder and deception have surrounded her since her birth, Nancy doesn't know much about death, except that people leave and never return. So much pain within one family, it's hard to differentiate their agony. Berthine sees Thomas III in Nancy, Nancy sees her father in Papa, Papa sees Teresa in Charles, and Charles sees himself in Christina. Berthine fights more tears, thinking about the coming finality in the Winniper family's saga—the affable prince will meet the electric chair.

"Berthine, I'm dying. Where...why is my son in prison?" Papa strains his eyes while apparitions of Olivia and Teresa fly throughout the room. The ghosts and illusions prance over Christina's head, passing two Sioux babies between them. Papa's eyes rest on Olivia's ghost, and he focuses on her face, that warm smile.

∞

Every dream came true with her, but she was never enough until she was gone.

∞

"Why's Thomas III...in prison? He's...a Winniper. He...doesn't deserve-"

"Thomas, please...try to rest." Berthine implores her brother sincerely, turning back toward him, leaning over his side, and placing her right hand over his weak heart. "You may have more time...if you just rest."

"No...I'm done. I'll...be resting...soon enough. Tell me, where...is my son?" Papa begs her in exhaustion, still fighting the darkness within.

"He's in the South Dakota Penitentiary." She confesses somberly and Papa feels his pulse weaken; a squeamish flutter passes from his toes to his head. The finale, he remembers; the betrayal, he recalls that, too. "He pled guilty; he's been sentenced to death."

"Why?" Papa Winniper asks knowingly but he's unwilling to accept the truth. He glances through the darkness, sees Nancy, and gently grabs her petite hand once again. "Nancy, what happened…to your father?"

"He's in jail because he killed my mother," Christina answers plainly; she's still an unfiltered child to some degree. She lacks bedside manners. Her frankness could have made her a successful doctor or scientist, but she never had the opportunity once she moved under Papa's roof. Secretly, she's hated her grandfather all these years, even before she learned the truth surrounding her mother's murder. Her curt answer exposes scars of anger that will never heal; these wounds have embedded themselves within her soul, questioning her importance within the world's determinism.

"Why…did…*my son*…kill?" Papa Winnipers continues to ask questions in delirium, tilting his head back against his pillow. "Why…would he do…such…a thing?"

"Please stop, Thomas. Just relax." Berthine wipes Papa's forehead with the lavender washcloth, hoping her brother can survive a little longer, just so he can find peace.

"You told him to kill her, Grandpa," Christina adds sharply, sitting up in her chair, awaiting her grandfather's end with a cold ambivalence. On his deathbed, she finally doesn't fear him and she takes the opportunity like Brutus. "Remember Kenny, too, Grandpa. You had him killed, too."

Christina quickly glances toward Charles to see if he approves of her brashness, but he just stares back at her, still unwilling to engage the family. Forgiveness only brings but so much resolution.

"But, why? Why…would *I*…do that? Why…isn't…*my son*…here?" Papa wonders aloud; tears fall from his weakening eyelids as he stares up to Berthine. "We're…Winnipers; we…don't…go to *prison*…do we? I thought…we own…that building…"

"Not for long, Thomas. You don't have to worry anymore." Berthine assures him with a comforting smirk, beseeching Papa to forget the trivial and tend to his eternal path. "But we're…"

"Why?" Papa interrupts, still only concerned with the son who betrayed him. He remembers the boy sitting in court, abandoning his loyalties to the Winniper name, and testifying about the brutal events surrounding the family's curse. "He...was...a traitor."

"He's on death row, Thomas." Berthine sobs, breaking apart from her solace. She falls to her knees, leans over, and hugs Nancy. "I know you don't understand, Nancy. But everything will be okay, I promise."

"*Death row?*" Papa Winniper repeats Berthine's words again, struggling to understand their meaning. "They're...going...to kill...*my boy.*"

"Yes." Berthine continues to sob and Christina joins her on the floor next to bed, wrapping Nancy and Berthine in her arms. The Winniper women hug one another as their patriarch drifts between life and death.

"He's...going...to die...like me?" Papa's mind abandons itself, unwilling to face his treachery. Confronted with the ghosts of his wife, his wife's killer, and his daughter, he also absorbs the knowledge that his son will soon join them. Papa clamors for excuses, still unwilling to admit his hand in his family's misery. "But...he's...a Winniper man...he...has...an empire...to run..."

"The *empire* will be fine, Thomas. Don't worry..." Berthine continues to hug Nancy and Christina tenderly; the mournful women can feel each other relax in their embrace.

"I feel...cold, Berthine." Papa shivers in bed, reaching out for his family but he only feels the still, damp air of the bedroom. "I- I'm...scared."

"It'll be okay," Berthine cries, wiping her eyes while rising to her feet and standing next to the bed. Christina stands by her side and Nancy steps closer to her grandfather's hand; with Charles standing at the foot of the bed, sheepishly watching the fall of a king, they all wait for the end to come. The ghosts continue to swirl around Papa's head, and he reaches out again as Berthine takes his hand.

"We've forgiven you, Thomas."

"I know...I know...but..." Papa freezes, stuck in a momentary lapse in reality, mesmerized by the familiar ghosts assembling around him.

Olivia, Teresa, Kenny, and the discarded Sioux newborns hover beside his deathbed silently, still seeking to the resolve the final moments when they wondered about the answer to the inevitable question: "*Why?*"

Papa Winniper glances frantically between his living and dead victims; tears pour from his all-seeing eyes.

"...I don't...think *they've* forgiven me."

"*Who?*" Christina asks, watching her dying grandfather stare fearfully around the bedroom. "Who are you talking about, Grandpa?"

"*Olivia...Teresa...Tilly...Kenny...all of the them...*" Papa Winniper whimpers in terror, seeing the ghosts surround him. The apparitions are living, breathing entities, haunting him in various illusions while transforming into their younger selves. He watches Tilly, Olivia, Teresa, and Kenny morph into children and begin playing and laughing throughout the room. Taking a break from their eternal torment and regret, his new neighbors have come to see him home.

"They forgive you, too," Berthine whispers reassuringly, but Papa sees his victims' sorrow. Their pale faces have replaced their childhood glee with sadness; even in their ghostly joy, they still miss the loved ones and the life that Papa stole from each of them. The thief must pay for his crimes in the afterlife and atone for his villainy. Feeling his unquenched soul, he fears his moment of judgment because he lacks the vital ingredient for absolution—acceptance. His mother appears across the bedroom, wearing the same dress from her portrait and standing next to the framed memorial; Ruby weeps for her dying son.

"No, they don't...forgive me...they don't...understand...what I've...been through!" Papa cries sadly as his heart stops in Death's grip. Ruby walks toward the foot of the bed while she observes Berthine, the Sioux daughter that she never knew. Papa stares between his mother and Berthine and, finally, he sees the resemblance. His words tremble on the edge of his lips as the light around him fades to darkness. "W-w-wait...y-y-y-you...d-d-don't go! I-I-I see her now, Ma'! B-b-ber-th-thine...y-y-you're...m-my... my...*s-s-s-sister.*"

He's simultaneously filled with joy and anguish, seeing his family's mistakes come full circle before his end, and he worries about what he may find on the other side. Olivia and Teresa smile next to Christina and Nancy, his mother sobs next to Charles, and Tilly and Kenny chuckle behind Berthine's back. All the ghosts stand amongst his living family, and he feels every sinister force in the universe descend upon him. He can no longer see; the darkness has won. His mother howls frightfully, but he can only hear her screams and he knows that all his hope is lost in this world.

"*Ma'? I can hear you, Ma'.*" Papa whispers with his final breaths. "Can you...save me...please? Please...please...save me, Ma'. I saved one...I saved one. June...is still alive."

NOVEMBER 1971

Sunday	Monday	Tuesday	Wednesday	Thursday	Friday	Saturday
	1	2	3	4	5	6
7	8	9	10	11	12	13
14	15	16	17	18	19	20
21	22	23 	24	25	26	27
28	29	30				

November 23, 1971
<u>Nancy Lucille Winniper</u>

Yesterday.

    Tomorrow.

        Now.

Gone.

    Forever.

        How?

Lost

    and

        Found.

Forgotten,

        Fated,

    and

        Proud.

Nancy Lucille Winniper hoists the strap of June's acoustic guitar over her shoulder so that the instrument rests against her back. She, Christina, and Berthine watch two massive steel gates slide open to reveal the entrance to the South Dakota Penitentiary. As they enter the cold, Pentagon-like building, Berthine holds Nancy a little closer, nestling the tiny nine-year-old under her left arm and shuffling past the gates' security guards. Nancy looks over her left shoulder and sees Christina's face glowing in the overhanging ceiling lights. Reaching up and squeezing Christina's hand, Nancy smiles during their trek and Christina returns her smile, content to help her little cousin survive this moment in her life. Nancy won't be the same when they walk back through those gates.

"We'll be okay," Christina whispers, forcing her cheeks into a modest smile that preserves the lie. She has learned to con through hardship and heartache. "Everything will be over soon."

"I don't want to go inside," Nancy protests to her cousin, but she turns her head to see if Berthine is listening, too. "I'm scared."

"I know, darlin'. I'm scared, too." Berthine confides softly, hugging Nancy and nodding to Christina as the three women continue to move through the prison entrance. "Your father needs to see you...*before*...he goes away."

"Why can't he leave tomorrow?"

"Darling, you know why..." Berthine explains with some hesitation, trying to choose her words wisely while glancing to the prison guards and penitentiary officials. "I told you, your father couldn't choose when to go."

"What about the day after tomorrow?"

"No, Nancy," Berthine answers, fighting tears and clenching her throat. "I'm sorry, please stop asking."

"Mrs. Lancaster!" An armed prison guard calls from the lobby and walks toward the family, flanked by several nosey employees. He raises his arm to his left and quickly ushers the women past the administrative wing. "Mrs. Lancaster, come *this* way."

"Excuse me…sir," Berthine steps away from Nancy and Christina and walks next to the guard as they march by three hallways leading to the cell blocks for inmates serving time in general population and solitary confinement. Duke sits silently within a cell down one of these hallways, but he will not allow anyone to visit him. As the prison personnel, Nancy, and Christina follow closely, Berthine and the guard reach the end of the lobby and enter a concrete corridor where more guards come to escort the family through the prison.

The Winniper family's protection is an utmost priority; although the press has deflowered and defamed the family's name, the people of Winniper County still hold the surviving members of the family in high regard. They are infamous; loved and loathed for the same reasons—their existence endures. Berthine addresses the guard comfortably, feeling Olivia's spirit guide her concerns.

"I was told we'd have time to speak with Tommy before…"

"Yes, Mrs. Lancaster, but we had to prep him in the medical office," the guard explains, moving aside and pointing down the corridor from which they came. He then nods over his shoulder toward a dark, concrete hallway behind him. "He's back in the row now. They're waiting for you. You can follow me."

"Okay," Berthine takes a deep breath and exhales. Her eyes dart between the prison guard, Nancy, and Christina; she reminds herself that these moments will come to pass. Berthine raises her chin and steps back between Nancy and Christina, feeling the comforting spirit of Winniper women. "Come along, girls."

Surrounded by a growing legion of inquisitive prison personnel, the guard leads Berthine, Nancy, and Christina down death row. To their right, sullen, solitary inmates sulk within their respective cells; they hardly raise their heads to acknowledge the passing procession. They have been warned that any misconduct will have dire consequences. As the family passes, Christina catches a glimpse of Earl, stewing in his cell. He doesn't look up as she walks by and she does not call to him. A little girl inside her stomach begs her to run to him, but she keeps her pace and continues alongside Nancy and Berthine.

They pass a few empty cells until reaching the last one on death row. Thomas Winniper III sits quietly on a thin, metal bed, wearing an orange prison-issue jumpsuit. The grease in his hair glistens under the cell's fluorescent light and he clenches his hands together tensely. When he raises his head and sees his daughter, his anxious face relaxes instantly and his spirit brightens.

"Daddy!" Nancy calls happily, running to the gray, iron bars and bouncing up and down with her guitar on her back. A prison guard opens the cell door and steps aside grimly. He has witnessed several last goodbyes.

"Hi, baby." Thomas III rises from his skinny prison bed just as Nancy runs into the cell. He lifts his daughter into his arms and holds her tightly in a hopeful embrace. The guitar on her back pushes into his fingers and, for a moment, he can feel June. "How's daddy's favorite daughter?"

"I'm your only daughter." Nancy laughs heartily and smells her father's greased scalp. "You smell funny, Daddy."

"I know, Nancy. The warden's got me marinated in lighter fluid." He jokes, looking at Christina and Berthine as they enter the cell slowly, leaving the guards, officials, and onlookers outside the glass jar. The Winnipers must remain within the menagerie, while they say goodbye to one of their own. "They're fixin' to cook me good, Berthine."

"Don't talk like that, Thomas. Think about Nancy." Berthine scolds Thomas III; he chuckles at her attempt to parent him. She still tries to replace Olivia and play his mother's role, but Olivia is still irreplaceable. His guilt is implacable. The paint has dried and Olivia's son is a murderer like his father.

"I'm sorry, Berthine." Thomas III cradles Nancy closely, still hoping to feel her in his arms forever. "I'm just...*scared*."

"Me too, Daddy, I was just sayin' the same thing." Nancy confesses softly, hugging her father tightly and whispering into his ear. "I keep pretending that I don't know, but I do."

"You don't have to be scared, sweetheart," Thomas III whispers back to his daughter, glancing again to Christina and Berthine. "Cousin Christina and your Great-Aunt Berthine are going to take good care of you, isn't that right?"

"That's right," Christina agrees promptly, trying to help her uncle console his daughter. She's been sober for a few days now; her spirit is in a bright condition despite this dark time. "We're going to travel during the summers and play games and do anything we want, Nancy."

"But, what about you, Daddy?" Nancy asks gloomily, wrapping her arms around her father's neck. "I'll miss you."

"I'll...uh...I'll miss you, too, b-b-baby." Thomas III whimpers, trying to hold back tears, but he can't. He moves his head to the side so that his daughter cannot see the salty streaks beginning to stream down his cheeks. "I'm so, sorry, Nancy. I'm so...so, sorry."

"Why are you crying, Daddy?"

"I-I..." Thomas III stutters; his eyes katrina into fervent floods. His forehead pounds, his sockets swell, his ears ring, and his mouth fills with saliva. "I just love you...all of you...so much."

"Tommy, take a moment," Berthine advises softly, peeling Nancy from her father's arms and lowering her to the floor so that the child stands next to Christina. "Have a seat, Tommy. We still have a little time...Nancy brought her guitar to play for you."

"*She did?*" Thomas III's face widens again as he sits on the bed, his arms shaking in fear; though this visit may distract his mind, his body can't ignore the coming end. "My little rock star..."

"I can already play three songs," Nancy announces proudly, pulling the guitar strap around her shoulder and throwing the guitar onto her knee like a pro. There's a small bruise on her knee that reminds Christina of June; the little blonde would spend hours playing her guitar and she would only stop when Duke or Christina picked on her. Christina remembers how she and Duke would terrorize June until she would scream and threaten to tell Kenny. The truth is that Christina and Duke were jealous that June had her father, but, after so many years and so much...tragedy, no...triumph, no...time, yes, time...after so much time, those childhood jealousies seem absolutely foolish.

"Wow, *'three songs'*? You really are a rock star! I'm so proud of you!" Thomas III gushes over his daughter, knowing these are the last moments to do so. "Can you play one for me?"

Nancy feels nervous, queer pulses course throughout her limbs, but Berthine gently nudges Nancy's left shoulder and smiles happily, while Thomas III scoops his daughter into his arms. Nancy lifts her guitar to her waist and sits on her father's knee before carefully placing the guitar into her lap and hunching over the strings. She searches for the proper fingering to begin a tune.

"Well, I'm not too good at two of the songs," Nancy admits with an anxious smile, clenching and unclenching her hands, trying to relax her fingers. "But I know one song pretty good."

"Play the good one, Nancy," Christina encourages while nervously locking eyes with Berthine. Both worry that the prison guards will retrieve Thomas III for their blood sacrifice before Nancy finishes her song, and another traumatic event will forever stain a Winniper childhood with irreparable pain. "I think we'll only have time for one song."

"It's one of Cousin June's songs…is that okay?" Nancy asks softly; she speaks in a muted tone when mentioning June. June's guitar has given Nancy an outlet during these hard times; the child can feel her cousin's joyful spirit throughout the family's mansion when she plays the guitar. While strumming the strings, Nancy senses her cousin's presence, and she believes that June's spirit watches over her and the family. She hopes that her father will do the same. "I can try another if…"

"No, June's song is fine, sweetheart." Thomas III smiles at his daughter while she fumbles through the strings. He soaks in every ounce of her image, her wheat-colored hair falling over her small shoulders and her youthful cheeks puffing up into little, red apples. Nancy is nervous even when the audience is so familiar; maybe the circumstances have rattled all their nerves. Everyone in the family is trying their best to keep it together. "Please play, Nancy. I just want to hear you play."

"Okay," Nancy concedes with a deep inhale and tries to begin, but her fingers are slightly stiff from the crisp, November air. Her index finger slips from the neck and her thumb collides with the E cord. "Whoops, sorry."

"Take your time, angel." Thomas III whispers solemnly, knowing that time is the last thing he has in abundance, yet he looks at his daughter, still trying to cherish these final moments as much as any dying father could. He feels time slow within the dark cell. His daughter sits in his lap with Berthine and Christina watching intently; she is the center of their world. "You really do look like a rock star, Nancy. You remind me of your Cousin June."

Nancy grins brightly, several baby teeth still peak through her gums. She's heard of a fairy that pays some children for sacrificed whites, but she has never received such rewards. Berthine and Christina ensure that she is neither spoiled nor disillusioned; Nancy knows more than any nine-year-old Winniper girl ever did before her. Taking turns explaining the bits and pieces and following up with extensive question-and-answer sessions, Berthine and Christina have explained all the secrets, the blood curse, the Sioux family members, and the murders.

Childhood fantasies are meaningless to a child without a childhood.

∞

Thomas III had planned to raise Nancy at the Winniper Family Estate, but the family's secrets turned their home into a place of turmoil and heartache. His sins mounted a battering ram of guilt that smashed through his privileged walls. Eventually, these sins eclipsed Thomas III and led to his confession, conviction, and a death sentence for the murders of his sister and his Sioux newborn.

∞

Soon, the story will culminate in his permanent absence from his daughter's life; yet, just maybe, he could inhabit a transcendent form as a fatherly ghost.

Except for a birthday visit to the Winniper County Zoo or a Christmas carriage ride around Winniper County Park, Nancy rarely leaves the family's sheltered estate. She and Christina still remain within their closed Winniper world, unable to face the public shame that still lingers over the family. There's more public vitriol for the murders than the miscegenation.

Although Berthine still visits Charles at her cabin, she has also become somewhat reclusive, remaining in one of the two places: the mansion or the cabin. The women spend holidays, evenings, and weekends, together—two women and a young lady trapped in spinsterhood, yet, compared to the dead, they are *triumphant overall,* no?

Now at age nine, Nancy knows very little about the outside world; she idolizes June, though she has never met her. Nancy and Christina still do not know that June is alive; Berthine has her suspicions and reliable sources. Tonight, will be the first time that she has seen Jazz since he left town. Nancy has never been beyond the county lines, a shortcoming, among many, that Christina and Berthine plan to correct soon. Neither of them has seen much of the world; they are planning a world tour that will rival Jazz and June's trips around the globe. The Winniper women have much to learn, and they have ample means and opportunity to do so; still, a few obstacles of recompense and reconciliation lay ahead of their path. The definition of family must evolve for their lives to be complete; retribution and reward be damned.

As Thomas III sits at death's door, still mimicking his father to the end, the Winniper family again offers another male sacrifice to a curse that once placed the entire bloodline in jeopardy. Something as simple as skin color threatened the lives of the innocent, like Nancy and June; once upon a time, Papa and Thomas III were among these ranks and then their hands tasted blood. Of course, a family with such sad songs to sing has produced notable musicians, entrepreneurs, and egomaniacs; yet, they are all haunted by the same misunderstood ghosts. So they sing and they lash out because they don't know any other way to express their pain…the pain of not being accepted…the pain of not feeling allowed to be one's self in one's own skin.

And now is the time when the family needs to sing and hear these songs, together, as Nancy resets her fingers and begins to play one of June's tunes, a melody that is familiar to Christina from their youth. She remembers fighting with little June and Duke, forcing her little sister to retreat into her room and hearing her strum that guitar behind the door—maybe, music was June's only friend until she met Jazz.

"I can't remember the words," Nancy admits finally, continuing to play the soft melody. Thomas III smirks at his daughter, mesmerized by her talent as if watching her ride a bike for the first time. She seems older than her years, a possible prodigy. Nancy stares back at her father's face before turning her head to Christina. "Cousin Christina, do you know the words?"

"Um..." Christina listens to the music for a moment and remembers June screaming from her room, threatening to run away. Outside of the cell, one prison guard coughs and breaks her trance; she turns to the lingering crowd and frowns as they watch the family through a looking glass. The display sign reads: *Winniper Family Moments from Death Row.* Christina collects herself and looks back to her uncle and cousin. "No, uh...I'm sorry, Nancy...I can't sing...*right now.*"

"Well, I...I think I can remember the melody..." Berthine adds shyly, hoping to preserve some joy in Nancy's last moments with her father. She steps closer to Nancy and Thomas III with Christina over her left shoulder. "Just keep playing, Nancy, and I'll...help you out."

Berthine begins to *la-di-da*; Nancy hears the lyrics in her melody, too, and hums along as best she can. They don't remember the words to June's song, or, at least, they pretend they have forgotten the lyrics. Maybe the words were, and still are, unimportant, because Thomas III smiles so brightly while hearing his daughter that death can't possibly be close. The end is not so near. Nancy glances over to Christina and stops humming when she sees tears rolling down her cousin's face. Christina notices Nancy's pity and tries to turn away, but Nancy stops playing altogether.

"What's wrong, Christina?" Nancy asks out of genuine concern. She is a young child with more care for another's well-being than her own, yet, she is still naïve to the effect of playing June's song in front of Christina. Berthine places her right arm around Christina's shoulders and softly pulls her close, knowing these times are tough for each of them. It is the empathy that makes the moment endurable; it is compassion that allows a family to survive as a family.

"She's alright, June." Berthine's tired, eighty-year-old mind mistakes Nancy for her cousin; sadly, the old Sioux woman's lapses in mental precision have become more frequent. "This was...a special song. It's one of Duke's favorites."

"Mine, too." Nancy adds, but there is another pause at the mention of another ghost. She knows that Uncle Duke is not dead; he is locked away somewhere within this prison, but Berthine and Christina rarely mention him unless they are answering one of Nancy's sporadic questions. Nancy understands just enough to know when not to ask more questions, so she remains quiet and allows the silence to fill the air until someone, anyone, says something, anything.

"I'm…uh…Christina, I'm sorry about Duke, too. I really am," Thomas III apologizes as his face reddens to match his daughter's rose apple cheeks. He lowers his head in shame. "I'm glad he won't be executed like me…I…I tried to help, but…I think I made things worse. Mama's gone. Tilly's gone. Papa's gone…I didn't expect…"

"We know, Tommy," Berthine interrupts, holding Christina's hand tightly. "We women are much smarter than you or your father ever thought. Olivia loved you both, and so do we. Women are much more forgiving than menfolk."

"I hope so, because…I got big plans from here on out." Thomas III pinches Nancy's nose and grins at her cheerfully. "I'm going to make sure my baby has everything she wants."

"*Really?*" Nancy muses as her mouth opens wide with faux-wonder; she's willing to play along with her father. "Like what?"

"Anything you want. Nothing's too good for you, Nancy."

"What about a zebra?" Nancy asks excitedly, raising her head to her father and strumming her guitar strings. "I saw one at the zoo."

"Then, I'll get you two."

"Thomas…" Berthine interjects, placing her hand on his shoulder. "Don't promise her that."

"Why not?" Thomas III counters, glancing up to Berthine. "My baby should have everything she wants. You have all the money in the world…even after closing up shop. Nancy should get her fair share."

"But there won't be any shares soon, Thomas," Berthine confides, looking at him as she once looked at Papa while informing him that the castle will soon crumble. "We've closed the oil refinery. You're right, we do still have more than we'll ever need, but the land…the businesses…it all has to go. When we're done, there will be no more oil profits from that land."

"You can't do that," Thomas III protests as he looks down to Nancy, who smiles back sweetly. She sits on her father's knee, listening closely inside his final holding cell. "What about Nancy?"

"She'll be fine. Your father left us...*all of us*...substantial trust funds. Nancy can have a fresh start. We're selling the mansion, and if we want, we can find a new home, in a new town. Christina and I plan to take Nancy traveling a bit. You and Teresa saw the world, once; I see no reason why we shouldn't have a look, too." Berthine beams over Thomas III, assuring him that his daughter will likely receive a better upbringing without him. Nancy releases her guitar and hugs her father around his shoulders; her arms slide against the excess grease from his scalp that has slid down his neck. Berthine places her frail hand under Thomas III's chin. "We'll have everything we need, but not everything we want."

"And the Winniper name dies..." Thomas III laments, brushing his daughter's hair with his hand. "We have no more male heirs."

"Tommy..." Berthine pauses, wanting to spare his feelings but she also wants to finally say the words which have festered within her soul for years. "Look how much pain that name brought us."

"What are you saying?" Thomas III asks, seeking clarification. "We're a family, now."

"Of course, we are, *now*. But we can still look back and see the casualties on the road to *this resolution*." Berthine burrows her insight into her nephew, softly holding his chin in her palm. She remembers her time as a housemaid at the mansion, when Olivia entrusted her to look after her children. Berthine has cared for Thomas III throughout his life, wiping crumbs, dirt, and tears from the face of a kind boy who has always found himself in trouble. "And we don't need a name in order to be a family."

"Time's up, folks," one of the prison guards interrupts, walking through the open cell door and shattering the fourth wall between the audience and the scene.

The guards and officials prepare for the trek to the execution chamber as several armed officers take their positions around the family, moving past Christina's right shoulder with subtle winks. Some of them can smell the booze in her hair.

"We're sorry you all couldn't have more time." There is a long silence that follows the remark and exposes its insincerity; these officers only have intentions to see justice fulfilled. Thomas III, Berthine, Christina, and Nancy silently agree that this moment should never end; though, staying within this cold prison cell isn't a just fate for dear Nancy. Berthine steps away from Thomas III and silently begs the prison personnel to be patient. Nancy watches her father's cheeks drop and his eyes fall to the floor.

"What's wrong, Daddy?"

"N-nothing, baby girl," Thomas III replies quickly, lifting his eyes and looking at his daughter with a smile. "Daddy has to go to Heaven now."

"Are you coming back?"

"Uh…of course, sweetheart." Thomas III folds his arms around her small back, cradles his daughter, and tells her what she wants to hear. His words wrap her within more fantasy as the reality crashes around them—he is never coming back. "One day…we'll be together again."

"*Soon*? Come to Thanksgiving Dinner on Thursday!" Nancy insists, tightening her arms around her father's shoulders and squeezing for dear life. She knows the truth, but she also knows the value of being a naïve child who loves her convicted and condemned father. "I always miss you at home."

"I…I miss you, too, Nancy. I…I always will." Thomas III continues to hold his daughter and he feels her weight against his chest. He remembers her as an infant and he refuses to accept that his child will grow without him. He shifts her weight in his arms and stares into his daughter's eyes. "You listen here. While I'm gone…you mind your Great-Aunt Berthine and your Cousin Christina, okay?"

"I don't want you to leave…" Nancy lowers her head, pouting with her guitar still in her lap; the vinyl strap hangs loosely over her shoulders, drooping awkwardly down her back. She removes her arms away from her father's neck, lifts the strap, and adjusts the guitar around her waist. She fiddles her fingers over the strings, while searching for any distraction from this traumatic experience. No daughter wants to remember her father's last steps down death row.

"Remember, Nancy, there's nothing…nothing more important than family." Thomas III places his hand under his daughter's chin and raises her head until her eyes meet his again. "You know, when you get older, you may become a mother."

"Ew! Christina already told me! Boys are gross!" Nancy pouts excitedly and turns her head to Christina and Berthine; both women chuckle together while nervously watching the security officers circling around them. Ignoring the officers, Nancy continues to lampoon her father's mention of motherhood. "Daddy, I don't want to grow up."

"Ha, no one does, dear." Berthine laughs along with Nancy, stalling amongst the officers and feeling the awkwardness in her trepidation. "But we all have to do it."

"And you may have children, too…" Thomas III pats his daughter's head lightly, trying to hammer a point home. This last visit must have a purpose; he's thought about this moment since his sentencing: his final words. "And when you have a family, Nancy, I want you to love…all your children…love and raise all of them, *together*. I'm…I'm sure…uh, you don't understand everything, but…"

"Time to go, Mr. Winniper," A prison guard barks gruffly, while a few others continue leering lustfully at Christina, thinking of superficial conquests. "You all understand, right? I have a job to do. They're waiting on him in the chamber."

"Okay, I…I'm sorry." Thomas III apologizes fearfully as he concedes to his end and he looks back to his daughter's face, trying to remember every detail for now and beyond. "I love you, Nancy. Please…please remember, if you ever have a family, if you ever have children, *love and raise all of them.*"

"Okay…um, I will, Daddy. I love you, too." Nancy hugs her father, unable to understand all his words; she feels his shoulders tense and she knows that her father is scared. Thomas III helps his daughter stand with her guitar hanging between them; he rises from his cell bed and hovers over her as Berthine moves closer to him.

"Don't worry, Tommy," Berthine whimpers, placing her hand on his cheek. "I will see you inside."

"No, Berthine. You don't have to come in." Thomas III protests in words only, leaning his pale cheek into her soft brown hand. He still seeks forgiveness while savoring these last touches. "I don't want you to see."

"Tommy, I'm not only here for them, but I'm here for your mother, too." Berthine smiles and rubs Thomas III's cheek, reminding him of his mother's warmth. His shoulders drop, his back relaxes, and she can see his body betray his pride. "I was there for your father. Now I'm here for you, too."

"This won't be like watching Papa die in bed." Thomas III grimaces, imagining his own charred end before pointing to his glistening head. "They've got me greased for fireworks."

"Don't be crude." Berthine pats her Thomas III's face with her hand, giving him a gentle strike that would be harder under different circumstances. The tears falling from her eyes distract her attention and displace her force; she needs all her emotional restraint to contain her sorrow. Soon, the state of South Dakota will execute Olivia's son for the murder of her daughter. "This is not justice…your mother lost both of her babies…"

"Please don't cry, Berthine." Thomas III begs, continuing to lean his face into her comforting palm and trying to console her as best he can. "I don't want to cause any more heartache."

"Who cares about heartache after so much bloodshed, Tommy?" Berthine responds swiftly, still crying. "This family may never recover from what you and your father put us through. What is one more wound after so much pain? Come along, children."

"Goodbye, Uncle Thomas." Christina steps around Berthine and hugs her uncle hurriedly, still uneasy with any physical contact with her mother's killer. The sins of the men in her life have infected all her relationships. She considers the conditions that led to the deaths of her mother and sister and she realizes the puppeteers who controlled these conditions were men who could have killed her, too.

"Goodbye, Christina." Thomas III lowers his head as his niece breaks their embrace. "I…I'll always be sorry…f-f-for…for what I did."

"Forgive yourself, Tommy. What's done is done." Berthine speaks tenderly to Thomas III as Christina joins her side and takes Nancy's hand. "Don't pass with regrets like your father did…try to make peace, so your soul can rest."

Berthine ushers Nancy and Christina from the cell with the prison guards surrounding them. Nancy looks back to see several guards remain within the cell and crowd around her father. A black-robed preacher enters the concrete cell, stands in front of Thomas III, and reads from the Holy Bible.

The women, guards, and officials march back through death row. Christina takes one solitary glance toward her left as they pass Earl's cell. This time, he raises his head from his bed, locks eyes with her, and grins somberly as she passes. She never breaks her stride; the family parade continues toward the execution chamber, weaving through the prison hallways.

Nancy lifts her head and gazes up at her cousin and great-aunt as they walk in silence; all three are trapped in fear and regret, carried along by the motions of familial duty. Time dissolves into contemplation and Nancy thinks of home, the safe gates of the Winniper Family Estate. She dreams of her household comforts as an oasis, the dreams of a would-be domesticate; but then, cold reality pricks her senses and her mind returns to the damp, concrete prison. Their grim procession reaches a narrow, concrete tunnel with an enormous steel door at one end and folding chairs lining the walls.

"Christina, Nancy, you two wait here, and I will be back after..." Berthine whimpers through her tears; a burly, black guard unlocks and opens the heavy door to the execution chamber. Nancy peeks inside and sees rows of similar folding chairs gathered around a solitary throne contraption. Berthine and several guards step inside the room and she looks back at Nancy while the steel door closes between them. Christina takes Nancy's hand and the two walk by another group of prison guards and staff officials. Nancy softly strums her guitar, thinking about how to forget.

"What's going on now, Christina?" Nancy asks as they sit in two chairs against the wall to the left of the chamber door, but Christina doesn't respond in words. She simply squeezes her cousin's hand gently and looks down to Nancy knowingly. Nancy squeezes back, and the two remain quiet; they hear footsteps turning down the concrete tunnel.

More guards and officials trudge toward the execution chamber, surrounding an assortment of shady figures. Within the group, several Sioux men in business suits carry briefcases and whisper amongst each other. A Creole man and a Sioux woman break away from the convoy with two children at their sides. The children, a Sioux boy and a blonde girl, listen to the adults' instructions before sitting in folding chairs across from Nancy and Christina. The Creole man and Sioux woman steal a few glances at Nancy and Christina before rejoining their group as an officer slowly opens the steel door and ushers the group inside the execution chamber. The two children take a few looks at Nancy's guitar, and whisper and giggle to themselves from across the tunnel.

"Daisy, I want a guitar like that!" The Sioux boy whispers excitedly.

Nancy watches them watch her before hearing more footsteps; she looks down the concrete tunnel and sees a small militia of prison guards escorting her father through the shadows in chains.

"Daddy!" Nancy screams, but the chains are so tight around her father's hands and feet that he can't lift his arm to say hello. He has no room to run. He shuffles through the tunnel, stuffed between the prison guards who hold his body in an upright position and force his legs to walk. Even if he tried to stop, they would only drag him to his death in more shame. Nancy rises from her seat with her guitar around her waist and she runs toward her father, but the prison guards stop her roughly and create a uniformed barrier between father and daughter. Nancy continues to push into the officers; her guitar clangs and strums, producing a sad song in the echoic tunnel. "Daddy, where are you?"

"I'm here, baby! I'm here! Hey! Don't touch her!" Thomas III yells from within the melee, still struggling in chains; his efforts to reach his daughter cause a stir among his pallbearers. "I'm here, Nancy!"

"Daddy!" Nancy shouts again, straining her thin arms, pressing her guitar closer to her body, reaching through the guards, and hoping to touch her father one last time. She imagines him reaching out to meet her, and their fingertips brush lightly before a giant, grisly guard picks her up by the waist, carries her back to her seat, and places her next to Christina with a loud thud. Her guitar bangs against her hips and Christina is unsure how to react; she wants to put up a fight, too, but she can't remember how.

"Keep her here! And keep her quiet!" The guard orders sternly with a threat behind his tone. Nancy stifles her tears, pouting for her father, but she fears the guard and she realizes that she is all alone; there is no one to protect her. The furious guard moves back into position as the death march passes and another guard opens the steel door with an ominous, deliberate chuckle.

"You better stay put, Nancy." Christina advices meekly, placing her arm over Nancy's shoulders, trying to console her distraught cousin. They watch as Thomas III steps behind the priest and pushes past a few prison guards in a last ditch effort to reach Nancy.

"Nancy! I'm here!" His face appears briefly amidst the uniformed wall and his frantic, blue eyes meet with his daughter's sad stare. "I'm sorry, sweetheart! Please, Father, let me speak to her a little more..."

Thomas III pleads to the minister as the prison guards grab the convict and push him toward the doorway.

"Just give me a second to..."

"I'm sorry, Mr. Winniper." The minister mumbles insincerely; the prison guards push Thomas III like a stubborn mule, tugging his orange jumpsuit and immobilizing his arms in their tough grip. Their overwhelming force muscles Thomas III into the execution chamber and he feels the cold air of the damp, dungeon setting. The minister gives the convict a grave look. "It's your time."

"No! I'm not ready!" Thomas III claws at the edges of the steel door, grabbing frantically at the hinges and sides. He struggles and strains against the guards who envelop his body in full, pushing him further into the execution chamber, past the precipice of any possible escape. Those within the concrete room stare in a mix of horror, pity, and applause while the four outside of the door watch in shock as Thomas III wrestles with the guards on the edge of darkness. He finds his daughter's eyes once again as the shadows of death close around him. She looks back at him blankly, unsure how to process this moment, especially after the guard's threats. She remains silent, but her heart cries for her father as he tries desperately to connect with her one last time. "Nancy! Nancy, I love you! I love you!"

The steel door closes quickly, leaving Nancy and Christina sitting in silence across from the two children. The world fades away during a deadly moment that Nancy has dreaded for the past few years, though she is too young to absorb the trauma completely. An eternity of time passes while they wait for the finality of her father's death. She cries and whimpers and angles her ear toward the door, trying to hear inside the sealed chamber—small murmurs, and then a switch flipped with a clank. The ceiling lights in the tunnel flicker…blink…blink…then shut off, placing Nancy, Christina, and the two children within total darkness.

"Ah! Darrel!" Daisy screams from her seat.

"What's happening, Christina?" Nancy asks in fear, finding her cousin's hand and holding it tightly until two ceiling lights glimmer slowly and offer some illumination in the dark tunnel.

"Uh…I don't know," Christina responds without moving to investigate; she hears screams from inside the sealed chamber and the steel door slides open suddenly. Charles rushes from the smoke-filled room and vomits into a metal trash can outside of the door. The grisly prison guard appears in the doorway, but his demeanor has changed from fierce to frantic; thin, gray smoke wafts from inside the execution chamber. Nancy tries to peek inside, but the petrified guard blocks her sight with his mountain range body while looking at Christina, Nancy, and the children as if he's just seen a ghost.

"Don't look in there!" He demands frenziedly, adjusting his body and trying to shield them from the gruesome sight.

"What happened?" Christina inquires sympathetically, as Thomas III begins to wail from inside the chamber.

"He's still breathing!" Berthine screams from within, while more smoke billows through the doorway. "Thomas!"

"We just had a…um, electrical…malfunction! It'll just be a moment!" The horrified prison guard explains loudly, trying to drown out the agony behind him. He looks back over his shoulder and wrinkles his nose in disgust before turning his head back to observe Charles, who still retches into the trash can. "You, um, are you coming back inside?"

"No! I've seen too much!" Charles gags, wiping his mouth with his coat sleeve. "Tell my sister that I'll watch the kids."

"Suit yourself." The prison guard cracks a nervous smile before closing the steel door carefully, still shielding Nancy and Christina from looking inside. He stares at them with a glimpse of sympathy until the door shuts completely, muffling Thomas III's cries for help; they are left in the tunnel with more questions and fears. Charles sits down next to Daisy, leans over her, and retrieves a red handkerchief from Darrel's jacket pocket.

"Thanks, Nephew." Charles grins wryly and wipes his mouth. "I just seen somethin' I may never forget."

"What happened in there?" Nancy inquires hastily, forgetting her place and staring intently at her cousin. Charles still hasn't made much of an effort to visit Berthine, Christina, or Nancy at the Winniper family's mansion. Although he speaks with Berthine often, he is still standoffish toward the surviving Winnipers, especially Christina.

"Nancy, don't be rude," Christina chides sharply, reprimanding her little cousin for improper social etiquette, though they rarely have a chance to practice. "Maybe, he doesn't want to discuss it…"

"No, it's fine…uh…*Miss.* I don't mind her askin'…it's just…it was downright disturbin' sh…uh, stuff." Charles explains, stopping himself from cursing in front of the children. He still refuses to address Christina or Nancy by name, so he readjusts his delivery and occupies his mind with trivial concerns by looking down and adjusting the buckle on his alligator dress shoes. "These *Gators* are too tight!"

"I like your shoes," Nancy remarks happily, and Charles smiles as if he hasn't received a compliment in a while. He's overjoyed to be noticed, or maybe, he's just a secret glutton for attention, even in moments of death.

"*You do?* Well, thank you, darling, you have good taste!" Charles chuckles softly and wipes his right shoe with the red handkerchief before folding it up. "My little brother bought 'em for me. I think he bought 'em for himself and then gave 'em to me. It used to be me givin' him the *hand-me-downs*, now, my little brother hands down to *me.*"

"Are you poor?" Nancy asks frankly, indulging in the distraction and capitalizing upon Charles's newfound openness; although, she is still unfamiliar with the rules of polite conversation. Though she rarely meets new people at the sheltered Winniper Family Estate, she has a natural curiosity and she feels a general affinity for the human family. When she does meet someone new, she questions them for an extended amount of time and prods her subject to provide personal details and authentic answers.

"Nancy, you're still being rude. He's your cousin; Papa left him just as much as he left you. You know he's not poor." Christina continues to chastise Nancy, though they both giggle along with Charles. Christina knows how ridiculous Nancy's questions can sometimes become, especially if she's excited. Her little cousin reminds her so much of June, boisterously loud and quick to ask or say whatever's on her mind. Nancy has a beautiful truth about her, a pure innocence in her devotion to understanding her surroundings so that her world makes sense. Christina looks to Charles and empathizes through her eyes, communicating an explanation that doesn't need words. "I'm sorry, Charles. She doesn't have much social skills."

"It's quite alright, Miss…uh…*Miss Christina.* No, I'm not poor, now, but I'm also not ashamed to admit that I was poor." Charles explains with a smile and points to his heart. Again, he leans across Daisy and places Darrel's folded handkerchief back into his jacket pocket. "I've been rich before, too, but I was also very sad."

"But if you're not poor, why does your little brother still buy you shoes?" Nancy continues to prod, content to take her mind off her father's execution. She engages in conversation with a person she has yet to explore, whose skin color, age, or gender has no influence on how she views him as a human being.

"Well, I have a good family and we help each other, look after each other." Charles pauses for a moment, thinking of Jazz, Lucy, his mother, and all the help he needed to kick his alcohol and gambling addictions. "When we were younger, my brother took my things and wore my clothes. Now that we're older, he gives me things and lets me wear his clothes. I like to think the Universe planned it that way."

"My father told me when I get older, I can have a family of my own, but...I still don't understand why he can't stay." Nancy confesses tearfully, choking up and looking down at her guitar before re-engaging her distraction. "I've seen you before, *Cousin Charles.* You were at the house when grandpa died. Why haven't you come back?"

"Uh, yes...yes I was there. It's...it's just tough...um...that was a sad day." Charles answers reverently, feeling guilty that he has not been strong enough to build relationships with Nancy and Christina. He looks across the tunnel to his cousin and sister and he feels compelled to make a connection, yet he's stuck within the awkward stage of not knowing how to address their situation. "I'm sorry we haven't spent more time together...since Papa passed."

"I'm sorry, too." Christina responds, staring at her brother keenly, communicating without words, and bringing together two lost souls from among Teresa's children. "I'd like to spend more time, *with you.*"

"Me, too...it's just...I can't believe...you're..." Charles pauses at the edge of confrontation, hesitating as he looks at Darrel and Daisy. He then glances at Nancy and locks eyes with Christina. Understanding their respective relationships, he resolves to set an example. Charles rises from his seat, walks across the dimly lit tunnel, wipes his moist palm against his slacks, and extends his hand to his sister. "I hope we can get to know each other, *Christina*...and you, too, *Nancy.*"

"I hope so, too." Nancy interjects eagerly; her small white hand plunges into Charles's large brown palm before he can connect with Christina. "Christina, why didn't you and Cousin Charles grow up together?"

"Well, uh…Nancy…that's another tough question. Charles and I…uh…we…didn't know about each other. All these years…I…we had no idea." Christina clarifies with a smile, explaining part of the truth to Nancy while knowing her little cousin will require more discussion. Although they have answered her questions to the best of their knowledge, Christina and Berthine still have not eased all of Nancy's worries. They doubt that the nine-year-old can even understand the answers that they have provided, because they all understand so little about their family. In moments of death, there have always been reciprocal times of birth and reconnection. While she sits, looking up to her twin Sioux brother, Christina finally reaches out to him and shakes Charles's hand for the first time; they feel an electric current pass between them that neither can explain. "I'm both sorry and happy to see you again under these circumstances."

"Hey, well, *'I'm both sorry and happy'*, too." Charles admits, before looking to Nancy and thinking about the circumstances which have led to this friendly interaction. His smile fades as he considers the botched execution inside the chamber, but he resumes a nostalgic realization that he and Christina are, in fact, twin siblings, born to the same murdered mother and a runaway father. "I'm afraid, without these circumstances, we may have never seen each other again. I don't really like going to that old mansion."

"Berthine said we're moving! We're going to see the world! Have you ever travelled, huh?" Nancy inquires excitedly, noticing Charles's brown skin for the first time. "You look like one of the Indians in the Lone Ranger. But they don't wear suits. Why don't you have a feather hat?"

"Nancy…please. If you're going to ask your cousin so many questions, at least give him a chance to answer one at a time."

"She has a lot of energy, huh? She reminds me of those two." Charles smiles, while looking over his shoulder to see Daisy and Darrel intently watching the conversation. Caught snooping, the twins turn to each other and giggle uncontrollably. Charles then turns his head back to Nancy and grins with wonder while seeing her resemblance to Daisy and realizing that she is his cousin. "I don't have a feather hat because I was raised Baptist. I've done a little traveling around the states, but I've never been out of the country though. My brother wants to take me to Brazil after we're done here, but I'm a little scared of planes."

"I'm scared of planes, too."

"Ha, well…that must run in the family." Charles laughs before noticing Nancy's her fingers fumbling over her guitar strings. "Hey, I like that box. Your guitar looks very *shop*."

"It's a Taylor Acoustic Limited Edition!" Darrel blurts out from his seat, having waited anxiously for a chance to enter the conversation. As a highly ambitious ten-year-old, he's already invested a considerable amount of time in learning about his parents' former business. He reads about fine art and researches appraisals for high-end musical instruments. His mother and father have detailed their modest, yet memorable beginnings in New Orleans, so he knows that he must work extra hard to surpass their accomplishments. "That guitar sells for $400 in Mama's catalogue!"

"Oh, hush, Darrel, keep it down." Charles commands calmly, placing a finger over his lips. He shakes his head and wipes the sweat from his brow; suddenly, he realizes his gaffe and points towards the twins. "Oh, I'm sorry. Please allow me to introduce my niece and nephew. This is Daisy and Darrel; they're your Cousin Lucy's kids."

"Nice to meet you," the twins respond in unison, tried and true, rehearsed over ten years of private dinner parties and secretive events amongst their small mountain community. The twins still rarely travel outside of Spokane, Washington. Their attendance is only mandatory when family duties supersede security, yet, Lucy and Marcus hope that the Winniper family's reconciliation will make their world safer, not only for Daisy and Darrel, but also for all the surviving family members.

"I swear Daisy and Nancy look just like June," Charles remarks, glancing back and forth between Nancy and Daisy and looking down at his caramel palm. "I don't know what it is about these Winniper genes, but we are an odd bunch to say the least."

"What do you mean *'genes'*?" Nancy questions inquisitively, hearing and dissecting the word. "Like jeans that you wear?"

"Ha, no, sweetheart, our *'genes'* aren't the same as *'jeans'*. Uh, genes… are…" Charles pauses, staring at Christina and forgetting the small amount of education that he had in the Sioux village. There was once a teacher who taught lessons in a school shack, but Charles can't even remember her name, let alone the definition of a gene. "Uh…maybe your Cousin Christina can explain."

"I never went to high school. So I don't remember much about anything. Nancy, just tell Charles about your guitar."

"Okay, it was June's guitar." Nancy explains proudly while working her fingers into an E chord. "I wanted to learn all her songs, but I only know three so far."

"Hey, that's good, though." Charles continues to smile at Nancy, remembering being young once; he often wrestled with Jazz inside Berthine's cabin, fighting over a similar acoustic guitar. "My brother started playing guitar around your age."

"You mean Jazz?"

"Yes, I don't think you've met him, but he's uh…" Charles pauses, unsure of all the implications in the information; Jazz has been very secretive for the past few years and Charles restrains himself from revealing too much. How tangled is their family tree? "Jazz is a complicated fellow…he performed music with your Cousin June."

"I know. I've seen some of Uncle Duke's videotapes of their performances. Have you ever seen them perform?" Nancy probes as her eyes grow wide again with wonder; she looks at Charles in a new light. He's a chance to hear about Cousin June's live performances. "I would've loved to see them perform in real life! Singing songs and dancing!"

"Yes, I…uh, I saw them live. They were great. I actually managed them when they started out." Charles beams smugly, sticking out his chest and remembering the past. He also remembers to stay humble; he looks at Nancy and smiles once again, seeing the light in her eyes. "Hey, Nancy, you're pretty smart, huh?"

"You think so? I don't go to school."

"Is that right? Why not?"

"I don't know."

"Well, school isn't all it's cracked up to be." Charles wipes his brow again, but this time, he exaggerates the gesture sarcastically. "My school had one teacher and no grade levels. I suspect I left right around the first grade."

"You left school?" Nancy wonders, while thinking that this conversation has paid for itself as both a distraction and an information session. "You can do that?"

"I did, but it wasn't the smartest decision I ever made." Charles waves his hand and points to Nancy's guitar. "Keep playing those strings, kid, but I need to talk to Mama, uh, I mean *Aunt Berthine*, about gettin' you some schoolin'. You're too smart not to get an education."

The overhanging lights flutter on and off, but they quickly resume full power. An eerie silence spreads throughout the grim tunnel—the world pauses as a soul flies away. Charles and Christina look down at the concrete floor, unable to turn their eyes to Nancy, knowing the finality of the moment.

"I guess it's over," Nancy murmurs sadly, forced to break the awkward silence that hangs over her father's death. The steel door opens and an exodus of awe-struck observers begins to leave the execution chamber. Limping awkwardly with a black, wooden cane, Jazz emerges through the doorway; Lucy, Marcus, and Berthine walk alongside him slowly. They move in hushed unison with their arms wrapped around one another.

"Hey, Lucy, Marcus…the kids are okay." Charles stands tall and steps forward, hesitant to address his brother. He smiles over his shoulder toward Daisy and Darrel before tilting his head and trying to read his brother's expression. "Jazz, are *you* okay?"

"Same…these people mean nothin' to me." Jazz mumbles angrily in a morbid tone; being so close to home makes him feel sullen and depressed, and he barely pushes the words out of his mouth. "I'm leaving."

"Just take it slow, Jazz," Berthine advises strongly, trying her best to cheer up her great nephew and adopted son. She hopes to pull Jazz out of a depression that has lasted since the attack.

"Give him some space, Mama," Lucy chides, placing her hand on Jazz's shoulder and leaning gently against his cane. "It's bad enough you can't outrun her, eh little bro? I'm going to get the kids, and then we'll leave."

She motions to Marcus and they begin walking toward Daisy and Darrel, but Charles stands in their way.

"But wait, Lucy. Let me introduce you, all of you, to Nancy…and Christina." Charles announces happily, ignoring the oddness of their congregation outside of the execution chamber. He waves his hand toward the family, imploring all of them to gather around. "Look Jazz, Nancy has June's guitar. I was thinking…"

"That's nice…I met Christina, years ago." Jazz grumbles, refusing to extend his hand, but, he does raise his eyebrows and observe Nancy; in a flash, she reminds him of June and he can't help but feel love. She still sits next to her cousin, staring despondently at her guitar, knowing her father is gone. "But, you, it's nice to meet you, Nancy."

"She's been through a lot today, Jazz," Berthine adds quickly, explaining Nancy's silence and sensing that Jazz doesn't fully grasp her current grief. "This is Thomas's daughter."

"His *'daughter'*?" Jazz repeats fully, finally lifting the clouds of his confusion. He understands that Nancy is one of his own. The look of sorrow and loss, he knows it well; they are truly kin. She returns his look with her own shock, meeting eyes with the mythical man. Berthine and Christina only speak about Jazz in whispers around the Winniper Family Estate. Jazz stares at Nancy and, again, he sees June, sitting with her guitar, writing a song or lyric about everything and nothing at all. "I…I'm sorry, Nancy. I…I'm sorry about your father."

"I know…but you don't have to be sorry. He's coming back." Nancy insists impatiently; she stands from her seat, guitar hanging across her waist, and she extends her hand with a confident smile. "It's nice to meet you, Cousin Jazz. I really like your music."

"Oh, well…I'm glad you do." Jazz balances himself on his cane and shakes Nancy's hand. For the first time in a long time, he feels a pull on his heart strings; he enjoys a momentary compassion for a white person other than June. His cheeks tighten unconsciously, reeling his lips into an unfamiliar expression—a smile graces his face. "How long have you been playing guitar?"

"Just a few years, but I'm not very good. I don't practice enough." Nancy looks down at her guitar, ashamed of her novice abilities as Lucy, Marcus, Daisy, and Darrel join the family gathered around her. Charles steps aside and helps Christina to her feet, grinning alongside his sister. Berthine places her arm around Nancy and pulls their colorful family together; they each hold one another in various states of sorrow and anxiety.

"Come along, June," Berthine orders sternly, continuing to mistake Nancy for the former idol. Nancy leans into Berthine's hip while holding her guitar.

"Aunt Berthine, I'm Nancy."

"Oh, I'm sorry, child." Berthine apologizes sheepishly, looking to each family member, investigating if they noticed her error. Her tired mind has been through so much lately; she feels a little dizzy, but she perseveres in the moment, knowing she may never have another chance to unite their family. "I want to thank you all for coming."

"It was hard to get them here, Ma'," Charles confesses, pointing to Jazz, Lucy, and Marcus. "They don't want no parts of it…'specially Jazz."

"I understand. But, like it or not, we're family." Berthine breaks her embrace with Nancy and stands next to the child so that the family faces another in a tight circle. Daisy and Darrel stand across from Nancy. Charles and Christina stand next to one another. And Berthine pleads with Lucy, Marcus, and Jazz, hoping that they will, at least, listen to reason. "Jazz, think about everyone we've lost. Lucy, think about why your family lives in the mountains? We can help each other and the children have a better life. And I think the Good Lord would want us to help Nancy, Daisy, and Darrel do better than we have so far. Whether you like it or not, Papa gave us each $40 million. I know you've been successful on your own, but…he made it so none of us ever have to work again. He wasn't a saint, but…"

"So *your brother* paid for our love, Berthine?" Jazz asks sarcastically, staring at the woman he disliked for years *before* he learned the truth. More prison guards and officials continue to peel out of the execution chamber, looking over the family's small huddle with a reserved nonchalance. The deed is done; all that remains are these final moments of familial conflict. "You lied to us the entire time. We knew you weren't our mother. Lucy, told me how Olivia brought us to you, but…you…you should've told us, excuse me, *Berthine*…turns out, you're our, what? Our great-aunt? The sister of the man who tried to kill me and my fiancée, who turned out to be…*tada*, my sister! And you want forgiveness? You want us to be one big happy family?"

"But, Papa didn't kill you…*or her*, did he, Jazz? I know more than you think…and it's long past the time for all our secrets to come to light. If we've learned anything, it's not right to keep family from one another and we've been living with too many lies for far too long." Berthine unburdens herself tearfully, her body shaking as she grieves for Thomas III. He is now the martyr who created such a public spectacle that he forced the truth upon the world and the family. She tries to choke her tears and hold back her emotions, still attempting to reason with her family. "I've apologized and apologized, but even once more, I'm sorry. I made mistakes but I have always tried to protect us."

"I could fill an ocean with everything you've tried to do," Jazz retorts, turning his head to Lucy and Marcus. "Get me out of here. I have a plane waiting."

"Jazz, wait." Lucy stops her brother by stepping toward him, placing her hand over his heart, and pressing firmly. Her tone and demeanor changes while she glances around the circle, feeling a genuine connection between Berthine, Charles, Christina, Nancy, Daisy, and Darrel. Lucy envisions a possibly peaceful ending, but she wants Jazz to see it, too. She is a powerful Sioux woman whose gifts have made her life easier; yes, being a brilliant tactician has made Lucy a talented mother with dreams and ambitions of seeing her children live a healthy, happy, and full life. "We don't see you anymore. You're taking Charles to Brazil but you won't let us and the kids visit. And I agree with Mama that we need to help our children. They miss you, too. Give us a chance."

"Why? You don't need me to raise your kids."

"Yes, we do; we're family, Jazz. You can run from that fact all you want, but it will always be true." Lucy steps even closer to Jazz and the family looks around to one another. They smile and nod silently, mentally trying to make amends. Lucy stares into Jazz's eyes and she bores into his soul, reminding him of those childhood moments when she would challenge him or scold him.

∞

She was a mute who started to speak and became a successful profiteer, a loving wife, and a caring mother.

∞

Her willpower is evident in her accomplishments, but, as she scrapes the recesses of Jazz's soul, she can tell that something is missing.

"I can look into your eyes and know you're hiding something…or *someone*. Mama…*Berthine* told me what Papa said on his deathbed. And I remember how you and June felt about Brazil. Even with her, you still need to be with us, too. And we need to be *with her*, too."

"No, I don't trust…anyone. And I have to protect her. I have to protect her this time." Jazz begins to tear up, thinking about his disabled twin.

∞

After visiting June in a Nova Scotian clinic, Jazz flew her to a hilltop ranch on a 4,000 acre estate that he had purchased for them in the countryside of Maranhão, Brazil. Although she was still in a chemically-induced coma in order to prevent further brain damage, he defied her doctors' orders and made the arrangements to safely smuggle *Jane Dorothy* through international airspace.

The estate's location is so remote that he had to charter a helicopter and transport June from the Machado International Airport to his rural property, along with a team of dedicated, and contractually obligated, medical professionals. Their silence and cooperation were guaranteed and insured.

∞

While looking at Nancy, he can see June in her mannerisms and he realizes that his twin sister may never be the same.

"She still can't speak. She can barely hold a spoon. She wouldn't want the kids to see her like that."

"Let us come to Brazil, Jazz. We can help you take care of her." Lucy vows, stepping closer to Jazz as the priest, the burly prison guard, and a few final guests exit the execution chamber. Their grim faces become intrigued when they glance over the family scene and pass by ever...so...slowly. "We don't have to stay if you don't want us to, but, at least, we could see her. She's our family, too."

"Lucy, we can never be a family, *not with them.*"

"But we already are family. You can't play God, Jazz. You don't have the right to keep her from us, from her family." Berthine interrupts, stepping next too Lucy and waving her right hand over their tribe. "Look around you, Jazz. We are the only family that we have left. From all the Winnipers, Robinsons, Lancasters, Bethunes, and Cashmens, we're all that's left of our five families. We can either join together or face the world alone. You may not believe it, but we can protect each other...better when we work together."

"I agreed with Papa to stay out of the public. We live a quiet life, not a camera in sight. The press would never leave us alone if they knew. Someone could follow you…it's just…easier for us to stay away." Jazz states his case toughly, no longer running from the truth, but rather, he turns and opens his frame to Berthine, boldly facing her with tears in his eyes. He stumbles over his brashness and glances down at Nancy, hoping that he does not wound her innocence, but, he knows that pain is inevitable. "How will you explain to Nancy and the world how I fell in love with my own sister?"

"Christina and I have explained a lot to Nancy. I think everything about our family takes a little extra time to understand. But we can get through anything, together." Berthine empathizes with his shame, but she wants him to see beyond himself. She places her palms on his cheeks, as if he is still her son, comforting him as only a mother can. "Let us come with you to Brazil, Jazz. Thanksgiving is a couple days away, and I want us to spend it together. I promise you'll be happier and so will we. Christina deserves to see her sister and Nancy deserves to be with her family…*all of us*. We have enough money to do whatever we like…but it means nothing if we can't be happy."

Jazz hesitates with Berthine's hands on his cheeks, embarrassed and relieved to still have a maternal figure in his life. He peeks at Nancy, who grins cheerfully amidst her despair. Nancy then looks up to Christina with a big smile and squeezes her cousin's hand, sensing an adventure in their future. Berthine removes her hands from Jazz's cheeks and reaches out to Christina, taking her hand and wrapping it around Jazz's right arm so that she can support his weight above his cane.

"Christina is your sister, too, Jazz. None of us are innocent, but none of us are without guilt." Berthine explains, hoping to ease Jazz's sorrow. She can feel him beginning to relax amidst the family, taking in her tender words and hearing her loving intentions. "We're going to have to forgive the past, Jazz. We've all made decisions that we regret."

Christina remains silent, unable to speak, given the circumstances; she has just learned that June is still alive, but she's still too weak to ask a question out loud. Gin, grief, and guilt have consumed her spirit, weakening her resolve after losing so many in her family. She leans into Jazz and accepts more of his weight, holding him up so that he can stand straight with his cane on his left side.

The tunnel seems completely empty, minus a few nosey, yet patient, prison guards who wait for the family to leave. There is no time limit for the Winniper Family Show; these guards are collecting stories for the next poker game. While holding her reluctant brother, Christina wonders if Jazz will allow her to see her sister. In addition, she feels shamefully, and pathetically, optimistic that she may also gain Jazz, Lucy, and Charles as siblings. She has missed Duke and since he will not allow visitors, she has longed for a connection with someone from her generation.

"I...I don't know what to say, really." Christina confesses while staring at Jazz in amazement; this meeting is a tragic miracle, it would seem. Kenny appears in his face, and she smiles brightly, remembering her mother's third husband for the good times. She holds her brother closer, places her free hand on Jazz's right cheek, and wipes away a stream of tears. "I can see your father in your face."

"My...oh...I...I never knew him," Jazz utters softly, looking down at the concrete floor. He is a private figure, forced into this uncomfortable, yet necessary, family confrontation. "June said his name was Kenny."

"Ha, yes...he was...*a character*. I can tell you about him sometime, *if you like*." Christina offers a rare chance, the opportunity for the fatherless to learn more about his roots, his blood, and himself. She pauses to assess Jazz's interest while remembering the last time she saw Kenny, lying in bed, amputated, weak, and scared inside of a dilapidated, Chicago apartment. Looking into Jazz's eyes, she still sees Kenny's happy-go-lucky sadness and she recalls his many failed pranks and lame jokes.

Kenny was a rapscallion from beginning to end, and Christina regrets that she didn't try harder to convince him to leave Chicago when he had the chance.

She regrets not going to her mother's funeral, and she regrets not stopping Duke and Earl the day that they attacked Jazz and June.

"Berthine is right, Jazz. We're family, even though we all have regrets. I have guilt and shame that I will carry for the rest of my life, too. But Nancy doesn't. She deserves a chance to have us all in her life."

"'*A chance*'? What about June's chance?" Jazz retorts tersely, instinctively responding with a sarcastic comment to deflect her pleas, but, he promptly relinquishes his ego as he raises his head and realizes that his family surrounds him with love and compassion. "I want you to see her…I have doctors tending to her. She may be able to speak soon, but…it's been hard to watch her fight to come back these past few years. She's in there, but…she's not the same."

"None of us are the same, Jazz. But, we are family. And we have to trust each other…or we will never be safe." Christina continues to encourage their reconciliation while they stand together after her uncle's execution. Berthine worries that the coroner may wheel Thomas III's charred remains into the tunnel, but she also knows that Jazz may soon board a flight and never return to the States. She is rolling the dice with fate, praying that her family does not crap out.

"I swear we have to be the craziest family in all creation." Berthine chuckles tearfully and her weary eyes begin to brighten while she looks to each of her family members. The gloomy mood amongst them begins to ease, and a calming aura moves throughout the dark tunnel. Lucy and Marcus hold their children closely to their hips and Nancy leans against Berthine while strumming her guitar and watching the scene with a forgetful smile. Music and family are welcome distractions. "Come along, Nancy."

"Yes, Berthine," Nancy answers tenderly, happy to leave the set of her father's death with four times as many family members. She takes Berthine's hand and moves next to her cousins. On cue, Christina accommodates Jazz's weight and begins to lead him down the concrete tunnel. Charles places his hands in his pockets and casually strolls beside his twin sister. Lucy and Marcus walk with Darrel and Daisy between them, holding the twins' hands while preparing to find a new home away from the isolated mountains.

The remaining prison guards and officials watch the family travel through the tunnel and they take a moment to whisper rumors and insults, but the family marches together steadfastly, striding slowly without shame and holding their heads high. Beaming from head-to-toe and brimming with childish ideas, Nancy carefully leads Berthine by the hand so that they close the gap and walk alongside Jazz. Nancy then releases Berthine's hand, raises her head, and stares up at Jazz with a toothy grin. "Cousin Jazz, can I have one of your songs for an audition Friday night?"

"What?" Jazz stops and pauses for a moment of déjà vu; he remembers the first time he met June.

∞

She had waited for him outside of *Teezy's Bar* and asked him to give her a song for an audition. Even then, he knew that she was special.

∞

With Christina still at his side, he emerges from this reminiscence and notices Nancy, Berthine, and the rest of the family waiting for him to join them and turn down a corner leading to the prison's lobby. He grins and nods his head, encouraging them to move forward. He shakes off his lasting trepidation and puts one foot in front of the other, continuing to walk with Christina. They turn the corner into a dimly lit corridor and Nancy still bops next to Jazz, strumming her guitar with Berthine at her side. Jazz looks down upon her blonde hair and tiny frame and, once again, he sees June.

"What kind of audition would a nine-year-old have?"

"Cousin Jazz, it could be a dance audition!" Daisy yells from ahead of them.

"We're ten, so we can try out for *The Gong Show!*" Darrel adds excitedly, beginning to gyrate before Lucy sternly grabs his shoulder and shakes her head. The boy promptly stops his dance and giggles with Daisy before continuing to walk through the corridor alongside his sister and parents, though he quickly turns back to Nancy. "What kind of audition is it, Cousin Nancy?"

"Berthine said I could audition for the Winniper County Founder's Day Parade!"

"We want to audition with Cousin Nancy, too!" The twins shout in unison, tapping into their natural harmony.

"Well…I'm not sure." Jazz smiles unexpectedly, thinking about music, performing, and June. "You kids can have any of our songs that you want. I haven't played any instruments in a while so…I doubt I could help you learn them."

"Oh, well I can help you play more and then, you can help me learn!" Nancy announces confidently, figuring everything out and strumming her guitar triumphantly. She adjusts the strap over her shoulder and holds the instrument close to her waist. "One day, I'm going to be really good and I'm going on tour like you and Cousin June!"

"*We want to go on tour with Cousin Nancy, too!*"

"You're going to have to practice a lot," Jazz states plainly, remembering how he and June spent months learning to play their songs and sing the lyrics that they wrote together.

∞

They worked tirelessly to get their sound just right, but once their harmony matched, their union became pitch perfect.

∞

"Kids, it takes a lot of hard work to be great at anything."

"*We'll work hard, Cousin Jazz! We promise!*"

"I'll work hard, too, I promise!" Nancy assures him with a big, wide smile and she continues strumming her guitar while waltzing through the end of the corridor toward the light of the prison's lobby. Berthine observes her family with a mother's view, happy to see them finally coexist, even under sorrowful circumstances. Jazz, Christina, and Charles walk side-by-side, chuckling to one another as Charles steps lightly, careful not to scuff his crisp Gators.

Darrel and Daisy bounce eagerly around Lucy and Marcus, begging their parents for matching guitars as the family reaches the light. The prison guards no longer surround them; the Winniper family's prestige no longer protects them, yet, now, they surround and protect each other while moving as a collective mass of love, compassion, and forgiveness. Feeling the heavenly glow of their union, the family passes through the light and Nancy thinks about one remaining problem, one lasting concern that still bothers her bright, inquisitive mind as she searches for a complete resolution.

"Grandpa said I can do anything I want when I get older, but…but…"

"*But what?*"

"I'd rather stay young."

www.ingramcontent.com/pod-product-compliance
Lightning Source LLC
Chambersburg PA
CBHW032248020726
47495CB00001B/13